Please feel free to send me an email. Just know that my publisher filters these emails. Good news is always welcome.

Adreen Fernando – adreen_fernando@awesomeauthors.org

Sign up for my blog for updates and freebies!
adreen-fernando.awesomeauthors.org

GW00647750

About the Publisher

BLVNP Incorporated, A Nevada Corporation, 340 S. Lemon #6200, Walnut CA 91789, info@blvnp.com / legal@blvnp.com

DISCLAIMER

Praise for The Heartbreaker's Dare

This book was one of the amazing books I've ever read. The
language used is so powerful and the author's technique of writing
had so much emotion. I cried on most of the parts. This was the
first book I read on Wattpad. Hats off to Addie AKA Adreen
Fernando for writing this beautiful book. I always end up crying and
I just love it when
an author makes me feel so much. This book was an emotional
rollercoaster and it was totally worth it. I recommended
this book to all my friends because I couldn't get over
the story and wanted to share this experience
with everyone.
-Ilma Ilham

This book was one of the most amazing books I've ever read. The
characters in this book seemed so real, and their feelings will
touch your heart. Once you start reading this book,
you will feel like you're taken to another world.
-Starcy Newman

Amazing book. Has a 21st-century view on teen
relationships and problems.
-Lilly M.

I really love THD. It's not just about love; it's also about
depression. When I first read THD, I thought it was going to be
your typical
high-school love story. But no! It wasn't like that at all. I also love
THD because I can relate to it! I was depressed when I read THD,
but the story made me feel at ease and made me even more
comfortable! I want to thank Adreen for creating THD!
You inspire me! God bless you!
-Harriet

The Heartbreaker's Dare

By: Adreen Fernando

ISBN: 978-1-64434-003-5

Table of Contents

*Mom, Dad, Rachel, my friends, my best friend,
and the Wattpad community.*

FREE DOWNLOAD

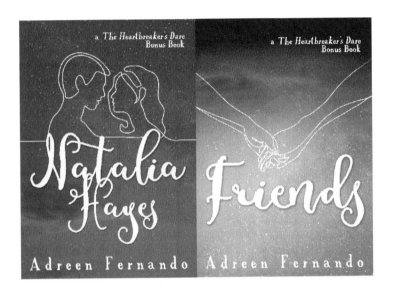

Get these freebies and MORE when you
sign up for the author's mailing list!

adreen-fernando.awesomeauthors.org

Prologue

Derek Matthews: known not only for being one of the sons of the eminent, worldwide billionaire who saved incalculable souls and lives, but also for his ghastly reputation in the small Canadian town, Peony Hallows.

He was the type of boy who everyone admired and wished to be friends with. He was carefree, comical, and devoted. He didn't give a damn about what the world could be like.

He *was*.

He changed.

Presently, all the girls have noticed how insensitive he can be, but they have no idea why. Why is he nothing but a straightforward, classic heartbreaker? They had this question in the back of their minds for quite a long time; they stayed away from him, knowing he's nothing but pure misfortune.

Everyone, girls and boys alike, has the misplaced optimism that they can change him—they believe that the whole "bad boy" vibe is a façade; that the genuine Derek Matthews is merely refusing to blossom.

Maybe they're right.

Maybe they're just dumb.

Derek has a bad temper. Bipolar? No. Bipolar doesn't even describe him. Using the word *bipolar* to describe someone's anger issues is incorrect, wrong, unfair, and illogical. It's a wicked judgment. He's solely bleak.

The boys abhor him. Nevertheless, clandestinely they crave to be just like him. Why wouldn't they? He has everything: he's a celebrity, he's wealthy, he's undeniably attractive, and he has a wonderful family.

He doesn't give a damn about people, except for the ones he adores. Let them bawl their eyes out. Let them tell their parents about him. Let them do *anything,* and he still won't learn his lesson. He seriously does not give a damn about people.

Obviously, if Derek is a heartbreaker—he uses girls. Then again, he doesn't use them for sexual tendencies. He just kisses them, dates them, and then breaks them.

He broke numerous hearts in his school. Various girls were blind to understand what a malicious player Derek Matthews is.

He broke their hearts and left them in despair. Just like how some people did to him – just left his heart there, in his ribcage, fractured and gradually shattering.

He's the callous, cold-hearted, bleak heartbreaker.

He has no heart. No feelings.

Right?

*   *   *

The music was ear-splitting, thundering, and presumably ached people's eardrums. I was leaning against a thick tree, sipping my Red Bull that's combined with pungent alcohol. The obscured sky permitted thin rays of the crescent moon to beam through, cunningly and graciously touching us. The trees were flourished with fairy lights.

People danced around like wild hooligans. They stomped the ground like aggravated elephants – howling, laughing and just enjoying the exhilarating occasion. They propelled their hands in the atmosphere compacted with reeking cigarette smoke, the fluid in their red cups leaping out and splattering their clothes. They didn't care. They preceded singing, some stumbling a few steps further and plummeting onto their faces. Hidden in the murky corners, various kissed their partners and hook-ups roughly, towing them somewhere more secure to pleasure themselves.

A nippy hand touched my shoulder. The leaves beneath me noisily crunched. I turned to see Hannah Smith, a girl only two months younger than me. She smiled blissfully, attempting to padlock our eyes romantically. I returned the smile. It was a fake one, of course.

I gulped down my drink, enjoying the sweltering sensation of alcohol sprinting down my throat. I threw the cup to a side, swathing my arms around Hannah's waist.

"Hey, baby," I whispered into her ear, my words vaguely stretching. I caught the eyes of my best friend on the other side of the bonfire, standing next to a girl. He shook his head at me with discontent. I knew he reviled to see me like this – getting wasted, getting rid of all the sentiments ensnared in me, wasting it on the girls…I knew he reviled to see me as a bully.

Hannah giggled and wrapped her arms around my neck. Honestly, I find it bizarre that girls are still attracted to me, yet they know that I'm nothing but bad karma. They consider that they can "bring the good out of me" and "destroy the badness of me". Ha, in their wildest dreams. They don't even know what's going on in my life.

I tugged Hannah into a kiss. She immediately kissed back. The kiss was meaningless like the other kisses I've encountered with other girls. They weren't passionate. Just hollow, insincere and inane. The kiss continued for several rapid minutes until I softly pulled away and lugged Hannah somewhere where no one was around. She giggled even more as I pressed her up against a tree and situated both of my hands on her hips.

I kissed her, pretending that I'm buried deep in this dull moment. She tugged locks of my black hair, and I muffled a phony moan into her mouth. Her hands dived underneath my shirt, mischievously tracing up my athletic chest.

I grabbed her surprisingly warm hands, not wanting her to do anything else. I leaned backward, her untamed pants wafting on my face, our hairs untidy.

Smirking at her, I took two steps backward, ticking my tongue, shaking my head as if she's a troubling kid.

"What?" Hannah demanded, confounded as to why I moved away.

"Hannah, really?" I said, crossing my arms over my chest. "Everyone knew I'm nothing but bad luck, and yet here you are, thinking that I love you when I wholeheartedly don't."

She frowned, registering the words. Her eyebrows drew apart, realization slaughtering her like an unmanageable train sliding over her body attached to a train track. "Derek—"

"Hannah, I don't love you. It was a game."

Tears unhurriedly flooded her eyes. She didn't shatter our gaze. She didn't feel mortified to weep in front of me. "I don't get it," she whispered. "Why are you like this? What did we ever do to you to make you resent us? What did we ever do to you to make you become like this?"

I shrugged. "The answer doesn't need to be mentioned."

"It does. Everyone hates you, but they don't want to because they loved you…they missed you as their friend."

"We're not in kindergarten anymore, Hannah. We can't all be friends. Friends come and go. They're not forever."

"Still, why? Why can't you go back to the Derek Matthews we knew? The *world* knew? Are you like this because of your—"

"It doesn't matter," I interposed. "I played you, Hannah. You were blind to see the tricks. I played you." She lowered her head, mortified. I took a large step forward, placing a finger underneath her chin and raising her head for our eyes to congregate. "Go. Run to your parents and tell them about your first break up."

Her lower lip wavering, her face suddenly hardened with antipathy. She raised her hand, attempting to slap me but I caught her wrist. She winced as my grip tightened, my knuckles whitening.

"You're a bloody arsehole," she snapped, her voice unsteady, her eyes pooling with tears.

"You're bloody late to realise that," I responded, mimicking her British accent.

"Don't you even care about people?"

"No."

"You don't even care about their feelings?"

"Why should I?"

She remained hushed for a minute, examining my face with her moistening eyes. Then, she whispered: "What the hell happened to you? Why the hell are you like this?"

I simply shrugged once again. "I dunno. I guess the feelings want to be seen."

"Feeli—" She was cut off by a yelp as I gently shove her rearwards, her back battering the bark of the tree.

"Just go, Hannah."

She scrutinized me once again, not whispering or making any noise. Finally, she moved away, silently sauntering to the elated cheers and the flickering flames of the bonfire. I didn't look at her, my eyes concentrating on how the leaves fluttered as the nippy breeze stroked past me. When I did turn to look at her, her eyes assembled with mine, and they held that one question I continuously see from everyone:

What the hell happened to this boy?

Chapter One

Dare

Derek Matthews

I chucked two tablets into my mouth to relieve and satisfy my brain from the horrible hangover, gulping it with water. I exited the kitchen, promenading through the various hallways and corridors, hearing Luke's loud snores from his bedroom.

Outside, I bounded to my golden Lamborghini, shimmering underneath the presence of the morning star.

A security guard standing by the grand gates protecting my mansion grinned at me. "Have a good day, Mr. Little Matthews."

I nodded my head in response and smiled, slipping into my vehicle and roaring the engine to life. The security guards were hired by my aunt. They work from mornings to evenings and sometimes sleep over in the mansion. I talk to all of them. They are all friendly and nice. The security guard pressed a button on the remote he's holding. The gates creaked forwards, formulating a vast space for me to ride through. The radio played *Mercy* by Shawn Mendes.

After a couple of minutes, the building of my school came into my eyesight. I pulled my Lamborghini into the parking area, jumping out, and slammed the door shut, locking it and sauntering towards the large entryway. People offered me smiles as I strolled past them with a cold-stoned face. Some eyed me warily. Some gossiped to each other. I rolled my eyes as a couple of girls approached me, attempting to begin a conversation. I muttered to them to go away and quickened my speed of walk to find my friends. Well, all of my friends are just bigtime assholes except for Theo Romano.

Up ahead, is the girl who was my greatest friend. Her head is facing downwards at some book she's reading. A wicked thought popped into my mind. *No*, my subconscious scolded. *Don't do it.*

I stuck out my leg, obscuring her path.

The girl who wasn't looking up stumbled over my foot and crashed to the floor. Everyone in the hallway watched the scene and cracked into snickers and howls of laughter. Her cheeks turned scarlet from embarrassment as she hunted the floor for her spectacles. She found them and rapidly slid them up her nose, stroking tresses of her dark brunette hair behind her ears. She blinked numerous times, and then gradually looked up to lock eyes with me.

I grinned as she gingerly rose up. My heart bawled with disenchantment. "Oops, sorry, I didn't see you." I winked.

April Levesque clenched her hands into fists. She grabbed her bag and smacked my head with it. I staggered backward, battering into a wall of lockers. I winced at the harsh impact, my backbone throbbing in agony at the slight pain.

I didn't see that coming.

"Oops, sorry, I didn't see you," April mimicked my voice. A few people snickered.

"*Ooooh!*" some guy in the hallway hollered, "that chick — don't know her name — brought down Derek Matthews. Awesome shit! Man, I should've recorded it on Snapchat."

April smirked at me, huffed, spun around, and walked away.

I scowled when April raised her right hand to flip me off with the middle finger, and I scowled again at the guy who made a comment. I straightened myself and slapped the guy's face (yes, I slapped him), and he timbered to the floor. He looked up, his nose soaked with blood. People's eyes widened and took fearful steps away from me as I walked through the corridor, the nerves in my arm quivering with fury.

That little brat...I'm going to get her back.

*   *   *

"Who was that little chick?" Theo Romano, my best friend, enquired around lunch time. We were both sitting in a park that is situated next to the school building, relaxing on the benches as the sunlight kissed our skin. This is our daily routine: sneaking out of school and just letting go of the distress by smoking—well, not Theo. He doesn't smoke. The refreshing, cool breeze tickled past us, shoving away the hotness. Trees swayed as if they're dancing. Birds fluttered above us, their shadows reflecting on the ground as they pass by, and traffic noises could be heard in the distance.

"What little chick?" I asked with no interest, taking out a cigarette packet. An old woman ambled past us, offering us confounded glances when she perceived the cigarette packet. She arched an eyebrow at me as if to say, *Boy, what are you doing?* I only rolled my eyes. That woman needs to get a life.

"The one you tripped her over," Theo reminded. Theo is fairly an attractive guy: his sharp cheekbones, curly, loose blond hair tousling his head, enthralling, light-hazel eyes along with a perfect tan complexion and his status as half Mexican and Lithuanian rewarded him the second position of the most wanted guy in Peony Hallows High School. It's a title he held with satisfaction. The first most wanted guy in Peony Hallows High School is, obviously, me.

"Oh, she's actually a little brat. She smacked me with her bag," I grumbled.

Theo laughed. "I've heard about that. Man, I never knew April Levesque could do something awesome like that. And then she just echoed your words: 'Oops, sorry, I didn't see you!'." A simple laugh escaped his throat. "That's so classic, man."

I glared at Theo. "Why are you even my friend?" I muttered. "Friends are supposed to help someone and stick up for someone, not to stick up with another person who nobody likes."

"Actually, I'm your friend because you pretty much begged me to be your friend because you don't want to look like a loner. And nobody likes her?" He arched his eyebrows, dubious. "Are you sure about that? I like her. She's nice. And something tells me that puppy-heart inside you likes her, too."

I threw a cigarette at Theo, avoiding his words. He caught it and threw it in the trash can near us.

"Thanks for the offer, Derek, but you know I don't smoke."

"That's why you're lame."

"And that's why you're demented. I love this talk, it's great."

"Because you're insulting me? Is that why you like this 'great' talk?"

"Pretty much, yeah," Theo admitted, smirking light-heartedly.

I poked the cigarette in between my lips and lightened up the end.

"How was the party last night?" Theo then questioned. "Did you have any fun? Because I certainly did."

"Really, what happened?"

"I finally asked out Natalia Hayes, man," Theo whooped, grinning like an idiot.

Natalia Hayes is a gorgeous girl. She's part of the popular girls, but she's much better than the others. She's not bratty. She's just a sweet and a feisty diva. I would date her, but I wouldn't because I don't want to hurt Theo's feelings since he's my best friend.

"Wow, you're lovesick," I muttered.

"I know, and I like it. The feelings you get when you're in love is heartwarming. When you fall in love, you will understand. Well, *if* you fall in love. Since you're the player, I don't think you'll ever fall in love. Nevertheless, I think you'll be a lone man in the future with no wife and kids."

"I will be married."

"To a bitch, yeah I know."

I exhaled my cigarette. A puff of reeking smoke escaped my lips and spiralled into the atmosphere. "Anyway, Hannah is gone," I said, looking at him. "I practically ripped Hannah Smith's heart."

"Now, do you see why you're demented, Derek?" Theo muttered. "You're too cold-hearted."

"I'm not demented. And I know that I'm cold-hearted. I like it, honestly," I lied, raking a hand through my black hair.

"You know there are other ways to get rid of it," said Theo. "Smoking won't help you, Derek. Drugs and hurting people, too! How do you think your parents would feel if they find out that their son is being a dickhead?"

"They're not here, so their thoughts don't really matter anymore." Saying those words caused a sudden brawl to palpitate in my chest, right where my heart is. Rude words, I know. But no one really comprehends what I'm going through. I loathe being like this but witnessing others happy with their cherished ones makes me envious and aggravated. I want someone to realise my true colours. I want someone to notice everything.

"What about Mike?" Theo said. "What did he say? He said that wasting the pain on others is worthless. It won't do anything good. It won't *bring* anything good."

"I can't control myself, Theo," I muttered. "I can't control them."

"Control what?"

"The demons."

Theo stared at me, pity cramping his eyes. He heaved an exasperated sigh, rubbing his head as if all of this is too much. "What about the angels?"

"I don't have any of them. They're not helping me."

"Mike said that the only angel who can destroy the demons is you. You gotta learn how to kill the demons."

"I don't think I can."

Demons are untameable. They're frenzied, delusional. They're the trigger of negative emotions — of misery, of anger, of death. Angels are calm and harmonic. They're the trigger of positive emotions — of happiness, of love, of freedom.

"Theo, I have no other girl to break."

"What about Samantha Moore?"

"Nope."

"Macy Harvor?"

"Nope."

"Daniella Willberg?"

"Nope." I tossed the cigarette into the bin closest to me. "Man, I think I destroyed all the girls in the school."

Theo's eyebrows twitched, considering for a long moment. He dramatically tapped his chin with his fingers. I knew he's only doing that to fake his deliberations. His eyes radically brightened, beaming a smile. "How about April Levesque?" he suggested.

I blinked. "What?"

"Consider it as a dare, Derek," Theo decided. "I dare you to make April Levesque fall in love with you. Once you did, break her or love her."

"Break her or love her?" I echoed.

"You can break her, or you can love her."

"What makes you think that I'll love her?"

He gave me an *are-you-kidding-me* look. "You had a huge crush on her when you guys were besties."

"And that makes you think I'll love her?"

"Definitely."

I scoffed. "I won't."

"Maybe you're blind to realise this, but we can't control our hearts, too. The heart wants what it wants. So, you gonna do it or not?"

I stared at him, contemplating.

Has Theo *seen* that girl? To be honest, I rarely see that girl around here, but I heard rumours that April Levesque talks to no one other than herself. People clap when they see her...but they clap their hands over their eyes, so they don't have to see her ugliness. She's destined to be alone. I can tell. Hanging out with her might humiliate my popularity, and people will start to think that I'm gentle, sweet, and weak, and not strong, dangerous, or bad.

Oh, who am I kidding? She's not ugly. She's actually really cute. April's parents and my parents kind of knew each other when they were in Peony Hallows High School, so April and I knew each other since we were babies. But it was her older brother, Mike Levesque, who properly introduced me to her when we were ten or younger. Plus, Mike was my brother's best friend.

Whenever I come over to April's house, I always see her reading at least eight hundred books at once, paper and online. Not joking. She's literally a bookworm, but cuter.

I had a profound, colossal crush on her. She never had a crush on me; she just saw me as a good friend. I was obviously not satisfied but seeing her every day made me feel as if I was the luckiest little boy alive. I always teased her, mocked her. I was always confident when she was around.

The crush wore off when…never mind. I'll just say this: as time bypassed, there was an extending distance between us, and we became frenemies.

"Why, though? Why do you want me to do that?"

"Because it'll be fun."

"But…"

Theo cocked an eyebrow. "Are you refusing? Dude, it's a simple dare. All you have to do is hang out with her for a couple of weeks, get her to fall in love with you and *bam!* You can break her heart and see her cry, or love her and let your heart be happy for once. And judging by the fact that she smacked you with their bag, if she ever comes to me and asks me if I know about this dare, I'll say no so I won't get hit by her bag. I'm very valuable to mankind."

"You're only valuable to the wall, not to mankind."

Theo rolled his eyes. "Derek, what do you have against April?"

"Nothing."

"Nothing? Is it because she's Derek-proof?"

"She's not Derek-proof."

"She is. And that's *very* rare in this world, you know?"

I scowled. "She's just smarter than the other girls. All the girls think that they can change me because my rudeness is a way of 'hiding my true emotions'."

"They're true, though," Theo muttered. "The true Derek Matthews is just refusing to blossom. I know you had a small crush on April when Mike was still here…"

"But that all changed," I snapped. "I don't like her. She's cute. But I don't like her. Too annoying and too rude."

"And you're not?"

I'm still wondering if it was really worth it to see the pain in April's eyes. I visualised a scenario of April Levesque crying tears of heartbreak. Thinking about it made my lips twitch into a smirk. I made a mental note to get that girl back after she smacked me with her bag, after all. This dare is payback.

"Deal," I finally decided. "This is going to be easy, dude."

"Great. You have five weeks to make April fall in love with you and break her heart."

The school bell buzzed, and we both groaned, straightening ourselves up.

*   *   *

I pushed the doors open. The hallway was bustling with chatter as students thundered out of the cafeteria, strolling to their next lessons. I roamed my eyes through the crowd of people, searching for the girl that I vowed to break her heart.

I padded my way upstairs to the Maths area. April is in nearly all of my period classes, and usually, when it's Maths, she's the first one in the line. However, I didn't see her there when I stopped next to the classroom door. Maybe she's going to be late?

A group of not-good-looking guys (geeks, I presume) walked up the hallway, chitchatting and guffawing. Maybe they'll know where April Levesque is.

"Hey!"

All four of them swerved to me in unison. One of them gasped, astonished that I greeted them with an enthusiastic *Hey* and smiled.

"Hi, guys. How are you doing?" I asked.

They all blinked, gaping at me with amazement.

"I…uh…" one guy stammered, swallowing.

I smirked, liking the effect I have on people. I am well-known in Peony Hallows—not as a player, but as the son of the illustrious worldwide billionaire who saved countless lives and souls. A billionaire who owned a prosperous company named after our surname: The Matthews Industry. The Matthews Industry aided many people as possible across the whole globe – the poor, the homeless, the hungry, etc, etc. My entire family is also a bunch of businesspeople who earn millions of money each year. So, I guess I would consider myself a lucky boy.

"You all good?"

The boys all gave me awkward responses to my greeting, only one or two able to look at me properly.

"You're Alex, right?" I pointed to the red-haired boy, who furrowed his eyebrows.

"My name is Sam," he muttered dryly.

"Okay. Whatever." I don't really give a crap about people, so it's kind of expected for me not to remember people's names in my school. "Have you seen April Levesque?"

One of the boys raised his eyebrows, bewildered by my question. He had a long, pointed nose that made me wonder if his name is Pinocchio. "Isn't she in your class?"

"I know that," I said. "But she's usually the first one to be in the line."

Then red-haired boy, Sam, analysed the line. "Maybe she's late? Why are you worrying about her?"

I frowned. *Is that what they're presuming?* "I'm not worrying about her."

Sam raised his eyebrows, sceptical. He then shrugged and sauntered away, his friends following after, not even bothered to say a polite goodbye to me. Assholes.

The door swung open, revealing the Nigerian teacher, Mr. Nelson. He told us to come in, and we obeyed, flopping down into our seats. The entire class, Mr. Nelson explained to us about God knows what. I didn't bother to pay attention.

It's funny that I was horrible at Science and English, yet I was good at Math. I was in the top set for Math. The top set only consisted of a small number of students. The rest were either in the middle set or in the bottom set.

Subsequently, the door creaked open. I turned my head around to see a girl standing in the doorway, her arms clutching her books; a pair of glasses resting on the bridge of her nose; her hair long and dark and cascading down her shoulders; her eyes so dark that it seemed black.

"Miss Levesque." Mr. Nelson was clearly annoyed that she was late to class just like other teachers. "You are twenty minutes late. *Twenty minutes.* Care to explain why?"

"Sorry, sir," April replied apologetically. "I…lost track of time."

Mr. Nelson arched an eyebrow while the class snickered because of her stupid excuse.

"This is the third time you're late, April, which means that I must put you in detention," Mr. Nelson said. "But I won't."

Teacher's pet, I thought.

I heard from a lot of people that April Levesque was liked by all the teachers in the school—even Mr. Taylor likes her, and he's the main cranky English teacher with a grim face. Some people envy April and scoff at her because whenever she's late to class or forgets her homework (which she rarely does), the teachers give her another chance and weren't even bothered to give her a detention. But when it comes to the other students or me, they instantly give us half an hour of deadly detention. I have to admit, that is unfair.

April smiled with delight. "Thank you, Mr. Nelson."

Mr. Nelson returned the smile. "You're welcome. Go on, sit down."

She approached her seat, her eyes locking with mine for a moment as she does so. I winked, expecting her to giggle or smile because that's how all the girls are like to me. But she just ignored me and slid down a seat behind me, taking out her exercise book and began writing the date and title.

"Aye, April, how was it like to get tripped over by Derek Matthews?" some guy asked.

April didn't even look up.

"Man, it was awesome when you smacked him with your bag," another guy howled.

This time, April smiled in agreement.

"And it'll be awesome if you just shut up," I growled angrily at the two boys. "Or else you will end up on the floor, bleeding." I offered them a sweet, innocent, naive smile. They rolled their eyes and continued their work.

*   *   *

Once class was over, I walked to my next class which is Science—my least favourite subject.

I spotted April walking ahead of me, and I increased my speed to catch up with her.

"Hey," I greeted once I have reached her.

Her long, crimped brunette hair cascaded around her shoulders as she looked at me. Her expression was instantly tedious and lacklustre when her eyes met mine. Normally, I have that effect on people when they stare at me is if I'm a famous celebrity—which I am since my father is a prominent billionaire. But April…she just stares at me as if I'm living in the trash can.

It's very rare for me to be this close to her. I see her every day in school, doing nothing but endless reading and listening to her own style of music. She never notices me, never meets my eye, while I just stand there near my group of friends or by the locker, gazing at her as if she's an angel descending from Heaven made only for me, an angel God sent to obliterate my wicked sentiments.

She's beautiful like always: her eyes are the colour of dark chocolate, and in the glow of the artificial lights above us, they shimmer and sparkle like jets. Her black-framed glasses make her look dorky yet cute. Yes, I called her cute. And I feel no shame calling her cute. I may have had a crush on her, and the crush may have died, but the side effects are still breathing in me.

There's always something remarkable about her that makes my heart quiver, waver, flutter…as if my heart is finally alive.

"Hey," she replied glumly.

"How are you?" I asked, flashing her one of my charming smiles. My voice trembled vaguely, but she didn't notice. An intoxicating, engaging, saccharine aroma molested me, and I furtively inhaled with no shame. Lavenders. She still smells of lavender. How gratifying.

April looked at me with a peculiar expression before saying, "Fine." She then returned her attention to the front.

A few people who passed gave us odd, suspicious, bewildered looks. They're probably wondering why the most-wanted, sexiest guy in the school is hanging out with April Levesque.

"So…" I said. The atmosphere was so damn awkward, I wanted to run away. Usually, it was so easy to make a conversation—especially when she is around. But that was before. "How's life?"

Instead of answering, April glanced at me. "What do you want, Derek?"

"What? Can't I talk to my friend?"

"I'm not your friend. Not anymore."

I clenched my jaw. "That's true, but I can talk to someone, right?"

"You can," she said. "But it's just weird for the school's asshole to hang out with the school's loner."

I blinked. "What did you call me?"

She never called me an asshole before. She mainly named me as an idiot, jerk, dimwit, or shitface. In fact, she's the first one to call me asshole. Except for my best friend, Theo.

"I just called you an asshole. Is that a problem?" she asked.

"No," I denied through gritted teeth, "It's not a problem at all. I just don't like the word."

"But it suits your personality."

I balled my hands into tight fists, composing the antagonism. April noticed this immediately, and her lips twitched up and down as she attempted to keep a straight face. I know she's enjoying this, and I hate it. Damn her.

"Please don't ever talk to me, come near me, or look at me," she said before I could reply, "I don't want to get infected by your viruses."

"I don't have any—"

She entered the Science classroom, not allowing me to finish my sentence.

*   *   *

I found myself gliding my gaze from the Physics teacher to the window, then to the board full of words that I don't understand.

Science is not my strongest subject, and that goes for all of the topics: Chemistry, Physics, and Biology. Physics is just Maths. The only reason I'm in all the top sets for all topics of Science is because I cheated in all the exams, and the teachers never realised it.

Sighing, I looked at the other students, who seemed as uninterested as me. I opened my bottle and chugged down the white wine. I closed it before my eyes drifted to the girl sitting on the left side in front of me.

April seemed to be expectedly focused on the science teacher as he explained about something that's related to numbers. Yet, I could see that exhausted glint in her dark eyes.

Her eyes are too dark. Almost black. It's as if her eyes are a warning of misfortune.

I got five weeks to complete this damn dare. I can do it. I know I can. It's not that hard, actually. Theo thinks I'll love her? Pfft, as if. My crush on her is long gone. It's dead. At the same time, my subconscious is laughing at me, probably thinking, *This guy is whipped*, whilst screaming at me to stare at April for a little longer.

I stood up. Several eyes immediately moved to me. I approached April, politely asking the boy next to her to move. The timid boy seemed frightened, and he gingerly and hastily moved away, flopping down in a seat at the back.

The science teacher raised an eyebrow. "Mr. Matthews?"

I sat down next to April. "I'm changing seats, sir. Permanently."

The teacher blinked, confused. Then, he shrugged and swerved around, continuing whatever he was doing.

I felt April's eyes staring at the side of my face as I placed my stuff on my table. I turned around. Our eyes convened. She's dressed in dark jeans and a long-sleeved emerald shirt which seemed too big for her. Her face is pale with an adorning, cerise flush painting her cheeks due to the nippiness.

"What are you doing?" she demanded.

"Do you need to change your glasses?" I asked her. "I'm sitting next to you."

She scowled at me. "Yeah, I can see that—"

"Then why did you ask me?"

"Why are you sitting next to me, Derek?"

The students were secretly eavesdropping on our conversation. From their expressions, I could tell we're more interesting than the teacher.

"Because I want to."

"Out of everyone in the class you chose to sit next to *me?*"

"Basically," I agreed.

The bewilderment in her dark eyes crawled out of her eyeballs and took over her features. She exhaled sharply, as if my presence is just a nightmare to her. She returned her attention to the teacher, and we sat together in silence. Here and then, April would jot down notes, and answer questions. The atmosphere lurking around us is too awkward to live in. Nevertheless, an idea came to mind.

My fingers uncertainly rose up to latch onto her hairband, pulling it. She tied her hair into a ponytail. It doesn't really suit her. I prefer if her hair is out and loose – it makes her more attractive. In my opinion, at least.

"What are you—" April was cut off by her hair descending onto her shoulders like a rock tumbling down a mountain.

Tentatively, I leaned forward to place a gentle kiss on her cold cheek. Her breath hitched up as my mouth warmed her skin, and the students that watched us echoed her gasp. A blush adorned her cheeks, and I leaned back in my chair, smirking. That probably would've given me a head start in my game.

"What the hell was that?" April asked, frustrated as she took out a tissue and dabbed her cheek with it hastily, her nose scrunching up in disgust as she shivered nastily as if my lips are a virus to her.

"A kiss, obviously."

April stared at me for a long moment, some type of emotion (which I'm sure I've seen before) wondering in her dark eyes. "You are literally asking to get slapped again, aren't you?" she muttered.

"Uhm, no. Not really. Why would you say that?"

She did not respond as the bell buzzed throughout the whole school building. April straightened herself up and cracked her hand across my face, catching me off-guard.

The whole class ruptured into hysterical laughter. One of them howled, "This shit is lit, man."

"Ow!" I complained, my hand reaching up to my cheek where she has slapped me. I rubbed my cheek furiously. She huffed and shoved past me, causing my ribs to crash against the edge of the table.

Maybe Theo is right.

Maybe she is Derek-proof.

*　　*　　*

"Aye, Derek." One of my good friends, Jackson, swung an arm around me as we walked the hallway. "I heard you accepted a dare to make April Levesque fall in love with you."

"Yup," I said, raking a hand through my black hair locks. "Don't tell anyone or else the game won't go right."

"Of course, I won't. It's just that I don't think it's—"

"Any success with Levesque, man?" Theo interrupted, popping his head in between Jackson and me.

"She called me an asshole," I grumbled. "That's progress, right?"

Jackson laughed. "No, that's called failing. Man, I love that girl. She is feistier than I thought she would be. Honestly, I never knew April would have the nerve to say that right in front of your face judging by the fact that you're a ruthless bull sometimes."

"She smacked Derek with her bag after he tripped her over," Theo said. "That's kind of expected from her."

"She also slapped me after I kissed her cheek," I added in a grumble. "She looks at me as if I'm a scum of the Earth. My looks, my charm, *everything* about me isn't affecting her at all!"

"I told you she's Derek-proof," Theo said for the second time today, grinning.

Jackson nodded in agreement. "Why would you kiss her, though? You should've given her time."

"I kissed other girls' cheeks before and it charmed them, but with April…"

"Derek-proof," Jackson and Theo said in unison.

"Can you two shut up?" I muttered angrily.

Jackson and Theo both grinned, winking at me before walking away to their classes.

When I entered the English classroom, I flopped down into my seat, sighing as I rested my head on my propped arm.

The English teacher informed us that he has to go somewhere for a few minutes. "No monkey business," he added before disappearing behind the door.

I looked over at April. Her head is facing downwards, calmly reading a book as the class exploded into rounds of chatter.

This is my chance.

Chapter Two

Daddy

April Levesque

I flipped to the next page of my novel. I utterly love books, especially adventure books with romance, drama, and mystery. I don't mind science fiction romance books. Whenever I read a book, my mind always wander off as I daydream about my very own fantasy world. I always daydream where I meet my true love and get poisoned by a villain so my knight-in-shining-armour would come to the rescue...yeah, I know, very lame and cheesy. I always wished my life has some romance. I wished I lived in the land of stories where everything is perfect — where I won't get bullied or insulted, where I could just relax peacefully and not get anxious about everything. I wish I could rest in peace...

Suddenly, a guy sat next to me. His skin was light brown and untarnished. He had droopy eyes. His lips were flabby, and his dark russet hair was coiled. His eyebrows were sleek and plump, and glistening on his right ear was an earring.

Carl Prot smiled at me. "Hi. I'm Carl."

I returned the smile. "Hi. I'm April."

"I know who you are. So, nice book?" He nodded at the novel.

I nodded.

"What's it about?"

"Uhm…adventures…death…"

"Sounds interesting. So, life's good?"

I felt uncomfortable with the way Carl scrutinized me. I wanted to cower backward, to hide myself, to stand up and walk away and read in peace, but I seemed to be frozen under his gaze. "Uhm…yeah. Life's good."

He grinned, his teeth remarkably white and shimmering. "Awesome. You're really pretty, by the way."

I subconsciously thrust my black framed glasses up my nose, something I typically do when I'm distressed and gauche. "Uh…thanks?" I'm not really used to these types of compliments. "You're pretty, too?" The compliment came out more of a perplexing question than I intended it to be.

"Your hair is really nice. Soft, right?"

I blinked. *What the hell is going on?* I'm so damn confused. I thought these compliments from guys only occur in dreams?

"Did you want it to be hard?" I responded derisively.

He bit his lip, and his legs suddenly trembled. My puzzlement intensified, and fear was combined with the look he gave me. He looked like a paedophile at the moment.

"Uhm, are you okay?" I nodded at his legs.

He laughed monotonously. "Yeah, I'm fine. Just not feeling good. I mean, I am good, but it's irritating and—"

Suddenly, he was cut off when a tan, muscular, smouldering arm slithered around my waist from behind. A hot chest was pressed on my back, and the fingers of a muscular arm coiled my hair.

What the...?

Abhorrence oozed on Carl's face, as he looked at the person behind me. People gave me odd looks as the person who has wrapped their arms kissed my head.

"Is he bothering you, baby?" he asked, his warm breath fanning my right cheek.

"No," Carl answered before I could. "She's fine. Piss off."

The person's grasp around me tightened. "Watch your mouth and leave April alone. She doesn't like you."

Carl crossed his arms over his chest. "You don't even know what she's thinking," he challenged. "Who are you to tell me to leave her alone?"

I tilted my head up to see who is behind me. I groaned. Great, another pervert!

It's the last person I wanted to see in the universe. Derek Matthews—son of the prosperous, prominent billionaire; the celebrity of Peony Hallows; the Heartbreaker; the Player; the Asshole; the guy who annoyed me ever since we were kids; the guy who used to be my best friend; the guy who constantly teased me whenever he was near me. He was *so* annoying, but I admired his frustrating charisma most of the time.

"I've been with her long enough to know what she's thinking, prick," Derek said brusquely, glowering at Carl, his celestial blue eyes intense. "You don't even know her like how I do. Or did. And she's uncomfortable by your erection, so I advise you to leave the girl and let her read her book in peace."

My eyes widened. *Erection? Oh, my God. Was that why his legs were quaking? Oh, my God...did I just give a guy a boner?* Holy unicorns, this is an April Levesque record! I mean, it is disgusting, but if you think about it...most girls get flattered if you give a guy a boner!

Okay, I sounded weird.

"She doesn't like you, too, Derek. So why don't you go away?"

"Who says she doesn't like me?"

"I don't like you," I muttered, but neither of them heard me.

"Why are you acting as if she's yours? She's not an object."

"I know she's not an object. I'm just telling you that she doesn't like you. And in her head, she thinks she's not mine, but in my head she is mine."

Derek pressed his lips to the skin of my neck and gently sucked on it. I gasped sharply, shivers trickling down my spine as his teeth nibbled on my skin.

Freaked out, I squealed in panic and jammed my elbow sideways into his chest. Derek collapsed sideways, plummeting to the floor. People started giggling at the scene as Derek hissed and groaned, rubbing the back of his neck from the impact and his ribs where I battered him.

"What the hell, April?" Derek grumbled. "Why the hell did you do that?"

"You just don't go around and kiss people's necks, pervert!" I snapped, rubbing the area where the shoulder connects with the neck.

"I was only trying to save you from *that* pervert," Derek snapped, heaving himself back to the seat next to me. Carl suppressed his laughter and stood up to walk away to his friends who were all laughing at Derek.

A faint blush coated Derek's cheeks from humiliation. Ha, take that.

I whined, a pained expression on my face. "Nooo. Now, I'm going to get STDs."

The whole class burst into endless laughter at my comment, and a glower rested on Derek's face. He compressed his hands into furious fists, maintaining his aggravation.

"Damn you, asshole," I muttered. "Damn you. Why does God have to curse me with you?"

The door swung open, and the English teacher came in. Derek continued to glare at me for a minute before he sauntered away, sliding down into his seat with an irritated expression. I smiled, glad that he went away.

*   *   *

I opened my locker, putting all the books in my bag inside and checking my homework diary to see if I have any homework left to do. Thankfully, I didn't—which means that I could just relax at home and watch TV. Hmm, *Teen Wolf* sounds great to watch again. Excitement bubbled inside me when I thought of that amazing TV show. I absolutely love Teen Wolf, and I am absolutely a true fangirl.

As I zipped my bag, my locker door suddenly slammed shut. I flinched and glanced up. In front of me are the last people on Earth I wanted to see—Brigit Sanders and her group of rich, popular, bratty girls.

"Hey, April," Brigit greeted, smiling at me.

I returned the smile, feeling anxiety filling my chest. I immediately knew they are going to humiliate me, cuss at me, and insult me. This is the one thing I hate about rich, popular kids— they think that they can do anything and pick on anyone they want. Well, not all rich and popular kids are like that, but Brigit and her clan are utterly brutal and horrible.

A girl behind Brigit took out her phone. The girl smirked as she turned her phone around, showing me a picture of me.

"This is a nice picture for my story on Snapchat, don't you think?"

"Just don't add a filter, Tiffany," Brigit said. "People need to know how ugly this bitch really is." She looked at me, a cruel smile plastered on her face. "I feel very sorry for you because you're so ugly, April. But I feel sorrier for myself and the people in the school because we have to look at you."

My jaw dropped slowly, my heart aching with hurt. I wanted to snap something harsh back at them, but the words wouldn't come out.

Brigit grinned. "What's the matter, April?"

"Nothing," I muttered, suddenly feeling the hurt vanishing, replaced by impudence. "I'm just thinking that you should post a picture on Snapchat to increase your reputation as the school's brattiest slu—"

My words were cut off by an astonished gasp from Tiffany. Tiffany's eyes widened, and she clamped her hand over her mouth, muffling the snickers. The girls inhaled sharp breaths in astonishment as Brigit's eyes glowered with antagonism

"Who the hell are you calling a slut, brat?" Brigit demanded, aggravated.

I mimicked a frown, tapping a finger on my chin. "Uhm…didn't you hear a thing I said? Or are you arrogantly deaf like Derek Matthews? Man, you two suit each other so perfectly! And who are you calling brat? At least I'm not the one who's going around, begging for a hookup and acting like an idiotic person who never experienced hospitality and kindness. So, I'm not the brat here, Brigit Sanders. You are." I then granted her a naive smile. "Have a nice day!"

I spun around and ambled away, grinning widely and proudly to myself, feeling blessed to know that I kind of kicked that girl's ass.

*   *   *

It was starting to get shady when I arrived home. I was still trying to find my keys in my bag when I realized the door was already unlocked. Frowning, I stepped into the shadowy hallway, reaching for the wall so I can switch on the lights. I noticed a silhouette in front of me, and before I could even react to that, my hand that was supposed to be on the wall was now on someone's face. *Who else is in here with me?*

My heart pounded faster as I let out a loud scream. But the weird thing is that I heard someone screaming back. I swiftly banged my hand on the light switch. The bulbs in the hallway flared a happy lustre instantaneously, killing the darkness. In front of me is my brother, Ethan, with a bat clutched in his hand, also looking terrified.

"What the hell, Ethan? You nearly scared me to death!" I yelled at him, my hand on my chest as I tried to calm myself.

"W-what, me? You're the one who made all the noise! I nearly killed you, April!" he yelled back with his eyes still wide open.

"With a bat?" I sneered.

"Yes!" Ethan exclaimed. "Bats may be a weak weapon for self-protection, but you never know!"

I rolled my eyes and bent down to take off my shoes. My younger brother is a year younger than me – he is fifteen going sixteen. I'm sixteen, turning seventeen in a couple of months. He tends to have a hobby to act like an immature, childish boy sometimes and doing ridiculous things like trying to smack me with a damn bat. Brothers are arrogant and juvenile. No lie.

"Where's Mom?" I asked as I entered the living room with him by my side.

"She went to the shops to get some groceries," my brother replied, sinking down onto the sofa and switching the TV on.

I cleared my throat. "Ethan, I thought you have a test in two days."

"Yup," he muttered, popping the 'p'.

"Then why are you not reviewing?"

Ethan looked at me. "Why are you acting as if you're my mother?"

"Just revise, Ethan."

"You're not the boss of me, April."

I raised an eyebrow. "Well, actually, I am since I'm older than you. And Mom did say you have to listen to me."

Ethan purposely ignored me. I sighed with frustration and snatched the TV remote off his hands.

"Hey!" he protested as he tried to get it back.

"Go and revise, Ethan. Then you can watch TV."

"It's in two days!"

"If you revise earlier you'll get better results."

"I'm a straight A student. I don't need to revise."

"Ethan. *Revise.*"

Ethan glared at me before he sighed with annoyance and stormed up the stairs. I hid the remote, just in case Ethan comes back down and try to watch TV without me realising.

I padded my way up the stairs and went inside my bedroom. I crashed onto my bed, sighing with boredom. I opened my book and started reading in an instant.

* * *

"Hey, Mom," I greeted as my mother pushed the buggy into the hallway warily, closing the door behind her.

"Hello, April," she replied, smiling at me tenderly. "How was school?"

"Good."

I picked up my baby sister from the buggy and held her in my arms. "Hey, Rosie."

Her reply was only a straightforward, tiny, adorable smile and she fidgeted with my heart pendant that was a present from my older brother.

We walked into the kitchen. Mom put the bags she was carrying on the kitchen island. "Where's Ethan?"

As soon as she said it, Ethan appeared in the doorway. He walked towards Mom, pecking her cheek as a greeting and walked to me, his eyes focused on Rosie. "Hey, Rosie."

Rosie held out her arms towards him, signalling him that she wants him to hold her. Ethan smiled, taking Rosie away as I felt disappointed, but I managed to get over it.

Mom took out the groceries from the shopping bags. She began putting most of them inside the fridge. "Your father called today," she announced.

Ethan and I both glance at her immediately.

Our dad is a soldier in the Canadian Armed Forces. He has been a soldier for seven years. We don't see him that very often. He only comes once a year to visit us and stays with us for a week or two, then he goes back to fighting in wars and battles. The last time we saw him was a year ago.

"What did he say?" I asked with pure curiosity. "Did he say he'll be coming back?"

Mom forced a smile at them; there was melancholy in her dark eyes. "He said that he might not make it to Canada, dear. You know how the civil war in Syria is like, honey. He admitted he…might not make it to Canada for a holiday."

My heart was shattered in disappointment at her reply. All hope was lost. *He might not make it.* I closed my eyes, forcing that thought to get out of my head before I start to sob. No. No, I believe that won't happen. I believe my father will make it and come back to us alive, healthy, and uninjured...but my hopelessness was rapidly taking over me.

What if my father doesn't make it?

Mom exhaled, her arms faintly shaking as if the tension at the thought of Dad not making it was pressuring her too much. "But he did say that he has time to Skype with us tonight." That made my heart flutter with appreciation and joy.

At least we get to chat with him.

*　　　*　　　*

As hours passed, it's finally time to Skype Dad. We all sat on the sofa, our shoulders brushing as we waited eagerly for Dad to answer the call. Rosie was sitting on my lap, fidgeting with my necklace. The necklace had a heart pendant, and my older brother gave it to me before he left.

The screen flickered for a moment. Then, the screen revealed our father with a bald head and eyes that were gleaming with contentment as we greeted him.

He grinned at us. "Hey, guys." His eyes leisurely drifted from Mom, to Ethan, to Rosie, and to me. "How's everybody doing?"

Mom was the first to reply: "We're doing great, Julian."

Dad's eyes focused on Ethan and me. "How's school, kids?"

"It's great," Ethan replied. "I won five medals for a sports event."

"Really? That's impressive, Ethan. What about you, April?"

"I got A for my Math, Science, English, Music and Art test," I noted. "And I got a job."

"A job?"

I nodded. "I'm working in a pet clinic. Temporarily."

"That's really good, April." His eyes darted down to Rosie. "Hey, Primrose. How are you, darling?"

Primrose. Reminds you of *The Hunger Games,* right? Well, let's just say that my older brother loved *The Hunger Games* and he wanted the second daughter in the family to be called *Primrose* because it sounded stunning and cute to him.

Rosie didn't do anything as a reply. She just stared at Dad in bewilderment as if she's trying to figure out who Dad was.

"Rosie," Mom said in a soothing voice. "This is Daddy. Say hi to Daddy, sweetie."

At that, Rosie smiled adoringly at Dad. She crawled over to the laptop. She touched the screen, as if expecting her tiny chubby fingers to brush Dad's face. But they didn't. We're just using a device to communicate with our father who's all the way in Syria. I felt my heart beat with wretchedness. Poor Rosie. She never saw Dad. She's only eleven months old. Dad was only at home when Rosie was in Mom's womb. He spent or month or two being with us while Mom was pregnant but then he, unfortunately, had to go back into the war and help the Syrians fight ISIS.

"Da-ddy," Rosie called out, making all of us widen our eyes with astonishment.

That was Rosie's first word.

"Did she just…"

"Yes, Julian," Mom said, smiling modestly at Dad yet so despairingly. I spotted her eyes glistening with miserable tears. "Rosie wants you, Julian. We want you." A tear falls from Mom's eye, and I, too, felt the tears threatening to escape mine.

Dad's eyes were glossy, too. He tried to smile, but his smile wavered. His finger hastily wiped his left eye before a tear could slide out. He sighed shakily, giving me the impression that this distance is an unbearable pain to him. "I know, sweetheart. I want to come back, too. But you know how wars are like. You know how ISIS can be. They are torturing the people – kidnapping them, raping them, killing them, making them slaves, going against the rules of a peaceful religion, trying to make a religion of their own. The victims need me to help them, to support them, to fight with them, to protect them. I promise that I'll find a way to come back to you guys."

Mom nodded, wiping her eyes. "Come back soon," she whispered, her voice shattering. "I need you, Julian."

Dad smiled at Mom with passionate, pure love and tenderness. "And I'll be there soon."

*   *   *

After the conversation with my father, we all went upstairs to sleep. I opened the door to my room and was about to go inside when Mom called me. I turned around to see Mom stop in front of me with Rosie in her arms, her head resting on Mom's shoulder as she breathed peacefully.

"I forgot to tell you something," she said.

"Tell me what?"

"Basically," she began, "I got a call from my best friend. She told me that her nephew is having some problems with his studies. He's good at Math, but he's really poor at Science and English."

"And…"

"She asked me if you could tutor her nephew," Mom continued. "And I said yes."

"Why did you say that?"

"Because—" Rosie whimpered in her sleep. Mom caressed her back by moving her hand up and down "—you always concentrate on your studies and review for your tests, and that's good, but I want you to be friends with someone. You never bring friends to our house, and I knew that you're lonely. I thought that if you tutor this boy, you'll be friends."

I pushed a strand of my dark hair behind my ear. "So you technically set up a study date for me?"

My mother smiled sheepishly. "It's not actually a study date…but you can think of it that way."

I sighed. "So, who's the guy?"

Mom bit her lip. "I-I'm not sure. Marline didn't say his name—"

"Mom, you're lying," I interrupted. Whenever Mom stutters, it means she's being dishonest. "Tell me who the guy is."

"If I tell you, you're going to freak out…"

"Am I supposed to know this guy?" I questioned.

"Yes…April, I won't tell you his name now. If I do, then you'll get mad at me and won't go. I'm only doing this because I know this boy is good for you and that you're good for him."

"Who are you? Cupid?" I muttered.

She did another sheepish grin. "You could say that," she admitted. "Anyway, my friend invited us to her house for a memorial event"

"A memorial?" I echoed.

She nodded. "I know it sounds odd for her to invite us to this memorial, but she's a businesswoman and business people are constantly preoccupied with work. Tomorrow is the only available day for us to meet her. And we can't decline her invitation, April. It's rude."

I agree with the fact that I'm so anti-social. I should change that. However, I keep on wondering who this guy is...Mom said that this guy's aunt is her friend...my eyes widened. "It's "Derek!" I blurted. My eyes widened. "Oh, my God. YOU WANT ME TO BE WITH HIM?"

Mom was puzzled about how I found out. Either way, she said, "Yes."

"Why?" I demanded. "Why him of all guys?"

"Because you two were so close," Mom explained.

"Things changed, Mom. We're not close anymore."

She sighed. "Okay, that may be true...but I have just adored you two ever since you both were babies! Your friendship was so strong and adorable and loving. You may not talk to each other that much in school because Mike left but I'm pretty sure you two are still close either way."

"How do you know that we're good for each other?"

"April...there are some things that you don't understand about him. Derek may seem rude, but he's just like a..." She bit her lip, searching for the correct words. "He's like a bulldog—" I snorted "—scary looking and fierce—" I snorted again "—but deep down inside, he just has a soft heart he's ashamed to expose."

I snorted again and suppressed the giggles. Really? A bulldog? Derek is nothing compared to a bulldog. He's not scary looking; he just looks like a troll. And fierce? Please. He's anything but fierce. And soft-hearted? Pfft.

Mom glared. "Don't laugh, April. You have no idea what happened to him and what he's going through."

I relaxed, stopping myself from laughing. "You're right, I don't."

"So…are you up for it? At least give it a try."

I momentarily considered. Derek and I were close when we were kids…now, we're not. Perhaps, hanging out with him might not be bad. I can handle him.

"Okay," I decided. "I'll do it."

Mom's eyes brightened with gratitude, and she kissed my forehead. "Wonderful. Hopefully, you and Derek might become good friends and…even better, become a couple!"

"Mom, that'll never happen."

"It might! You never know—"

"Mom…"

My mother giggled. "Sorry. Just a bit excited. I've always wanted to see you date at this age. It'll be fun, you know? Seeing you grow up with a man, hugging a man, making out with a man…I mean, you cannot have intercourse yet because you're too young, obviously; if you do, I will literally come after you with a stick and slap you—"

"Mom!" I cut her off.

"Right. Sorry." She cleared her throat. She kissed my forehead again. "Good night, darling."

"Good night," I echoed as I kissed my sleeping sister.

I went into my room, flopping down on the bed and pulling the duvet over me. I gazed up at the ceiling which was speckled with glow-in-the-dark stars. Yes, it's childish that I have them, but my older brother gave me them when I was so young. I cherished them as if they're diamonds, more precious than stars.

I thought about Derek Matthews who I will have to tutor.

It's going to be torture.

But I can handle him.

I am strong even though I'm weak.

I can handle him.

He can be an asshole sometimes…but I know that he's nice, sweet, and funny because that's the Derek Matthews who I admired.

I'll just give this tutoring thing a try for three days. If it doesn't go well, then I'll end it.

However, Mom said that this guy is good for me, and that I am good for him.

How was the last thing I asked myself before I closed my eyes, turning over and releasing a sigh, and went to sleep.

Chapter Three

My Angel

April Levesque

The radiant rays of the morning sun peeked through the windows and the curtains, beaming on my face. I groaned, turning around so the rays won't come in c my eyes. I felt myself drifting off into my dream world again when the alarm clock beeped insistently, causing me to jolt upwards and fall off my bed.

I groaned loudly with frustration. All the damn time, I keep on falling off the bed. My hand banged on the on mute button. My eyes were fuzzy for a minute. My hands searched for my glasses on my nightstand, and I put them on. Instantly, my eyesight is clear. I tucked strands of my hair behind my ear as a yawn widened my mouth.

Rubbing my eyes, I wandered around the room to the bathroom. I locked the door behind me and gazed at my reflection in the mirror sleepily. I look half dead.

I squirted toothpaste on my toothbrush. I began scrubbing my teeth though I paused abruptly when I noticed a pink reddish mark on my neck. My fingertips touched the mark, feeling the firmness of it. It took me a minute to realize what this could mean. I read a lot of romance stories before…They ruined my innocent mind…

Oh, God. Please don't tell me it's what I think it is. Please, please…

"Mom!" I shouted. I don't know why I'm calling her. I shouldn't be. But I'm panicking. A RED MARK IS ON MY NECK, FOR DAMN'S SAKE! SOMEONE BIT ME! NOT A VAMPIRE BUT SOMEONE ELSE! "Mom, can you come here quickly?!"

"Where are you?" I heard her ask a minute later from my bedroom outside.

"In the bathroom!"

The door creaked open slightly, and Mom's head popped through the gap. "What's wrong, honey?"

"What's this?!" I pointed a finger at the red mark plastered on the skin of my neck.

Mom furrowed her eyebrows, perplexed. Then, her eyebrows shot up. "Uhm…" Mom mumbled. "Well…April, can I ask you a question?"

"What?"

"Are you dating?"

"No, why?"

"Because that mark is a hickey…"

"A WHAT?!" I shrieked. Ugh, why does life have to torture me like this? "I KNEW IT! I KNEW IT…WAIT, IS THAT BAD OR GOOD?"

"Uhm…I don't know… Depends on who the guy is…wait, did a guy bite your neck?"

"Yes," I replied, my eyes fluttering close. Yesterday, in English, Derek Matthews was biting my neck… Oh, that dumbass is going to get the part where the sun doesn't shine kicked! "This idiot bit my neck, Mom."

"I'm pretty sure he isn't an idiot," Mom objected. "He must be a good person who's crushing on you. You know, hickeys mean that you belong to someone and you're taken—"

"Mom, how do you know this stuff?"

"Uhm...I'm not that old, honey. Besides, we're in the 21st Century; people should know what hickeys are by now..."

*　　*　　*

After I took a shower, got dressed, and ate breakfast, Mom dropped me off at school. I gave her a quick hug, thanking her for the ride, and said goodbye as I closed the car door, sauntering away. I strolled through the corridors to my locker, swinging it open and taking out the books I need today.

A figure leaned against the lockers next to me. I glanced sideways, my expression instantly going dull as Derek Matthews smirked at me, enhancing his good looks.

"Hey."

"Goodbye." I closed the door and walked away, hoping that he'll just leave me.

Sadly, he didn't. "So, we have Maths next, right?"

I nodded, not even glancing at him.

Derek sighed, muttering something about how annoying I am. He seized my shoulders with his hands from behind, twirling me around. I can't lie, he is attractive. His jet-black hair is messy, falling over his mesmerising ocean blue eyes. If someone meets him for the first time, they would consider him a sweet and kind boy judging by the fact that his face was nothing but cute and innocent-looking. That's what I thought he was when I met him for the first time. Looks can be deceiving.

"April, I'm sorry about yesterday," he said.

I batted my eyelashes. "Am I going crazy or did I just hear Derek Matthews utter an apology?"

Derek rolled his eyes.

"Don't roll your eyes at me, asshole," I snapped.

"I just said sorry. It's not a big deal."

"For a heartbreaker, it is. I thought you don't have a heart."

"I do have a heart. It's beating. If I don't have a heart, then I will be dead."

"And everyone will come to celebrate the death of Derek Matthews."

"I may be a heartbreaker, April, but I'm not that bad."

"I find that hard to believe."

"Well, let's just say that I'm not an open book. Just like how all readers say: *Don't judge a book by its cover.*"

I snorted. "Lame," I muttered. "And your apology is not accepted."

Some people in the hallway sent us perplexed looks. I ignored their stares and realized that Derek was too close to me. I took a step further to create some distance.

"Why?" he asked.

"Because you gave me a freaking *hickey*," I hissed in a low tone, flicking my hair to the side to show him the redness of the bite mark.

His lips widened into a satisfied, cocky smirk. "Good. Now everyone will know that you're mine."

"I'm yours?" I echoed. Irritation boiled in my nerves. "Listen, Matthews. I don't belong to anyone—not even you. I'm not a freaking toy that you can use to satisfy yourself. I am a human being just like you. I don't belong to *anyone*—"

Derek put his finger over my lips, forcing me to stop talking. He took a step closer. His breath fanned my face with his unwavering lopsided, smug, attractive grin. "We'll see about that, angel," he whispered, his face travelling downwards to leave a gentle kiss on the hickey. I gasped. Sensational tremors tickled down my back. My heart beat promptly in my chest.

He strode backwards, clearing his throat to shout, "Attention!"

The chatter in the hallway hushed as pupils turned their attention to Derek.

What was he doing?

"I just want to clarify that I am dating April Levesque," he declared. People arched their eyebrows, shocked and baffled. "She's mine, not yours. If you try to hurt her, I'll know, and I'll hurt you. I know, I know, April is like a cute little kitten, but if you try to touch her, flirt with her or talk to her, I will be informed about it and I will...well, knowing April, I won't kill you. I'll probably just break your nose. Did everyone get that?"

The students were speechless; blinking numerous times as if they were dreaming. Then, one guy stepped forward, sniggering. Carl Prot.

"You?" he asked. "Dating her?" He pointed at Derek, then at me. He snickered at full volume, clapping his hands together frantically. "Priceless. We all know that's not true, Derek."

Derek glared at Carl. "Why do you think that, Prot?"

"Because you're the heartbreaker," the boy retorted. "You're probably using her."

"What if I'm not?" Derek snapped, rage penetrating his voice. *Why is he getting angry all of a sudden?* I know he has anger issues, but this brief chitchat shouldn't cause him to go furious. "What if I actually changed? What if I actually love her?"

"I won't believe you," Carl said. "None of us will. Your momma probably will. Oh, wait! She isn't here! Do you know why? Because she's in he—"

Wrath consumed him. The rage was too hard to tame, I could tell by the look on his face. Derek grabbed the collar of Carl's shirt and slammed him into the wall nearby.

"You little piece of shit," Derek growled. He looked like a predator with that perilous glint in ocean-blue eyes. He does, indeed, look dangerous. "Don't you *ever* talk about my mother like that." With his other hand, he punched Carl in the stomach. Carl did a fusion of howling and groaning; his teeth gritted in soreness. "Got it?" When Carl didn't reply, Derek roared, "GOT IT?!"

Carl bobbed his head up and down hastily, trepidation crawling into his eyes.

I couldn't stand this. I couldn't watch Derek hurting another person. It makes me sick. I don't know why the boy's words affected Derek, but I assumed something happened to his mother. There were rumours about his mother: some say she moved far away to a different country, leaving her kids and husband behind. Others say she's dead.

"Derek," I called out. "Derek, let him go."

Derek's posture was rigid He turned his head, his eyes locking with mine as if the key unexpectedly got lost. He held my gaze for five seconds before letting go of Carl. The boy fell to the floor, groaning while clutching his stomach. Derek glared at everyone in the hallway and shouted, "Turn around and go back to your business!"

They obeyed.

"What was that?" I demanded as Derek walked away "Why did you hurt him?"

"Because he insulted my mother," he grumbled. "I can hurt someone back if they insult my mother."

"No! You can't just punch them!" I grabbed his arm and spun him around.

He shrugged. "I don't give a damn. They get what they deserve."

"Why did you tell everyone that I'm yours?" I asked next, getting irritated.

He stared at me, a soft smile gracing his lips. "Because you are."

"I'm not!" I objected. "And I'm not a kitten!"

He chuckled huskily. "It was just a metaphor, April." He then frowned. "Or was that a simile?"

"You humiliated me by telling everyone that I am yours!" I snapped. I stretched my fingers, attempted to slap him for being such an idiot. But judging by the fact he punched that guy, I was afraid he would hurt me.

"If you want to slap me, then slap me," Derek said, as if he could read my thoughts.

"How did you know I was thinking about that?"

"Because you pout whenever you're thinking."

"I do?" I baffled.

"Yes," he said. "It's cute, by the way."

I cracked my hand across his face. Derek stumbled two steps backwards, his hand touching his left cheek.

"Ow..." He rubbed his cheek. "That actually hurts."

"Did you expect it to hurt?"

"No..." He fixed a fierce look on me. "Do you like slapping me?"

"Yes."

"Why?"

"Because you deserve it."

"You know that's abuse, right?"

"But you allowed me to slap you, so technically it isn't." Derek's glare deepened. He clenched his delicate jawline as I say, "I still don't accept your apology."

*   *   *

All through Math, I paid attention to Mr. Nelson. Sometimes, I drifted off into space, staring through the window as I daydream about many things.

Then, we had to make a cluster of three for a Maths activity. Mr. Nelson always put us into pairs, so I didn't mind working alone. Albeit, right now, I have to work in a group. The class went feral as they bounced off their seats, running all around the room for group members. I was motionless in my seat, still staring out the window.

A shadow fell over me. I looked to see Derek and a blond boy called Theo Romano.

"What do you want?" I asked before they spoke.

"You're going to be in our group," Derek said, sitting next to me. His shoulder shoved mine tenderly. The strong aroma of his sweet manly cologne attacked my nostrils; the only revolting scent was the odour of cigarettes.

"What if I don't want to participate in your group?"

"It's just for now, April. Jesus, can't we be together for once?"

"We can't be together. That's an actual impossibility."

"How?"

"Because you're a virus to mankind."

Derek's friend snickered. "Ouch," Theo sniggered. He placed a hand on Derek's shoulder. "Don't feel hurt, man. She's right."

Derek shot a fierce glare at Theo. "And you're a worthless scum of the Earth," Derek snapped at me.

"I know that's true, so stop reminding me," I snapped back.

My remark seemed to trigger a surprised expression from Derek. "April, I didn't really mean—"

"Hi, Theo," I greeted, smiling at Derek's best friend.

"How do you know who I am?" Theo asked, perplexed.

"We were in the same biology class for three years, and I was your partner last year for a science project. Good talk," I muttered sarcastically. "Plus, Derek and I were friends when we were kids, and he always blabbed about you, and I think we met each other at Derek's ninth birthday party. Double plus, all I ever do is listening to everything that's going around in Peony Hallows High School rather than socialising with people. The only people I talk to in this school are the people over there." I nodded in the direction where Brigit is with her group of girls.

"I'm really sorry about them," Derek said with no sympathy visible in his voice.

"Wow, this must be my lucky day because Derek Matthews, the school's number one banana head, apologised to me *twice* today," I said in a dry tone.

"Theo, now you know why this girl is annoying." Derek complained.

Theo smirked. "Nah, she's amazing. Aye, April, thanks for smacking my best friend with a bag and slapping him. Hopefully, his common sense is back."

"Derek Matthews never has common sense, which explains why he's an idiot."

"Exactly!" Theo agreed.

"Theo, you're supposed to be my friend, for Christ's sake!" Derek retorted.

"I am your friend. April, did you know that Derek begged me to be his best friend, so he won't be a loner?"

I arched an eyebrow. "Never knew Derek Matthews was that desperate. All I know is that he's desperate to get lung cancer to kill himself."

"I don't want to kill myself."

"You're practically killing yourself."

"No, I'm not. Maybe you are."

"And how am I killing myself?"

"By just being you."

"Derek!" Theo snapped. "Cut it off with the rude shit, man!"

"She was being rude to me first," Derek protested like a fuming child, somehow pouting in the most engaging way possible.

"She was only telling you the truth. Smoking will damage your organs, which means that you can die. How is that rude?"

"No, Theo, it's okay," I murmured. "I get that a lot, anyway."

Derek sighed brusquely, rubbing his forehead with his fingers as if he's having a headache from this chat. "Look, April, I'm sorry about that. I didn't mean it. I just get angry easily."

"I know that. I know you have bipolar disorder. To be honest, it's kinda obvious."

"Yeah, whatever. Anyway…do you have any plans for today?"

"Yes, I do. Why?" I asked, tapping my pencil.

Derek shrugged. "I was thinking about taking you out tonight."

I raised an eyebrow. "As in…as in a *date?*"

Derek nodded. "You want to go out with me?"

"No."

"What?"

"Are you deaf? If so, then go and get some hearing aid. Even an old man can hear better than you."

Theo laughed at my remark while Derek scowled at me. "Shut up."

"Okay." Silence hung thick in the air. Our eyes met: blue eyes locked on to dark brown ones. A few people glimpsed at us. Theo was grinning with amusement, his eyes never moving away from us, glancing back and forth, pleased by our interaction.

Derek was the first to break the staring contest. "At any rate, will you go out with me?"

I remained silent.

Derek cocked an eyebrow. "Are you going to answer or not?"

I didn't reply. He told me to shut up, and I was obeying him.

Derek clenched his jaw in vexation. "Stop being a smartass and answer my damn question, April."

At that, I smiled at Derek and said, "Okay. I won't go out with you because we're busy today. I have to go and meet you in your house, remember?"

"Oh, yeah," he mumbled. "I forgot about that. We can skip it."

"We can't. It's rude."

"It's my house—"

I cut him off by continuing: "I won't go out with you because I don't even know you—"

"Of course, you do. We personally met yesterday. Plus, we were best friends. We knew each other ever since we were kids."

"Yeah, but you pushed me away and became the world's second asshole."

"You pushed me away."

"When you became the world's second asshole."

"Wait, who is the first?"

I stared at him, incredulous. "Seriously? You're really asking that?" He still seemed bewildered. I sighed. This boy...dimwitted as I remember him to be. "Donald Trump."

Derek's mystification died. "Ah, I agree. He's an asshole. But why am I second?"

"Because you are. You have a problem with that? Well, go to the White House and make a deal with Trump about taking his place of being the world's number one asshole."

"Is that the only reason?"

"I have many: you are really stupid. Did aliens come and brainwash you or something?"

"Well, you see—"

"You and I don't really get along—"

"That's true but we will eventually."

"You're just plain rude—"

"It's a flaw. Get used to it."

"I don't even like you—"

"You're lying. Everybody loves me. I'm the most wanted guy in school."

"Dead or alive? I hope it's dead."

At that, Theo ruptured into laughter. He guffawed like a hyena, his snickers cracking every second as he snorts profoundly. Tears pooled in his eyes, and he grasped his stomach, wheezing. "Man, this is gold," he puffed breathlessly. "I should've recorded this on Snapchat."

Derek rolled his eyes at his best friend as I grinned. "Yes. You should've. I would love to see Derek getting humiliated by the girl he pushed away because he's nothing but an idiotic asshole."

"You pushed me away, too," Derek snapped. "Stop putting the blame on me."

Anger boiled inside me. I wanted to rant out everything—about how he was the first one to shove me away, creating this tension and this misery between us, making us strangers once again. Instead, I responded to his statement about being the most wanted guy in the school, with a hint of antagonism: "I still find it hard to believe. Not everyone loves you, Derek. You think that you're so perfect just because you're rich, just because your father was a billionaire who was respected by millions of people in the world, that you have the perfect family, a perfect future ahead of you and that you will get everything…"

"I don't have the perfect family," Derek interrupted.

"Well, news flash, Derek: not all of us are perfect! Not everyone will love you! Everyone will get hated one way or another. That's how life is!" I rammed my black framed glasses up my nose. "Plus, you are famous because of your father. Your father was a billionaire who owned one of the world's greatest companies that saved so many souls. Do you want to hear something, Derek? Your *father* will always get more *respect* and *admiration* and *friends* and *love* than you. Do you know why? Because he was like you, yes, but he learnt quicker than doing all of this — breaking hearts and being a sadistic jerk, loving to see girls getting hurt because you think it's 'entertaining' — is wrong."

He might've been my best friend, someone who I trusted and adored as an awesome partner in crime, but that doesn't mean that I won't consider about his reputation as an asshole. He breaks girls, ripping the human heart as if it's plain paper. I have no idea why my mother wanted me to tutor him—I get it that he's dumb, but I will probably die after the first five seconds just by being so close to him.

"I won't give you a chance and I never will. I will never trust you or love you. I *hate* you."

*   *   *

After school, I went to the pet shop because that's where I'm working—and today is my first day, so I hope the customers will, at least, like me.

"April!" Alan said, the manager of the pet shop. He was also the only vet in the shop and the only other person who's working here. I always saw him so exhausted whenever I pass by, and I felt sorry for him, so I decided to help him by asking him if I could work with him.

Alan is in his forties. He has bushy eyebrows, a bald head with strands of grey hair and compassionate, gentle, beautiful blue eyes. He's wearing a sweatshirt and a pair of jeans.

"Hi, Alan," I greeted, taking my coat off and hanging it on a hook. I put my bag next to a chair and walked towards the counter. "So, how can I help?"

"Well, you can feed the pets," Alan suggested, nodding towards a door that led to the pets' room. "Or you can help me with my next patient who's coming in thirty minutes."

"I'll do both."

I smiled at him as he gives me a huge bag of pet food. I opened the door to the pets' room and closed it behind me, turning around to observe a small amount of dogs and cats.

I knew that the shop was low in business, but I didn't expect for the shop to have so little pets. I sighed, walking to where the bowls were. I ripped the bag open and poured the food in each of the bowls as I felt the animals' eyes focused on me. Once I've finished, I turned to the animals, noticing them still staring at me attentively and waiting keenly for me to say it.

"You can eat now," I told them, smiling soothingly.

The animals dashed towards the bowls and gobbled their food. I giggled. I love animals.

At the corner of my eye, I saw something fluffy. I looked to the left. A small, furry snout was peeking out from the back of a chair—an appealing, golden puppy with charcoal eyes.

I ambled to the puppy, though that only caused the little fella to whine with apprehension, sinking backwards as its back pressed against the hard wall.

I crouched down. "Hey, I won't hurt you." My thin fingers reached out to stroke its fur.

The puppy whimpered. It raced to another part of the room, hiding underneath the table. The puppy's eyes were cast down as it whimpered and howled.

I heard someone chortling behind me. Alan was standing in the doorway of the pets' room. "I see you met the little lad." Alan grinned, winking at the puppy. "I found the dog in the streets. The poor lad was filthy and bruised, so I decided to bring it to the pet shop in case anyone wants to adopt it. The Golden Retriever is still getting used to his surroundings, so don't be disappointed if he won't go near you. The little guy is still scared of everyone."

He. The puppy was a male. I averted my attention back to the Golden Retriever. He was still gawking at me thoughtfully, as if wondering if I was a good person or a bad person. I meandered to where the food bag was. Scooping up a handful of dog food, I approached the terrified puppy.

"Hey, boy," I whispered, crouching down to my knees. "I won't hurt you. Are you hungry?" I held out my hand that's full of dog food.

The little dog gaped at the food hungrily. Silent, considering minutes passed by and the little guy hobbled over, slightly hesitating and sinking down, staring at me with thoughtful eyes. The puppy finally munched the food in my hands, his tongue licking my palm as he does so. I grinned, picking the puppy up and sitting down on a chair.

"Does it have a name, Alan?"

"No."

"Then Lucky should be his name."

"Why?"

"Because he is lucky to be found by you."

Alan smiled with appreciation and admiration at my answer, lines appearing at the corners of his eyes.

After I fed Lucky, I cleaned up the pets' room with a bit of help from Alan. I helped Alan with his patient, which was a cat who nearly scratched my hand with her sharp claws. I hate cats.

Alan paid me thirty bucks, and I thanked him before saying goodbye to Lucky and the pets. I was about to leave the room when I felt something furry brushing my ankle. I glanced down and noticed Lucky wagging his tail, looking at me with gregarious, glistening, beautiful charcoal eyes. I crouched down. He lifted his front two paws, resting it on my chest, whining as if he doesn't want me to leave.

"I have to go, Lucky. I'll be back soon."

*　　　*　　　*

The cold was like an evil spirit, horribly invading my body as it creept under my clothes and numbed my skin. My teeth chattered uncontrollably as the wind gracefully howled past me. If it's this cold today, then I'm absolutely sure that it'll snow eventually.

Since it was November, the sky was darkening swiftly, and the streets were already speckled with ravishing Christmas decorations. The fairy lights flickered around each house, rapidly changing from one colour to another. Some shops displayed their Christmas tree with dazzling ornaments and jewel lights. Mom said we cannot decorate our house for Christmas yet because November is the month of the Saints. She promised that we'd start decorating our tree on the first day of December. My family is very religious.

I stopped at the porch of my house and rummaged around my pockets, searching for my house keys. I got in, closing the door behind me before sliding my shoes off my feet.

"Mom, I'm here!"

Mom walked out of the kitchen and smiled humbly at me. "Hello, April darling. You better get yourself washed up and dressed." I furrowed my eyebrows, bewildered. Mom noticed my expression because she said, "We're going to my friend's house to meet Derek, remember?"

My eyebrows slowly slid away from each other. "Oh yeah, I totally forgot about that. Did they invite us to a party?"

"No. Marline's brother passed away six years ago. His brother's wife passed away seventeen years ago. She wants to bring everyone to this memorial event. She and a couple of her family members will be coming to her house to celebrate the anniversary of her brother's and sister-in-law's death. Now, go and dress in something nice and formal to this memorial."

"Celebrate?"

"Mourn!" she corrected. "Sorry, they want to *mourn* her death. Not *celebrate* her death. Like, why would someone celebrate someone's death? Unless you're from New Orleans because I heard they celebrate the deaths and—"

"Mom, you're rambling again."

"Right. Sorry." She scratched the back of her neck. "Get dressed. Look…*beautiful* tonight because I want you to catch Derek's eye."

"Mom…this is only tutoring."

"Yeah, but I did say that I want you to date. I want you to be happy with a man… or a woman." Mom narrowed her eyes. "Are you lesbian or bisexual? Or trans? Or are you unsure?"

"Mom!"

She giggled. "Joking, joking. But I won't mind if you're homosexual or trans. Jesus never talked about the LGBTQ+, so it's not really atrocious or a sin. Plus, even if it is a sin, Jesus comes for the sinners, so he is going to come for the homosexuals, the bisexuals, the trans, the questioners."

"Mom…I know that. You keep on saying that all the time. And Mom, you don't know Derek like how I do."

"You don't know him like how *I* do, April. I've known Derek for a long time. Longer than you. I've known his parents. If he does anything, then I'll rip his balls off. Simple. But I know that this boy will be a good influence for you." Mom frowned. "Or is that the other way around?"

Hours later, I'm already refreshed and smelled like daffodils. I observed myself in the mirror. The dress was a rich shade of ebony that came up to my thighs. As always, my dark hair cascaded down my shoulders and I wore a pair of new glimmering black ankle-strap heels.

"April, are you ready?" Mom shouted from downstairs.

"I'm coming now," I shouted back. I closed my bedroom door and descended down the stairs.

"You look very beautiful, darling," Mom complimented with an approving smile.

"Thanks, Mom."

Ethan wore a black shirt that was neatly tucked into his black trousers. "C'mon, let's get this over with."

*   *   *

Everyone knew that the Matthews mansion was very posh. I've been to his mansion before, but that was a long time ago, so the memory was only a blur, until it finally came into view.

A humongous, deluxe mansion emitted incandescent lights to show off its affluence, fortune, and potential.

It didn't surprise me that men dressed in black clothes stood in front of the prosperous gates with earphones attached to their lobes. Mom told the men that she's a friend of the woman who owns this house. One of them pressed a button after talking to someone over the intercom. The gates automatically jerked backwards, leaving a large space for Mom to drive through.

The house was glorious. It's your typical dream house. Inside, the building was jammed with people, dressed in wealthy attires — exquisite clothes, bags, jewellery — and they had that high-class, posh way of carrying themselves. Classical music hummed faintly while people chitchatted among themselves. If it was the Victorian Era, I bet these people will be in First Class.

"Is that you, Mia?" a voice called.

Ethan, Mom, and I looked to see a woman with long dark hair winding behind her back. She wore an elegant silky, tight white dress, and her diamond earrings jingled as she approached us. The woman's eyes widened. "Oh, my God! It is you!" She threw her arms out and embraced Mom in a tight, loving hug as they both laughed with delight.

"How are you, Marli?" Mom questioned as they pulled away from the cuddle.

The woman groaned. "It's the usual, Mia. Work, aunt duties, more work, more aunt duties…" she sighed. "It's so tiring, but I'm quite energetic than on normal working days. I guess it's because I managed to sleep for 10 actual hours like normal people."

"So you still didn't find a man?"

Marline scoffed. "I don't need any man in my life. I am strong on my own. I like to be independent. Besides, I have my two nephews, so I guess that's enough." Marline momentarily looks at Ethan and Rosie, and gasped. "Oh, my, Ethan! Wonderful to see you again after a long time!"

Ethan smiled. "Hi, Miss. Good to see you, too!"

"My, my, you've grown so much! Look at you, looking so ravishing, dashing, and handsome!"

Ethan looked uncomfortable by her compliments. "Uh, thanks. You look ravishing, dashing, and hand . . . beautiful, too."

Marline's gaze averted to Rosie, who was shifting around in her buggy, her eyes glancing at every direction with that gleam of desperation in her eyes, as if she wants to discover the whole house. Marline cooed.

"Aw, so this is Rosie!" Rosie looked up at Marline and grinned. Marline returned the gesture.

"And this is April, Marli."

Marline's eyes settled on me. She took a few seconds to run her eyes up and down my appearance, a kind of sentiment dazzling in her familiar pair of blue eyes. "Oh, my God! April! I miss you so much, honey!"

She hugged me. I awkwardly returned it.

"Uh, yeah, nice to see you, too!"

Marline was always nice to me. It's actually enchanting to see her again after a long time.

"Wow, you're so beautiful! Now I know why Derek kept on blabbing about you."

I blushed. *Derek kept on blabbing about me?* I thought we hated each other.

"Speaking of Derek, where is he?" Mom asked. "My daughter is very curious and excited to meet him."

I silently gasped, nudging Mom's shoulder and hissed, '*Mom*' with an embarrassed blush. She only granted me a sly smile as Ethan rolled his eyes.

"Oh, he's coming later. You know how he is." Marline sighed heavily, misery substituting the jovial radiance in her eyes. "This isn't the first time he was late to the memorial. I know he can be a jerk sometimes, a heartless one even, but I wish he could at least try and let somebody in."

The world knew that Derek's father died. He died in a car crash. Some people believe his mother moved away after a divorce, but the fact that this memorial was dedicated to both of Derek's parents, she died. Then, I remember Mike mentioning to me that Derek suffered from his parents' death. How come it never occurred to me?

"His parents?" Empathy flooded my chest. I'm a very sensitive person and I always feel sorry for anyone who lost their loved ones. "I'm sorry to hear that."

Marline smiled at me. "Thank you, April. It's hard for my nephew to live without them especially since they were so close to him. Well, technically his father was closer."

"I know what you mean, Marline," Mom mumbled lowly. "We lost someone close to us too."

Marline's sad smile faltered. She knew about our elder brother who tragically passed away. In fact, everyone in the entire town knew about Mike. Mike was Peony Hallows' hero. He still is.

Marline sighed. "Why must life be so cruel?" she muttered, to no one in particular. She pushed a ringlet behind her ear. "Anyway, I'm glad that you made it here and please do get comfortable in my house. Would you guys like a…" Her voice trailed off all of a sudden when her eyes settled on the main exits. "Ah, he's here!"

Just like this morning, he is lightly tanned with messy, lustrous, soft jet-black hair as if he raked his hair with his hand multiple times. His eyes are the colour of the deep, majestic, mystical ocean. A conceited smirk appeared on his face as he approached us.

"Derek! Theo!" Marline smiled at them. "I was wondering where you've been!"

Chapter Four

Insecurity

April Levesque

"Hey, Aunt Marline," Derek greeted.

"Derek," Marline greeted back. "You look handsome."

"I agree," my mother chirped in. "You look like a polite, loyal, presentable gentleman, dear."

Mom acknowledged Derek's reputation in Peony Hallows. I snorted loudly at her compliment. Derek being polite, loyal, and presentable? Derek as a gentleman? Ha. He's nowhere near gentle.

Mom glared at me, sending me a silent message to behave. I cleared my throat as silently as possible, pursing my lips and trying not to giggle.

The thing I don't get is: *why him?* Out of all the guys in this town, Mom decided that I should tutor this guy? Everyone knows how Derek Matthews can be like. I just don't get why Mom wants him and I to be together. We don't even have anything in common! We're complete opposites—he's the bad boy and I'm the good girl. It won't be like those bad boy / good girl stories! Those stories are too good to be true!

"Thanks," he replied in a dull tone, as if he's used to that comment.

"Derek, remember when I told you that you will have a tutor?" Marline enquired.

"Yes."

"Well, April will be your tutor!"

Derek's gaze settled onto me. His lips twitched, as if he's trying to preserve a smile. His celestial eyes softened. "Nice to see you again," he said, his voice slurring slightly.

"Uh, nice to see you again, too," I responded, my voice coming out as a fractious mutter. The others might've not suspected the distaste that lingered in my throat, but from the way Derek finally permitted a smirk to beam on his face, I knew he heard the frustration. He always loved to see me uncomfortable when it comes to teasing.

"I have no idea why you two don't communicate anymore. I thought you're both best friends. I understand that...*certain* deaths can separate people, but I never thought it would separate you. You're inseparable! I remembered how clingy Derek was with April—always standing next to her, shielding her, being so overprotective. Oh, and the way you always blab—"

"I have no idea, too, Marline," Derek interjected, dropping his stare bashfully.

At that moment, a tinge of pink made its way up his neck, climbing onto his velvety, fair, delicate cheeks, as if Marline's words humiliated him. Yet, regardless of the blushing, the way he verbalized his interruption prowled with despondency, as if he was contemplating the answer to Marline's declaration nearly his whole life.

Ethan, who's standing near me awkwardly, uneasily cleared his throat, detained Derek's attention. He nodded firmly at Derek as a salutation, and in return, Derek's blushing immediately vanished, and was substituted with nuisance. Ethan and Derek were never on good terms. When we were all younger, they constantly squabbled back and forth.

Marline's eyebrows scrunched together as she observed Derek's scarlet cheek. "What happened to you?"

Derek was baffled by his aunt's question. He touched his cheek, feeling the soreness of the reddish mark. I reminisced to earlier this morning when I slapped him after he affirmed everyone that I'm his.

"N-nothing," I countered rapidly at the same time Derek says: "April slapped me."

Snake.

Mom's eyes widened. "April!"

I held up my hands. "It's not my fault! He was the one who was being annoying!"

Marline waved her hand at me. "Oh, it's fine. Derek probably deserved it, anyway."

Derek rolled his eyes at his aunt's comment. He muttered something under his breath — probably angered profanities — and then took a swift minute to move his eyes up and down my attire. "You look gorgeous."

I would've scowled. I would've rolled my eyes. He's nothing but a sadistic liar. Though, this time, I didn't do anything boorish. I perceived the undeniable integrity from him, triggering a blush to blister my face. I lowered my head a little, my coiled hair curtaining my face vaguely, so he won't distinguish my pinkness. It's too late. His smirk amplified into an exultant, cheery, goofy grin at my flushed face. He chuckled, amused.

"Thanks," I replied gracelessly. "You don't."

I took a minute to examine his clothes. He's wearing a white shirt with the top two buttons disengaged, exposing his smooth collarbone; his sleeves are rolled up, marvelling his light-tanned arms. His jeans are loose, as if he's not bothered to constrict them around his waist. His black tie is undone and a cool, silver, spangled watch seized his right wrist. His jet-black hair is attractively cluttered, the endings plummeting over his shimmering eyes. He looks devilishly handsome, but not handsome enough for me to drool over; not handsome enough for me to fall for.

He shifted, and my eyes assembled with his. I noticed he's still smirking. The blush I tried to expire revisited, only darkening this time. He unquestionably saw me checking him out. He winked swiftly, and I resisted the urge to bark a discourteous remark at him.

"I think April will be a good influence for you, Derek," Marline proclaimed with an appealing beam.

Derek's face muscles are stern, his lopsided smirk unmoving. The way he gaped at me caused odd chills to course through my body.

"Maybe, Marline," he whispered. "Maybe."

*   *   *

Mom and Marline walked deeper into the throng of people cramming the mansion, chitchatting nonstop. Derek is nowhere to be seen. Ethan and I are sitting on the sofas, feeling utterly discomfited.

"This is so weird," Ethan mumbled next to me.

I looked at him. "What do you mean 'weird'? Ethan, we've been to memorials numerous times."

"Not really. Just once or twice."

"Still, it's not really that weird."

"These people are strangers, April."

"Strangers came to Mike's funeral."

"Yeah, but...all these people are so *expensive,* whereas we are just...*normal.*"

I snorted. "And they're not? They're humans like us, Ethan. They're just better off financially."

"You know that Derek dude?" Ethan asked.

"Yeah..."

"I don't trust him."

"I know that. You and Derek were never on good terms."

"He was annoying. I don't know why Mike invited him to our house all the time."

"Derek's brother was Mike's best friend, and Mike helped Derek. I don't know how, though."

"He was so annoying. He broke my Xbox, you know?" Ethan crossed his arms over his chest.

I laughed. "And you still hate him for that? That was years ago."

"I don't care," he stated simply. "But I feel sorry for him that his parents died."

"He shouldn't behave like this, though," I murmured. "If this is a memorial for his parents, then why is he being such an ass?"

"He must have a reason, April."

"I know...but still, it's wrong to disrespect a—"

I was disrupted by the speakers squeaking a little. The chatter died down. We all gazed to the front. Marline, Derek and another boy stood there. Luke. He looks slightly different. He still has the same jet-black hair, blue eyes and athletic body, but he seems sadder. Lost.

"Hello, everybody." Marline smiled at the audience. "Thank you so much for attending this memorial service for my brother and his wife: Samuel and Alexandra Matthews. I am going to pass the microphone to my nephew, Derek, who will be reading his eulogy. But firstly, let's say a sweet Hail Mary to Alex and Sammy."

The audience immediately started reciting the Hail Mary, emphasizing the words beautifully with intense faith and adoration, infusing meaning in each word. Then, Marline and Derek's older brother, Luke, took a step back to make room for Derek. Derek stood behind the microphone, clearing his throat.

"Good evening, everybody."

"*Good morning.*"

"I, uh, don't really know what to say for this year's memorial," he began. "I managed to write some crap, so bear with me.

"I don't know if my parents loved me. They always told me they did, and back then I believed them, but now I don't really know what to believe anymore. I mostly knew my father more than my mother, so I'll try to tell you some facts about my mother.

"Samuel Matthews: he was annoying, too cocky, too self-confident, a jerk, dumb, and, undeniably, a bastard." Chuckles reverberated from the crowd. "But who cares if he was a bastard, right? Everybody hated him, but eventually, everybody loved him! Why? Because he helped millions of lives—he saved them, hugged them, smiled at them. A lot of people idolized him. He was happy from his success, but his rough past still brought him down and changed him, turned him into a devil...until he met my momma.

"The way they met is cliché, I suppose. Momma was a nerd. Dad was a bad boy asshole. They met at a party. Momma drank too much and bumped into Dad. She vomited on him — literally, she *did* — and Dad went crazy and started cussing at her. He gave her a ride home, though, and from that day, Dad knew he couldn't stay away from Momma. 'She was too innocent', Dad told me. 'So innocent, that I wanted to protect her every second of my life. It's crazy, annoying, and exhausting. I don't know what the hell that woman did to me. Is she a witch or something?'"

The chuckles transformed into laughter. I smiled when Derek laughed an unadulterated, genuine, heartwarming laugh. The way he laughed made him seem so innocent, so pure…For a moment, it was hard to believe that he's nothing but an asshole.

"She was his life. She helped him get over the distress of his past. He was so happy that she was his, and his happiness strengthened when they married. Then came along my older brother, Luke—" Derek glanced over his shoulder at Luke, who granted an uplifting smile "—and after a couple of years, I came along. And…" He drifted off, pausing temporarily. Something flashed in his eyes. Heartbreak? "Well, when I came into this world, that's when Momma left."

Derek heaved a shaky sigh, stopping once again. He looked at his aunt, shaking his head. Marline encouraged him with a smile, mouthing *You'll be okay.* Derek looked back at the audience, who all gazed at him intently, waiting for him to proceed.

"Yeah…finding out that my mother died because of me was never the best thing. It broke nearly everyone in the family, but the death affected dad the most.

"Dad still talked to Luke, Aunt Marline and me. Eventually, he stopped and started returning to his old habits— going to clubs or bars, drinking, and smoking, and just destroying himself. Every night, I heard him crying himself to sleep. The love my parents had for each other was unlike anything on this planet."

Derek closed his eyes, composing himself. The nerves in his neck pulsated, as if the pressure of this eulogy is too much for him. Nevertheless, he reopened them and continued. "And that is why I want to speak a few words to Dad. Dad, I don't think you love me because of everything I did, but if you still care — even the slightest — then listen to this: I'm sorry. Sorry that Momma left. Sorry that you had to leave. I hope you're happy up there in Heaven. Just make sure not to make Big Guy angry enough to kick your ass."

Small chortles once again resonated from the audience, yet, I saw tears glimmering in the guests' eyes.

"Now, Momma was beautiful. I never saw her, but I saw plenty of pictures to back up that statement. She was undeniably and outstandingly beautiful. She was the dork, the chatty person, the one who constantly read books and complained about her favourite characters dying; the one who fangirled over Harry Potter and Ron Weasely, debating who was better suited to be her fictitious boyfriend; the one who believed that God took her to Heaven so she can become my guardian angel."

My eyes watered. I blinked harshly, pushing them away, and caught a few other people in the horde hastily wiping the corners of their eyes.

"My parents' death affected me deeply. I would say it lowered my self-esteem, but then again, you'll probably snort and not believe me. I know none of you will. Because none of you understand. None of you understand what it feels like to know that your mother died because of you, because you had to come into this damned world. I never saw her. I never heard her voice. I never touched her. I only heard good things about her, which makes me jealous to know that people knew her and not me.

"No matter what I do to move on from this pain, deep down inside I will always know that I'll never get to hug my mother, talk to her, hear her sweet voice, feel her warm embrace, or get told off because I didn't do my homework or because I got suspended. I miss her. So damn much.

"I get *so* jealous when people around me, people that I know, have mothers whereas I don't. It's completely unfair that you all have a woman — a woman who carried you for nine months while enduring the pain of pregnancy — cherishing you so profoundly and passionately. And then you look at me: a jerk who was never mothered before.

"I know you are all disgusted by me because of my, uh, reputation. But it's not that easy to be happy all the time. Sometimes, you just have to allow yourself to experience the pain, so it can numb the insides of your body; so you can be empty for a while. Other times, people want to express their pain to others because it's their way of saying 'Help me, please'. But people don't really get it, you know? They don't get it because they don't understand, and they don't care.

"I may remain like this forever. Or maybe not. God knows what He has planned for me. I believe He's real, so I don't know about you. I believe He's real because Momma believed Him. I can feel Him around me sometimes, other times He's distant. I guess that's His way of testing me.

"Anyway, to end this eulogy, I want my parents to remember this: I hate you for leaving me. I wish you can come back. Though, Big Guy just wants you in Heaven beside Him."

*　　*　　*

Derek's eulogy made me feel sad for him. I can say I pity him. No, I sympathize with him. I understand how he felt because I lost a beloved person too. I know each word he said is sincere and candid.

His parents are dead. He has no one except for his aunt and his older brother. The whole world knew that Derek's dad died in a car crash. Some believed his mother moved away, but actually, the ones who said she died are right. She died during labour. The whole world knew he is a cold-hearted, soulless, impolite jerk with troubling issues. The world, however, doesn't realise that his bad boy persona is just a mask, a façade, to cover his true sentiments, his true pain, his true colours.

Yes, what Derek does is wrong, but no one really knows what he went through. No one really knows him properly. We all don't know what others suffer through. We all don't know if the suffering can alter a person's charisma.

People who are rude are the ones who are feeling insecure, Mike whispered to me one time. *Their rudeness is a way of saying 'Please help me, I can't handle this pain any longer'.*

Derek is insecure. My chest constricted painfully at the theory. Sure, he's an asshole. But he was my best friend. And regardless of the times he was rude to everyone, regardless of our quarrels, regardless of his bad boy facade, I still care about him.

I took a swig of my fizzy drink. Notwithstanding the fact it's November — and it's one of those wintry months — the atmosphere in the mansion was filled with humidity. I decided to go outside for the chilly breeze to freshen me.

Sauntering towards a set of glass doors, I slid them open and stepped outside. The nippiness destroyed the heat crawling on my skin. It rustled my hair backward, and I shivered. The sky above was clouded with no signs of stars or the moon.

"Aren't you glad to see me?" a deep, husky male voice spoke.

Startled, I whipped around. Derek is sitting on a chair, with a cigarette in between two of his fingers. His legs are propped up on the table in front of him. He inhaled the cigarette and exhaled, the smoke hissing out of his lips and nostrils, filling the air.

"No," I replied. "I needed some fresh air. It was hot inside."

"Mm-hmm." His arched eyebrows specified to me that he didn't believe my response. "Or you were just looking for me because you missed me?"

I rolled my eyes. This boy is so arrogant.

I hate witnessing people smoke. It's repellent, nauseating, and dreadful. I seriously speculate how girls can stand to be near Derek Matthews when he's smoking—or any bad boy, for that matter. How can they kiss him when he has a smelly breath? Do they just go with it or gag? Honestly, if he kissed me, I will literally gag in his mouth.

"Are you going to stare at me or are you going to sit down?"

I scowled. "I was *not* staring at you."

He smirked at me. "Keep telling yourself that, angel."

"Don't call me that," I snapped.

Angel was the nickname he gave me when we were best friends.

"But it suits your personality."

"No, it doesn't."

"It does."

"It doesn't."

"It does."

"It doesn't."

"It does."

"It does—"

"You are an angel. You are my angel. So, shut up and go with it."

"I am *not* 'your angel' thank you very much," I corrected. "So why don't *you* shut up and go with it?"

"What are you going to do if I don't shut up?" he challenged, cocking an eyebrow. "Slap me again?"

I ignored him and twirled around to gaze below me. We were both silent as smoke spiralling from Derek's cigarette and mouth veiled the atmosphere. My eyes are mesmerised by the view of the town, Peony Hallows. Peony Hallows is located in the North-West of Canada. It's a pretty safe place—not that much of crime, no murder, no bad reputation except for Derek Matthews.

"You know smoking isn't good for your health," I mumbled, not looking at him.

"I didn't know you care about me."

"I don't care about you." *I do. I still care. You were my best friend, for God's sake. You may be a jerk, but everyone deserved some care from others, no matter how little.* "I'm just telling you facts about health. Smoke damages your lungs and your life."

"Don't really care."

This time, I looked at him. "Derek, this is a memorial for your parents. *Your parents.* Why are you being like this?"

Derek shrugged. "It's a free country. I can do whatever I want."

"It's disrespectful."

He shrugged again. "I do the memorials every year. It's getting boring so…"

I stared at him, my jaw dropping gradually. "Why are you like this? Why are you an ass?"

His eyes rallied with mine. "I think you already know the answer to that."

"You allowed the pain to change you, to make you become a heartless jerk. What do you think your parents would feel about this? What would your mother feel about this?"

"They're not here. Their thoughts don't really matter."

Fury consumed me. "It's better they're not here so they won't see your horrible face."

At that, Derek stiffened. His grasp around the cigarette tightened, and he clenched his jaw, his delicate cheekbones hardening. "Shut up," he hissed.

"You don't tell me to shut up."

Derek stood up. His shoulders sharp. His breathing heavy and intense. He took a threatening step forward, glowering at me. "You don't have the right to be rude!"

"Well, you're being rude to your parents! You said the memorials are getting boring because you do it every year. Your parents would feel horrible, Derek!

"I'm sorry for my comment. That was rude. I didn't mean it. It's just that I *hate* seeing you like this—being so rude and disrespectful. I know everyone has flaws, but you're taking your flaws too far!"

He chucked his cigarette to the floor and stomped on it. His hands are in fists, specifying to me he's endeavouring to tame his antagonism. "You rarely talk to me, April." His voice is dangerously calm. "How can you say that I'm taking it too far?"

"Yes, I don't talk to you that much. But we were friends. I know well enough that this—" I waved my hands at him, hinting to his heartless facade "—isn't you." I took three steps closer to him. His head hovered over me, his lips inches away from my forehead. "And you *know* I'm damn right."

He remained silent. His breath wafted on my face, creating tingles on my skin. Beneath the clouded sky, his questioning eyes glittered like aquamarines.

"Tell me you still care," I whispered.

"About you?" he said. "Because yes. I still care about you."

"No. Tell me you still care about your parents. Tell me that the Derek I knew is still in there—" I jabbed my finger into his chest, right where his heart is. I can feel the pulsing and the battering against his ribcage, as if it wanted to leap out.

His lips are thinly pressed together, reflecting his answer.

A minute later, I exhaled and took a step back. "Your eulogy may be true, but it can be lies too. Maybe you will remain like this forever—bad, heartless, and careless—"

"I do care!" he roared, slamming me into a wall roughly. I groaned at the harsh impact, my backbone tingling with pain. "I'm human too, April! I care just like everybody else! I care about my parents, but I hate them for leaving me! I hate my father for making me like this."

He closed his eyes, swallowing deeply. A puff escaped his lips, his body slanting forward and slightly compressing into mine. He placed both of his hands on each side next to my neck. His eyes opened, and they're full of resentment, desolation, and…tears?

Yes.

Tears.

He's crying.

He stepped backward, his breathing unsteady. He rubbed his eyes with his fingers. "I-I do care about my parents," he whispered, not bothered to look at me. I've witnessed Derek being vulnerable many times, but I never thought I would see him this vulnerable again. Especially now. "And the Derek you still knew is in me, okay? I just don't trust him."

"Why?"

"Because if I become him again, I'm going to get hurt. Just like I always do." He's so defenceless, like a fuming, cheerless bulldog, begging for a hug. "I hate my parents for leaving me. For making me feel lonely and...*guilty*." A tear slid down his nose. "And I hate seeing people happy. It makes me feel even more lonely."

"You have Marline and your brother..."

"I need someone else," he muttered, and I actually heard the pain in his voice. "I need someone who understands me more than anyone else; someone who understands the pain I'm going through; someone who understands why I'm an asshole; someone who trusts me."

"How can people trust you when you're just a bully?"

"You know, Mike was the only one who was there for me," Derek said, pushing my question to the side. "He was like a true father to me. He helped me, he understood the pain I was going through, he healed my wounds. He did so many things for me, and every time I kept on asking myself 'Why did Mike help me even though I was and still a bad person?'" Derek finally looked at me. "Why did he help me, angel?"

"Because he loved helping people," I countered.

"He said that he saw something beautiful inside me," Derek said, particularly to himself. He chuckled humourlessly. "There is nothing beautiful inside me but a black heart."

"If Mike was here, he would get angry and scold you for saying that. He doesn't like it when people insult themselves."

Derek flicked a tear off his cheek. "I missed talking to you." His eyes never left mine, and a sudden, affectionate sentiment enclosed around us. "I missed you...so much."

I stared at him. His words were mostly unbelievable. Derek and I were awesome friends. I think Mike's death was the main reason our friendship to shatter. Derek grew distant. I tried to help him, but he pushed me away, begging me to leave him alone.

So, I left him alone.

For far too long.

And every time, I wish I could just hug him.

I missed Derek's hugs.

I missed his annoying personality.

I missed him.

I loved him.

"I wished I didn't push you away." His voice is still hoarse from his blistering tears. "I wish I allowed you to help me. I thought you wouldn't understand the pain I was going through when Mike died."

"I felt pain too, Derek!" I burst. "I missed Mike. I want him back just as much as you do. I know how close Mike and you were. You should know how close Mike and I were too. You're right—you shouldn't have pushed me away! You should've just allowed me to hug you, to help you, to comfort you because you were the second person I was closest too. I…needed you too."

His eyes were full of shock at my choice of words.

"Derek, if you want someone to understand you, to love you, and to help you, then you shouldn't have hurt those girls. How can people trust you when you're just a bully?"

"Do you want to know why I hurt girls?" he questioned. "I hurt girls because *I* don't want to be hurt. I hurt girls because I don't want to feel miserable. I want them to feel miserable."

I wanted to snap at him, *That's a lame excuse*, but I thought otherwise. The reason why Derek is a player is because if Derek abandons the girl before she abandons him, he can't get hurt just like the way his mother left him.

"Derek, that's irrational. There are other ways to get rid of the pain."

"Like how?"

"Like…thinking happy thoughts?" My suggestion came out more like a question.

Derek snorted. "That's what everyone says," he muttered. "They just don't know that it's hard for people like me to think happy thoughts. It's too difficult."

I didn't say anything as a reply. Derek is a hundred percent right. I'm sick of everyone saying to people who are hurting to think of happy thoughts. Can't they see that it's hard for people who are depressed? The only way for someone to be truly happy is if he or she receives help and understanding.

"I hate saying this but do you think your parents and Mike would be happy to know that you hurt girls?"

My question only caused Derek to look guilty, ashamed, and sad. His eyes wandered away from mine, not even bothering to look at me. Gradually, he lowered himself to the chair, placing both elbows on his knees and running his hands down his face.

"No," he finally answered. "No. They'll be disappointed."

"Exactly." I walked toward him, sitting down next to him and placing my hand on his. "This is why you need to stop."

Before he could say anything else, the door to the balcony opened, and Ethan's head peeked through the white curtains.

"We gotta go," he informed. He noticed Derek and a glare settled on his features. "What were you two talking about?"

"None of your damn business," Derek snapped.

Ethan's glare deepened. "It is my damn business if my sister is involved in it."

"Ethan, it's nothing," I said.

Ethan looked at me. "Are you sure?"

"Yes."

"Right, then I'll go." He glowered at Derek one more time before leaving.

I glanced at Derek once more. He smiled at me and I returned it. I swerved around, making my way to the doors, feeling his gaze smouldering on my back. My hand grabbed the knobs of the balcony doors, twisting them...

"April, wait."

I turned around. "What?"

"April, I know this sounds crazy, but recently, I've been having these thoughts that you could be that person who knows me and understands how I feel."

I blinked. "I...uh..."

"I want you to go out with me."

"I...uh..."

"Please. Just one date. And if it goes great, then it's great. If it goes bad, then it's bad."

"But...you broke other girls though."

"So? Maybe I can change if I am with you."

I stared at Derek. "I don't know, Derek...You're a player. A heartbreaker. I don't know if it's best if I go out with you, especially since my life is shitty as well."

"Then...can we go as friends?"

I raised an eyebrow at him. "Friends dating? This isn't friends with benefits."

In less than a second, he's unexpectedly standing in front of me. His jet-black hair fell over his ocean blue eyes, obscuring them yet giving a glimpse of that enchanting shimmer. "Please? Just one date?"

Don't. Don't do it, my mind told me. But my heart was telling me: *Yes, go with him. He's hurting just like you. Go. Make yourself happy for once.*

No! He's using you! He's playing with you!

My mind's words are getting stronger than my heart's words.

"Fine," I decided just when an idea popped into my head. "I'll go out with you."

Derek grinned. "Awesome."

"We're going to the cinema," I noted. "I'll meet you there around seven in the evening."

"Awesome," Derek echoed.

Chapter Five

Date

Derek Matthews

"Aye, Derek," Theo's voice sounded from my phone resting on my bed; the loudspeaker is on.

Other than the extravagance of my bedroom, it isn't really enchanting: white walls with huge windows facing the yards surrounding my humongous house. The floor is wooden with a fluffy square-shaped grey carpet that holds my bed. My bed is a white mattress with thick black sheets and pillows, facing the large TV screen that's glued to the wall with a small white sofa placed underneath it.

"Theo, success is on my side, man," I said, grinning as I took out a dark shirt. "I asked April out and she said yes."

"Huh? That easily? But you guys were, like, enemies in Math. How come you're, like, good all of a sudden? That's odd, don't you think?"

"Yeah, whatever. But, dude, on this date I will—"

"Wait, wait, wait...what did you do to make her go out with you? I thought she's Derek-proof?"

"Well, you're wrong about that."

"Derek, what did you do?"

I pulled my shirt over my head, throwing it on the bed. "She came to the memorial yesterday. She heard my speech—"

"To make her feel sorry, right?"

"What? No! To be honest, I wasn't really thinking of her when I was saying my eulogy. Anyway, we had a talk. I got angry at her because she said something rude about my parents. I told my true feelings: that I was feeling guilty and lonely."

"Basically, you were being yourself."

"Yeah. I...I confessed my anger to her."

"So, she knows why you're a douche?"

I chuckled. "Yeah."

"Man." The phone resonated with Theo's sigh. "I never thought you would be so open to her. To anyone, actually."

"Same," I mumbled.

"How do you feel?" Theo questioned. "How do you feel about confessing?"

"It feels..." I spent five seconds to consider the right words. "It feels good. Confessing isn't really that bad. But what if she tells the whole school that I'm, you know...weak?"

"April is the perfect person to confess to, dude. She won't tell the whole school. She can be snarky, but she isn't that rude. She's the perfect girl for you, Derek."

"No, she's not."

"She is," Theo argued. "Even Jackson admitted it."

"It's not like I'm gonna fall for her."

"What if you did?"

"That's impossible."

"It's not, actually. Have you ever heard of the phrase 'opposites attract'?"

"Yeah. But it's not actually true."

"Sometimes it is."

"The heartbreaker doesn't fall in love."

"But he can if he finds the right girl," Theo said. "You never know what God has planned for you. He allows the bad things, the challenges, in our lives so we will learn how to overcome them. God is good, bro."

"I do believe in God," I admitted. "I can feel Him around me. I think it's because most of the time I pray to Him and ask Him to take away the pain. But sometimes I feel as if He left us all alone…"

"He didn't. He's the Invisible Superhero. His way of not being seen or heard is His way of testing us. My man Jesus is my hero, too. Derek, don't worry. He will take the pain away. We just got to wait."

"I don't know if I can wait."

"Time goes fast, man."

I put on my shirt. Theo is correct—my pain will go away. I just need to give life some time to verify to me that God does have something great for me. No matter how heart-breaking it can be, I know that He knows I am in so much pain. "At any rate, on this date, I will *crush her*. I'm telling you, it's going to be epic."

"Bro, when are you gonna stop doing this unnecessary shit? Don't you even feel ashamed that you're doing this to April? You had a crush on her, and she's Mike's little sister, for Christ's sake!"

"I don't have a crush on her. Not anymore."

"Bro, why you lying? You promised Mike that you won't hurt her."

"Then why did you give me this damn dare?!"

Theo sighed. "It's…complicated."

"Tell me."

"No."

"Then do you think I'm gonna be lit on this date?"

"I don't know, man. I smell something fishy about this. And I can literally smell fish because my Dad is making some fish, so… Ugh, I think I'm going to puke…" I heard Theo make a nauseous noise. "Yup, I'm going to barf. Gotta go now. Good luck on the date. Bye." He ended the call.

I glanced at the time. Shit, twelve minutes left.

*   *   *

I finally finished dressing up. I didn't bother to wear something nice since this date isn't really going to be an actual date.

I hopped into my car and drove to Peony Hallows Cinema. Once I arrived, I parked the car, got out, and waited in front of the building for April to come. The November coldness dug deep into my skin, numbing my bones. I shivered, shoving my hands into my pockets as I looked down at the pedestrian sidewalk, still waiting for April to arrive.

After some minutes, I took my phone out to see that it's ten past seven. I frowned.

Where is April?

I decided to call her.

"April, where are you?" I demanded once she answered the call.

"What are you talking about?" she asked.

"I'm outside the cinema for the date, remember?"

"Oh, the date…Well, Derek, the thing is that I wasn't really planning to date you in my entire life. This date was just a game."

I clenched my other hand into a fist. "You mean you—"

"Yup. Derek Matthews, I, April Levesque, tricked you and played you." I heard April laugh. "Man, this feels good."

"You're going to pay for this, April," I growled. "One day, I'm going to make your life a living hell."

"I have to tutor you. My life is already a living hell."

"I'll make it worse."

I ended the call and threw my phone into my pocket. I grabbed my hair with my fingers and pulled it in frustration.

That girl…That girl is annoying as hell. She's full of surprises. Some of them are good. Some of them are just plain maddening.

Chapter Six

Mike Levesque

April Levesque

The next day, someone decided to pay me a visit.

I was sitting on the couch, glued to the TV screen which was playing an episode of Teen Wolf season six. The doorbell rang, leaving me puzzled.

"Are we expecting someone?" I asked in a raised voice.

"Uhm, I think so!" Mom replied. "Check the door, honey!"

I groaned with laziness. I just started watching TV fifteen minutes ago, and I'm finally starting to feel relaxed. *For once, why can't I be at peace?*

I walked to the main door, swinging open to be greeted by that arrogant, annoying smirk that triggers me to slap his face.

My greeting was an irritated, whine as Derek said "Hi."

"Honey, who is it?" Mom asked from the kitchen.

"It's my worst nightmare!" I yelled back.

"Beautiful nightmare, actually," Derek corrected cockily.

In less than a second, Mom emerged from the kitchen door. Approaching us, a smile appeared on her face. "Derek!" my mother greeted. "How great it is to see you again."

"Good to see you too, Mrs. Levesque."

His eyes landed on me, and he opened his mouth, attempting to start a conversation with me, but I abandoned him and went upstairs to my bedroom, ignoring my mother's instructions to come back.

I shut my bedroom door behind me and flopped down onto my bed, exhaling a fractious sigh. I rubbed my eyes with my fingers gently.

"Oh, boy…" I glanced at a picture frame of Jesus Christ and hauled myself into a sitting position. Staring into the eyes of Jesus, I said, "PLEASE TELL ME I WILL NOT HAVE TO SUFFER HIS PRESENCE FOR THE WHOLE WEEKEND!"

I was about to echo the same words, begging Jesus to make my weekend splendid, when a knock sounded. Thinking it was my mother, I muttered "Come in."

The door swung inwards, revealing Derek who was clutching an exercise book and a pencil case.

"What are you doing here?" I asked.

"Your mother told me to start my lesson now." He flopped down onto my bed. He raked a hand through his black locks, his blue eyes fixed on me. "You hate me, right?"

"Absolutely. Although, I am a little happy that I tricked you." I grinned when I remembered our last conversation on the phone—when I told Derek that the date was just a trick. That was awesome.

Derek's jaw hardened. "That was just luck."

"I know. I am full of luck and you're just full of bad karma."

Derek rolled his eyes. "Can't we at least be friends, April?"

I titled my head to the side. "Can we start the lesson, so you can get your ass out of my house?"

His jaw clenched with annoyance again. I have to admit, he looks cute when he gets aggravated. Wait, what? Cute? *Cute?* Seriously?

"Derek, write down the title of the topic we're learning which is called Smoking and Drugs."

He didn't obey. He just stared at me. "Why don't you like me?"

I glared at him. "Is it necessary for you to ask that?"

"Yeah."

"Well, the reason why I don't like you is because you're just a messed up bipolar douche. You have some troubling issues, and you are a cold-hearted ass who doesn't even care about what others feel. Yes, I know why you're being a heartbreaker, but there are other ways to cope with the misery. But, as expected, you decided not to be mature and intelligent and listen to the dumb voice living in your head."

Derek blinked at my words.

I yelped when he suddenly thrust himself forward and fell on top of me, pressing his warm body onto mine. He then leaned forward, and his breath tickled the skin of my neck, sending tingles down my back.

"I'll admit, what you said is certainly true. But one day you'll love me," he whispered huskily in my ear.

I clenched my hand into a fist as anger boiled inside me. *How dare he touch me?*

I jammed my elbows into his ribs, and he groaned faintly. I took this as an opportunity to ram him off of me and he fell to the floor with a loud *thud*. I wanted to slap my hand across his cheek to wipe off that ridiculous smirk. He knows that he's irritating me, and he likes it. I straightened myself up and stormed out of the bedroom, slamming the door behind me. I ran down the stairs, running both of my hands through my brunette locks in frustration.

"Hello, April," Mom greeted as I entered the kitchen. Her brunette hair is tied up into a messy bun, with strands hanging down. Her bun dangles as she sliced a carrot on the chopping board. "How's Derek?"

"He's an asshole," I muttered in reply.

Mom glared at me. "Language, April."

"But it's true, Mom. He's a complete asshole."

"You'll get used to it, trust me."

"You sound as if you've been through stuff like this."

"I have been, actually," she admitted. "Your father was a dick. He still is sometimes."

I raised an eyebrow, cracking a smile. "Really?"

"Mhmm. He was the jock in my school. He stole many girls' hearts and blah, blah, blah." She glanced at me. "But whenever he's with his family, whenever he's out of school, he's a completely different person. He's so nice, so sweet, so charming."

"So, are you saying that people are different at home than they are at school?"

Mom nodded. "For example, you're an introvert at school. Yet at home, you're such an extrovert." She began slicing a vegetable again. "Give Derek a chance, April. You have the authority to boss him around whenever you're tutoring him, but you have to be nice to him as well. Get to know him and make a mental list of how he's like at school and at home."

"But Derek isn't nice."

Mom sighed. "That's what everyone thinks," she muttered. "I've known Derek ever since he was a kid, honey. His mother and I used to be good friends…"

"What are you trying to say, Mom?"

"He may be a jerk," Mom admitted. "He may need a few slaps once in a while. But he's…he's hurting. You know what happened to his parents. He feels lonely. Marline and I always saw how close you two were. We thought that if he spends time with you, he won't feel lonely anymore. He'll be more himself. He'll get better." Mom looked at me. "You don't know what type of past he had. You don't know what he saw. One day, he'll confess everything to you."

"How can you say that?"

"I know that ever since Mike left," Mom said, "you feel hurt, shallow, and miserable. It's the same with Derek. One day, you and Derek will realise what you both have in common and he'll confess everything to you."

"He already did," I said. "He told me why he's the heartbreaker. It's because of his Mom. But don't you think that's a lame excuse?"

"It could be a lame excuse…But he's still learning, April. He hated his mother for leaving him. He hated *God* for taking her away. He lost his dad, too. And Mike. You know that Mike was so special to Derek. Sometimes, people are more likely act out or to inflict their pain on others so that others know what it feels like. So that they can feel better about themselves. Derek doesn't like showing weakness, so he is doing all the player-act to channel his anger, insecurity, and pain. Just give him a chance. He's not that bad."

Mom has a point. People are like that—they project their pain onto others. That's one of the main reasons why there are bullies. I thanked Mom for the pep talk and exited the kitchen.

When I entered my bedroom, I found Derek sprawled out on my bed, looking at my sketchbook, causing me to let out a shriek. Derek flinched, startled. He slammed the sketchbook shut.

"What are you doing?" I snatched the book off his hands.

"I remember you loved to draw," is all Derek said. He somehow managed to grab the sketchbook back and opened it. "You've improved." He kept on flicking the pages over, analysing each sketch. "April, even when I'm not bored I can only draw stick figures. But *these*...these are *beautiful*," he confessed, looking up at me and smirked. "Are you...blushing?"

"No. I'm not."

"Yes you are. It's cute, though."

That made my cheeks burn even more.

"This is Mike," Derek whispered, staring at my sketch of a young good-looking man — around his early twenties — with high cheekbones, a sharp jaw line, and dark shaggy hair.

I stared at the picture of my older brother as bittersweet memories flashed in my mind. "Yeah." My eyes roamed over Derek's face, detecting a hint of tears prickling his eyes.

"I miss him," Derek murmured, his eyes full of sadness.

Sitting down next to him on the bed, I hesitantly put my arm around Derek. He involuntarily leaned into me, resting his head on my shoulder as he stared at my sketch of my older brother. "I miss him too," I whispered. Tears stung the back of my eyes.

Derek had known Mike for a long time. He properly met him when he was eight or ten. I knew that Derek was in a bad mood when he first met Mike—Derek was crying (I don't know why, though) and he told Mike what was going on. Mike helped Derek.

"Tell me a story of him," Derek suddenly demanded. "Please." He hastily wiped his eyes vulnerably. "And maybe telling me stuff about him will make you feel better."

"Why should I tell you?" I asked. "You don't care about me."

"I do!" Derek burst out, looking up at me with cold eyes. "Don't you ever say that! I always cared about you...even when I needed you the most." His last words came out as a soft, heart-wrenching murmur. "We were good friends, April. Now we're not. We don't talk anymore."

"We're talking now."

"April. Please. You know how much I miss Mike."

"I miss him, too."

"I just want you to tell me a story about him...like the good old days." I smiled at his last words, remembering our times together as younger kids when we were cuddling in my bed and I was telling him stories.

"Will you tell anyone?"

"No. I won't."

To be honest, I miss this Derek Matthews. This is the Derek Matthews I knew—vulnerable, sweet, and so funny and caring. It's a shame that he has to be a player to mask his true self.

"Besides, your mother wants us to be friends again," Derek said. "Maybe opening up to each other will be best."

I snorted. "My mom thinks we can be a couple. She's blind."

"I don't mind, though," said Derek. "But I'll probably get abused, judging by the fact that you like slapping me."

"You deserve it."

"No, I don't."

"My mom admitted you deserve some slaps."

"No wonder where you got your I-like-to-slap-people trait from."

"Hey, my mom isn't that bad."

"Neither was mine."

Derek's head is still in the crook of my neck, his warm breaths tickling my skin. I lowered my gaze to my sketch of my older brother. He's grinning at me. His grin gave me the feeling that he never left me, that even though he's gone, he's still there for me. The way I drew his eyes, the way they gawked at me, gave me the impression that Mike is watching over me from Heaven.

"Once upon a time, there was a boy," I began, "his name was Mike Levesque. My brother and my best friend. He always wanted to do something memorable for this world — to save the poor and the innocent, to fight the wickedness—"

"He wanted to become like Superman," Derek interjected. He laughed, reminiscing.

I laughed too, feeling his tears falling on my skin. He swung one arm over my waist and held me tightly, as if he's afraid to let me go. "That's right—he wanted to become like Superman. He decided to become a soldier. He fought for a few months. Sometimes FaceTime us and told us what he did. Then, three years ago, he got shot and lost a lot of blood. The soldiers tried to save him, but it was too late…" I blinked my eyes rapidly to push away the tears.

"He was a good soldier," Derek said. I actually heard the empathy in his voice, which made me smile a little. "May the soldier rest in peace with the Lord and protect us from all danger." He patted his chest with his palm as an act of respect.

That's what everyone says when they hear Mike's name.

"I wish he could be here," Derek mumbled into my neck. I am a little bothered by our position yet at the same time I'm not. This is how we're always like before when we're telling each other stories in bed. "I wish he could see how people are like whenever they hear his name. He got what he wanted—he is finally a hero."

"A hero of Peony Hallows. Not of the whole world."

"Well, eventually the whole world is going to hear Mike's story."

We spent a long hour embracing each other in bed in beautiful serenity. Here and then, Derek would draw lazy circles on my stomach, curl my hair with his fingers, or close his eyes and have a small nap—just like old times.

Then, I woke him up and told him to write down the title for today's lesson. He listened to me carefully as I taught him, jotting down brief notes and asking me questions. Sometimes, he goes on his phone without my permission, but I didn't hiss at him to pay attention to me. I let him do it. If he doesn't listen to me then he's going to fail in his tests, and when he does, he'll be on my doorstep and yelling at me that I'm a bad tutor. But hey, this is a lesson that he must understand.

Finally, the session is over, and I said goodbye to Derek. I padded my way up the stairs and crashed onto my bed, drawing the quilt over my body to keep me warm and comfortable.

I grabbed my sketchbook that was resting on the desk next to me. I flipped the pages over to a clean one, grabbed a pencil, and started sketching a person: my father. As I started drawing the shape of his head, the memory of when a soldier knocked on the door and informed us about the tragic, heroic death of my older brother played in my mind.

Lying on my cozy bed, my eyes were wide open, gazing at my ceiling that glimmered with Mike's glow-in-the-dark-stars.

For three hours, I've been waiting patiently. My patience ran out an hour ago, and I am now eager to hear that sound that will reverberate throughout my whole house. I need to hear that sound that will signal me he's finally home. I need that sound, so I can dash downstairs and crash into my older brother, cuddling him tightly as he embraces me back. I need to hear that sound for my brother to wish me a Happy Birthday *even though my birthday occurred three days ago. I need to hear that sound, so I won't feel lonely in my room anymore. I need to hear that sound for me to weep tears of contentment because he is finally here after several torturous months—*

DING!

I let out a screech of glee as I bolted upright in my bed, scrambling off the sheets and leaving my bedroom. I hastened down the hallway, my foot brushing the topmost step of the staircase. I descended hastily, but I slowed down when I perceived who was standing there. Mike isn't there. Instead, it was my father and another soldier with dark eyes, dark skin, and tiny coiled hair sticking out of his skull. They appeared grief-stricken, dressed in their uniforms.

My mother (she wasn't pregnant with Rosie that time) was crying, and my younger brother, Ethan, bit down on his lower lip, as if trying to keep from crying.

Dad's watery eyes met mine and I froze. I stood on the last step, motionless, as I tried to figure out what was happening.

"What's going on?" I finally asked after a moment of silence.

My mother looked at me, her cheeks dripping with tears, her drenched eyes puffy. "April…Oh, April…"

"Mom? What is it? Why are you all crying?"

Mom glimpsed at Dad and the dark-skinned soldier, not murmuring anything. I was about to call my mother again when the dark-skinned solider cleared his throat. He looked at me. "You're Mike's little sister, right?"

"Yes."

The soldier sighed, shoving his hands in his pockets. He seemed to be thinking what to say. "Kid," he started saying. "I'm sorry but your brother passed away…"

Silence. I can only hear silence. The birds that were serenading outside paused suddenly when the soldier said those tragic, heart-wrenching words. The atmosphere was thick with tension and misfortune.

I staggered backward, as if an invisible spirit callously pushed me. My bottom hit the step. I clamped my hand over my mouth as tears brimmed in my eyes. The menacing tears gushed out as I stopped myself from blabbing incoherently.

I can only feel grief and misery. The problem with these two sentiments is that they combine together, creating a sort of emptiness in your chest, yet at the same time, it feels as if your heart and lungs are on fire. It's a way of manipulating you, bullying you, killing you. It's a way of dousing the positivity.

"No," I managed to choke out. "No, no, no. Mike can't be gone. He can't. How can he just leave me like that?"

My father stared at me. A tear glided down his cheek. He advanced towards me, sliding his arm around my shoulders, pulling me into his loving embrace. He smoothed my hair with his quivering, stiff fingers. "April…"

I can't help this anymore. I was shivering. Not from the frostiness lurking in the house, but from the cynical emotions inside me. These emotions are like incurable viruses. I couldn't feel anything. I couldn't breathe. In fact, I was gasping for sweet air.

"April," Dad said when I pulled away from his arms.

I sprinted up the stairs. Wailing quietly, I slammed my bedroom door shut.

The gloom rose up like tidal waves, crashing over me, devouring me. It felt like I was drowning—my lungs hewing, my throat restricting oxygen to rescue me, my stomach churning with pain. There's a murderous throbbing in my brain as I hammered my head into the wall. The salty tears flowed in a frenzy down my scratchy cheeks.

Mike's death is just engulfing me, drowning me, pulling me away from the unnoticed brightness. My legs buckled. My knees plummeted to the carpet. I covered my face with my hands, all alone in my gloomy bedroom.

Storm clouds are now veiling the sky. The wind is roaring, howling with wretchedness. Silence invaded the room like unheard demonic spirits, capturing the light and hurling it away, only permitting the darkness to enter. Relief, comfort, and peace denied to embrace me and endorsed this pain to abuse me.

How can Mike just leave me like that? I feel more miserable. I just want the pain to leave my body. But there's no way. Unless…

My eyes settled on the shiny object, glistening underneath my pillow. I've been self-harming for two months. It was last week when I decided to stop and slaughter the temptation of cleaving my skin.

I stood up, approaching the knife. I threw my pillow across the room. Picking the knife, the sharp blade sinisterly sparkled in the darkness, as if Satan himself absorbed his body into the blade.

No, April, I tried to convince myself. April, don't do it. It's bad.

But I want to do it.

I hacked my arms and my legs. Over and over again. Again. Again. And again. Again until so much blood leaked out of the deep disfigurement, snaking down my tingling, numb skin. I looked at my reflection in the mirror, my hands clamping onto the sides of my desk. I gasped, my eyelids sliding over my eyeballs. I feel light-headed. My arms and legs stung…

My body collapsed to the floor. The blood saturated the carpet. I sighed one more time before I felt myself leaving my body and drifting off into a state of unconsciousness.

A tear dropped onto my sketchbook as I thought of him. My older brother meant a lot to me. He always looked out for me; always defended me from the people who were bullying me;

he encouraged me to try things that I haven't done. He kept our family happy until he died in the war in Syria.

Ever since he died, my whole family is now depressed. I sometimes hear my mother crying in her bedroom, looking at a picture of Mike as she sobs, muttering things, and saying a sweet Hail Mary for him.

I shut my sketchbook and thought about many things— but it was mainly about my older brother who sacrificed his life for the world, for the poor and the innocent. For Syria. For the Muslim victims of ISIS. Sometimes, I just wish that wickedness isn't real, that the Devil isn't real. But he is, and there's no way to stop him. He controls ISIS—he manipulates them, he gives them false theories, and dominates them to make fun of a peaceful religion. He's their boss now, even if they couldn't realise it.

Every day, I always ask myself this one, small question that doesn't always seem to have an answer: *Why is life so unfair?*

Chapter Seven

She's My Game

Derek Matthews

"So, how's it going with April?" Theo asked as I sat down next to him, placing my tray on the surface of the round cafeteria table.

"Yo, Derek, I heard that April tricked you," Jackson greeted, sitting down next to me, grinning so hard. "Why do all the good things happen when I'm not around?"

Word does spread fast in Peony Hallows High School.

Theo grinned as well. "I've heard about that as well. You guys were supposed to meet up, but she didn't. That girl has some balls, you know?"

Jackson frowned. "She's a woman...she doesn't have balls...she has a—"

"It was just an expression! God, Jackson, you're more annoying than Derek, actually!"

Jackson rolled his eyes before moving his attention to me. "Is luck on your side with April?"

"Luck is never on his side, Jackson," Theo muttered. "Bad karma is just ruining his life."

It was my turn to roll my eyes. April said the same thing, and now Theo did. Ugh.

"Everything is going fine with April," I grumbled.

"Doesn't look like it to me. Last time I checked, April still looks the same." Theo pointed to April who's standing in line, looking through the window, her hand fidgeting with a pendant attached to a black thread. "I don't think I spotted her giving you lovey-dovey stares."

"I have it under control, man."

"You have four weeks to make her fall in love with you and crush her, dude," Theo reminded.

"I said I got it!"

Theo didn't flinch, but Jackson did. Jackson exhaled, placing a hand over his chest. "Jesus Christ, Derek, calm your balls," Jackson muttered. He looked at the table next to him where his twin sister, Jasmine, is sitting alone, tapping his fingers on the desk, impatiently waiting for her friends. Jackson looked back at me. "Derek, I don't like this dare. It's cruel. April is a freaking human being like you for God's sake."

"Why are you against this dare?"

"Because my sister wants to be friends with her! Plus, I like April Levesque even though we never talked that much. I don't know why people hate her. She's normal like us. Sure, she might have some issues, but everyone is different."

"Exactly," Theo agreed. "People need to leave that girl alone and let her live her life."

I raised an eyebrow at my friend. "Then why did you give me the dare to make her fall in love with me?"

Theo stared at me for a long moment before saying, "I have my reasons."

"Care to tell me them?"

"When the time is right, I will."

I raked a hand through my black hair. "April is also impossible to get," I added in a mutter. "One time she's shy and the next she's so hissy and angry."

"Maybe it's because of Mike," Theo guessed.

"Oh, yeah, that guy who died in Syria, right?" said Jackson. "I never met him, but people in the town said he was a good guy."

"There are still posters of him in the town, you know?" Theo said. "*They Call Him Fearless For A Reason* is always on all of the posters."

"I knew him," I said. "I knew Mike ever since I was a kid. He was Luke's best friend."

Theo's eyes met mine, and I silently begged him to change the topic. Mike is always a vulnerable subject to talk about. Not only for me, but for other people.

"My older sister, Chloe," said Theo, "knew Mike when they were both in high school…"

"Wait, were they dating?"

"No. Well, I think Mike liked her, but Chloe didn't feel the same way. Chloe found out about Mike's death. She was sad, of course, and she told me that the Levesque family…sadness changes your mood sometimes."

Jackson bit his sandwich. "How did he die again?"

"He got shot by an ISIS soldier," Theo explicated. "He got shot after he saved a little girl. That's what everyone says."

"Whoa, that guy must be hella brave," Jackson mumbled, his mouth full of food. "That's sad, though." He looked at me. "Derek, go easy on her."

"I am going easy on her!" I protested. "She's the one who's not going easy on me!"

"Then tell her something," Theo suggested. "Anything that might make her fall in love with you."

"You mean…lie to her?"

Theo nodded. "Why the odd look, Derek?" he asked as he bit on his homemade pizza.

"It's just…won't lying make her upset?"

Jackson grinned. "Derek," he said in a teasing voice. "Do you have a crush on her?"

"What? No!"

"Then why do you look worried? What's up, man?"

"It's nothing…"

"Derek…"

"April just looks a lot like my mum," I blurted. "I have this urge not to hurt her and just to help her, but at the same time I want to win this dare."

Jackson's nose scrunched up in disgust. "That's disgusting…"

"No, it's not what you think it is." I rolled my eyes at Jackson's disgusted expression. Sometimes, Jackson can be nasty in so many ways. "I mean that April sort of reminds me of my mother: they both love books, they both wore glasses, they both have dark hair, and they both wear long sleeve shirts."

Before Jackson could say anything, Theo said, "Who cares if April looks like your mum? April is your game, Derek. This is a dare that you accepted. You promised to break her heart after she falls in love with you."

"And I will," I said, looking at April who is now walking out of the cafeteria with a packet of sandwiches and a water bottle. "I'll rip her heart out while she's crying."

Chapter Eight

Pain Is Temporary

April Levesque

"April?" a voice called from outside. Knocks hammered the door. "Little Sis, open the door."

I sniffled. "No. Go away."

I heard Mike sigh. "April, I didn't mean to yell at you."

My eyes fluttered closed. Another tear gradually glided down my cheek. My brother's crush, Chloe Romano, came over to our house so Mike can help her with her homework. I was too timid to make new friends. However, I was suspicious of this Chloe girl. When I first saw her, I didn't like her. She seemed one of those rude girls who think they are way superior to others. However, Chloe and I were surprisingly on good terms. Mike, on the other hand, was frustrated that I had Chloe's attention. He lost it and scolded me to go away. I was frightened at his sudden anger that I never witnessed before. He never shouted at me. Today was the first.

A thought came to me that Mike in all probability likes Chloe more than me; a thought transpired that Mike cares about Chloe more than me.

I was in my bedroom. Gawking up at the glow-in-the-dark-stars peppering the ceiling, another tear rolled down my face, dampening the pillows. The glow-in-the-dark stars looked enchanting in the night. They're like fireflies, flying in the air, shining down at me as if I'm the most valuable, most precious human in the entire universe.

"April," Mike called again. "Please, open the door."

"What's wrong?" Mom asked Mike.

"April is not letting me come in."

"Why not?"

"I shouted at her."

"What?"

"I got annoyed that Chloe was talking to her more than to me. I got jealous."

"So you shouted at her?"

"Yeah..."

"I got scared," I murmured, knowing they could hear my quiet, quaking voice. "Mike never shouted at me before. Mike is going to leave me, Mom. Mike is going to leave Dad, Ethan, you and me. He's not going to care about us anymore. He's going to care for someone else."

My fingers were shaking, so I dipped them underneath me, sitting on them to stop the trembling. I loved my brother. So much. He's so sweet, so caring. I couldn't imagine my life without him. Just couldn't.

Mom sighed. "April, honey, that's not true."

I wiped a tear. "It is."

"April, stop saying bullshit!" Mike snapped. "There is no way in hell that I will care about someone more than you."

"Mike, language!" Mom scolded.

Mike exhaled. I heard him bang his forehead against the door. "April, please let me in. I don't like seeing you cry. I don't like knowing that you're crying because of me."

"Go away, Mike," I retorted.

"April—"

"Mike, love, let her be," Mom insisted. *"She needs space."*

"But she's crying..."

"She'll stop. Just give her some time."

*   *   *

Scurrying along the hallways as fast as possible to my next classroom, I did not care who stopped me to bully me. I was not getting late for class again.

I sensed a presence behind me and stiffened, peeking over my shoulder to see Brigit Sanders advancing towards me, a cruel smirk plastered on her face. My heart battered with anxiety as I increased my speed of walk, though Brigit grabbed me by my arm, her sharp fake fingernails piercing my skin, and yanked me backwards callously.

She thumped me into a wall nearby, her other hand seizing my neck ruthlessly. "What's this about Derek?" she demanded in a hiss.

For a moment, I thought she's talking about me tutoring him. I was pretty sure I warned Derek not to tell anyone about the tutoring.

"People say he's trying to get with you," Brigit continued. "Apparently he kissed your neck."

Oh, that, I thought.

"Yeah," I said. "He did, and I punched him. I told him not to do it again and he didn't."

Brigit leaned forward. "Stay away from my boyfriend, April," she hissed.

I raised an eyebrow. "Wait, he's your boyfriend? But how come nobody knows?"

Brigit released her grip from my neck. She snatched strands of my brunette hair and yanked it unkindly. My head banged the wall and I wheezed in pain. "Promise me that you'll stay away from him," Brigit growled.

"Brigit, I don't even like him. I'll stay away from him."

"Good," Brigit said, releasing my hair. She leaned forward and whispered another insult, "You're so ugly that Hello Kitty said goodbye to you, you little bit—"

I cringed. *Wow, what a great insult.* Note the sarcasm. "Do you need lessons on how to be a high-class spoiled girl?"

Brigit can be embarrassing sometimes. She could act like a brat, but she always managed to lower my self-esteem. She treated me horribly in the past...thrashing me around, pushing me into the lockers, slapping me. She stopped for a while, which made me happy but worried at the same time.

I should tell a teacher. But I have no idea how. It's hard for me to confess.

The sad thing was Brigit and I were best friends. She and I were always there for each other until that one time when a boy decided to interfere in our lives.

Brigit's lips tilted up into a sneer. It looked like she wanted to slap me again. Though, she thought otherwise. She let go of me, her eyes like daggers as she eyed me one more time before pacing away, doing her "sassy walk", her hips swaying from side to side as her fine blonde hair swung behind her back.

She paused in her tracks and peeked over her shoulder to look at me one more time. "And it's a good thing that your brother died. He deserved it. You deserved it. He probably died in the battle because of your ugliness. And when you die, April, I do hope you go to hell."

She walked on and disappeared behind a wall, leaving me all alone. Now that rudeness burned me powerfully...

Tears blurred my eyes. Everyone in town knew Mike. However, Mike passed away three years ago, so the chatter about

Mike decreased leisurely. He was a hero. I loved him. I would do anything to have him back, even if it's only for one second.

Why do I feel as if Derek told her?

*   *   *

My eyes opened as I heard the noise of feet shuffling in the small corridor outside. I jolted up in my bed. Darkness lurked in my room except for the light of the moon behind the clouds that crawled inside, dancing around and killing the shadows. The glow-in-the-dark stars were still dazzling like jewels budding in the ceiling.

Knock.

"April?"

Knock.

"April?"

"Yes, Mike?"

"Can I come in, Little Sis?"

I hesitated. Then, I slithered off my bed and walked to the door, unhurriedly and gently opening it to see my older brother, dressed in his pyjamas; his brown hair messy with spikes poking out. Glistening on his right ear is a ring.

Mike pulled me into a hug.

I wrapped my arms around his waist as I buried my face in his stomach. He's taller than me. Taller than Mom. Nearly taller than Dad.

Mike crouched down, buckling his knees, his face levelled with mine. His fingers fondled my hair. "I'm sorry for shouting at you," he whispered, smiling apologetically. "I didn't mean to."

My lower lip trembled, and I wanted to slap myself for being such a coward. "I'm sorry for making you jealous."

Mike only laughed. "And being jealous was unnecessary since I always have you."

My trembling lips managed to beam a smile at him.

"Come on, I'll read you a story," Mike decided, pulling me to my bed.

"But it's one o'clock in the morning."

Mike shrugged. I sighed. Mike was always the ill-disciplined one in the family. He got his good-humoured mischief from Dad. It's flawlessly evident.

I slid underneath the covers next to Mike. He wrapped an arm around me, and we both gazed at the ceiling.

"Mike?" I whispered.

"Yes?"

"What I said is true, isn't it? About the fact that you will have to leave us?"

"Yes, Little Sis," Mike responded. *"It's the same for you anyway."*

"I don't want you to leave."

"I'm not going to."

"You will."

"No. I won't."

"Mike?"

"Yes?"

"How does it feel like to fall in love?"

Mike only grinned at me, winking. "Why? You have a soft spot for someone?"

"No. I'm just asking."

"If you do like someone, tell me who the person is so I can see if he's a worthy guy for you."

"Are you really that overprotective?"

"You're my sister. Of course, I have to be overprotective of you. At any rate, falling in love is amazing. You get this fuzzy, warm feeling inside your chest and you're always happy whenever you think about the person you love. You can actually talk about your crush, but whenever he or she is around, you're speechless."

"But love doesn't always work out," I mumbled. 'Some people cheat. Some people break hearts. Why is that?"

Mike struggled to find the right words. "April, love is like a test. Love is like a creature. It knows you more than we know ourselves. It knows who is right for us and who isn't. It's testing us in a way that we will never understand. It's cruel, abusive, and dangerous. It's not always the best thing in the world. It's a healthy sickness. It's like a bright smoke enclosing around you. It's like an awful joy clouding your feelings. It's confusing."

"God loves us," I said. "He loves us no matter what we do."

"That's right. God loves us."

"Mike?"

"Yes?"

"Why are people insulting God? Why don't people believe in Him?"

"There are other religions, April. Not everyone believes in the same deity. Some people find it hard to believe that there is a Higher Power out there, watching from above, testing us. People find it hard to believe in God because nobody has ever seen Him. There is evidence of him: the Bible…his Son who came to Earth two thousand years ago… When Jesus was born, the timeline split: BC ended, and we're now living in AD. But people want scientific evidence. The world is all about science, after all."

"Science doesn't know everything," I muttered.

"It doesn't. The knowledge of science is ninety-five percent of the truth. The other five percent…well, I think they just don't want to believe there is a God. Personally, I think that people struggling to believe Him is just a test, a test to see if we're wise. Besides, God gave us free will."

"What do you think about the people insulting God?"

"I don't mind them. They're okay. But the thing is, some of the nonbelievers try to persuade others not to believe in God and Jesus Christ. That's the thing I hate. Why can't people just leave everyone alone and let them believe in whatever they want?"

"What happens if you don't believe in Him?"

"Nothing. He'll still be there for you, but He'll realize that you don't need Him anymore, so He'll back off from you."

"But isn't that a sin?"

"What? Not believing in God? Yeah. In our religion, it is. But He won't mind, though. He'll be upset, He may not accept us during Judgement Day, but I think He won't mind."

"Some people don't mind us. Some do. Why is that?"

"The people who don't like us...they just find us...idiotic."

"It makes me cry, sometimes. It hurts me."

"I know."

"Do you think we're idiotic?"

"Nah. I mean, we can believe in whatever we want, and the rest can believe and not believe in whatever they want. I just don't like it when people don't like people like us because of our belief."

"Someone tried to punch me for believing in God and Jesus."

Mike tensed. "What? Who?"

"You already talked to him. It was that guy you met yesterday."

"Oh, that guy."

"Did you talk to him nicely or...?"

"I talked to him nicely. I didn't do anything to him. I just told him to leave you alone and to allow you to believe in whatever you want to believe in."

"Why do you believe in God, Mike?"

"Because I do. I just love the feeling of knowing that there is someone out there who will love you no matter what you've done. Because that's what everyone needs right now: unconditional love. I love the feeling of knowing that there is someone out there looking over you. I also believe that the explosion of energy and light, the Big Bang, was part of God's plan. Because, come on, something can't happen randomly. There's a reason for everything, and I believe God let the Big Bang occurred. Besides, in the Bible, God did say 'Let there be light'. The Big Bang could be that light."

"Mike, why are there bad things in the world? Why does God let bad things happen?"

"He can't interfere in our lives unless we call Him, April."

"Why?"

"Because He gave us free will. He promised us that He will not interfere with our lives unless we call Him."

"Does He answer immediately?"

"He will hear you, but He won't answer immediately. He will test you first, analyse you, and then that's when He will embrace you. He has a plan for all of us, but only if we ask Him. Sometimes, His plans can be painful and hard, but I believe that if our journey is unbearable, that's when the good comes. You just got to wait. When He's silent, that's when you know His plan is gonna be good."

"What would you do if you meet Jesus, Mike?"

"I would hug him. What about you?"

"I would cry and hug him, too. Mike, you know Jesus is going to come back one day, right?"

"Yeah. He will."

"What happens when he comes back again?"

"He's gonna kick Satan's bloody ass."

"And?"

"He's gonna…give us holy donuts?"

"What?"

Mike chuckled. "Kidding."

"Mike?"

"Yes?"

"Are you scared of God?"

"Yes."

"Why?"

"He's powerful, April. He's more powerful than anyone and anything in the universe. He is full of love, but he's also full of anger. He wants justice. He can test us, but we can't test Him. He's stronger than us."

"Mike, I'm scared if I'm not going to be one of those people who will be saved from God's wrath."

"Don't think like that, Little Sis. As long as you say 'Jesus, I love you, I trust in you, I believe in you. Please save me and forgive me' then you won't suffer."

"I say that all the time, Mike. I can actually feel Jesus in my room whenever I say a prayer."

"Me too. I guess it's because we're the Levesques—we come from a strongly religious family that's why we can actually feel him."

"Mike?"

Mike sighed. "Yes?"

"I love you."

Mike smiled. "I love you too."

*   *   *

After school, I walked home.

I closed the door behind me, slid my shoes off, and strode to the kitchen. I realised it was quiet, which was peculiar because every day I always hear the TV or music coming from Ethan's room upstairs. Ethan should be home by now. Maybe he came out of school late? Or maybe he's in detention. Mom and Rosie must be out shopping.

I was about to turn on the TV when the doorbell rang. I groaned. Every single time, whenever I watch TV, there is always something or someone who interrupts my free time. I ambled to the door, opening it to see the last person I wanted to meet on Earth. Derek Matthews.

Derek grinned. His attire was only a pair of jeans and a white shirt with a blue, denim cardigan warming him. His jet black hair was tousled, touching his eyelashes attractively. "Hello, my angel, how are—"

I ignored him. I kicked the door in an attempt to close it, but Derek immediately stepped inside. Why did he come here after he told Brigit about my brother? I felt my eyes sting as Brigit's words echoed in my mind. *And it's a good thing that your brother died. He deserved it. You deserved it. He probably died in battle because of your ugliness.* What if her words were true?

I grabbed a can of juice from the fridge.

"Why are you so rude?" Derek demanded, pouting.

I nearly laughed. "I'm rude? What about you? You're rude like a demon. In fact, you could be one."

As expected, his jaw tightened, his blue eyes glared. "Stop insulting me, April. At least be nice to me!"

"I cannot do that."

"Why not?"

I spun around, banging the juice can on the marble counter next to me. *Was he really serious?* "You told Brigit about my brother when I specifically told you not to tell anyone!"

Derek furrowed his eyebrows. "I never told anyone, April."

"That's a lame excuse, Derek!"

"I'm not lying, April. I swear to God, I never told anyone about Mike."

"Then if you didn't tell Brigit then how come she knows?" I demanded. He didn't reply for a moment, so I said, "Well?"

"Theo has a sister," Derek started saying. "She knew your brother when they were both in high school."

"Who is Theo's sister?"

"Chloe Romano."

I raised my eyebrows. So that's who Chloe Romano is. "My brother knew her. He apparently had a crush on her or something. Anyway, so are you saying that Theo told Brigit?"

"No," Derek replied instantly. "Theo would never do that. Look, April, maybe Brigit somehow overheard us in the cafeteria. Plus, everyone in town knows who Mike is. So why are you looking at me as if you want to slap me again?"

"She's taking advantage of Mike's death, Derek. She told me that he probably died in the battle because of my ugliness."

"And I'm pregnant."

The liquid fizzed through my lips, splattering on Derek's face. Derek's lips curled up into a sickening sneer. I wiped my mouth with my sleeve, staring at Derek with wide eyes.

"WHAT?!" I shrieked slightly.

"I'm only stating the things that are impossible," he said calmly.

It took me a moment to realize what occurred for the past few minutes. I felt heat going to my cheeks. That's sweet of him.

"It's a quote from Google, by the way," he added in a mutter.

I shook my head, a serene sigh sounding from me as he angrily wiped his face. This boy…

"April, you and I both know how Mike died," Derek continued speaking. "He died saving a child's life in the Syrian War. He was shot and lost a lot of blood, and his soul went up…literally. He's a blessed man. Everyone knows that."

I smiled, my heart aching at the thought of my beloved brother. "Yes. He is a blessed man. He risked his own life to save a woman; he pushed the woman to the other side of the road, and the truck hit him instead. He was dead for a minute then he came back. Miraculously."

"Because God knew he cannot die yet," Derek mumbled, smiling at that heroic time. "He brought Mike back because Mike had to accomplish his destiny for Him."

That's what everyone said. No one really knew how Mike came back to life after the incident. He was dead for a minute before the paramedics came. Then he suddenly gasped and his heart continued pumping.

That time, it felt as if I wasn't dead, Mike told me when I went to meet him in the hospital. *It felt as if I was sleeping. It was the most peaceful sleep I've ever experienced.*

I exhaled sharply, swallowing the hard lump that formed in my throat because of the tears. "Let's just get on with today's lesson. Come on, let's go."

When we entered my bedroom, Derek sprawled over my bed with me next to him. He opened his book and wrote down the date and title. He listened as I told him about the human body, about how the human DNA was structured, and about all the systems in our body. He wrote brief notes and listened to me carefully.

After long explanations of the human body, I decided to have a break, and he let out a sigh of relief, closing the book and resting on the bed.

There was a long silence, and it was awkward.

I decided to start a conversation because I couldn't bear the awkward atmosphere. "So...how's life?"

"Shit," he muttered, and then he asked, "Are you going to the Black and White Masquerade Ball?"

The Black and White Masquerade Ball was held in our school every Christmas term. The students have to wear black and white along with a mask. It's like prom. I never went to the Ball, mainly because I didn't have someone to go with.

"No."

Derek looked at me. "Why not?"

"I have no one else to go with."

"You know, you don't *have* to go to the Ball with a date. You can go with a friend."

"But, I…don't have any friends."

Derek straightened himself up, crossing his legs. "Why don't you have friends, April?"

I shrugged. "I want to have friends, but everyone treats me as if I'm a contagious disease. It's as if they want to project their pain on me. I hate being alone, Derek. It's terrible. Mike was the only true friend I ever had. Now, he's gone, and every night I cry to myself… Every night I complain about my life… I hate the bullies at my school."

"You could've told me, you know?" Derek's eyes suddenly raged with anger and…disappointment? "You could've told me that you're getting hated, and I could've handled the situation!"

I stared at him, incredulous. "Told you?" My voice reverberated with rage. "TOLD YOU? Derek, you hurt me too!"

Derek sighed, closing his eyes and rubbing his forehead firmly. "I know, and I'm sorry about that… It's just that everything went downhill… Things were just messed up for me…I started to get angry at myself for not keeping Mike's promise."

"Mike's promise?"

Derek shook his head. "Nothing…never mind. But I'm sorry for being such a jerk. I just miss us being friends…just like the old days. Can you forgive me?"

"For tripping me over or leaving me or giving me a damn hickey?" I asked.

Derek chortled. "All of the above."

"I'll forgive you for tripping me over and for leaving me, not for the hickey."

"So…are we friends, again?"

I smiled unwillingly. "For now. I still don't trust you."

"You'll trust me soon."

"Maybe."

"Is Brigit the only one who's bullying you?" Derek then questioned. "Or there is someone else?"

"No. It's just Brigit."

"But I thought there was someone else? Mike told me that a bastard abused you in school because of your faith."

"Yeah...but he's gone now, so it doesn't matter."

"How did he abuse you?"

"He slapped me sometimes...pushed me into lockers...gave me some scars... Mike dealt with him, though." I felt relieved that I finally confessed to someone. I confessed to Derek... Derek can be a jerk sometimes...but no matter what he did, no matter how annoying and rude he was, I still didn't mind him. "I can still feel the pain today...even though the abuse happened years ago."

"Life can be a pain," Derek spoke softly. "But the pain is only a challenge. You cannot give up on life no matter how hard the challenges can be. You need to keep on going, to keep on feeling and fighting that pain, in order to achieve something great."

"I don't think I can hold on."

"Well, I'm going to make sure you will hold on. Your pain will end, April. Pain isn't endless. It's only temporary."

My eyes stung. His words were so sweet, so heartwarming. The fact that he understood my misery, that he was feeling the same way, made my heart flutter graciously. "What will you do if I gave up?" I whispered.

"I don't think you will. Since we're going to be together more often because my aunt and your mother want us to, I'll make sure that you won't let go."

He ran a hand through his black hair, glancing at the clock on the wall. He stared at it, watching how the red hand moves swiftly with a considering look. He then looked at me. "When it's five, come to my house."

"What if I don't want to?"

"Then I'll come here and drag your pretty little ass into my car."

"That's not a good excuse."

"April, don't test me. You know how I can be like."

"I know, but…"

"If you don't come, I will give torture you horribly."

I raised an eyebrow. "How will you do that?"

He angled his head to the side, aiming to look menacing. Since I am lying down and he's sitting up, he unpredictably fell on top of me, seizing my wrists with his big right hand and pinning them above my head. His face was inches away from mine. His warm breath that smelled of cigarettes fanned my face, and I resisted the urge to gag. Our chests were practically brushing, and our noses were touching. I was extremely aware of our closeness.

"Are you ticklish?" he suddenly asked.

My eyes widened. "DON'T YOU—"

The fingers of his left hand attacked my stomach, teasingly caressing his fingertips against my skin in haste. My laughter was the only noise in the room. That exasperating, funny sensation flooded my gut. I wheezed and wheezed, inhaling deep breaths and screaming at Derek to stop. Derek ignored me and carried on torturing me, grinning goofily. I tried to slither out of his grasp, but he's too strong. I even tried to lift my knee so I could hurt him, but he acted fast and pressed more pressure onto my body.

"O-O-k-kay!" I stuttered in between giggles.

He smirked, satisfied with my answer. He rolled off me. I wheezed, breathing in some oxygen. Derek lifted his head and placed it on his propped-up arm.

"So, are you going to come? Or do you want to get tickled more?" His fingers scuttled under my shirt and I smacked it away.

"Derek, I don't know…you're not a very nice person, and I don't want to be seen with you."

Derek rolled his eyes. "Who cares what others will say about us? I just want to show you something."

"Like what?"

"Something personal." He got up and stretched his arms above his head, a yawn escaping from his lips. His muscles flexed, the bottom of his shirt rising up to expose his set of abs and V-line. "Please come. And don't be late. Bring you sketchbook."

With that, he left my room.

At least he said please.

Chapter Nine

The Meadow

April Levesque

The largest building in this town is Derek's mansion. Everyone could see it from such a distance.

The vast front yard of the three-storey mansion was coloured in a rich dark tantalizing shade of grassy green as the walls of the mansion dazzled as if it's been polished every day. The windows were immense enough to view the insides. There's a big, deluxe pool. Enclosing the mansion were gates with men dressed in black clothing standing in front of them.

One of them eyed me. "How can I help you, ma'am?" he asked, offering me a gentle smile.

"Uhm, Derek asked me to come," I replied in a timid voice.

He blinked, seeming surprised. "Mr. Little Matthews?"

"Uh, yeah."

"Funny. This is the first time Derek asked a girl to come over."

"Really?" I said. "But isn't he, uhm, a player—"

"He is," the guard admitted in shame. "That sadistic guy could be cruel, but he's got some problems that he couldn't solve. He may be a player, but he doesn't bring girls to the mansion unless it's a party…"

"Oh," is all I could say.

He took out a device and pressed a button. The gates automatically creaked open, allowing me to enter the front yard. I thanked the guard and advanced to the large front doors.

I stopped at the doorstep and knocked on the door. In an instant, the door swung open, revealing a beautiful woman who I've seen before: Marline, Derek's aunt.

Marline's blue eyes lightened up. "Hello, April!"

I smiled. "Hi, Marline. Is Derek here?"

"Yes. He did notify me that you'll be coming here." She stepped aside, gesturing me to come in.

The receiving area is grand and efficiently decorated with beautiful, artistic designs painted on the walls. Poles supported the ceiling which is round with a blue mosaic in the centre; hanging from the centre of the mosaic is an enthralling chandelier. Two curving, long staircases on each side of the room reach to the top where the second floor begins. There wasn't a single speck of dust on anything, just glamour blinding my dark brown eyes.

Marline led me to the living room. To the right side is a staircase that also leads to the second floor. The balcony of the second floor is visible, and I could see security officers roaming around. They all smiled down at Marline politely. The floor is marble. Two long sofas and four individual ones stood on top of a blue-grey rug with a glass (that's holding a vase of white flowers) in the middle. There are picture frames of two boys and a man on the walls—Derek, Luke, and their father. The rest are of Derek, Luke, and Marline.

This wasn't the living room I was in for the memorial. Marline seemed to notice my puzzled look because she said, "We have two living rooms. We use one of them for important occasions."

Two living rooms? Seriously? I know Marline is a businesswoman who runs a famous industry but damn, this is too much even for a millionaire. "Let me guess, you have two kitchens?"

"No. Just one. But we have about ten bedrooms in this house in case there are guests."

I sat down on a sofa just when a tall male entered the living room. Luke. His features are exactly like Derek's: messy jet-black hair, eyes the colour of the deep blue ocean, light tanned skin. Luke gave me a soft smile. "Hey, April."

"Hey."

"I'm going out, Aunt Marli."

"Okay," said Marline. "Bye, love."

"Bye. Bye, April."

"Bye."

"So how is everything going, April?" Marline asked once Luke disappeared behind the door.

I looked at her. "Fine."

"What about Derek? How is he like when you're tutoring him?"

I bit my lip. "He's okay."

"He never invites a girl to his house unless it's a party. He rarely does parties, though. He's always wrapped up about…" Sadness suddenly crawled into Marline's eyes. "His parents."

"Really?"

Marline nodded. "He is independent, you could say. Secretive."

"He isn't that secretive."

Marline smiled gently. "Maybe not to you."

"What do you mean?" I asked, curious.

"I don't know if you know this but before Derek was really...*fond* of you. He always told me how beautiful you are, how much he wants to hug you, how he wants to annoy you just to get a snarky comeback, how he wants to embarrass you just to see that gorgeous blush of yours...He was so happy when he met you. He thanked Mike so many times because Mike was the reason why you two were close friends..." Her eyes abruptly saddened again. "But then suddenly you're not friends anymore..." She looked at me. "Do you miss him?"

"Uhm..." I searched for the correct words to answer. "Before, I used to," I admitted, "because his company was...nice. I still do miss him. Though, he can be..." My voice trailed off.

"Bothersome?" Marline suggested. "Because of his reputation?"

I nodded unwillingly.

"I know," she mumbled. "He got his attitude from his father."

That could be true. Samuel Matthews was a player, too. Though, he learned from his mistakes and became a man admired by more than ten million people.

"His father was exactly like him...until he met Alexa. He changed. He became a good man. So, I thought that if you and Derek are together, or friends even, then it will..."

"Make him better," I finished. "Make him himself again."

Marline nodded sadly. "I'm sorry if this is offending you in any way—"

"No!" I objected. "No, Marline, it's *fine*. That's very nice of you but...I don't think I'm that girl for him."

Before Marline could respond, Derek appeared in the doorway, dressed in a black T-shirt and black jeans. He smirked when his eyes fell on me. "Hey."

"Hi," I greeted, straightening myself up.

Derek looked at his aunt. "I'm going to take April somewhere."

"Where?"

"To the meadow."

Marline's eyebrows shot up. "Really?"

Derek smiled gently at his aunt. "I'll be fine, Aunt," he assured. "Don't worry. It won't affect me." He approached her, offering her a humble kiss. "I'll be back soon." Marline smiled gently at his actions and told him to come home before nine o'clock.

Outside is a dazzling deluxe golden Lamborghini. Derek approached his car with pride, opening the door and gesturing me to get it. "Ladies first."

"If you're trying to be a gentleman, then it's crap."

He rolled his eyes at me, and I got in. Derek got into the seat next to me and placed his hands on the wheel.

"So, we're going somewhere personal. I don't want you to tell this place to anyone. okay?"

"It's a meadow, right? What's so secretive about a meadow?"

"You'll see. And did you bring your sketchbook?"

"Yes. Why did you ask me to bring it, anyway?"

He smirked. "Because I want you to draw me when we get there."

I glared at him, and a low gorgeous laugh delighted my ears. I nudged his shoulder good-naturedly, and his car roared to life, turning the wheel as we hit the road.

*   *   *

Derek pulled the car to a complete stop, the wheels of his golden Lamborghini running over the soft grass. We both got out, witnessing a marvellous vastness of chilly green grass freckled with dying flowers, swaying as the nippy gentle wind swept past us. The meadow undulated like a sea of jewels, going up and down as if imitating waves. The everyday birds of Peony Hallows flapped above us, serenading melodies from every direction as the sun grinned down at us, its rays kissing us passionately.

"It's beautiful," I marvelled.

Derek smiled. "Like you," he complimented.

"Stop flirting with me," I snapped, still amazed by the beauty of this meadow.

He shrugged. "What can I say? I just can't help it. It's fun annoying you."

"Just like old times," I muttered.

Derek chortled. "Just like old times. I want to show you something. Come." His fingers entwined with mine, gently tugging me forward through the long grass. His hand is warm, as if I'm grasping a radiator. I felt an unfamiliar sensation tingling up my arm.

"Where are we going?"

"You'll see soon enough."

We circumspectly jogged down a small hill as the birds' melodies soothed my eardrums. The grass moved in waves, the dying flowers surging down the grassy slope. I jumped over a small stream to reach flat land.

Derek was walking slower. Ahead of us, I could spot something shimmering and reflective. As we got closer, I realized that it's a large body of water with land enclosing it. Flowers floated across the surface—blood red poppies, pink roses, peonies, beautiful daffodils, primroses, bluebells, and water lilies. They're all organised into the perfect colour order of the rainbow.

"Wow," I breathed. I inhaled the refreshing air as the pleasant smell of water took over. Even though my eyes were absorbed to the lake, I could feel Derek gazing at me with a charismatic grin.

"I knew you'd like it," Derek said. "Dad calls this the Lake of Miracles because from what he said, he witnessed so many miracles."

"Like what?"

"He proposed to Momma here and she said yes. To him, that's a miracle.

"Dad also said this is where Jesus is mostly present in Peony Hallows because there was a church over here in the olden days, but it got destroyed during WWI. It was right beside the church. People would come here and swim in the lake because apparently the priest said it's where your sins get cleansed, it's where your prayers are properly heard and answered."

To the right side of the lake, there are ruins spread out across the long, thick stalks of grass. All of them ashen brown. Some of them standing on top of another block. There was even a cross sticking out from a curved rock.

"The flowers are ordered in the colours of the rainbow because it represents hope, peace, humanity, joy, and compassion. Plus, it's sort of a symbol for the LGBTQ+ community."

"I can see that. My mother told me that Jesus never complained about them so there is nothing wrong about homosexuals, bisexuals or Trans."

"Yeah, but people focus on the Old Testament more, April."

"I know."

"To be honest, whenever I'm really trapped in my darkest times," he murmured, "I come here not only because I can feel peace but because of my parents."

"Parents?"

"They're buried here."

"Oh."

"My Dad died in a car crash," he mumbled, his eyes narrowed as if he's lost in his own deep thoughts. "Before that, Dad, Luke, and I always used to come here, have picnics, swim in the lake, have fun, and make wishes—most of them came true. Miraculously." His ocean blue eyes met mine. "I never told anybody about my parents before or about this place."

"Not even Theo?"

"Theo knows about what happened to my parents, he knows he about this place, but he never came here."

"So…I'm the first?"

"You're the first."

I smiled at him tenderly and gazed at the stunning lake. "Is this why you asked me to bring my sketchbook? So I could sketch it?"

Derek nodded. "But before you do that, I want to show you something else." His hand once again swallowed mine and I let him drag me forward.

The path Derek and I took is covered with beautiful, radiant leaves. Eventually, ahead of me, I noticed two gravestones planted in the ground.

The gravestone on the right read:

IN LOVING MEMORY OF
ALEXANDRA G. MATTHEWS
AGE 35
LOVING DAUGHTER, FRIEND, WIFE, AND
MOTHER

The other gravestone on the left said:

IN LOVING MEMORY OF
SAMUEL J. MATTHEWS
AGE 45
LOVING SON, BROTHER, FRIEND, HUSBAND,
AND HERO

"We buried Momma and Dad here because this meadow is a very private place, I guess," said Derek. "This place makes me feel protected." He then chuckled sombrely. "Sometimes, I come here and start a conversation and imagine them listening to me."

His eyes watered. My heart bawled in commiseration for him. He blinked, and a tear fell from his left eye. At first, I thought he was faking it, but then I thought about my brother Mike. I cried whenever I went to his grave. The way Derek expressed his feelings through brief words gave me the explicit thought that they're genuine. That *he's* genuine. Mom said Derek is a lost boy. He is.

My thumb reached up to his cheek, licking off the tear. I wiped his eyes, surprising Derek. Then, he just smiled gratefully at me.

"I guess we both have something in common," Derek noted. "We lost our loved ones."

I nodded, looking at the gravestones that belong to his parents. I said a silent prayer for them before we both went back to the Lake.

"Don't tell anyone about my parents." He led me to a large willow tree. Letting go of my hand, he sat down and patted the place next to him for me to sit. "Or about the memorial. Please."

"I won't," I promised.

A chilly breeze brushed past us. The emaciated branches of the willow swayed above us, as if they're protecting us, yet at the same time they permitted a beautiful view of the miraculous lake with stunning flowers floating on its surface. The autumn leaves formed shadows to spread out beneath them, cooling us from the sun.

It was silent between the two of us, but it was a relaxing kind of silence—the one where you can settle down and take in all the striking, assuring sounds that nature is creating.

I took out my sketchbook and flipped the pages over to a clean, fresh page. I started sketching the lake first, glancing up at it multiple times as the pencil in my hand skidded around rapidly. Once I've finished outlining the lake, I felt Derek's eyes focused on me as I drew the flowers on the lake's surface.

As I was sketching, Derek said, "Look up."

I did. The clouds that vaguely veiled the sky sprinkled water. Tiny raindrops splattered everywhere, drenching nature, drenching the flowers floating across the surface of the water. Gorgeously, thin radiant rays of the sun seeped through the joyful crying clouds and gradually, I noticed colours appearing in the air.

A rainbow.

Highly curving over the lake.

I gasped. "It's beautiful!"

Derek was smiling and so was I. Water dripped from the long leaves of the willow tree and hit our skin. He shifted closer to me and his arms hovered above us, as if trying to shield us from the water. "Yeah."

"I've never seen a rainbow this close before."

"It's rare for these rainbows to happen. They mean good luck, you know. We can make wishes."

Contentment bubbled inside me. "Let's go and make wishes!"

My sketchbook was abandoned on the floor and I sprinted towards the lake. Derek laughed, jogging after me as the rain soaked us. I heaved into a stop right in front of the Lake of Miracles. Derek and I closed our eyes.

There are so many things in the world to wish for. I could wish for the sadness to go away. I could wish to have a good future. Though, I wished that my father is good and healthy, and that he'll come back very soon with open, embracing arms. The wish was followed by a brief Hail Mary.

When I opened my eyes, Derek was gazing at me with . . . affection? His wet jet-black hair glued to his forehead, slightly covering his thick eyelashes that quivered over his celestial blue eyes. He was spinning a white flower between his fingers.

"What?" I said, copying his smile.

Derek shook his head. "Nothing." Still twirling the flower, he surprisingly pushed my drenched hair to the side to place the flower on my ear. Then, he grabbed my hairband and gently tugged it off. My hair cascaded down my shoulders. "There. To be honest, you look beautiful like that."

My cheeks smouldered and I giggled timidly. Derek laughed, as if he loved seeing me smile. His eyes lit up with elation as he flicked a strand of hair off my face. I am touched by his compliment. No one called me beautiful, other than my mother, of course—but mothers are like that, aren't they?

Suddenly, he leaned forward, his warm breath fanning my face. His nose moved closer, closer, and closer to mine. Water dripped down our faces. His eyes hastily darted to my lips. My heart throbbed. My wet hands somewhat felt sweaty regardless of the fact that the rain intensified.

The rainbow faded.

There was only a small space between us.

His lips brushed mine.

I wanted to move away. I couldn't. I was paralyzed. Frozen. Motionless. And I hated it. I hate being like this in front of him.

He abruptly pressed his soft, moist lips on mine, closing the miniature gap between us.

He stiffened, perhaps shocked like me.

Then, he moved his mouth rapidly against mine, as if they were endlessly rehearsed to dance elaborately. Second by second, the wet heat from his lips blistered mine and sent such sensational tremors to my body. One hand cupped my face as the other draped around my waist, pulling me closer, closer, and closer for our chests to mould together.

It was hot. Fiery. Demanding.

It was passionate. Innocent. Gentle.

I wanted to pull away. I can't seem to.

I don't know if I'm doing this whole kissing thing right because this is my first time—

Oh...

Oh, fudge.

Derek stole my first kiss.

He's my first damn kiss.

MY FIRST DAMN KISS!

WHAT AM I DOING?

I pushed him away. He stumbled backward, tumbling into the lake behind him. The water crashed over him, engulfing him until he came out, gasping. The rain continued to drench us more.

"What the hell, April?"

"You *kissed* me! Derek Matthews, you freaking *kissed* me!"

"So, what?"

"So, what?" I echoed. "I don't want a jerk like you to kiss me!"

A negative sentiment flashed in his eyes. "You could've pushed me away, idiot."

"I was caught off guard! Are you trying to play me?"

"I'm not. I just...wanted to kiss you."

This time, I don't believe him. "Whatever. I'm going." I whipped around.

I yelped when a cold hand grasped my ankle. Derek jerked me into the lake and my shriek was muffled underwater. I punched a hand through the surface and burst forth, water surging down my body. Gasping, the lake came up to my waist.

I glowered coldly at Derek. He exploded into laughter. "Asshole," I muttered.

"No bad language, baby,' he said in between snickers. "I thought you're a good girl."

"Oh, just because I'm a good girl doesn't mean I can't swear."

He cocked his eyebrow. "Feisty, huh? To be honest, I find feisty girls attractive."

I rolled my eyes. "That's what every guy says to get a girl, and honestly, it's so lame. They need lessons. But..." I pushed myself closer to Derek, a thought coming to mind. "Is it only attractive?"

He leaned into me. "No. I find them hot."

I did something that I did not expect myself to do: I traced my hand down his wet shirt. The rain and the water of the Lake soaked his shirt, outlining his abs. He looked at me, trying to read me. There was something peculiar about his eyes—behind that cockiness is a broken boy, weeping and finding a way to escape his misery. He's all alone. I almost felt sorry for him again.

Almost.

My fingers then traced his cheekbones and he released a sharp breath. His arms wrapped around my waist. I leaned closer into him...

"What are you doing?'" he asked but his words were subdued when I kissed him.

I wrapped my weak and numb arms around his strong neck. My mind was blank. My cheeks red , my body was flushed with heat when he kissed back and immediately deepened the kiss, continuously tugging me closer. Wrapping my legs around his waist, he pressed me to a curvature wall of the lake.

I stopped the dance of our lips by untying my legs and floating an inch away.

Derek ran a hand through his damp black tresses. "Damn, April," he mumbled, his voice hoarse. "You can kiss."

After a second or two, I managed to compose myself. A smirk played on my lips. "And damn," I said, "I never thought Derek Matthews is that daft."

He frowned. "What do you mean?"

I leaned and whispered into his ear, "The kiss meant nothing. I just played you, Derek Matthews. *Again.*"

Chapter Ten

What's Wrong With Me?

Derek Matthews

I should still be infuriated, aggravated, and frustrated that April played me *again*. But I'm not. Instead, I am confused. Confused about what's happening to me.

I've been considering the previous days I spent with April, and I realized that every night I wasn't able to go to sleep because of *her*. I can't stop thinking about her and her humble, gracious, gorgeous smile. I can't stop thinking about the way she pushed her black-framed glasses up her nose. Everything about her – from her beautiful, dark-brunette hair that cascades down her shoulders, to her dark eyes that gives me an uncomfortable warning yet a miraculous serenity, to the feisty way she stands up for herself – was too impossible not to think about.

The past few hours, I kept on rewinding every single second, minute and hour I spent with her in the meadow today. And this is giving me a wild headache as three questions flooded my mind:

What's wrong with me?

What does this mean?

Am I going crazy?

The way I felt when I was with her…the way she listened to me carefully and understandingly with solicitude as I explained to her about my parents made my heart pound with pride and felicity. *Felicity.* Something I haven't had for a long time. And when I say a long time, I mean a long, long, *long* time.

When my hand touched hers, I felt a spark erupting inside me, as if a firework was planted in my heart for years and was waiting for the correct time to ignite. I only experienced that spark when my father was alive and happy…at least, I thought he was.

And the kiss…the kiss just made me feel alive as if I was dead inside for the past six years. I secretly enjoyed the kiss, and I was secretly disappointed and unhappy that she only did that to trick me…I thought she meant it. I thought the kiss was true and passionate. But nope. It had to be a joke. I supposed I deserved it judging by the fact that my past kisses with other girls were meaningless and worthless.

I moved off my bed, running a lazy hand through my hair as I let out a loud sigh, closing my eyes. "What the hell is wrong with me?" I mumbled to myself.

April reminds me of someone who (I hope) I know very well yet I have never seen or met in my life before.

My mother.

I don't mean that in a disgusting way, of course. It's just…Momma died when I was born. She left me. From the stories I've heard from other people, Momma was described as a very feisty nerd with high spirits and a stunning smile. She was described as a beautiful woman with fair skin, long wavy hair, and dark eyes with glasses. I always cherished Momma in my heart.

I sort of see her in April, if that makes sense.

I ambled through the dark hallways. A security officer was sitting on the floor, leaning against the wall, snoring. I always felt pity yet gratitude for the guards—every day and night, they have to keep an eye on our mansion, inside and out. They get tired and I asked my aunt if she could reduce their working hours.

I walked to the kitchen to get some water or anything that will calm my headache. I was surprised to see my older brother, Luke, sitting there with his chin on his folded arms. His eyes are droopy with sleep, he was yawning.

He looked at me. "What are you doing up?" he asked.

"I couldn't sleep," I responded. "What are *you* doing up?"

"Just thinking…"

"About what?"

"Whether I should propose to my girlfriend or not…"

"Did you talk to Aunt Marline?" Luke nodded. "What did she say?"

"She told me to go for it."

"Then go for it."

Luke sighed. "I'm scared."

I rolled my eyes. I hate how men get nervous of proposing. "Luke, how long have you been dating her?"

"Six years."

"Do you love her?"

"Of course, I do."

"Does she love you?"

"Uhm…I don't know…"

"If she doesn't, then you won't be together. She does love you since you're together. You have no need to be scared about proposing to her."

Luke narrowed his eyes. "Since when did you become a love expert?"

"I'm not being one. I'm just trying to help—"

"Since when did you start to help?"

I blinked. "I help people because I care—"

Luke snorted. "As if."

"I'm being honest, Luke. I care about you. You're my freaking brother. I have to care about you."

"So do I," Luke muttered. "Now, why are you awake?"

"I told you. I couldn't sleep."

"Why?"

"I can't stop thinking about something."

Luke was silent for a moment. Then, his lips widen into a playful, teasing grin as he said, "Or *someone*?"

I rolled my eyes. "I'm not—"

"You're turning red!" Luke pointed out. "You *are* thinking about a girl. Holy crap, this is a freaking miracle."

I frowned. "What do you mean?"

"You're in love!" Luke exclaimed. "I never thought you will actually fall in love with someone. I never thought you actually have an actual human heart!"

I felt as if a brick was slammed into my face. "Huh?"

"You love a girl," Luke said slowly.

"N-no I don't."

"You're stuttering. You do love someone."

"I don't love anyone!"

"Then why are you blushing?"

"Because it's hot!"

"The girl you like, what's her name?"

"April Levesque."

Luke grinned. "You just admitted you like her."

"I-I didn't."

"You just did."

"Shut up."

Luke chuckled. "It's okay to be in love, Derek," he said. "But wait…you said her name is April Levesque?"

"Yeah."

"Mike's sister?"

"Yes."

"Weren't you and April best friends when you were young?"

"Yeah."

"Didn't you have a crush on her?"

"Uhm..."

"She's tutoring you, right?"

"Yeah."

Luke grinned harder. "She's ugly."

My hands clenched into balls of fist at his words. "No, she's not. She's freaking beautiful."

My eyes widened when I realized the words that tumbled out of my mouth.

Luke laughed. "Aw, dude, don't be embarrassed. It's nice to be in love."

"I don't love her," I said through gritted teeth, incensed about the fact that Luke could be right about my anomalous emotions. "I don't love *anyone*. So, shut up before I stuff my shit down your mouth."

Luke held up his hands in surrender, his lips fighting back a smile.

I slammed the door behind me and stormed up to my room.

I love April? Do I? Do I actually?

What about the Dare?

Those four questions replayed over and over in my head. I flopped down on my bed, my back facing the ceiling, my arms folded beneath my face. The last thing I thought about was April, and then everything around me turned black.

Chapter Eleven

A Granted Wish

April Levesque

I entered the cafeteria, which was bustling with loud chatter. Students were howling with laughter, whispering the latest gossip, chitchatting about celebrities, and cracking smiles at each other. Some were kissing, which I think is gross. *Don't they feel ashamed about making out in public?*

Through my black spectacles, my eyes settled on Derek Matthews. He's sitting on a round cafeteria table, conversing with Theo Romano and Jackson Gray. They seemed to be having a serious conversation due to the stern expressions they all have. As I paused in line, his ocean blue eyes instantly met mine. I rapidly looked away, my mind flashing back to what happened yesterday.

The way he leaned forward, the way his sexy yet charming laugh thrilled my ears, the way he smiled…everything he did made my heart flutter so fast. I could still feel his warm, soft lips against mine. I could still feel his arms wrapped around my waist.

I frowned, unfamiliar with these strange sentiments. I was pretty sure I could be developing a teeny tiny crush on Derek Matthews. I know: What. The. Hell. But, maybe I could be wrong. These feelings were totally different to the one I experienced for this guy who used to be my next-door neighbour.

I hate my ex-crush. So much.

He abused me.

I don't want to have a crush on another person.

If I do, then I want him to be worthwhile.

*   *   *

As soon as the bell rang in the corridors, I padded my way up the stairs to my art class. Art class is in the attic. It's pretty cool. I love art. Mainly because I have a passion for art and I love how peaceful it is in the classroom.

I walked through the open door and put my stuff on the table, sighing. I rolled my aching shoulders backward.

"Hello, darling." My mother smiled at me. That's another reason why I love art. Mom is the art teacher. Everyone knows that. And everyone loves her because she's so nice, caring, and sweet. And then everyone looks at me…and they treat me as if I'm a contagious disease. Art was the only lesson when no one is bothering me with disgusted looks because of Mom.

It's the only lesson I can survive from the cruelty of this high school.

For three days a week, half of the day she's the art teacher, and she spends the other half of those three days as a nurse. For the rest of the week, she is a nurse and mostly works night shifts.

"Good morning, Mrs. Levesque." Jasmine Gray, one of the popular girls, sauntered in with her twin brother, Jackson Gray. The twins are both sandy blonde with big vivid eyes.

Jasmine smiled at me as Jackson waved his hand in my direction. I smiled back at them. I have always liked the Gray Twins. They're so sweet and entertaining. They're the only ones who actually like me.

Soon enough, the place was packed with students. Mom clapped her hands together, hushing everyone. Once they did, Mom began speaking about the lesson for the day.

"Today is different. We won't be doing any class work." Mom received a few sighs of relief and whoops. "Today, we will be drawing posters for the Black and White Masquerade Ball that is coming up in a couple of weeks. You will be in groups of four. Please do make the posters colourful and eye-catching in order for them to look brilliant on the walls of the school. Before we begin, I know that all of you are rushing around and trying to find dates. I will be allowing you all to ask people out for the Ball."

Everyone grinned at my mother, appreciating her offer. Mom returned the smile, and we all started looking for group members, wildly screaming people's names while I remained silent in my seat, tapping my pencil as Mom played some music faintly in the background.

"Hi!"

I looked to see the Gray Twins standing before me, both beaming with pleasant smiles. I blinked, amazed. I glanced behind me to see if they're looking at anyone else, but when I turned my eyes back to the Gray Twins, I was proved wrong.

"Was that for me?"

"No, we said 'hi' to the wall behind you," Jackson muttered sarcastically. "Do you need to change your glasses, April?"

Jasmine jammed her elbow into Jackson's ribs. "Shut up." A hiss escaped Jackson, and he rubbed his right rib roughly, glowering at his twin sister. "Do you want to work with us?" Jasmine then asked me.

I blinked, astonished. "Me?" I asked, pointing at my chest. "Why me?"

"Because you're the only person who isn't in a group and we don't like seeing you alone," Jackson responded. "Plus, my little sister wants to talk to you about something."

Jasmine scowled at him. "I'm not your 'little sister', thank you very much. We're both the same age."

"Yeah, but I was born earlier."

They brought their chairs over and sat around my desk.

"Aren't we supposed to have four members?" I asked them. I regretted saying it immediately because a tall familiar figure stood in front of us.

Derek Matthews.

"Hey, guys." Derek smirked at us, sitting down on the chair next to me.

"What are you doing here?" I demanded.

Derek glanced at me. "I'm going to be in your group. Why, is that a problem?"

"Yes," I hissed. "It is a problem because that girl over there is glaring at me murderously." I pointed at Brigit, who, indeed, was glaring daggers at me.

Unexpectedly, Derek gave Brigit the middle finger. Brigit's eyes widened, shocked that he would do that to her, and whipped her head around.

"She's a brat, anyway," Derek mumbled.

I furrowed my eyebrows. "Isn't she your girlfriend?"

Derek snorted. "No. She never was. Who told you that?"

"Brigit."

Derek rolled his eyes. "Don't believe anything she says, April."

Jackson cleared his throat, making both of us look at him. He gestured to the large plain piece of paper resting on the surface of the table. "We should get started."

I nodded and sharpened my pencil. "What should we do?"

Jackson shrugged. "I dunno. And I'm not good at drawing. Seriously, the only things I can draw are stick figures."

"Same," said Derek.

I looked at Jasmine, who's staring at me intently. "What about you?"

She shook her head. "I am better than my brother, obviously, but my art skills aren't that great.'

I sighed. 'Look, guys, everything isn't about perfection, okay? You need to try your best. Jackson, just draw stick figures."

"With dicks?" Jackson asked hopefully, causing Jasmine to smack his head. "Ow!" he complained, rubbing his head. "What the heck, Jas?"

"I've seen your Instagram page, April," Jasmine told me. "You post some amazing artwork. You should draw."

That compliment made me blush with pride.

Derek nodded next to me. "She's a natural beauty, isn't she? She's amazing."

My cheeks burned even more, causing Derek and Jackson to break into amused grins.

"She's even cute when she blushes," Derek stated.

I banged my hand on the table. "Stop it! My head is already as red as strawberries; I don't need it to be red as a tomato!" My words only made the boys crack into laughter while Jasmine flashed me a hysterical smile. I rolled my eyes.

I started moving the point of my pencil across the paper, visualising an image in my mind to sketch. I drew a figure of a girl wearing a pretty, long, white dress with her hair flowing as she dances with her date. After I shaded her hair dark, I started drawing the boy, wearing a handsome suit with his arms wrapped around the girl's waist. Jackson and Derek started chatting about stuff that seemed quite unnecessary to talk about while Jasmine blurted out ideas to me for the poster.

"Why is it called the 'Black and White Christmas Masquerade Ball'?" I asked in wonder.

"Well, my aunt planned the Ball," Derek answered. "She wanted it to be a great time for Peony Hallows High School. It's in Town Hall. It's exquisite over there, but it's a good place for the Ball."

"Why is the theme black and white?"

Derek shrugged.

Jasmine did the fancy writing. She wrote down all the information about the Black and White Christmas Masquerade Ball as I leaned backwards in my chair, flashing my mother a smile, and stretching my fingers. I felt warm fingers brushing my right cheek. Derek was playing with my hair, curling it in between his fingers, his chin on his folded arm, his eyes signalling me that he's bored. I would've told him to stop touching my hair. I don't want to. It feels nice, actually.

"Are you two dating?" Jasmine asked out of the blue.

I blinked. "Who? Me and *Derek*?"

"Yeah."

"No!" I hissed at the same time Derek beamed a "Yes!"

Jasmine narrowed her soft bright blue eyes at us. "Complicated relationship?"

"No, we're dating—" Derek began explaining, but I stopped him by kicking his shin underneath the table. Derek grunted at the sudden impact, glaring at me. "What the hell was that for?"

"Derek and I are *not* dating, Jasmine," I informed her, ignoring Derek's glares.

Jasmine pouted. "Aw, that's a shame."

I blinked, surprised at her words.

"Honestly, in my opinion, I think you two will be adorable together and will be relationship goals," Jasmine added quickly.

From the corner of my right eye, I could feel my mother's gaze focusing on us. I could feel my mother's lips breaking into a humble smile, eavesdropping on our conversation with no shame. Redness coated my cheeks.

Derek was staring attentively at me; his ocean blue eyes hazy with thoughts, his stunning smirk never seemed to falter. Our eyes never seemed to drift away from each other. It's as if our eyes are *destined* to be locked to each other forever. This uneasy feeling bubbled inside me—it's the type of feeling you get when you're on a rollercoaster: your gut is simmering with anxiety, happiness, and excitement. Confusion is another word that describes my emotions towards Derek. I'm unsure about these emotions.

"But April is Derek-proof."

I snapped out of my reverie immediately when Jackson's voice crawled into my ears. "What?"

"You're Derek-proof," Jackson said. "You are the only girl in the school who can resist Derek and his charms and everything. Jasmine, Derek and April are enemies."

Jasmine scoffed. "April's the only girl who can resist Derek Matthews? Please, Natalia, Sophia, and I can. The other girls are just dumb."

"Hey, that's not nice, Jasmine."

"I'm sorry, but they're just baiting themselves to get hurt. I'm glad April is not that blind to fall for Derek's charms. I've heard that you played Derek twice, April: ditching him when you both 'planned' a date, fake kissing him...that's what I call asshole-proof."

How does she know about that?

Jackson grinned cheekily. "But Derek is April's asshole."

I shuddered. "Ew, Jackson. Please stop."

"What? I'm just saying..."

"And I wouldn't say that we're enemies," Derek blurted. "April and I are friends too."

"Derek and April are *frenemies*," Jackson corrected. "Have you seen the way they bicker? Theo said it's hilarious."

"Bickering is a sign of an upcoming relationship," said Jasmine. "Sometimes, enemies become lovers."

"Kids, I will be going to get something from the staff room," Mom announced. "Please don't do anything silly. I will be back in a minute." Mom hurried out of the art room, the noises of her feet pounding the highest floor of the school building. I heard the creaking noise of the door opening and slamming shut.

Chatter jammed the art room once again as everyone returned to their posters and conversations.

From the corner of my eye, I spotted Brigit glowering at me, her lips lifted up into a nasty, loathing sneer. She leaned sideways to Tiffany and whispered something. Tiffany glanced at her, her hand clamped over her mouth, her shoulders shaking, her snickers muffled.

Brigit smirked viciously at me. She ripped a piece of paper from her book, hastily scribbled something, crunched it up into a ball, and chucked it at me. The note smacked into my face, falling onto the surface of my desk.

Derek glanced at where the paper came from. A second later, he looked at me, baffled. "Who threw that?"

I didn't answer. I fearfully unfolded the paper, reading her fancy writing:

I think Hell has a place for you, April. You know, since Mike died from the war, I think I will be happier if someone else in your family dies. Your dad, maybe? He's in the war, fighting against ISIS, right? When he dies, I will be so glad to see the tears on your face.

Water prickled my eyes. A dreadful scenario came to my mind: my father lying on the floor, blood saturating his uniform and pooling around him, shallow gasps resonating from him as he wheezes from the pain of a bullet submerged deep in his chest.

I fluttered my eyes closed. *No, no, April, don't think like that. Dad won't die. He won't.*

"April?" Derek's hand touched my shoulder. I opened my eyes and flinched at the contact, frayed puffs breaking out through my thin lips. Derek's hand withdrew; disenchantment in his eyes. "Are you okay?"

The tears are wedged in my throat. I stood up, unable to endure in this room. Jasmine, Jackson, and Derek enquired what's wrong when I scurried out of the attic, running through the petite hallway and pushing the white, wooden door open. I hurried down the stairs, the tears dropping from my eyes agitatedly.

I scampered through many hallways, light-headed. I want to go outside. I want to be alone and just cry for as long as possible. I panted, panted, and panted, the breaths sounding as if

I am the one who's going to pass away. An ache scorched my chest, and I wheezed, my speed becoming gradual. I slammed my eyes closed at the soreness, the blistering tears scuttling down my cheeks.

Panic attack.

I'm having a panic attack.

I hate panic attacks.

Faint footsteps jogged behind me, catching up. *Whoever it is, leave me alone*, I wanted to scream. The words died in my throat. I could not speak.

"April?" His hand grabbed my arm, alarmed, twirling me around to face him. "Baby, are you okay?"

I would've told him not to call me that. Instead, I exploded into irrepressible sobs. I shamefully cried, cried, and cried in front of him. I hate crying. All the time, I block the hatred, the horrible visualisations. But truthfully, inside, I endeavour so hard not to break, not to fall on the floor and curl into a blubbering ball.

"April?" His finger seized my chin, pushing my head up. My watery eyes met his worried ones. "What's wrong?"

"What if my Dad died?" I whispered.

"Your Dad?" he puzzled. "Wait, is he still fighting ISIS?"

"Yes. What if he died, Derek?"

His eyes softened sympathetically. "He won't," he assured in the most soothing voice. "Why would you think that?"

"Because anything is possible." A tear slid down my right cheek.

"He won't die. There's no such thing as death, you know?"

"That's what Mike said," I mumbled. The tears stained my spectacles. "He believed that there is no such thing as death—only the body dies. Because there are so many religions, because he was a Catholic, he believed that the soul will take a journey to its afterlife. He believed that you won't rot on earth because that would make you feel worse about yourself."

"Exactly," Derek murmured. His hands cupped my face. "Your dad won't die. He'll always be there for you."

"What if he goes away sooner?"

"He won't."

"How can you say that?"

"Because I know." Derek stroked strands of my coiled hair off my face. "Tell me, why are you crying? Is it because of the note? I tried to find it, but I couldn't. What happened?"

"Nothing," I lied. "I'm just negative all the time. It's how I am."

He narrowed his eyes. "You're lying."

"I'm not."

"You are. I can see it. Your face is getting hot."

"It's because of my body temperature and the warmth of your hands."

"Did Brigit do something?"

This time, I couldn't answer.

"I knew it," Derek muttered. His hands fell off my face, and he spun around, moving away with a stiff posture. "I'm going to murder that little whiny, desperate, idiotic, bratty, dumb, stupid, unforgiving—"

"Whoa, Derek." I grabbed his hands and pulled him backward. "You're not going to do anything."

Derek pouted like a baby. "But I will be happier if I punch her face and break her nose."

"You're not going to break her nose."

"She deserves it, though. April, what did she say?"

"It doesn't matter."

"April…"

"I said it doesn't matter."

"To me, it does. If Brigit hurts you, I need to know why and I need to know what she said. So, tell me what she said."

"Derek—"

"April!"

"Okay, okay, I'll tell you!" I exhaled sharply. "She said that she thinks hell has a place for me and Mike and that she will be happier if someone else from my family dies, like my dad, maybe… She will be so glad to see me cry."

A vein visibly pulsated in Derek's neck. His eyes blazed with odium. His shoulders were straight. He inhaled three deep breaths to calm his anger. "That's it." He spun around. "I'm gonna go and break her damn nose."

"What? NO!" I ran around him to stop in front of him. "No. Stop! This is so irrelevant!"

"The only thing that is irrelevant is someone saying something so rude like that to you," Derek muttered. "April, I may be rude sometimes, butI don't cross the line like Brigit."

"Derek, if you hurt Brigit then she's going to hate me more. I don't want that."

"You said that everyone is going to get hated one way or another."

"I know! But…" I struggled to think of the accurate words. "I just…I just…"

"You just get down easily by the hate, but you don't want to show it, so you mask your negativity by standing up for yourself and acting like a feisty kitten with sharp claws?" Derek guessed.

I blinked. "How do you know that?"

"It's obvious, April. I'm the same, you know?"

I frowned. "So, you're a kitten?"

"What? No! Well, technically, Theo says I'm a bulldog, but that's not the point! What I'm saying is that people like Brigit deserve to get a broken nose. So, can you move to the side please?"

"Derek, just let it go."

"I won't let it go. I'm not Elsa."

"That's not what I meant!" I snapped. "Please, forget about this."

Derek stared at me, considering. Then, he sighed, muttering, "Fine. But if she hurts you again, I will not hesitate to break her nose."

*   *   *

"Hey!" Jasmine ran up to me, astonishing me by yanking me into a friendly hug. I smiled and hugged her back. Jasmine hooked her arm through mine, leading me towards her table that was occupied by her group of friends. Luckily, I knew the people sitting over there.

"Where were you?" Jackson asked me as we both sat down.

"I was in the bathroom," I replied.

Derek slid his tray over to me. "Saved you some food."

I thanked him for doing that. The chatter in the cafeteria subdued and people sent our table confused frowns, bewildered why I am sitting with the popular clique.

Jasmine noticed how uneasy I was with everyone staring at me. She stood up and shouted at everyone to return back to their business. They obeyed immediately. Except for one: Brigit.

She bounded up to us, her eyes glowing viciously with that deadly gleam.

"What the hell is she doing here with you lot?" Brigit demanded, pointing at me as if I've done something bad.

"Brigit, go away," Theo groaned.

"I'm not going to go away until you tell me why this little bitch is sitting with you."

Derek's jaw hardened. "She's a bitch, and you're not?"

Jasmine stood up, her face level with Brigit's. "What do you have against April, Brigit?" she growled like a predator. Jasmine's bright eyes moved onto everyone else who decided to eavesdrop on our argument. "Why does everyone hate April Levesque?"

Everyone was silent.

Jasmine continued, "April Levesque is nice, people. She's caring and sweet, and you're treating her as if she's a bug destined to be squashed. She's pretty, she's silently smart, and she's secretly a talented artist. I just don't understand why you're treating her as if she's a contagious disease."

"She's weird," someone called out.

"Everyone is weird!" Theo snapped, standing up and joining Jasmine. "It's technically a characteristic for us, humans, to be weird. Did you all forget that her brother is Mike Levesque?"

Silence.

"That shut you up, doesn't it? You guys are cunts. If Mike was here, if Mike knew that you guys are treating her like shit, he will get hella pissed. You all know that. You all know how much Mike loved April.

"If our hero was here, he will be sad. He'll be angry at all of you little punks. Do you want that? Do you want someone who sacrificed his life for someone else's to be angry at you?"

Some people shook their heads. Others didn't respond.

"Exactly. See. You guys are cunts."

"If someone tries to insult her," Derek spoke up, loud and vicious, "I will know, and I will kill you. Brigit, go away. None of us like you. If bullying April is all you can do in your life, then get a damn life. The only person here who has a high chance of ending up in hell is you."

Brigit was silent. She glared at all of us and was fuming with anger as she walked away.

I was dumbfounded. Speechless. My jaw was hanging open. *Did they really just defend me? Am I dreaming?* I pinched my arm hard, just to make sure that I'm not imagining this. *Ouch.* Yup, I'm not dreaming.

Jasmine put her arm around me. "We are officially best friends," she announced.

I blinked. "What?"

Jasmine looked at me. "I've been keeping an eye on you and started thinking that you'll be a good friend. I have other friends, but I don't feel that connection with them, you know? However, whenever I'm with you, I feel that spark between us. Like a spark of friendship. Do you feel that too?"

"Yeah."

"I want us to hang out after school."

"I would love to, Jasmine, but I have work after school."

"I'll come with you. Where do you work?"

"In the Pet Clinic."

Her eyes widened. "Really? Oh, my grandpa works there!"

"What? Alan is your *grandpa?*"

They both nodded.

"I think he mentioned someone volunteering to work with him," Jackson mumbled, looking down at his lip, giving me the impression that he's on his phone because Derek is too.

The bell buzzed, and we all stood up, but Jasmine's arm was still wrapped around me as if she's afraid that she'll lose me forever.

My eyes stung with tears of joy. I've never had a friend in my life before. I couldn't imagine having a friend. My only real, true friend was my brother, Mike. But now he's gone...

"Thank you," I whispered to Jasmine. "For being my friend."

Jasmine smiled at me and hugged me tightly. I hugged her back. My tears dropped onto her shoulder, and I could feel her resisting the urge to cry again.

Could today be one of those wishes I've been wishing that came true?

*　　*　　*

The school bell rang. Students packed the hallway as they strolled out of the school building. The teacher in my last class annoyingly left us behind for ten minutes. So, by the time everyone and I went out, the hallways were practically empty.

I hummed a song to myself, ambling to the bathroom because I cannot hold it in anymore. My phone vibrated in my pocket. So, I took it out to see a message from Jasmine. Jasmine and I exchanged phone numbers around lunch time.

Jasmine sent me six messages for the past ten minutes:

Hey, April, do u want to go to McDonald's first?

April?

Hello?

R u there?

Hello?

April, r u there?

Me: *Hey*

Sorry 4 not replying

My history teacher kept us behind

Jasmine: *Oh*

OK

I thought u got kidnapped or something

Anyway, we r going to the pet clinic?

Me: *Sure*

Yeah y not

Jasmine: *Where do u want to meet?*

I wasn't able to reply because someone slammed me into the wall, cornering me in the bathroom. I inhaled a flabbergasted breath, groaning a little at the collision of my head with the solid wall. I blinked swiftly to clear my darkening vision. My phone was on the floor, buzzing and buzzing as Jasmine sent me incessant messages.

Brigit was in front of me, her hands pinning my arms to the wall, a predator-like twinkle in her cold-hearted eyes. "I told you to stay away from Derek, April."

"I am staying away from him!"

"You're not! Derek kept on touching you in art class today. He ran after you when you decided to be a cry baby when you heard me saying that your dad deserves to die! He *defended* you!"

"Why don't you go and tell *him* to stay away from me?"

"Because he won't listen to me! He kept on ignoring me and being rude to me. He said that I'm a whiny, desperate, idiotic—"

"Why are you like this, Brigit?" I cut her off. "Why are you so rude to me?"

"You know why!"

"Because of Owen?" I asked. "Seriously? Owen liked you, for goodness sake!"

"But he left because of you!"

"It's his fault for being a psychotic asshole! It's your fault, too! He left because you both were abusing me in school!"

"I loved him!" Brigit screamed. "I loved him, and you took him away!"

"I didn't," I whimpered. "Brigit, why can't you let this go? Why can't you stop bullying me?"

"Because you deserve it!" Brigit hissed. "You deserve to get stabbed a thousand times slowly and painfully. You deserve to die. So why can't you die already?! Don't you realize that *no one* loves you in this school? Don't you realize you don't belong here? So just leave and kill yourself already!"

"We were best friends, Brigit," I whispered. "We were so close when we were young. But everything changed when you and I got a crush on Owen. Owen liked you more than me. It hurts, yes. I was so damn blind to even think he would even like me. Then, he insulted me so many times. He punched me. He's crazy. I don't even know why you loved him!"

"Because he understands me," Brigit growled.

"He doesn't. He's only using you!"

My phone on the floor began vibrating as Jasmine calls me. Brigit ignored the sound and continued to glare at me. She yanked me forward, lifted her knee and jammed it into my gut. I groaned, my knees buckling and hitting the floor roughly.

"Go to hell," she snarled, walking away and slamming the door close.

The tears that blurred my eyes fell to the floor one by one, hot and restless. Sobs filled the bathroom as the pain in my stomach increased, spreading all over my body like a virus that couldn't be stopped.

I pushed back the long sleeves I wore a little, exposing the wounds, the scars—long, short, thin, big, healing, or still dry with blood. Most of them seemed old whereas the others seemed to be new.

I wanted to cut myself again. I know, I know, cutting yourself is bad and dangerous. I can't help it, though. I cannot resist it. It's too addictive. It makes me so numb that I cannot even feel anything — no emotions, no sadness — other than physical pain.

My eyes settled on a loop of a key ring, dangling from the corner of my handbag. I grabbed it. I took the charm off, dropping it the floor as I unlooped it, straightening it so the ends stick out. I unrolled the long sleeves of my shirt, exposing my scarred arms. There were so many scars; you cannot even see any unharmed skin.

I dug one end of the metallic stick into my skin and lashed over the other scars with so much force. A groan resonated inside the bathroom. Tears kept on running down my cheeks as I slashed my right arm again and again and again... Blood seeped out of the wounds.

"Oh, my God!"

Startled, I spun around, the metal object escaping my grasp and falling to the floor.

There, standing in the doorway, was Jasmine with her hands clamped over her mouth as her eyes travelled to unlooped key ring on the floor and then to the newly fresh scars.

"April, what are you doing?!" Jasmine screamed, dashing towards me, grabbing my right arm in her hand and gawking down at the scars. Her other hand gripped my left arm, gently pushing up the sleeve. She ripped off the bandages to reveal the old scars. "Oh, my God...Why are you self-harming?"

I yanked my arms off her grasp. "Come on, let's go to the clinic."

"Not until you tell me why you are doing this!" Jasmine demanded.

"It doesn't matter," I mumbled.

"It does matter!" Jasmine corrected. "Tell me why you're harming yourself."

I stared at Jasmine. I just met her. I don't even know anything about her. I don't want to tell her the reasons. In fact, I don't think there are many reasons to explain why I'm self-harming. I'm self-harming because it's addicting. I'm self-harming so I can get rid of the pain.

"I'm going to tell a teacher," Jasmine said. She turned around, but I latched onto her arm, yanking her backwards.

"Don't!" I begged. 'Please, don't tell anyone."

"Why not?" Jasmine asked.

"B-because," I stammered. "If you tell, no one will believe me."

Jasmine gave me an incredulous look. "People will believe you. April, you know self-harm is dangerous. I hate it when people self-harm. I know people go through bad times, but self-harm isn't the solution to everything. It doesn't help. I need to tell an adult. An adult will help."

My eyes moistened. "Jasmine, even if you tell someone they'll think I'm doing it for attention."

"They won't."

"They will. You know how people can be, nowadays."

"April, not everyone is like that..."

"Jasmine, please don't tell anyone!" I said in a cracking, hoarse voice. "Please. If you want to be my friend, please don't tell anyone. No one will understand. No one will believe me. People will just stare at me as if I'm crazy. I don't want my parents to know because it'll hurt them even more and I don't want that—especially after Mike died. Dad's in the Syrian War, and he doesn't need to get more stressed by finding out that his daughter has been cutting herself. I'm scared they'll get angry."

Jasmine's eyes saddened. "April, telling someone will help."

"That's what everyone says." I sniffled, wiping my nose with my sleeve. "But I'm just scared to confess why I am cutting myself. I feel as if my life will go downhill."

"It won't. April, confessing is not that bad."

"That's what Derek said," I whispered.

Jasmine's eyes widened, as if a thought occurred to her. "Derek," she murmured, her eyebrows furrowing in thought.

"What?"

She blinked. "Nothing. Are you sure you don't want me to tell anyone?"

"Yes. Please."

'But, April, you cannot hold your secret forever. Secrets will eventually be revealed one way or another. Your parents will find out eventually."

'Jasmine, please promise me…"

Jasmine managed a sad smile. "I promise I won't tell anyone."

*   *   *

Jasmine and I had a great time at the pet clinic. We helped Alan with the patients—Jasmine helped her grandfather inject serums into the patients' veins while I tried to pull the pets that were waiting outside in the small reception into the doctor's room. A cat scratched my hands, and now I have a cut. *Did I mention that I hate cats?*

Here and then, Jasmine looked at me concerned, as if terrified I will cut myself again. Since Jasmine came into my life, she's attempted to always be there for me and to stop me from self-harm.

"You are banned from knives, scissors, and anything that is sharp," Jasmine declared. "If I catch you cutting yourself one more time, I will tell someone."

"But you promised…"

"April, like I said: self-harm is not good. So please, stop it. If I catch you doing it one more time, I'm going to tell your mother. Got it?"

"I don't know if I can stop…"

"I'll help you, okay?'

"Okay."

After my work hours in Peony Hallows Pet Clinic, Jasmine and I walked to my house.

When we arrived, we rushed upstairs and crashed on the bed, sighing with relief as we relaxed. I looked at my bedroom deco. In a few days, I am going to give my bedroom a makeover. It's been years since I've decorated my room. The walls were resplendent with different images that I've painted—one wall was an image of a flower; another was an image of the beach and a sunset, with radiant colours streaked across the sky; and the other wall was just an image of me.

This time, I'm hoping to change the paintings: one of the paintings could be of Lucky, the Golden Retriever. Another wall could be of my brother and my father, standing next to each other while doing the salute. The other walls: I'm not sure.

"Are you going to the Black and White Masquerade Ball?" Jasmine suddenly asks.

I looked at her. "I don't know, honestly."

Jasmine bit her lip. "But I thought you're going with Derek."

I groaned. "Jasmine, we're not together."

"But the past few days I've seen you two together. And the way he talked to you when we were in our art class...I just had a feeling that he loves you."

"No way," I said. "Trust me, if we're a couple, he will be the one who will end our relationship."

"True," Jasmine agreed. "I know he's the heartbreaker of the school but...the way he looks at you, it looks like love. Maybe I'm hallucinating or something, but I swear its love."

"It's not love, Jasmine. And I will never love him," I said. "I've heard that he has hooked up with hundreds of girls in the school and broke their hearts. I don't want to get upset, especially since I'm...you know."

Jasmine pulls herself up to stare at me. "April, now I found out you're — well, *was* — self-harming, I want to know the reason why. I know we just met, but we've known each other ever since kindergarten. We talked to each other rarely, but I'm not like Brigit. I won't hurt you. I'm not one of those 'popular girls' who make fun of you. Even if you are self-harming or not, I will still be your friend no matter what."

"Why are you my friend, anyways?"

"Because I need a true friend," Jasmine explained. "All the friends I have are sweet and nice, but they're not really there for me, you know? They use me because of the money. Jackson's different; his best friends are Theo and Derek. I'm the only one who has been praying for a true friend my whole life."

"So...you thought that I will be your best friend?"

"If you want to..."

"Of course, I want us to be friends," I said. "I always wanted to have friends, too."

Jasmine smiled. "As long as we're friends, I will be there for you and help you no matter what, starting with you telling me why you're self-harming."

I stared at Jasmine. She's just like me: praying for a friend endlessly. Nevertheless, our prayers have been answered. Mike once told me that if you pray really hard, your prayers will be answered eventually—no matter how long it will take, your prayers will always get answered. *Just don't give up*, he said.

"I cut myself because…" I inhaled a deep, shaky breath; my fingers fidgeting with the ends of my right sleeve. "Because I feel as if I deserve to get hurt. Cutting takes away the pain."

"Is Brigit bullying you?"

"Yes."

"Why?"

I explained everything to her—what happened in the past, the argument between my next door neighbour; how I tried to convince Brigit that Owen was a bad influence; how I tried to stop Brigit from smoking and taking drugs; how Owen hurt me and how he left.

"Brigit is bullying you because of that lunatic?"

"Basically," I agreed.

"That's dumb."

"Is it? But don't you think I deserved it? I ran home crying after Owen punched me—"

"Because of your faith," Jasmine said, "so Owen deserved to get punched by your older brother. Honestly, if someone is rude to me for believing in God, I will also do what Mike did." Jasmine scooted closer to me, leaning backwards against the headboard, our shoulders brushing against each other. "Your parents don't know about this, right?"

"No."

"Do you…" Jasmine exhaled. "Are you tempted to kill yourself?"

"Sometimes."

If Jasmine wants to be my friend, then I have to be completely candid with her. I have to tell her. I can't keep everything to myself. If I do, it'll affect me and destroy me even more than before.

"I complain," I whispered, my eyes moistening whilst hurt surged through me. "I cry every night. I don't know what the hell is special about me, about what purpose I have to fulfil. There's nothing good about me. All I do is weep and moan about life. I yell at God a few times, demanding what He sees in me and how He finds me special. Because all I get is losing people I love, getting bullied and insults from everyone. And it sucks: feeling like you're not good enough. The scars hurt but I'm used to it.

"You see, I find it strange that people fear death when life hurts a lot more—at the point of death, the pain is over. I had enough of life, Jasmine. I want to kill myself. I want to get away from this hellhole. I just want to die. I don't freaking care. I just want to stab myself and say goodbye. I want to reunite with my brother, Mike, in Heaven.

"After a few months, my faith in God faded. I didn't believe in Him. And one time, I actually tried to kill myself—I was in the kitchen, it was dark, I took out a knife from the drawers and pointed the tip directly to my chest. I was about to stab myself, straight through the heart, when I thought: *Do you really want to do this? Is it worth it, taking your own life?* It was so sudden—the second thoughts, I mean. Almost as if—"

"As if God's talking to you," Jasmine murmured, completing my sentence. "It was your conscience; your conscience was speaking to you. Jackson told me that the conscience is God's way of communicating with you, but you gotta educate it, train it, and tame it so it would be helpful. What else did your conscience—I mean, *you* thought?"

"That's it; I kept on repeating the same questions in my head. And while I was, I felt sad. Like, my heart was squeezing and breaking, as if…"

She put her hand over mine. "I'm not really religious. I'm an atheist. Jackson's a Christian, and I remember one time he told me 'If you kill yourself, you won't go to heaven'. I think what you felt — the sadness, your heart squeezing and breaking — was His way of expressing His emotions. I think He was trying to tell you that if you kill yourself, He won't be able to save you because you committed a sin."

"But why am I going through this? Why do I feel so sad? Why do I feel so unloved? I prayed to Him a lot—"

"His ways can be beautiful, April," Jasmine whispered, smiling softly, "but it also has to be painful and hard for you to appreciate its beauty. Every good thing comes from something bad; it's life's way of teaching us a lesson.

"And why do you feel unloved? There are many people who love you—your family, Alan, Jackson, Theo, me…we all love you. You just don't realise that, do you? And have you forgotten about your God? Isn't He an unconditional, all-loving, mysterious dude? He loves us, April. But if we commit a sin, His love will still be there, but He will walk away from us because He's disappointed. He'll be in agony that we decided to give into the temptations of the bad guy.

"God will never forgive you if you commit suicide. Life is a gift from Him. He wants us to cherish it, to live it. However, He also wants to test us, to give us challenges in order to make us stronger, not weaker. He knows how tough and hurtful these challenges can be, but He'll help us through our struggles if we *ask* Him. April, you want to meet Mike again, right? Then don't kill yourself. Or else you will never see your brother again. God will forgive everyone who asks Him for His redemption, but He will never forgive us if we kill ourselves.

"So, don't kill yourself. You're worthy. You don't see it, but I see it. You are important to so many people. So please just don't self-harm."

"Should I continue to ask Him?"

Jasmine nibbled her lower lip, contemplating about her answer. It must be hard for her to talk about Someone she doesn't believe in, though I am full of gratitude that she's willing to aid me with religious advice. Luke, Mike's best friend, is an atheist.

"Jackson told me that God answers when you least expect it. He said not to worry about anything because Big Guy has special plans, and his plans are ten times cooler than your dreams." Jasmine stroked her fingers across my knuckles. "Hold on, April, because I guarantee you your pain will end. You have to face the challenges first for the good to come. God will help you through your struggles, okay? Just believe and have hope."

Hot tears streamed down my cheeks. Nobody has ever said anything sweet like that to me before. Her helpful advice made my heart throb with unfamiliar feelings, but my instincts were telling me that the feelings are happiness and hope.

My instincts were telling me that the sentiments are God's way of telling me:

Jasmine's right.

I do have special plans for you.

Just bear with me, OK?

Don't give up and have hope.

Chapter Twelve

I Want You Back

April Levesque

People say cemeteries are too dull and sad. They're right. Yet, sometimes, cemeteries are good places to confess your feelings to the deceased.

The cemetery in Peony Hallows is like a vast lake of the dead. Everywhere, to your right and left, behind and in front, are gravestones, new or ancient, both small and large, cuddled in the soft soil with flowers leaning against them.

I'm not the only one here because I always stumble across a middle-aged Ghanaian man called Elinam Abban. He helped us bury Mike.

"Elinam!"

The kind-hearted man spun around. Elinam moved to Syria to help the refugees. He came across my brother when my brother set up a refugee camp for the victims of the civil war. Elinam helped Mike and they were very close friends. He was also a victim of an ISIS kidnapping. Obviously, he's a survivor, and burying Mike was an absolute honour to him.

Elina's humble dark eyes lightened. "April!" He smiled, lines appearing at the corner of his eyes as we offered each other a heartwarming hug. "Beautiful as ever, kid."

"Thanks, Elinam. You look great as well."

He chuckled. "I'm old, April. Old people tend to have unattractive wrinkles. How are you, though? Everything alright with your family?"

"Yeah. We're all fine. I, uh, have to go. I want to talk to someone."

Elinam nodded, understanding, and said goodbye to me. I sauntered over to the small white fence with a blue balloon clutched in my right hand.

The fence enclosed a private area of the cemetery. In that area, a large, opulent white cross was tenderly embraced in the soft, exuberant ground. Huddling around the luxuriant cross were millions of vibrant flowers, cards and letters from most citizens of the Canadian town. So many people loved him. Behind the white cross is a statue of a soldier, saluting, with an inscription below it which says:

"This hero sacrificed his life to defend the innocent from danger and wickedness. This hero understood the responsibilities, advantages and consequences of fighting in wars,
yet he did not give a damn."
MIKE T. LEVESQUE
CANADIAN ARMED FORCES
LOVING SON, BROTHER, FRIEND, AND
INSPIRATION

I walked to the white cross, bending down to replace the old wilting flowers with new lush ones I bought from a shop. I kissed the tips of my fingers and brushed them against the firmness of the blessed cross.

"Hey, Mike," I whispered. The sombre, funereal wind howled past me. The sky looming above was crammed with dark clouds.

I lifted my gaze to stare at the statue of my brother. Mike was very famous in Peony Hallows. Everyone in school knew him. He did have his haters yet he cared about them anyway, which is very inspiring if you think about it. Here and then, I would always hear people murmuring to each other about Mike, saying how he was so sweet, so kind, and so caring. Mike was hilarious, sarcastic, and always full of mischief. He loved to prank people. He loved to help the feared. He just loved to help people in general.

My brother meant a lot to me. He shaped my young life. First, he taught me how to walk by grabbing my small hands and yanking me up to my feet, guiding me around the house as Mom and Dad cheered. Then, he armed himself with sticks and snakes that I thought were real, and chased me, and I learned how to run. My first word was his name. We were truly close. We still are. Even though he left me here in this wicked world, I will never accept that he died because he didn't die in my heart.

Mike always loved me. He read me bedtime stories. He thundered into my room whenever I woke up from a nightmare, screaming. He wiped every tear off my cheek. He made every bad feeling I had go away. He healed my wounds. He teased me. He caught me when I fell. He defended me from all the hate. He told the bullies to leave me alone, and they did. He always told me that there is nobody as special as me.

Every night, I would always say a sweet Hail Mary for him. Every night, I would close my eyes and imagine that he is in my bedroom, sitting on the edge of my bed, smiling at me;

running his fingers through my hair; singing me a sweet song; or whispering a bedtime story. Sometimes, I actually thought that I felt his presence because I would always feel this warm feeling touching my arm, leg, or cheek, as if Mike was there. As if he's trying to tell me: *I'm here, please don't cry.* I would always feel this heartwarming feeling lingering on my forehead, as if Mike is giving me a peck.

When my eyes are close, *closed* that's when I can see him..

I love him. He was the only one who kept my heart beating, the only light that shined *shone* in the room of darkness I was trapped in.

I inhaled a shaky breath. My eyes ached with scorching, inconsolable tears. I cleared my throat, regaining my voice.

I sang *Happy Birthday* to Mike softly as my voice slightly cracked. I closed my eyes to stop the distressing tears. It's no use. They tumbled down my cheeks like a furious waterfall, each and every one of them full of unspoken, indescribable negative emotion.

When I opened them again, I read some of the letters from the people in the town.

I love you Mike.

Come back Mike.

I want to be like you Mike.

Thanks for saving me Mike.

All these notes were too much for me. It just made it worse. Knowing that so many people — more than a thousand — depended on a young son, a young brother, a young *man* made it ten times more sentimental.

Why, God? Why did you have to take him away so soon?

"Happy Birthday," I whispered, my breathing slow. I released the blue balloon. It spiralled up into the air, ascending and ascending as the dull wind suddenly seemed to come alive, kicking the blue balloon up and up until it disappeared above the ceiling of clouds.

I reminisced that time when a soldier knocked on the door and informed us about his heroic, tragic death. I felt a part of my heart dying. I felt all the elation, all the hope, every good feeling that was breathing in me shatter into a thousand puzzle pieces. I felt an invisible harsh presence, sinisterly shoving me into a room of darkness, pain, misery, and loneliness and trapping me there until I die.

I closed my eyes as more tears rushed down my cheeks. I hate crying. I don't want to cry.

But how can I not when I'm such a pessimist?

*   *   *

A stupendous variety of different people from all over town — strangers and relatives — came to the funeral, dressed in their most sophisticated black and white clothes. They came to offer their respects to the young man who they either have heard of or knew very dearly.

They came to say their final goodbyes to my beloved older brother, Mike Levesque.

There was no sun. Only colourless clouds, crying heaving rounds of tears. The wind mourned miserably, as if God was weeping Himself.

There were thin rays of sunlight, scraping through the thick clouds miraculously, as if it was a sign that Mike was well and secure in heaven, safe with Him. The thin lights could be a sign that Mike was joyous to be with his eternal hero, knowing that he did not die, but still living with his inspiration.

The church was beautifully colossal with curved ceilings that held a cross and a ringing bell. Inside the church, there was a fresh natural fragrance of roses and the poles supported the vaulted ceiling as mosaics coloured the plush windows. .

There were rows of benches, encircling an open space and the casket. The coffin was open, exposing the hero wearing his army uniform, with his hands clutched around a rose and a crucifix resting on his chest.

"April...Ethan..." Mom gradually approached us after whispering her farewells to Mike. "Go and say goodbye." Her eyes were swollen and her makeup was messy from crying. Dad, who's dressed in his Canadian army uniform, placed a tender hand on her shoulder.

Ethan advanced to the coffin with me by his side. My fingers gripped his arm. There was an empty hole in my chest, as if I was dead.

The Matthews were here. Samuel Matthews stood behind his two sons, Luke and Derek. Luke looked devastated, his hands shoved into both pockets of his black jeans. Derek looked sad, too; though his eyes were red and puffy with a trickle of tears. Marline Matthews had her hands on the boys' shoulders.

Derek's eyes met mine. He bit his lower, trembling lip and managed to a mournful smile, mouthing, "Sorry."

I smiled sadly. I turned my attention to the coffin, stopping right in front of it with Ethan beside me.

My older brother's eyes were closed, slumbering peacefully. Yet, I could not hear him breathing. I pecked my unmoving brother's forehead, and regardless of the fact that he is gone already, I murmured a goodbye.

I tried so hard to keep the pain inside. I failed. Tiny beads of sweltering, restless water slid down my cheeks, one by one. My heart felt as if it's burning.

Not from a fire.

From the loss of my brother.

From grief.

My breathing slowed. I felt light-headed. All the voices in the room were incoherent.

I couldn't stare at Mike's serene face anymore. It's too much. I swallowed the sobs roughly, turning around to run out of the church. My vision turned fuzzy.

That's when I notice a blurry figure of Derek Matthews, dashing towards me with a concerned look on his face as I felt myself falling to the floor.

"April!"

Firm arms swathed around me before my body hit the floor. My head throbbed with more pain. The boy I knew ever since I was a baby, the silent boy who comes to my house all the time, the boy who was my best friend, the boy who pushed me away, suddenly exposed a soft heart and whispered...

"I got you, April. I got you."

A loud sob escaped me, freeing me from the bleak memory.

"I miss you Mike," I blubbered. "People say your spirit is with us, but I want to *see you physically*. I want you back, Mike. I want you back.

"But I can't. You're gone. You're dead. You left us. Left *me*. You will never come back. And I'm suffering in school. Everybody is treating me like I'm a disease, a disease destined to die. Someone actually threatened to harm me and I don't know why. I don't know why people hate me so much. I never did anything. Even Ethan is getting hurt.

"Sometimes...it's better to be alone so nobody can hurt you. I'm so broken that I can feel it. Physically. The sadness never seems to go away.

"You said that you care about me. You said you loved me. Yet, you left me alone to cry. I hate you for leaving me. For leaving us. Mom is crying all night and praying to God for you. Ethan is quiet. We talk, but we don't talk that much. And Rosie is...well, Rosie. She doesn't even know that you're her brother. Dad is constantly telling us that he'll be back soon, but he won't. He's too busy in Syria. How long do I have to wait, Mike? How long? We're not the same anymore. We're all distant, yet we love each other."

I released a shaky sigh, brushing off the grass as I got up. "I love you."

I kissed my fingertips once again and stroked them against the cross-shaped gravestone. I strolled away, looking up at the sky and watched how the clouds parted.

I have an angel protecting me: my brother.

Chapter Thirteen

I Do Care About You

April Levesque

As I ambled along the sidewalk of a very quiet street linked to the humongous, beautiful park, a familiar masculine voice called my name. Derek was jogging towards me, dressed in dark blue jeans and a white shirt with a cardigan covering his arms.

"Hey."

I didn't greet him back. I just said, "Are you stalking me?"

Derek furrowed his eyebrows. "No, I am not stalking you. Why?"

"What are you doing here, then?"

"I'm taking a walk. Is that a problem?"

I shook my head. "No. It's not. Anyway, it's great to see you — not really — but…"

"Are you…" Derek narrowed his eyes. "Are you *crying?*"

"No," I muttered, turning around. "I'm not."

"Why are you always lying?" He sang in the most horrible voice I have ever heard. Well, truthfully, his singing voice wasn't that bad, but I don't want to admit it to him because it'll just bring out the arrogance again.

I was about to walk away when I felt his warm hand covering my cold wrist, swinging me around to face him. His touch sent tingling sensations up my arm, causing my heart to throb swiftly.

"April, why are you crying?"

"Why would you care?" I asked. "You don't even care about me."

"Lies. I do care about you. Even if you don't see it, I still care about you." He did something I did not expect—he stroked his thumbs across my cheeks and the bottom of my eyes, wiping away the tears and warming my skin. "Now tell me, baby, why are you crying?"

"Don't call me baby, please," I grumbled, not in the mood for his nicknames.

"I'll stop calling you that if you tell me what's wrong."

"I went to meet my brother," I answered, my voice suddenly whispery. "It's his birthday today. I went to greet him."

Derek's ocean blue eyes softened, mixed with commiseration. He tugged me into his hard chest, wrapping his warm defined arms around me. I would've struggled to pull away or hiss or cuss at him to let me go. I didn't. Instead, I embraced him back. My head on his chest, his chin on my head. His lips stroked my forehead, granting a swift kiss. I found this comfortable yet uncomfortable at the same time. I guess it's because I'm not used to these types of hugs. In fact, I never experienced these types of hugs.

"Those we love don't die." His warm breath fanned my forehead. "They live forever. They're always there for us, even if we don't realise it. Mike didn't die, April. His body did, but not his soul. I know it's hard to lose someone. I lost two people, too, so you don't have to be afraid to talk to me. I will understand."

"But you can't fix them," I mumbled into his chest.

"Fix what?"

"My problems."

The gentle wind tickled past us, chilling my body. "What if I can?" he asked. "What if I can help you face your problems? Won't that be nice?"

"I don't know. I don't deserve any help."

"You do."

"We all don't deserve something, Derek," I muttered. "You know it's true."

"True," he agreed. "But sometimes we can make that false. Besides, I don't deserve you."

"You're damn right about that."

He laughed above me. His laugh thrilled my ears and caused a smile to beam on my face. I pulled away, my hands still flat on his chest. "I never knew you had a heart, Matthews."

Derek raised an eyebrow. "What does that supposed to mean?"

"Well, I've heard things about you."

"Ah, that," Derek said, scratching the back of his neck. "Well, people don't know me very well—even Theo."

I took my hands off his chest. "I have to go."

"Where?"

"Why are you asking?"

He smirked, enhancing his handsome looks. "Cause I'm gonna follow you."

"Are you serious?"

"Yes."

I groaned. "Asshole. Stupid, annoying asshole."

He chuckled. "I'm your stupid, annoying asshole."

I rolled my eyes, spinning around and walking to the pet clinic.

"You know I'm right, April!" he shouted. He laughed when I offered him an irritated scowl and the middle finger, winking attractively as he bounds after me, swinging an arm around my shoulders.

"Let go of me," I snapped.

"It's only for this walk," he said. "Promise."

"I still don't want to get infected by your virus."

"I don't have any damn viruses!" he snapped, and I laughed, amused by his sudden fury.

It only took us a few minutes to arrive at the pet clinic. Alan was leaning against the counter, glasses on, reading a newspaper. He glanced up when the door opened and grinned when he saw me.

"April!" His eyes focused on Derek next. "Oh, my! Welcome, Mr. Matthews!"

Derek smiled. "Hi, sir. I'm just tagging along with my girlfriend. I hope I'm not interrupting anything."

"No, no. You're not." Alan raised his eyebrows at me. "Boyfriend?"

I rolled my eyes. "Don't believe anything he says, Alan. He's not my boyfriend. Just a friend."

"Oh, so we're friends?" Derek asked. "Since when?"

"Since we were kids," I responded.

Alan made a *tsk tsk* sound. "Pity." He narrowed his eyes at Derek and me, glancing back and forth as he murmured to himself about how correct Jackson was that we both suited each other. "Anyway, a patient is coming in less than an hour, so you could just relax or just clean the pets' room."

"We'll clean the pets' room," I decided, and Derek looked at me. Before he could protest, I dragged him into the pets' room, closing the door behind me.

"There's no way I'm cleaning!" Derek objected, crossing his arms over his chest like an angry child.

"Then why did you follow me?"

Derek opened his mouth to say something, though the words didn't come out. Then, he groaned and cursed, "Damn it!"

"It's just cleaning, Derek," I said. "Not that big of a deal."

"I don't want to clean up shit," he groaned. "I don't want to touch it either."

"But you're already shit, so I don't know what you're talking about…"

Derek went to the storage room to get the food. I sat down on the couch, sighing with serenity. Suddenly, a petite, furry dog dashed towards me, its tail wagging in excitement.

"Lucky!" I squealed as I picked him up.

"Who's that?" Derek asked as he returned from the storage room, dropping a large bag of dog food.

"Lucky," I answered. "He's a rescued puppy."

Derek walked over and sat down next to me. Lucky's charcoal eyes were fixed on him.

"Hi," Derek said to the puppy. Lucky only opened his mouth, his tongue sticking out. "Can I hold him?"

"Sure."

He gently took the Golden Retriever from my hands. Derek brushed his fingers through the dog's golden fur.

"I love dogs," Derek stated.

"Then why don't you have one?" I asked. "You're rich, and your house is very huge."

'I had a dog. But he died a few years ago," Derek said. "I'm hoping to get a dog for Christmas."

"Lucky would make a good dog," I said, ruffling the puppy's fur.

"Yeah," Derek agreed.

Once Derek and I poured the food into the bowls and cleaned the room, we went to help Alan with his patient. After that, we left the clinic and strolled along the sidewalk to my house. I had to tutor him again today. Honestly, tutoring isn't that bad. Mom and Derek were on good terms. Ethan and Derek, however, weren't.

"I don't like that big idiot," Ethan muttered once.

A droplet of rain fell on my forehead lightly, gradually running down the bridge of my nose. I wiped it away, gazing up to see a blanket of clouds covering the sky. The weather forecast did mention that there will be a storm today. It started to rain more, not very hard, but quite like a drizzle.

I observed Derek walking slower. "What's wrong?"

"I just realized that I have to visit my grandma."

"What, now?"

"Yeah. You can come if you want. She's in the care centre. It's not that far."

I've been to Peony Hallows Care Centre a couple of times just to visit the staff members and offer them money. I liked to be generous. The last time I visited the place was in September and I kindly gave the centre three hundred dollars so they can develop their property.

"I'll come." I decided, and he smiled.

*　　　*　　　*

The place was great. The elderly rested on the lounge, conversing with their neighbours, cracking smiles or bursting into laughter. I admired the people because they were so nice. They had so many interesting stories to tell. Some of them were Holocaust survivors from Europe who came to Canada for a better life. The atmosphere in here was marvellous and generally jam-packed with luxuriant life.

Derek advanced to the reception desk. "Hi, Kofi," Derek greeted a familiar-looking guy — perhaps in his twenties — sitting on a red chair.

Kofi looked up at the sound of his name. He grinned at Derek and stood up. "Derek, my man." The two males hugged and patted each other on the back. Kofi's eyes landed on me. "Who's this?'"

"I'm his friend" I responded at the same time Derek said "She's my girlfriend."

I glared at Derek. He smirked and winked at me in reply.

Kofi laughed, as if Derek and I were in a comedy. "That's cool. Lovers lost in paradise. And I was kidding, April, of course I know who you are."

"You do?"

Kofi has a short afro with a stubble on his jaw line. "Yeah, bruv. I was your brother's partner in the Syrian War. I'm the African guy from England. We were both fighting against ISIS together. Mike was awesome, man. He was a good soldier."

I remember now. He was the guy who informed my family and me about Mike's death.

Kofi picked up his Bible. "I didn't really believe in God. Back in England all the mates insulted me coz I'm gay. They said that I'm gonna end up in hell and God will never accept me into heaven. My mum was Muslim and she was my only hero. She helped me when Dad left us coz he's ashamed to have a homosexual son." His fingers drummed the surface of the Bible. "Thanks to Mike, I understand some things now. I feel happy because I can feel this Sky Dude all around me. He really had a way of making people hopeful again."

I smiled. "I know." I had a rocky faith journey. Sometimes, I believe in God. Other times I don't. When Mike started taking me to church, however, when he introduced me to Jesus Christ and to everyone else, that's when I finally started to believe. That's when my faith in God strengthened. That's when I started to feel God around me.

Kofi turned his dark eyes to Derek. "Are you here to meet your grandmother?"

"Yeah."

"She's in Room 29."

"Thanks, man."

"See you later, bruv."

We both said goodbye to Kofi and walked away. We strolled through a series of corridors and climbed a small flight of stairs. Finally, we stopped in front of a door.

Derek turned the door knob to the right. It swung inwards. His hand found mine and he pulled me along with him into Room 29.

Chapter Fourteen

She's Crying and I'm Breaking

Derek Matthews

Grandma was resting by the windowsill, humming a soft tune to herself as she read a novel. Her temporary room was vintage. White curtains were pulled apart and there was a picture of a my parents with their arms wrapped around each other as Luke and I stood in front of them, smiling into the camera. There was another one of my grandma and momma.

Grandma's emaciated fingers drew her gold-framed spectacles off, her blue eyes dancing as I stepped inside the room, my hand interlinked with April's.

"Grandma." I smiled and walked towards her to kiss her wrinkled forehead.

"Derek, my little warrior." Grandma kissed both of my cheeks after setting her book down. Her eyes averted to April. For a moment, she blinked, speechless as she just gaped at April, as if she's a beautiful phenomena. "You look a little like Alexandra," she said to April.

I glanced at Gran. She said my mother's name. I then looked at April, and I realized why Grandma said that. From the pictures I've seen and the stories I've heard, April has a small resemblance to Momma. As I mentioned before, Momma was described as a beautiful woman who was a dork, a nerd, a geek, a bookworm. April has all of the aforementioned qualities.

"Gran," I whispered, my chest tightening at the thought of my mother. I always get this sentimental scorching sensation inside my chest whenever I reflect about her. "This is April Levesque."

"Oh," Gran mumbled. "Oh! You're Mike's little sister, aren't you?" April smiled, nodding. Gran grinned. "I must say, Mike was a lovely boy! Derek told me how sweet and caring he was. If Derek liked him then so did I. I met him once, actually. He was such a gentleman. He's with the Lord, I know. I know the Lord is proud of the work he has done." She held out her wrinkled hand. "It's nice to meet you, April. I am Sandy Matthews. Old but alive. Surprisingly."

"She's ninety-five," I stated proudly.

April's eyes widened, amazed. "It's nice to meet you, too, Sandy. How are you?"

"I'm splendid." She then asked: "Are you two in a relationship?"

"No," April replied promptly before brusquely muttering, "Why does everyone think that we're a couple?"

"It's a shame, though," Gran said, "you two will be *adorable* together. I remember clearly now—you are the girl Derek had a crush on when he was a kid. He kept on talking about you on and on and on. It was annoying although it was endearing. I never saw Derek that happy before."

April opened her mouth to respond to Gran's statement, though the words didn't tumble out. She was gobsmacked at Gran's declaration about my crush.

She glanced at me and quickly looked away. I glared at my Grandma who cunningly smirked at me and shook her shoulders innocently. A sweltering blush seared my cheeks.

I stared at April. Ever since I took her to the meadow, I've been feeling these peculiar sentiments—like when I hugged April, I felt intense, heartwarming sensations. My heart pounded in my chest whenever I see her. This was exactly how I felt when I had a crush on her.

I can't stop thinking about her.

And when I think of her, I can't stop smiling.

It's bewildering.

I glimpsed at her pale bruised lips. They're soft. I remember how soft those lips were when they were pressed against mine. I want to close my eyes, pull her into me, and just *kiss her*. I want to forget about everything — life, insecurity, pain, my parents — and just *be with her* and *hold her in my arms*. Forever. If that's possible.

I exhaled sharply, raking a hand through my hair and tugging at them with nuisance. *What the heck is happening to me?*

"Plus, it will be nice for a beautiful girl like you to be with my little warrior," Gran continued. "My little bear is hurting, I know, and it will be nice if he's in a relationship with you."

Gran narrowed her eyes at the sight of us, as if trying to brainstorm the state of our relationship. Her gaze dropped to our interlinked hands. April looked down and instantaneously pulled her hand away.

"Derek needs a break from everything," Gran continued. "He's breaking inside, I know."

"I'm not breaking," I muttered, "I'm not a damn mirror."

"Darling, I mean your feelings and your sorrow—it's breaking you. You know that, so stop denying it. It doesn't make you look weak if you accept it. It just gives you a hint of who you are." Gran smiled at both of us. "Marline could be right. Sometimes, any type of love can be miraculous. Perhaps you both could help each other in a way."

Ignoring my grandmother's words, I turned to smile at April. "See, even my gran wants us to be together."

April scowled, not looking at me. "Us? Together? That's impossible, don't you think?"

I shook my head. 'April, for the past few days we've been together, we've been talking to each other nonstop. I know you felt that bond with me."

"A bond of friendship," April admitted. "Not a lovey-dovey bond."

"That will soon turn into affection."

"No, it won't."

"Yes, it will."

"How can you say that?"

"Because two friends of the opposite sex will eventually start dating."

"Unless if one of them is gay."

"We're not gay—"

"How do you know that?"

Gran laughed. "This girl is funny. She has a good sense of humour. Maybe she can give you tips, Derek, since your humour can be dead sometimes."

I rolled my eyes.

"Sandy, how is everything going?" April asked Gran.

April and Gran talked about books. I rolled my eyes again. I knew they would start a nerd chat. They're both geeks. I sat down on Gran's bed, staring at the two females who were chatting and chatting persistently. Gran laughed at something April said, lines appearing at the corner of her blue eyes. Her laugh made April crack a smile. Eventually, she started giggling. I grinned too. It's nice to hear April laugh. It's attractive.

April Levesque is the type of girl who is continuously grinning. You never know if her smile is fake or not. You think that she's okay, with everything that has happened to her— Mike's death, her pain. *Everything*. But when you get to know her properly, you will realize that she's not what people say she is. She's not a brat. She can be annoying sometimes, but then again: we are all annoying one way or another. She's mean, but she's only mean so she can stand up for herself, to prove to everyone that it's not affecting her when you know that deep down, it is. She feels as worthless, unloved, ugly, and always lonely. She doesn't know what *I see in her*: a beautiful, beautiful girl with a beautiful persona, so talented with great courage.

She's crying inside.

And I'm breaking inside.

Funny coincidence, isn't it?

I stared through the window. Heavy droplets of rain smacked the casement, racing down the glass.

"Are we boring you?" I heard Gran ask me.

I looked at her. "To death," I agreed light-heartedly.

Gran rolled her eyes, a sly smile on her face. She glanced at the clock and then at us. "We can chat later. I have TV shows to watch."

"What shows?" April asked, inquisitive.

"Teen Wolf, The Flash, Shadowhunters, Supergirl, Stranger Things, Legends of Tomorrow, 13 Reasons Why…"

Gran sang all her brief list of her favourite shows, a gleeful glint beaming her blue eyes.

lit

April's dark brown eyes ~~lightened~~ up. "I watch all of those shows!"

Gran smiled again, offering me a rapid glimpse. "I like this girl. Date her, please."

"I *love* Mason and Corey from Teen Wolf," April stated, seeming to ignore Gran's last sentence. "They are *so* cute!"

Before Gran could reply to April's statement and start fangirling, I blurted, "I'll come back next week, Gran."

Gran looked at me and nodded. "Okay, Derek. Goodbye, my little warrior."

I kissed Gran's forehead lovingly. I grabbed April's hand, snaking my fingers through hers. Both of us said goodbye to Sandy Matthews before we exited the room.

"I like your grandma," April announced, a happy smile on her face. "She's cool."

I smirked. "I knew you'll like her. She's a nerd like you."

April rolled her eyes. "Just because we both read books and watch the same shows, doesn't mean we're nerds! Everyone read books."

"I don't," I stated.

"Then that explains why you have weasel very dim-witted brain."

It was my turn to roll my eyes as I opened the main doors.

The water heavily streamed down from the leaden clouds. The wind howled cordially. Beads of water hit my face, trailing down my skin as I shivered.

"You must be cold," I noted, analysing April's attire.

She scrutinized herself, as if just apprehending what she's wearing: a long-sleeve purple shirt, jeans, and a pair of shoes with no hoodie or jacket. She shrugged, waving agitatedly.

I shrugged my hoodie off. "Put this on."

She blinked at the clothing in my hand and then at me. "Derek, thanks, but I'll be—"

"Put it on," I commanded. "I'd rather see you warm than freezing to death."

"What about you?"

"I'll be fine. Don't worry about me."

"And you should worry about me?" she said.

"Basically," I agreed.

"Gentleman much?" she muttered. "But I'll be fine…"

"You are so stubborn," I grumbled, grabbing her and tugging her toward me. "It's annoying."

"What are you—" She was cut off as I seized her arms and dipped them into the arms of my hoodie. I twirled her around, her chest facing me, and zipped it up, yanking the black hood over her head and shoving all the tufts of her brunette hair inside.

"There." I wiped the water off her glasses and put it back on her face. "Perfect."

In that moment, I was desperate to kiss her again. I had no idea why, though. It's maddening, aggravating, and draining to have this atypical sentiment of need just to *be with her, hold her in my arms, hug her,* and *just kiss her.* I could easily crash my lips on her just by cupping her face with my hands and bringing our trembling lips together. I had to be cautious, though. I know how April is like. If I ever try to kiss her, she would expectedly slap me or kick my balls. Or, if Karma really hates me, I'll get both.

She's your bad karma, I thought and chuckled at the truth.

"Thanks," she whispered.

I only smirked at her. "Baby, you don't need to thank me. I would do anything for you.'

April groaned. "Derek, please don't even start. I'm not in the mood for flirting."

I grinned. "Oh, so you want to *flirt?* Okay, then let's flirt—"

"Derek, stop."

"Why, not, babe?'

She shivered. "That just sounds so weird and cringe-worthy."

"What? 'Babe'? Nah, it doesn't." A comical thought popped into my head and I opened my mouth to sing, *"And I was like baby, baby, baby, oh, like baby, baby, baby no, like baby, baby, baby oh. I thought you'd always be mine—"*

"Derek, stop it *please*," April whined, infuriated. "Let's go. I'm starving."

I chortled at her childishness before I kissed her forehead swiftly, earning a surprised gasp from her precious lips. I smirked approvingly as she glowered at me.

"Stop kissing me whenever you feel like it!" she grumbled.

"Baby, I know you love it." I winked.

"I *don't*. How many times do I have to repeat that?"

"Whenever I kiss you. Trust me, it'll happen again."

"Then I'll have my hands prepared." She cracked her knuckles and stretched her fingers, sending me the silent message that if I kiss her, she'll slap me.

However, I thought about something else when she said that...

I grinned harder. "Prepared for what?"

April batted her eyelids at me, befuddled. Then, her lips rose up into a disgusted sneer as she exclaimed an "EW!" She closed her eyes and cringed. "Ew. Ew. Ew. EW!" She smacked my arm. "Why did you have to bring that thought to my head, damn it!"

erupted

I ~~ruptured~~ into laughter as she shivered revoltingly.

"*Ew, ew, ew, ewwwwwwwww*. I will make sure that my hands will *never* be prepared for that!"

That only caused me to laugh harder. My hands seized my stomach. I wheezed and wheezed, trying to gain some breath but I laughed again when I saw her infuriated expression.

"Do you need to have a bath of holy water?" she mumbled.

"Definitely," I snickered. "And you need to be there too."

"Me? Why?"

"Because you were thinking dirty. So you need to come."

"But you are dirtier than me!"

"Doesn't matter. Still need to come."

She huffed. "And when will this bath of holy water take place?"

"In…three or four years' time," I countered.

"Why?"

"Coz we'll be together…" Her eyes widened, knowing exactly what I will say. "…in bed and performing the—"

"DON'T YOU DARE SAY IT! DEREK, DON'T YOU FREAKING SAY IT!"

"The *elaborate dance*."

"DEREK!"

I held my hands up in surrender. "I'm sorry!" I said in between laughs. "I just can't help it!"

"You disgusting, dirty, nasty, horrible, ghastly, rude, annoying, arrogant, dim-witted, brainwashed—"

"I don't need a whole dictionary of my personality, angel. Oh, and I'm sorry for this."

She frowned. "Sorry for—WHAT THE HELL!" She screeched when I kicked some muddy water at her. She balled her hands at her sides, her eyes full of light-heartedness.

I stuck my tongue out at her before I spun around and fled. Droplets of rain splattered on my face, but I didn't care. I was grinning helplessly as April sprinted after me, yelling rants and curses at me. I only laughed as the cold licked my skin.

"Come back here, asshole!" April shouted with a blissful expression. For once, I couldn't see that well-known wretchedness in her eyes anymore, as if her desolation had been shattered. Well, for now.

Chapter Fifteen

It Happened Again

Derek Matthews

April shut the door. She heaved the black hood off and her dark hair, damp and strikingly curly cascaded down her shoulders. She unzipped my hoodie, took it off, her teeth clattering as the chilliness devoured her.

"That was a nice run," I muttered.

April squeezed the hoodie over my head. The water sprinkled out of the material, splattering onto my already-soggy hair and dampening me more.

"What the hell, April?" I whined as April smirked.

"You kicked muddy water at me," she muttered, "so you deserve the payback."

I mumbled about how annoying she can be. My hands shook my hair, the liquid slapping April's cheeks. She doesn't seem to care. Surprisingly, April riffled my black tresses, stroking her fingers through them. My eyes half-closed, I secretly enjoyed the soothing touch of her fingers smoothing my hair. It relaxed me and sent abnormal tingles all the way to my abdomen. Her fingers accidentally wrenched them, causing a low, hoarse moan to break out.

"If you don't stop then I'll lose control over myself," I said huskily.

April halted briefly, furrowing her eyebrows, puzzled. It was truly adorable how innocent April is, and annoying her with dirty phrases was the best. It just makes me laugh. I remembered when I used to come to her house back then; I always had this way of infuriating her all the time. April begged her older brother to take me out, but Mike only just laughed and was amused by our childish behaviour. I recalled a time, when Mike admitted that April and I will be good for each other...

*　　　*　　　*

I chased April to her older brother's room. Mike and Luke were sitting on the bed, playing an action game as packets of crisps were sprawled messily in front of them. The game instantaneously ended when April swung the door open and whined:

"Mike, Luke, can you please tell Derek to go away and leave me alone!"

Luke only mumbled a, "Derek, leave her alone. She doesn't want you."

Mike, on the other hand, said with an amused smirk, "Derek, continue to bother her, please."

"What?!" April complained. "That's unfair! I want to read, Mike, and this...this idiot here keeps on asking me to play with him!"

"Hey, I'm not an idiot, idiot," I snapped. "And you are always reading in your room or drawing. It's annoying. I want you to play with me!"

"Why does he always have to come to our house, Luke?" April whined again.

Luke shrugged. "Apparently he likes you."

"I don't!" I objected. "I will never like her! She's too annoying. I just want to play."

Mike's smirk widened. What he said completely shook April: "You know, I won't mind if you and my little sis will date in the future...or marry. I know you two will be good for each other."

As Mike said this, Luke was drinking his coke. He spat his coke out, the liquid splattering on the floor as Luke coughed and coughed, patting his chest roughly. April's eyes widened with horror, presumably envisioning her and me as a couple in the future. Mike sniggered at Luke's red face and smacked Luke's back. That only caused a pained groan to break out from Luke.

"That will be..." she shivered in repulsion. "A nightmare."

"A beautiful nightmare," Mike and I corrected in unison.

A glower rested on April's gorgeous face. She shoved her black-framed glasses up her nose and huffed. "You two are so alike. So annoying."

"But you love us," I blurted out.

"You're annoying too." Mike leaned forward and kissed his little sister's forehead lovingly. "But, I also think you are beautiful as an angel." Then, Mike leaned into me and whispered into my ear: "If you do like her, and if you do want to be with her, then promise me that you will take good care of her and that you will never hurt her. Understand, Derek?"

"Yes. I understand."

"Promise me that you will make sure no one hurts her."

"I promise."

*　　　*　　　*

Mike helped me. When I went into depression due to my parents' deaths, and since Mike was Luke's best friend, he perceived that I was very despondent one day. He asked me what's wrong. Without hesitating, I spilled everything to him—how my parents' death affected me, how envious I get whenever

I see people with their parents, how I wish I could just hear my momma's voice, how I wish that dada never died. Mike listened attentively. I was crying when I finished explaining everything to him, and he pulled me into a cuddle and whispered: "*We lose people so we can meet others who will bring a difference to our lives. That difference can be good or bad or, perhaps, both.*"

My reverie shattered when April scrunched her nose in antipathy at me. "You are nasty, Matthews!"

I shrugged. "It's my nature, Levesque. Get used to it." April rolled her eyes.

April's mom, Mia, smiled at us once we walked into the parlour.

"Hello Mrs. Levesque," I said, greeting her with a beam.

"Derek, please call me Mia," April's mother insisted.

"How are you, Mia?"

"I'm exhausted, and I want to go to sleep. Unfortunately, I couldn't. I'm working on night shift." Mia rushed to the shoe rack, taking out a pair of trainers and putting them on. "Since you are here, Derek, you and April are in charge of the house. Ethan is upstairs doing God knows what. He's really rebellious and annoyingly rude sometimes, so please excuse his attitude and please don't hesitate to shout at him. Oh, and take care of Rosie while I'm gone." Mia gave April a peck on the cheek and walked over to the sofa, kissing Rosie's forehead before she sprinted to the main door. "Goodbye, darlings!"

"BYE MOM!" Ethan shouted from upstairs just when Mia closed the door.

April glanced sideways at Rosie, who's lying down on a mat, playing with a toy. Then, she spun around to face me. "What do you want to do?"

"I want to change." My hands grabbed the hem of my shirt to slide it off my body. My six-pack stretched and so did my biceps and triceps. Once I took it off, I observed April's beet red cheeks. I instantaneously smirked.

She batted her eyelashes, pulling her out of her hazy reverie. She scowled at me, her eyes meeting mine. From the way she blinked hastily, and the way her cheeks heated up, I understood she is refusing to look down at my stomach. "You can't just take your shirt off whenever you feel like it!"

"Your mom said that I'm in charge of the house too, so I can do whatever I want whenever I feel like it. Now, are you going to stand there all day, trying not to gawk at my awesome body, or are you going to get me a suitable shirt to wear?"

April scoffed. "I am *not* trying to look at your 'awesome' body, idiot."

"Mhmm." I winked at her. "Stop denying that I'm awesome, angel."

"Stop calling me that," she retorted.

"What are you going to do if I don't?" I challenged, cocking an eyebrow. "Slap me again? You know, your slaps have no effect on me. It doesn't really hurt sometimes."

"Perhaps," she admitted. "But maybe you can change Rosie's diaper…"

This time, I blinked, caught off guard. "Come again?"

April took one, large step towards me. I swear to God that my heart rate seemed to quicken because of the thin line of space between us. April tiptoed up to my ear and…

"CHANGE ROSIE'S DIAPER!"

I flinched and pushed her away. I rubbed my ear and glared at April. "Jesus, woman, I don't wanna be deaf."

April offered me Ethan's clothes. The last time I met Ethan was in the memorial. Before the memorial, I always see Ethan when I came to Mike's house. Ethan and I were never on good terms. Constantly arguing back and forth. Mia allowed me to play with his toys, but Ethan objected.

I followed her upstairs and stopped in front of Ethan's bedroom door. April was about to knock when we heard Ethan mumbling permission for us to come in.

"Ethan, Derek's here," April announced.

Ethan groaned. "Great. The asshole is back again."

"I'm right here, idiot," I grumbled, anger penetrating in my voice.

"I know. That's why I insulted you. *Idiot.*"

"You haven't changed a bit, Ethan," I said. "Still the same annoying boy version of April."

"At least I'm better than you. I'm not a player like you." Ethan swerved around in his chair as we closed the door. "How can I help you?" he asked in a dull voice before he took a sip of his apple juice.

"Derek needs clothes," April replied.

Ethan averted his eyes to me. He noticed that I'm shirtless and he spat out his juice, his eyes wide with disgusting dreadfulness.

"Were you two hooking up in the shower?!" he exclaimed, his expression full of repulsion.

Our eyes widen in disgust.

"What? No!" April hissed. "What the hell, Ethan?"

"He's shirtless, though!" Ethan pointed out.

"Why would people make out in the shower with their clothes on?" I rolled my eyes at how senseless he is. "And why would you think that we were hooking up? I mean, don't get me wrong, your sister is outstandingly beautiful and attractive, but she will literally kick my balls to make me childless in the future if I ever try to hook up with her."

Ethan frowned. "You find my sister attractive?" he asked, narrowing his eyes at me.

"*Yes*," I breathed, smirking as I witness the fair shade of strawberry-pink crawling up April's face.

"You cannot date my sister," Ethan snapped.

I was taken aback. "I'm sorry, what?"

"You're an asshole," said Ethan. "I know you very well. Everyone in Peony Hallows does. Your reputation is shameful, man. I don't trust you with my sister. She deserves a true man unlike you. She needs a man who will love her, care for her, look after her no matter what happens, protect her, be there for her, and be her shoulder to cry on. Certainly, that man isn't you—"

"Ethan, Derek needs clothes," April interrupted, sighing as if she's wondering how the hell a conversation was suddenly so awkward and nasty at first and then it's the *you-don't-deserve-her* chat.

"No. If Derek really finds you attractive then I need to talk to him and get some sense into him. If that doesn't work out then I'm going to call Dad for help and he'll definitely beat the shit out of him and will give you, April, a lecture about—"

"Ethan!"

Ethan held up his hands in surrender. "Okay, okay." He took out a shirt and jeans, handing it to me. "But, just a note Derek: if you ever hurt her, I will literally kill you. Heck, maybe Mike might haunt you for the rest of your life."

"Mike gave me his blessing to marry her. He won't haunt me. He's nice to me."

"Yeah, but he won't be if you hurt April. You know how overprotective he was of his baby sis and baby bro."

Ignoring his words, I snatched the clothes from his grasp and examined it. "They might not fit me."

April groaned with rage. "Just put it on."

I did as told and went into the bathroom with the spare towel she offered me. After I was done changing, I walked to the staircase, whistling a song softly to myself. I remembered that April ordered me to change her little sister's diaper. I cringed. Nope, I will not do that. April cannot make me do that. She's not the freaking boss of me. I don't want Rosie's poo to smudge my fingers and clothes. I shivered uncomfortably at the thought. I spun around, heading to her room.

"April, there's no way in hell I'm going to—" I, without delay, frozen in place after I swung the door open.

April was dancing around to a song playing moderately high and low. A wry smirk danced on my lips and I recovered from my frozen stance. I leaned on the doorway, shoving my hands in the pockets as I watched her dance. When she swerved around, she yelped at the sight of me, abruptly stopping her odd, horrible dance and silencing the song.

I erupted into laughter as April scowled at me, folding her arms over her chest, obviously humiliated.

"Shut up," April grumbled.

I laughed harder, clutching my stomach as I wheezed, trying to catch my breath to speak. April glared at me, a gleeful friskiness roaming in her dark eyes. She grabbed her pillow, and smacked me with it, causing me to abruptly stop laughing. April slammed her pillow onto me relentlessly until I finally grabbed it, jerking it off her hands.

For the first time, April was smirking in front of me, giving me the message.

"Oh, baby, it's on."

April backed away, grabbing two pillows from behind her to shield herself as I charged towards her like a ruthless bull, a light-hearted smile on my face.

I collided into her. April shrieked, laughing, as we toppled to the carpeted floor. She panted beneath me. The only thing between us was the pillows. I tossed them away, closing the gap even more. April calmed herself, her relaxing breaths wafting on my face.

I looked into her eyes. I couldn't help but stare down at her lips, recalling how velvety they were. I wanted to bridge the distance. I wanted to kiss her.

And I did.

Chapter Sixteen

She's Still Here

Derek Matthews

April was motionless beneath me. Then, I felt her eyelashes stroke my eyelids, indicating she closed her eyes and went with the flow of the kiss.

This kiss was better than the last one. Unlike the last time, it filled me with contentment, knowing I achieved my ambition: to kiss her. Fireworks seemed to ignite inside me, its spark sending quivers throughout my whole body.

The heat spread everywhere, triggering such wild thoughts. My hands cupped her delicate face, kissing her hungrily as if she gives me energy.

My heart was always broken. It still is because I know I caused my parents' deaths. I am guilty. I should get killed. I deserve to die. However, kissing her gave me second thoughts—that I am special one way or another, that I deserve to live and experience the bad and good things in life, that I am not culpable. The way we kissed glued back pieces of my shattered heart together, like forming a puzzle.

It's as if I'm the depressing blackness of the sky, and she's the moon and all the stars. She brings light to my darkness. She always did. Surprisingly, she still does.

This unusual need of just taking her here right now overwhelmed me. Never have I ever encountered such strange intense, passion with other girls before. I never had experienced the need to just protect a girl, to claim her as mine, to just kiss her all the time, and to just be the loving, perfect guy...

BANG!

"April, Rosie is crying, and I have no idea what to— HOLY *SHIT!*"

Ethan's voice caused April to instantaneously shove me off her. I tumbled backwards, my back and head hitting the floor harshly, a low grunt resonating from me. April breathed heavily, her eyes widened, her lips red and swollen. We turned our heads to a very wide-eyed Ethan, his hands scratching the back of his neck.

"I, uh..." Ethan looked at April. "You're *so* screwed. April."

April didn't reply for a minute. Then, she spoke, "Ethan, don't you dare—"

"Nah, I won't tell Dad," Ethan mumbled, an impish leer forming on his lips. "I'll tell Mom first and then Dad. Shit, April, Dad is gonna come here and gonna cuss at you about how young you are for guys and will probably beat the crap out of Derek—"

"Ethan, go and check on Rosie," April grumbled.

Ethan looked at me, hastily saying a "I will not pray for you when you die, Derek Matthews" before dashing out of the room, leaving us alone.

I unhurriedly averted my eyes to April. She's staring at me. Her hands were balled into tight fists as if she's furious.

"April..." I started to speak but was instantly cut off.

"I. Hate. You." She stood up and grabbed a pillow randomly, attempting to smack me with it but I grabbed her wrists, feeling the smooth material of her long sleeves.

"Listen," I insisted. "I didn't mean to kiss you…"

"Just because you're the most wanted guy in Peony Hallows doesn't give you the damn right to kiss me and mess with my feelings!" April screamed with aggravation.

"I wasn't trying to mess with your feelings!" I protested, getting up so I'm looming over her.

April tilted her head upwards. "Yes. *You are.*" Her eyes flooded with frustrated tears. "Listen, Derek, if you're trying to use me as game, then you need to stop and reconsider. My life is already messed up and I don't need you to ruin it even more by playing with my goddamn feelings. Hell, I'll probably hang myself so I can die and go up to God and ask Him to kick your damn ass and to haunt you with ghosts for the rest of your freaking damned life!"

Her last sentence…the way she said it with such intensity, plunged deep into my throat, nearly sucking the air out of my lungs and leaving me breathless and gasping like a fish. *I'll probably hang myself.*

I fumed. "Your life is messed up?" My voice was incredibly calm, and judging by the way the colour drained from her face at my sudden calmness gave me the indication that she knows I'm furious. She took three steps backwards. I advanced towards her. "April, all our lives are messed up. My life is messed up because I know I murdered my beautiful mother. My life is messed up because I'm the one who caused my father's death. My life is messed up because I know that I'm causing everyone to get miserable and I wish I can stop myself from continuing to spread this sadness, but I can't because I get so jealous seeing people with their parents whereas I'm here, all alone, with nobody who understands me." Tears scorched the brim of my eyes; I blinked rapidly in order to get rid of them. "I know not everything is about me. But you have no idea how lucky you are to have great parents, great siblings, and a great family. I have Marline and Luke, but Marline is constantly at work and Luke is always in his bedroom ever since Mike died. And Mike...when he died, I felt as if I lost my best friend because he was always there for me. He was like a father to me. He gave me everything—hope, dreams, happiness. But when he died...everything changed. I lost control. I continued to blame myself again and again, telling myself that I deserve to die . . .'

"You don't," April whispered.

"I do," I snapped. "I do deserve to die. Everyone hates me because I'm the player. No one loves me. I know everyone experiences pain one way or another, but I just can't hold this pain in any longer, you know? No one understands what I'm going through. No one understands what I did in the past. No one does."

"I do," April echoed. "I understand."

"Yet, you said that it's better that my parents are dead since they don't have to see my horrible face," I muttered.

April's eyes saddened. "I'm sorry about that," she murmured. "It's just that I know you do the memorials every year, and I know you find it boring because every year you always have to bring up the fact that your parents are gone and you know that no one will understand the pain you are going through, but I always know that there will be someone to help you ease the pain...like how Mike did. I just got triggered."

"Were you on your period or something?" I asked.

"What? No."

"Are you on your period now?"

"Why are you asking me this?"

I shrugged. "Just asking." I stroked a thick strand of her dark hair off her face. "Also, I'm *not* trying to play with your feelings because I know you don't deserve to get hurt, not after everything that happened in your life. I agree with Ethan—Mike will haunt me for the rest of my life if I mess with you. April, you're so innocent and it's funny to annoy you with things that make you uncomfortable. You are so sweet, and you deserve happiness, not sadness. But just like Mike said, we have to experience the bad things in life first in order to achieve the good things. I'm not going to hurt you. If someone hurts you in *any way*, tell me and I'll take care of them. Because no one hurts my girl."

April's eyes widened, shocked at my unexpected words. I did too. I clearly wasn't expecting myself to say that. Big time.

"I'm *not* your girl," she corrected, "and never will be."

"I just claimed you in front of everyone," I mumbled, ducking my head downwards to the right crook of her neck, my eyes settling on the fading hickey. My arms wrapped around her waist. "You are my girl and my angel. If someone tries to take you away from me, flirt with you, or touch you, I will beat them." I peck the red pinkish mark, nibbling on it slightly.

April tensed. She shoved me away from her, glowering at me yet a hazy gleam clouded her dark eyes. "Why did you kiss me?" she asked, changing the subject, her hand still touching the hickey.

I shrugged. "Just felt like it. I mean, I can't resist kissing you. And no, I didn't kiss you just to mess with your feelings. I just…felt like it."

"You shouldn't have kissed me."

I smirked at her. "True. But why didn't *you* push me away when I kissed you?"

She opened her mouth to give me a logical explanation. The words didn't come out.

I winked at her. "Already crushing on me?"

"When you said that you murdered your mother," April vocalized, noticeably changing the subject *again*, "what did you mean?"

I didn't expect her to ask me that question. I didn't want to answer, too. However, she went to my memorial and she heard my speech. Plus, we were best friends.

I press my forehead against hers. "I killed her, April." My voice came out low and subtle. Sudden tears came to me.

"Derek…" April's fingers reached up to cup my cold cheek. I fluttered my eyes closed, loving how warm her fingers are. "You didn't."

"I did," I whispered, reopening my eyes. "I killed my own mother because I had to come into this damned world. If I was never born, she would still be alive here today."

"Derek, are you hearing yourself? You're speaking trash. Just think for a moment; you said that your mother was sweet, caring, and loving. If she was like that, then don't you think she will be distressed to know that her son is upset? Don't you think she will be heartbroken to know that her son is blaming himself for causing her death? Derek, you told me that those who die never leave us. They are next to us, above us, and around us for eternity. So your mother is still alive."

The tears uncontrollably slid down my cheek. I felt as if my heart skipped a beat with such strong contentment.

"My mother isn't dead?" I asked, a little too hopefully.

"No. Your mother isn't dead. She's here. She's around you, Derek. You just can't see her. The only way to feel her presence is to visualize that she is here. Then, you will feel that warm sensation in your chest, which is a sign that your mother is here."

"How do you know if it will work?"

"Because Mike told me to do that if someone dies. I did it when I was at his funeral, and I felt his presence. It was so magical. I loved it."

"But...do you think she loves me?" I questioned, optimism penetrating my voice.

"Duh. You are her son after all. Plus, I don't think she wants you to be miserable all the time. She certainly wants you to be happy and have a good life because that's how mothers are like. But, personally, I presume your mother is upset at you."

I frowned. "Upset at me?" I echoed. "Why?"

"Because you broke other people's hearts, Derek," April said carefully, as if afraid that her words will go in a wrong direction. "You played with girls. You were...a bully."

A blazing feeling suffocated my heart. "But..." Another tear dropped from my eye. Truthfully, I felt so embarrassed. I was in my most vulnerable with April. Though, the way she comforted me...I liked it because I never experienced someone helping me for the past six years. "I didn't mean to," I murmured. "I didn't mean to make my momma upset. I was just so angry at her for leaving me alone. I was just so angry at myself for killing her."

"Derek, let's be rational. You didn't kill her. She sacrificed her life to give *you* a life. That's the best thing in the world. No one will be that brave enough to die for someone else. It's rare to have good, brave people."

"My mother was a warrior, then," I mumbled. "She's my warrior—"

"APRIL!" Ethan shouted from downstairs, cutting April off. "COME HERE. ROSIE WAS PEEING ON ME AND IT WENT IN MY MOUTH! I THINK I'M GOING TO DIE!"

April rolled her eyes. "I'm coming!" Before she went, she attacked me with a hasty, heartwarming hug and whispered, "You are never alone, Derek. I know that we're always arguing and annoying each other, but I just want you to know that you have me."

She stood on her tiptoes and gave me a peck on the cheek. My cheeks burned. Hers did too. It's so cute. She turned around and fled out of the room.

Your mother isn't dead. She's here. She's around you, Derek. You just can't see her. The only way to feel her presence is to visualize that she is here. Then, you will feel that warm sensation in your chest, which is a sign that your mother is here.

I bit my lip, feeling some tears threatening to come out. I rubbed my eyes. Dad always told me: *A man doesn't cry.* However, when Mike saw me crying once, he just scoffed at me and said: *Men who cry are real men. They're the type of men that every woman wants. So, don't feel ashamed.*

I sighed unevenly, deciding to take April's advice.

My eyes fluttered closed. I imagined that my mother is right here in the room with me. I visualised her dark hair is curling around her shoulders. A soft smile graced my lips at the thought of me hugging her for the first time.

I can feel it.

My momma.

I can feel her.

I can feel that warm feeling blooming in my chest, spreading throughout my whole body. Goosebumps formed on my right arm, as if invisible fingers are touching the skin of my arm.

I opened my eyes, knowing that I cannot see my momma but that she's here. She's right next to me.

I looked to my right. Another tear glided down my left cheek.

"Momma?" I called softly, knowing that I won't get a reply, yet I don't give a damn. I want to talk to her for once. "I'm sorry for being such an ass. I love you, Momma. Don't ever leave me. Please, Momma."

(To those who have mothers: remember to love them always. Because you will never know when God will take them to heaven.)

Chapter Seventeen

Arguments and Miracles

Derek Matthews

I walked into the living room. April was sitting on the couch with her little sister, Rosie, on her lap. Rosie was fidgeting with April's brunette hair as April traced soft, lazy circles on her back. Ethan was there too, talking to her in hushed tones. When he saw me, he offered a sarcastic grin. He stood up, advancing to the doorway, smacking my back as he does so. The smack was harsh.

"We're going to talk later, okay?" Ethan told me, his eyes oddly menacing as if he's trying to resist ripping me into bloody limbs.

"About what?"

"You know what I'm talking about, idiot," Ethan grumbled. "About my sister. You kissed her—"

"It was a simple kiss. Not a big deal."

"It is to *me*," Ethan snapped. "She's my sister. You should know what it is like for her ever since Mike died. You don't know what happened to her in the past. Mike was always there for her whenever she got bullied. Since he's gone, I will be the one who will protect her from everything. Including you."

"Mike gave me his blessing to be with her."

"Well, that doesn't mean you will have my blessing too," he muttered. "Without my blessing, you cannot date her."

I cleared my throat, ready to imitate Donald Trump. "Wrong!" I objected, pointing a finger up at him.

Ethan rolled his eyes. He glanced at April (who was staring at us intently) before looking back at me. "Sis, I'm going out with my friends," he announced, still glowering at me. "I told Mom about this. I think she forgot to mention it to you. So, I'll see you later." That's why he's dressed up so nicely today. Usually, Ethan never cared about what he was wearing.

Ethan shoved past me, ambling into the small, slender entrance hallway. I heard the thud of the door closing.

I sat down next to April. "Your brother is nice," I grumbled.

April smiled awkwardly. "Sorry about that. He's very…overprotective of me."

"I know. You're a very fragile human being. Of course, guys are going to be overprotective of you."

April frowned. "What's that supposed to mean?"

"Ethan is concerned and protective of you because he knows that you're very timid, April. It's the same with me. Theo and Jackson, too. Don't be surprised when I tell you that all the guys in the school will soon be fond of you and will be keeping a close eye on you."

"Everyone hates me," April mumbled.

"I don't think so. Since Jasmine, Jackson, Theo, and I stood up for you, I presume everyone is trying to find some way to be nice to you. Eventually, they'll know what a great girl you are to hang out with. It's annoying that you said thanks to Jasmine, Jackson, and Theo when you didn't thank me."

April giggled softly. "Thanks, Derek."

I shrugged. "What can I say? I'm nice like that."

My eyes darted down to Rosie. The chubby little girl was gawking at me with a befuddled pout.

"Hello," I cooed, raising Rosie from April's lap and placing her on mine. My left arm encircled her and I held out my index finger. Rosie curled her tiny hand around it, shaking it tenderly and I ruffled her hair. The young girl giggled. Then, her mouth formed an *O* as she yawned. Her eyes quavering, she surprisingly rested her head on my chest and went limp, falling into a deep slumber. I caressed my hand up and down her back and noticed April gawking at me.

"What?"

"Who are you and what have you done to Derek Matthews?" April demanded, narrowing her eyes at me and Rosie.

I rolled my eyes. "I'm not always cold-hearted, April."

"I know but…I never thought you like kids."

"Oh, I love kids," I stated.

April cocked an eyebrow. "What else do I not know about you?"

I considered for a moment, still running my fingers up and down Rosie's back. "When my father was still alive, I was a total nerd like you. I loved books because I found out that my momma loved books. I loved to study. Basically, I wanted to be just like my momma because I thought it will help me to understand her more, to connect with her more…but then everything changed when…" A lump clogged my throat.

April immediately knew that what I was about to say is too heartbreaking. She placed her hand on my shoulder hesitantly. "You don't have to tell me."

No. I want to confess to her. She may be different, but we have so many things in common. We knew each other when we were kids. She's the only one in this world whom I can trust. She's the only one in this world that I need to endure. She's the only one who I know can destroy the pain I've been suffering from.

I heaved out a small breath. I have to tell her the truth. I can't keep the secrets to myself anymore. *Confessing to someone who understands you will help*, is what my therapist told me. "I told you that my father died in a car crash, right?"

"Yeah..."

"That was a lie," I whispered, unable to look into her eyes because if I do, I know I'll cry. I don't want to cry in front of her. *Damn it, Derek, stop being such a freaking baby and be a freaking man.* "Dad didn't die in a car crash, April."

"Hmm?" she baffled.

"Before Dad died, he was still bothered and traumatised by Momma's death. Luke and I knew that because we overheard one of Dad's doctors diagnosing him with major depression. We also found out that Dad was cutting his wrists, legs, and chest with anything sharp and burning his arms. Aunt Marline was emotionally furious when we found out about Dad's self-harm and scolded him.

"One night, I heard Dad shouting at Aunt Marline, telling her everything. He was telling her his pain, his sorrow. He said he couldn't handle life anymore. He said he wanted to be with Momma again."

Tears bristled in my eyes. April entwined our hands together as an act of comfort. Her eyes told me that I don't have to continue, that I can tell her another time or never.

I can't keep any more secrets.

I need to tell someone.

Someone I love.

"He drowned himself, April," I whimpered, and I erupted into melancholic sobs.

April eyes widened. Her other hand clamped over her mouth to muffle the gasp. The tears dripped to my chest. I inhaled profound, frayed breaths to calm myself, but my nerves were twitching from the distress.

"Oh, Derek..." April whispered after a moment of silence.

"He drowned himself." I wiped my blazing eyes. "In the bath tub."

Tears prickled my eyes. April's hand caressed mine, entwining our fingers together as an act of comfort. Her eyes told me that I don't have to continue, that I can tell her another time. Though, like I said before: I can't keep any more secrets.

"He never thought about Luke, Aunt Marline, and me. He just took his own life."

*   *   *

"Luke?"

My brother was sitting on the floor of the balcony near the staircase, his head inclining against the wall as he gawked downwards at our aunt and our father, eavesdropping on their conversation.

He whipped his head around at the mellow sound of my voice. "Derek? What are you doing out of bed?"

"I can't sleep," I replied, "because of Dad's and Aunt Marline's argument."

Luke exhaled. He patted the space next to him, indicating to me to sit.

The arguments between Dad and Aunt Marline began not so long ago. First, it took place in the kitchen. Then, in the garden. Then, in the living room. Then, everywhere in the entire mansion. Then, everywhere in the entire town, including the harmonious meadow. I wanted to clamp my hands over my ears and screech at them to hush. I hate witnessing their quarrels. Families are supposed to be loving and caring, despite the difficulties. They can't be angry at each other and bicker every single day!

Right?

Or is it the other way around?

Luke wrapped an arm around me lovingly. He rubbed his thumb up and down my arm comfortingly as we both concentrated warily on the altercation. It's dark in here. Faint light blazed from the bulbs vaguely and the flicker of a winsome candle. The windows were closed yet the cold seeped inside and pricked my skin.

"Samuel, you can't say that!" Aunt Marline screamed. I could hear the tears in her voice.

"Marline, please go to sleep," Dad muttered, incensed. I, too, can hear the tears in his deep voice.

"I can't go to sleep when you keep on going around, finding something dangerous to harm yourself!" Aunt Marline snapped. I noticed there were no guards. Dad and Aunt Marline must've restricted them from coming in here. "How do you think Alexa will feel about this? To know that her husband is harming himself? She'll hate you!"

BANG!

"Don't you dare talk about my angel like that!" Dad hollered.

Aunt Marline ignored Dad's comeback and repeated the same questions: "How do you think Alexa will feel about this? To know that her husband is harming himself?" Dad didn't reply. Therefore, Marline continued: *"She will be devastated, Sam. You and I both know that she doesn't want you to be depressed for the rest of your life. You know that she will appreciate if you try to be happy."*

"It's not easy, Marl!" Dad barked. "Can't you see that? I can't be happy, knowing that the love of my life is gone!"

"Are you saying that Derek and Luke aren't the loves of your life?"

Dad exhaled sharply. "No...I...Th-that's not what I..."

"Your sons are becoming suspicious of your behaviour, Sam. They're asking me why you're smoking and drinking again. They're wondering why you're not playing football with them or taking them to the meadow or just spending time with them. Sam, they miss you. They barely see you. This...It will bring pain to them...Especially to Derek. Have you forgotten about your second son? He's feeling miserable. It's bad enough that he's blaming himself for causing Alexa's death. And if you...If you..." Tears dribbled from Aunt Marline's eyes. "It will make Derek even worse. It will make all of us worse. Cutting, burning, taking alcohol and drugs aren't the answer to your pain!"

"Then what is?" Dad snarled. "Find another woman and be happy? Marline, you don't understand. There isn't any other woman like Alex."

"You don't have to find another woman! You have me. You have Luke and Derek. You have Mike. You have Mia and Julian and their kids. You have God. You have Jesus. You have all the angels and saints. You have the entire world. We all love you, but you don't see it! You won't accept it!"

Dad groaned. "I hate this pain, Marline," he whimpered. "I hate living in this world. I want to die."

"And leave your two boys alone? Fatherless?"

I was so engrossed in the conversation that I never felt the salty tears on my cheeks. Luke was weeping, too. He bit his bottom lip roughly, as if to prevent it from quivering. He closed his eyes and furiously and despondently slammed his head onto the wall, permitting the tears to flow.

My fingers were quaking with fear. With sadness. With disappointment. I stood up.

Luke instantaneously glanced at me. "Derek," he began though I was already descending the stairs stridently.

My face was still dirty, and my throat tightened because of all the crying. Luke and I knew there was something wrong with Dad, though we never suspected Dad was suffering from suicidal thoughts.

"Dad, don't leave me!" I implored, running towards him, the salty tears leaching through my lips. His shoulders stiffened at the sound of my voice. Aunt Marline's eyes averted to me and she erupted into a series of thunderous sobs and nodded in agreement at my next words: "Please, don't leave us."

Dad's eyes were puffy. His jaw clenched like always—he always gets angry when he cries. He said that crying is only for girls and for little children. He said that grown men shouldn't cry and just keep their feelings to themselves. That is toxic masculinity, I know. Marline tried to correct him by saying that it isn't childish to cry a few tears, because it just makes you more lovable.

It makes you purer. More human.

Aunt Marline looked at my father. "Sam...Listen. Please, listen: you have a huge family who loves you. I love you. Derek loves you. Luke loves you. Don't forget about God...He loves you. Your company is so popular. Do you know why? Because you help people. Despite all your insecurities, you sacrificed everything to help everyone—victims of rape and sexual harassment, victims of war, victims of poverty, the hunger, the thirsty, the lonely, the refugees...And the people working in your company love you. You still have Alexandra. Sam, if you believe that she is still alive in your heart, then that's when you can finally push the pain away. She's not dead. She's alive in your heart. That's better than nothing, right?"

"Dad, you said that Momma always told you something," I whispered, wiping my eyes with the back of my hands. "What did Momma say?"

"That she will always love us and be with us, dead or alive," Dad responded, his mess of jet black hair tousling over his puffy ocean blue eyes.

"And what did you promise Momma, Dad?"

"To be there for you and Luke; to protect you, to hug you, to love you, and to never leave you."

"Exactly," said Marline. "She'll be so heartbroken if you broke her promise, Sam."

Outside, it's crying. A subdued drizzle yet it vibrates a vigorous gloom to the town. There was no light. Just murky.

Luke, who was standing near the stairs, finally emerged from the shadows. "Don't leave us, Dad," he begged. "Please. You don't want to hurt Momma, do you?"

Dad stared at Luke, then at Aunt Marline, then at me.

I saw them.

His sleeves were rolled up, exposing his scars and burns—all thin and large, deep and shallow, red and white, all healing. Self-harm scars. Self-harm burns. Now I know why Aunt Marline always cooked and hired a chef; why she protested that Dad should never cook again. Now I know why Aunt Marline panicked whenever Dad was caught holding a knife or anything razor-sharp. Now I know why there were security guards every day except for the weekends—they're here to keep a close eye on him.

"Kids, go to sleep." His voice mellow and stony. He's exasperated, exhausted. I could tell by the dark bags under his eyes.

"Dad, please don't leave us," I pleaded.

"Sam, if you leave, you know what your death will do," said my aunt. "It's unforgivable. Even to whatever deity you believe in. It will…" Her eyes met mine, and then hastily looked away with more tears.

Dad exhaled huskily, knowing what Marline meant. "I won't," he decided. "I won't leave you."

"*Promise?*"

Dad smiled forlornly. He tottered to me, boosting me up into his arms. His other hand clamped Luke's shoulder. "I promise."

I am very serious when it comes to promises. I always knew that whenever Dad promised about something, he'll never break it.

However this time…

I was damn wrong.

A shriek.

That's what I woke up to.

A shriek.

I bounced in my bed; my eyes half-open. All the lights in the mansion breathed their radiance once again. I could hear thudding, strident footsteps from the corridors outside, along with screams and demands.

The snivelling rain that was once a drizzle intensified into a heavy, sombre downpour, whacking the casements of the mansion, and the wind howled despicably, as if the earth itself was in excruciating pain.

When I scuttled out of my room, the security hastened towards the reverberating screeches. They pushed past me with concerned, anxious expressions. I scampered after them and saw all the men crowding around the door of one of the bathrooms. All of them held horrified and grief-stricken.

"Auntie?" I jostled through the small mob. "Aun—" I paused, revolted and doleful.

I wish I never came inside. I wish I closed my eyes. But I couldn't. My eyes, my vision, my mind, were already horrified by the heart-breaking scene in front of me.

"Dad?" I whispered, crestfallen.

My father was inside the overflowing bathtub. His damp dark hair was drifting around his head like a black halo. His eyes were wide open and unmoving, gazing up at the tiled ceiling. A rope ruthlessly seized his neck, causing the colour to drain from his face. The veins in his neck were bulging.

Blood from his blood-soaked mouth, leisurely seeped down his neck and mixing with the water, turning it into a dark vermillion shade.

Marline tightened her clutch around her mobile. The loudspeaker was on and her body was shaking with distress.

"911, what is your emergency?" a deep voice asked from the phone.

Marline squeezed her eyes shut, two tears hurrying down her cheeks. "H-he's dead."

"Ma'am, I cannot hear you."

"He's dead," she echoed.

"Sorry, who?"

"Samuel Matthews...he drowned himself."

It wasn't that long when the police and the ambulance services arrived.

Inside, I peered from a distance at the paramedics, perceiving how they unhurriedly raised my father's body from the bloodied bathtub and into the large blue bag on the floor. One of them closed Dad's ocean blue eyes. They zipped the bag shut, carrying it and lugging it outside to the ambulance.

The cops and other people helped to clean up the blood staining the bathroom. They drained the water and used rags to wipe the bathtub, making sure to scrub miniature blemishes of my father's blood.

Luke was on his phone, snivelling. "He drowned himself, Mike," he whimpered, wiping his eyes slowly. "He left us."

I couldn't help it. I can't watch this. I can't witness my brother crying and watch how the guests scoured my father's blood off the tub. I bolted through the hallways, scuttled down the stairs, and dashed to the gardens. I fell on my knees and slammed my hands on the saturated glass, crying and crying as my sobs transformed into desperate wheezes. The droplets of rain fused with my salty tears.

"Kid?"

A policeman was there, observing me with a curious face. His curiosity immediately wore off when he saw my features, realising that I am

Samuel Matthew's second son, the boss of the most famous organisation that saved millions of lives from countless tragedies.

Yet he couldn't save his own.

My lips quaked. "He left me," I grieved. "He left me and it's my fault!"

The cop squatted in front of me. "What are you on about?"

"Dad," I bawled. "It's my fault he died...If I was never born, then Momma will still be alive, and Momma and Dad will be happy together with Luke. I'm the one who deserves to die, not Dad! I don't know why I'm in this world. I don't deserve to live. I'm such a horrible, worthless, ugly, weak boy...Life for Momma, Dad, Luke, and Aunt Marline will be so much better without me—"

"Hey, hey, hey." The man rested his hands on my shoulders. "This isn't anyone's or your fault."

"Then why did he die!" I snapped. "Why did he drown himself?"

He didn't answer. Sympathy shimmered in his eyes.

"He promised me that he will never leave me. But he did. He broke his promise. He left me. And I hate him for doing that."

*   *   *

"Derek, I'm so sorry," said April.

I tittered solemnly. I don't understand why people apologize for others' loss. I understand it's a way of showing sympathy, but I know that deep down, they don't fully understand the feeling of losing someone. It's different for everyone. "None of it is your fault, April. Why are you apologising?"

April crawled closer to me. Her fingers rose up to wipe away the tears. My arms bind her waist, jerking her to me, and I embraced her. Rosie slumbers on the sofa opposite to us. April put her there whilst I was explaining everything that occurred in my callous past.

"Dad broke his promise, April," I whispered into her neck, my breath caressing her skin. "He broke Momma's promise, too. And I hate him. I hate him so much for leaving me. But I hate myself more."

April leaned away from me, gazing at me with uncertainty. "Because you caused your father's death?"

"Yes."

Memories of the things I endeavoured to do invade my mind. Memories of my time with my therapist—how he tried to help me and how he listened to me. Memories of the doctors diagnosing me with major depression. Memories of myself duplicating my father's deeds. "Can I show you something?" I asked.

"Of course."

"Okay. Get off me."

She did as she was told and stood in front of me. I took my shirt off and unbuckled the button of my trouser, heaving it off.

"What are you—" April discontinued the second her eyes noticed them.

Wounds scarred my arms, my waist and below. Each and every one mending. There were so many. Ten. Twenty. Thirty. Forty. Fifty. Sixty. I couldn't tell. I lost count. I used to graze myself incessantly after my father's suicide. Day by day, minute by minute, I would filch something razor-sharp — a scissor, a shattered window piece, you name it — and just slash my skin.

April put her palm to her mouth. "Oh, Derek."

"A-after my father's death, I wanted to die." My voice wobbled. Tears filled my eyes. "I wanted to kill myself. Life will be better without me, to be honest. I took my mother's life which sent Dad into depression and suicidal thoughts. The doctors diagnosed me with major depression. Marline sent me to therapy classes, but they were no use. The therapist gave me sweet advice, but it didn't mean much to me. It didn't help. I started cutting my legs, feet, arms, waist, and most of my chest ever since I was ten." My eyes fluttered close, the tears soaking my eyelashes. "Then, one time, I…"

"No." Tears brimmed in April's eyes. "No, please tell me you didn't."

"I tried to drown myself. On my birthday. Because that's when Momma died."

April didn't say anything. She let out a quavering sigh and stared at me as I explained to her how I tried to do it, how I attempted to die…

*   *   *

When I was young, all kinds of people liked me. I was so contented and free. People loved me. They loved my sarcastic, comical personality. They loved the way I burned the teachers with rude, savage comments. They loved playing with me. Basically, I wasn't a demented asshole back then.

Nonetheless, after my father's suicide, I grew distant from everyone. They all understood my grief, and asked: "Derek, are you okay?", "Dude, you look so down. What's going on?", and "You're not talking to me anymore. What's wrong?"

Even my teachers, who all loathed me, were irresolute about my cheerless state, wondering why I haven't cracked any jokes, made people laugh, and goofed around.

"Can't you just go away?" I retorted at everyone. "Leave me alone and mind your damn business." They were flabbergasted by my uncouth words, hurt evident on their faces. I regretted it. I wish I could take it back, though this melancholy just caused me to become so aggravated all the time.

One day, during lunch, my best friend, Theo, asked me, "Derek, are you okay?"

"Can you please go away?" I barked.

Dissatisfaction washed over his face. He crossed his arms over his chest. "Look, dude, you may have forced me to be your best friend, but that doesn't mean that this whole friendship is fake. I care about you. I love you. I worry about you. You skipped classes about ten times this week. What's going on?"

"It's none of your—"

"Don't say it's not my damn business. Your damn business is my damn business. That's how friendship works. So, spill it."

The students in the lunch hall eyed us enquiringly. I felt uncomfortable by their stares, so I said in a timorous voice, "Another time."

Theo noticed my self-consciousness. He nodded, gave me a hug, and whispered: "I'm always there for you, okay? Even though you're gonna be annoying in the future, I will always be there for you."

I smiled. "Thanks, Theo. Maybe forcing you to be my best friend wasn't so bad, after all."

Theo chortled. "Actually, it's fun to be your best friend." He paced away, his eyes sending me an unspoken message: Talk to me when you can.

I nicked a sandwich to eat and ambled to the exits. I merely want to be alone for a while and reflect about my life.

Outside, the sunlight welcomed me in its warmth. The school grounds are stunning—so many bushes speckled with roses and a cherry tree with shadows illustrating under the hefty leaves and branches. I love the cherry tree. It's usually a calm place to sit and think in peace.

As I neared the cherry tree, I realised that someone was already sitting beneath it. It's a girl with dark hair winding down her shoulders. Dark-framed spectacles were placed on her cute nose. A book was on her lap, an apple in her right hand.

April Levesque: the little sister of Mike Levesque, my brother's best friend and the guy who saved a woman from getting hit by a truck three *days ago. I also know her because she's my best friend. We've known each other since we were babies.*

A leaf crunched underneath my feet. April peeked up. The first thought that popped into my head was: She's so cute. That's a fact. *Her cheeks were rosy. Her eyes were abnormally dark — almost the colour black — yet they glisten like jets. The way she wore those glasses instantaneously reminded me of my mother (people said that Momma wore dark glasses and she had dark eyes. She always read books).*

I felt shy all of a sudden. The wind that was rustling past us abruptly became moderate. The wind swept up a leaf from the ground, whacking it onto my face. Mortified, I hastily peeled the leaf off, my face red from humiliation.

April wasn't bothered to suppress her loud laugh. I smiled. Hearing her laugh is always so heartwarming. I love her laugh.

When she managed to stop, she kept a straight face and the giggles died. "Are you going to sit here?" she asked.

"You seem peaceful there. I don't want to disturb you."

"So, you're just going to stand there and watch me read?"

"Y-yes."

April tilted her head, arching her eyebrows at me. She patted the space next to her. "Come, Derek. Sit."

I sat down next to her, my shoulder stroking hers. "Twilight?" I observed the book on her lap. "You're reading Twilight? Aren't you too young for that?"

April shrugged. "My mother allows me to read whatever I want."

Her mother is very nice. I like her. Her father is in the army, so I haven't seen him except last year. Up ahead, a squirrel hurried across the grass with something in its mouth. It scampered up a tree, disappearing into the branches and leaves.

"I heard about what happened to your brother, angel. I'm sorry about that."

"He's okay now," she said, "has a few injuries, but he's fine."

"He's really brave to do that: to save a woman from getting hit from a car and risking his own life. What did your parents say?"

"They were worried. But then they were like 'That's our boy'."

"Your parents are awesome." Saying this, resentment blazed in my chest. I always get jealous when I see kids with their parents, full of high spirits and pleased that they have at least a mother or a father.

April smiled with pleasure. "They are awesome."

"You're very pretty, you know?" I always tell her that, and each time I do, I blush, yet I don't regret it. Because it's true. "Like a flower blossoming. Like an angel. And you're very cute."

Pinkness flared April's cheeks. "Uhm…thanks."

For the rest of lunch break, we chitchatted endlessly. Long minutes later, the bell rang. I said goodbye to her and tottered away.

Classes went by rapidly. The teachers kept on pestering me to confess what's wrong. My classmates were the same. Fury, combined with irritation, boiled me. I appreciate their concern, but I just want to be alone for a while. Is that too much to ask? See, the thing about people is that they're too nosy. I know, I know, it's nice to have people who are always concerned about you, but I'm afraid that if I declare what's wrong; they'll gossip it to everyone in the school. I don't want that. I'm accurate that no one does, either. That's why, other than Theo, I don't trust anyone in my school.

After school, I walked home with Luke.

"Are you okay?" he enquired. Tufts of his jet-black hair stuck out from underneath his hood, plummeting over his eyes. Headphones covered his ears.

"Yeah. Why?"

"You look down. Your eyes are red. Were you crying?"

Yes. I was. "No," I lied.

I had a headache the whole day. I still do. My mind was fuming with pessimistic thoughts that kept on recurring every day—thoughts about guilt, suicide and how life will be much easier without me. For each statement *and question, a faint, scrawny, positive response endeavours to battle the negativity:*

> **I don't deserve to live in this world.**

Yes, you do.

> **Momma and Dad are gone because of me. Because I came into the world.**

Momma wanted to give life to you. She still loves you. And Dad had a choice: to live or die. He chose the wrong choice by leaving you. He chose a choice God will never forgive. Either way, he and Momma will always be with you.

> **If I didn't, then they'll still be alive with Luke as their happy child.**

Luke will feel lonely, though. You know how much he begged to have a sibling before you were born. And what about April, Theo, Ethan, Mike, Mia, Julian, and your family? It won't be the same without you.

> **Besides, what's so important about me? What's my purpose in life?**

You are important to many people. Everyone is. You just don't realise it. You will realise what your purpose is. You just have to wait. Waiting can be tough, but that's the main point of living a life—we need to go through our own storms to reach the rainbow and the light; we need to wait for our destiny, for our success, for us to accomplish our goals in life.

Think happy thoughts, *I told myself.*

I snorted. It's challenging for me to be optimistic. When you're uncontrollably and vulnerably cheerless, you cannot have power over the thoughts invading your mind, your emotional state, your mentality...they seem to be verbalizing from an actual voice that can only be heard in your mind. You don't know who that voice belongs to: a ghost, a demon, the devil, or all of them.

I feel so empty. It's bizarre. I can feel my heart beating, but at the same time it's as if it's not there. It's as if each beat will get softer, and softer, and softer until you can't even feel it anymore.

So, this is what Dad felt.

At home, I locked myself up in my bedroom. Aunt Marline was at work. Since Dad's gone, she's now the head of the Matthews Industry. She recruited a team of guards to protect the mansion. We don't get robberies or anything, but we all know how envious the citizens of Peony Hallows can be. They're jealous of us because of our fortune.

I was cuddled in my bed, the duvets swathed around my body. The casements were sealed. My eyes flickered from one page to another of an album—an album of my parents. In each photo, they're beaming with their arms around each other. One of the images was of Momma, pregnant with me, and of Luke. Momma and Luke were so close. That's a reason why I hate Luke sometimes – because he knew my mother, hugged her, kissed her, and was scolded by her. He's so lucky.

Tears bristled in my eyes. I slammed the album shut, hurling it across the room. The album hit a frame of my parents. The glass shattered, splintering into miniature pieces.

I rolled off my bed, collapsing to the floor, sobbing vociferously. I gripped my hair, wrenching hard enough for my scalp to sting and released an aggravated scream.

My hand felt something chilly and thin. A hanger. The hook of the hanger dazzled beneath the light of the bulbs, the sharpness tempting me.

"Momma died because of me." My quaking fingers grasped the sinister-shining hanger. "Dad died because of me." I overturned my wrist, locating the prickly ending of the hook above my flesh. "I deserve to die." I jabbed the ending deep into my skin. "No one loves me." Wrenching the metal down my arm, all the way to my elbow. Restless, sweltering, weeping blood percolated out of the large fiery wound, diagonally leaching and dripping to the floor. "Everyone hates me." I rambled so many sentences, all true or false. All depressing. Each of them encouraged me to do it—to die.

The hanger clattered to the floor, the end smudged with my dark red blood.

I want to die.

I want to die.

I want to die.

I deserve to die.

Right?

I am a bad person after all.

I killed Momma. I killed Dad.

That makes me a bad person.

Tottering out of my room, I scuttled through the hallways to a bathroom, my blood dribbling and tarnishing the deluxe, polished floor. The door wide open, I grabbed the tap of the tub and turned it. Water deluged the bathtub whilst I peeled off my clothes.

Scars. That's what I can see. Scars. Wounds. Lacerations. Marked on my pelvis, my legs, my feet, my arms, and my chest. The hacks were all new and fresh, bright and red, all healing.

The water overflowing the tub, I switched the tap off. With no hesitation, I dipped my feet into the wintry water, quivering as the chilliness numbed my skin and sizzled my slits.

The water inched up to my chin, mixing with my salty tears. "Momma." My voice was so low, it was nearly inaudible. "Give me a reason why I shouldn't kill myself. Please. God, give me a reason why I shouldn't kill myself. I'm sorry I killed Dad and Momma because of my existence. I know taking my own life will hurt you, God, but I suppose that this is the best way. I don't know what You see in me but I deserve to die..." Ranting, my words were muffled as I ducked my head into the glacial water.

Nothing happened for a moment, until my head throbbed. My lungs were heavy with no air. It's like they're cleaving. A part of me dreadfully implored for oxygen. Dark dots blemished my vision, my head woozy.

The reddening water was tranquil and I involuntary permitted it to travel up my nose, causing the throbbing in my head to transform into a deadly sting. The bulb planted in the tiled ceiling flickered, as if it's giving me a vital sign that I was close, close to death. My heart palpitated severely, pleading for divine, saccharine oxygen. My throat drummed at the ominous, disastrous, appalling feeling of ambushed air, as if a knife was plunged unfathomably into my throat.

Suddenly, I was heaved out of the bathtub.

My eyes flew open; my eyesight blurry.

I wheezed, inhaling deep breaths of air. I collapsed to the floor. Water oozed from the ends of my black hair, saturating the white, tiled ground. I quaked as more iciness hospitably and sadistically numbed me.

My vision finally cleared. Standing in front of me, was my older brother with a disturbed expression. "What the hell were you doing?" Luke yelled, frightened.

I didn't answer. Instead, I cried, deliberating why death didn't overtake me. I curled into a ball; the tears would not stop. Luke squatted to his knees in front of me, his warm arms jerking me into an embrace.

"What the hell were you doing?" he echoed, this time softly. "Drowning yourself?" I didn't answer. "Don't do that, Derek! Don't do what Dad did. It's bad!"

"But I deserve to die."

"You don't! Don't you ever say that again! You don't deserve to die!"

"Momma died because of me."

"She died giving a life to you. She never regretted carrying you for nine damn months. It doesn't make you a bad person."

"It does. I'm a killer."

"Derek, shut up."

*   *   *

"Ever since my suicide attempt, Aunt Marline found out. She cried, of course. I felt guilty. Back then, I didn't like seeing people cry. I was always there for them. I was the one who always questioned someone if they were down. I knew that Aunt Marline was so stressed—with work, with Dad's suicide, and with so many things. Her finding out about my suicidal self caused me to feel disappointed, ashamed that I even tried to kill myself.

"Marline sent me to therapy. They didn't help at all. The therapist never understood the pain I was going through. But Mike…"

"I know what he did," April interjected. "He told me."

"Your brother gave me hope, angel. He gave me hope that pain will end eventually. You just got to endure the bad things first. All I have to do is wait." I looked at her. "And that is why you shouldn't cut yourself, April." Puzzlement was clear on her face. "Because when someone who loves you find out, they'll feel so horrible and they'll cry so hard. You will feel guilty for cutting yourself. People say that cutting yourself takes away the pain, the stress…it doesn't." I inched closer to her, grabbing her arms and pushing the sleeves of her shirt up, exposing her scars. "Jasmine told me that you were self-harming."

April stared at her scars. Anger showed on her face. She jerked her arms out of my grasp. "And I told her not to tell anyone," she retorted.

"But it's a good thing she told me," I said.

'Why would she tell *you*?" she asked, furious.

"Because I will understand. Jasmine knew that you and I have so many things in common. She thought that we will be good for each other. Plus, she also knows about what happened to me since we're good friends because of Jackson. I trust her. She's a good friend."

April scoffed. "That's bullshit—that we're good for each other."

"Well, it's her opinion." I can still see the scars hidden beneath her sleeves. Some were emaciated and pale. Others were deep and long. Most were burgundy as if they've been there ever since this morning. "You should try a therapist. Sometimes they're no help, but other times they are. Or you should tell your parents."

Her face hardened. "No."

"Why not?"

"I just can't," April replied. "I tried to tell Mom, but the words wouldn't come out. Plus, I don't want to add to my parents' worries and make them more nervous. They already suffered too much, especially about Mike's death. Finding out that I self-harm will be horrible to them."

A thought occurred to me. "Do your parents know that you're getting bullied?"

"No. But before, Mike was the only person who knew about it. He was the one who defended me from everyone. But when he saw me crying, when I told him that I wanted to die, he told Mom and Dad. Mom and Dad were upset that I didn't tell them. They went to the school and scolded them, saying that they couldn't believe that the school didn't suspect any bullying at all. The head of the school was fired. Though, when Mike died..."

"The bullying happened again," I guessed.

April fidgeted with the ends of her sleeves. "Yeah."

"When did you start self-harming?"

"Ever since Mike died."

"And that was...three years ago, right?"

"Yeah."

It's still raining; the water smacking the blurry windows. Blurry lights of vehicles blazed as they drove by.

"From now on, you will stop self-harming."

"What?"

"You won't self-harm again. If you do, I will tell your parents"

"You can't do that!"

"Yes, I can!" I snapped. April jumped at the loudness of my angered voice. "I can, and I will!"

"Why do you care so much if I stopped?" she demanded. "You don't even care about me."

"Can you shut up?" How can she say that? I know I may seem mean, but she should know that I still care about her. I started to care for her when we were kids. "April, I care about you. I care about you so much that when Jasmine told me about your self-harming, I cried. That's right. I cried. Why? Because…" My voice trailed off. My mind flooded with thoughts if I should confess or not. It's too late to stop now, anyways. "B-because you mean so much to me."

Disbelief was evident on her face. "I-I am?"

"Yeah." My voice is apprehensive and low. My cheeks burned. "When we were young, we were good friends and I…had a crush on you. That caused me to become so concerned about you, to care about you so much. Then, we grew distant though the crush never faded away. It was small, but it never went away. It was still here—" I patted my chest, right where my heart should be. "I promised Mike that I will be there for you, to make sure you're alright. Knowing that I'm not being true to my word, makes me ashamed. Mike was always there for me. He was such a good person and not keeping my promise is awful. He promised me so many things and kept those promises, yet I didn't. Now, I realised how lucky I am to have you back in my life. You understand me more than anyone else…"

Again, my voice trailed off. This time, it's because of April's tears. They were attentive. Very attentive. Gradually, they glided down her cheeks, running over the corners of her thin, soft lips.

"Why are you crying?" I asked.

Her lower lip quivered. Her fingers cleaned her eyes quickly. "I…" She inhaled a shaky breath. "I never heard anyone telling me that they care about me." The tears rasped the quality of her voice. "Other than Mike, of course. But ever since he died…I thought I'll never find someone as sweet and caring as Mike. It's funny because I realised that when we started talking to each other after a long time, good things were happening to me." She spoke the last sentence in a quiet tone, that I nearly misheard it. "I found a good friend. I'm starting to realise that in order to get happiness, you need to walk a dark path in order for that happiness to find you—no matter how long that dark path will take to walk, the happiness will eventually come to you. You have to go through your storms to reach the light and the rainbow."

I snatched her wrists and wrenched her to me. Her rear fell on my lap; a sweet, surprised gasp came out of her mouth.

Without any hesitation, she placed her head in the crook of my neck and silently cried. My arms caged her elusive body, shushing her, rocking her in my embrace in a composed amorous behaviour.

"Shhh, angel," I whispered. "Don't cry."

"I hate crying," I heard her mumble. "It makes me feel weak."

"Crying doesn't make you weak. It just makes you human. It makes you who you are. It just tells people that you need help, comfort, and love. And I'll give you all of that. I will help you. I will comfort you. I will love you—"

"In a friendly way, right?"

I chortled. Yet, I feel disenchanted that she friendzoned me. Perhaps, if I want her to love me, I have to wait. Waiting isn't my thing. I'm very impatient. "Yeah, in a friendly way." I kissed her forehead. "I will do all of those things. For Mike. For you. And for the sake of myself."

Sometimes, there's nothing great about life.

We all know it.

The world is just too cruel.

We were given the freedom of speech, yet we take that to our advantage to hurt people.

The world breaks us until we're dead.

Sometimes, there's no one to talk to about your pain, about your sorrow, because you can't trust anyone.

I don't tell people about my emotions, my insecurities, and my dilemmas because I don't rely on anyone. I just express my grief. I give it to others, so they know how I feel. Before, I knew that I will never tell anyone about my pain because all the humans in the world are big-time assholes. They'll never understand. I learned that the hard way.

A good friend will always betray you...All the good things in this world turn bad because there's no point in being good anymore. Next thing you'll know is that earth is completely and utterly destroyed with only a small amount of humans as survivors.

Life is only a wild game of survival.

Some people are strong enough to face the challenges and the brutality of this world and just wrestle to stay alive.

But others just give up because they can't see the good in life anymore.

That's what I thought before: I can't see what's so great for me. I can't see why I should live.

Until I met April.

Our friendship was rebuilt by the pain we're both experiencing, the tears we're sharing, and the hugs we're giving. We both realised that even though we argue a lot, it's not too late to be friends again.

I am glad I told April everything. I trusted her the minute she told me about her life and her depression. I trusted her the minute I met her when we were kids. Because I knew that I found that person I've been waiting for my whole life.

I know what's so true about her:

She's the miracle in my life.

Chapter Eighteen

Craving for Her

Derek Matthews

The rain outside has now turned into a sweet drizzle; the soft droplets pitter-pattering on the glass of the sealed windows in a catchy rhythm.

April and I sat in silence, staring at each other. The silence around us was...serene, surprisingly. Not awkward.

"We should start studying," she recommended, ending the peaceful silence. Her eyes weren't dark brown like the soil—they're just really dark, so dark that her black pupils were not obvious.

I agreed. I need to take my mind off my past and just calm my nerves. We decided to leave Rosie where she was because she looked so peaceful in her tranquil nap.

April taught me about religious things—about the Nativity and other subjects linking to the birth of Jesus. It's nearly Christmas so she considered telling me some spiritual facts that would be worthwhile.

Before I met Mike, my faith in God wasn't really that strong. I was always mesmerised by the wonders of the earth and the universe, always questioning myself how the views can be so perfect. I was a Deist (just like my father)—meaning that I believe God created the universe but left us to run the world ourselves. Though, eventually, I became Catholic, and my family respects me for that.

April respected my reasons and didn't brag about it. "I respect everyone's opinion. I respect if you think that God left you alone. But just because nobody has seen Him, doesn't mean He left us alone. He might still be out there, watching us."

"That's what Mike said." There was a time when I met Mike in the park. He noticed me crying and asked me if I was okay. Without hesitation, I told him everything—about my father's suicide, about my thoughts of dying. He took me to the church. He was so understanding, so sweet, so caring, so funny. I was miserable when he left. "He helped me with my faith."

"I know he did. He told me."

"What did he say about me?"

"Nothing much, actually."

"Mike made me believe that there are good people out there in the world," I mumbled. "We just don't notice them. We just think that they're full of themselves—"

"When they're not," April cut me off. "People being good doesn't make them annoying. It just makes them...pure."

"Like you."

A blush tinged her pale cheeks. "I-I'm not really pure."

"You are. You gave the Care Centre about three hundred dollars so they can develop their property. That's call being pure. No one would do that April. They'll just spend their money on fast food and stuff. Most people in the world won't do that."

"But being pure is being perfect."

"And imperfect." My hand strokes her cheek, jostling a thick strand of hair out of her face. "I prefer imperfect than perfect. Imperfection is beautiful."

"But some people—" She gently pulled my hand off her cheek "—find religion offensive, which makes me sick. That's why I hate our world, Derek; some people hate our beliefs and won't even accept that we're all different, that we all believe in different things. I just don't understand why everyone can't accept. I don't like the way that people won't leave us alone and just let us believe in whatever we want to."

I could hear the resentment in her voice. I immediately knew something happened to her. Something terrible. "What happened?" I asked softly.

"My uncle — well, *granduncle*, technically — was a priest. He was a very strict person when it comes to Christianity. He was a good priest, too. But…I know there are different atheists out there; you get the ones who don't mind religion, but you get others who do. So…this atheist, who really hates all kinds of religion, murdered my uncle because he believed in God."

"What…?" I couldn't even say anything other than that simple word. Mike talked a couple of times about his granduncle. He told me that his uncle was the reason why Mike had such a strong faith.

Anger raged inside me. How can some people be so callous and heartless to even do that? I mean…I broke hearts, but I don't kill people! Especially about their faith! April was right to be confused about the fact that some people won't even accept that there are different kinds of religion on this earth, and that they just won't let people to believe in whatever they want.

April exhaled shakily. "It's fine now," she mumbled. "The police arrested him. Twenty years in jail."

* * *

After long hours of studying, I closed my book and lay back on the sofa, closing my eyes and realising a swift sigh of relief. A long comfortable silence was around us. Rosie is in her baby room upstairs, sleeping.

"Are you going to the Black and White Christmas Masquerade Ball?" I asked April after a minute or two.

April shrugged, not looking at me. "I might not."

"Why?"

"I have nothing to do over there—just stand, drink juice, and watch people dance. It'll be boring."

"You can dance."

"Alone?" she asked, dubious.

"There's nothing wrong about dancing by yourself—"

"I hate dancing. And I prefer to dance with someone rather than dance on my own."

"Then a guy will ask you to dance." My lips pressed into a tight line. An ominous jealousy burdened my lungs at the thought of April being with someone else. Someone who is not *me*. The hatred intensified as I visualised her arms around a guy's neck and the guy's hands on her waist. My jaw tightened. My bitten nails were jabbed painfully into my palms.

I'm perplexed about why I'm feeling so...*jealous*.

Why the heck am I jealous?

"I don't think that's possible since I'm not really attractive." Her voice was full of clear doubt. Her eyes darkened with misery, probably getting negative thoughts about her appearance.

I frowned. Why would she insult herself like that? Girls are never ugly. They're always beautiful. Besides, everyone can't have the perfect looks. Life isn't perfect. Perfection is fake.

"You're not ugly. You're actually so beautiful. Honestly. So, shut up."

April is beautiful. I love the way ~~he~~ her dark hair cascades down her shoulders in perfect wavy curls as if they're the waves on the sea. I love how she shoves her glasses up her nose, scrunches her nose up in disgust at my witty comments, how her cheeks blush so observantly whenever I compliment her and tempts me to pinch them and grin at her helplessly. I love the feeling of her soft skin...the feeling of her lips...

Her lips tentatively curved upwards into an appreciating beam. "Thanks."

Her smile made me smile. Her smile is so contagious...it made me wonder why everyone dislikes her. "Don't let anyone's words get to you—they are not worth it. You don't need any more negativity in your life."

April suddenly bit her lip. I instantly and involuntarily stared at them. A sensational prickling-like feeling tickled my lower parts. I balled my hands and hardened my jaw. Oh shit...I slowly looked down to see a protuberance...

Oh, crap.

"Don't do that!"

April blinked, bewildered. "Don't do what?"

"Bite your lip," I muttered. "Don't bite your lip."

"Uhm...why?"

"Because it's making me feel sick."

April looked unconvinced. "Biting your lip makes you sick? Are you kidding me? Are you joking around or—"

"You're giving me a damn boner, April!" I hollered in a subdued tone. ? ??how can a holler be subdued???

Her eyes widened. Her eyebrows crept all the way up to her forehead. Her jaw dropped. She looked at that area, a flush revisiting her cheeks, and looked away in discomfiture.

"Sorry," she apologized awkwardly.

"I thought you read romance novels?"

"I do."

"Then how do you not know that when you—"

"I don't think about that stuff all the time!" she interjected. "I'm not dirty like you."

"I'm not dirty. I don't have soil or mud all over me. This is the last time I am going to ask this: do you need to change your glasses?"

"I can see perfectly clear with these glasses, idiot. Anyway, about the Black and White Ball…"

I find it amusing how April tries to change the subject in an awkward situation. It's more amusing when she blushes.

"I don't really know how to dance," she said. "Once, my dad admitted that I dance like a retarded chicken."

I laughed. "Your dad sounds cool."

She smiled with pride. "He is. But Mike's dancing was way worse." She giggled. "Everyone kept on telling him that his dancing is horrible, but he didn't care."

"If Mike wasn't afraid of anything — even his dancing was embarrassing — then you shouldn't be either."

Her smile dropped. "Mike's different from me, Derek. I wish I could be like him sometimes—brave, fearless, nice."

"You are nice. You are brave. You are fearless."

"I'm not."

"You are. You keep on standing up to the bullies even when you're breaking down. That's what I call bravery."

"You're the same, though."

"But I give my pain to others." Saying this, despondency deluged me. I always regretted seeing others in pain. Though, witnessing others full of high spirits makes me so jealous and sadder. Everyone's life is so messed up, true, but they have parents. I don't. Seeing kids with their parents – of how their parents hugged them, kissed them, scolded them, and laughed along with them—just makes me want to cry all the time.

April detected my sudden melancholy. "You should apologize, Derek."

"Apologize?"

"Yeah, to the girls you've hurt. To everyone, actually."

"It's too late for that now, don't you think?"

"It's never too late for anything."

"What if they won't forgive me?"

"Some won't. Some might. Either way, it's better to say sorry sooner than later. Saying sorry might…destroy most of the pain. I know you have your own insecurities, but you shouldn't use them to bring others down, to take that pain off your chest, because it won't do any good. Even if you feel relieved, sooner or later you are going to pay for the people you've hurt. That's how life is like.

"Just give it a try. I don't like seeing you so sad."

Instead of considering about the suggestion, I smirked. "Aw. You do care about me." I patted my chest, right where my heart is, in mock affection and appreciation.

April rolled her eyes. "You never take anything seriously, do you?"

"Nope."

April admitted she's horrible at dancing. I stood up in front of her and held out my hand. "Come on, I'll teach you how to dance."

Confounded, she opened her mouth to object, but I grabbed her hands and pulled her to her feet. Her hot touch sent desirable tingles up my arm, just like how Bella always get those electric tingles whenever Edward Cullen touches her.

Yes. I read the Twilight series. Don't laugh at me. April read it, so I read it.

I dragged her to the large, open space of the living room. I drew out my mobile, tapping on the YouTube app. "What song do you want?"

April shrugged. "I don't mind. You choose."

"Do you like Shawn Mendes?"

Her eyes brightened. "Oh, my God, YES!"

"Good. I like him, too. I met him."

"WHAT?" she hollered. Eyes widened. "SHUT UP. You're lying!"

"Angel, I'm not lying."

"You are!"

I went on my gallery app and showed her a picture of myself and Shawn Mendes himself. April's eyes widened more (if that's possible) and she crossed her arms over her chest like an angry child. Jealousy flared on her face. "You are *so* lucky!" she whined.

"We can meet him one day," I said. "I can book a ticket to a concert of his, if you want."

"You will do that?"

"For you, anything." I went back to YouTube, scrolling down my recommendations list until I noticed a song that I really like. *Imagination* by Shawn Mendes. I clicked the song and waited for it to load. I put my phone on the arm of a sofa and turned back to April just when the first few seconds begun to play.

I wanna tell you how beautiful you are from where I'm standing. The song is so relatable. I just want to tell April how beautiful she is. I don't want her to feel so negative about her appearance. "For the Christmas Ball, slow songs will be played for the dates to dance. For slow dancing, you have to put your hands on my shoulders or hang them loosely around my neck."

April attempted to contradict my instruction, though I grabbed her hands, raising them up to my shoulders and locking them around my strong neck. I bet without a doubt that she can feel the pulse in my neck pounding erratically in a twitchy rhythm. My fingers skimmed down her body. She shuddered at the ticklish touch. I smirked, my hands on both sides of her curved stomach.

"Next?"

"Feet positions: if you are slow dancing very closely, you have to put one foot in between your *guy's*—" I emphasised the last word with venom, though I was accurate she didn't suspect it "—and your other foot on the outside of the person's feet."

April blinked. "What?" she baffled.

"God, April, are you really that dumb?" I crouched down to place her feet in the correct positions.

"You're not a very good teacher."

"Whatever." Finished putting her feet in the correct position, my lips met hers as I rose up, broadening my shoulders. "Right, next is head placement. It actually depends on your and your partner's height. Since you're a midget, you could rest your head on your partner's chest…"

She scoffed. "I am not a midget."

"Small people are midgets to me."

"You are very rude."

"Wow, you're damn late. Now place your head on my chest."

"Do I have to?"

"If you want to build a romantic relationship, then yes."

Hesitantly, the side of her head was pressed to my chest. My breathing involuntarily paused. My rapid heartbeat was unquestionably loud. I wondered if she could hear them.

"Next, you can invite your date to twirl you." My voice came out more of a whisper than I intended it to. We efficiently swayed from side to side in a deliberate pace. "Just take a step back, hold your date's arm up in the air so that your date knows you want to twirl."

She took a step back, holding my left arm high in the air with her right. Her dark hair whipped around as she did a simple 360 turn. We returned to the starting position: arms around each other, swaying with grace.

"What if no one asks me to dance?" Her eyes are, once again, doubtful.

"Then I'll ask you to dance."

"You would?"

"To make you happy, yeah."

Sceptical, she said, "I don't believe that."

"You trust me, right?" I asked.

She opened her mouth to respond. Nothing came out. Closing her mouth, she temporarily considered the answer to my question. Finally, she said, "Yes. I do trust you."

I smiled. Relieved. "You trust me enough to believe me, right?"

"Yes."

"So, believe me when I say that I will ask you to dance with me at the Ball."

"But...what if someone else asks me?"

"I'll...you know what I'll do." She rolled her eyes, knowing what I was thinking. Of course, if someone asks her to dance, I will punch them. That's quite expected from me. "Besides, I did tell everyone that you're mine, angel, so they know well enough to stay away from you and not to ask you out."

"I am not yours," she balked.

"One day, you won't deny it."

"In your dreams."

"'Dreams can become reality'," I quoted.

We spent minutes rehearsing the routine. Meanwhile, I heard perturbed breaths coming from her. I told her to relax. She protested, grumbling many complaints like her stepping on the guy's toe in the ball. I know she's clumsy from the day I saw her falling down the stairs with a book in her hands.

"You won't mess it up," I lied.

"I will!" she whined. "You of all people should know that!"

"You only fell down the stairs with a book in your hands, didn't notice the wet floor once and slipped and banged your head, tripped and fell on me when we were in the park when we were...eleven, I think. You stepped on poo once...on Mike's birthday, your face fell on his cake and—"

"Okay, okay, STOP! I get it!"

I chortled. "I was just messing with you."

"But they're all true." She closed her eyes, panic creasing her forehead.

"Hey, look at me." My hands cupped her face. Her eyes fluttered, those dark irises of hers gazing deep into my ocean ones. "You'll be fine. We'll just practise and we'll get better. Meanwhile, calm down. If you keep on panicking all the time, then *that's* when something goes wrong. So chill and just...have fun."

"I can't stop panicking."

"Okay then..." An impish idea occurred to me. "Here's what: every time I notice you panicking, I will kiss you."

Her eyes widened. "*What?*" she squeaked. "Oh, hell no!"

"Then calm down. Besides, everything can't be perfect. Life is full of ups and downs, full of embarrassing moments. If you flop this dance, then who cares. Everyone embarrass themselves. For example, three months ago, I fell down the stairs. Theo laughed like a hyena and recorded the whole thing and posted it on Snapchat."

"But you don't care if you embarrass yourself. You're one of the guys who are light-hearted and goes with the flow. You don't care about what others think. Me? I do. I care about what others think."

"I thought you don't?"

"I want people to think that…but deep down, I am always curious about what people think of me. It's just the way I am."

"What makes you calm?"

She shrugged. "Reading?"

I grunted. "Of course, you'll say that."

"What? I like reading. It's fun."

"It's not."

"It is."

"It's not."

"It is. Shut up."

For twenty minutes, we practised the cadence of the dance. Every so often, she unintentionally stepped on my feet a few times, and I resisted the urge to groan as she apologized repeatedly. She started breathing normally.

Eventually, the dance was faultless She started getting used to my actions, to how my feet stepped back and forth. She didn't step on my feet anymore. She would laugh as I whirl her around. When she laughed, I smiled, my ears loving the merry ecstasy of her mirth.

Imagination by Shawn Mendes never stopped. We replayed it continuously. The lyrics of the song were imprinted in my mind, echoing and echoing nonstop. The words of the song are so true. I want to keep on telling her how beautiful she is.

"*I keep craving, craving you don't know it but it's true,*" I sang in a whisper. I know she can hear my singing because she's listening carefully, a gracious, mesmerising smile adorning her beautiful features.

"Sing louder," she insisted. "Please. You have a nice voice."

I grinned, glad. "*Can't get my mouth to say the words they want to say to you; this is typical of love; can't wait anymore, won't wait; I need tell you how I feel when I see us together forever.*"

My singing voice was so low and soft, so gracious that it soothed my nerves. "*In my dreams, you're with me. We'll be everything I want us to be. And from the there, who knows, maybe this will be the night that we kiss. Or is that just me and my imagination.*"

Want to know what the funny thing was?

My eyes were burning with tears.

I didn't think she noticed them, but I was close to crying, and there was a lump in my throat.

The lyrics of the song were so significant. So relatable, it makes me want to cry. It makes me want to cry because I just want to tell her my true feelings…

I want to tell her that I love her.

She didn't know that I'm craving for her.

She didn't know that I need her in my life. Forever.

I wanted to hold her in my arms, hug her, compliment her, smile at her, kiss her, and hear her laugh as long as possible.

There's one thing preventing me from confessing.

The Dare.

I nearly forgot about it. In fact, *I did* forget about it until I remembered about the Dare just a minute ago.

I realised that ever since Theo gave me the Dare, after a few days I wasn't so motivated to accomplish the Dare, let April go, and just keep on living my life as the heartless player.

That's just the point:

I didn't want to let her go.

Her company was…invigorating. The bond we had when we were kids was so different to the one I'm feeling right now. Back then, I had a crush on her—just feeling butterflies in my stomach whenever I see her, blushing so hard whenever she speaks to me. Now…it's different. I feel tingles. I feel urges. I have wild desires.

It's so different. It's crazy.

Is this what it's like to be in love?

I was never this happy with anyone else before. I only felt this outstanding happiness with my father, when he was still in high spirits. Though, when he died, I was lost in darkness. Pride, joy, hopes, dreams, goals—*everything* was shattered into puzzle pieces that cannot be solved.

Then I met her.

April Levesque.

All those puzzle pieces were starting to fit back together, restoring my pride, happiness, hopes, dreams, and goals.

To me, April was pure, rare, special, enchanting, extraordinary . . . the list goes on. In fact, the list is infinite, endless.

One day, you will find that person who will take your breath away just by looking at her, make your heart throb uncontrollably just because of her beautiful laugh, and this urge just to be with her every single day of your life, my father told me once. *You will find that person who you want to cherish. You will find that person who will be your treasure.*

April was that person—just looking at her takes my breath away, makes my heart throb uncontrollably just because of her beautiful laugh. She gives me this urge just to be with her every single day of my life.

April was the person I wanted to cherish. She was the treasure in my life.

I wanted us to be together, even as ghosts. I wanted her to be my girlfriend. I wanted to marry her. I wanted to have kids with her. Heck, I wanted to have grandkids with her.

I was starting to doubt the Dare...

Chapter Nineteen

It Was All a Set Up
Derek Matthews

The doorbell reverberated in the house. April threw her arms in the air. "FINALLY!" she exclaimed. "PIZZA, MY BABY, I'M COMING FOR YOU!"

She skipped out of the living room with a happy face, her hair swaying from side to side as she sang. April has the most *horrendous* singing voice in the entire universe. She agreed with me with no indignity or mortification. Her horrible singing voice is one of the things I love about her; her voice is out of tune, yet it has that saccharine humility lurking in it. She's so appealing.

Rosie was still asleep in her room upstairs. Ethan has returned from his time outside. I was suspicious about where he has been. April's mother did mention that Ethan was starting to become rebellious a few times, so I thought about the unruly things a rebellious kid would do: smoking, drinking, and drugs? Nah, Ethan is not like that.

My eyes landed on the large Christmas tree. April's mother sent a message to decorate the tree without her. April told me that it's a tradition for everyone in the family to decorate the tree.

"Decorating without her is like living without Nutella," April muttered, her face horrified at the thought, making me laugh and pinch her cheeks.

"But you still have me," I told her.

April scowled at me. "Nutella is better than you. You have to agree with me, Derek."

"I taste better than Nutella." I winked at her.

She shivered in abhorrence, and I laughed harder. It definitely was amusing to mess with her.

I remembered the good old days of my childhood. When my father was still alive, he, Luke, Marline, and I would always sing Christmas songs, cracking puns at each other, and wishing Momma a Merry Christmas once we finished decorating the tree. I would do anything to relive those memories every single year of my entire life.

Before Ethan came back, we spent a good hour or two decorating April's tree. We were both laughing constantly, strengthening the bond between us. I made fun of her. She made fun of me. I teased her. She teased me. We danced and waltzed around the living room, our smiles never fading.

Spending time with her was like living in Heaven. No lie.

April returned to the living room, carrying two boxes of pizza. Ethan came downstairs and took one box, kissing April's forehead before going back to his room. April placed the remaining pizza box on the small glass table in front of me. She propped it open. The sweet smell of hot dough, tomato sauce, and melted cheese filled the air. Our stomachs rumbled loudly.

"What do you want to watch?" April asked as she took a pizza slice from the box. Strings of cheese hung from the corners of her pizza slice. She sucked them into her mouth as if they're noodles.

I shrugged. "You put on something to watch."

April grinned like the Cheshire Cat. "TEEN WOLF!" she squealed.

I groaned. "*Nooooo*," I whined.

"*Yesssss*," she whined back.

"Teen Wolf is shit."

April froze abruptly at my choice of words. Her eyes flared with sudden anger. I radically gulped. *Oh, no, Derek, why did you say that?* I thought.

Her foot kicked my shin harshly and I winced at the sudden pain.

"How dare you say that!" April mocked her anger. "Damn, I wish Peter could snap your neck right now."

"Who is Peter?" I rubbed my shin, the pain rapidly fading.

"I'll be right back," was all she said.

She walked out of the living room, leaving me mystified. Then, she came back, clutching a long, large bat in her hands. She charged at me and smacked my arm with the bat gently, yet hard enough for me to yelp.

"Ow!" I moaned, rubbing my arm. "What the hell, April? Where the hell did you get a bat?"

"It's not just any bat, Derek Matthews," April said slowly. "It's Stiles Stilinski's bat."

"Who the hell is Stiles Stilinski?"

"He is the man of sarcasm," April replied, a pensive grin dazzling her face. "He's the man of this bat, too. He's the friend of the adorable Scott McCall. He's the boyfriend of—"

"Let's just watch the show."

April smiled with hilarity. She switched the TV on and went to a website.

"What do you want for Christmas?" I asked, taking another pizza slice. Her answer was just a simple, short shrug. "C'mon," I said, "Everybody should know what they want for Christmas."

"I want my Dad," April whispered, the smile plummeted, and apprehension crawled into her eyes. "I haven't seen him for months, Derek."

"Is he coming back, though?"

April shrugged once again. "I don't know. Mom said that it might take time for him and the other soldiers to return to their families. Dad has been in the army for a long time. Plus, have you seen how Syria is like nowadays?" April put down the TV remote after choosing the first episode of Teen Wolf season one. "I'm scared about Dad. I'm scared of losing him too."

I placed a tender hand on April's shoulder. "He'll make it," I assured.

"I hope so." Her voice was low just like the hope that vibrated from her.

I ate a third piece of pizza, biting the crusts, crumbling it into small pieces. We watched ten episodes of Teen Wolf so far. April laughed at the hilarious scenes; she even fell off the sofa, laughing to death. I admit I'm getting infuriated and jealous whenever she swoons about the males in the TV show. I nearly stood up and smashed the TV. Like, hello, I'm more attractive than them? Why can't she just turn around and swoon about me like normal girls?

April reached to her box of pizza, her dark brown orbs glued to the TV screen, and searched for a pizza slice. She glanced at the white box, perplexed, realizing that it's completely empty.

"Did you eat all the pizza?" she groaned.

"Mhmm." I brushed the crumbs off the corners of my mouth.

She sighed, closing the pizza box. "It is truly amazing," she muttered, "about the fact that teenage boys are able to eat without getting fat or making themselves sick."

"I only had eight slices," I protested.

She rolled her eyes, muttering "Pig" before returning to watch the show. We watched the whole first season of Teen Wolf. Man, you have no idea how happy I am right now. I don't have to resist the urge to shout at April, telling her to stop making me so livid whenever she calls Stiles her baby.

I reached over to grab the TV remote, switching it off. "I admit, the show is good—" I stopped.

April's head was on my left shoulder. Her eyelashes whisked over the dark bags hanging beneath her eyes as she slept with grace. I flicked her hair to stare at her stunning face. I couldn't help it: a smile blossomed on my face. I like this position...

Ethan walked into the living room. His eyes immediately met mine. Straight away, his lips turned into a tense line at the sight of April sleeping on me: her arms around my waist, her legs over my legs, my arms around her. Her warm steady breaths tickled my neck as I traced lazy circles on her back, my lips caressing her forehead.

"I'll take her to her room," Ethan declared in an unyielding tone.

I raised one hand to him. "It's fine, man. I know you're weak. I'll do it."

"I'm not weak, asshole. April is my sister. I'll carry her to her room. So shut up."

"I don't give a damn if she's your sister or not. *I'm* carrying her. End of conversation."

Ethan crossed his arms over his chest. We glowered at each other.

I respected the fact that he hates me because of my reputation. I don't blame him if he is troubled about my presence in his house. For once in my life, I feel ashamed of the horrible things I did in my past. Right now, I wish I could travel back in time and fix my mistakes. I wish I wasn't a player. I wish I wasn't a heartbreaker. I wish I didn't put my pain on others.

Maybe April was right—maybe I should apologize to everyone in school.

Then I thought of something – if I weren't a player, then Theo would never give me the Dare to make April fall in love with me.

I nearly laughed. I was supposed to make *her* fall in love with me.

Yet, *I* fell in love with her.

I failed the Dare.

And I don't give two flying shits.

"You said you wanted to talk to me," I said to Ethan. "So, spill it."

"Stay away from April."

"No." My grip around April tightened selfishly.

"I mean it, Derek," he said brusquely. "Stay away from her. Stay out of her life."

"Why?"

Ethan arched an eyebrow. "You're really asking me that? I know you, Derek. I think that *this*—" Ethan pointed at April and me "—is just a game to you, isn't it? You, the heartless jock, just want to have fun with *my* sister."

"You're wrong."

"No. I'm right."

"Look, Ethan, I get it: you hate me, and you deserve to hate me. But I won't hurt April. She's too fragile—"

"That's the reason why I want you to stay away from her!" Ethan shouted.

April mumbled something into my neck, tensing slightly at Ethan's outburst. Therefore, I softly kissed her forehead, whispering, "I'm still here, angel." April smiled thankfully, her shoulders relaxing at the sound of my voice as her slumber deepened.

"April is fragile," Ethan told me. "She's too sensitive. She has panic attacks. She has anxiety. She's scared to cross the freaking road because she thinks that she'll get hit by a car. She's scared to go on the plane because she thinks the plane will crash. She's scared to go to school because she doesn't like being in public places. She's scared to sleep at night because she knows she'll have nightmares about Mike's death. And I'm *worried* that you'll make her life worse because of your devil reputation. Derek, *every night* I have to wake up, go to her room to make sure she's fine. Every day, I have to check up on her in school to make sure she's fine—"

"I understand you, Ethan. Honestly, I would do the same. But I'm telling you, I won't do that to her. You can stalk me every day to make sure I'm being honest. Ethan, if you were me, you'd understand that April would be the death of me. You'd understand that she changed me."

"Changed you?" Ethan echoed.

I nodded. "She changed me. *Being with her changed me.* It made me realize that holding back the pain for so long will only break me. So, I let the pain go. I'm so grateful that I met someone like her. She's my miracle. Honestly. She is. Just give me a chance, Ethan, please."

Ethan composed himself, breathing in and breathing out. He stared at me considerately. Then, he stepped forward, an ominous twinkle in his eyes. He leaned and whispered with an insensitive, intimidating, morose tendency, "If you hurt her, not only I will hunt you down but my father, my uncles, my cousins, and my friends. Got it?"

I nodded, not the slightest bit terrified by his threat.

Hearing the thud of Ethan's bedroom door closing, I carefully raised April into my arms, placing one hand underneath her legs and the other arm curved around her petite body bridal style.

Hmmm.

Bridal style.

I like the sound of that…

Her head lolled on my chest as I ascended the stairs. I kicked the door of her bedroom. It swung open. I strolled inside. Lowering her on her bed, I realised that it stopped raining, yet the clouds were still covering the sky. April rolled over, releasing a sigh. I tugged the sheets over her delicate body.

I kissed her forehead. Then I kissed her right temple. Then I kissed her cheek. Then the corner of her lips. She stirred, and I froze, immediately contemplating if she's awake when I spotted a smile falling on her lips.

After a minute, she was still breathing serenely, and I decided that she's still asleep.

Careful not to wake her up from her gracious siesta, I stroked her hair for a couple of seconds. "Good night, my angel."

*　　*　　*

Outside, clouds still obscured the night sky. I rested in my bed, my laptop on my thighs. After a few minutes, the screen revealed my best friend. Theo unenthusiastically yawned, his blonde hair cluttered like a rat's nest, his eyes foggy with fatigue.

"What the hell, man?" he grumbled. "It's freaking midnight. What happened? Did someone die?"

I frowned. "No. Why would you ask that?"

"Because people call others late in the night when someone died." Theo rubbed his eyes. "What's up, Derek?"

"Uranus."

Theo glared at me. "Shut up and tell me the reason why you called me at 1 am."

"I don't want to do it," I riposted nonchalantly.

Theo grudgingly yawned again. "What are you talking about?"

"The Dare. I don't want to do it."

Theo's eyebrows shot up, stunned. "Why not?"

"Because April doesn't deserve to get hurt," I said.

Theo seemed incredulous. "Or maybe because Cupid shot his arrow at you." His smirk was egotistical and teasing.

"No, that's not it—"

"You don't have to lie to me, dude," he interposed. "We're best friends." The grin never vanished from his face. "Come on, admit that you're lovesick. Admit that you're in love with Aril Levesque."

"No. I'm—"

"Admit."

"I love her," I retorted.

Theo's grin turned into a delightful, contented smile. "I thought it'll take you an hour to admit your love, but it's good you admitted straightforwardly."

My eyebrows knitted in confusion. *"Good?"* I baffled. Honestly, I was expecting him to tease me about it.

Theo nodded, his contented smile never weakening. "Look, man, there's something I haven't told you. The main reason why I gave you the Dare was because I know that April can help you with your problems. I know that you will fall for April because you will realize that you and her are so unbelievably alike."

"So, you set me up?"

"Yes."

"How did you know the Dare will work?"

"Because you're like the sad, angry dog who's looking for his adorable kitten. You're a devil searching for his angel. Plus, I hate seeing you so angry at yourself, blaming yourself for your parents' death. I hate seeing you projecting your anger on other people and not knowing how to confess. I want to see you happy."

"How did you know that I'll do it?"

"I know that you want to prove to everyone that you're not a coward. I knew you're going to do the Dare anyway."

A question occurred to me. "Wait, you said we're meant to be. How did you know that?"

"I knew that ever since you both became best friends," he explained. "I knew that you and April were meant to be together ever since I saw how close you and Mike were, and how close you and April were at Math when you were arguing with each other."

A happy smile made the muscles in my face ache. "So…you're cool with it?"

"If she makes you happy then it makes me happy," Theo enlightened.

Uncertainty clouded my happy mood. "What if April doesn't feel the same way about me?"

"I think she will. You just have to be patient."

"Thanks, man. You're an awesome asshole."

"So are you. But, since I did you a favour by inventing the great Dare, I want you to do something in return for me."

A groan puffed out of my lips. "And that is…?"

"Eat a ghost chili."

"Huh? What?"

"Do it."

"No."

"You're a coward."

"Of course not."

"Then do it. Just imagine its April's v—"

I left the bedroom before he could complete his nauseating sentence. I ran down the stairs and entered the kitchen to see Aunt Marline eating her late dinner. She always came home from work late at night.

"What are you doing out of bed?" She asked, still wearing her formal clothes.

"I want to eat a chilli."

Mystified, she asked, "Why?"

"Because I'm in the mood to eat it?" My reply came out more of a question than an actual answer.

She eyed me disbelievingly and curiously as I opened the cupboard, taking out the bottle of ghost chillies. You may be thinking, *Derek, don't pee your pants* or you may be wondering how there are three bottles of deadly chilis in my kitchen. Well, Aunt Marline loves spicy food; if she loves spicyfood, then she obviously loves chilis.

I took out a small ghost chili diffidently. Without hesitating anymore, I sank my teeth into the chili, the fiery juice mixing with my saliva. I swallowed it, whole. In the next second, I fanned my hand in front of my mouth, exhaling unsteadily, dashing for water. I gulped the fluid down my throat, but that only made it worse.

"Shit!" I cursed.

"Drink milk," Marline snickered. "And language, darling."

I glared at her before yanking the fridge door open. I took out the milk bottle and drank the white liquid. The milk and the spiciness smouldered my throat. It wasn't enough. It didn't destroy the hot sensations inside me. Hence, I drank more.

I stopped to inhale short breaths. I looked at my aunt, who was smirking at me.

"Okay?" she asked.

I gave her a thumbs up, and she chuckled, leaving the kitchen. I went up to the bedroom with the milk bottle and sat down on my bed.

"Did you do it?" Theo asked optimistically.

"Y-yeah." I panted, coughing when my throat ached. "Spicy…very spicy. Damn you, Theo Romano."

Theo ruptured into hysterical laughter. He laughed so hard that his laughter sounded like a hyena's. Everyone does say that Theo laughs like a hyena and snorts like a dying pig. I just don't know why girls find his embarrassing hilarity so adorable.

After a minute, he wheezed, gaining deep breaths to calm himself. Then, he said, "I'm going to sleep. Good night."

"Good night, asshole. Oh, and thanks for being my best friend."

Theo grinned. "No problem. I will always be your best friend, even if you're so annoying."

My smile never vanished. "I just don't know why you're my best friend, though."

"You begged me to, remember?"

"Yeah, but you could've denied it."

He shrugged. "At first, I found you annoying. But then, I got used to you. I didn't want to leave you. Friends shouldn't leave each other."

"I always thought I never deserved anyone," I mumbled. My eyes prickled with tears. Damn it. I had enough tears for one day. "I thought I don't deserve help."

Theo's eyes saddened at the sight of a tear involuntarily dripping from my left eye. "Whoa…April really did change you."

"I know," I grumbled, hastily and angrily cleaning my eyes. "She's making me weak. I hate it."

Theo smiled softly. "Nah, she's just making the true Derek Matthews blossom—the one who was always full of joy, constantly smiling, and always mischievous. I prefer that Derek Matthews than the cold-hearted player."

His last two words caused reminded me of something. "April said that I should apologise to everyone. I don't think it will be worth it, though. It's too late."

"It's never too late for anything."

"That's what April said."

"And that's what Mike said." Theo shifted in his seat. "Derek, I agree with April—you should apologise. It will only make you more…loving. Asking for forgiveness will make everyone realise that you're not that bad. Asking for forgiveness will bring miracles. Besides, you've changed for the better."

"They won't believe me."

"True. But some will. Just give it a go, man. It won't be the end of the world if you say sorry." Theo rubbed his eyes, another yawn escaping him. "What would your mother want you to do?"

"She wants me to be a good man." My heart bawled at the statement. "I'm not a good man. I'm a bad man."

"Derek, please shut up," Theo said brusquely. "I told you. I don't like seeing you so negative. So please stop and just be positive for once. I know it's hard for you to be positive, but it hurts me to see you so miserable. It makes me feel as if I'm a bad friend."

"You're not," I protested. "You're a great friend."

"Then please—just try and think happy thoughts no matter how hard it can be," Theo rationalised. "Please remember that your parents are always with you. They want you to be happy, to do something great. Don't repeat your father's actions because his permanent solution was a permanent mistake. It's unforgivable and inevitable. Nobody can forgive that, not even God. Can you believe that? Not even God will forgive suicide. He will never accept you because life is a gift; we have to use that gift to produce something amazing.

"Death isn't the end, but it will be if you give up. Don't act like it's the end of the road when your parents aren't here. Trust me, the ride isn't over yet.

"I know you feel lonely sometimes. Therefore, I want you to never forget this:

"You have Jackson, Jasmine, your brother, your aunt, your family, your parents, April, and her family. You have Jesus and God who will always love you. They will never leave you. Even though that you cannot see Jesus, God, and your parents doesn't mean that they left you. They are always there for you. Besides, you promised Mike that you'll never leave April. So please don't try and kill yourself ever again. Please."

His words hit me like a brick. They caused a wave of indescribable emotions to fill my chest and more tears prickled my eyes.

"I love you, man." Theo's voice quaked a little, revealing to me that he, too, was full of tears. "You're my best friend. Jackson loves you. Jasmine loves you. Mike loves you. His whole family loves you. Your parents love you. Your brother and your aunt love you. April loves you. Her family loves you. Jesus loves you. God loves you…" he chuckled, a tear running down his cheek. "The list goes on."

"Why are you crying?" was all I asked.

"Why are *you* crying?"

"Because no one ever said those words to me before," I whispered, feeling like a child lost in darkness. "Except for April."

Theo managed to smile. "'There will always be that one person who will understand you more than others, love you more than others, and will be there for you more than others'," he quoted. "'We have to wait for that person…and the waiting will be worth it'. Do you want to know who told me that?"

"Mike."

Theo nodded. He patted his chest with approbation, closing his eyes. "May the soldier rest in peace with the Lord. R.I.P Mike Levesque," he mumbled. I heard many people say that whenever they hear Mike's name. It's an act of gratitude. Theo reopened his eyes. "Good night, Derek. Remember: you'll never be alone."

I smiled. "Good night. Thanks for the talk."

"Anytime." With that, he ended the chat.

I closed the laptop, putting it on my nightstand. I switched off my lamp and cuddled deeper into my duvet.

Staring at the ceiling, I made the sign of the cross and murmured a brief prayer: "God, Jesus, I know there are many people out there in this world who need your aid more than I do, who need your attention more than I do. But, if you are listening to me, I just want to say this: I thank you for giving me life. I thank you for those horrible storms I've been through because I think I finally reached the rainbow and the light. I thank you for Momma because she sacrificed her own life for me. I thank you for Dad even though he committed suicide, and I know that you will never forgive a sin like that but I hope you will forgive Dad's...He's a good man regardless of his moments. I thank you for providing amazing people to be an important part of my life and for the love they give me. I'm hoping life will get better and that April will be mine forever."

My eyes roamed the ceiling as I tried to feel His presence in my room. "I just wish that you will give me a sign to prove me that you are listening and that you love me…"

I stopped speaking, my eyes still roaming the ceiling, waiting for that sign. A minute passed by and I felt discouraged. Sighing, I was about to make the sign of the cross again to finish the prayer when I heard an impulsive, clamorous *THUD*.

I flinched, jolting up in my bed at the abrupt crash. My eyes roved my room and they landed on the floor.

There, on the floor, was a Bible.

Mike's Bible.

He gave it to me before he left to fight in Syria.

I switched the lamp on, scrambling off my bed, and scuttled to the holy book. It's open to a particular section. I saw a particular passage encircled. I recalled a time when Mike told me that he always evaluated the Bible, drawing on it and adding connotations to toughen his faith.

Picking up the Bible, I read the text with the circle around it.

You are precious to me,
You are honoured in my sight
And I love you

-Isaiah 43:3

For the hundredth time today, an extra tear trickled down my cheek. I couldn't help but let a harmonious laugh to break out and reverberate in my room—a laugh full of relief knowing that He still loves me no matter what I have done or what I will do.

"He answers in the most mysterious ways," Mike told me once. *"And in those mysterious ways, they will always bring a certain joy and hope into our hearts."*

I stared at a picture of Jesus that's stuck to my wall. "Thank you for still loving me even though I have sinned," I said. "Please forgive me for my sins."

I went back to my bed, placing Mike's Bible on the nightstand next to me. My eyes closed, and darkness benevolently invaded my vision as I felt myself drifting into a serene slumber.

For once after so many years of misery, I can finally feel the presence of my Saviour in my room, protecting me from all evil ghosts, spirits, demons, and Satan, temptation, evil and sin, and just bringing tranquillity to me.

Who knew miracles can come from dark times?

Oh, wait, I know. Hope. Miracles come from hope and love.

Chapter Twenty

Apology

April Levesque

Dreams. Some are better than reality. Some are weird. Some are horrible.

I stretched my arms above my head, sighing. The sunlight trickled through the curtains.

I didn't want to get up. I want to stay in my bed a little more. The sheets were so thick and comfortable. I love my...*bed?*

I jolted up, my eyes roaming my bedroom as I remembered what happened last night: Derek taught me to dance...we had fun...he told me about his past...we cried together...we watched Teen Wolf and ate pizza...I obviously fell asleep. *Did he put me to bed?* Or was it my brother?

My phone vibrated. I grabbed it. It's a message from Derek. A smile instantaneously danced on my lips.

Derek: *Hey, angel*

Had a nice sleep?

Me: *Yeah*

U?

Derek: *Meh*

Fine, I guess

Me: *Did u put me 2 bed?*

Derek: *Yeah*

Ur annoying little brother didn't want me to, tho

Of course, Ethan would refuse. He's so overprotective of me. Sometimes, it's annoying. Other times, I adore it. *Thx*, I replied.

Derek: *I know what ur thinking: u wish I was in ur bed with u*

I scrunched my nose up in disgust. *Ew, as if. Why would I want that?*

Derek: *Cos last night u couldn't seem to stay away from me.*

Ur head was on my shoulder

Ur leg was over my legs

Ur arms were around my waist

When I tried to move, u knitted ur eyebrows together, as if ur afraid to lose me.

Angel, if u want me, u can just ask, u know?

I felt my cheeks burn. He's calling me angel. His father used to call his mother that name, too. *Angel? What happened 2 'sweetheart', 'darling' and 'midget'? And no, I don't want u.*

Derek: *Angel suits u*

Ur the angel in my life ☺

My cheeks burned more. *Uhm, thanks...?*

Derek: *Y don't u want me, angel?*

Me: *What's up with u and ur flirting, tiger?*

Derek: *Idk*

I'm in a happy mood

Me: *So that gives u the right 2 flirt with me?*

Derek: *Come on*

U know u like it ;)

I bit my lip. *No. I don't.*

Derek: *Yes, you do.*

Me: *Nuh-uh.*

Derek: *Yuh-uh.*

Me: *Nope.*

Derek: *Yup.*

The door swung open. My turning-sixteen-year-old brother ambled inside, offering me a morning grin and a gentle kiss on my right cheek. "Good morning, beautiful sis. Breakfast is getting cold, so I suggest you get your ass downstairs."

"Mm-kay," I mumbled, not really listening to him properly as I was busy messaging Derek.

Ethan narrowed his eyes at my phone. "Who are you talking to?"

"Derek."

"That asshole? Really? I thought you hate him?"

This time, I looked at him. "I don't hate him," I protested. "In fact, I never hated him. I just found him annoying."

Ethan's cheekbones hardened. "You seem very fond of him." Each word seeped with malice. "Are you crushing on him?"

Horrified, I barked a "NO!"

"Good," he retorted. "You better be friends with him. I don't need that annoying asshole hurting you just like he did to other girls."

I groaned. "Ethan, seriously, he's changed."

"That's what he said. And you know what? I don't believe him."

"When are you going to start liking him?" I demanded. "He's not bad, Ethan, he's just hurting."

"Everyone's hurting, and everyone isn't dumb enough to project their pain to others." The resentment in his eyes never weakened. "I don't know what Mike saw in him! I don't know why Mike loved him!"

This attitude of his is getting on my nerves. "Mike taught Derek so many things to be a good man."

"Did Mike tell Derek to break girls?' Ethan demanded. 'No, he didn't. That's why Derek is a demented bastard."

"That's it. GET OUT!" I shouted, scuttling off my bed and standing in front of him. I was panting in irritation. 'You don't disrespect Derek like that. You have no idea what he went through. So shut the hell up and go downstairs!'

"April, I know that you and Derek were friends," Ethan said. "But he changed…"

"He. Changed. For. The. Better! If you don't accept that then go away!"

His eyes cold, he spun around and stormed out of my bedroom, the door slamming shut loudly. I sat back down on my bed, the antagonism watering my eyes. I never had an intense quarrel with Ethan before. This was the first.

The screen of my phone lit up. I unlocked my phone to see twenty texts from Derek, asking me if I'm still there.

Me: *Yh, I'm still here*

Derek: *What happened?*

Me: *Just an argument with my brother*

Derek: *Was it about me?*

I frowned. *How did u know?*

Derek: *Ethan doesn't like me*
Ofc he'll have a talk about me with u.

Me: *Ik, but the way he talked about u was very rude. His behaviour irritated me.*

I don't know why he can't like u.

Derek: *He's just scared for u, April*

He's scared if I'll hurt u

Me: *But u won't...will u?*

Derek: *Of course not*

Anyway, I decided to apologise to everyone

I smiled. *That's good. Are u going 2 apologise now?*

Derek: *Yh*

Do u want me to pick u up?

Me: *Yes pls*

Derek: *OK*

I'll see u in 10 mins.

Me: *Bye*

Derek: *Bye, my angel*

Me: *Derek. Stop with the flirting*

Derek: *You love it ;)*

Me: *I don't*

Derek: *Lying is a sin, baby*

Bye

I shook my head, smiling to myself.

Ten minutes later, I was dressed in black jeans and a long-sleeved blue shirt. My hair was tied up in a ponytail. Mom was downstairs, feeding Rosie. Ethan sat by the table, devouring his cereal. His eyes met mine. They were filled with regret. Thus, he looked down at his bowl of cereal, stirring the spoon.

"Mom, Derek is giving me a ride," I informed, kissing Rosie's cheek.

Mom's eyes brightened. "Are you two dating now?!"

"No." I grabbed a cereal bar from the cupboard and bit it. "We're still friends."

Mom pouted. "That's good," she said disappointedly.

A horn honked outside. "That must be Derek." I swung my bag over my shoulder, kissing Mom's cheek. "I'll see you later."

"I'm coming, too." Ethan stood up from the chair, walking to the sink and chucking the bowl. He washed his hands and grabbed a kitchen towel to dry them.

"Derek's presence might suffocate you, little brother," I muttered. "I'll be fine."

"I'm coming."

Outside, the pavements were damp, and the after smell of rain enchanted my senses. I love the smell of drenched dirt. It's one of my favourite smells like the odour of petrol.

Derek leaned against his dazzling deluxe golden Lamborghini. He smirked as I stepped down from the porch, but his smirk abruptly died at the sight of Ethan. I heard him mutter different profanities with dissatisfaction.

"Ethan," he greeted with an uneven tenor, his jaw clenched. "Good to see you again."

"I love that sarcasm of yours." Ethan faked an alluring smile.

"Why is he here?" Derek looked at me, not even bothered to be courteous to my brother.

"Because he's still concerned about me being around you," I responded. "Guys, can't you just try and get along?"

"That is impossible," the boys snapped in unison.

"He's damn demented," Ethan grumbled.

"And he's damn annoying," Derek grumbled back.

"At least I don't break girls."

"At least I give your sister freedom."

"What are you talking about? I give April freedom."

"No. You won't allow her to see me."

"Because I don't trust you."

"I don't trust you, too."

"Go and die in a hole, please. It's one of my favourite dreams."

"Why don't you?"

"Boys!" Derek and Ethan turned their concentration to me, their shoulders sharp and broad. "Both of you please shut up. Be nice to each other."

"Ethan was rude to me first," Derek said absurdly.

I rolled my eyes. "Let's just go."

Derek kindly opened a door for me. Ethan, infuriatingly, told him: "Nope, nice try dumbass. She's sitting next to me." Derek balled his hands into tight fists, frantically slapping the door shut. He opened the door of the back seats, letting us in. However, when I crawled inside, Derek insolently closed the door, stopping Ethan from getting inside. Ethan swore under his breath, jerking the door open ungraciously, getting inside and folding his arms over his chest with aggravation.

The ride was awkward. None of us spoke. Derek sporadically glanced at me through the rearview mirror. Most of the time, he smiled softly at me, and I reluctantly returned them.

Finally, we reached school. Derek parked his car, and then opened the door for me.

"Thanks," I said as I got out. "Are you going to drop us home?"

"Sure."

Ethan groaned at Derek's answer.

"What?" Derek seemed exasperated by my brother's behaviour. "If you don't want me to drive you home, then why don't you walk home in the cold? I'll be so happy to see you freeze to death."

"Derek," I warned. "Enough."

Ethan decided not to comment on Derek's words. He kissed my forehead, informing me that he'll see me in the afternoon. He walked off, leaving Derek and me alone.

"Your brother is so annoying. I want to punch him sometimes."

I looked at him. "He's just concerned about me, Derek."

"Too concerned."

Derek threw one arm around my shoulders, tugging me into his affectionate embrace as we walked to the opening doors. We ambled through the hallways, earning astonished stares from students as if we're celebrities. Derek raked a hand through his hair, not bothered by everyone's mystified stares. I wanted to tell Derek to let go of me. The truth was I liked it. When we were twelve, we always used to do this: walk the hallways with his arm around me. However, people didn't stare at us.

I inched nearer to him. "Derek," I whispered, "they're staring at us."

He smirked. "Let them stare. I want everyone to know that you're my girl."

I glowered at him. "I don't like being stared at."

"Just ignore them." Surprisingly, Derek kissed my forehead, and gasps reverberated in the hallway from shocked pupils.

"*Derek!*" I hissed. He only laughed, pleased by my flushed cheeks. I couldn't help but smile at his attractive laugh. I shook my head, feeling magnificent sentiments overwhelming my senses.

I love this.

Classes proceeed in a haze. I hung out with Jasmine during my break. She's gorgeous today—her blonde hair made into two French plaits; her attire was a pink sweater with sequins, jeans, and fluffy boots.

"So…" Jasmine wiggled her eyebrows at me. "You and Derek, huh?"

I rubbed my gloved hands together to keep warm. "It's not what you think it is."

"Really? Then why is everyone gossiping about you two being a couple?"

My eyes enlarged. "WHAT?!" I obtained uncanny expressions from other students at my outburst. "Is that what they think we are? A couple?"

"Mm-hmm." Jasmine bit her apple. "Brigit is jealous, but don't worry. Theo, Jackson, Derek, and I are protecting you from her."

"What else are people saying about us?"

"That's just it. They think you're a couple. Some believe that you changed him because, for the past two classes, he was his light-hearted self. Just like the old Derek everyone knew when he was young." Jasmine smiled favourably. "You brought Derek back. Thank you for that."

I felt pride swell in my heart. Despite the fact we're inside, and the heaters were on, we're still shivering from the cold. So many people were glued to the heaters, their hands flat on the surfaces with relieved looks, sighing at the sweet ~~warmness~~ warmth.

"Did Derek find out about your…" She leaned forward and whispered, "*self-harming?*"

"Yes. Jasmine, you shouldn't have—"

"I know!" Jasmine seemed culpable. "I know. I am sorry for that."

"It's fine. Why did you tell him, though? Did you know that he was…"

"Self-harming?" she rubbed her hands together, shuddering. "Yeah. Derek told Jackson. Jackson told me, but with Derek's permission. Although Derek didn't tell anyone why he cut himself. Only Theo knows…and now, you do."

The bell resonated throughout the whole school. Jasmine and I said goodbye, sauntering away to our classes. For my last lesson before lunch (which is Science), Derek sat next to me as usual. Since he's exhausted, he put his head on my shoulder, letting a yawn out.

At the end of the lesson, Derek's head was still on my shoulder. He's asleep: his eyelashes fluttering captivatingly as he dreams with endearing tranquillity; his lips pouting faintly; his chest gracefully rising up and sinking back down. To my surprise, the teacher didn't notice Derek sleeping.

"Derek." I patted his cheek tenderly. "Derek, wake up."

"Hmm?" His eyebrows knitted together, his eyes opened. They roamed the Science classroom. Students were still leaving. Most of them glanced in our direction in stupefaction.

"I thought you had a good sleep," I said.

"I did." He pulled himself to his feet, putting on his beanie and pulling tresses of his hair to stick out delightfully. "I'm just still tired."

We met Theo, Jackson, and Jasmine in the cafeteria, sitting in their usual places at the roundest table located in the far back of the hall.

"You go, I'll get you lunch," said Derek.

"I'm not hungry."

"Nuh-uh." Derek wiggled his finger in front of my face. "You, baby, need to eat."

Baby girl. I flushed frenziedly. He laughed quietly, quickly kissing my cheek. I gasped at the sudden movement. Derek winked, spinning around and sauntering to get food. Still blushing furiously, I sat down next to my friends.

Jackson narrowed his eyes at me. "Why do you look like a tomato?"

That caused my blush to brighten. Jackson glanced at Derek, who was still standing in line with his arms crossed over his chest. Girls gifted Derek with flirtatious winks, stares, and smiles. Derek rolled his eyes, turning his back to them.

Jackson's attention returned to me. "Is Deril finally sailing?"

Theo grinned. "It finally is!" he whooped at full volume, earning strange looks from other students. He danced in his seat with a satisfied smile, singing: "Deril is sailing. Deril is sailing. Soon they'll be banging—"

"Theo!" I reprimanded.

Theo ruptured into frantic laughter. "*Soon they'll be banging.*" He snorted at his made-up lyrics. The Gray Twins sniggered along with him. I just sat there, silent and mortified. The blush never went away.

Finally, Derek came back with a tray of chips and nuggets. He sat down next to me, putting the plate in between us. He picked up a chip and devoured it, munching as his eyes roamed his friends' snickering faces. "What's so funny?"

"Oh, it's nothing," I responded at a fast pace. "Theo just told a joke—"

"Do you want to hear it?" Theo asked.

"No!" I squeaked.

Derek stared at me with a strange expression. "If April said no then that means it's very embarrassing…" he ingenuously smiled at my imploring eyes. "Sorry, baby. I want to hear it." He looked at Theo.

Theo stood up, clearing his throat. He opened his mouth and sang: "Deril is sailing, Deril is sailing. Soon they'll be banging and moan—"

"Alright, enough!" I cut him off. I don't like being trapped in dirty moments.

Theo sniggered. "I love making innocent people uncomfortable." He shook his head at my red cheeks. "Ah, the amusement is awesome."

Derek nodded in agreement. "But, Theo is right," he chirped with a grin. "Soon, we will be—"

I did not need to hear what Derek will say. Hence, I interjected, "In your wildest dreams."

"*Wildest dreams, ah-ah,*" Theo crooned. He noticed my glare and rapidly apologised, "Sorry. I'll shut up now."

"Are you drunk?" Jasmine asked Theo.

Theo looked at Jackson's twin sister. "No."

"Then why are you acting as if you are?"

Theo shrugged. "I'm just in a happy mood."

Jackson contracted his eyes. "What happened?"

"I'm just in a happy mood," Theo echoed.

"Did you hook up with Natalia?" Jackson guessed, tilting his can of Fanta up to guzzle down his drink.

"Theo didn't lose his innocence, Jackson," said Derek, popping another chip in his mouth.

Derek's best friend glowered at his phrase, humiliated, as Jackson spat his drink out in surprise. This drink splattered on Derek's face. Luckily, I slid away before the liquid could hit me.

"You never hooked up with anyone?!" Jackson exclaimed, a little too loudly. The students didn't hear Jackson, though, which was a relief to Theo.

"No," Theo said lowly.

"Damn," Jackson muttered.

"It's not a bad thing," I spoke, sniggering as I watched Derek irately wipe his face with a large tissue.

"Exactly," Theo agreed.

"So...are you going to do it with Natalia tonight?" was Jackson's second question.

Theo shrugged. "Maybe. Now can we please talk about something else? I don't like getting embarrassed. Why don't we talk about how adorable Derek and April will be as a couple?"

Derek looked at his best friend, a devious, charming grin on his face. "I know, right? We will be the best couple ever." To prove his statement, he kissed my cheek. I didn't scowl. Instead, I blushed yet again.

"Can we talk about something else?" I implored. I glanced sideways at the blue-eyed, black-haired boy. "Derek, didn't you say you're going to apologise?"

Derek stiffened at my enquiry.

"You should do it," Jasmine persevered. "It'll be good."

"It might not be worth it," he muttered. "No one likes me. The apology will be useless."

"Every apology is worth it," Theo retorted. "And don't say that no one likes you. Jackson, Jasmine, April, and I, and so many other people like you."

"No one will forgive me."

"Some will."

"And some won't."

"Derek, just do it," Jackson persisted. "Do it right here. Right now. It won't be the end of the world. It'll just be the beginning of something new, something greater. Saying sorry will reward you with great things in life."

Derek fleetingly ogled Jackson, Jasmine, Theo, and then me. "*Fine*," he finally decided after a minute of consideration. "I'll do it."

We all smiled with satisfaction. Derek climbed onto the table, clearing his throat and shouting at people to turn down the noise and pay attention to him. Everyone in the cafeteria gawked at Derek. Most of them groaned, rambling numerous profanities directed at him.

"Okay, so… First of all, sorry if I interrupted your lunch. I just wanted to apologise." Frowns were now visible. "I want to apologise for being such an asshole. You know, being a player, a cold-hearted dumbass, and all that. I know that none of you will believe me for this apology, but my friends—" He smiled at us with gratitude "—encouraged me to say sorry to everyone who I hurt and broke." His eyes focused on one girl and then on a boy, then a girl, then a boy. They're probably the people he bullied. "What I did — breaking girls and hurting others — was wrong, obviously. But, the thing is, I thought that projecting my pain on others…it'll take the pain away I felt all my life.

"I was so jealous seeing people being so happy with their parents. I don't have parents. Sometimes, I find it very…*childish* that people don't like their parents because of simple things like, they don't offer you a smartphone or won't allow you to go out…it's their way of protection. They passed our ages, so they knew what was best for us.

"I don't have parents. My momma died. My dad…well, his actions weren't very good. He was like me — a heartbreaker and all that — but then he was a good man…I didn't like seeing people with their parents. It makes me jealous and makes me want to punch something closest to me because I'm…"

He swallowed roughly. He swiftly glimpsed at me, an anxious gleam in his enchanting eyes. I nodded my head, encouraging him to continue.

"Because I felt alone…" he prolonged. "I felt alone and I felt so sad. I just wanted to give my pain to others because I thought that the pain would go away." Derek chuckled sombrely. "I know that's dumb. But no one really understands." His gaze roved the students. "So, yeah…that's my way of saying sorry. Which is pretty lame but…I'm sorry."

The stillness in the room was excruciating for Derek, I could tell. He ineptly got off the table and sat next to me, sighing unsteadily and timidly. He closed his eyes, muttering how dim-witted that request for forgiveness was.

Then, the teachers in the hall capriciously smiled at Derek's apology. Some students rolled their eyes as expected, whereas others clapped or stood up and approached Derek.

Derek peeked over his shoulder at the students huddling around him. Most of them are girls…

"We forgive you," they said.

Derek's eyes widen, gobsmacked. 'Y-you do?" They nodded.

"We're glad you've changed," one of them said.

Subsequently, they meandered away, returning to their seats.

Derek was still frozen, his jaw opened in disbelief. "How…" He closed his jaw. Tears gradually filled his eyes. "How is that even possible?"

"I told you people are going to forgive you," I said, swinging an arm around him and wiping the tears from his eyes.

"But…I thought it will be harder for them," he mumbled, still flabbergasted.

"Derek, who is the hero in Peony Hallows?" Theo asked.

"Mike," Derek answered unfaltering.

"Why do people admire Mike nowadays?"

"Because he did good things. He was one of those rare good people."

"What did Mike always say?"

Derek's silence told Theo that he had no idea.

"'Saying sorry because of something awful you've done is good—it will reward you so many wonderful opportunities; but, forgiving someone because their sins and flaws is purer'," said Theo. "Nowadays, forgiving is very hard because of how messed up the world is. What Mike tried to say that if you forgive a person who had done brutal things, then it will make you pure and admirable. Everyone in town knew Mike and what he did, but those kids who forgave you admired Mike just like how I do. They understood Mike's advice about living a good life."

"I was really stupid." Derek folded his arms on the table and buried his chin in between them. "About being a player."

"Everyone is stupid." Jackson drank his fizzy drink. "Besides, I don't care if you're a player or not, I believe that everyone should be loved no matter what they've done. Well, except for rapists, murderers, and those lot."

"'Forgiveness is also a way of destroying insecurity'," Theo, Jackson, Jasmine, and I rambled in harmony.

Derek smiled enthusiastically at us. "You'll never stop quoting Mike, will you?"

Theo shrugged, smirking cheerfully. "What can I say? The dude was awesome."

Everyone in the table, including me, patted our chests, feeling our hammering hearts, and said with pride: "May the hero rest in peace with the Lord. R.I.P Mike Levesque."

Chapter Twenty-One

Mike's Letter

April Levesque

A week went by in a blur. After school, Jasmine and I would normally take a serene stroll in the park, chitchatting here and then, and then say goodbye to each other when we reached the porch of my house. On weekends, we ate at McDonald's, confessing secrets and things about each other just to strengthen our bond. The scars on my body were fading awfully slowly.

This Saturday, Jasmine and I planned a shopping spree to find dresses for the Black and White Christmas Ball that will be held next Friday. I decided to go because why the heck not? The Ball might be a superior experience for me. I might even get a date. Plus, I'm very excited for this dress hunt; every Christmas, the shops were selling beautiful clothing and deco. It'll be entertaining.

My tutoring with Derek was good. Derek never stopped teasing me endlessly by twirling my hair with his finger, here and then kissing my cheeks, forehead, temples, jaw, and sometimes the corner of my lips. He offered Ethan and me a drive to school and back home. During each ride, there was always that hateful tension between the two boys. I seriously wonder how my brother and Derek will finally get along. For most classes, he sat next to me with his head on my shoulder, listening intently to the teacher. Occasionally, the teacher scolded Derek for being too close and touchy towards me, and we were made to sit apart as consequence. Derek pouted like an angry child.

"Can you *please* stop kissing me whenever you feel like? Damn it!" I rebuked him one day.

Derek only smirked superciliously. "I know you like it, baby." His warm velvety lips skimmed my rosy cheeks.

"I *don't*," I denied.

The snow commenced two days ago. The footpaths were breathtakingly concealed with magnificent whiteness. My shoes chomped the snow underneath my feet, leaving my footprints as I walked the hushed roads to my house.

My house was just like every other house in Peony Hallows: simple and sweet. My house was a two-storey building. It has a slight wiggling pathway to the porch that has four poles supporting the roof. The entire roof was grey. There was a garage with a white door. A lamppost was sticking out in the middle of a flower bed.

Derek was sitting on the couch in the parlour, tapping the screen of his phone. He looked up just when I closed the door. "Hello, my angel." He smiled, arising, advancing to me and kissing the corner of my lips.

"How many times," I said slowly, "do I have to tell you to stop?"

Derek inclined his head, mocking innocence. "Baby, I don't know what you're talking about."

"Stop with the names."

"What names?"

"Sweetheart, angel, baby…"

"You can call me names."

"I don't want to."

"Why?"

"Because I find them…cheesy."

"I thought you were cheesy because you were saving your first kiss for 'the one'." His cocky smile never receded. "But, angel, don't you realise that the one is me?"

"Stop with the flirting," I retorted.

"What flirting? I'm only calling you names."

I groaned and rubbed my forehead with my fingers. "Damn you, Derek. You're so annoying."

"So are you."

Ignoring him, I took off my shoes.

"Are you darlings together?" Mom stood in the doorway, smiling amiably.

"No," I responded. "He's just being an ass."

"But I don't mind being together," Derek chirped with a happy grin.

"Aw," Mom cooed, "you two are so cute. Just like when you two were kids."

Mom went to work, leaving me alone with Rosie, Ethan, and Derek.

I decided to bake cookies—generally because Ethan begged me to. I went into the kitchen and took the ingredients, placing them on the counter. Derek offered to help me—by help, he means tasting the cookies to see if they're appetizing or not.

My playlist turned on. I poured the flour into the bowl. In the next second, I tensed, feeling a hot chest pressed against my back. I nearly flickered my eyes closed, enjoying the sensation of his sturdy stomach muscles taunting my spine, transmitting quivers.

"Hurry up," Derek grumbled, enveloping his arms around my waist, "I'm hungry."

My shoulders were pushed back to straighten them. "Let go of me."

His nose skimmed my neck and along my shoulder. "Nope."

"Derek—"

"Can I just please hold you?"

"*Why?*"

"Because I like it. Please?"

No matter how many times I may reject it, I know that he won't listen. "Fine."

He cuddled me as I made the batter for the cookies. I stirred the mixture in the bowl as Derek's chin was on my left shoulder, his fingers curling a tress of my hair as his other hand rests on my stomach, massaging my belly in an affectionate, tingly, comforting manner. I blushed frenziedly at the position we're trapped in. I don't mind it. I love it.

I gasped, shocked because Derek's lips lingered on my shoulder—kissing my skin, sending heat that went through my body. My jelly knees almost buckled as if I liquefied at his touch. He left a humid trail of butterfly pecks up my neck, before kissing underneath my ear. I failed not to quake, and now I can feel him smirking against my skin.

"Derek," I said. "*Stop it!*"

"Do you want me to?"

I gnawed my lip as his teeth found my earlobe. He suddenly and roughly turned me around, tenderly trapping me between his hard body and the counter. His hands on each side of me, his head above me, his eyes hazy with desire as they travelled from my orbs to my lips.

He kissed my forehead. "Hmm?" He kissed both of my temples. "You seem as if you don't want me to stop."

Then down my jawline…

Then both of my cheeks…

Then the corner of my mouth…

My eyelids soared open. Shoving away the mistiness, I pushed Derek away. He staggered backwards.

"What was that for?" My cheeks scorching and my gut flurrying with affection, I turned my face to the bowl, refusing Derek to notice my red face when I know that it's too late—I caught him smirking conceitedly.

Half an hour later, I slid the tray (that holds 20 large pieces) into the oven.

"Derek, can you help me clean up?" I requested, turning to him.

He's playing a game on his phone; his eyes narrowed in concentration, his fingers speedily tapping the screen of his expensive mobile.

"Derek?"

He either didn't hear me, or he ignored me on purpose.

"Derek, I burnt my finger!" I cried.

Still, he didn't look up.

I huffed.

My gaze settled on the flour sprawled across the surface of the counter. I gathered the smooth flour into my hands and chucked it at him.

Derek's phone dropped to the kitchen island and he shouted, "What the hell?"

I erupted into laughter as I threw more flour at him, which snowed his face.

Derek glared at me. "I was playing a very important game, you know?"

Twenty minutes later, I took the tray out of the oven with my baking gloves and put them on the kitchen island. The mouth-watering smell of fresh, baked cookies assaulted the air. Derek suddenly appeared by my side, picking a hot cookie by random. He let go of it in the next second, yelping.

"THAT MOTHERFU—" He paused, noticing my glower. He cleared his throat "I mean THAT MOTHERTRUCKER NEARLY BURNED ME TO DEATH!" He glared at the cookie. Derek pouted, blowing his red fingers, his forehead creased with pain.

Either way, he tasted them.

"Very good!" he said with a certain level of surprise. "I thought these were going to taste like shit, but you proved me wrong."

I frowned. "You tasted poo before?"

Derek returned the frown. "What? No. Why?"

"Because you said that you thought these cookies are going to taste like shit. Shit is poo, so you must've eaten poo before."

"No. I haven't. Now, leave me alone, angel, and let me enjoy these amazing cookies. *But* I'm sure you taste better than them."

I groaned, tenderly and lightly smacking his arm. He mocked an "Ow!" before moving away to the parlour to sit and eat in peace.

Seriously, Jesus needs to come down from Heaven and throw Derek into a lake of Holy Water.

*　　*　　*

"I'm hosting a party tomorrow," Derek declared when I sat down next to him on the sofa. Ethan and Rosie were sleeping. "I want you to come."

"I'm not a party person."

He rolled his eyes. "I don't give a shit. I want you to come."

"Everyone's gonna get drunk."

"Yeah, so?"

"Someone could harass me."

"No one will." He let out a sigh. "Why are you always negative, April? Why do you always think negatively?"

"Because that's me. That's who I am. And there's no one who can make the misery go away."

"No one? Not even me?"

"No one," I admitted. "Except for Mike. But he's gone. And there's nothing that can change that."

His eyes softened sympathetically.

"Maybe someone can change that." His face was now in front of mine, our noses brushing. "Someone like me."

"You?" I baffled, slightly touched by his words. "Please. That will be impossible."

"Anything is possible."

*   *   *

The windows were sealed. The sheets of my bed sheltered me with peaceful heat. The wind hollered outside like wolves. I heard the creakiness of the trees. Through the soft see-through curtains, the sky was clearly visible—dazzling with an significant quantity of stars.

I couldn't sleep. For me, those relaxing sleeps are always rare. Normally, my eyes sting with exhaustion, and if I try to close them, my consciousness won't slip, which was very frustrating.

My eyes roamed over my dark room. They settled on my computer desk where I can see a yellowish-brown envelope — the envelope that protects my older brother's letter.

Before, when Mike was still in the army, we would write letters to each other. It's the same with Ethan and Mom. That letter on my desk was Mike's last letter for me before he was shot to death. Every time I read the letter, I cry. The crying never gets old. Not when it came to Mike.

I swung my legs to the side of my bed to get the letter. I grabbed the envelope, opening it and taking out the letter. I sat on the cushions of my bedroom windowsill.

Dear April,

Hey, Little Sis, how are you?

Is Mom okay? Are Ethan and his friends okay? Are Luke and Marline okay? What about Derek? Is he fine?

It's been such a long time writing a letter to you —three weeks, right? I'm sorry if you got disappointed because of my absence. I've been busy with things lately.

In the last letter, you asked me how things are going over here in Syria. Well, it's bad. The war is horrible, Little Sis. The view is devastatingly heart-breaking —the buildings are in ruins, crumbling into dust and flying off into the air, some of the leftovers obscuring the roads. Mainly, the sky is clear and sunny, but the sun doesn't beam in that joyful manner, you know? It glows with so much depression that I bet people can sense the emotion from other countries —or is that just me?

That guy who hates me eventually grew fond of me. I don't blame him for loathing me. I'm from Canada, which is literally above

America, and Syria don't like the Americans because of America's lack of respect to them. The Syrians think the Americans don't care, that they don't even bother to help them and their children during the war. To be honest, I think the Syrians should ignore people's disrespect and at least appreciate the others and me for helping them to endure in the war because nowadays, no one really risks their lives to save others. Nearly everyone in the world is selfish.

I recently built a refugee camp for the survivors to shelter in. The soldiers and I also set up a small school for the kids and we taught them all the subjects you get in school. However, everyday, in the Camp, I hear the babies wailing. I see the teenagers crying due of the death of their parents. I sensed the adults trying to calm them down but it's no use - they had no hope. It's so clear in their eyes. In wars, there will never be hope.

Dad and a few soldiers are escorting the people of Syria — they're using ships to relocate the victims to France or England or any country that's the closest. So far, five ships have reached England. Six were supposed to go but, unfortunately, one of the ships was attacked by a bomb. The ship sank. The rescue team managed to gain a small number of survivors.

I knew this woman called Rima. Her husband was stuck under a collapsed wall of a building. I saved the husband. He had a few fractures in his bone. Rima was on one of the ships with her husband. The husband were one of the dead victims of the bomb attack. And I haven't heard any news of Rima recently so I'm getting apprehensive. She's pregnant with twins... God, I hope she's okay. I hope she survived the attack.

See, this is the thing I dislike about this earth—people don't really believe in themselves. I know, I know: life is hard to endure, although people should know that there must be challenging moments in our lives in order for us to find the solutions and overcome the difficult times—the solution can be the help from a person, a deity...anyone or anything. We just got to believe in ourselves, and if we do, that's when the good comes.

When I found out that there are such things as heroes, I wanted to be one. That's my ambition in life: to become a hero. Maybe I will be one, maybe not. Either way, I'll always be proud of the work I've done.

There are two things I'm afraid of:

1) Not able to save many people

2) You

I'm scared about you, April. Heck, I wish I wasn't here in Syria because I know what you're going through—you're in despair that I'm not there for you. I'm angry at those idiots for bullying you. I dislike anyone who hurts you.

I wish I was there. I wish I could beat the shit out of those bullies. N

Nobody hurts you, April—emotionally or physically. No one deserves to get hurt in life. People are different, but it's their differences that make them beautiful and imperfect. I wish society will accept that—that people are different from their own faiths, opinions, appearances, race, and personalities.

Nope, we have to be dumb and just take things too far.

It's so sad to know what the world is now. A hectic place. A place where people give up. Where people lose trust, hope and dreams. Where they close their eyes and just cry because of the insults and the horrible cusses.

I want to help everyone in this world. I want everyone in this world to know that I love them, no matter what they did. The biggest flaw, the biggest mistake, the biggest error in their lives will be the most invisible to me.

Man, your birthday is coming soon, isn't it? I know you're twelve—so you're going to be a teen in a few days! I want to come and surprise you on your birthday.

However, I can't...

April, I have to tell you something. Please, please, please don't do anything dangerous.

One of my friends volunteered to be a spy and secretly inform us about the enemies' plans. Before he sadly died, he informed us that one of the ISIS groups found the location of our Refugee Camp. If you don't remember me mentioning this: the camp normally moves from one place to another so we can be unidentified. Since they found our location, we're preparing ourselves to defend the Syrians from them. Emergency teams are on their way to quickly transport the remaining people to other countries for safety. Hopefully, they'll arrive soon.

I won't make it. Some of us will make it. Some of us won't. Either way, I'm pretty sure I won't survive this horrendous battle.

My little sis, I am ready to die. My body will die, but my mind and soul won't. It will be lifted up to the heavens and shall rest with my Everlasting Hero, Jesus Christ, and the Creator of the universe and my life: God, the Almighty, Loving Father.

I know that it's time for Jesus to take my soul.

It's time for God to take me.

You're crying. I know you are. So desperately, I wish I could wrap my arms around you, hug you so tight and whisper, "Shh, little sis, it's okay. I'm here. It's okay."

I can't. Because I won't be there anymore. You will never see me. Mom and Ethan won't see me. Luke won't see me. Derek won't see me. No one will see me speak, walk, laugh or smile. Not anymore.

Though, remember that I will speak, walk, laugh and smile forever.

Life is eternal.

If you believe, it's eternal and you will never die.

My Little Sis, I know you will believe life will be shit for you since I'll be gone. Beautiful sister, remember that I am NEVER gone. I will STILL and ALWAYS walk by your side, put my arm around you, hug you when you cry, kiss your forehead when you go to sleep, laugh when you laugh, smile when you smile and just have a small chuckle at your stubbornness.

Our bond will never break. God knows that.

While I'm gone, please please PLEASE...

Don't harm yourself.

I know you, April—you're very pessimistic. I know that when you find out I'm gone, you will slit your skin. Please don't. Little Sis, if you love me don't do it. You will be precariously weak. Cutting yourself will become an addiction. Not only will you scare yourself, you will scare others. Don't do it no matter what happens to you.

You are not alone. You are always loved by God and His son, who are greater than everyone, and me. You are loved by your family and your friends. Never forget that.

You are not ugly. Don't listen to others. You are beautiful. Don't listen to Satan's negative words. You are the prettiest imperfection in my eyes and in the Lord's.

Don't worry about other people's opinions about you. Jesus never told you to impress people, now did he?

If you ever feel the need to talk to someone who understands you, talk to God. He knows your feelings. Your hopes. Your dreams. Your fears. He'll listen to you. He'll answer you in the most mysterious ways possible. His silence is His way of telling us that He is planning us the answers to our prayers. He's planning a good life.

Just don't lose hope.

Don't take your own life.

Promise me you won't.

Take care of Derek, Mom, Dad, Ethan, Luke, and everyone else. Remind our new baby sister that I will always love her. I'm sad that I won't see her, but remind her that I'm there for her.

While I'm gone, remember my promises:

I will ALWAYS kiss you goodnight.

I will ALWAYS walk by your side.

I will ALWAYS wipe your tears.

I will ALWAYS hug you tight.

I will ALWAYS call you my first love. You stole my heart, after all.

I will ALWAYS thank Mom and Dad for giving me you, Ethan, and the new baby girl in the family (remember to call her Primrose. You know how much I love the Hunger Games.)

Just remember, that I'm ALWAYS there.

Don't cry when I die. Look up at the sky, say "Hi" and I will say "Hi" back.

Goodbye, little sis,
Mike

My eyes held back the hot tears. I gazed through the window next to me, lifting my gaze. A large cloud drifted away gradually, exposing a single star. I hugged Mike's letter to my chest. A hot tear glided down my cheek.

"Mike?" I never looked away from the star. "Hi. I miss you."

At that moment, the star miraculously and magically twinkled—as if Mike heard my greeting. However, I know that I will never hear his. I could imagine what joy he brings to the heavens above us.

I missed the way he smiled at me. I missed the pleasant sensation of his hugs. I missed the way he wiped my tears and kissed me good night. I missed his sweet words and helpful advice. I missed him.

If I tell someone how great Mike was, he or she won't believe me. Because Mike sounds too good to be true.

It's our fault that the world is so ghastly, he always used to say, *we take freedom for granted to harm people, to kill them, to misuse them.*

He's so right.

Chapter Twenty-Two

The Party

April Levesque

I descended the stairs, to get something appetizing to eat. I saw Mom holding the door wide open for Jasmine Gray to step inside. Just as my feet thudded across the floor, they both looked at me.

My good friend smiled. "Hey, April."

"Hey, what are you doing here?"

"We're going to change."

"Change?"

"Yeah, for Derek's party."

"Oh," I was confused for a minute, but then recalled that he invited me yesterday to his house for his seventeenth birthday party.

"Mrs. Levesque, you can come," Jasmine encouraged. "It'll be nice—you are, after all, a good friend of Derek's aunt and mother."

"Thanks for the invite, but no. Marline and I planned to go out tomorrow."

"But I thought Marline Matthews is off today?" Jasmine baffled. "For Derek's birthday?"

"No, she's not. Anyway, do you want me to make you something? Sandwiches?"

"No, thank you, Mrs. Levesque."

"Okay. And please, dear, call me Mia." She sauntered away, shouting at Ethan to get dressed for Derek's birthday.

In my bedroom, Jasmine threw her large bag (which she has been carrying) on my bed, zipping it open to reveal a treasure of clothes, accessories, shoes, and makeup. Jasmine separated the equipment into neat piles, a glitter of exhilaration swirling in her bright blue eyes.

"How long did it take you to arrange this?" I asked her, marvelling at the paraphernalia.

"About fifteen minutes," she replied nonchalantly. "Now, come on, girl. I need to dress you up."

"I'm sixteen turning seventeen in a few months. I'm not a baby."

"I know that. But, no offence, you dress up like a hog sometimes—always shirts and jeans with your hair up in a ponytail or let out. It's boring. I want to make you look splendid for your lover boy's party."

"He's *not* my lover boy."

"Don't you get tired resisting?" she enquired. "Of refusing that you love Derek?"

"No…"

She stared at me, sceptical at my answer. Then, she let go of it and ordered me to try on different dresses.

For the next thirty minutes we dressed up—well, to be precise, *me* dressing up. Jasmine needs to clarify if the dress was too bad or too inappropriate for me to wear for Derek's party. I complained like a cranky kid.

"This is just an ordinary party," I whined.

"It's Derek's *birthday party*," Jasmine corrected. "So it's *not* ordinary. You need to wear something that will capture his attention."

"It sounds as if you want us to be together."

"I do," Jasmine admitted with a furtive grin. "Theo, Jackson, your Mom, *lots* of people wants you two together."

"Well, tell them that it won't happen because I don't like him," I mumbled. "I'm a hundred percent sure he doesn't like me too."

Jasmine raised an eyebrow. "You sure about that?"

I didn't answer.

What if Derek does like me? I mean, I'm a hundred percent sure he likes me as a *friend*...though, perhaps not in *that* way.

I like him, too. In a friendly way.

"This dress is too tight," I complained, sauntering out of my closet, tugging the dress down, "and it's *too* short."

Jasmine bit her lip in thought as her orbs ambled up and down my body. "Hmm, you're right. It doesn't suit you. You need to wear something nice and hot..."

I groaned. "Jasmine—"

"Hush, April, and let me think," Jasmine snapped.

I exhaled, crossing my arms over my chest, infuriated as Jasmine went through the clothes she brought. Her eyes averted to my closet. Humming a song to herself, she skipped over to my wardrobe and spent a good five minutes in there.

I heard her say to me, "Damn, April, you have some pretty good clothes here."

"Thanks, my nana sends me clothes four times a year."

"Your nana has good taste in fashion because all these clothes are *cute* and *sexy!*"

"Just make sure to find something that will cover my arms!" I noted.

In the next minute, Jasmine jogged out of the closet, bouncing up and down elatedly as she waved a dress in her hand, squealing: "Oh my God, try this on!"

I puffed, snatching the dress and stomping back into the closet for the twentieth time. Jasmine told me she'll change in my room while I change in the closet. I slid my clothes off me. My eyes self-consciously assessed my appearance.

Scars. That's what I can distinguish on my naked body. Scars. Some were deep. Some were not. Some were long. Some were short. All of them were healing.

Forcefully, I pulled my eyes off the mirror, wrenching the dress on. The dress was flexible and soothing for my slender body. It's long-sleeved, plunging up to my knees; glistening with sequins and gems, and coloured in a dark blue and blackish shade. I decided to wear the gorgeous dress with tights.

Jasmine was already dressed in her pink dress that exposed most of her bare back. She's wearing gold, ankle-strap heels along with gold bracelets; her honey blonde hair curled down her shoulders to make her look fair and trendy. She's applying makeup. She stopped as soon as I cleared my throat. She swerved around and...

Her jaw dropped. Her soft, vivid cobalt eyes widened, gawking at my appearance.

"Uhm..." I fidgeted with a lock of my hair apprehensively. "Do I look...?"

"You look hot!" Jasmine screamed with joviality, clapping her hands together with a bright and breezy grin. "Damn, all the guys are sure going to try and catch you tonight. Though, I doubt Derek will let that happen..." Jasmine stood up from the chair. "Sit down. I'm going to do your hair and makeup."

Jasmine began straightening my hair, gently singing a song to herself. I tapped my fingers on my knee-caps, feeling fretful for this party. Nowadays, people get drunk; they get horned up and act like fanatical, feral hooligans. I'll be one of those people standing in the corner of the room, drinking a fizzy drink and glimpsing around at the people in the party. That's what I normally do. If it's a party with my family, then I am composed and bright. If it's a party full of students from my high school, then I'm going to be edgy and uncomfortable.

"So, Jasmine, you keep on teasing me about Derek and me," I said. "I need to tease you. It's only fair. Do you like anyone?"

Jasmine shook her head.

I raised my eyebrow at her through the mirror. "You don't have to lie to me. If you don't want me to make fun of you then I won't."

"No, it's not that," Jasmine said, "I just don't have an interest for any guy. Jackson said that I should get a boyfriend, even my Mom suggested that, but I don't know. I guess now isn't the time for me and boys. I'm not lesbian or anything—there's nothing wrong with that."

"You mean you're not ready?"

Jasmine shrugged. "I don't know, April. My parents divorced because things weren't working out between them; that made me have second thoughts about romance, boys, and relationships. I mean, I like to see people together and being affectionate to each other, but I'm pretty cautious when it comes to love. Sometimes love works out. Other times it doesn't." Jasmine put down the straightener, smiling at me through the mirror. "Done. You look nice with straight hair, you know?"

My fingers raked through my hair vigilantly. I smiled back at Jasmine. "Thanks, Jas."

"Anytime. Now, come on. Let's go."

*   *   *

"You girls look gorgeous!" Mom squealed, admiring our attires. "Oh, April, you're growing up so fast. I remembered how young and adorable you used to be as a baby—crying, giggling, shitting, and—"

"*Mom*," I hissed, temperature burning my cheeks.

Mom smiled cunningly at me. "Have fun, girls. Take care of each other. Don't do anything stupid tonight."

"And I'm coming with you."

Jasmine and I tilted our heads up to see Ethan thudding down the stairs, dressed in a low V-neck shirt, loose jeans, and a comfortable cardigan. His brown hair is slightly drenched.

"Why?" I asked him.

"Because," Ethan says, walking towards me, "this is your first time going to a high-school party and I'm worried if something bad might happen to you. I need to keep a close eye on you, especially since this party is hosted by Derek."

"I don't think you can survive, though," I said, "him and you are enemies."

He chuckled. "I'll survive."

I smiled. I'm grateful that I have Ethan by my side—he's not like Mike but he's a faultless brother with a caring heart. Sure, he can be annoyingly overprotective, but he cares about me. We all need at least one true caring person in our lives.

Ethan eyed Jasmine. "Hi," he greeted. "Are you two friends?"

"Yup," Jasmine responded. She held out her hand, a faint blush colouring her pale cheeks. "Nice to meet you, Ethan."

Ethan granted a smile, his teeth glittering under the lights of the hallway bulbs. "You too. You look beautiful tonight, Jasmine."

My friend's blush darkened. Ethan observed this and smirked with self-satisfaction. I rolled my eyes. Just like Mike, Ethan was admired by many girls in his grade. It's irresistible due to the light hazel eyes, hardened cheeks, arched eyebrows, stunningly carved jaw line, and sturdy body.

Ethan was fond of the attention he obtains from girls. However, he's not ready to go out – at least, that's what he says. He mentioned to me once that he wants to find the right girl. He doesn't want to experience heartbreak.

I dangled my arm around Ethan's shoulder. He's one year younger, but he's taller than me by three inches. "Let's go!" I pulled my brother and my friend out of the house as Mom waved us goodbye.

"Tell Derek I wished him a Happy Birthday!" was Mom's final holler.

*　　*　　*

In the dimness of the awakening night, Derek's house was the only burnished building in the town.

The security officers opened the gate that encircled Derek's house. They bobbed their heads at us in salutation, compassionately smiling. Jasmine unhurriedly drove through, parking her car in the humongous lot.

Our eyes widened as we take in the display before us.

The imposing, polished, reflective building's windows were illuminating enchantingly, and I could see shadows of

Wandering

people ~~wondering~~ inside. The garden is outrageously vast—the grass was beautifully dark and green with artistic-shaped bushes and leafless trees that hold tiny coloured fairy lights from one branch to another. Tables were stocked in random places of the garden with refreshments. There's a lavish pool where people swam, floating around, chitchatting with one another, dancing or playing water games. The DJ played booming music, pumping a fist in the air with one hand as his other hand controlled his devices. People danced and laughed. Some slurred and stumbled. The thick scent of alcohol filled the air.

"This dude is *rich*." Jasmine gasped, marvelled.

"Have you been to his house before?" I asked.

"Nope. He never really hosted a party. I think this is the first party he arranged after his father died."

"When his dad was alive, his father always used to throw good parties," Ethan added, "but then his father stopped and…he died."

I was surprised my brother even knows the tiniest information about the boy he resents. "How do you know this stuff?"

"Everyone knew Derek's father is a good host."

"I don't."

"I wonder what happened to Derek," Jasmine speculated. "He's always so…secretive. Before, he used to be so happy and funny and caring. Then he was just…*glum*. Now, he's okay, I suppose."

"During those five years, the dude was a doofus," Ethan suggested.

I smacked his arm. "Derek is not that bad, you know."

Ethan looked at me with raised eyebrows. "Are you…*defending* him?"

"Yes, I am. Do you have a problem with that?"

His already hardened cheekbones tightened with antipathy. "Yes, I do have a problem with that. I don't like him. I told you to stay away from him."

"Ethan, honey, April and I love you, but please don't ruin any Deril moments," Jasmine uttered.

Ethan's eyelids twinkled. He stared at Jasmine temporarily, ogling up and down her body then back to her face. "I'm sorry but I don't like seeing my sister hurt. In fact, I don't like seeing *any* girl hurt, *honey*."

I don't think Jasmine noticed the soft flush skulking to his cheeks.

The corners of Jasmine's lips slanted upwards into a timid smile. I copied her though my smile was much wider than hers. If she has a crush on my brother then *ew*, although I can adjust to it.

The three of us immediately whipped our gazes to a boy who sang a One Direction song: "*Nobody can drag me down.*" The boy was twirling around drunk, one of his eyelids closed and the other open, an impish grin on his face. "*Nobody, nobody.*" Then, he fell face-first on the floor.

I snickered. Well, the guy is right. Nobody can drag him down but alcohol can.

My giggles died when I saw the stares of puzzlement from people. Others sent me modest smiles. A few eyed me up and down with jealousy and desire. Self-conscious, I neared my tall brother, hiding the left side of my face in his chest. Ethan protectively wrapped an arm around me securely, taking in the sight of people slurring, stumbling drunkenly, and kissing desperately.

I looked at up at him. "It's okay, Ethan. I'll be fine."

"And I need to make sure of that," he told me.

A boy winked at Jasmine. "Hey, beautiful."

Jasmine snapped a "Piss off" at the same time as Ethan. The boy flinched at their retort — mostly affected by Ethan's threatening glower — and held his hands up in surrender, speed-walking away.

Jasmine and Ethan exchanged an expression. Jasmine bit her lip, moving her eyes to the building. "Let's go find Derek," she recommended with a sigh.

We strolled inside the deluxe mansion of Derek Matthews.

Chapter Twenty-Three

Mine

Derek Matthews

"Happy Birthday, Derek" was everyone's greeting as they enjoy themselves in my mansion.

Aunt Marline was at work, unfortunately. However, Luke was upstairs on the vast balcony with his friends, laughing and joking around. Even from beneath, I could see the despondency on his face. Mike was Luke's best friend. They depended on each other too much. They attended countless parties together. A party without Mike made Luke feel weird, yet he hid it by putting on a stunning smile.

Security guards were everywhere, enjoying themselves, their earpieces dazzling from the luminosity of the mansion. People from my school were somehow drunk and I don't care where they got the drinks from. I was sort of drunk, too—staggering the gardens, slurring at people, here, and then dancing uncontrollably. People made out in the corners. Music deafened my ears temporarily.

"Aye, Derek." Theo's arm was hurled around a young, gorgeous girl. Natalia Hayes. The girl Theo has been crushing on ever since fourth or fifth grade. I think. I don't know. I can't think properly. "Happy birthday!"

"Thanks, man."

Theo lugged me into a tight, warm, friendly hug, patting my back. I backed away to gulp down my drink, my eyes closed in satisfaction as the burning sensation of alcohol sprinted down my throat.

"Don't drink too much," my best friend said.

"Toooo late for th-that."

Then I saw her.

April.

She's walking on her silver heels with Jasmine Gray and her younger brother, Ethan. My body went rigid as I examined her dress. It's alluring with dark blue and black gems, extending down to her tight-clothed knees; her dark hair wasn't curly as I expected it to be; it's straight, stopping right below her breasts. She wasn't even wearing her glasses. I frowned. She looked different without them.

I noticed countless boys gawking at her. Their eyes, full of yearning, travelled up and down her body, nibbling their lips. Antagonism got on my nerves. Those idiots. Didn't I tell everyone that she's mine? She's all mine. Not theirs. They can just piss off and die.

I approached April. She's talking with her brother as Jasmine stood suspiciously close to Ethan. Jasmine caught my eye. I placed my finger over my lips at the blonde-haired girl, silently shushing. My footsteps were soundless.

My hands covered her eyes. "Guess who?" I murmured into her ear, smiling blithely.

Her lips involuntarily smiled. "Hmm…I don't know." She frowned good-naturedly. "Are you an idiot?"

"Yup." The grin never vanished. This was how things were like when we were kids—we would always play this *guess who* game and just tease each other.

"Are you an asshole?"

"Yup."

"Are you a dimwit?"

"Yup." My other arm found her waist. She tensed at the sudden movement, and then relaxed. "My angel, you are gorgeous as always."

I uncovered her eyes. She hastily spun around with an adorable blush at my compliment. She threw her arms out and embraced me in a tight grasp.

"Happy Birthday!" she beamed.

I hugged her back. "I'm so glad you're here." I kissed her right cheek, and to my surprise, she didn't scowl at me.

Her neck is blank. The hickey I gave her must've vanished, hence I cunningly placed my lips on her skin and affectionately kissed it. April gasped.

"Derek!" she hissed. "Stop it!"

"Baby, you're mine."

"I'm not."

"You will be."

"In your dreams."

"The Matthews will always get what they want."

"What a rubbish motto."

"I wrote that for my Art exam and I got a B+."

"Unbelievable."

"You're so cute, you know?" I cooed, pinching her cheeks.

She rolled her eyes, not bothering to smack my hands away.

I kissed her forehead. "My baby."

"Let her go."

I looked at the person disrupting us. Ethan was obstinate with nuisance, his arms over his chest, his cheekbones visibly hardening more with fury.

I pulled April closer to me, pressing her body to mine. "No!"

Ethan rolled his eyes. "Dude, don't make this difficult."

"I'm not going to let her go! I already let her go when we were kids and that broke me! She was the only one I ever needed! This time, I will never *ever* let her go. Not again! Go away!"

"Derek," April said carefully and softly. "I told you how Ethan can be like."

"I'm stronger than him."

"Derek, stop acting like a child and let her go." He moved forward once. "I warned you—"

"Didn't you give me a chance, Ethan?" I reminded. "A chance to prove that I can be the best man for her? That's what I'm trying to do. Shut up and leave me alone. She's mine. All mine."

"Damn, possessive huh?" Jasmine failed to whistle. "Ethan, that's pretty hot. Am I right?"

Ethan didn't glower at Jasmine to shut up, but at me. "See, you're trying to gain other girls' attention." He looked at April. 'He's a player. Why can't you *see* that?"

"Why can't you see that he has changed?" asked April.

"I don't want you to get hurt," Ethan explained. "This idiot here is the perfect example of impending gloom." He offered me an extra glare. "You are nothing but gloom. You are irrelevant."

'What are you, then? What's so good about you?" I held up my hand before he could answer. "Oh, wait, never mind. I don't need to hear it since you're irrelevant."

I seized April's hand tightly, tweaking her away to the area where everyone was dancing.

"What was that about?" April stipulated.

"Nothing," I grumbled back. "It's just that Ethan is annoying."

"Hey, that's my brother you're talking about."

"Like I didn't know."

"He's only looking out for me, Derek."

We halted somewhere in the crowd of dancing drunk teenagers.

I lugged her arms around my neck. My hands relaxed on her hips. "I know but sometimes his 'looking out for you' is getting really annoying."

Before she could respond, a whistle interrupted our dance.

Theo suddenly stood next to me, eyeing April up and down. He released another, sharp whistle. "My, my, April Levesque. I must say you look *ravishing* tonight."

April smiled in gratitude. "Thank you, Theo. You look handsome."

Theo smirked. "Well, duh. Of course, I do."

I gritted my teeth. *Did she call Theo handsome?* That little asshole doesn't even look attractive. Let alone handsome.

Theo sensed my childish jealousy and resentment. He guffawed and smacked my shoulders. "You get jealous too easily."

"You said that my best friend is handsome but not *me?*" I growled, fuming.

Theo was not the slightest bit anxious about my anger. He continued laughing. "April, you have changed him so much." He wiped the corners of his already watering, laughing eyes. "I never knew he could get jealous because of one damn compliment."

"You're not even handsome, Theo," I barked. "Shut up."

Theo gasped dramatically, whacking his chest with his hand. "How *dare* you insult me! Derek Noah Matthews, take that back!"

"No."

"Take it back."

"Nuh-uh."

"Are you here with someone?" April enquired of Theo, interrupting our small juvenile squabble.

"Yeah, I'm with my girlfriend, Natalia. I'm just going to get her and me a drink. She's talking to Jasmine. You should meet my girl, April. I think you and her will be great friends." Theo glanced at me quickly, bestowing me a swift wink before whispering, "Try not to get too angry of the guys looking at your girl, Derek."

I smirked at Theo's choice of words. *Your girl.* Nonetheless, my sneer dropped when a guy approached us. My lips were a thin tight line as the guy smirked flirtatiously at April; his eyes focusing on the parts that turned him on.

I muttered incalculable vulgarities. Theo perceived my blasphemy because he asked, "What?" and peeped over his shoulder. He discharged an "*Ah, that*" as the lust in the boy's eyes never subsided.

"April Levesque, right?" He stopped right in front of her, not perturbed by my presence. He looked familiar; I must've seen him before. "Mike's little sister? Brigit's former best friend?"

There's only an insignificant line of propinquity between them.

This guy was unmistakably begging to get killed by me, wasn't he?

"Uh…y-yeah," April stammered nervously, hastily glancing at me. "That's me."

His hands were now placed on her stomach sides. "Do you want to dance?" His hands coasted down to her…

I lunged at him.

And I was yanked back by two pairs of dense hands: one belonged to Theo and the other belonged to Jackson Gray.

"*Move* away from her," I commanded.

The familiar-looking guy stared at me. "Huh?"

This guy is deafer than me. "Let me go," I addressed to Theo and Jackson. "Let me go. I want to kill him."

"No, dude," said Jackson. "I know you have some anger issues, but you need to calm yourself down."

"That bastard is touching her," I growled in a dangerously lowtone.

"You need to calm down," he reiterated.

My eyes locked with April's. If I need to calm down, then I want to hug her. Holding her always composed me—not just holding her, but talking to her, smiling at her, listening to her laugh, looking into her eyes, kissing her…so many things that were related to her calmed me.

"Hey, dude," I called to the guy touching her. "Let my baby go and I promise I won't hurt you.'

The guy appeared to be angry. "Why should I listen to you? Who the hell are you, anyways?"

I arched my eyebrows. *Did he just…? "Who am I?"*

Why would this dumbass come to my party then?

"Yeah." He crossed his arms over his chest. At least he's not touching her now. "Who the hell are you?"

"He's Derek Matthews," Theo answered before I could. "My best friend. I advise you to back away because you're already on his bad side. He's strong and can break you in seconds."

"Oh, right," he said, "forgot who you were for a sec, Matthews. Romano, I think you forgot that he's a demented asshole who lost his mommy."

His last sentence instantly ~~instantaneously~~ rings a bell. He was that guy who insulted Momma. I was in the hallway of the school with April. That's why he was so familiar. He's also the guy who was flirting with April during English.

"What's your name again?" I ask him.

"Carl. Carl Prot."

Theo snorted. "Nice name," he said sarcastically. "Anyway, Carl Fart or whatever, please move away from Derek's girl."

"Or else what?"

"You're gonna get busted," responded Jackson.

"Bullshit."

"What? You don't believe us?"

"I don't. Just because he threatened me doesn't make him dangerous."

"You're seriously asking me to hurt you, aren't you?" I muttered.

"Nope, I just want to dance with April."

April, who has been standing there, hushed and listening to our quarrel, moved away from Carl to me. Jackson and Theo immediately let me go, knowing for a fact that whenever she's near me, it calms me in the most unbelievable ways. April leaned her head on my shoulder.

I kissed her forehead. "Okay?"

"Yes." She sighed. "This is why I hate parties—guys just try to get with you."

"Don't worry. I won't let him hurt you," I assured.

A chill soared past us. April quivered at the wintriness. I wrapped my arms around her, my temperature warming her.

"Carl, she's mine," I proclaimed.

"I'm not yours," April whispered stubbornly, low enough for Carl not to hear.

Carl gritted his teeth. He didn't move for a minute or two. His eyes travelled down her body, concentrating on the most seductive parts.

"Dude, seriously, if you're that desperate go and find a prostitute," Theo snapped, irritated at Carl's need.

Carl rolled his eyes. "Whatever. She's ugly, anyway."

April tensed at his remark.

Oh, he went too far. Too far.

I liberated April's waist and hushed a 'Turn around. I don't want you to see this.'

Her forehead creased with worry. "Derek," she warned. "It's okay. I'm fine—"

"Turn around."

"You little cunt," I sneered at Carl. "All girls are beautiful, dumbass. You're too dumb and blind to realise that!"

I walked to Carl, stretching my fingers, prepared. Theo and Jackson barked at me to stop. They tried to latch onto me, but I jostled them away. I grabbed Carl by his collar and whacked him in the face.

Carl howled in pain, staggering backwards, his lips splitting open. Blood oozed down his chin.

"Little bastard," I blasphemed as Carl breathed deeply with fear. "First, you insult my beautiful mother. Then, you insult my beautiful girl. You need to learn to keep your shitty mouth shut."

Carl only sniggered dully. "Oh, come on, Derek. Do you *really* think April is yours? She doesn't even like you!" This stupidity of his is noxious. "I bet your mother doesn't, either. You're a bad person, Derek. Too bad. You are stupid, too. Projecting your pain to others, making them feel horrible."

"I apologised."

He guffawed sombrely. "And you think that will solve everything? You think one damn apology will make people realise that you're a good person? Hah! In your dreams."

A crowd enclosed us, watching absorbedly.

"You deserve to lose *everyone*!" Carl hollered. "You deserve to lose your mother and father. Heck, I wish April will *leave* too so you can suffer more pain! Even Mike deserved to die."

I leaped at him. He fell backwards as I landed on him, hammering limitless punches into his stomach. He groaned at the brutal sensations from the collisions. The people huddled around us inhaled sharp breaths.

"Mike never deserved to die!" I yelled, tears blurring my vision. "He deserved to live! He sacrificed his own life to save someone else, not just once, but *twice*! He risked his own life to save a woman from getting hit by a truck. He gave a thousand dollars, which was his college fund, to the homeless. He did great things. What did you do? Nothing. And my parents were amazing! Shut the hell up before I really mess up your mouth."

Tears still flooding my eyes, I dragged him through the swarm of onlookers, shoving my way through until I saw April standing with Jackson, Theo, Jasmine, and Natalia Hayes. Ethan was there, and when he saw me dragging Carl, his eyes immediately hardened. I thought his glower was directed at me, though when he advanced to us and punched Carl in the stomach more than three times, I was proven wrong.

"Dickhead," Ethan remarked as I grinned with appreciation. "Good thing Derek screwed you up big time."

His sister's eyes widened, her hand clamping over her mouth. Theo and Jackson, on the other hand, simpered in approval. They both offered their middle fingers at Carl Prot.

I threw the boy right in front of April. "Apologize," I commanded as Carl hauled himself to his feet. "Apologize to April. Now! Or else…"

"I'm sorry!" Carl apologised hastily, his voice high-pitched with trepidation.

"Admit that Mike did not deserve to die and that he was an awesome person."

"He didn't deserve to die. He was an awesome person. Your parents didn't deserve to die, too, Derek. I'm sorry!"

My eyes met April's dark ones. "Accepted or not, angel?"

She sighed. "You didn't need to punch him—"

"He insulted my parents. He insulted your brother. I don't care if I looked like a psycho, but seriously – what this cunt said was too far. I will fight for you, April. And I'll hurt anyone who hurts you."

"—but thanks, anyway. Oh, and apology accepted."

I blinked. *Did she just give in that easily?* I thought it'll take a day for me to persuade her that the punches were worth it. "Good." I looked at Carl. "Don't ever insult girls again."

Not so far away were two security guards. I beckoned to them.

"Yes, Mr. Little Matthews?" one of them enquired.

"Get this guy out of here. I don't ever want to see him again."

They both bobbed their heads in unison. Carl's eyes widened. He started to protest, thrashing around as the guards captured his arms. He shouted numerous obscenities. Theo and

Jackson helped disperse the crowd. They retreated, although I heard small whispers from them discussing the scene that occurred. Theo grabbed Natalia's hand and pulled her to one of the refreshment stalls. Jackson and Jasmine went away too, leaving me alone with April and her brother.

I grinned at Ethan. "Punching the shit out of that guy was awesome. I'm guessing we're good?"

Ethan's glare still masked his face. Then, his lips formed into a grin, and he slammed a hand onto my back, causing me to let out a wheeze of air. I took this answer as an agreement.

"I'm still cautious of you." He walked away, leaving me alone with April.

I held out my hand to April. "Dance?"

"Sure."

*   *   *

The fat speakers resonated the song *Fetish* by Selena Gomez. I pulled April nearer to me, pressing our chests together. My heart clobbered promptly with ecstasy—a horrible ecstasy that triggered passionate thoughts and the need for intimacy.

Frankly, she's stunning. She can be bratty every now and then, but aren't all girls bratty from time to time? In fact, everyone, men and women, can be bitchy. April is magnificent, gorgeous, and endearing.

I crave her all to myself.

I crave to take her on long walks, amorous dates, put my arm around her shoulders, kiss her…

I crave to spend every particular second, minute, hour, day, month, and year with her for my entire life.

Although, I know I have to be patient for that to happen.

Patient. I hate that word. So, so much.

We all do, don't we?

We hate waiting for the future to arrive. We hate waiting to eat food. We hate waiting so much.

Waiting is torture. It's excruciating, I know.

I hate waiting, particularly if it's a situation linked to April. For example, having her all to myself, calling her mine, kissing her lips incessantly…I want to prove everyone that we're together, that we're inseparable, no matter what challenges lie ahead.

I want to kiss her. Good Lord, this yearning just to *kiss her* is killing me painfully and awfully slow.

Now, I know how Theo felt about Natalia Hayes.

It's weird to know that you like someone who is exactly the opposite of you. It's weird to know that you are attracted to someone who you are scared of hurting. It's bizarre to know that you unintentionally fell in love with someone yet *she* is *supposed to fall in love with you*. It's so weird to know that an ordinary girl with problems like April can make you feel so *good* by just smiling.

Now I know how Dad felt when he was in love with Momma.

I snorted quietly. Dad was a heartbreaker. Like me. He fell in love with Alexandra who was fascinated by books, TV shows, and continuously studied to achieve fabulous results.

I suppose April's parents' past was the same. Mia was Marline's best friend. They were both dorks. Because of Marline, April's mother was introduced to my momma, and from that time, they became the "three musketeers". At least, that's what people used to call them.

April's father…he was a member of the popular clique, I suppose. He fell in love with Mia just when Momma fell in love with Dad.

It's as if history was repeating itself...*again.*

I wonder if it's going to be the same with my son...or daughter...or both...

"What are you thinking?" April asked. My arms enclosed her waist. Her arms dangle around my neck. The space between us was invisible. She's shorter than me—my lips are touching her forehead, granting me easy access to kiss her and rest my chin on her head. Other than the ear-piercing music, our breathing ~~were~~ was the most audible.

"Nothing." We twirled through the hectic horde of dancing teenagers.

"You were frowning," she mumbled below me. "You looked...surprised."

"Was I?"

"Yeah."

"Well, then...I'm just surprised that you would allow me to be this close to you."

Astounding me, she laughed. "That's why you were so surprised?"

"Yeah. Usually, you would slap me."

"I thought my slaps don't hurt you."

"Sometimes they do. Remember when we were twelve, you used to give me wedgies?"

She laughed again. "Yeah. You always whined..."

"You always laughed along with Mike and Luke."

"You tried to get me back."

"I succeeded."

"Most of the time."

"Most of the time?" I echoed, looking down at her. "Baby, don't deny that you can get pranked easily. I placed a spider in your room and you got scared just by stepping on—"

"I thought it was real!"

"It wasn't, though. And remember the time when Mike and I scared you for Halloween with clown masks?"

"That was so rude, you know!"

"You fell down the stairs."

"I could've injured my back."

"But you didn't."

I held my arm above April. She took the signal to twirl under my raised arm. I rapidly pulled her back into my chest. My hands travelled down to her waist.

"You're so gorgeous. It's actually impossible to know that you never dated anybody, let alone kissed anybody before me."

She blushed. "Thank you. Are you going to keep on saying that the whole night?"

"Yes. Are you going to keep on calling me handsome the whole night?"

"No."

I pouted.

She giggled. "Of course, I will."

Her giggle made me smirk. "Well, someone is very flirtatious today," I noted.

She rolled her eyes. "You started it."

"You could've stopped it."

She bit her lip, her vulnerable silence is making me titter. People quickly glanced in our direction. Some whispered to others, pointing at us. April noticed their looks — looks of admiration, puzzlement, jealousy, happiness — yet she was not bothered by them. Not anymore.

"Stop it," she suddenly whinged. "Stop doing this."

"Doing what?" I baffled.

"I don't know," she snapped. "I don't what the heck you're doing—"

"I'm not doing anything!"

She heaved an exasperated sigh. "I know, I know. But recently, you're making me feel weird. The things you do to me...it's odd. I feel as if I should know why I'm feeling this way. I just think I don't want to accept it."

"Accept what?" I urged. My heart pulsated in an irregular pace. *Does she have feelings for me?*

She didn't reply.

"Do I have to apologise for making you feel weird?"

Cuddled in my arms, she shrugged her shoulders.

"Is that a yes or a no?"

She chose not to answer, leaving me hopeful.

Hopeful because perhaps she was falling in love with me...

I thought about the Black and White Masquerade Ball. Then the word *date* immerged into my head. April doesn't have a date. I don't have one too. Perhaps I should ask her? I frowned. Nah, she'll smack me with that bat if I ask her to be my date for the Ball. My lips formed a thin, hard line; if I don't then she'll probably be with a guy who's not *me*. Nope, I'm not allowing that to happen. I earned Ethan's trust to be with April. I *must* be with her. I must ask her to be my date for the Ball.

I have to.

Maybe, just maybe, she'll give me a chance.

She believes in me, right?

Even when we separated, even when we saw each other in the hallways, even after Mike's death that impacted us so miserably, even if I am an asshole, she never gave up on me...

Well, she found me annoying, but she still loved me, right?

I loved her ever since we were kids.

And I left her.

It was the cruelest thing I've ever done—cruel to her, cruel to myself.

Leaving her felt as if my soul has been ripped and torn into shreds.

Leaving her felt as if my heart died.

Leaving her...

I regretted leaving her.

She was the greatest person to be with, and still is now.

She was the light to my darkness.

That's why Marline themed the Ball "black and white". *The blackness meets the light. Without darkness, there will be no light, no stars, nothing.*

Her reason was so beautiful. So passionate.

On the other hand, I was worried if April trusts me.

Because I don't trust myself.

Never did. Presumably, never will.

I always had second thoughts about myself. Since I reconnected with April, since we're practically together all the time, I had more second thoughts.

I'm not the type of guy everyone wants, personality wise, I mean.

I allow this vindictive, big-headed, merciless character to mask my true emotions, my true persona, my misery. *Everything.*

Why would a unique girl like her fall in love with me?

Why?

What's so special about me?

Exactly. Nothing.

Nothing is special about me.

I only have money, a few friends, and a slowly recovering broken heart.

Why would April fall in love with me?

God? Can you hear me? Please answer me: why should April fall in love with me?

Was it because she changed me for the better?

Was it because You destined us to be together forever?

Was it because You know she is good for me?

I don't understand why April trusted me. I don't trust myself nowadays. Even after my apology for my callous behaviour, I still don't trust myself.

Because I never forgave myself for the brutal actions I've committed. And probably never will.

I'm changing, though. Changing for the better. Changing for April. If I want to have her, then I must be the best I can be. I must be more positive. I must be nice. I cannot be rude. I cannot be stubborn. I cannot allow that heartless player to manipulate me.

And I will never be that heartless player.

I'm not that cold-blooded, impenetrable, malicious Derek Matthews anymore.

I'm a different Derek Matthews.

The old one.

You know: the one who was in high spirits? With a mischievous personality, always known as the class troublemaker, with a big heart and a big smile?

The good one before his father committed suicide?

Yeah, that Derek Matthews.

I'm him now.

I'm him only for April.

Chapter Twenty-Four

I do

April Levesque

The morning light stung my eyes. I groaned, edging closer to the warm pillow. For a pillow, it's really hard and it's vibrating with rapid harmonic throbs. I can feel the pillow rising up and sinking down...

I jolted my eyes open at the resonance of a husky chuckle.

Derek Matthews' warm muscled, graceful arms lovingly seized me. He carried me upstairs, bridal style. His unkempt velvety black hair dropped over his ocean blue eyes that were dusted with exhaustion.

"Derek?" I whispered, drowsy.

"Hmm?"

We reached the hallway, and it's filled with shifting shadows.

"What's going on?"

He kicked the door to his bedroom open. We moved inside. The curtains dangled tightly together, blocking the view of the night sky. I felt him lower me to his cosy bed.

"Everyone left the party," Derek explained. His puffs heated my face. He scooted underneath the covers next to me, pulling the sheets over us and making sure that I'm cosily wrapped. "Theo, Natalia, Ethan, Jasmine, Jackson, and Sophia were in the mansion, sleeping."

Still sleepy, I noticed something shimmering smudging the ceiling of his room. They leisurely shimmered from one colour to another magically, taking my breath away.

"Mike gave them to me," Derek said, placing his head on my shoulder; one of his arms fell on my stomach.

"I have some too."

"I know that." His firm fingers pleasurably caressed my head, stroking my hair. "Sleep, baby."

"I don't feel comfortable in my dress, though."

"Go in my closet and get a shirt."

"Okay."

I swung my legs over the side of the bed and walked to the white doors of his closet. I gasped. His closet is like another room, a small room. I scanned the closet, my fingers feeling the materials of each clothing as I hunted for a shirt. I zipped out of my long-sleeved, thigh-length dress and put on a large shirt that fell to my knees. I was wearing tights underneath this, so I guess I'll be fine.

Stepping back into the room, my cheeks flared.

Derek was bare-chested. The sheets were pushed down to his waistline, exposing his sturdy abs and his V-line slightly. His eyes were closed, slumbering peacefully as he snored lightly.

I silently tiptoed to the bed, crawling underneath the covers, alarmed not to wake him up. I spent a minute staring at him with my head on my propped-up arm.

He's so adorable when he sleeps. I should freak out because I'm sleeping in a guy's bed, particularly since the bed belonged to Derek Matthews. Though, I'm too exhausted and happy to complain.

This reminded me of when we were kids.

When we were there for each other.

When we trusted each other.

When Mike was still alive.

Derek always slept in my bed after we read a fairytale to each other.

It felt as if the good things were happening again. And it brought happiness that scorched my lungs.

My head hit the humongous fluffy black pillows. When I turned around, I stifled a scream when a warm arm snaked around my waist. He jerked me into his hard, defined chest and dropped his head into my neck, kissing the juncture.

"Good night, my angel."

I'm so glad to know that his room is dark enough to cover my radiant flush. In the party, he was so overprotective of me: persistently putting his arm around me, barking countless blasphemies to any guy approaching me. He was so charming, too: he embarrassed me but made me laugh and smile.

I didn't stop him. I allowed him to be affectionate in public. It's infuriating to know that someone can make you so weak.

I deliberated about the conversation I had with Mom this morning:

"So, April." Mom was cooking as always. Her hair made into a bun; her hands grasping the hilt of the knife and the food, chopping them in a rapid tempo. "Do you love someone?"

"No. Why?"

"Just asking. I thought you love Derek."

"Ew, no. He's nasty."

Mom heaved a sigh. "April, just because he has a horrible reputation doesn't mean he's nasty. He's sweet. You of all people know that. Even Mike knew that! Besides, he's not a player anymore—he apologised to everyone, right? Everyone makes mistakes and commits actions that they will regret. Do you want to know why we make the wrong decisions? It's because the mind manipulates us; it gives us false theories and convinces us to do the wrong. Even with such horrible, brutal emotional pain...even if you're smart...one way or another, you will inflict your pain to others. It's just how some people are...and you can't be judgemental about that."

"Mike hated when people are so judgemental," I said. "He said that it only causes more pain, sorrow, and brutality. He admitted that the reason why people who have been raped, harassed, or assaulted keep their stories to themselves is because they know they will get judged. He said that people must stop and think twice before they say or do something because even the tiniest action and simplest words could cause callous things."

"It's so sad and true. I hate it." Mom shook her head, disappointed at how vicious society was today. "Anyway..." With her hands, she slid her sliced vegetables into the frying pan; steam hissed. "Marline and I have been talking about Derek recently. She told me that Derek is doing well with letting go of the past...all because of you. You know the reason why I agreed to the tutoring idea, right?"

"Yes."

"Are you still mad with me for setting you two up?"

"Nope. He's fine. I actually miss him."

"You two were adorable when you both were kids."

"That's what Marline said."

"She's right.' Mom stirred the frying food with a wooden spoon. "Derek needs a true friend, April...and perhaps a true...girlfriend..."

"Mom!"

She threw both of her hands up in surrender. "What? I'm just saying. Marline messaged me about Derek blabbing about you all the time. He changed, April – he's turning back to the old Derek. To the happy one. The humorous one. All because of you."

"Mom, he doesn't like me," I muttered.

"You're right. He loves you."

"He doesn't love me and I don't love him," I said. "Okay?"

"Yeah, yeah...whatever."

What if Mom was correct? Does Derek like me romantically? If he does, then why? Why would he love me? On the contrary, I understood that he needs me because we're exactly alike. We were there for each other ever for years. Apart from that, there were other girls who were better than me and way, way, *way* prettier than me.

He kept on kissing you all the time, was one of my contemplations. *You're sleeping in his arms. He's being so charming to you. Of course, he loves you.*

Maybe Mom was right. Maybe Derek does love me. He didn't literally admit it, though. So, I can't get my hopes up too much. If I do, it's a high possibility for them to get crushed.

Nevertheless, one theory was correct:

I love him way more than a friend.

*   *   *

When I woke up, Derek wasn't sleeping. The space next to me was empty and wrinkled.

I headed to the bathroom. There's a note on the sink: *Baby, rise and shine! Had a good sleep?* I smiled, picking up the packet that held a new toothbrush. Derek must've brought it for me. I ripped the packet open, pressed toothpaste to my toothbrush, and scrubbed my teeth, humming a song to myself.

After that, there's another note in his bedroom that informed me to put his cardigan on since it's cold. Without any hesitation, I shoved my arms through the armholes, zipped it up, and went outside.

The corridor was short. I was immediately welcomed by the satisfying fragrance of breakfast wafting from downstairs. My stomach rumbled impatiently. I tried to find the kitchen. For each door downstairs, it's either a bedroom or something else. *Seriously, how many rooms does this mansion have? A hundred?*

I reached the front room and, as expected, it was still adorned with stunning, creative designs painted on the walls, columns supporting the ceiling that holds a dazzling chandelier and two staircases on each side. I'm astounded and mystified at how clean it is. Last night, it was jam packed with teenagers. I guess Derek hired cleaners who cleaned the whole mansion overnight?

Downstairs, Ethan was talking into his mobile, murmuring quietly. He looked in my direction as I descended. He nodded his head as a morning welcome, muttering something into his phone before ending the call and shoving it into his pocket. His dark brown hair was untidy from sleep. He swung out his left arm, engulfing me in a loving hug.

"Morning, little brother."

"Morning, beautiful sister. Had a nice sleep?"

"Mm-hmm," I hum into his chest.

"Are you wearing Derek's shirt?"

"And his cardigan." I eyed his expression. "Don't get mad."

"I'm not."

I felt my face brighten with joy. "Are you and him okay now?"

He shrugged. "Meh. I suppose we can get along."

"Yay!" I exclaimed. "No more annoying banter that will deafen me!"

Ethan rolled his eyes.

He led me to the kitchen. Theo, Jasmine, Jackson, Natalia, and another girl were sitting around a large kitchen island, talking to one another in low voices. Luke and Marline were also there. The surface of the kitchen island was stacked with plates and food: sandwiches, omelettes, glasses of juice.

Jackson grinned at me. "April!"

There's an empty seat between Jasmine and another unknown girl. The unfamiliar girl is oriental. Her eyes were chestnut brown. Her skin was flawless. Her eyebrows were perfectly straight. Her nose was faintly chubby, and her cheeks seemed to be smooth. Her waist-length hair was silky, and the endings were dyed in a luxuriant, eye-catching, gorgeous tone of dark red. Jackson had his arm over her shoulders. This must be Jackson's girlfriend, obviously. Sophia, was it?

Ethan sat down opposite to Jasmine. He reached to grab a sandwich from Jasmine's plate.

"Oi!" Jasmine tried to grab it back, but he already devoured it, giving Jasmine a thumb up. Jasmine shot him the middle finger.

Something hard and humid brushed my back, and I glanced up to see Derek smiling down at me. He kissed my forehead, and my face flushed immediately not only because he kissed me in public, but because of the fact he's shirtless with a pair of light grey sweatpants loosely hanging around his waist, revealing a part of his V-line.

I squealed when he lifted me up effortlessly and placed me on his lap, sliding both of his arms around my waist. I saw everyone looking at us with thrilled smirks, even Ethan. He interlaced his fingers with mine and sighed into my neck.

"Did I miss something?" Jackson asked, still grinning. "You two dating now?"

"No!" I protested. "Derek is being so touchy lately and I hate it! Ethan, tell him to get off me!"

Ethan shot Derek a mocking glare and then continued to steal food from Jasmine's plate.

"Okay." Jackson frowned at Derek. Derek shrugged, silent. "Anyway, April, this is my girlfriend, Sophia Lee."

Sophia and I exchanged smiles.

No more words were spoken for the next minutes. The silence was soothing as we all ate in silence; here and then, whispering to the person next to us.

Derek was feeding me, shoving food into my mouth and making sure I swallowed them.

"I can feed myself, you know!" I retorted. "I'm not a baby!"

He smirked, satisfied by my anger. His answer was short, simple and infuriating: a shrug.

He attempted to shove another piece of omelette into my mouth. I smacked his hand away and grabbed a small piece of strawberry. I bit it. The sweet juice made my taste buds vibrate in pleasure. I leaned into his chest. He kissed the sides of my cheeks and then lay his chin on my hair, his fingers tenderly massaging the soft skin of my legs.

"The Ball is coming up in two weeks," Sophia proclaimed. "I want Natalia, Jasmine, April, and me to go shopping for dresses today afternoon. And no boys, you can't come because this is a girls' day out."

"April, you have never been to the Ball, have you?" Theo asked me.

I shook my head in answer.

"You're coming, right?"

"Maybe."

"Come," Jackson, Theo, and Derek insisted in unison.

The three best friends exchanged funny looks and ~~ruptured~~ *erupted* into laughter. Jasmine smacked Ethan's hand away from her plate for the hundredth time as Marline shouted a goodbye at us and left the house for work. Luke was silent.

I stared at Luke. Sympathy filled me. Luke was Mike's best friend, and without him, Luke was obviously miserable. After Mike's death, Luke was like Derek; he walked away from my family and me, just spending time alone.

He met my eyes. I instantly gave him a soft smile. He smiled back and looked down at his bowl of cereal.

The laughter died after a minute. The three boys had hysterical tears smudging the edges of their eyes.

"That's not even funny, boys," Sophia muttered. "I don't know why you're laughing."

"Baby, it's a guy thing." Jackson wiped his eyes. "Get used to it."

"Luke wasn't laughing," Natalia Hayes pointed out. "Neither was Ethan."

"That's because Ethan was too busy flirting with Jasmine and Luke was busy eating his food," said Derek.

Ethan was drinking water as Derek spoke, and when he mentioned the word *flirting* Ethan choked, the water sprinkling through his lips. He coughed and coughed, banging his chest.

Jasmine's face was flushed.

Ethan's face was the same.

I couldn't help but smirk at my brother's awkwardness.

"I proposed to my girlfriend," Luke declared, catching our attention. Ethan and Jasmine sighed in relief at the sudden change of subject, their faces still red.

Theo's girlfriend smiled. "Aw, that's wonderful."

"When's the wedding, Luke?" Jackson asked.

"In a couple of months."

Derek beamed. "This wedding will be great."

"Yup," Luke agreed. The light in his eyes was abruptly replaced with woe. "There's nothing I could ask for to make the wedding better." His last sentence came out in a husky manner, as if they're hurting him.

"You miss him, don't you?" asked Theo, referring to Mike.

"Of course, I do, Theo. How can I not miss Mike?"

"True." Theo put her arm around Natalia. "It's ~~irresistible~~ to miss Mike." *impossible not*

Ethan put his hand on Luke's shoulder. "You were a great friend to him. And still are."

"I want him back," was all Luke whispered. Painfully.

He stood up and walked out of the kitchen. I caught the glistening tears streaming down his cheeks.

"Leave him," Derek said when nearly all of us attempted to go after him. "He needs his space."

Sophia sighed. "I never met Mike, but I heard that he was an awesome person. People described him as an angel from heaven, a hero, a martyr." Her eyes averted to Ethan and me. "I'm sorry for your loss."

"It's fine," Ethan answered for me. "We know he's still with us."

"Always."

Another silence enveloped us until I ended it by questioning: "What else do you do at the Ball?"

"Well," Jasmine began, "you get the Christmas King and Queen. People vote for a male and a female to become the King and Queen. It's like prom but the Ball is way better."

"Who's promoted to be the King and Queen?"

"From what I've heard, Derek and this other guy are nominated. Brigit and Tiffany are nominated for the Queen…and so are you."

"W-what?" I stuttered, astounded. "*Me?*"

They all nodded.

"Why me?" I demanded. "Who suggested me?"

"We did," Jackson answered.

"Why?"

Derek curled a strand off my hair with his pinkie. "We want this Ball to be the best first Ball ever for you."

"But…what happens if you win?"

"The King and Queen must dance in front of everyone and sometimes they kiss," said Derek.

*　　*　　*

The next day, Natalia, Sophia, Jasmine, and I went to the mall for a dress hunt. I was exceedingly excited. I rarely go to the mall, especially with friends. Plus, I didn't know half of the trendy stores. It'll be a fun experience with the girls.

Couples passed by, seizing hands and large bags. Children skipped around, eating appetizing treats. Music hummed from the speakers seeded in the ceiling. Lights scintillated on the walls. Christmas trees were displayed in the small shops.

We entered several, different stores, scrutinizing the dresses and mocking here and then. Laughing. Chatting. Smiling. Just having fun. Annoyingly, none of the dresses fascinated me——well, to Jasmine at least. The clothes were appealing to Natalia, Sophia, and I. Though, Jasmine was revolted by our taste in fashion.

"What are you? A fashion expert?" said Natalia.

Jasmine's lips lurched up slightly. "You could say that. I'm very serious whenever it comes to shopping. I want to become a fashion designer."

"That makes sense," Sophia uttered.

In the next shop, I walked through the store, easily astonished by anything exquisite (which was everything) I gazed at. The only unimpressive thing was the prices. *Why do they have to be so expensive?*

Sooner or later, I found a dress. It's black with a transparent lace sheet that's stitched around a belt stunningly. Jasmine's remark on the dress, on the other hand, was identical to the last one—it's not perfect enough.

"A simple black or white dress will be fine, Jas," I grumbled.

Jasmine shook her head impatiently. "April, the Black and White Masquerade Ball is a big deal to every student in Peony Hallows. We want to look pretty, right? Plus, I want this Ball to be a wonderful time for you."

"Not everything has to be wonderful." Sighing, I put the dress away.

Alas, the girls found delicate dresses. I haven't, until I saw that one dress that made it impossible for me to look away. It's a white halter lace dress along with a white skirt enclosing the belt.

Jasmine must've noticed my scrutiny because she squealed, "That's perfect!" She grabbed the dress and looked it over. They glanced at me, back at the dress, and repeated it twice. "This will suit you! I can tell!"

The dress was too expensive. Annoyingly. Therefore, Jasmine spent the rest of her money to buy the dress with mine, too. Her wealth made me consider about the fact that her parents co-operated with the Matthews Industry. Her family were just like Derek's family: a humongous group of millionaires and billionaires, successful in their jobs, never giving up no matter what blocked their paths.

We spent another good ten or fifteen minutes finding accessories and shoes. After that, our shopping spree sadly ended. We decided to get food.

The food court was packed with people. The noise was fairly high and music played from the speakers planted in the ceiling.

After we ordered, we gathered around a clean table. *clear*

Sophia was the first to start chitchatting: "Let's talk about dates." She clapped her hands with glee at the topic. "So, as you all know, my guy is Jackson and Nat's guy is Theo. Jasmine, who is your guy?"

Jasmine shrugged.

Natalia cocked an eyebrow. "What about Ethan?"

Jasmine looked at Natalia. "There's nothing going on between us."

Natalia snorted, incredulous. "You two were flirting this morning."

"Derek pointed it out and you two blushed," added Sophia.

"That's different," Jasmine denied. "There's nothing going on between us."

"You can date him," I told Jasmine, in case if she's nervous about dating my brother. "He does seem to like you. In fact, he's been talking about you a lot recently. Well, while we were in your car, he was messaging me and we were talking about you." It's true. In Jasmine's car, Ethan annoyed me with a hundred messages regarding Jasmine Gray—about how beautiful she is... He even surprisingly confessed that he had a crush on her...

Jasmine appeared to be astounded at my statement. She smiled a little. "He's younger than me, though."

"So? Who cares about age? Ethan is only a year younger than us. It's fine if you two go out. Mom will be glad, too. She always wanted to see Ethan dating."

"Justin Bieber is younger than Selena Gomez," Natalia uttered, "and they were together – probably still are."

"I don't know... What if he likes another girl?"

"He doesn't. Trust me, I know," I said. "I can tell him that you like him too..."

"No!" Jasmine's eyes enlarged. "Please don't! What if he—"

"Relax, Jas, everything will turn out awesome. Trust me."

"But—"

"Jas." I place my hands on her shoulders. "Relax."

Natalia diverted her focus to me. "Jasmine's love life: sorted. Now, it's time to talk about yours."

I blinked. "There's nothing—"

"You and Derek." Sophia's interjection was full of great enthusiasm. "You two *have* to be together. Jackson wants you two to be together. Theo does. Jasmine does. Natalia does. *I* do. Your mom does. Derek's aunt does. Luke does. So many people ship you two. Even the birds and the bees!"

Natalia gave Sophia a look. "Birds and bees? Really?"

"It's obvious he likes you, April," said Jasmine.

"What? *Pfft*...No, he doesn't like me. He's way out of my league. He isn't my type, anyway," I ranted, knowing for a fact that my face was already heating up.

"Who says that a guy needs to be your type to become your boyfriend?" Natalia asked.

"He isn't my boyfriend, Natalia. He might be crushing on another girl anyway."

"What if that girl is you?"

Sophia went to get our meals as I muttered, "That's impossible."

She frowned again. "Why do you say that? Because you're ugly? If so, April, no girl is ugly. We, girls, are beautiful in our own way. Everyone sees beauty in all the girls. They just don't know it because they're criticising themselves too much. Beauty is in the eye of the beholder."

Sophia came back with our food. I lifted my large glass of strawberry-and-banana-smoothie for a sip. The sweet flavour amazed my tastes. "If he likes me, then what does he see in me?"

Jasmine shrugs. "How can we answer that? You need to ask him. There might be a million reasons why he loves you."

I sulked. "He doesn't love me."

"Yes, he does," Jasmine retorted.

"How do you know that? Are you a love expert now?"

"I know love when I see it." Jasmine took out her phone from her jeans. She placed her mobile in front of me. The screen displayed her messages with De3rek. "I talked to Derek. This is what he told me. Read it."

Jasmine: *Derek, can I ask u a question?*

Derek: *Sure*

Jasmine: *Do u love April?*

Derek: *Yes*

Y?

Jasmine: *I just wanted to make sure*
You seemed really into her this morning
Derek: *She's just beautiful*
Jasmine: *Why do u love her?*
Derek: *Because she was there for me when no one else was. She understood me. She can easily relate to the negative feelings I've been secretly hiding for these past, long years. I can't stop thinking about her because she's always on my mind every second, every minute, every hour, and every day. When I do think about her I couldn't help but smile. She's the angel God created only for me.*
Jasmine: *Why haven't u asked her out yet?*
Derek: *I'm nervous*
Jasmine: *Why?*
Derek: *There's a high chance she'll say no, Jas*
She might presumably slap me too or smack me with the Stiles bat
Jasmine: *Before, she might. Now, she won't.*
Derek: *Idk...*
I'll just wait until the time is right
Jasmine: *Don't wait too long*

"He loves me?" I whispered, ogling at the boxes full of Derek's shocking, touching, amorous words.

"Oh, my God." Her groan was filled with exasperation, her forehead clouting into her palm. "Are you really this naive?"

"Sorry," I apologised timidly. "I'm just not used to these things. I never thought that any guy will like me...let alone love me."

"Well, Derek loves you and he's super nervous to ask you out." Jasmine stashed her phone in her pocket. "The question is: do you?"

Derek confessed that he had a crush on me when we were kids. His crush slowly died when we stopped talking, at the time when we both realised that we needed each other more than anyone to commiserate our emotions, to understand our depression, to console each other.

I never deduced that Derek would have a crush on me again.

I wanted to know what Derek sees in me.

I wanted to know why he likes me…well, *loves* me.

He could be playing me. He was the cold-hearted player.

On the other hand, he changed. He's the good Derek who I loved as a friend.

Now…he's the Derek who I love more than a friend.

A part of my mind was hollering at me to stop my feelings for him. The other part persisted for me to go on with my affectionate sentiments for him.

"Yes," I finally replied. "Yes, I do."

Chapter Twenty-Five

I Need You

April Levesque

A week went by in a haze. There was only two weeks left until our break for the Christmas holidays. People talked about the Ball with strong enthusiasm. There were posters everywhere about the Ball, all colourful and captivating.

Every morning, Derek kindly drove Ethan and me to school and then back home. The childish grudge the boys had for each other died. Every morning, they chitchatted incessantly, grinning, snickering, and having their man talk while I sat next to my brother, staring through the window.

Today, Derek's golden Lamborghini was parked in the school's parking lot. Derek threw his arm around me and we walked through the crowd of curious onlookers. Unlike before, I'm not troubled by their jealous fury, their curious eyes, or their disgusted sneers anymore. Being near with Derek created a protective, relaxing barrier around me.

After school, I approached Derek's car to see Ethan and him leaning against Derek's deluxe vehicle, talking in low voices.

They both smiled at me as a greeting, and in addition, they pecked my cheeks like always.

"Can you please stop doing that in public?" I hissed one time, my cheeks heating up intensely.

The boys shrugged, smugly smirking.

"We like embarrassing you," said my brother.

"It's cute when you blush," Derek added.

Mom welcomed Derek into our home with open arms, giving Derek a tight cuddle and kissing his forehead in a motherly way. Sometimes, when Mom was at work during the night, Derek offered to babysit Rosie with the help of my brother and me. Other times, when Mom was having a day off, Derek and Ethan played videogames in the living room while I sat diagonally on the couch, reading a book or watching YouTube videos.

The next day, I was walking down the corridors with Derek, Jackson, Sophia, Theo, Natalia, and Jasmine. We're really close now.

Ever since I discovered Derek's true feelings for me, I blush uncontrollably whenever I see or talk to him.

"I'm fine," I muttered for the tenth time when he asked me if I'm OK because I was blushing furiously.

"You don't look fine." Derek's hand caressed my smooth beet red cheeks. "You're turning red."

Sophia, Jackson and Natalia walked ahead, not bothered by our pause, as Theo and Jasmine kindly stayed closer to us, eavesdropping our conversation.

"Because of the heat," I responded naively.

Jasmine raised an eyebrow in scepticism at my idiotic response.

Derek echoed Jasmine's scepticism. "Angel, it's cold."

"It's always hot inside."

"The school doesn't even put the heaters on!" He cupped my face tightly, puzzled at my flushed cheeks. "Are you sure you're okay? Every day you're a tomato and it's making me worried about you. Is your temperature high? Are you ill?" His knuckles stroked my forehead, feeling the temperature. "You are slightly hot. Maybe I should take you home…"

"Derek." I softly held his hands, tugging them off my face. "I'm fine. Don't worry."

He interlaced our fingers together. "I always worry about you."

Jasmine and Theo decided to leave us alone with smug smiles.

"You shouldn't," I said. "Relax. I'm just hot…"

"Don't lie to me."

"I'm not!"

He widened his eyes, reading my expression. "Are you sure you're okay?"

"Yes!"

In English, the teacher explained to us about this story written by…I don't even know. I wasn't paying attention. My eyes were heavy with drowsiness. Derek detected my exhaustion because he tenderly pushed my head onto his left shoulder. I didn't object to his movements. I allowed myself to at least be in this position for a few minutes.

His hand suddenly dived under the table and touches my clothed left thigh.

My head shot up straight away, and I smacked his hand. He sniggered.

"Idiot," I hissed, a light-hearted smile on my face.

"Midget," he hissed back.

"Jerk."

"Bitch."

"Asshole."

"Pussy."

"Banana head."

"Kitten."

"Shit head."

"My miracle."

"My nightmare."

"My angel."

"My bad boy."

He raised his eyebrows at my choice of words, taken aback. I nibbled on my lower lip. My cheeks heated.

I shouldn't have said that.

I cringed.

Me and my big damn mouth.

Derek simpered smugly. "My baby girl," he murmured, his husky voice profound with love. His eager eyes glanced at my mouth.

"Mister Matthews and Miss Levesque," the English teacher snapped, causing us both to look at him. He placed his hands on his hips. "Do not make out in my room, thank you very much. You can do that in your free time."

My cheeks reddened. Ugh. I NEED lessons to stop blushing! "We-we're not dating," I stammered, mortified.

His lips shuddered. "Then why were you flirting?"

"We weren't flirting!"

His eyebrows heaved. "Do I have to move you two?"

"No!" Derek and I objected in unison. The whole class sniggered at our childish hostility. The teacher was, obviously, entertained.

"No more kissing," the teacher ordered with a hint of glee. "Or else, I will give you detention."

*   *   *

Walking along the hallway, I heard the tales about me. People called me atrocious words. Some agreed that Mike was only in the Canadian Armed Forces to get away from me. Some agreed Mike died in Syria because he hated me and was revolted for having an ugly sister.

Despondency clouded my perception. I lowered my head, my thick hair concealing my face from everyone. Vindictive, sardonic, painful laughter deafened my ears.

Everything reminded me of the abominable days of torture.

The bullying started when I was ten. People hurt me emotionally. They spat insults at me, telling me that I'm an ugly bitch; saying that I don't deserve to live; convincing me that I should be thinking about something more necessary like killing myself; saying that I deserve to be in Hell with the Devil.

Eventually, the bullying turned into physical torture. The school bullied me with words, but two people always grabbed my hair; pushed me into the lockers; kicked me; punched me; slapped me hard enough to leave a scar or a bruise on my cheek. That's why I always wore too much makeup: to conceal the marks. And that's why people called me ugly, because of the makeup. I wasn't really good at make-up; they had a reason to laugh at me.

The dreadful problem was that nobody knew the bullying lowered my self-esteem and gave me manipulative, negative, immoral theories.

I wanted to tell someone.

I couldn't.

I felt as if no one would believe me.

Whenever I see a teacher or an adult, I would go near them and open my mouth to tell them the horrible treatment I got in school, yet it felt as if a dark invisible, domineering spirit wrenches me back, stopping me from confessing.

Nobody knew.

It hurts to keep this dark secret.

It forms a shallow hole in my chest.

"Where do you think you're going?" a boy called Owen taunted spitefully one day.

I closed my eyes in trepidation. Ethan has detention and I was waiting for him. I texted Mike about the simple issue, and he told me that he'll come when the detention is finished.

The hallway was noiseless. No one was here except for the two bullies and me. I heard evil chuckles next to my ear.

I gulped. Unhurriedly, my fretful eyes looked up to find the bullies staring at me.

"D-don't hurt me!" I pleaded, horrified.

"Aw, but why?" Brigit asked in an acerbic, sweet tone. "Scared?"

"I-I will run to my brother!" I threatened.

Owen snorted. "The little shithead?" He laughed gravely. "Please. He can't even pick up a log, let alone a stick."

"He's stronger than you think! He will beat you!" It's true. Ethan was just like Mike—he may look young, but he was terrifying once you get on his nerves. He's strong for a reason, and that reason is to protect his loved ones from anything.

"Okay, then," Owen mused. "Run."

I twirled around and hastened away from ~~them~~ them. In an instant, Brigit seized my arm violently. Her grip was so tight that I whimpered, panicked.

"P-please!" I begged, the tears trickling down my cheeks. "Leave me alone!"

"Are you going to cry like a baby?" Brigit's eyes saddened with phony sympathy. "Are you going to run to your mama and papa and tell

them about us? Nah, we need to give you the best shit first. Happy Birthday, April."

I thrashed in my ex-best friend's grip. Owen smirked pitilessly and his balled fist pummelled my stomach.

"Ethan!" I cried out, hoping he could hear me. His detention classroom was upstairs. "Someone help me!" My screams wobbled with pain. "Mike! Mom! Dad! Derek…"

Brigit pressed her palm to my mouth, muffling my shrieks. Owen continually struck my stomach. My lungs constricted and scorched. Gasps didn't come out. In fact, I couldn't breathe properly. Brigit was squeezing my nose, restricting air flow. My fingers clawed at her hands, endeavouring to wrench them off me for divine air.

Owen kicked me into the wall. Brigit grabbed a fistful of my hair. My scalp stung. She tossed me around as if I was a bag of dirt. My legs and arms scraped against the floor and I snivelled, knowing that I have wounds on my legs and arms. I can feel the blood oozing down my skin.

Brigit thumped my stomach. I groaned. A bittersweet liquid puddled in my mouth. Dark spots danced across my vision…

"April!" a voice bellowed.

I cried in relief as footsteps thudded toward us. Brigit and Owen froze. They glanced in the direction of the thunderous footsteps. I can feel the resentment vibrating from the person.

Slowly, I turned my head to the other side. My vision fuzzed, but I can see him clearly. I know it's him.

Mike thundered to Brigit and Owen, his body quivering with fury at the sight of my injured body. Behind him, another figure came into my line of vision: − Ethan. His forehead was creased with concern as he stared at me. But when he looked at Owen and Brigit, his figure was identical to Mike: shaking with rage, shoulders stiff, the muscles in his jawline tight.

Owen and Brigit attempted to sprint away. Mike grabbed them before they could and slammed them up against the wall.

"You little pieces of shit," Mike growled.

Owen and Brigit whimpered in panic.

"You dare hurt my sister?" he demanded, vehemence infiltrating his voice.

His feet cuffed their shins, and they both bawled in pain.

"Brigit, I'm disappointed in you. You were such a sweet girl. A great friend to April. Now, you're nothing but a…a ruthless individual, following the footsteps of this…this cold-hearted boy." He glowered at Owen. "I told both of you to stay away from April, or else you the pain you gave to April will now go to you. Yet, you are still idiotic enough to not listen."

Ethan crouched in front of me. "Sis?" His eyebrows knitted together in alarm. "Are you okay?" He pulled my body up and wrapped his arms around me protectively.

I shook my head, hiding my face into his chest, my pained tears soaked his shirt.

"You dare hurt my sister?" Mike repeated, his voice loud. Brigit and Owen flinched, cowering backwards.

They didn't answer, which seemed to provoke Mike.

Mike took intimidating steps forward. "You know what: I'll beat the shit out of you. I don't care if I go to jail. No one hurts the people I love. No one hurts my parents. My brother. And no one hurts my baby sister. Got it?" The kids were too frightened to counter. "No. One. Hurts. MY SISTER!"

Brigit broke into a sprint. Mike grabbed before she could move any further, hauling her back. She screamed as Mike bent her arm behind her. Owen tried to punch Mike, but Mike seized Owen's wrist before he could. Mike took martial arts classes which explained the sleek and impressive reflexes he had.

My face still buried in my younger brother, I slowly turned to Mike's direction. "Mike…"

"Don't you ever think that you can continue to hurt my little sister," my older brother presaged. "You're both screwed. Go and tell everyone that."

He let them go. They dropped to the floor. They scurried away, and soon enough, they disappeared.

"Are you going to let them go just like that?" Ethan grumbled, his arms still caging me.

"No."

My older brother crouched in front of me, his face level with mine. He saw my tears and immediately yanked me into a heartwarming, loving hug.

"Shh, Little Sis," he whispered into my ear. "It's okay. I'm here. It's okay."

My arms tightened around my older brother, my sobs muting into his chest, my tears moistening his shirt. Mike fondled with my hair.

"April, since Dad is back, I need to tell him everything," he said softly. "Okay? No more secrets. It's not fair."

"Wait…" Ethan was confused. "How long has this been going on?"

"A few weeks," Mike answered.

"Weeks?!" my younger brother exclaimed. He looked at me. "And you never told me? I could've helped you, April! I could've beat the shit out them!"

"Ethan, don't shout at her. It's hard for victims of bullying to tell anyone. Don't blame her."

"I'm not. I just wished I knew about this…I could've helped."

"I know, Ethan, I know. C'mon, let's go home."

Mike carried me to his jeep. Ethan hauled the door open and Mike placed me in the back, pulling the belt to secure me. He wiped the tears from my cheeks. "Don't worry. Everything will be fine." He kissed my forehead.

"Should we take her to the hospital?" Ethan suggested. "She got bruises all over her body."

"I'll heal her, don't worry."

"Can we get McDonald's?" I asked quietly.

Mike peeped at me through the rearview mirror with raised eyebrows. "Two kids just hurt you, you're in bad shape, and you're asking for McDonald's?"

I shrugged. "I'm hungry."

Mike's laughter brightened the atmosphere immediately. "Oh, April." He shook his head, smiling. "Even in serious situations, you can be naive sometimes. But we can go. My stomach rumbled and Luke thought I farted."

Ethan snorted. "Usually, when I'm hungry, I burp."

Mike frowned at Ethan. "What?"

Ethan shook his shoulders. "I'm weird, Mike."

"You don't have to say that twice," Mike agreed. I giggled in the back, causing Mike to enlarge his smile. "There's your beautiful laugh, Little Sis."

I smiled back at him. My brother made me smile in the most horrendous moments. This was why I love him. He's just simply amazing and I just couldn't imagine my life without him...

*   *   *

A subdued sob escaped my throat. I slammed my mouth shut to prevent more from erupting. I wiped my eyes swiftly and walked faster, ignoring every single person in the school corridor.

I pushed the door to the girls' bathroom open, and it swung close loudly. I strode into a stall and sat down on the commode, hearing the door opening and swinging shut. I heard a group of girls coming inside, laughing and snickering.

"She's so ugly," a familiar voice gossiped with resentment and envy. Tiffany. "April, I mean."

"She's so weird, too," another familiar voice groused. Brigit. "No wonder everyone hates her. I can't believe she's part of the popular clique now. Like, what do they see in her?"

"Maybe they're using her?"

"That is a high possibility. What about Derek? He's been so fond of her lately…There are rumours of him flirting with April in English this morning…"

"He's using her. He's a player, you know."

"He changed. Apparently."

"Or not. He may be faking it. You know how he can be like."

"I hate that bitch so much. Why can't she just kill herself already?"

The school bell rang. I heard their footsteps shuffle out of the door. A minute later, I heard silence. Just silence. I opened the door and went back outside to stare at myself in the mirror.

My eyes were puffy and brimmed with redness. My lips were trembling and quivering downwards as tears continued to come out, hot and uncontrollable, full of depression, and draining the happiness out of me.

The bullying stopped once Mike told Brigit and Owen to leave me alone. Everyone heard about Mike defending me and decided wisely to stay away from me because they knew what Mike was capable of. Mike told Mom and Dad about what was happening—the bullying, the beating, and the torture. Mom began crying, begging me why I didn't tell her and Dad sooner. I cried too. I cried because of guilt. I hated seeing Mom crying. I hated it. Dad was angry, not at me, but at my school. He went to the headmaster and gave him one damn of a lecture. The headmaster was fired, and Dad had the help of the authorities to deal with the bullies.

I had a temporary period of blissfulness until it suddenly ended when Dad returned to his soldier duties. And when Mike joined the Army. Some students in Peony Hallows High took this opportunity to ignore me again.

I didn't know why, though.

Why were they so bent on making me feel so wretched?

What did I do to them?

I wanted to tell someone. I desperately wanted to.

But I can't.

It's like my shadow was yanking me back to prevent me from telling the truth.

Only a few people in the world will understand me.

I was scared that if I confess about the abuse in school, my life will go downhill. I didn't know why I can't just confess. I was just too weak, emotionally and physically.

"Why did you leave me?!" I screamed, banging my hands on the white sink, the tears dropping from my eyes. "Mike, why did you leave me?"

I looked at my reflection in the mirror. Brigit's words echoed in my mind: *Why can't she kill herself already?*

My hands still clutching the white sink tightly, my fingers still quaking frenziedly, more tears escaped my stinging, smouldering, desolate eyes. I seized fistful of my hair and wrenched them hard. My scalp throbbed and stung with soreness. I paced back and forth, insufflating unfathomable, profound, pained breaths, trying so hard to calm my nerves. My heart beat loudly and remorselessly. My vision blurred. My mind roared with manipulative, negative, immoral thoughts.

I sank to my knees, not caring about the dirty bathroom floor. My wails reverberated.

I didn't know how long I've been in the bathroom, but I could tell that I've wasted a lot of time panicking. Clouds covered the sky, and the howling wind banged the windows unkindly. My lungs were aching. I felt as if a million knives were stabbing me again and again and again until I was numb.

I closed my eyes. I remembered everyone's ruthless words that isolated me for years. Their words ricocheted in my mind.

I had enough.

I had enough of everything.

I had enough of life.

What's the point of me being here anyway?

I spent so many years convincing myself that I will get better, that my life will get better, but now I'm realising that I'm not better and never will be.

I'm tired of telling everyone I'm fine. I'm tired of feeling so lonely sometimes. I'm tired of hating myself. I'm tired of the bullying. I'm tired of everything.

I can't take it anymore.

I slammed my hand into the mirror, hearing it crack, and I hissed as my knuckles burned with pain. I slammed my fists into the glass again and again until it's cracked enough to shatter into shards, all big and small. I grabbed a large piece of broken glass from the floor and clutched it tightly, feeling the sharpness of the object ripping the skin of my palm.

I brought it to my arms and began cutting. I scraped my skin, gashing it open. The blood leached out of the fresh blistering wounds, dribbling down my arms and leaking from my fingers. Tear-shaped drops splattered the filthy floor. My tender arms implored me to stop as they stung spitefully.

I looked up at the ceiling, another tear running down the side of my face.

"Mike," I wailed, "God, Jesus, angels…give me one damn reason why I shouldn't kill myself! Because I can't see it. Mike, I promised you that I won't leave, but I cannot handle it anymore. I cannot handle the pain. It's unbearable. Please, give me a reason why I shouldn't kill myself…"

I raised the glass piece, ready to leave this world, and—

The door banged open.

"APRIL!" It's Derek, jogging to me with a look of concern and apprehension in his eyes. He froze, gobsmacked.

"Oh, my God." His words tumbled out in a pained tendency, each word vibrated with disbelief and anguish. He saw the blood soaking the white floor, pooling around my feet. His eyes met mine. More melancholy filled those mesmerizing, enchanting, ocean blue irises of his. "Theo, call the ambulance!"

"What? Why— oh, shit." Theo was behind Derek, looking shocked. He took in the sight before him: me standing in a puddle of my own blood, my eyelids drowsy, my lips parted, my weakened breaths. "Oh, April." He was appalled and sad.

Derek clutched my wrist and gently took the glass piece out of my grasp.

"Guys! Is she here?" Jasmine stormed inside. In the next second, her eyes widened like Theo's, and she slammed her hands over her mouth as her eyes observed the blood emerging out of my fresh scars.

And she screamed.

She screamed and sobbed as Theo called the emergency services, raking a shaky hand through his hair. Jasmine collapsed to the floor, tears rolling down her cheeks.

My eyesight blurred. I feel light-headed. My whole body was numb. Derek enclosed his warm, muscled arms around me before I could hit the floor, swinging me up into his arms. Theo told him that the ambulance was nearly there, and that Derek should take me outside.

That's when I started protesting. I fought to get free from Derek's grip around me, yelling: "No, let me go! Please, let me die!" I cried as Derek ran out of the bathroom. "I don't want to live. Everyone hates me, Derek. I want to die. Please. Let me give up."

I kept repeating the same words. I punched Derek, kicked him, slapped him, did anything that would free me from his hold. When I felt something sweltering dropping onto my forehead, I glimpsed up to see wet lines on both of his cheeks. His eyes were glossy and poignant. My head was pressed into his chest; I could hear his heart beating with misfortune.

He's hurt.

He's crying.

I heard sirens in the distance. By the time Derek kicked the main doors open and sprinted into the front yard of the school building, I caught a hazy glimpse of the ambulance. Paramedics rushed out of the vehicle, pulling out a stretcher.

"Come on, hurry!" A paramedic shouted.

I felt so cold. The beating of my heart was weakening as if my last breath will escape me at any moment. My eyes started to close, and I wished to leave the world.

Derek lowered me into the stretcher, and the paramedics hastily pushed me inside.

"I'm coming with her," Derek confirmed.

A man swerved around to him to object. "Sir—"

"I'm coming with her," Derek snapped, "whether you like it or not. I am never going to leave her side."

With that, Derek leaped inside the vehicle before the man could rationalize. I felt the ambulance move and charge into the road, the siren wailing raucously. I whimpered and cried incessantly as the paramedics inspected my scars.

Derek was sitting close to me, clutching my right hand tightly and anxiously, as if he's frightened to let me go. His fingers were interlaced with mine, his eyes never abandoning my face.

I was getting drowsy, and I concentrated on not going to sleep because of him. Because of how shiny his red cheeks were due to tears. Guilt hit me as another tear ooze from the corner of his left eye.

I cannot control the drowsiness anymore. I let slumber take control of me, to take me away from this world. But not before I heard his words:

"Why did you do that, angel? Baby, why? I don't want you to leave me forever like how my parents did. Don't you know I need you in my life?"

Chapter Twenty-Six

Stay With Me

Derek Matthews

I looked curiously through the window of April's hospital room. The sheets were pulled over her body, although both of her arms were exposed.

Bandages.

That's what I saw.

Bandages.

Bandages concealed her new scars; all of them white with smudges of redness.

Other than her new scars, I can see other ones. They were dark, old, and mending—the cuts that she done after Mike's death.

I don't blame April for harming herself.

Mike was a great person.

Everyone loved him.

He was so sweet and understanding.

He was flawless.

Losing Mike…it's like you lost a part of your heart.

Because of Mike's death, I also tried to take my own life. But then I thought, *Hang on, will Mike like that? Will he like it if I killed myself because he left? No. He won't. He will want me to live my life to its fullest, no matter how hard life can be.*

I've been inside the hospital for a couple of days. Those days were angst-ridden. And still is. Until April wakes up, that's when I can calm my nerves and my fretful heart.

I don't blame April for taking her life without thinking clearly. Judging how wicked the world is today, people would take their own life without having second thoughts. Our minds…our minds are full of voices—negative voices that we cannot control; negative voices that manipulate us, isolate us, provide us with false information.

For people who are depressed, we have to battle that negative voice every single, freaking day.

The heart rate monitor beside her was beeping, lines spiking up and sinking back down, up and down, up and down, up and down. Jasmine, Jackson, Theo, Natalia, and Sophia were here with me along with April's mother, Rosie, and Ethan. April's mother finally contacted April's father. She's standing in the corner of the hallway, sobbing into the phone, explaining what happened.

Three police officers were here too, only for a small conference. They asked us what happened to April. I told them the truth: I found April in the girls' bathroom, holding a shard of glass from the shattered mirror, and cutting the skin of her arms.

"Do you have any idea why she would do that?" An officer asked us.

I exchanged a look with the others. "Yes," I responded.

"The students in our school were bullying April," Jackson said next. "I don't know for how long, but I can tell it was for a long time."

"The bullying caused April to spiral into depression and have suicidal thoughts," Jasmine murmured. "So, she harmed herself. She thought that cutting herself will take away the pain and the sadness."

"How long has she been doing this?" the policewoman asked.

"Three years until I found out and told her to stop," I countered before my friends could. "But then she must've started doing it again."

"Is it just the bullying?" the redhead officer asked.

"She had an older brother," Theo joined in. "Mike Levesque."

All three cops looked wounded with wretchedness.

"Ah, the good lad who unfortunately died," one of them mumbled, managing a weak smile. "I knew him. He was a nice kid."

"April told me that when Mike died," said Jasmine, "she wanted to die because she loved Mike so much. Their relationship was so strong. Now, ever since she lost him, she's completely broken. Mike always defended April from the bullies. Since Mike is gone, she's trying to stand up for herself, but I know that she could break down any second even if she tried to."

"We'll talk to the girl when she wakes up," the policewoman told the two men. "And then we'll check up on the bullies."

"What are you going to do with the bullies?"

"That's for us to decide," the redhead countered. "For now, I want you kids to keep an eye on your pretty friend. Make sure she doesn't repeat the same mistakes. Guard her against all the hatred."

We all nodded, and they strolled away, discussing to one another in hushed tones.

I could hear Mia speaking to her husband. Hence, I looked in her direction and listened to what she's saying:

"She was bullied, Julian. And those bullies caused her to have suicidal thoughts…No, dear, we can't move towns. Even though she had horrible experiences in this place, I know she doesn't want to leave because there's someone here she cares about… Julian, she needs you now. You have to come back…Yeah, the doctors said that she's perfectly fine, but her body is poor and too weak from the amount of blood loss, it will take her time to recover…Three days, Julian. She's been in the hospital for three days…"

"I just don't understand why she did that," Jasmine whispered next to me, catching my attention. "Why would she try to take her own life? I know she's having a hard time, but doesn't she know that she has us by her side?"

"Depression isolates you slowly," I mumbled to her. "It's like another voice living in your head – it only tells you the negative things and tries to push away the positivity in your body. Depression makes you feel alone and worthless and makes you think that there's no purpose for you to live. It's hard to fight it."

"Do you have it?" Jasmine asked.

I nodded.

"How do you fight it?"

"I thought about what Mike said: to reach the light and the rainbow, you have to go through some tough storms. I'm fighting depression for my friends, for my family, because I feel if I did anything permanent, anything inevitable, then it will bring some pretty nasty stuff into their lives. I'm fighting depression for April because she's my best friend. I love her. We both share the same pain and…Hopefully, we can help each other. It's better to be with someone who understands you, to be honest."

"Is it going away?" She sounded concerned. "The depression, I mean?"

"Usually, it takes time. For me...it's going away *slowly*."

Jasmine smiled, contented with my answer.

"When April wakes up," I heard Theo speak in a serious tone next to me, "we're all going to make her feel safe and then we're going back to that school and give everyone shit."

*   *   *

Word travelled fast in Peony Hallows about April Levesque's suicide attempt. I heard that all the students in the school were culpable, and some even cried. They regretted making April feel so worthless. When I heard this from Jackson, his teeth were clenched firmly and so were mine. Good. Good that the students felt guilty. They deserved it. They nearly took away the only person I need.

Ethan was gazing through the window, engrossed to the slumbering April, his arms crossed over his chest. I approached him and patted his back. He didn't glimpse at me. However, I caught the sight of tears on his cheek.

"I promised Mike that I'd take care of her," he murmured, wiping his eyes. "And I did. I tried so hard. Now I failed."

"You didn't," I protested. "You're a great brother to her."

"And yet, I didn't even know about her bullying life," he muttered.

"She thought no one would understand, Ethan. She thought things wouldn't work out right if she confesses. To be honest, you can't even describe how you feel. One minute you feel sad, the next you feel empty and shallow. There are a lot of people out there with depression who open up about being bullied to adults."

"I'm guessing you were the same?"

"Yeah."

"And how are you doing now? Do you still have your depression?"

"Yeah, depression doesn't go away quickly. It takes time. Mike knew about it, so he helped me. When he died, everything went downhill. I have my friends and my family. I never realised their love for me. Now, I do. And I'm very grateful for that.

"For April, though…I did my best to help her. She's not really a person who can let go of the past. I guess people like her cannot escape the darkness of the mind."

Ethan finally looked at me. He seemed to be remorseful. "I shouldn't have underestimated you, Derek. I'm sorry. Maybe you can be the man for April. All you need is my father to like you."

"He likes me. Everyone loves me, Ethan."

He chuckled. "Well, this is my father we're talking about. Besides, you only met him a few times in the year…once or twice. You don't know him like how I do."

"How is your dad like?"

He narrowed his eyes in thought. "Funny," he answered. "Mischievous, playful, romantic, loving, caring, overprotective, dirty-minded…"

"Dirty-minded?"

Ethan snickered. "Very. Don't take that in an uncomfortable way, though. I meant it in a funny way."

"So, he's like the typical teenager type?"

"Yeah, I guess you can describe him in that way."

"Is he coming back? You know, because of April's attempt?"

"Hopefully, he will."

* * *

My friends demurred when the staff instructed them to go home. Mia went home with Ethan unwillingly. I, on the other hand, refused like a naive child and managed to stay in the hospital for three more hours.

I looked at the clock. One hour left until midnight. Luke texted me, asking me where I am. I told him that I'm in the hospital.

Don't be late, was all he said.

Sitting in the chair for long hours caused me to become lethargic. Here and then, my head dropped as my eyes reluctantly closed. A few nurses eyed me suspiciously, wondering why I am still here.

It was only ten minutes past midnight when the doctor (who inspected April) approached me and said, "Sir, you should go home and rest."

"How many times do I have to tell everyone?" I grumbled, stifling a yawn. "I will *not* go away until she's awake."

"Sir, you are tired," the doctor remonstrated. "I could tell by the *very* dark circles under your eyes. April Levesque is special to you, I know, but you should at least get some sleep. Come back tomorrow. She's going to be okay."

I deliberated his words temporarily. "Am I allowed to see her?"

* * *

I silently and carefully pushed the door closed behind me. The odour of medicines and chemicals harassed my nostrils.

I slowly spun around. April was sleeping peacefully, the heart rate monitor detecting her heartbeats as she inhales and exhales.

I brought her hand to my lips. I kissed each fingertip and then interlaced our hands together.

Witnessing her like this — vulnerable and wounded — it stung my heart with grief. The sight was ghastly. Luckily, she's getting better—her skin was normal, and her lips weren't plump blue like before.

"Why did you do that, April?" I whispered. "Why did you try to leave me? Don't you know you're my miracle? Don't you know you're my angel from God? Don't you know I need you?"

I lowered my head. "Don't you know I love you?" My lips stroked hers as I murmured those words.

I blew the hair out of her face. "Don't ever leave me. Don't be like my dad and leave me without any thought. Stay with me."

Chapter Twenty-Seven

You Make Me Feel Wanted

April Levesque

My eyes adjusted to the white light above me, stinging for a second. I perceived blurry figures hovering above me. Just as my vision finally cleared, the nurses smiled compassionately.

"Welcome back, Miss Levesque." A woman with a stethoscope greeted me. Lines appeared at the corners of her eyes as she beamed benevolently. "We've been waiting for a long time for you to recover. How are you?"

I scrutinized my surroundings. A hospital room. I'm in a hospital room. White floor. White walls. Few cabinets. A blue curtain concealing the casement. I scrutinized my body. My skin is dry and vaguely pale. Plasters — new and old, white and red — covered my wounds.

"What…happened?" My voice was hoarse.

The woman ~~enlightened~~ explained everything: a young man found me in the bathroom (Derek, I assumed) along with two other kids. They witnessed my arms, blemished with bloody scars; my blood oozing to the floor and pooling around me as I gripped a large, glass piece. My suicide attempt. My first suicide attempt.

"Your body lost a huge amount of blood," the doctor appended as the nurses removed the old bandages from my arms and legs, replacing them with new ones. "Your body was weak. Not only did you cut the skin of your arms, but you also cut your legs. It took you a couple of days to recover from the incident."

A lone tear seeped out from my left eye and trekked. The curtain exposed a small part of the casement, and I saw my friends and family—Theo, Jackson, Natalia, Sophia, and Jasmine, sitting on the chairs next to Mom who's cradling Rosie; standing right behind the casement was my one-year-younger brother, Ethan. Their eyes were wide and bloodshot, holding apprehension and angst, as if they had difficulty sleeping. I can feel the severe stress weighing on their shoulders—and it made my heart bawl and ache to see them like this. Guilt consumed me. I shouldn't have tried to take my own life. I shouldn't have. I was so clueless, so stubborn.

I realised that someone wasn't there: Derek.

"The police organized a conference with you once you wake up."

My attention returned to the woman. "A conference? What for?"

"About the bullying you experienced and your depression. Your friends told them a few things, but the police prefer if they hear everything from you so they can conclude their investigation."

"Oh, okay. Will I have therapy?'"

"Well, the thing is, the hospital staff and I recommend you to take therapy because it'll be good for you. However, you don't have to do it. You can give therapy a try. If it doesn't appeal to you, then just end it."

"Thank you."

The woman smiled. "Any time, dear."

The doctor allowed my family and friends to come in. Jasmine dashed inside and threw her arms around my shoulders, jerking me into her chest as she cried tears of joy. My hands pressed on the back of her shoulder blades. I closed my eyes tightly and cried into her neck, mumbling that I was sorry for doing something so unintelligent, something so egotistical.

"You scared the crap out of us!" Theo said brusquely.

"You could've told us about everything!" Jackson reprimanded next. "You know we will help you!"

"I'm sorry!" I bleated, disappointed.

Their eyes saddened when they sensed the despondency penetrating my voice.

"Don't say sorry." Theo hugged me tightly. "Just don't do it again. As Jackson said, we will help you through everything. That's what friends are for, right?"

I smiled against his shoulder. "Thanks, Theo."

"Why didn't you tell us, though?" Jackson asked despairingly, embracing me next. "You should've told us about your depression. We could've helped you."

"I found it hard to explain, Jackson. Explain about everything. It's hard for me to describe my depression; it's indescribable. I thought no one would understand. I thought people would call me an attention seeker."

"Attention seeker? Why would we think that?"

"Because whenever the public hears about self-harm from a person, they mostly think it's for attention. That's one of the reasons why I didn't want to tell."

"April, whenever you are tempted to cut yourself, tell us and we'll help," Theo solicited. "There are alternatives to self-harm: you can wear a rubber band and smack it against your skin, hold an ice cube for a long time, scream, cry, etc."

"I tried them. Didn't work."

"We'll find something else that is *less* harmful and *more* useful. For the sake of your health."

I smiled. "Thanks, Theo. Thanks, Jacks."

Jackson ruffled my hair. "We're glad you're okay now, midget. Don't make me cry again. Please. I cried nonstop. That deserves a world record, to be honest."

"I won't."

"You can tell us anything, okay?" he added.

"Yeah, I know."

"Pinky promise?" He wiggled his little finger.

I giggled. "Pinky promise." Our pinkies curled around each other's. "Anyway, where's Derek?"

"He's coming," replied Theo. "We told him you're awake. He'll be here soon."

"He had a hard time sleeping more than us," Jackson acquainted. "He never left your side, April. He cares about you a lot."

Natalia, Sophia, Jasmine and I shared a few tears. I embraced Rosie, Mom and Ethan.

"Sweetheart," Mom said in a hushed, insecure tone, "why did you do that?"

My eyelashes were still damp and bulky with sweltering tears. Hearing Mom's word and hearing the despair in her voice, more water stroked them. "I-I'm sorry, Mom. I'm so sorry."

She hugged me again. "Don't say sorry. It's not your fault. Please don't do that again. If anything bad is happening, you can always tell me—you know that, right?"

It's not that easy, I wanted to say. *I can't tell people everything because they won't understand. They'll either get confused or judge you, laugh at you or roll their eyes at you. I did it because everything hurts, because the words hurt, and I cannot hold this pain inside me anymore. I want it to leave me, so I made it leave. Cutting myself may not be the best answer, but what's the point of not doing so? Nobody realises how much words can impact someone. Nobody realises how severe depression is.*

Don't tell me to get over it. Because it's difficult. Can't people see that?

I kept my mouth shut and just nodded.

Ever since Brigit left me for Owen, changed for Owen, I always acted like everything was fine when in reality, it's not. Mike's death stabbed me harder than a damn knife. He was the only one who understood me—who understood that people with mental illnesses shouldn't be judged; that we aren't crazy and insane; that we deserve help; that we deserve sweet, candid words and heartwarming hugs every day.

But that's how people treat us. No matter what we do, that's how people will always treat us.

They will always judge.

They will always tell someone to kill themselves carelessly.

My family and friends told me that I have them, but it's funny about the fact that I still feel lonely.

Mom left with Rosie. Ethan walked in.

His dark hair was messy. His eyes were swollen, red, and drowsy with dark circles under. He leaned forward and bound his brawny arms around my fragile body, squeezing me as if he's frightened to let me go.

"I love you," I spoke before he could. "I love you, Ethan. Don't ever say that you're a horrible brother because you're a great brother. I know we haven't been talking properly ever since Mike died, but I always knew that you're always there by my side. I always knew I could count on you. I'm sorry."

"I feel as if this is my entire fault," he muttered, his chin resting on my head. "If I knew what's been happening, then I could've taken care of it, and you won't be in the hospital today."

"It's not your fault. It's mine."

"No. It's not your fault. You were in a depressed state. No one should blame you for that. I won't say that you could've told me what's been happening, because I know you get that a lot, but I promise to help you heal your depression.

"And I thought the bullying ended?"

"It did. For a while. It started again after Mike died."

"Oh."

Mom strode inside with her phone. "April, it's your father—he wants to talk to you."

Ethan and Mom left the room. I pressed the phone to my ear. "Dad?"

The phone resonated his relieved sigh. "*Hi, my darling. Are you okay?*"

"Y-yeah. I'm fine. What about you?"

"*I'm fine too.*"

"Dad, I'm so—"

"*Shhh. It's fine, April, it's fine.*" I heard him heave another sigh. "*Your mother and I have been discussing something...*" he explained. "*We were considering — well, I was considering — if you wanted to move towns.*"

"W-what?"

"*I presume it's best if you move towns, sweetheart. After what I heard about your school, I don't trust that place anymore. However, I won't force you to move. I'm giving you a choice. I thought about moving to England and living there forever. It's pretty safe. So, are you up for it?*"

My entire body felt numb.

Should I move?

My eyes wandered around the room, as if trying to find the answers written on the white walls. They landed on my great friends — Jasmine, Jackson, Theo, Natalia, and Sophia — who were all wrapped up in each other's arms, staring at me with affection. Jasmine smiled. Theo did that self-confident wink of his. I grinned. They are the friends I've been praying for—the friends I've been desperate to have. If I move to another place, I'll be the new girl, and it'll be hard for me to build new bonds and relationships.

My mind ghosted to Derek.

I don't want to leave him.

I reminisced to when I was in the ambulance with Derek sitting near me, holding my hand in his. He told me: *I don't want you to leave me forever like how my parents did. Don't you know I need you in my life?*

He needs me in his life. I need him in my life.

"No, Dad," I finally answered. "I don't want to move. I found great friends here."

"*Your mother said the same thing. She also said that there's someone else you care about. Is this a guy?*"

I bit my lip. "Maybe…"

"*April, you're sixteen—*"

"Turning seventeen."

"*Don't you know boys are dumb?*" he snapped.

I sighed. "Dad, this boy is different."

"*Who is he?*"

"Derek…"

"*Matthews?*"

"Uh, yeah…"

"*Are you crazy?!*"

"Dad, Derek isn't that bad. You know Derek and Mike were close. You know Derek loved Mike just as much as I do. I know that you love Derek too. Don't you remember the times when you both played football together? When you taught him basketball?"

"I've heard stuff about him. He changed. He changed badly. He uses girls. I don't want him to use you."

"He changed again, Dad, for the better. He's the Derek you and I love. The happy one. And I know he won't use me. We're closer. We're friends. Best friends..."

"I don't care! He is a bad influence for you—"

"Funny. Mom said he's a good influence over me."

"—and he cannot be trusted!"

"When you come back, you will meet him properly, and you will realise that you've misunderstood him. On the outside, people see him as a rude person. But once you know him, you'll realise that he's soft and breaking inside. Dad, he's nice, arrogant, funny, sweet, and mischievous, and sometimes is a dick like you."

"Did you just call me a dick?" Dad grumbled.

"Well, Mom calls you a dick—"

"She what?"

"—so, I guess I can."

"What else did Mia say about me while I was gone?"

"Oh, I don't know...Stuff...Funny stuff...Gross stuff...Stuff." Mom and Dad always had a witty relationship – constantly squabbling tediously with a bit of humour, or sometimes they would express their love for each other around Mike, Ethan and I just to frustrate us. "Are you coming home soon?"

Dad sighed on the other end. *"Yeah. I'm coming home soon. Maybe in a month."*

"A month?" I echoed, all the optimism draining out of my body. "But what about Christmas? A Christmas without you is like living in the world without Stiles Stilinski, and much worse."

At this point, I could tell my father rolled his eyes at my choice of words. He knows I'm a mega fan of Teen Wolf. I remembered the good old days when he and I used to sit in front of the TV and watch the latest movies and TV shows while Mom scolded at us to go outside and have some fresh air.

"I'll try to find a way and come there as soon as possible. It's just that Syria is getting worse every day."

"What happened?"

"Stuff. Bombs. Death. Shooting. Injuries. And more death." Dad exhaled deeply. *"It's horrible, April. ISIS has no heart whatsoever. They don't even think before they do something. It's like they want to be in Hell."*

"Whoa, Dad, that's a bit too much..."

"It's not! They kill kids in front of the parents. The Muslims are suffering because of the torment, and I hate it. Muslims and other people shouldn't get killed. The fact that the world is calling ISIS Muslims angers me the most—Muslims are NOT terrorists. ISIS do NOT follow the Islamic religions and rules, they are rebelling against them. Trust me, I know.

"Before I joined the army, I had a best friend. He's a Muslim. And this guy in our class told my pal to kill himself because of his religion, his identity. I got so mad, I broke the guy's nose. Muslims are not terrorists. These people need to shut the up and realise that."

Never have I ever heard or witnessed my dad being so angry before.

He's true, though.

Muslims are not terrorists. Not all of them.

When we see Muslim in the streets, we shouldn't edge away from them or give them disgusted looks, we should smile at them, Mike told me once. *But no. Humankind is too dim-witted to do that. Why can't people realise that not all people are evil? You get good people and bad people. It's not that hard to comprehend.*

Knock. Knock. Knock.

A cluster of police officers was standing behind the door.

"Dad, I got to go now. The police are here."

"*Why?*"

"They want to question me about getting bullied."

"*Oh, okay. Take care, baby.*"

"Come home soon," was the last thing I said before I hung up.

The police saw my smile as they entered.

"Miss Levesque!" A man with a fluffy beard and prickly hawk-like nose beamed at me. "It's good to see you awake." Just like the other two authority figures, he sat on the chairs huddled around the room. "The doctor told you we're here to question you, right?"

"Yes."

"Good. Please answer the following questions honestly. We want to come up with a conclusion to our case."

They asked me as many questions as they could think of: when the bullying started; why was it caused; have I done anything to anyone to make them feel hatred towards me; who knew about the bullying before I told Derek and Jasmine; how did the depression occur; how did I survive atrocious years of violence and affliction. They paid attention to my answers very carefully and deliberately. I told them that Brigit Sanders and another boy called Owen Fall abused me the most. I told them that one day, when I was fourteen, Brigit used to have a knife in her bag and used it to cut my legs, not too deep, but thin enough to keep me anaesthetized. They asked me why I haven't reported about the bullying I experienced to an adult. I told them that it was hard for me to confess. I couldn't open up because I was terrified no one will believe me or understand how I feel.

"What are you going to do?" I asked them once the questionnaire was over.

They all exchanged contemplating glances.

"Arrest them."

My eyes widened. "You can do that?"

One of them raised an eyebrow at me. "Of course, we can. We're the police."

"But…wait, bullying is a crime?"

"Yes. Bullying is a crime. Even telling someone to kill yourself counts as a crime. Brigit Sanders harmed you. You are a victim. We're going to send Brigit Sanders to jail, and maybe that Owen Fall guy—wait, is he in town?"

"No. He moved."

"When we find him, we'll arrest him. We will also charge the school with heavy fines."

My eyes blurred with tears. "Thank you," I whispered. "So much."

A life without bullying…

Amazing.

It's another wish granted.

*   *   *

Jasmine, Natalia, and Sophia's arms wrapped around me devotedly as we ambled through the parking lot. Jackson was mumbling something into his phone, his eyes occasionally looking at me with a warm-hearted smile. Theo and Ethan exchanged a conversation. Strangers offered us curious looks; some were relieved to see me awake.

Guilt. That's what I felt. Guilt. Guilt for causing my friends to feel immense, intense sentiments.

I was so stupid. I wasn't thinking properly. The thoughts of suicide were getting stronger. They consumed me, manipulated me. They were powerful, more powerful than positivity. They isolated me, made me feel insignificant, and hypnotised me that there was no purpose for me in this world.

I thought about Derek's grief-stricken words. He needed me, yet I tried to leave him without any second thoughts like his father. Leaving him will only trigger his emotions, his mind, and his frenzied darkness to control him once again.

"We'll leave you alone," Sophia whispered into my ear, smug. Natalia and Jasmine giggled as Theo, Jackson, and Ethan smirked. Jasmine walked into Ethan's arms, and he kissed her forehead as they all left me with a confused expression.

Are Jasmine and Ethan finally going out?

The baby hairs on the back of my neck stood up, and tiny bumps formed on my skin as a warm breath exhaled behind me.

I turned around.

His blue shirt and dark jeans were wrinkled and worn out, as if he hasn't changed for days. He's wearing a beanie that concealed his ears with tufts of his jet-black hair. A strong whiff of cigarettes hit me as the wind sang past us.

My nose twitched at the nasty smell. I don't want him to smoke. It's not good for his lungs, for his health. He knows that; he just doesn't care.

"Derek," I whispered, my dry lips sloping into a wary smile.

"Why did you try to leave me?" he asked. His voice firm, filled with disappointment. My heart, my mind, my lungs blubbered at me for being so clueless to damage him so insensitively.

I couldn't answer.

His fingers curled around my chin when I refused to look at him, lifting my head up for our gazes to meet. "I need you, April. You knew that, yet you tried to leave me?"

Another round of scorching tears returned. "I-I'm sorry!"

"Sorry?" he snapped. I saw the swift pulse in his neck, thudding with fuming desolation. "You're sorry? Do you have any idea how everyone was feeling? They were devastated! Your brother was cursing himself for being a horrible brother. Your mother had more than two panic attacks a day. Jasmine hasn't been eating properly. Jackson and Theo kept on punching every single person in the school because of what they did — they deserved it — and they were suspended. You have a little sister, for Christ's sake! If you died, it would affect her mental health. I have been losing my mind and was slowly breaking to know that I could've lost the only person I ever wanted. And all you can say is *sorry?*"

My lower lip quivered at his harsh words. I stopped a sob from escaping my throat. He saw my tears and muttered blasphemy. He took a step back, swallowing big gulps of the chilly air to calm his raging nerves. He rubbed his eyes, wiping his wet cheeks.

"I didn't know what to do, Derek," I retorted. "I didn't know what to do when I know that I will break at any moment. I hate this stress. I hate feeling so worthless and lonely. I know there are people who love me, but I don't feel it, you know? I don't feel it. And I hate it.

"Whenever I cut myself, that's when I feel actual pain. I can't see anything good about this world. There are terrorists everywhere. People hate others because of their faith and beliefs. In fact, they *kill* them because of their religion. All the good people will have a little bit of darkness inside them. A friend will always leave you. And every time, I tell myself that everything happens for a reason. But I don't know what the reason is. This world is messed up. I'm tired living in it. I'm tired of trying to *survive* in it.

"Honestly, I couldn't imagine a world without you. It's just too hard. I called you an idiot, a pig and all, yet deep down I cared about you so much…I loved you so much… When Mike died, you just left. You never came to my house. In school, you always saw me, but you just looked away quickly as if I never existed. You pushed me away. You gave me a thought that you never wanted me. I was sad. I cried all night. Every morning, I prayed you would come back to me. I prayed you would hug me again, mess with me again, for us to read each other bedtime stories before we went to sleep.

"We both changed. I became a bitch—standing up for myself whenever someone insulted me. You became an asshole, playing with girls, being a bully. Then, we reunited and…everything changed for the good. I have good friends. That hope I felt when we were best friends returned. But when I heard Brigit say that I should just die, I lost it. I completely lost it. I started cutting myself as I thought of every bad memory I had. When you found me and took me to the ambulance, the words you said caused me to break into tears with guilt because I finally found someone who needs me more than anyone in this world. When you said those words, I feel *wanted* after three years. I decided to live only for you.

"I was all wrapped up in my emotions, Derek. You of all people should know that it's tiring to have a constant, repeated battle with depression every, single, damn day!"

Everything I said was factual and straightforward. They're all the feelings I've been keeping to myself.

Derek was silent for a moment. Then, he advanced towards me. His arms slithered around me, heaving my chest to his. Our hearts hammered in our ribcages at the sensation of this sudden closeness. The proximity between our faces was nearly invisible—our noses touching, our lips caressing, but not entirely locked together. I received a big close-up of his eyes: coloured in the shade of the blue ocean with that everyday arrogance in them, yet that sentiment masked the real Derek Matthews—the sadness, the hope, the glee, the light-heartedness.

"You're right," he whispered. "I'm sorry. It was wrong to shout at you. I was just so scared to lose you…"

"But you didn't lose me."

"And I thank God for that. Losing you," he cupped my face in his hands, "will be unbearable. It's like not seeing all the stars in the sky, only the darkness."

I could see Ethan in Jasmine's car, and Natalia, Jackson, and Sophia in Theo's car. Theo's head was poking through the window, gazing at us with a smug smile.

"I want you to be mine." Derek's irises somehow glimmered underneath the gloom-veiled sky.

"What?"

"I want you to be mine, baby. I want to kiss you every day. I want to hug you tight, call you beautiful every second, and just make you happy. I want to be your guy." His fingers stroked my cheeks softly. "I want to live my life with you; have a family with you; be proud to have you as my wife."

"Did you…Did you just *propose* to me?"

He smiled. "Yeah."

"Derek—"

My response was consumed in a sudden intake of breath that was muffled by his velvety lips with an immense, undeniable fervour. For a minute, my eyes were wide open, and then I closed them, and that's when his lips moved over mine, performing in an elaborate, intimate, and breathless dance; fervent, fanatical, and frenzied.

He kissed me as if I was the light to his darkness. No matter how breathless I was, no matter how resilient the pain of no air tightened my lungs, we never diverged; never stopped. We just continued…

His grip tightened around my face, alarmed to let me go, as the kiss renovated into an impulsive calmness and gentleness. Yet, it's still contented with fervour, commitment, and heat. Warm-hearted and deliberate, as if he's spilling all his emotions — his misery, his panic of losing me, his love, his heartbreak — into me, bestowing me a better insight of him.

That moment, I heard Theo shouting, "Oh, *damn*, the ship has officially sailed! Deril is finally happening!"

We broke the kiss.

"Why did they stop?" I heard Theo say. "DEREK, APRIL, WHY DID YOU STOP?"

My cheeks blazed a rich shade of strawberry pink as Derek glowered at Theo, silently growling at him to shut up.

"Does this mean she's your girlfriend?" Jackson shouted.

Derek's jawline tightened, his attention returning to me. He glanced at me fleetingly, opening his mouth, attempted to say something, but nothing came out of his mouth. I wanted to say something too, but I couldn't find my voice, as if my voice was yanked down my throat.

"I don't know," he finally murmured, his eyes once again turning sad.

"What?" I managed to say.

"I don't know," he repeated.

"Don't know about what? About me being your girlfriend?"

"Yes."

"Why?"

"Because I've done bad things."

Chapter Twenty-Eight

Love Isn't Easy

Derek Matthews

Three more days left until the Black and White Christmas Masquerade Ball.

Theo, Jackson, and I went to get suits for the Ball. Luke came along since he had nothing to do. His soon-to-be-wife was organizing everything for the wedding — the decorations, the DJ, the food — leaving Luke with no duties. He's dissatisfied not having any responsibilities. He wanted to help since it's also his wedding.

"Are you okay?" he asked me when we were at the mall. Theo and Jackson are ambling ahead of us, dressed in tight jeans and loose shirts that caught the eye of countless girls.

"Yeah. Why?"

"You look down."

"I'm fine."

He looked dubious. "Is this something to do with April?"

I sighed. No matter how distant we can be, Luke always seemed to know my thoughts.

"It is about April. What's up?"

I explained everything—the time in the parking lot, her words and my words, the kiss.

"So, you rejected her?" said Luke.

"Yeah."

"Why?"

"Because I'm not a good person."

Luke rolled his eyes. "You are not a bad person anymore."

"I've done bad things."

"Like what?"

"Bad things," I echoed. I didn't want to tell Luke about the Dare. In fact, I didn't want to tell anyone.

That's the thing holding me back from having a relationship with April: the Dare. Our feelings were developed from the Dare, and now they will get crushed because of the Dare *if* April finds out.

People have been talking about the exciting, merriment ball, waiting in anticipation. They were all nattering about who might become the Christmas King and Queen. Some even concurred that I have a high chance of becoming the King. Others were unsure about the Queen because Brigit was now arrested due to the vicious bullying.

I had been the Christmas King a few times. I always danced with the Queen and just left her alone because the ball wasn't even that thrilling. However, since April will be there, this year's ball will be different than the previous ones.

Ever since my conversation with April, I had this feeling that I had to avoid her a little. We've been talking to each other regardless of what happened …yet, that one thought always occurred to me several times which urged me to ignore her.

I was not good enough. I know, I know. I've been telling everyone she's mine, that she belongs to me. However, after everything she and I had been through, if we're in a relationship, then it will most likely be the death of us. If she finds out about the Dare, she's going to get suicidal, and she'll leave me. And when she leaves me…

"What's wrong?" April asked me one day. Natalia, Jackson, Theo, Sophia, Jasmine, Ethan and his friends were sitting with the both of us on the grass, chitchatting with each other as we ate our lunch. The circle was huge, and since Ethan's friends were here, I got to know them properly. They're fairly nice.

Theo, on the other hand, didn't like it when one of Ethan's friends stared at Natalia. Therefore, Theo muttered blasphemy at the boy and protectively wrapped an arm around her. "She's mine, asshole."

The guy held his hands up. "Alright, alright. Sorry, dude."

"Why have you been ignoring me?" April demanded.

I looked at her, still munching on a sandwich that I stole from April's lunch box. Damn, her mother can make great sandwiches. "I'm not."

Disappointment overflowed her eyes, yet she decided to let it go.

Not only Theo, Jackson, Natalia, and Sophia, but also Ethan and his friends had been huddling around April continuously. She began to feel frustration at our protectiveness. She even admitted that Jackson and Theo kept on texting her every night to make sure she's okay.

"Like, I get it you're looking out for me — I appreciate that — but I don't want you to stalk me every day," April grumbled one time when we were meandering in the hallway. "Can't I have some personal space?"

"Nope."

April groaned.

The students in the school apologized for their behaviour. April only mumbled small things like "It's fine", "It's alright", "Don't worry about it". Though, we could tell she's uneasy around the pupils. I heard rumours that nearly everyone in the school was fined for the bullying.

"I never knew you could get arrested for bullying," Theo said another time when he and I were headed to our Math class.

"Same. It's a good thing that the police are taking action for bullying."

"Yup."

We're nearing the door of the Math classroom. I saw April standing there in line, alone, her head facing downwards, her dark hair falling down either side of her face like a curtain as she read a book.

Theo followed my gaze and enquired, "Why aren't you two together? You two kissed, didn't you?"

"Things didn't work out."

"Tell me."

"It's complicated."

He snorted. "Everything is complicated when it comes to you. I'm used to it. Tell me."

"Well, we kissed," I explained, "and she told me that she wanted to be mine. I rejected her…"

"No." He gasped dramatically. "Did Derek Matthews reject the girl he *always* loved and still do?"

I rolled my eyes. "I was thinking about why I'm not good enough for her."

"Really?" He seemed suddenly exasperated. "Dude, for the past weeks you've been blabbing about April. Even when we were kids, you've been chatting about April nonstop. Why the hell are you being so negative and self-conscious about this?"

"It's not easy, Theo. You of all people should know that."

"I know love isn't easy—there are always ups and downs. But, Derek, that's the *main point* of love. Besides, I was scared about asking Natalia to be my girlfriend…"

"Theo, you're Theo. You're a good guy. Everybody likes you. Everybody hates me, even from the beginning."

"Wrong!" Theo argued. "Everyone admired you when we were kids! Everyone wanted to be your friend…"

"And I changed because of Dad's suicide."

"And you changed again—you became the old Derek Matthews, not only for yourself, but for April Levesque. You want to know how many men in the world do that? 40% of men. And the other 60% don't even try to prove their true feelings. Changing for April is what I call dedication. So, shut the hell up before I punch your face. You guys are destined for each other. Heck, even the birds and the bees want you two together! Get that into your shitty head!"

Despite his anger, he laughed at his own *birds-and-the-bees* joke.

"But what do you think will happen if she finds out about the Dare?" Theo's smirk faded. "She's going to break, man."

"True," Theo agreed. "However, she's going to come back to her senses and forgive you. I know April, too, Derek. She can be a bitch, but she's nice."

Hope crept into my face. "She'll forgive me?"

Theo nodded. "Wait…are you going to tell her *now*?"

"What? No!" I scolded. 'Not now. Perhaps, not ever."

"Are you going to ask her out?"

I shrugged.

"Well, you better do it soon."

*　　*　　*

My fingertips tapped the surface of the table.

Every five seconds, April caught my attention. She's secretly reading a book; her head on her propped-up arm, her book on her lap under her table.

"Mister Matthews!" the Math teacher barked.

"Hmm?" I hummed, not taking my eyes off April.

"Look at me."

Why should I look at you? The sight of you horrifies me."

The students gasped. Some clamped their hands over their mouths, stifling the laughter. Theo shot me a "serious" glare, and then he laughed.

"Do I have to send you out of the class?" the teacher said, angered.

"For saying something that's true? Didn't we learn from kindergarten not to lie? Lying is a sin."

"Alright, that's enough!" the teacher shouted. "Get out!"

"Before I do that…can I ask a question?"

"No! Get out now!"

I rolled my eyes. "I'll ask the question anyway."

I hauled myself up from my seat, striding around the table and approaching April. She's still reading the novel. Her shoulders tensed, sensing me behind her. She lifted her head, staring at me with confusion through her black framed, dorky but adorable glasses.

Smiling softly, I lowered my head to place my lips over hers.

She gasped into my mouth, and the students in the classroom echoed after her.

"Yes!" Theo whooped. "Give us a scene, man! Show everyone that Deril is official!"

I smirked, our lips still connected for a long moment. My hand cupped her cheeks, pecking her lips a few more times before I left her.

I asked her loud enough for everyone to hear:

"April Levesque, will you be my date for the Black and White Christmas Ball?"

"No."

Chapter Twenty-Nine

Yes

April Levesque

A fabulous book called *Starcrossed* by Josephine Angelini was on my lap underneath the table as I secretly read. I only started reading the story yesterday, and I'm halfway through the novel. It's so captivating.

I must've been too absorbed with the story because I jolted when I felt something stroking my back. I lifted my head to see Derek above me; his hair messy, his lips smiling.

I blinked, dazed by his enthralling grin. "Uhm…can I help yo—"

He smashed his lips tenderly onto mine, and I inhaled with astonishment at the sudden movement.

I didn't see that coming.

Helplessly, I kissed him back, and he smiled with gratification, his hands cupping my face.

"YES!" I heard Theo hoot. "GIVE US A SCENE, MAN! SHOW EVERYONE THAT DERIL IS OFFICIAL!"

Derek chortled, his vibrating chest caressing my back.

Our lips moved in the most faultless, beautiful, sophisticated sync as his firm hands relaxed on my cold rosy cheeks.

Derek pulled away. I pouted at the removal, and Derek chuckled, amused. Then, he turned serious.

"April Levesque," he said, "will you be my date for the Black and White Christmas Ball?"

I slightly gasped, my eyes widening in shock.

I didn't see that coming too.

Not replying for a moment, Derek now appeared concerned, his eyes full of panic. So, I offered him a modest smile.

"No."

Everyone gasped. Derek's eyes fell in shock and sadness. Theo, being himself as always, didn't feel gobsmacked or sad at my response. Instead, he laughed and fell off his chair, his body smacking onto the floor. He was guffawing so hard that he was wheezing, yet he still managed to hold his phone. "Need...to...record...this...on...Snap..."

"What?" Derek asked, disbelieving.

I snickered. "I'm kidding. Of course, I will."

He sighed heavily. "Oh my God, April. Don't ever do that. I nearly had a heart attack." He shook his head, smiling. "Will you also be my girlfriend?"

"Yes," I replied immediately.

Chapter Thirty

The Ball (Part 1)

April Levesque

School was finally over.

The Christmas Holidays have begun.

Today is the day.

Today is the Black and White Christmas Masquerade Ball.

I'm tense because…honestly, I don't know. Perhaps it's because I get anxious whenever I'm in communal places. Yet, I was in high spirits for the Ball because I'm Derek's date…and his girlfriend. I smiled. *I'm his girlfriend.* We've been chatting to each other persistently. Derek couldn't defy the urge to keep on kissing me. When he does, I always blush. When I blush, he laughs with glee and kisses me again, telling me he's so glad that I'm officially his.

It's one o'clock in the afternoon. The Ball is beginning at six o'clock. Natalia, Sophia, and Jasmine arrived at my house with the boys, thrilled.

Ethan kissed Jasmine's lips. "See you at the Ball, baby."

Mom beamed at the amorous action, satisfied that Ethan was dating. She wanted something amazing to happen to us. She was depressed about Mike's death, and still is, but she became more cheerless when she sensed the loneliness lurking around Ethan and me—the melancholy, the heartbreak. Hence, she's been praying that both of us will find something beautiful. Since Ethan and Jasmine were together, and Derek is my boyfriend, she was more than exultant.

"You're all going to Derek's house, right?" Natalia asked the boys.

"Yup." Theo heaved his lips to Natalia's forehead. "Can't wait to see you at the Ball."

"See you girls later." Derek hugged me tight and kissed me until someone squealed.

The girls and I scurried up the stairs. While we were getting prepared, I discovered several facts about my friends:

Natalia Hayes has two sisters — one is younger, one is older — and her family paid more attention to her sisters than her, which planted jealousy in Natalia's heart.

"It's like I'm invisible and I hate it. I can't wait to go to college with Theo and start my own family with him."

"Don't get your hopes up too high, Nat," Sophia said.

"It's good to be hopeful," said Jasmine. "Hope is the main thing that encourages you to keep on going, to fight the evil, to find the light. Or, if you're religious, perhaps, God/Allah, Jesus, The Holy Spirit, Buddha, Prophet Muhammad — peace be upon him — and other religious people or deities can be the hope in your life."

"My hope is Buddha," Sophia stated proudly. "I am a proud Buddhist."

"I believe in God, and I am proud of that."

Jasmine grinned at my choice of words. Even though she's an atheist, she was clearly contented to know that I haven't given up on God, didn't deny His existence, and kept on using Him as my hope to live my life to the fullest.

"And I am proud of that, too. I don't really believe in God or Buddha, but I like to learn more about other religions because I find them interesting. It's very sweet to know that people find a certain person or god that grants them with hope and helps them to conquer their fears. Religion is beautiful."

Natalia grinned. "I know religion is beautiful. I don't understand why some people say that religion is disgusting. It just helps each individual in life. Like, I get that there might not be any scientific evidence, but science isn't everything. I wish that people could just accept that and just move on instead of trying to persuade others to stop believing in God, Jesus, Buddha, Allah, guru, and other gods and entities…Just let everyone believe in whatever they want."

Sophia's previous relationship was horrible—her ex abused her continuously, making her body weak, pushing her self-esteem down. When she met Jackson, she unintentionally told Jackson everything and was worried if Jackson would think otherwise in a negative way. She was wrong. Jackson did his absolute best to help Sophia and reported her ex to the authorities. Sophia's ex was charged and arrested.

"Jackson is my hero," Sophia said. "He saved me."

I already knew some facts about Jasmine's past: only bibs and bobs. Although, today she explained everything in her life in full detail: her parents always argued brutally every night. It broke her heart to see their parents fight. One time, her father cheated on her mother.

"We're fine now," Jasmine assured. "We're happy without Dad."

"You're also happy with Ethan, aren't you?" said Natalia.

"Yeah."

"You guys are using protection, right?" I blurted, attempting to lighten the mood.

Jasmine's eyes widened. Sophia and Natalia laughed as Jasmine bit her lip, glaring at me, mortified.

"Oh, my God." My expression was full of disgust and horror. "You and Ethan are actually doing it?!"

"Doing what?" she asked stupidly.

"You know what!"

"No, I don't."

"You're doing this—" I made a circle with my thumb and index finger, and jerked my index finger inside the circle. This caused Natalia and Sophia to laugh harder.

"It's not like you and Derek aren't going to do it!" Jasmine retorted.

My eyes widened. "We're together, yeah, but it's not like we're going to hook up right after the Ball."

"That's what everyone does!" Sophia said through sniggers.

"Well, we won't!"

"Are you sure about that?"

Natalia suddenly frowns. "Wait, Derek was a player, but he didn't sleep with girls…in fact, I don't think he ever did."

Sophia's eyes widened. "He's a…" She looked sceptical. "No. That's impossible. Jackson slept with three girls. Theo…well, Theo only did it with Natalia. Ethan did it with Jasmine. Derek—"

"Didn't do it with anyone else," said Jasmine. "Jackson told me."

"Aw, that's actually cute. Derek and April will lose their—"

"OKAY," I interrupted Sophia. The girls giggled at my discomfort. I smiled. I have great friends.

Natalia went into my closet to dress herself as the girls and I took out our makeup and organised them on my bed.

Natalia's wearing a black background crop top with white flowers. She beamed with ecstasy as the sunlight shined *shone* through the sealed casements, dazzling on the shiny black material around her waist. Her bare left leg was exposed.

Sophia was wearing a crop top and a long black skirt which exposed only a thick line of her bare stomach. Her crop top was stunning with designs made from white stones. Her shoes were black with gold gem straps, making small diamonds.

Jasmine's dress was a V-neck. From the waist up, it's flower laced; from the waist down, it's just black that vaguely fades to a lighter shade of black. Her black platform heels had a black-and-white dotted bow.

It was my turn.

I walked into my mini ~~closest~~ *closet* with my white dress. It took me about ten minutes to put the dress on. After I was done, I took a quick moment to gaze at myself. It's a high-low dress. From the waist above, it's just a halter neck lace top of striking flowers that made me wonder how long the designer took to work on. A long attractive sheet of white was draped around the halter top, transparently covering my legs.

"Are you done yet?" Sophia asked impatiently.

"Yeah."

I tentatively stepped out of the closet with my deluxe white ankle-strapped gold heels. Jasmine, Sophia, and Natalia were doing their makeup and hair, humming to Christmas songs. They all froze when they turned to me. Their gazes never faltered, which made me nervous. *What's wrong? Do I look bad?*

"You look amazing!" Sophia squealed. "Oh, my God, I can't wait to see Derek's face when he sees you!"

I blushed. "Thanks."

"We just need to cover your arms and legs," Natalia suggested.

I nearly forgot that the dress was sleeveless, exposing the scars on my arms. The dress was long enough to conceal the scars, yet Jasmine decided to cover them with foundation and concealer.

One hour later, we're magnificent and ready. Sophia's hair was tied up into a gorgeous curly ponytail with white long earrings. Natalia's hair was made into two plaits that took a journey to the back of her head to create a beautiful flower; the rest of her hair was waving down behind her back. Jasmine's platinum blonde hair was styled into a plait bun with tresses of her smooth hair falling at the sides of her face. My hair wasn't that fancy; my curls were gathered into a high bun as a plait surrounded it; at least two tresses of my hair delicately curled down right next to each of my ears.

The sky outside was dotted with thick and small clouds as the sun sets into the horizon. Snow still cloaked the roads, the trees, and the pavements.

We walked into the living room. Mom spent a moment to look us up and down. Then, she squealed, delighted, jogging to us with her arms held out. Jasmine, Natalia, Sophia, and I screamed along with her, embracing each other tightly.

"Beautiful!" Mom complimented. "Absolutely and outstandingly *beautiful!* You will take every person's breath away tonight, especially the boys!"

"Thanks, Mia," responded Natalia.

Mom stared at me, and for some reason, her eyes moistened a little. "Oh, April," she whispered, "if only Mike was here to see you...he will be so happy!"

I smiled. "He is here, Mom. He is happy."

"I know, I know, but..." She examined my white dress. "This dress of yours reminds me of your future wedding..."

I groaned. "Mom...please..."

A horn honked outside. There's a glossy exquisite black limousine parked on the pedestrian sidewalk. We all said our farewells to Mom. The gentle freezing breeze tickled our skin as we walked to the limousine. A man in a black suit was leaning against the sleek car, nodding at us in greeting, and opened the door.

"Who is he?" I whispered to Jasmine as I was the first to get into the car.

"He's just a driver Sophia hired for us," Natalia answered before Jasmine could. "We needed an escort to the Ball."

"Is it really that fancy?" I asked in marvel.

"It's hosted by the richest woman in town — Derek's aunt — and it's a beautiful event to spend with your friends and loved one. Of course, it's going to be fancy! It's going to be magical!"

*   *   *

Finally, we arrived.

I gave the girls the masks Mom had made for us.

We all stepped out of the limousine, waving goodbye to the driver. Hooking our arms through each other's, we approached the open doors with security officers standing beside them.

"Why do I feel as if we're living in those Disney movies?" Natalia whispered.

We're in the entrance hallway of an ostentatious building. A large Christmas tree was placed in the centre, shimmering with tinsel and flickering lights, and a staircase curved around the Christmas tree.

"I don't know, but I'm feeling the same way," Jasmine whispered back. We ascended a ~~case of~~ marble ~~stairs~~ *staircase*, hearing thunderous music up ahead.

The hallways were carpeted with poles supporting the ceiling above us. On each side were Christmas trees, decorated with red balls and sparkling with gold lights; plastic vines with lights wrapped around them coiled above our heads, chandeliers hanging from the ceiling.

The ballroom was vast, spectacular, and flamboyant. Columns held the vaulted ceiling with a snowflake-shaped disco, emanating countless rays in many directions as it twirls. Strings of Christmas lights dangled from one wall to another, twinkling like stars.

The music was so loud that it made me feel as if my lungs turned into mush. The ear-splitting, booming beat thumped in unison with our hearts.

Circular tables were scattered across the immense room, adorned with cutlery and vases. In the centre of the ballroom was an enormous space for students to dance. I expected them to be slow dancing. They're not. They're all dancing like frenzied hooligans with uncontrollable grins.

Natalia glanced at us through her masquerade mask. "Ready?"

People glanced at our direction, oddly amazed by us.

"Ready," I said along with Jasmine and Sophia.

Our arms still linked, we descended the ten-storey marble staircase with elated smiles, positive energy raging inside us. Four handsome boys approached us. One of them stared at me with fervour in his ocean blue eyes.

Perhaps, Jasmine was right. Perhaps, tonight will be the best night ever.

Chapter Thirty-One

The Ball (Part 2)

Derek Matthews

Ethan's eyes meandered around the living room with an astonished face. The floor was marble. Two bulky and elongated sofas, and four undersized ones stood on top of a blue grey carpet with a glass table that holds a vase of peonies in the middle. On the walls were family pictures. To the right was a staircase that glided up to the second floor which had a protective fence. The security officers weren't working today since Marline was busy continuing the preparation for the Ball.

Cuddling on one of the elongated sofas were Luke and his fiancée, Neyara Nadasiri. Neyara was leaning backwards as Luke rested his head on her stomach, their eyes glued to the action movie they were watching.

Neyara was a gorgeous Sinhalese girl with upturned nut-brown eyes, perfectly arched eyebrows, thin lips and smooth skin. Her deep brown hair was outstandingly curly, falling below her shoulders.

"Hi, boys!"

"Aye, Ney," Theo beamed back.

"Getting ready for the Ball?" asked Luke.

"Yeah."

"Do you want a ride?" he asked. "I can lend you my car…"

"Nah, our cars are in the parking lot," Jackson countered.

Luke looked up at his fiancée. "Remember when we went to the Ball?"

Neya's grin widened. "Oh, yes!"

"We went with Mike and the boys…"

"Makayla came too…"

"Makayla?" I echoed. "Mike's ex, right?"

"Yup."

"Where is she?" Ethan asked, bewildered. "The last time we saw Makayla was…" He thought for a moment. "I couldn't even remember."

Makayla's cousin, Neyara, shrugged.

I've seen Makayla before. She's very beautiful. Mike and Makayla were a great couple until Mike joined the army… I think stuff was very complicated between the two lovers when Mike joined.

"I don't know," Neya said. "The last time I contacted Makayla was two years ago. She told me she visited her family in Sri Lanka, stayed there for a while, and went to Australia to find a good job."

"Did you try to call her?" asked Ethan.

"Yes. A couple of times. She never answered."

Puzzlement filled all of our faces.

"Maybe she changed her phone number?" Jackson guessed.

"Maybe," Luke agreed. "But she would've told Ney before she changed her phone number. Ney and Makayla are close cousins."

"I liked Makayla," Ethan muttered, "but when she left Mike, I stopped liking her. Mike was literally crying when Makayla left him. I never saw Mike cry before."

After our conversation, we went up to my room and changed into our suits. Ethan was wearing a black suit with a black bow and a silver watch. Jackson was wearing a white buttoned-up shirt, a black cardigan, and a black bow and so was Theo except he has a tie. I'm wearing a black suit with no tie or bow; the first two were buttons undone, exposing my flawless collarbone.

The Ball was exactly what I expected it to be: the atmosphere exploding with euphoria. The music bellowing from the large speakers made my heart race. Everyone chatted with their friends, smiles on their faces. The dance floor changed colour every fifteen seconds as the snowflake-shaped disco rotated leisurely, blazing petite squares of light everywhere.

Theo, Jackson, Ethan, and I formed a circle; glasses clutched in our hands. I secretly brought a flask of alcohol and asked them if they wanted some. They all nodded except for Ethan.

"Come on, man," I told Ethan. "Live a little."

"Nah, I'm fine."

I sighed. "Lame."

Ethan looked taken aback. "What did you say?"

I looked at him and smiled ingenuously. "I just called you lame. Is that a problem?"

Ethan rolled his eyes, a good-natured grin on his face. "April won't like you drinking."

"I'm not a drinker…"

Jackson snorted at my sentence.

"You're a smoker, though," said Ethan. "April won't like that. Why do you smoke, anyway?"

I shrugged. "It helps me, sometimes."

"It kills you," Theo said. "That's why I don't smoke. That's why I hate it when people smoke—they think it can help you, but it won't. It just destroys you. Yeah, I get that life can be a pain in the ass, but that's how life is like. Everyone's life is a pain. It doesn't mean you should increase that pain by smoking or drinking too much because you feel so 'relieved'. It's like magic—wicked, devilish, and a trick."

"I don't mind you being April's boyfriend," said Ethan, "but if you want to be hers, then stop smoking. You can drink, just not all the time."

"You're not the boss of me, Ethan."

He rolled his eyes once again. "Jeez, I seriously wonder how April can kiss you when your mouth smells worse than garbage."

"Shut up," I grumbled.

Approximately thirty minutes passed, and still, the girls haven't arrived. The guys and I watched couples dance, smile, laugh, and kiss as impatience filled our chests—well, my chest.

Where is April? Seriously, does it take that long for a girl to get dressed?

Jackson called Sophia with his loudspeaker on. "Hello?" he said when the call was answered. "Sophia, where the hell are you?"

"We're nearly there," Sophia replied. "Jeez, calm down."

"You're thirty minutes late."

"We took our time."

"Of course, you did," Theo muttered. "You're girls. Girls always take their time to piss the guys off."

The girls tittered.

"We're not that far," Jasmine replied.

Ethan grinned at the sound of her voice. "Come soon, baby. Is April okay?"

"Yeah, I'm fine," April responded.

"You booked a ride, didn't you?" Theo asked.

"Yeah."

"Tell the driver to hurry. The announcement for the Christmas King and Queen will take place soon."

"Yeah. Okay. Whatever."

The call ended.

"Ladies and gentlemen." Heads veered to where the principal was standing on stage, a microphone in his hand. "Please give your votes for the Christmas King and Queen to the teachers over there." The principal pointed to his right where a long rectangular table was occupied by three teachers, fair and elegant in their fancy clothes.

Everyone returned back to their business. My friends went to give their votes.

I walked to the table stacked with refreshments and poured myself more punch. I took out my silver flask and opened the cap, pouring ten drops of the alcoholic drink. Closing the flask, I rapidly shoved it back into my pockets. Taking a swig of my drink, the liquid scorched my gums sensationally.

I thought about Ethan suggesting me to stop drinking and smoking. I wish I could. I don't think I can. It'll be hard for me. My body was already used to the toxins. Trying to endure the addiction will be unbearable.

Do it for April.

I can do it for April. I'll give it a try. Perhaps I'll fail, but I won't stop trying until I fully found a way to get rid of the addiction. It might take a couple of days, weeks, months, or years for the addiction to die. It'll be worth it, though.

Anything for April is worth it.

"Hey, Derek," a feminine voice squeaked.

I puffed a sharp breath, perturbed to see Tiffany next to me with the rest of her friends. Since Brigit was expelled and arrested, Tiffany took the role as the leader of her squad. They huddled together beside me, with long dresses that blatantly exposed their chests.

I groaned. "Please, go away and find some other guy who will miraculously like you." I looked away. My friends were still standing in queue at the voting table. I sipped my drink again.

Soft fingers touched my cheeks, forcing my face to look at her.

"I'm nominated as the Christmas Queen," she said in that awful high-pitched voice of hers. I instantly cringed at her horrible flirty actions. "You're nominated as the Christmas King, right? Hmm…I think this is a sign that we're meant to be together."

"Or maybe it's a sign that you're going to become the evil queen and I'm going to become the good king where I kill you and send you to the underworld to become Hades' new wife."

The girls behind Tiffany gasped at my rude comment, muffling their snickers.

Tiffany's smiling face never faded, and I started to get irritated. "It's funny to know that your date is…what's that girl's name again?"

"April," I answered. "April Levesque. She's much better than you. So beautiful. So funny. So adorable. So nice."

"I'm beautiful, funny, adorable, and nice," Tiffany blurted out.

I chuckled sarcastically. "To me, nah."

Tiffany's eyes seared with fury. "What the hell do you see in her that you don't see in me?"

Not even looking at her, I said loudly, "I see an angel in April. In you, I see a bitch. Bye."

I walked away from Tiffany and her group of girls. Their jaws dropped with shock. Some of them guffawed at my savage words. Tiffany's eyes watered.

I could say that I regret being rude to her. However, her friend nearly caused my girl to kill herself. Therefore, I will not like her.

I passed the thickening mass of dancing students. I saw Jackson, Theo, and Ethan standing together in the same place as before, glasses in their hands, mumbling conversations.

Jackson's eyes randomly averted behind me and his jaw dramatically dropped, the glass slipping out of his grasp and hitting the floor, splintering into pieces. The people around them glanced at them in confusion, noticing they're all staring in one direction. They followed their gazes, and so did I.

Four girls unhurriedly descended the stairs, captivating and fascinating people's concentration. The four girls were dressed in the most opulent dresses. Three of them in black, one in white. The girls looked absolutely magnificent.

However, the girl with the white mask enticed my eyes. She's more stunning than the others. Her brunette hair made into a messy bun with tresses drooping at the sides of her oval-shaped face. She had a high-low dress on. From the waist above, it's a halter neck top, laced with creative flowers and leaves. From the waist below, it's just a white sheet transparently concealing her legs.

"C'mon," Theo said behind me, letting out a prickly breath as his eyes wandered down his girl with solid desire lurking in his eyes. "Let's get them before the other bastards can."

Chapter Thirty-Two

The Ball (Part.3)

April Levesque

"I hate you," Theo muttered as he wrapped his arms around Natalia's waist.

Natalia frowned. "Why?"

"For wearing that dress," he whispered, placing a hand on her bare leg exposed through the parting of her fine-looking black dress, and at a snail's pace, he slides it up her skin.

Jackson, Ethan, and Derek joined our small huddle. Jackson and Ethan were the same height, one inch shorter than Derek. The two boys were wearing attractive tuxedos except that Ethan's tuxedo was plain black. His hair was made into a quiff. Jackson's hair was combed to the side.

Jasmine bit her lip, examining Ethan. Ethan noticed her stare and smirked conceitedly.

"Something wrong, baby?" Ethan said smugly.

Jasmine's eyes met his. "Nope."

Ethan arched an eyebrow. "Sure?"

Jasmine blushed. "I'm sure."

Ethan's smirk never faded. "Okay. By the way, you look beautiful."

Jasmine's blush darkened. "Thanks."

Derek's suit was plain and midnight black with no tie or bow. The top two buttons were undone, exposing his flawless collarbone and I strangely had this urge to feel his skin. The holes of his simple curved mask exposed his blue eyes that were startlingly, mesmerizingly divine tonight, much brighter and beautiful than the majestic sea.

He scrutinized my dress, my hair, my heels—everything. He wrapped his arms around my waist. "You are beyond gorgeous, baby," he whispered, his warm breath tickling my cheeks and spreading tingles across my face. "You are the pure, accurate definition of imperfect uniqueness. It's torturing me."

"Thanks," I replied rather nervously. "You look gorgeous, too."

He cocked his eyebrows at my compliment. My eyes grew large when I realized what I said.

"I mean handsome!" I quickly rephrased. "You look handsome!"

Derek laughed and kissed my forehead.

Jasmine, Sophia, Natalia, Ethan, Jackson, Theo, Derek, and I joined the colour-changing dance floor.

Derek placed his hands on my slender hips. Derek chuckled into my ear when I shivered. I wrapped my hands around his neck, my back moulding with his rough muscled chest. Here and then, he twirled me underneath his right arm, just like how we practised. We murmured conversations, and our position changed—we're now facing each other, his arms around my waist, my arms around his strong neck.

Our eyes locked, his blue eyes and my brown ones. Just like before, I saw something behind that cocky glint masking his inner emotions and secrets: a boy with the same background as me, struggling with problems, life, and depression.

At that moment, I wondered why no one takes Derek seriously. I understand that he can be a jerk sometimes, horrible and savage. Yet, I wondered how no one could notice that whenever someone was rude and spiteful, it meant that the person was hurting inside, but doesn't know how to confess the pain.

Derek can be rude, annoying, and too self-confident, but that's just the shell of his personality. Inside that shell was the true Derek—the one who has trust issues and who was begging for someone to notice his pain.

The subject made me deliberate about Brigit. Brigit and I used to be best friends; we were so close. Sadly, that friendship was destroyed because of one boy who I thought was sweet and kind, and in the end, I found out that his looks were manipulative. Brigit was tricked by Owen's false words and promises. Brigit was just controlled by Owen's looks. Plus, she and I were twelve. We were too naive and juvenile.

"You're so gorgeous," Derek whispered.

I broke out of my thoughts and smiled. "You already said that."

"I know. I can't stop saying it. It's the truth: you are *very* gorgeous tonight."

My face burned at his sweet compliment.

His right hand moved downwards, pulling me closer. His rough lips fondled mine but not entirely. His gaze dropped to my mouth, focusing on them long enough for me to get the message.

I leaned in…

"Ladies and gentlemen."

Derek groaned at the interruption.

Everyone in the ballroom diverted their attention to the principal. He's standing on the stage, a microphone in his hands with an energized grin on his face. In front of the principal was a small stool that had two cushions which held two stunning, glimmering crowns and two envelopes.

"It's time to announce the Christmas King and Queen!"

Everyone cheered, nearing the stage.

Jasmine wrapped her arm around my shoulder, whispering to me, "It's going to be Derek and you. I can guarantee it."

I bit my lip. A part of me egoistically agrees with her. A part of me doesn't, and that part hissed at me not to get my hopes up. It could get crushed in a matter of seconds.

I saw Tiffany glaring at me, her arms folded over her shamelessly partly exposed cleavage, her eyes raging at the sight of Derek's arm around my waist. Tiffany was also nominated for Christmas Queen.

The principal picked the black envelope. "The King of this year's Black and White Christmas Masquerade Ball is…" He peeled the black envelope open, pulling the cute, iridescent card out. "Derek Matthews!"

Everyone erupted into cheers and whoops. Derek seemed surprised at the sudden enjoyment of the students and at the genuine happy expressions. Perhaps, because of Derek's apology, everyone was starting to like him again.

A smile of gratitude finally settled on his lips. He swiftly kissed my forehead before pacing through the throng of people to the stage.

The principal raised the black crown when Derek stopped in front of him. "Derek Matthews everyone!"

Everyone applauded.

The noise subdued.

The principal took out the card from the white envelope. "The Queen of this year's Black and White Christmas Masquerade Ball is…"

His eyes narrowed at the card.

"…Tiffany Anderson!"

Chapter Thirty-Three

The Ball (Part 4)

April Levesque

All my hopes were crushed. Jasmine, Sophia, Natalia, Theo, Jackson, and Ethan drop their shoulders in disappointment, bemused.

"I don't understand," Jasmine muttered to the others, "it should be April. Not Tiffany."

Derek froze. Tiffany shrieked with enchantment, slapping her hands together in glee as she skipped to the stage, jogging up the three-storey staircase and bounding to Derek. She threw her arms around him and embraced him tightly. Derek grunted, his lips curving downwards into a sneer.

His eyes met mine. I saw the dissatisfaction in them.

Disillusionment filled me. I puffed a sharp short breath of displeasure as the principal places the white crown on Tiffany's skull.

"One more round of applause for the new Christmas King and Queen of this year's Ball!"

Everyone rooted for Derek and Tiffany. However, I perceived the thwarted expressions from a large amount of the people in the room. Several took a quick glance at my direction. Hardly any of them seemed to be contented by the prospect of Tiffany Anderson.

Tiffany hooked her arm through Derek's and wrenched him down the stairs. Everyone formulated an immense space for Derek and Tiffany to dance underneath the mistletoe. Derek's shoulders were rigid with ~~irate.~~ *anger.*

Tiffany turned to slam her chest into Derek's, looping her arms around his burly neck. Derek diffidently put his hands on the sides of her stomach, and they started to dance elaborately.

Intently watching them dance, I became aware of the fierce jealousy roaring in my lungs. The scene hurt me. A part of me quietly told me not to be sad. It's only for today. Besides, Derek loves me more.

The other part manipulated me, telling me that Tiffany was more beautiful with her flawless skin, her hourglass body shape, her beautiful Dove hair, and her beautiful eyes. The manipulation told me that Derek must have liked her more than me.

No! I protested. *Don't think like that!*

I hated myself for being such a weak-hearted person. But how can I not control the negative thoughts when I have been negative nearly all my life? The negativity was unbearable to control. Even in the happiest moments, the tears will fall and the smile will break.

Living in a repulsive, appalling, atrocious world…It is not easy not to be cynical, hesitant, and distrustful.

"Are you okay?" My brother, Ethan, was suddenly next to me, his arm around me in comfort.

I nodded, swallowing the lump in my throat. "Yeah. Fine."

Incredulous, he said: "Do you want to go out? I know that this..." he ogled Derek and Tiffany dancing. Their faces were so close. Too close for my liking. "...hurts you."

"Ethan, it's fine. I've been through stuff that is much painful than this."

"Jealousy can be more painful than anything else in the world, sis."

"I'm not jealous—"

"You are. If that was Jasmine and a guy dancing, I would be jealous. I will question myself. I will feel hurt."

People joined Derek and Tiffany, dancing around like flowers floating on a lake.

"April, you should go outside and just have a little alone time," Ethan advised. "If you stay here, you're going to cry."

"I'm *not* going to cry!" I hissed. "Not for some stupid couple dance!"

Ethan sighed. "Alright, you won't cry. But you'll feel more pain. At least, have a moment to yourself."

"I can stay here and watch them dance," I snapped. "I won't feel pain. I've been through worse. Now go and dance with Jasmine. Please."

He obeyed and went on to dance with Jasmine, leaving me alone. The throng of people jammed the dance floor, and I couldn't see Derek or Tiffany until I caught a glimpse of their faces too close for my heart to break.

I turned around and ascended the stairs. A sudden, strong chill came over me, leaving goosebumps on my skin. I shivered, my teeth chattering. I glanced over my shoulder, observing the eyes glued to me as I neared the large open doors. I saw Derek staring at me. He was shoving through the crowd, attempting to get closer to me, but I had already left the ballroom.

Walking along the decorated hallway, the windows rowed the walls, displaying a view of the snow falling from the sky. The gentle icy wind seeped through the windows and caressed my skin. The soft, romantic, slow music still reverberated from the ballroom.

Outside, snowflakes landed on my hair, my face, and my dress. Unusually, I'm not bothered by the wintriness that numbed my skin. In fact, I was surprisingly pleased by the coldness. The way it snowed, the way the floor was covered with whiteness, made me feel as if I was in a magical land, like Narnia. The sky was concealed, yet stars were noticeable.

I breathed in the chilliness, calming my veins.

"It's beautiful outside, isn't it?"

Startled, I swerved around.

Derek's body was inclined against a tree, the snow-covered branches stretched out above him. His crown rests on his head; his hair dishevelled; his eyes a celestial blue.

"It's rare to get a few stars on a snowy night," he uttered, staring above as snowflakes fall on his cheeks. "Dad told me that a snowy, starry night sky is a sign of good luck, a sign of imminent happiness."

"What's going on?" was all I asked. "Why aren't you dancing with Tiffany?"

"It didn't feel right dancing with her." His hands were behind his back, which made me inquisitive. "It should've been you, wearing that crown, dancing with me underneath the mistletoe, proudly showing off to everyone that you're mine." He approached me. My heart thundered frenziedly underneath my ribcage. "But it wasn't. And I hate it. I want to make sure everything is perfect."

My eyebrows drew together in uncertainty. "What do you mean?"

He removed his hands from behind his back. In his hands was a tiara. A tiara made out of white flowers. It's beautiful. *Did he make that?*

Derek tenderly placed the flower crown on my head. "I want to be with my true queen."

He held out his hand. "May I have this dance?"

Grinning like a lunatic, I interlaced our fingers together. Derek brought them around his burly neck. He wrapped his arms around my small waist, his face slanting down for our noses to touch.

Suddenly, he was grinning.

"What?" I asked at his grin.

"This just makes me think of our marriage," he said, a bit too timidly to my surprise.

"Our marriage?"

"Yup."

"Too young to be thinking that, don't you think?"

"Time flies fast."

The snow continued to fall on us. It's cold, but the warmth radiating from his body pleased me. Therefore, I edged closer, leaning my head in his shoulder.

"Do you want to know something else?" he whispered, his hot breath spreading tingles across my cheek.

"What?"

"I love you."

I froze. Then, I said, "Really?"

"Of course."

"Why?"

"Because...you are so stubborn, frustrating, smart, amazing, talented, and so beautiful. I don't know how I could not love you when you're pretty much all I can think about every single day. Even when we were kids, I couldn't get you out of my head, and it was driving me crazy.

"Tell me that you feel the same way," he implored. "Tell me you love me."

"I love you," I countered immediately.

He kissed me with his blissful smile. I kissed him back. Unlike the other kisses we shared, this one was unhurried, supple, and comforting—his hands cupping my face, our hearts racing, our breaths colliding. All my senses dispersed—everything around us disappeared. I couldn't concentrate on anything but his lips, his heat…him. Just him. It will always be him.

He just makes me happy in a way nobody else can. Yeah, I have my parents: they make me happy. Jasmine and the others: they make me happy. My brother, Ethan: he makes me happy. My brother, Mike: he may be dead, but his soul is always around us; the love he gifted me with is endless and will forever make me happy. But this happiness from Derek was stronger than the others—purer.

If the love is strong, it brings positivity no matter how long the negativity has been breathing inside you.

Love provides hope and faith, and it withstands everything.

It gives us a certain rare stamina for us to endure everything.

It can look beyond numerous sins.

It can heal broken hearts, dry crying eyes, repair shattered smiles, guide you through life, and teach you lessons.

It gives you a reason why you are not worthless; it makes you realize you are unique, and extraordinary.

Love existed from the beginning.

Even in the end, it shall continue living.

Love is great and infinite.

As we strolled back to the ballroom, I heard the last lyrics of the song that delighted my eardrums and made my heart throb with the most warming sensation ever. A sensation that gave me feelings, indescribable feelings...

In the darkest night
I will be waiting for you
I will shine for the both of us
I will carry you through
I will be your fire when everything goes dim
I will burn for the both of us
We'll let the light back in

"Yeah," said Derek. "The singer of this song describes exactly what I want to do for you: *In the darkest times, if we ever break apart, I will wait for you to come back to me because even God knows that you're mine. I will carry you through the times that are the most painful, the hardest, the saddest. I will be your fire in your dim life. I will do anything for you.*

"We both endured the darkness. We both had enough of the darkness. It's time to let the light back in. For the sake of our lives."

Chapter Thirty-Four

Quadruple Date

April Levesque

"Derek, *stop!*" I'm infuriated, releasing an aggravated huff as I leaped up to grab the remote.

Derek only laughed, hilarity shining in his ocean blue eyes as he stood on his tiptoes, the remote high in the air. I jumped again, trying to seize it, but I'm just too damn small.

"Derek, this isn't funny," I snapped, getting more furious.

"But baby, it is—"

He was cut off by me harshly hitting his shin with my foot. A hiss escaped his gritted teeth, yet that arrogant smirk of his was still visible on his enthralling face.

"Besides, you had the TV yesterday! It's my turn to have it!" His childish retort only reminded me of our juvenile arguments when we were kids.

It's been a week and a half since the Ball. It's been a week and a half since Derek and I confessed our true feelings towards each other.

I'm happy for Jasmine and Ethan; they were so adorable together. I'm glad that my younger, protective, tall brother found love. I'm definitely happy he's not relentlessly alarmed about me anymore.

Theo and Jackson frequently teased me about my relationship with Derek. For example, they lightheartedly asked when we're going to bed, and I smacked them for saying something repulsive. They're like Derek's clones. They're like two extra brothers God gave me.

Sophia, Natalia, Jasmine, and I have been relishing our free time together; mocking each other, organizing sleepovers— basically, the stuff that usual friends do.

It's heartwarming, though. After a long time of suffering and agony, my life finally twisted into unexpected happiness. I have amazing friends; an amazing boyfriend who was and always will be my best friend; an amazing brother who's in Heaven; an amazing Father who's powerful and can make your life greater just by calling His name. I have a therapist now. She's nice. She went through depression too. She wants to help people who have been desolate like her.

I can finally feel the depression dying. Slowly. It's still beyond amazing. Miraculous.

If you have depression and finally overcome it, you will know how remarkable it feels. A few negative thoughts, but a large number of positive thoughts. No guilt and shame overpowering you. No theories of worthlessness. Just happiness.

Mike once told me: "*Happiness is always eternal. However, there's a catch: you must go through the bad times first. You can either chase after it, or let it find you. You may feel it's not worth it, but trust me, everything is worth it. It's how we live.*"

"The Flash is going on!" I argued. "Please, Derek, you have no idea how much The Flash means to me! It's my life!"

Derek raised his eyebrows. Mom, Ethan, Dad, and Mike accepted the fact that I'm a crazy fangirl. Theo, Jackson, Natalia, Sophia, Jasmine, and Derek also got used to my being a vivacious, wholehearted fangirl. Derek admitted it's hilarious and endearing whenever I scream with exhilaration every time I go crazy over a certain character. He also admitted it's annoying and he gets envious whenever I became affectionate over a male character. Well, he should know that it's not my fault that there were marvellous TV shows.

"You can watch it some other day."

"The waiting will kill me, Derek. *Literally.*"

"You're such a drama queen," he muttered.

"And you're not?"

I whined and thought about how I could convince him. *Maybe if I kiss him…*

"Fine," I said. "You can have it because I love you."

"I love you more."

I pressed my smiling lips to his. He lowered his arms, kissing me back passionately, pulling me into him to bridge the space. I took this as a chance to snatch the TV remote out of his grasp and gently push him away.

He fell backwards on the sofa, surprised. Then he pouted, crossing his arms over his chest. Oh, my God…it's so cute whenever he pouts. "You're not fair, April."

"Life isn't fair."

"You two are *so* adorable!" Mom stood in the doorway of the living room, delighted as she walked inside with Rosie in her arms. "I'm so happy you're in a relationship. You're good for each other. You both will hopefully heal each other's pains."

"She already has." Still sitting on the sofa, he gazed up at me as he binds his arms around my legs, heaving me onto him. I squealed, falling on top of him. "From the moment she kissed me in the meadow, she healed me."

A blush tinted my cheeks. He kissed me in front of my mother. *Oh, my God...this is so embarrassing!*

Rosie squirmed in Mom's grasp. She's starting to say a few words and mumbles. "Dek!" My little sister swung her small fragile, chubby arms towards Derek, grunting, her fingers wiggling at him. "Dek!"

Derek grinned at Rosie. He took Rosie from Mom's embrace. Rosie giggled adoringly, smacking his head with her hands as Derek made kissy noises into Rosie's stomach.

I couldn't help but beam admiringly at the scene. Derek was so good with children. I was unquestionably confident he will do well with our kids...

Wait...

What?

Kids?

KIDS?

What the hell, April! I hissed at myself. *Already planning your future with him? You can't just do that! Anything can happen! Plus, we're still in high school!*

"There's only a year left." Derek's voice interrupted my train of thought. "It's not too late to already plan our life as parents."

I blushed. "I said that out loud, didn't I?"

Derek laughed, nodding.

"*Hmmm,*" Mom hummed. Her dark eyes dilated as they bounced from Derek to me. "A mini Derek...a mini April..."

My eyes begged her to be silent. "*Mom.*"

"I want to name my son Isaac," Derek blurted out.

Mom and I stared at him.

"Why?"

"Because it's my father's middle name," Derek answered. "I know I said that I dislike my father because he left me, but I still love him. That's how family is like, I guess. No matter what happens, you always feel this tinge of love for them. It's endless."

"Isaac means 'laughter' in Hebrew," I said.

"What's Mike's middle name?" Derek questioned.

"Travis," I responded. "Mike Travis Levesque."

He held Rosie with one arm as his other arm glides around my waist, heaving me to his side.

"Isaac Travis Matthews," he said. "That's what we'll name our son if we ever have one."

The same, dark, bright blush returned to my cheeks. He chortled at my flush, kissing my forehead. Butterflies metaphorically fluttered in my stomach, providing me with indescribable feelings as I closed my eyes and reluctantly imagined a son called *Isaac Travis Matthews*. A boy with the same personality as Mike: benevolent, sympathetic, supportive, understanding, loving, fearless, heroic, humorous…

"If Mike was here, he would feel as if he won the Grammys when he knows that his nephew's middle name is the same as his," Mom said in a hushed tone. I heard the crack in her voice when she said my brother's name. The mention of his name always had an effect on us.

I laughed; my eyes stinging once again. "Yup," I whispered. "He would."

"He'll be a bit rebellious if he knows that you belong to a man." Ethan walked into the living room; his hand intertwined with Jasmine's. "Though he'll say, 'My little sister is growing into a beautiful young woman'."

Derek's eyes were moistening uncontrollably.

A tear slipped out of my eye. A tear was on Mom's right cheek. I averted my gaze to Rosie. She seems bewildered by our glistening eyes.

She never met Mike. She never knew about him. My heart ached with agony. I remembered one time, when Mike and I were playing in the park, he asked me if I wanted a younger sister. I told him that I do want one. He also said the same.

If we have another sister, I want to call her Primrose, Mike had said. *Because I love the Hunger Games.*

That's why we named our little sister Primrose.

Mike once told me that he named me April because…well, I was born in April.

Derek seemed to know what I'm deliberating about because he said to my little Rosie, "Hey, Rosie." Rosie looked at Derek. "Want to know something amazing?"

Derek turned his attention to a shelf in the living room, a shelf that held pictures of Mike. He approached it and took a picture of Mike wearing his army uniform, beautifully grinning into the camera with his arms wrapped around Ethan and me.

Mike trained in the army for three months. He came back to Peony Hallows. Mike, Ethan, and I took this picture before Mike went to join Dad's fight in Syria.

"This," Derek bobbed his head at the picture, "is your eldest brother, Mike. He was an awesome dude. Always fearless. Risking his life for others. Even *dying* for the sake of others. He was everyone's best friend. Everyone loved him, and still do. He died, Rosie, but his soul and mind haven't. He is still alive, and as he continues to live, he will guard everyone—including you—until the end of time."

Rosie's frown faltered. Her fingers stroked Mike's face. "Ma-i-ke," she pronounced. She repeated his name again, but this time in a questioning manner: "Mike?"

"He is here," Derek said softly. "You may not see him, but you can feel his presence."

"What do you think he's doing right now?" Jasmine asked in wonder, sad.

"He's in heaven—that's a definite fact—though he is on earth, watching over you, over us. He can be everyone's guardian angel."

"I know he is," Ethan whispered. "I just wish I can see him."

"Ethan, darling, you know that in the end, we will be happy together once again," Mom whispered back. "Mike is up there, waiting for us to meet him at the end of the road, so we can throw our arms out and hug him tight; say how much we miss him and how much we love him. He's waiting…" Another tear glided down her cheek. "Waiting with Him." She whispered the last word with pain and happiness, as if the thought of meeting Mike and Him will be beyond outstanding. "Mike once said: *'If war kills me, do not grieve because I was smiling. I pledged myself to fighting for the innocent, and even in death I will continue that fight'.*"

Mom couldn't help it. She couldn't fight back all the tears any longer. She fell onto the sofa and broke into tears. Ethan sat down next to her, putting an arm around her as Mom's snivels shook her shoulders. I bit my lip, allowing the tears to flow down my face. Jasmine must've felt our pain because her eyes were glossy with tears. She smiled sadly at me, embracing me tightly in her arms. I buried my face in her neck, crying into her shoulder.

If Mike ever saw me crying, he would say this: *'Shh, Little Sis; it's okay, I'm here. It's okay.'*

*   *   *

"Have you guys been on a date yet?" Jasmine asked me.

Sophia, Natalia, Jasmine and I were in my bedroom, relaxing on my bed, checking on our phones and listening to the music. The snowflakes continued to sprinkle down, concealing the ground with remarkable whiteness. Through the windows of other houses, the lights of the shimmering Christmas trees were very visible.

"Derek and me?"

"Yeah."

"No…"

"You should."

"Well, he hasn't really asked me out…"

The door swung open, and the boys spilled into my room. Jackson and Theo were munching on crisps. Ethan lifted Jasmine, and she yelped in surprise. Ethan lowered her onto his lap, kissing her neck from behind. Derek crawled toward me on the bed. I parted my legs, and Derek rested his head on my lap, my fingers massaging his scalp and playing with his black hair.

"We've been thinking about something," Theo announced. "Well, *I* was thinking about something. We should go out. Together."

"Like a quadruple date?" asked Theo's girlfriend.

"Yeah," Ethan answered before Theo could. "It'll be nice. The eight of us. Together."

"Where are we going?" I enquired.

"To the ice rink," Derek responded. "It'll be fun."

"Do you boys even know how to skate?" Jasmine said to the boys.

"Of course, we do. We're not that dumb, Jas."

"It's been a long time since I skated," I mumbled, meeting my brother's gaze. "I think it was two years ago we skated in the ice rink. Right?"

"Yeah. And, big sister, we're still awesome at skating.

"We're always awesome, Ethan."

"So, when are we going?' Natalia asked.

"Tonight, at six. Then we're going to the restaurant," Theo replied.

"We'll see you in three hours." Jackson straightened himself, Theo and Ethan echoing after him. "You girls do your girly dressing up shit. We'll be in Derek's house—"

"And do your boy shit?" Sophia guessed. "You know: playing video games, watching nasty shows, having nasty talks, and doing nasty things?"

Jackson lightheartedly rolled his eyes. He kissed Sophia goodbye and left my bedroom with Theo and Ethan.

I stared down at Derek. He brought his firm fingers up to stroke my cheeks. He cupped my face and brought it down for our lips to meet, holding them together until we heard a cough.

I broke away, and Derek rolled his eyes when Sophia coughed again with a smug smirk.

"See you later, baby." Derek crawled off the bed, closing the bedroom door.

The girls turned their faces to me with conceited smirks.

"Stop looking at me," I snapped.

They giggled and returned to their phones. I stayed still on my bed, my legs sprawled on top of the sheets and over Jasmine's legs, my arms behind my head, my eyes glued to the glow-in-the-dark-stars scattered across the ceiling.

*   *   *

"Darlings, the boys are here!" Mom shouted from downstairs.

"We'll be right there!" I shouted back.

Jasmine, Natalia, Sophia, and I took a moment to inspect ourselves in my bedroom mirror. We're in cosy sweaters and jeans with our hair down. I was so excited for this quadruple date. With my friends, my brother and Derek, anything can be amazing. That's what true friendship provides—true friends always make the worse better.

Downstairs, the boys wore coats with sweaters and jeans, their hair covered by the beanies, their hands gloved. The boys beamed at the sight of us.

Derek held out his hand. "Ready?"

"Ready."

Theo drove Sophia, Ethan, Jasmine, Jackson, and Natalia to the ice rink. I stayed in Derek's golden Lamborghini for the entire ride. I just found out Derek gave his car a name: Gorghini.

I erupted into laughter at the ridiculous name.

"It's a good name," he said in defence.

"It's horrible," I guffawed. "So horrible. What's this car's name?"

My hand rested on my thigh, and Derek put his hand on top of mine, caressing my skin softly as he turns the wheel with his other. My head leaned against the window next to me, watching how the small flecks of paleness seep from the concealed glum, shady sky. Buildings blurred past.

Suddenly, the radio broadcasted a Korean pop song. In an instant, a scream full of glee blasted from me. Derek jolted at my euphoric shriek. He placed a hand over his heart, murmuring: "Jesus Christ, this girl is going to be the death of me."

I ignored him and started dancing in my seat, singing along to the song *Blood Sweat & Tears* by the phenomenal BTS. I sang my heart out loudly, attempting to annoy Derek since he always found my singing repulsive. It made him cringe him apparently.

To my surprise, Derek smirked, entertained. He shook his head, sighing as he pressed on the gas pedal, driving on.

The song ended. I pouted, sad.

"What was that?" Derek asked, hilarity flickering in his burnished eyes.

"BTS!" I exclaimed. "THEY ARE SO AMAZING AND SO CUTE! I LOVE THEM SO MUCH!"

Focused on the road, he raised an eyebrow. "Love them more than me?"

"Yup."

I expected him to take my response playfully. Instead, jealousy permeated his face. "Well, then…BTS are assholes."

I gasped. Okay, he has gone too far! First Stiles Stilinski, now BTS? Who does Derek think he is! Who gave him the right to insult the stupendous BTS?

I slapped the back of his head.

"Ouch!" he hissed. "That actually hurts—"

"You deserve it. First, you insulted Stiles Stilinski, who is purely amazing and handsome. Now, you insult BTS, who are absolutely remarkable, sweet, and adorable."

"You have no taste in men."

I ran my eyes up and down his appearance. "Apparently."

He rolled his eyes. "Do you even know what they're saying?"

"Yes. Their music videos have English subtitles."

"They have no sense in fashion."

"They do! Their style is so sassy and sexy! I love it!"

"They can't sing."

"And can you?"

"Of course, I can. Can you?" Before I could reply, he held his hand to my face. "Oh wait, you can't. You sing like a mouse. Anyway, BTS is horrible, rubbish and trash."

"If the whole ARMY heard you that," I mumbled, "boy, you are *dead*. Not even God can save you." I looked up through the window next to me. "No offence, God. But you know it's true, isn't it, God?"

"Who else do you love more than me?"

I contemplated on the answer. "Hmm… Gosh, I don't know! There are so many hot and sexy guys…"

Derek's grip on the wheel tightened. I grinned. To be honest, it's hilarious to witness the jealous side of Derek. Yeah, he can get over-the-top when he's jealous, but when he gets jealous because of fictional characters, it's just too comical.

"…Percy Jackson…Four from *Divergent*…Alec from Shadowhunters…Edward from *Twilight* — Jacob is okay, but I prefer Edward more — Elijah and Klaus from *The Originals*…Damon and Stephan from *Vampire Diaries*…Mike, Will, Dustin, and Billy from *Stranger Things*…Clay from *13 Reasons Why*…Stiles, Scott, Isaac, Jackson, Derek from *Teen Wolf*…"

"There's a Derek and a Jackson in Teen Wolf?"

"And there's a Theo."

"Is that why you love me? Because there's a Derek in Teen Wolf?"

"No. I love you because…because you're you. You have anger issues, you're an asshole sometimes…but deep down inside, there's this sweet, charming, handsome Derek who really cares about people and regrets the pain he caused everyone. Deep down, you're the Derek I knew when we were kids, including the asshole part. That's why I love you."

"I love you, too. But what do you hate about me?"

"When you smoke, I don't like it. It damages you, and you know that, but you don't care. Which hurts me. You drink too. I don't like that side of you. I wish you can get rid of it—"

"I will," Derek interjected. "For you, I'll stop. I actually stopped smoking and drinking a week ago. It's hard, but hopefully, I can avoid my previous addictions."

A thought occurred to me which made me wonder. "Derek?"

"Hmm?"

"Did you love anyone before me?"

"No. You're my first love. What about you?"

"*Uhh...*" I let out a nervous laugh. "I won't say love—a crush. I had this crush on this guy. He used to be my neighbour. Mike never liked him. He was always aware of him. Mike always glared at me whenever I blabbed about him.

"One time, Mike said he doesn't want me to see the guy anymore. I was annoyed, and I shouted at him to leave me alone. I walked outside and...I thought the boy liked me. I was wrong. I saw him kissing a girl."

"Who's the girl?"

"Brigit."

"Of course, it's Brigit," Derek muttered.

"You know Brigit and I were best friends."

"Honestly," he said, "if I never met Brigit and if I heard about what she has done to you, it will be impossible to imagine that there was a friendship between you two. It's too hard. Brigit is so...rude, and you're so...sweet and innocent. Anyway, what happened when you saw your crush kissing Brigit?"

"I felt disappointed. I cried a little. But the crush went away. Brigit started blabbing about him, about how he's so gorgeous and stuff. Because of him, Brigit became distant from me. She never really talked to me anymore. That's why you would always see me underneath that cherry tree, reading and reading, just letting time fly and burying myself in a world of books. Books are so much better than reality. It's unfair."

"What's the guy's name?"

"Owen."

Derek pulled the car to a sudden stop. I screamed, bouncing in my seat. I blinked, inhaling deep breaths, gradually spinning my gaze to Derek with wide eyes.

"What was that for?!"

Each heavy breath breaking out from him was profound with loathing. His eyes fumed with resentment, his knuckles becoming pale from gripping the wheel too tightly.

"Owen Fall?" Derek hissed. "Is that him?"

I nodded slowly. "Do you know him?"

Derek chortled sombrely. "Oh, I know him. He and I were never on good terms."

"Did something happen between you two?"

"Yeah. April, why, *why* did you have a crush on him? There are thousands of people in Peony Hallows, and you liked *him*? That little cunt?"

"What happened?"

He gnashed his teeth. "You know about Matthews Industry?"

"Yeah…"

"His family's business was having a shadow war with my aunt's business. My father knew Owen's parents. He never liked them. He thought they were selfish. My father was the one who started the agenda. Owen's parents wanted to lead the agenda when Dad died, but Aunt Marline took it. Ever since then, they're always bickering. Back and forth. It's tiring.

"Owen is not a good person. He's like the male version of Brigit. He's more heartless than me. He was my bully. He insulted my parents, saying it's best they died…or it'll be better if I died along with them."

I put my hand on his shoulder, knowing that my touch calms him. His irate expression died hastily, the incensed lines on his forehead vanishing, his teeth no longer gnashing. He grabbed my hand and brought it up to his lips, kissing it.

"Have you met him again?"

I shook my head. "Owen started bullying me."

"Wait…was *he* the one who physically abused you with Brigit?"

"Yes."

The vehemence returned.

"Derek, calm down."

"I am calm. Tell me what happened."

"You need to stay calm…"

"Just tell me what happened!"

"Okay, okay. Mike found out about the bullying, so he warned Brigit and Owen that if they don't leave me alone, they'll experience the pain they inflicted on me, only that it'll be ten times worse. But Brigit and Owen didn't listen, so they harassed me again. Mike saw me, and he saved me with Ethan. Mike took me to the hospital because I had bruises and wounds all over my body. Then, I heard the news that Owen left Peony Hallows…I think Mike actually beat Owen."

"Good," said Derek. "Good. Owen deserved it. But, damn it, Mike could've called me to help. I would've loved to punch his teeth out." He exhaled the anger out sharply.

His eyes brightened, as if another thought occurred to him. "Where's Makayla?"

I frowned. "I don't know actually…"

"Didn't she go to Australia?"

My frown weakened. "Oh, yeah. I remember now: she went to Australia to find a nursing job. Apparently, a few of her family members live in Australia, so she went there to stay with them."

"How did Mike and Makayla break up?"

"Makayla didn't like the idea of Mike joining the army. She can be negative sometimes. She thought that if Mike joined the army, she would lose him. Permanently. And she doesn't want that pain. Especially since her parents died."

"That's stupid! She shouldn't have left Mike! In fact, why would a girl or guy leave Mike? Honestly, I would turn gay for him." I gave Derek a strange look. "What? Just saying... Have you talked to Mike's ex?"

I shook my head. "Mom did, though. But Makayla never answered."

*　　*　　*

Derek and Theo parked their cars. We all walked towards the immense ice rink and stopped to take in the sight.

It's beautiful—absolutely, stupendously, outrageously beautiful. Two artificial silver branches curve to craft an entrance. The colossal spherical polished ice rink was dappled with snow. Tinsels bandaged the fence guarding the rink. Incalculable filaments of big and small, searing, iridescent, and incandescent lights with mistletoes hung above our heads. A large Christmas tree was planted in the centre, cobwebbed with tinsels and lights, dotted with ornaments. People glided across the ice rink, guffawing, snickering, spinning, holding hands, hoping, and singing along to the Christmas carols. Next to the ice rink was a small cafe with people bustling inside.

After my friends and I put on our skates, we all stared at the ice rink.

"It's not hard. It's not hard. It's not hard…" Jackson repeated, nervousness crawling into his voice. "It's not hard…"

Sophia arched an eyebrow at her boyfriend. "I thought you know how to skate?"

"I do," Jackson protested.

"Mhmm. Come on, I'll teach you."

She seized Jackson's gloved hands, hauling him to the surface of the frozen water. In an instant, a high-pitched shriek escaped Jackson's throat as he stumbled forward, waddling his arms around like a chicken, and fell backwards, landing on his bum.

We all laughed. Jackson scowled at us to shut up, rubbing his bum, pouting.

Sophia snickered, offering her hands. "Are you okay?"

"What do you think?!" he hissed.

That only made us laugh harder.

I looked at Derek. He sniggered, his shoulders shaking up and down. Eventually, his laughter died, and only a smirk was visible on his handsome face. At the same time, his eyebrows were creased with worry as his hands moved backwards to hold on to the fence. He stared at the floor fretfully.

"You don't know how to skate, do you?" I skated toward him, my hands held out to help him.

He looked at me and sighed in defeat. "Theo knows though. He told me it's easy. It's just like surfing, only without a board."

"You know how to surf?"

"Yeah. It's easy."

"Surfing isn't really like skating."

"Well, Theo says it is." Derek tried to grab my hands, but when he leaned forward, his feet skittered, and he yapped, plummeting to the floor on his stomach and sliding further.

I giggled. "Not bad for a beginner."

"Thanks for the comfort," Derek muttered sarcastically.

I clutched his hand, tenderly lugging him to his feet. Once he did, his feet slipped, and he tumbled backwards. I screamed as I fell along with him, my chest smacking onto his, my forehead hitting his chin. Derek panted apprehensively, his arms outstretched on the pallid surface.

"I'll die. Baby, I'm gonna die," Derek whined childishly. "God, help me, please."

I rolled my eyes and scuttled off him. "You won't die when you have me. Now, come on."

"No," he objected. "I'll stay in the cafe and watch you all skate."

"While we're having fun and you're not? No way."

"April—" he tried to reason.

"Get. Up. Matthews."

Derek groaned. "Yes, ma'am."

*　　*　　*

Coaching Derek Matthews how to skate was far from hilarious. He knew it. He hated it. He used foul blasphemies whenever he falls, slips, or fails while I laugh at him. He glared, muttered, spouted sarcasm, and swore while I attempted to suppress a grin.

"Are you okay?" I asked for the hundredth time when he fell on his bottom. Amidst all the absurdity of witnessing my boyfriend fail, I feel bad. He tries so hard, yet he fails.

"Fine," he retorted brusquely. He glared at the ice, muttering numerous foul languages at it for being so slippery. "Shitty ice rink; it deserves a shitty reward for being the shittiest, most slippery rink in the entire universe."

I smirked at his childish behaviour. Cute and funny. There are seven billion humans in the world, and out of all of them, God gave me Derek Matthews.

Theo helped Derek at his ice skating. Derek tried to sashay on the ice rink with Theo by his side. He suddenly tripped. Anxiety spreading across his face, he grabbed Theo's hands as if to prevent his fall. They both shrieked and fell on the arctic floor, Theo landing on top of Derek.

"Why does everyone have to fall on top of me?" he grumbled. "I'm not a damn pillow!"

Theo slapped Derek's head. "Stupid asshole. My bones are too precious to get broken!"

"I'm the stupid asshole? You're the stupidest asshole I know!"

"Oh, shut the hell up. We all know that you're the stupidest asshole, Derek." Theo looked at me. "Isn't he, April?'

"Uhm…" I wasn't able to say my honest opinion because the two best friends continued to argue.

Boys.

Finally, after several minutes, he managed not to fall and glide.

He grinned delightfully, releasing a whoop as he pushes himself forward, the ice sprinkling behind his skates as he moves with grace. He swerved around and gave me a thumbs up.

"I'm doing it!" he exclaimed. "I'm doing it, April!"

I grinned back. "Keep it up, Derek!"

"Do you think I could do a back flip?"

"If you want to die then go for—" My eyes expanded when I saw an obstacle behind him. "Derek, turn around! You're going to hit the fence!"

His eyes widened whilst he spun around. He tried to skid to a stop, wobbling his arms like a penguin, but couldn't. "April, how do you stop—*AHHHHH!*"

He hurtled face first and plummeted backwards, collapsing on his bum.

I burst into laughter. I laughed so hard that I clutched my stomach, my knees buckling to the floor, my face leaning downwards to the frosty ground. My lungs ached and burned for oxygen. My stomach tightened.

Wheezing to maintain myself, I glanced at Derek who's rubbing the back of his butt, fiercely staring at me for tittering at him.

"Shut up," he snapped. "It isn't nice."

"But…it's…funny…"

"It *isn't nice*," he echoed, getting up and yet falling back on his bum once again. "Damn it!" he cursed, and I laughed harder.

*　　*　　*

After our fun in the ice rink, we walked to our cars.

Derek was still grumpy hat he's the only one who's still bad at ice skating. He was on the verge of shouting at us when I interlaced our fingers, balancing on my tiptoes to give him a kiss. His anger vanished, and he kissed me back, snaking his arms around me.

He's the first one to break the kiss, smiling softly. "I love you."

I mirrored his smile. "I love you, too."

"You're my girl."

"I know."

"Promise me you'll never forget that?"

"I pro—"

Something wintry and ivory hit my face. I squealed, detaching myself away from Derek, hastily brushing the icy snow off my skin. I glanced at the direction where the snowball came from. Jasmine was standing next to a tree, smirking as she crafted another ball.

"SNOWBALL FIGHT!" Jackson shouted.

A hand taps me on the shoulder. I spun around...

SMACK!

I lurched backwards, duplicating my previous squeal. I scoured my face, and through my quivering eyelashes, Derek gave me a juvenile, impish, devilish grin as he tossed a ball up and down with his right hand.

He winked. "Girls versus boys."

"Girls, time for bitch power!" Natalia screamed as the girls stood in one huddle, while the boys were standing in their group across from us.

"Boys, time for dick power!" Jackson screamed back. We giggled as the boys crossed their arms over their chests, trying to look frightening and determined.

Laughter and shocked shrieks were the resonated in my ears. Snowballs soared through the sky from every direction. People passed by with entertained expressions; some joined us.

I had plenty of snowball fights with Mike and Ethan. As always, I won. Sometimes, Mike won as well. Ethan...well, he was good, but he was the first one to get hit by countless snowballs before getting the chance to run and hide. I remembered Ethan screaming like a girl and plummeting into a huge pile of snow as Mike thundered towards him, falling on top of Ethan and tickling him until he was wheezing.

Promptly, I dashed to a tree and hid behind it after I battered Derek with three snowballs. My heart hammering roughly in my chest with exhilaration, anticipation, and worry, I cautiously peeked around.

I screamed with absolute panic when I spotted Derek sprinting towards me. I crouched down, clutching the snow in my hands, and threw it at him. He ducked as the snowballs soared above him, smacking the back of Theo's neck instead.

Theo screamed as his body shivered, muttering profanities. "Shit...It went down my back...Shit, shit. F—"

I turned around and ran…

"Nuh-uh." Strong arms surrounded me, and my back whacked into his muscled chest. His husky chuckle excited the veins in my neck and created hills on my skin. "You're not going to run away from me. Not now. Not ever."

He turned me in his embrace, hiding the both of us underneath the vast white branches of a tree.

He kissed me. I kissed him back.

Abundant, heartwarming, euphoric sentiments ignited my body, mind, and soul. Holding my face with his cold hands, he slanted my head to intensify the kiss.

I was trapped between the tree and his body. The branches arched over us, hiding us as Derek's lips found my neck. He pecked the juncture and sucked it, once again marking me as his. Only his. To warn everyone that if they take me, they'll regret it. To make sure that no one can emulate the way he touched me, kissed me, and made me feel ecstatic and pleasured.

I suppressed a moan. However, when he discovered another of my weak spots, he bit on it gently, and a moan spilled out of my throat, delighting his ears, manipulating him.

"Derek…" I closed my eyes at the sensational pleasures. "St-top. We're in public."

He froze at my words, comprehending them. He sighed into my neck. "Fine. But we'll resume this later."

*   *   *

Jackson recommended staying in a restaurant for a while. He was cold after the snowball fight, and all the energy he used to make his girlfriend lose left him famished.

The restaurant was a fairly nice place. Not too fancy and exquisite, not too dull and cheap. It's the perfect place to eat. We sat around a globular table — our cardigans, gloves, and hats off — permitting the heat to warm and pleasure us.

I leaned into Derek just as the waiter arrived at our table with plates of food.

As we enjoyed our time in the restaurant, I was ~~merely~~ really surprised to receive brief ~~phases~~ words from people in the restaurant. Everyone was familiar; I suppose I've seen them at Mike's funeral. Their speeches were full of condolences:

"You're Mike's sister, aren't you? I'm sorry for your loss."

"Mike was an amazing man, kid."

"He deserved better, kiddo."

"I admire him. He's a great friend and a great inspiration. Love him to the bottom of my heart."

Even though Mike died three years ago, he's still famous and loved due to his heroic actions. I should've expected those sincere dialogues from strangers.

I finished my meal and told Derek I'm going to the bathroom. I weaved through the labyrinth of tables to the girls' bathroom door. I was about to push it open when I heard a small, boyish voice.

"No!" I saw a small boy with fair skin, shaggy velvety caramel brown hair, stunning curved cheekbones, chiseled jaw line, and cognac eyes sparkling with bliss, tomfoolery, and hilarity – pouting at his mother, his arms crossed over his chest. He looked three or four. "Mama, I want that toy!'"

The mother shook his head. "Honey, you had enough. Let's go home. It's getting cold."

"Gimme that toy and we go home!"

I'm aware of how familiar the features of the young boy were…

"You can ask Santa for that toy." The mother lifted her son into her arms.

"No, Mama, I want that toy!" Her son struggled to get free from the young woman's hold.

The woman turned around.

My smile vanished.

"*Makayla?*" I said loudly with disbelief.

Her eyes moved at the sound of her name. They widened as they settled on me.

My God…Makayla was ten times more gorgeous since the last time I saw her. Her eyes were still the same colour: nut brown. However, unlike the previous time, her velvety coiled, brown hair was not longer, falling to her waist beautifully. It's shoulder length now. Her figure was slimmer and more curvaceous than before. Her cappuccino-tan skin was shiny and faultless as always.

A profound grave, heavy hush enveloped Makayla, the boy, and me. A bewildered frown on my face, an astounded one on hers. Curiosity overwhelmed me.

The boy…

My eyes swiftly diverted to the young boy cuddled in her arms. My heart clobbered. Various theories and unspoken demands immerged in my head.

Oh, my God...The boy looks just like...

I exhaled sharply, asking, "I-is that my nephew?"

Chapter Thirty-Five

Papa

April Levesque

"Mama?" the adorable little boy looked up at Makayla, intrigued by my presence. "Who is that?"

Makayla swept her hand up and down the boy's back. "This is your aunt, baby," she whispered, her eyes suddenly moistening, as if I was the cause for her despondency. "She's your papa's sister."

The boy returned his eyes to me. His eyes...those sweet beautiful eyes...cognac ...just like his...

Oh, my God.

I was too flabbergasted to even mumble a word, not even a sound. My lower lip quivered. My eyes filled with tears. His hair, his eyes, the structure of his face...everything about this boy was so identical to Mike as if this boy — this beautiful young, charming boy — was Mike himself, reincarnated.

"How?" I finally whispered. "H-how? When did this happen?"

"After I left Mike," Makayla whispered back, her voice fracturing when she said his name. "I found out I was pregnant with his baby."

Mike's son writhed in her embrace, wincing and grunting. Makayla lowered her son to the ground. The little boy frowned, gaping at me with such intense curiosity. Then, his lips broke into a grin, and he squealed childishly, closing the space between us.

"Papa sister!" he exclaimed.

I wiped my eyes, crouching down in front of him, endeavouring a shaky smile. "Hello," I said lovingly. "What's your name?"

"Cody," he replied. "You name?"

Cody. It's an Irish name. It means *helpful*.

"April. My name is April."

"Where Papa?" Cody asked, his eyebrows furrowing. "Papa with you?"

My heart pulsated with woe. My gaze diverted to his mother. "He doesn't know?"

Makayla shook her head agonisingly. "I was planning to tell him when he's older. Like seven or so. He asked me every day where his father was, and I repeated the same words: 'He's working, honey. He'll come back soon. Don't worry'. It was bad enough that Cody read Mike's letter for him—"

"Mike's letter?" I mused. "Wait, Mike knew about Cody?"

"Yeah. When I left Peony Hallows to visit my family in Sri Lanka, I stayed at my aunt's house for a few weeks. During those weeks, I found out I was pregnant. My aunt helped me. She promised not to tell anyone because it's bad for a young woman to get pregnant in Sri Lanka.

"I got a call from a company in Australia. They wanted me to work there. My aunt said not to go because it's dangerous, especially since I was pregnant. I didn't care. All I could think about was how I could raise my baby. I couldn't raise my baby in Sri Lanka because...it's really a good place to live in. You don't get that much of opportunities over there.

"I decided to tell Mike about Cody. Mike said he'll meet me soon. He met me when I was in the hospital, ready to give birth. After my labour, Mike came into the room, and we talked for a while. He told me that after this — after he properly meets his son — he will leave Australia and go to Syria. He didn't want to, but he has to because he promised his father he's visiting his friend and will come back. Your father doesn't know about Cody. Mike kept it all a secret.

"He stayed with me for a week. Before he left, he wrote Cody a letter..." A tear dropped from Makayla's eye. "Cody is very intelligent, but he can't read the entire letter. So, I read it for him. He told me it gives him hope. Right, Cody?"

Cody nodded, though his perplexity was still evident.

Listening to Makayla's brief story, I imagined everything: Makayla's struggle through pregnancy; her fear of getting shamed; her disappointment and regrets of not telling Mike sooner; Mike's face when he saw Makayla; Mike staying only for Makayla and his son; Mike writing a letter to his son.

"Papa?" Cody asked. I came out of my reverie. Cody's fingers vaguely caressed mine, capturing my attention. "Where Papa?"

"April?"

I turned to see my younger brother and my dear friends, huddled together with bemused expressions.

"Who is that?" Jasmine asked, nodding to Mike's ex.

"Makayla," Ethan, Derek and I answered in unison.

The bewilderment disappeared from their faces and astonishment took over.

"What are you doing here?" Ethan demanded with a firm tone. From the time Mike announced he and Makayla were no longer a couple, and from the time Ethan saw the heartbroken tears on Mike's face, a robust antagonism built up inside him. He resented Makayla.

"I live here."

"No, you don't. You went to Sri Lanka and then to Australia for a job," Derek said brusquely, uncomfortable by Mike's ex's company.

"Who told you that?" befuddled Makayla.

"Neyara did," Derek responded.

"Neyara?" Makayla echoed. "She's here?" A certain hope and happiness crept into her voice.

"Yes. Why are you..." Ethan's words died in his throat as he finally noticed Cody. He was silent for a moment, his eyes flickering from Makayla to Cody. I could tell by the expression on his face that his mind is flooding with theories. "Who is this?"

"Mike's son," I declared.

Their eyes widened, astounded.

"W-what?" Ethan stammered. "Mike's *son*?"

"Ethan, just look at him. Doesn't he look like Mike?"

Ethan stared at Cody. Then, he answered, "Yeah."

"Mama?" Cody tugged on Makayla's fingers. "Who they?" he pointed at my friends.

"They are my friends," I contradicted before Makayla could. "And that guy over there—" I pointed at Ethan "—is Uncle Ethan."

Cody immediately seemed to be blissful. He trotted to Ethan. "You know Papa?"

Ethan crouched down in front of him, his eyes hazy with astonishment. He took in the features of Mike's son, presumably comparing them to our eldest, treasured brother. "Yeah, I know your papa. He's my big, annoying, cocky, funny, loving brother."

"Papa brother!" Cody exclaimed, enclosing his arms around Ethan's neck. "Where is Papa?"

Ethan was muted, despondent.

Cody turned to Makayla. "Mama? Where Papa?"

"He's busy with work, honey," Makayla explained. "He'll come back."

"When?"

"Soon."

"How soon?"

At that, Makayla's eyes glimmered with grief. She shifted her focus to the ground, hesitant to meet her son's eyes. I saw tears sliding down her cheeks, and I heard the echo of a silent sob.

"Cody?" He turned to look at me. "Cody, Papa isn't here."

Cody frowned. "He coming?"

I opened my mouth to say something. However, nothing came out. I looked at Derek and Ethan. "Should I?" I asked him.

Derek and Ethan exchanged glances with Theo, Natalia, Jackson, and Jasmine. They stared at me with forethought.

"I want Papa!" Cody demanded. "I want Papa!"

I met Makayla's watering eyes. "Makayla, do you want me to tell him the truth?"

She shook her head. "It will only break his heart."

"But if you keep the truth from him too long, he'll get more heartbroken to know that his mother has been keeping the truth about his father. Won't you get tired repeating the constant lies?"

"He's too young... It will break him."

I sighed. "Fine. But he will continue demanding where his father is and repeating the lies will become exhausting. The more lies you say, the stronger your grief becomes."

"We won't force you to do anything," Ethan furthered. "It's just...Mike will be happy to see you again. Have you met him after he...died..."

Makayla's mouth quivered as she shook her head.

"Do you want to meet him?" Theo asked. "To at least talk to him?"

She contemplated.

"Mike would love to see you again," Derek reasoned. "He loved you so much, Kay. Why did you leave him?"

Makayla's silence enlightened the answer: *I don't know. I was scared to feel the pain if I lose him when he's in war.*

I don't blame her. Even from the time we were granted free will, we weren't clever enough to dominate our mind and its oppressive thoughts. Our minds are the most dangerous organ in the human body. It gives us absurd pessimistic thoughts to change our behaviour, to slaughter the optimism. Our mind is our lifetime tyrant.

Makayla was too oppressed at the visualisation of losing Mike. She was apprehensive imagining Mike in the war, fighting ISIS — a dangerous major group of people, murdering people because of their faith, and trying to obtain power from all over the world — and getting shot numerous times. She lost her parents...losing Mike will be an absolute devastation.

"I'll go," she finally decided. "I want to meet Mike." She looked at her son. "Cody?"

"Yes, Mama?"

"Ready to meet Papa?"

His eyes brightened with resilient enthusiasm and optimism. "Yes!"

"I'm sorry it's not going to be what you expect it to be," I heard Makayla whisper, but Cody was too cheerful to concentrate on his mother and her words. He's more absorbed by the idea of finally meeting his father.

His much-loved, comical, compassionate, valiant father.

*   *   *

I opened the door of the fence that enclosed a private area of the cemetery—the private area where Mike was buried. Makayla carrying Cody, we approached the white cross devotedly embraced in earth. Behind the cross was a statue of Mike saluting.

So many loving things filled this area. There were flowers, some old and new. There were all letters. There were hearts. And regardless of the snow, regardless of the gifts shrouded in the whiteness, I can still feel the love and the compassion from the offerings.

"*This hero sacrificed his life to defend the innocent from danger and wickedness. This hero understood the responsibilities, advantages, and consequences of fighting in wars yet he did not give a damn*,'" Theo read the inscription printed below the statue, his arm around Natalia.

Jackson smiled forlornly next to Sophia. "He already sounds awesome."

"He is awesome," Theo whispered.

Makayla dropped Cody to the ground carefully, and hurriedly advanced to the white cross. Cody trots to me, seizing three of my fingers with his tiny ones. Makayla sank to her knees, staring silently at the large cross, not bothered about the snow sopping the grass. Her tears fall to the ground, her hushed wails echoed throughout the cemetery. No one else seems to be here.

"Mike," Makayla sobbed. "I'm so sorry."

Suddenly, there was a moderate, calm, kind-hearted waft of air, full of tranquillity, benevolence, and ardour as if the earth is trying to communicate with us, hissing at us that Mike heard Makayla's sobs, and that Mike is pleased to see her once again.

Cody is staring at the large pale gravestone cross, his eyebrows gathered together in bafflement.

"That Papa?" he asked, pointing at the cross.

Makayla's lips moved swiftly, as if she's talking to Mike.

"No, he's underneath the cross, Cody," replied Ethan. He squatted next to his nephew. "He's buried under the cross."

"Why?"

"He died, Cody," Ethan said tenderly and carefully, placing his hands on Cody's shoulders.

"Died?" Cody echoed. He looked up at the clouded sky. "He there? With God?" Ethan nodded. "God care Papa?"

"Yes, God is taking care of your dad," I murmured.

Derek hunkered down next to Ethan, in front of the cute little enthralling boy. "Cody, I met your father. He was the most remarkable human being I know. He's quite the celebrity in Peony Hallows: everyone loved him — and still do —, they talk about him, telling everyone how great and kind-hearted he was."

"Papa saw Jesus," Cody mumbled randomly. "Papa told me."

"Told you?"

"Mike wrote a letter to Cody before he went to Syria," I explained to Derek.

"Oh." Derek returned his eyes to Cody. "Your father saw Jesus?"

Cody nodded. "Papa said dat Jesus want him to swave people."

For a three-year-old (Makayla told us his age), he sure can speak intelligently.

"Jesus told your Papa to save people?"

Cody nodded as tears filled my eyes again.

Derek grinned. "He told me that, too."

"I see Jesus!" Cody elated.

"Really? When?"

"No when." Cody jabbed his finger into Derek's chest, then into Ethan's chest, and then pointed his fingers at my friends. "I see Jesus n evwione!"

Sophia awed at Cody's heartwarming words.

"Do you want to know something else, Cody?" Theo enquired, bending his knees. "About your father?"

Cody nodded his head, thrilled to hear anything about his father.

"He's the bravest man in the entire universe."

He gasped, eyes widening. "He superman?"

I laughed. "He is superman. He's brave, tough, strong, funny, sarcastic, and caring."

"He flies?"

"Well, now he's flying," says Derek, "since he's an angel."

Ethan straightened his figure. "Cody, do you want to say hi to your dad?"

Cody hastily nodded. Ethan and I held his hands, guiding him to the delicate pale white gravestone cross. We let go of his fragile chubby fingers and Cody ran up to the cross, embracing it in his small arms.

"Hi Papa!" Cody said. "Me Cody!"

Ethan wrapped his arm around me. I cried into his chest, my tears dampening the material of his shirt. It snowed once again, melting on our clothes. My eyes wafted up to the statue of Mike. He's saluting, with a dauntless jovial grin, a long gun attached to his back.

I reflected on how Mike saw Cody for the first time before he went to join the soldiers in the war. I could already visualise the stunned, ecstatic smile as he turned his cognac eyes at to his little boy, his fingers caressing his son's velvety cheeks, his lips lingering on Cody's forehead as he whispered countless wise, unforgettable phrases and promises.

If he was still alive, he would make Cody feel like the luckiest son alive. He would play with him, wipe his tears, stand up for him, give him wise advice, thunder into his room whenever Cody wakes up screaming from a nightmare, beat up the bullies, and tell stories every day about great superheroes such as Spiderman, Iron Man, etc.

"Luv you, Papa!" Cody said to the cross as we guided him away from his father. "Bye-bye, Papa!"

* * *

Jasmine, Jackson, Theo, Natalia, and Sophia went home. Derek drove the rest of us to my house. Snow coated the roofs of my house and veiled the grass.

Makayla met Mom inside. Regardless of Makayla leaving Mike, Mom was utterly contented to see her again. Mom swung her arms out and embraced Makayla in a tight heartwarming hug.

When she saw her grandson, she was baffled, rapidly batting her eyelashes as if she's trying to wake up from a bewildering dream. Then, she broke into tears, murmuring about how much Cody looks like Mike. "Oh, my God…" Mom raised her quivering fingers and stroked Cody's soft cheeks. "If only

Mike was here." Mom shook her head, desolated at the thought that Mike won't be able to see his son.

"Papa is here!" Cody argued. "Papa no die. He there." Cody pointed at the casement, indicating to the concealed dull sky. "He with us."

Mom smiled, poignant. She kissed Cody's forehead.

All of us assembled in the living room. Mom sitting next to Makayla; Rosie resting on Makayla's lap; Cody sitting next to Ethan; and Derek sitting next to me. We talked about a variety of things: what happened to Makayla for the previous years, how are things going, if everything is alright, etc. Cody met Rosie. Immediately, he loved her like a little sister even though he knew Rosie is his aunt.

I was aware of the loss of Makayla's parents; they tragically died in a car crash. Makayla lived in her uncle's house (her father's brother) in Peony Hallows for a couple of years. Her uncle, based on her story, was abusive, merciless, and judgmental. Her uncle judged Makayla, comparing her to other members of her family, how great and prosperous they were. Mike was the one who comforted Makayla; the one who was there for her. When Mike declared he would become a soldier, Makayla was worried about the worst that could happen: Mike dying. She didn't want to experience death. Stubbornly, she left Peony Hallows, lived in her home country for a few months, and then went to Australia for a job. I wondered how Makayla coped with taking care of Mike's son.

"Why did you leave Mike?" Ethan demanded.

I kicked his shin. Ethan did not wince, and I muttered vulgar language of how weak I was. He shot me a glare. I glared back. *Don't*, I mouthed.

"I didn't want to." Makayla's fingers caressed Rosie's brown hair. "I never wanted to leave him. When Mike wanted to join the army...I couldn't help but think that he could get killed easily. I know he's strong — he had martial arts classes and he tells himself philosophical, strong stuff to keep himself going — but the fear of losing him made me so stubborn, so dim-witted. I thought that if I left him before he leaves me—"

"You won't have to feel the pain," I finished.

"That's stupid," Derek said brusquely. "Very stupid. Beyond idiotic. Why would you leave Mike because of his choice? His dream?"

Mom glared warningly. "Derek, be nice." She took Makayla's hands. "Darling, I understand. The negativity manipulates the mind, gives us false information and urges. I understand. Don't worry."

Makayla smiled, grateful for Mom's benevolence. "Mike was shot to death, right?" she asked, just to make sure.

"Yes. He died three days after my birthday."

Makayla didn't say anything else.

An hour later, Derek went to his house. Mom organized a spare bedroom for Makayla. She gifted Mike's room to Cody, promising to the little boy that the room and everything in it are all his and his mother's.

"Cool!" Cody beamed.

Ethan and I took Cody upstairs, sharing a beautiful moment in Mike's room. I haven't been in Mike's room for a long time. Attending to his room attacked me with memories, memories that were too miserable to reminisce and reflect on.

We changed Cody into a shirt and a pair of boxers. We tucked him under the covers of the comfy bed.

"What that?" Cody pointed at a frame stuck on the wall. It's the frame with Mike's speech.

"It's what your father said once," I spoke.

"What say?"

"'I believe life is about perpetrating the good and praying for the bad. I am aware of your woe for my absence recently, but just bear in mind that I am always there.

Forever and ever.

Do not grieve when war kills me. Instead, smile because I was smiling since I pledged to fight for the innocent, for everyone who has a special place in my heart.

And in even in death, I will continue that fight.'"

"Papa brave," Cody stated, smiling boyishly.

"He is,' Ethan agreed, sitting on the right edge of the bed.

"I want Papa,' Cody whispered, tears suddenly brimming in the eyes identical to Mike's.

"He's here, Cody," I said quietly. "He's alive in here." I pat his chest, right where his heart is. I wiped his dampening eyes. "Don't cry, Cody. Your dad won't like it if you cry."

"What Papa like?"

"He will like if you know that he is still alive. He will like if you be happy and keep your mother safe."

"I'll do dat," Cody stated. "I make Papa pwoud."

"He's already proud," Ethan said. "He's proud to have a child."

Ethan's hand dropped into his cardigan pocket, drawing something silver, beguiling, and sparkly: a necklace with a design of a dragon safeguarding a cross with its wings and tail.

Mike gave Ethan, Dad, Mom, and me necklaces. He surprisingly got one for Rosie even though he never met her. Before, he always asked Mom and Dad for another sister to cherish. They were considering it, so Mike got another necklace in case we have another sister.

Mike's necklace for Rosie is a fascinating, beautifully designed heart locket with a picture of him inside. On the picture was a text written by Mike: *I'll forever love you, I'll forever be with you. Love, Mike.*

Ethan's necklace is adorned with two lions, one of them said *Lil bro* whilst the other was *Big bro.*

Mom's necklace is a gold heart with a silver circle enfolding it with a passage: *I love you to the moon and back, Mom.*

Dad's necklace is a circle which says: *My Dad, My Hero.*

My necklace is a heart with wings. On one side, it says: *Little Sis, God Gave Me You; You're Forever In My Heart.* And on the other side, it says: *Shh, Little Sis. Don't cry. It's okay. I'm here. It's okay.*

"This was your father's necklace," said Ethan. "He always wore it. He told me the necklace provided him with strength—it reminded him of who he wanted to be. He wanted to give this necklace to his son, so the strength and hope he had will be passed on." Ethan attached Mike's necklace around Cody's warm neck. "Don't lose it. Okay, buddy?"

"Yes, Oncle Ehan," Cody promised.

Ethan chuckled. "It's *Uncle Ethan.*"

"You can call him E-man," I suggested.

Ethan smiled at me when I said that. *E-man* was Mike's nickname for him.

"Or Eth," Ethan suggested. He shrugged. "Call me whatever you want, kiddo."

"E-man," Cody pronounced. He grinned. "Nighty night, E-man. Nighty night, Aunty April!"

"*Goodnight, Cody,*" Ethan and I said in unison, smiling as we watched Mike's son close his eyes.

*   *   *

Dad talked to us on Skype; mostly talking with Cody and Makayla. He was laughing and crying and was angry, wishing he could return to Peony Hallows sooner.

Things have been hushed and peaceful. Cody has been leaping up and down, exhilarated for Christmas, complaining about how far away the merry event was.

Derek came over to my house there and then. I met Neyara, Luke's to-be-wife. She's really pretty. When Neyara met Makayla, she cried. When Luke saw Mike's son, he was too stunned to even mumble a sound. Eventually, he cried and hugged Cody tightly. Makayla declared that Luke was now Cody's godfather, which was a pleasure to him.

Derek and I went out on numerous dates—sitting in cafes, holding hands, chatting with each other, laughing, and just having that everyday romantic staring contest. My heart warmed and fluttered with joy whenever we're together.

Ethan helped Cody write a letter for Father Christmas.

"Don't know." Cody shrug his shoulders when Ethan asked him what he wants for Christmas.

"Do you want a toy?" I asked, sitting down next to my younger brother, placing my arm around Cody.

Cody narrowed his eyes in thought. "Star Wars!"

Makayla laughed, entering the parlour. "Him and Star Wars," she mumbled, shaking her head with a smile.

Cody picked up the pen and scribbled on the lined-sheet of paper. "Dear Santa," Cody muttered, tapping his chin with his pen. "Me name Cody! I love you, Santa. I sowy I'm bad boy 'cos I pee-pee on Mama! Fogive me, Santa! I want Star Wars!"

Ethan and I exchanged grins as we admired Cody writing his letter to Santa. He's such a cutie. And the more he smiles, the strong. Mike's presence in the house becomes.

* * *

"Did you get me a Christmas present?" Derek asked inquisitively.

We're in Starbucks, sitting on the curved sofa near the large casement. Petite mesmerising ivory flecks of snow oozed from the heavens. Cars drove by noisily, whiteness sprinkling from behind their wheels. Kids sprinted around, throwing snowballs at their families, squealing with happiness. Some were shopping. I heard the echo of choirs singing carols in the streets.

I nearly spat out my coffee. Oh, shit. The Christmas present… Damn it, what type of girlfriend am I? "Uh, y-yeah."

"What is it?" Derek demanded, not suspecting my apprehension. He's very handsome, wearing a fluffy back-sided cap, a grey sweater along with worn-out jeans. His clothing only made his blue eyes more visible and divine.

"I can't tell you."

Derek pouted. "Why not, angel?"

"Because I don't want to. Now shush, Derek, and let me enjoy my coffee." I sipped the delicious Starbucks coffee. I closed my eyes. Starbucks' coffee always made me feel good. All I needed was Stiles Stilinski, and there will definitely be hearts levitating around my head. Though, I doubt Derek will be pleased to witness that. "Did *you* get me something?"

Derek nodded. "The gift is still in process."

"Still in process?"

"Mm-hmm."

I wanted to ask him what's my gift, but then again, I can't tell mine.

A silent ambience gripped us. If I blocked out the traffic noises, the screaming kids, and the music broadcasting from the speakers buried in the ceiling, the silence was peaceful and harmonic, as if angels have spilled into Starbucks and hummed a serene tune.

Derek suddenly grinned, staring at me intently.

"What?"

He shrugged. 'You always make me smile." He leaned forward, his hands reaching out to my black-framed glasses. My vision blurred as he took them off, putting them on his face. 'What do you think?" he asked.

I blinked. "Idiot, I can't see."

"Oh, right, I forgot." My vision cleared once he returned my glasses.

Derek showed me a picture of him wearing my glasses. "What do you think?" he asked. "I look cute, right?" he then chuckled. "You know what, don't answer that. I'm always cute, sexy, handsome, and drop-dead gorgeous."

I rolled my eyes at his self-confidence. Derek smirked and leaned forward to kiss me. Smiling, I kissed him back. A second later, I realised that we're in a public place. I pulled away, coughing gently, my cheeks blistering.

Derek tilted his head. "There is no need to be shy, baby."

"We're in public…"

"So? Everyone needs to know that you're mine." He glided around the curved sofa to my left. Putting an arm around me, he rested his chin on my head. Both of us watched as the snow fell, listening to Christmas carols.

* * *

In the car, Derek sang melodiously to the song *Happier* by Ed Sheeran. I tenderly smiled, paying attention to how tantalizing and dainty his voice was.

"You have a nice voice," I complimented.

"Better than yours."

I rolled my eyes. "Whatever."

My phone screen brightened. A notification regarding a message was sent from the group chat that included Sophia, Natalia, and Jasmine.

Natalia: *Babes, we're going out!*

Sophia: *Where?*

Natalia: *To the mall*

I haven't got Theo a gift yet!

Me: *Sm*

Jasmine: *OMG, u girls r horrible girlfriends*

No offence

Natalia: *Stfu*

Jasmine: *Make me*

Derek swerved the car into another lane. "Who's that?"

"The girls. Natalia planned a shopping spree."

"Now?"

Me: *Nat, when z the shopping spree?*

Natalia: *Now*

"Yup, now."

Sophia: *Smh, I'm still in my pjs.*

Natalia: *It's 2 in de afternoon*

Who r u, Sleeping Beauty?

Sophia: *I am beautiful when I sleep*

So I guess I am.

Jasmine: *Nat, Sophia s in Jackson's bed*

Natalia: *Ooooo*

Jasmine: *Was it nice, Sophia? ;)*

Me: *U guys r so dirty-minded*

Then again, so am I...

Kinda

Jasmine: *Blame my brother 4 making me lose my innocence.*

Natalia: *I lost my innocence when the skl taught us about reproduction. I thought school is supposed to be a good place?*

Me: *Ikr*

I lost my innocence by reading books…

Sophia: *Yeah…I lost my innocence by maturing. I'll meet u girls in the mall in an hour. Bye.*

*   *   *

Jasmine, Natalia, Sophia, and I had a tough time finding fantastic presents for the boys. Well, Jasmine already got a present for Ethan.

Natalia groaned. "*Ugh!* None of them are perfect! This shop deserves a one-star rate for being so boring and unorganised!"

"Get Theo a watch," Jasmine recommended.

Natalia arched an eyebrow at Jas. "A *watch*? Are you kidding me? Theo already has a watch! I need something better!"

In the next fifteen minutes, Natalia's complaints and rants were absolutely unnecessary since she finally found the perfect present for her boyfriend. Sophia also found something for Jackson. On the other hand, I, unfortunately, haven't.

My eyes wandered the shelves, objects, and clothing of the next shop, deliberating what will be terrific for Derek. He's seriously affluent—he can get anything in a second. He got everything —a room of clothes, ten bedrooms, two living rooms, a kitchen… Pondering on what to get for Derek was gravely complex.

I wanted my Christmas present to be at least memorable and affectionate.

came up

An idea ~~immerged~~ in my head, and my eyes widened. I pointed a finger up as I exclaimed, "That's it!"

Sophia looked up. "The ceiling? The ceiling is your present to Derek?"

I lowered my finger. "No…something else…"

"What is it?"

I told them my idea. They all agreed that it's a good and sweet present for him. My present for Derek is going to be Lucky, the Golden Retriever puppy Alan rescued from the streets. It'll be a nice present. Derek mentioned once about how desperate he wanted a puppy, but never really had time to buy one. I will get Lucky for him.

After our shopping spree, we hooked our arms through each other's, striding towards the automatic doors.

I received a text from my mother. She demanded to know where I am. I told her that I'm with the girls. She asked me to be safe and come home with a bright smile. As I was typing "Okay, I will" to Mom, I unintentionally bumped into someone.

"What the hell?!" the person I accidentally walloped into stared furiously at me. "Watch where ya going, bitch!"

I raised my eyes at the boy, endeavouring to mutter a succinct apology. The words were trapped in my throat. My eyes widened. My jaw vaguely dropped. Resentment burned me. My hands curled into raged, tightening balls.

He's the same since the last time I saw him: sleek blond hair; greyish-blue orbs; that lopsided, impish, repulsive egotistical grin of his; flawless skin and revolting dimples (that I once thought was beyond handsome).

"Hey!" Jasmine hollered at the boy. "Mind your language, asshole. She accidentally bumped into you. No need to snap about it. Jeez."

The boy's glare became callused. "Listen here, you ugly bitch—"

"That's enough," I retorted brusquely, my gaze hardening at his obnoxious features. "I am *sorry* that I accidentally bumped into you, you dumbass banana head. However, I will not apologise for my friend calling you an asshole, because that's what you are—a complete, undeniable asshole, Owen."

If this life was a cartoon, I visualised steam sizzling from his nostrils and ears.

My friends' eyes widened when I said his name, and they flooded with antagonism.

"So, this is Owen," Sophia murmured. "The crazy guy Brigit loved."

Owen understood Sophia's phrase, and then took a moment to examine me. His eyes widened as realisation hit him. "*April?*"

"Did you bang your head onto something so hard that you had memory loss?" I muttered derisively.

Owen chortled. "Of course, it's you. Your sardonic attitude never leaves." His British accent was very thick and sharp.

"And that horrendous smirk never leaves your ugly face."

"Don't be rude."

"Why shouldn't I be rude when you were the devil in my life?" I swore, his smirk tingled at my words, as if he enjoyed the memories of torturing me. "Shouldn't you be in jail by now? Mike did report you and Brigit to the cops."

"I was in jail longer than Brigit. Brigit had six months, I had twice the time, unfortunately."

"Fortunately," Jasmine rectified.

"Where did you go after your jail time? England?" I guessed based on his British accent.

"Yes. I now live there with my parents. We came here for a business trip."

Natalia arched her eyebrows. "Business boy, huh?" She leaned in and whispered to me: "That's kinda hot." I glared at Nat. "What? Just saying."

"You know, I came here a day ago, and I already heard gossips about you," said the boy I admired before. "I heard that Brigit was arrested for nearly half of her life for brutally bullying you. I also heard about Mike's death; there were literally posters everywhere about the lad even though he died, like, three years ago. The lad's already dead, don't need to mourn about him for another three years. It really is unnecessary."

At that, Sophia snapped, "Just because Mike was better than you, had friends unlike you, was loved unlike you, doesn't mean you should say something impolite about his death. He died saving Muslims and innocent people from terrorists."

Owen shrugged. "Muslims are bad people. I don't see why Mike risked his life to save them."

Sophia's mouth dropped at Owen's vulgar words.

She cracked her hand across Owen's face so roughly, that a sharp sound of friction emanated.

"Shut the hell up! Mike was a great person. And Muslims are *not* bad people. Not all of them are! There are good Muslims and bad Muslims, good Christians and bad Christians, good Sikhs and bad Sikhs, good Buddhists and bad Buddhists, good Hindus and bad Hindus, good atheists and bad atheists. There are always a good side and a bad side, so that doesn't give people the right to assume that an entire group is evil."

"Religious people are idiotic and disgusting," Owen grumbled, rubbing the side of his face. Strangers from around us glimpsed at our direction, focusing on Owen's triggering words. "They believe in a God that is so stupid and doesn't even exist. Catholics, Christians, Muslims, Protestants, Sikhs…they are all idiotic and deserve to die! They should realise that there is no God or Jesus. They are myths! Even homosexuals, bisexuals, transgenders are disgusting."

Fury crawled into faces of strangers around us. This was why I hated Owen when I finally saw his true colours. He was very racist, atrocious, and callous. I don't know what bad things happened in Owen's life, and I don't care. Owen's persona was a hundred times more evil than anyone I knew.

"I wish Mike was here," Jasmine said irately. "He would've kicked your ass ten times harder for saying that."

"Mike deserved to die," Owen muttered.

"He's not dead. He's alive."

Owen rolled his eyes. "Spirituality is shit. Get that into your head."

"April, I cannot believe you had a crush on this devil," said Sophia.

"Same." I suppose it was the looks that deceived me. "Thank God that Mike beat the shit out of him and reported him and Brigit to the cops."

"You deserve more time in jail," Jasmine spoke. "Just like Brigit."

"My time in jail is over."

"That can come back because of that offensive mouth of yours."

"This is a free country. I have been given the freedom of speech. I can say whatever I want."

"You do realise that anyone's words — a joke, an insult, *anything* — can make someone suicidal. You *can* get arrested for that. Lifetime, even."

"Whatever."

My phone in my pocket vibrated. I took it out to see Derek's name flashing on the screen.

Owen noticed and said, "Ah, Derek Matthews. How is the lad?"

"'She's Derek's girl now," Natalia declared to Owen. "If you steal her, you're going to have more than one broken bone."

Owen seemed dubious. "You're dating that son of a bitch?"

I clenched my hands into fists. "Okay, 1) his mother isn't a bitch. She's an angel. And 2) you have no right to insult my boyfriend like that!"

"What the hell do you see in him?" Owen hissed. "I understand you both were best friends, but I thought you both got separated after Mike's death, at least, that's what Brigit told me before we lost contact."

"I see the true Derek Matthews. That's why I love him."

Chapter Thirty-Six

Devilish

April Levesque

"Who's back?" Ethan spun in his chair to face me. His hair was damp from his encounter in the shower, and that overwhelming odour of manly soap emanated from him.

I sat down on his bed. "Owen Fall."

Ethan seemed gobsmacked. "That asshole?"

"Yes. That asshole."

"He's back?"

"Sadly."

"Why?"

"For a business trip, apparently."

"Wait...I think the Matthews Industry hate the Falls, right?"

"Yeah. I think the Falls wants the Matthews Industry all to themselves."

"Are you still scared of him?" he suddenly asked.

I was silent.

Ethan sighed and seized my hands. "You shouldn't be scared, sis. I'm here for you. Derek is there for you. Luke is. You have so many people who will protect you."

"He abused me, Ethan," I whispered. "He hurt me so much. Even today, I can feel the pain from three years ago. His return to town...it's like a nightmare that came true. What if he hurts me again, Ethan? What if he punches me? What if he insults me? He's racist, Ethan. You know that. He's so racist, psychotic, and rude. He hates religious people. Those callous eyes of his...they're devilishly frightening. I think my words are my only defence. I don't even know how—"

"Hey, hey, hey." Ethan's cold hands cupped my face. "Don't worry about him. I know you're scared because of what he did to you, but since Mom and Dad know about the bullying, you have a bigger army that will protect you. Don't worry, sis. I promise to beat the shit out of him if that psychotic asshole comes close to you or walks into this house. I got your back. Promise."

"You know Owen bullied Derek?"

"Yeah. Owen was the main one who made Derek believe that he deserves to die. Remember when Derek pushed you away when you begged him what's going on?"

"Yes." Derek and I had a little squabble. I demanded to know what's happening to him... He insisted for me to leave him alone, although my distress for him was so immense that I never stopped demanding. Finally, he snapped and pushed me away, and I hit the wall. That time made me blubber badly. Mom told me that Derek was having a tough time, and that Derek will tell me everything eventually. But after that quarrel, we never spoke.

The door suddenly slammed open. I jolted at the sudden sound. Cody jogged inside Ethan's room, bouncing up and down with glee, waving a sheet of paper in his right hand.

"Santa!" he exclaimed, handing the paper to me.

"He replied?"

I grinned at my brother. His return was a cunning wink. Ethan was the one who wrote the letter.

"Yes! Aunty, read!"

"*Dear Cody,*" I read. "*In spite of your misbehaviour to your mother and peeing on her, you have been a good boy. You are on my good children list! I will get you a Star Wars toy! Take care of your mother while my fellow elves prepare your present. Best wishes, Father Christmas.*"

Ethan raised his hand and Cody smacked it with his own. "Nice, buddy. Did you show this to your mama?"

Cody bobbed his head up and down rapidly. "Mama laugh! She pwoud!"

Ethan and I chuckled. We pulled the three-year-old boy into a bear hug, and he beamed, hugging us tightly in return. We kissed his forehead. He ran out of the room, screaming, "Granny! Santa gave letter!"

"He has Mike's looks," Ethan spoke softly. "He has his personality. Cody has your kindness and my wittiness."

"Just imagine him when he's older," I said in wonder.

"He'll be a good man. That's for sure."

*　　*　　*

"Derek!"

Cody raced to Derek. Derek grinned, swinging his arms out as Cody leaped into them. He threw the three-year-old boy into the air. Cody shrieked boyishly, and then Derek approached me after catching Cody.

I tiptoed to kiss him; my fingers on his cheeks.

"Ahh!" Cody clamped his hands over his eyes. "Ew! Eyes! My eyes!"

We broke away, guffawing.

Cody peeked through his fingers. "See?"

"Yes, it's safe to see."

From the time of our conference with Cody and Makayla, the atmosphere in the house became merrier and brighter every day. Everyone was laughing and smiling. I couldn't detect a trace of misery on anyone's faces, eyes, or smiles. I couldn't sense sadness. Everyone was blissful.

"E-man, Aunty, Derek," Cody says as we went into the parlour, "hide and seek?"

"Okay." Ethan rises from the couch. "Who's going to count?"

"I will," volunteered Derek.

Cody tittered. Derek covered his eyes, beginning his count. Ethan hurried out of the living room with Cody and me. Mom gave us confused expressions at our playful snickering. I hastily informed her that we're playing a game, and she smiled, enchanted to see my light-hearted side after so many years.

Ethan hid downstairs. Cody and I hid upstairs.

"Ready or not, here I come!" Derek shouted.

I shushed at Cody to be quiet as we hid in his bedroom. A nerve-wracking silence occupied the room. Cody was concealed under the bed. I'm sheltered inside the closet, peeking through a linear hole to inspect.

"Aw, man." Ethan's voice grumbled from downstairs.

I heard Derek snigger. "Cody, April, I'm coming for you!"

His footsteps noisily battered the stairs, and they hammered through the hallway. My heartbeat increased its velocity. Cody shuffled a little under the bed, sending me a vexed expression.

The door lightly opened. He appeared into my line of sight, scanning the room. His gaze paused under the bed. He chortled. "I know you're there, Cody."

"Aw, man." Cody shuffled out from under the bed and huffed at Derek.

"Where's April?" Derek asked.

Cody's lips widened into a cheeky grin. He pointed to his right.

Damn it.

Derek progressed to the closet. Stubbornly, I burst out of the closet, dashing out of Mike's old room before Derek could catch me. Derek laughed, sprinting after me with Cody by his side. I peeped over my shoulder, permitting a childish shriek when I scanned the small proximity between us. My legs shifted faster...

Stalwart, strapping, slender arms ensnared me. My back was condemned into his rigid chest. I wormed out of his grasp, but then exhaled sharply in defeat, frustrated.

"Ha-ha. Got you, Aunty," Cody said, grinning.

I glared at Cody playfully. "You betrayed me."

Cody shrugged and skipped away.

I spiralled in Derek's hold.

Derek rapidly looked down at my lips, and then into my eyes. "I want to kiss you."

Immediately, my arms went over his shoulders, wrapping his warm neck. Our mouths feverishly impacted. An unexpected, unusual current went through our bodies, from my nerves to my lower stomach where an immense fire sensationally smouldered. My fingers pulled tresses of his black hair at the feeling.

Derek inadvertently moaned.

Damn...that was so hot...

His tongue skimmed my lower lip, begging for permission   which I granted. His tongue dipped into my mouth. We engaged in a ~~dominant~~ battle, both of us sounding eager.

dominance

He rammed me to the wall forcefully, his body compressing into mine so tightly that I couldn't breathe. His hands ambled down my body until they gripped my legs. Effortlessly, he hoisted me up. My legs wrapped around his torso, my hair covering the stimulation of our lips.

He pulled his mouth away, going down my jawline to abuse my throat…

"Aunty! Derek! Come donstairs now!"

His sweet, innocent voice made me push Derek away from me, realizing what could've happened if we continued.

Cody appeared from the stairs. He skipped to us with Ethan behind him. Cody frowned at the distance between Derek and me, and at the fact that our hair was dishevelled, our mouths were bruised, and our clothes were wrinkled.

"What happened?" the innocent boy enquired.

Ethan became conscious of the situation. He suddenly glares at Derek. "Did you two just…?"

"Shut up," Derek grumbled. "We haven't. Just had a moment. Besides, it's not like you haven't done it with Jasmine."

Ethan's cheeks turned a shade of cherry. "Shut up."

Cody tugged on Ethan's fingers. "E-man? What happened?"

"Nothing," I responded. "Ethan, what's wrong?"

A loathing spark appeared in his brown eyes. "He's here."

"Who's here?" asked Derek.

Not answering, my fifteen-year-old-brother glanced at Derek and sauntered downstairs.

In the parlour, Cody leaped onto Makayla's lap. Mom spoke to a wealthy pale woman.

Derek's body tensed behind me. I fluttered my eyes once I saw my boyfriend look daggers at him.

"Derek," Owen acknowledged.

"*Owen*," Derek hissed at the devilish boy.

Chapter Thirty-Seven

Christmas

April Levesque

"What are you doing here?" stipulated Derek.

"We came here for a business trip, mate." That infuriating, impish lopsided smirk of the devilish boy returned to his revolting face. "I see you haven't changed the slightest bit, Derek. Still have that cruel heart?"

"Oi!" Cody hurdled off his mother's lap and thundered to Owen, fiercely glaring at him. "No rude to Derek! He is good dan you!"

I snorted with appreciation behind my boyfriend. Derek's mouth curved into an agreeable grin.

Owen's irritating grin by no means disappeared. "You have quite the tongue, little man. Just like that dead father of yours."

Cody's anger subsided at Owen's harsh words. Makayla's eyes saddened when Owen said *dead father*. I saw liquid filling Cody's sudden eyes, and for that reason, Derek's jaw clenched with fury.

"Owen," his mother warned, "enough. We didn't come here to start an irrelevant argument."

"Then leave," Derek snapped gruffly.

Owen's father glowered. "You are not the adult here, boy. Respect your elders."

"I give respect to those who give me respect."

Mom stood up, glaring at the Fall family. She loathed them. "Please leave."

"We came here with kindness, Mia. Merely to meet you and your family."

Mom rolled her eyes, irate. "The kids and I don't want you here, Robert. Get that into your damn head."

Robert's face muscles tightened at her attitude. "You're siding with the Matthews, huh?" He ticked his tongue. "I am appalled, Mia."

"The Matthews and the Levesques are close. You all know that. You don't know anything about the Matthews. Why are you judging them, then? Because of Derek's reputation?"

The man opened his mouth to respond, but Mom was still ranting.

"Derek is actually a respectful, sweet boy. You may not believe that. I don't care if you don't. I do not tolerate criticism *especially* if the denigration is regarding a child. I enormously do not abide by your disrespect. I completely do not accept your presence at my house after what your son did to my daughter! Do you really think I will still be fond of you after your son maltreated my April?"

"We apologize for our son's behaviour," the mother said with...shame? "We just want to be on good terms again."

Mom laughed sombrely. "I do not accept your apology. I heard the fake sympathy in your voice. Falls, you all are too full of yourselves. Even from the first time I met you, I had this feeling about you. You are selfish. You think more about yourselves. Your business is redundant. You will leave this house otherwise I will call the cops!"

Derek, Ethan, and I blinked in unison, astonished at my mother flaring up. I knew my mother was a very kind-hearted woman. She rarely shouts at Ethan and me. When she shouts, then it means she's utterly livid. The Fall family also looked taken back by Mom's outburst.

"Granny z badass!" Cody remarked. "Go Granny!"

Mom gifted a humble smile, and then her face went serious again toward the Falls.

They all stood up, adjusting their clothes sophisticatedly, and left the house with rigid postures. Derek cussed at Owen when he winked at me.

Derek secured me selfishly in his arm. "She's mine, Owen. Only mine. Piss off."

That glimmer of mischief crept into his grey-blue orbs. "It really is a mystery how you two are together, isn't it? Enemies cannot be friends, even a couple!"

With that, he left, and apprehension showed on my boyfriend's face.

"*Damn*, Mia." Makayla smirked at Mom. "That was epic."

"Yup. Way to go, Mom." Ethan held out his left hand and Mom smacked it with her own, smiling. "If Dad was here…" Ethan whistled, "…he'll get hard."

Mom's nose scrunched up in abhorrence. "Ethan!" she hissed. "That's nasty! Since when did you become like this?"

Ethan held his hands up in surrender. "It's Mike's and Dad's fault for telling me dirty things!"

Mom arched her eyebrows. "Your father told you irrelevant stuff? Why?"

"Man talk, Mom," Ethan replied, stomping up the stairs. "Man talk."

Mom sighed, shaking his head. "If Julian gets back... Heck, I'll be having more than a serious chat with him." She sauntered to the kitchen with Makayla. Cody remained in the living room to watch TV.

Derek and I were in the living room. He exhaled sharply, massaging his nose with his rough fingers, leaning into the white wall. I rested my hands on his biceps, his muscles immediately relaxed at my touch. He stared at me through his thick, long, quivering eyelashes.

"I have to go and tell Marline and Luke about the Falls, but I don't want to leave you."

"You always see me every day." I wrapped my arms around his neck. "And you always have me. You won't ever lose me."

An impulsive, wary expression ambushed his face. "Y-yeah...I won't ever...lose you."

I was bamboozled at his stammering. Hence, I decided to let it go. "Ethan told me that the Falls wanted to steal your family business."

"Yeah. They're trying to."

"Wait...will you take over the business?"

"Yes. When I officially become an adult."

"You mean when you're *eighteen*?"

"Yeah...or twenty. It depends if I want to do some things first before I take over the business."

"So...you're going to have your own office and security guards?"

"And the paparazzi. Unfortunately. The Matthews Industry is very famous."

*　　*　　*

I was in my room, humming along to the music, drawing on a clean page of my sketchbook. I went on my mobile when the girls' group chat beeped with a text.

Jasmine: *Hey*

Natalia: *Sup, chica*

Sophia: *Aye*

Me: *Hello.*

Jasmine: *April, Ethan told me Owen came to ur house and ur Mom went all badass.*

Natalia: *Oh, the business boy?*

Me: *Yh*

Sophia: *I don't like him*

Natalia: *He's cute*

For a suspicious guy, tho

Sophia: *Omg, Nat, don't tell me u like him!*

Natalia: *I don't!*

It was just an observation!

N I didn't say that I like him! I find him weird 2

Jasmine: *Owen's family business dislikes Derek's family business, r8?*

Me: *Yup*

Sophia: *So the war has begun, ladies*

Get ur wands

Summon Hogwarts for help

Call the demigods to kick some ass

And let's fight them to death!

Me: *Don't forget about the Shadowhunters!*

Sophia: *YEAH. LET'S CALL THAT SEXY JACE HERONDALE*

Jasmine: *R u drunk, Soph?*

Sophia: *No*

Natalia: *So straightforward…she's drunk, chicas*

Sophia: *I'm not!*

Natalia: *Theo gave me a text when he was drunk last night…it was disgusting. He was like "Hey, babe, want to ride tonight? *wink wink*"*

Sophia: *Lmao*

That horny pig

Natalia: *Ikr*

Jasmine: *We need to keep an eye on Owen*

And the boys

We all know everything will become terrible when they meet

Me: *True*

Sophia: *Operation-stalk-Owen-and-the-boys begin!*

Natalia: *…Sophia, what's happening to u?*

Sophia: *I'm in a good mood, okay?! Don't ruin it*

Natalia: *K*

Jasmine: *Um…Guys, y is Ethan sending me weird messages?*

"CODY, GIVE ME BACK MY PHONE!" Ethan shouted.

"Give later!" Cody's insignificant voice responded.

"DON'T TALK TO ANYONE!"

"Um…" I heard Cody nervously snigger. "Me did."

"Who did you talk to?"

"Jas—"

"Oh, Lord."

"Ahhh, Mama!" Cody shrieked. Pounding, rapid footsteps echoed in the hallway. "Mama, save me! Tell Ethan stop!"

"Cody, come back here!" Ethan commanded.

"No!"

"Cody…"

"Na, na, na, na, na…Ethan slug!"

I snickered and told Jasmine that Cody was playing with Ethan's phone.

Jasmine: *Makes sense*

The messages have grammar errors and r confusing 2 read

Cody is asking me if I watched the Star Wars movies

Sophia: *Cody is SOOOO cute*

Natalia: *IKR! MIKE AND MAKAYLA MADE A WONDERFUL BOY!*

It's so sad that Mike isn't able to father Cody.

Dammit, why did he have to die?!

Sophia: *He's not dead. He's alive. Isn't that what Christians/Catholics believe? That death isn't the end?*

Me: *It actually depends on what u've done. If u want 2 receive eternal life, it depends on the good deeds u've committed. If u have done very bad deeds – like murder, rape – etc, then you will suffer in Hell for a short period or a long period. It's God's decision.*

Sophia: *Oh…okay*

Buddhists believe in reincarnation

Does God do that?

Me: *Yeah, ig*

Jasmine asked if we're excited for Christmas since Christmas Eve is tomorrow.

Sophia: *Meh*

Me: *Cody is*

He's bragging about Star Wars.

Natalia: *What r u getting for Christmas?*

Me*: Idk*

Jasmine: *Sm*

Sophia: *Sm*

For the rest of the afternoon, the girls and I talked for hours. At nightfall, we went to bed as the sky dimmed in haste.

I could hear Makayla trying to get Cody to bed. I giggled softly at the sound of my brother's loud snores next to the door.

I closed my eyes, unquestionably eager and prepared for tomorrow's Christmas Eve.

*　　*　　*

My body lugged upwards in my bed due to a raucous, clamorous, vociferous *BANG!* A modest, delectable, beaming boy bounced inside my room, leaping up and down, clapping his hands together with a gleeful smile. He jumped onto my bed, and I groaned when he unintentionally fell on my stomach. He didn't apologise as my fingers hunt for my black-framed glasses on my nightstand.

I put them on. "Morning, Cody."

"Up!" Cody exclaimed. "Christmas Eve!"

I simply smiled at the three-year-old boy. I collapsed back into my bed, fluttering my eyelashes close, groaning. I want to sleep.

"Help Granny cook," Cody informed. "Come now."

"Yes, sir," I mumbled.

"Sir," he duplicated. "Hmm...I like that!" He scrambled off the sheets and skipped out of the room, singing a Christmas carol under his breath.

Mom cooked the food for tomorrow's Christmas party. Normally, we always have our Christmas party at my house, and our family members would come over to celebrate. However, this time we were invited to Derek's mansion for the grand occasion.

I approached the bathroom door. I grabbed the doorknob, twisting it to open. It's locked. I groaned.

"Ethan, hurry up."

"I'm in the shower!" Ethan shouted.

"Hurry. Up."

Twenty minutes later, the door abruptly unlocked. My brother emerged from~~out of~~ the bathroom with a white towel firmly clenching his waist. His chest was bare and moist with beads of water falling down his abs; his dark hair drenched.

"Finally," I muttered, slamming the door shut behind me.

It's chilly inside the bathroom. Jeez, how much cold water did my brother use? Did he have a boner or something? Hmm, probably. He might've had a dream of Jasmine last night…I shuddered at the thought.

Changed in jogging bottoms and a thick comfy ruby Christmas sweater, I helped Mom in the kitchen. Makayla also assisted in chopping a few vegetables for fried rice. Ethan's there, too—he's stirring the fruitcake mixture. All of us were wearing Christmas sweaters since it's a tradition. Christmas music boomed from Ethan's mobile. Through the windows~~casements~~, I can see thick immense layers of white making colossal lumps and bumps. People were shovelling the snow out of their driveways with irritation.

Cody appeared in the doorway. He noticed me not doing anything. Therefore, he unhurriedly advanced to me with open arms.

I lifted him into a loving embrace. "You okay?"

"Yes."

A thought occurred to me. "Cody, is it okay if I read your dad's letter?"

"M-kay.

"Mama, Granny, I'm hungry."

"Sweetheart, we're nearly done. Why don't you have some juice and watch a movie in the TV?"

"Mkay."

Cody tugged me to the living room to switch on the TV. I left the remote to him and went upstairs to his room.

On Cody's bed, was a very worn-out opened envelope with the letter inside. Sitting on Cody's bed and folding my legs, I drew the letter out, unfolded it, and read Mike's letter:

Dear Cody,

Hi. My name is Mike Travis Levesque. I'm your father who will love you for eternity.

I don't know what age you will be when you read this letter, but when you do, please keep this letter with you forever because this letter might be the only object that can draw you closer to me, to my soul to feel my presence.

Cody, I do not know where life will take me or what obstacles will impede my path, though I want you to remember me as the distance between us extends However, in my heart, the distance will never extend, it will continuously fade.

I am sorry for my absence from *in your life. The reason why I won't be there — to embrace you in my arms, to kiss you good night, to shush you soothingly whenever you cry, to give you piggy back rides, to read you bedtime stories about my favourite superheroes — is because I will be in the army, fighting for the innocent.*

My fight in the army will go for a short while or longer. Either way, I am not afraid to admit that my life is now in God's hands, and I will accept anything that happens to me.

Sometimes, soldiers endure wars. Other times, they, unfortunately, don't.

I'll be honest with you. I think I won't survive the war because the war is very tough. Too tough for surviving.

There's this man I know...his name is Jesus. A great man with great power, great compassion and great, infinite, never-ending love. His love for everyone is indescribable!

You might know this, might not: Jesus died on the cross for everyone, for our sins, for our violence. He died to save us. Now, just take a moment to deliberate: would anyone in this world — an immoral, cruel, selfish world with an unfair, unequal society — do that for the entire, global population? No.

Eventually, you will realise that it's so sad to acknowledge what society has become, all because of the free will we misuse.

I want to be like Jesus. I want to make Him proud. He did so many things for us, sacrificed so much only for us, suffered so much only for us. I want to return the favour.

That's why I chose to join the army, to fight for the innocent. I considered that if I did this, Jesus would be tremendously proud to welcome me with open arms into His Father's Kingdom, to save my soul from Satan.

I think I will sacrifice my soul for the blameless people, for the people I have always loved.

Speaking of Jesus, I'll tell you a small secret. Derek (this boy who you will, hopefully, meet one day. He's awesome), my siblings and my family know this, and they believe me. I don't want to tell this secret to anyone else, because I straight away will expect the incredulity from people. No one will believe this stuff since they consider it's solely impossible.

I saw Jesus.

Basically, when I was hit by that truck, people said that I was dead for two minutes. But, from what I remember, I felt as if I wasn't dead but sleeping.

Yes, I believed that I was sleeping and dreaming. And in my dream, I was in unbearable pain. Blood was oozing down my nostrils and ears, my ribs were aching from the damage.

Then, I heard this voice, telling me to come closer. At first, I was confounded, and when I heard the voice again, I was uneasy. The voice said: 'If you are scared, I should leave'.

I was suddenly frightened when it said leave. So I begged the voice not to go and followed where it's reverberating from.

And I saw Him. Jesus. He was standing there, grinning widely at me with pure love glistening in his beautiful eyes. His arms were held out. 'Mike, come,' He implored, 'I want to hug you.'

Without hesitation, I dashed into Him, attacking Him ferociously and hugging Him so tightly, I swear He couldn't breathe. He staggered backwards and laughed jovially; His laugh relaxing my senses, creating an unexpected, particular peace in the atmosphere enfolding us.

He hugged me. Can you believe it? HE FRICKING HUGGED ME. And when He hugged me, all the pain, all the injuries...vanished. Completely and utterly vanished.

I was so happy, I cried. I cried so hard into his neck, my grip around Him tightening. He batted my back with His subtle hands, shushing me benevolently. Jesus whispered to me that He was proud of my valiant act: risking my life for a woman who was about to get hit by a truck.

Little Monkey, if I die...don't be afraid. It might seem that I'm gone forever, but if you want, you can believe that I'm always there for you. You may not see me, hear me, touch me, or smell me, but you will feel me. Trust me, you will.

I haven't joined the war yet. I was only training in the army not so long ago to prepare myself for the unruly, appalling, ghastly war. I am here, in Australia, quickly writing this letter as I watch you sleep in your crib.

Your gorgeous mother is also sleeping in the bed.

Now...I want you to promise me something, okay?

Promise me that you will take care of your mother, that you won't hurt her, leave her, or shout at her. I know that sometimes parents can be a pain in the ass, but your mother is actually new to parenting. Her memory of her parents is only a blur.

Don't break the promise, okay?

Now...let's talk about girls. You cannot date a girl until you are sixteen! You can have a few crushes, but make sure they don't get too excited! Also, don't use girls like how most assholes in this world do. It's not moral. It will only break them. Therefore, control your hormones! Plus, if you become a player (I doubt that), you won't ever find true love. And trust me, son, true love is the most miraculous, marvellous, and remarkable thing in this entire universe.

Now...puberty. Puberty can be odd, confusing, and maddening. I hit puberty when I was ten — which is very early for a guy — and everything took a sudden twist. Puberty can be a pain in the ass too, but that's how life is like. Sadly. Just be glad you don't have periods. Jeez, April used to whine all the time about her cramps, back pains, bellyaches, and headaches. Unlike Ethan who physically cringes whenever he knows about April's or Mom's (Granny to you) periods, I am mature about it.

Cody, perhaps I am wrong, perhaps I won't die, but survive the war and come back to you with a huge grin, chuck you up into the air and just cuddle you tight. Perhaps we will meet each other. Properly.

But, if not, then don't cry. Please don't cry. I don't like seeing people cry. Don't cry, Cody, don't cry. I'm always here, always by your side, always protecting you at night. I promise.

Remember and keep my promise about taking care of your mother. Okay?

I'll meet you at the end of the road, son.

I love you so much,
Papa☺

"April?"

Ethan was standing in the doorway, immediately disturbed when he noticed my tears. He sat down next to me, snaking his arms around me, wiping my soggy cheeks and my stinging eyes. "Are you okay?"

"I read Mike's letter to Cody," was all I said.

His eyes wafted to the letter in my hands. "Oh…I read it, too. It's sad, I know." He carted me into his body, cradling me.

"I hate crying," I grumbled, sniffling. "I'm tired of crying because of Mike. I should be happy for him since he's safer than all of us."

"I know, sis, I know." He kissed my forehead softly. "But sometimes, crying is good. It heals your soul. It drains the pain. Besides, we're going to meet him at the end of the road."

"That's what he said in the letter."

"He's right: one day, everyone will unite at the end of the road. It's how life is meant to be, I guess."

* * *

Roughly at four, the cooking was done. We rested in the living room, watched TV, cuddled underneath the bulky, cosy blankets. Cody drowsed, his head on my lap, soft exhales leaving him as he dreams.

Mom wanted us to help her wrap the presents. Ethan carried Cody upstairs to his bedroom. The rest gathered around the large table. Ethan joined us, and soon enough the surface of the table was messy with Christmas wrapping papers, gold bows, and ribbons.

At six o'clock, we used the free time to have a small siesta. When we woke up, we have to be prepared for midnight mass.

"Mama, I'm tired," I heard Cody whine when Makayla patted him awake.

"I know, baby, but we have to go to church."

Cranky tears flooded his eyes. "I don't want to."

"Cody, when we come back, we'll see Santa's presents under the tree," Ethan chirped.

Cody's eyes widened. He hastily wiped his eyes and bounced off the bed. "Let's go!" He rushed to his coat, wrenching it on, tied a scarf and grabbed his beanie.

Makayla guffawed. "You have to wear something nice, Cody."

Cody blinked. He glanced at his clothes and looked back at his mother. "Oops."

Twenty minutes later, I'm wearing a red flower-laced knee-length dress with tights. A dark fluffy cardigan warmed my arms, falling all the way to my knees to keep me warm tonight.

Mom was beautiful as always in her white long-sleeved dress. Her dark hair was made into a messy bun. Rosie just wore a fluffy pink dress. She's sitting in the buggy, her eyes blinking sleepily. Ethan's clothing was just a square-checked shirt, black jeans, and a denim cardigan. Cody was wearing something similar to Ethan's attire.

Before I could close the door to the house, Mom went inside quickly. Obviously, she's setting up the presents underneath the Christmas tree. We always open our Christmas presents after we come back from church.

Finally, she graciously sauntered out of the house with a festive smile. She locked the door and joined us in the car.

"What do you think we're getting for Christmas?" Ethan asked me as Mom rode the car to the church.

I merely shrugged. "What do you think?"

Ethan also shrugged. "Though, deep down I get this feeling that this Christmas is going to be the best Christmas of our lives."

I smiled at him. "You always say that for *every* Christmas, Ethan."

"Yeah," he agreed. "Though, this time, I *know* I'm right. Since Cody and Makayla are here, everything is going to be different. This Christmas will be different. I know it."

* * *

The mass was only an hour long. We used white candles in some parts for the mass. It's a tradition. Anyway, did you know that the 25th of December isn't actually Jesus' birthday? Nobody knows when his birthday is because it wasn't mentioned in the Bible. In 350 AD, Pope Julius I, Bishop of Rome, proclaimed that December 25th is the official celebration date for Jesus Christ's birthday. Mike told me that. So, of course, I'll always remember it.

Mom parked the car in front of our house. We got out, my hands diving into the pockets of my coat. It's chilly. I don't really like winter. I like spring. Spring is neither hot nor cold. It's also beautiful—the rebirth is breathtaking, the way the flowers fall from above is beautiful.

I unlocked the door, tenderly shoving it open. Regardless of the lack of glow in the entrance hallway, I could see the luminous Christmas tree lights from the parlour, flashing and twinkling as if they're imploring me to come closer.

It's moderately dim in the parlour if you block out the Christmas tree lights. Silhouettes were contrasting from objects, dancing as the lights shimmered in a recurring pattern.

Though, something was off. I concentrated on the tree properly; the emerald branches attempted to veil an unusual shadow.

Initially, I assumed it's Ethan hiding behind the tree since he always scares us for Christmas Eve. He presumed that scaring us will put us in good spirits before we go to bed, and it pleasures him.

Ethan was standing next to me, though, holding a sleeping Cody. He followed my perplexed gaze.

"Derek?" I whispered. Derek has our house keys. He could come into our house whenever he wanted to. I knew that he also loves to prank people, especially me.

No answer, no movement.

Ethan whacked the light switch on with his other hand.

The light bulb sputtered into an intense illumination.

A *figure* bounded from behind the tree.

It was a man with a bald head, eyes that were so dark that it seemed like the colour black; elusive, god-like structured high cheekbones; and a tantalizing, chiselled jawline with tiny spots of facial hair beautified his humble appearance. He's wearing an army uniform, a Canadian Armed Forces uniform.

I was frozen in place. I couldn't believe what I'm seeing.

Then, at a snail's pace, tears deluged and blissfully blurred my eyesight. My fingers wobbled, my whole body quivering with happiness. A smile formed upon my lips as the tears glided smoothly down my wintry cheeks.

My father's lips curved into a smile as he held out his arms. "Merry Christmas!"

Chapter Thirty-Eight

Christmas Day

April Levesque

I screamed.

That's my impulsive response to his words.

A scream.

I screeched, elated. My screeches vibrated with euphoria. I scurried to him, bouncing onto him, my legs wrapping around his waist as he tightly embraced me in his muscled arms. The tears outrageously spilled, soaking his left shoulder.

"Merry Christmas, darling," my precious father whispered. I, too, heard the bliss

"I miss you," I sobbed. All that fear of permanently losing my father died. Completely and utterly died. I don't have to worry about him anymore. I won't have recurring nightmares of worst case scenarios. I'm finally free from my miserable panic.

I shed extra tears of gladness. The tears showed my father how much I miss him and how happy I was.

Dad soothingly and quietly put me back on the ground. I untangled my arms from his neck, wiping my eyes. He gifted another affectionate, loving kiss on my forehead.

His gaze diverted to Ethan, who was still frozen in place. Makayla carefully pulled Cody into her arms. Ethan's shuddering fingers rumpled his dark brown hair, his silken eyes full of disbelief and astonishment.

Dad's shoulders shook in laughter, scrutinizing Ethan's flabbergasted expression. Then, Ethan darted and pulled Dad into a hug. Dad lurched back, laughing harder, returning the hug. They both swayed from side to side, and I discerned tears sparkling on my younger brother's cheeks. Dad patted Ethan's back, subtly speaking to him.

Makayla shook her son awake. Cody whined, grumbling to his mother, demanding why he's awake.

"Look who's here." Makayla pointed to Dad.

"Santa came?" Cody enquired. His head rotated and gasped. "GRANDPA!" Cody soared out of his mother's grasp, and the little boy hastened to the soldier.

Dad lifted the three-year-old boy into his arms, throwing him into the air, laughing with delight and then hugging the child tightly. 'How's my little grandson?'

"Good!" beamed Cody.

Dad turned his smile to Rosie. Rosie was wide awake in her buggy, gawking at Dad with bafflement.

"It's Daddy, honey," Mom whispered merrily. "Daddy is home."

Rosie's lips curved upwards into an enchanting smile. She lifted her arms. "Daddy," she called. "Daddy." She snivelled, her body shaking.

Holding Cody, he managed to wrench Rosie into his arms by effortlessly lifting her up, holding her. He kissed her forehead.

That's when I saw the tears in his eyes. This is Dad's first time meeting Rosie. Dad was only here when Mom was pregnant with Rosie.

Dad lowered Cody to the floor, still carrying Rosie. He drew nearer to Mom, wrapping his free arm around her. "The surprise went well."

Mom slanted into his body. "Mm-hmm," she hummed in agreement, and ardently kissed him.

"Wait…" It dawned on me. "Mom, you knew about this?"

Mom broke away from the kiss and nodded.

"You said that Dad wasn't able to make it back home for Christmas!" said Ethan.

"He wasn't, actually," Mom admitted. "But last week, he called me and told me that he could make it—"

"—And we both thought about surprising you, Cody, April, and Rosie for Christmas," Dad finished. "Also, I'm not going back to the army anymore."

"What?!" Ethan and I squeaked.

Dad contentedly grinned. "I finished my years in the army. I wish I could continue them, fight in the Syrian War a little longer, but every day I get sad because of the distance between us. The experiences in the war made me stronger, but they made me fretful if I…I'm not like Mike. I'm afraid of death. Mike isn't. That's why I'm proud of him.

"From now on, I'll be at home, taking care of all of you—" He kissed Mom's lips "—to be the perfect husband and father, to spend every, single moment of my life with you." He returned his gaze to us. "Is that fine?"

"Of course!" Ethan, Makayla, Cody, Mom, and I squealed.

Dad guffawed at our outburst. I wiped my scorching eyes once again. I glanced at Ethan, who was also rubbing his wet eyes with a goofy smile.

"You're right," I whispered. "This is the best Christmas ever."

*   *   *

"Up!" yelled Cody. "Everyone, up, up, up! Christmas day!"

I would always grunt on Christmas Day. People always make a fuss about Christmas — I get that — but we get to celebrate it every single year. On the other hand, since Dad is back, I bolted upright on my bed energetically, scrambling off the mattress and jogging to the window, pulling the curtains aside. Dots of white sprayed from the cloudy atmosphere. The trees, the roofs, the cars — *everything* — were covered in snow. Everything looked like a fantastical, mystical world. It's a White Christmas. Beautiful.

Outside in the hallway, Cody hammered on each door, hollering at everyone to get their asses up. You may be wondering, *He's three, how can he cuss at that age?* Please ask my parents that! Please ask them why I always get in trouble and scolded because of my cussing whereas my little nephew doesn't!

I heard groans from the other rooms. They implored to wake up later.

"Nuh-uh!" Cody protested, crossing his arms over his chest. "It's Christmas. Up, up, up!"

After minutes of grunting, everyone finally came downstairs gruffly, their eyes filled with exhaustion. In front of the radiant Christmas tree were presents, each and every one of them covered in fine-looking papers with bows and labels.

Ethan got a TV for his room. Mom received the latest, modernized cooking set. Rosie's present was a humongous teddy bear. Cody was gifted with a set of Star Wars toys, which he bounced up and down with glee, exclaiming, "Santa is awesome! Luv him!" Dad got a new phone. I got a new laptop. Makayla got an Apple watch.

After marvelling at our gifts, we had our Christmas breakfast.

"Let's get fat!" Cody remarked, falling onto his seat and clutching his fork and knife tightly.

Dad laughed, shaking his head and sitting next to Cody. "Let's," he agreed.

Christmas food is unquestionably my favourite part of Christmas. First: the big luscious chicken with mouthwatering roasted potatoes and vegetables and the delectable gravy. Then, the scrumptious pudding.

We ate in pleasure, guffawing, giggling, and telling stories, humming along to Christmas songs. We then tugged on the crackers, cheering just as the swift *POP* sounded.

For the next couple of hours, Mom and Dad spent some quality time. Makayla, Cody, Rosie, Ethan, and I lounged on the ᵇofas, glued to the TV which broadcasted the first Nativity movie. We cannot eat for lunch. For Christmas, my family must have two meals: Christmas Breakfast and Christmas Dinner (which will be held during the party).

Given the fact that Dad was back home, unharmed and elated, we're full of euphoria. Although, everything would be merrier if Mike was still alive; if he's in this living room, intently watching his son and his Makayla, his arms around Ethan and I…

"Merry Christmas, Mike," I quietly whispered. My eyes closed, and I drifted into slumber with Rosie relaxing on my stomach.

*   *   *

More or less around seven o'clock, Mom, Dad, Makayla, Cody, Rosie, Ethan, and I went to Derek's house for the celebration.

Dad wore a simple red Christmas sweater with printed snowflakes with LET IT SNOW printed on it along with dark jeans and black Nike shoes. Mom wore a gold blouse with a long white skirt; her brunette locks are made into a messy bun. Ethan wore a square-checked shirt and classy jeans. Makayla's dress is a glistening gray halter neck. Me? I'm just wearing a simple, snug long-sleeved crimson jumper, cream heeled boots, black jeans, flower-shaped garnet ruby earrings, a cream scarf, and Mike's necklace.

From the outside, the sophisticated, sleek building's windows beguilingly brightened with tinsel, veiling them, yet I can see moving silhouettes. The superior, vast jade garden and the bushes are covered with snow.

Inside, a colossal, tree was positioned in the grand, immense entrance hallway, and the shimmering tinsel, suspending from the ceiling with Santa Clauses glued to the railings of the stupendous staircase, made the hallway more stunning.

In the living room (the one Marline opens for unique occasions), it's different since the last time I've been here. In fact, it's utterly altered, as if Marline hired interior designers to reconstruct the entire living room. Unlike last time, the living room was ten times more massive…more luxurious.

The floor was made of marble and wood. Spherical dark peach cream sofas surrounded a hole, and unknown people descended down the five-storey staircase through that hole. Stiff poles maintained the ceiling from which a chandelier hung, and there was a reflecting curved staircase leading to the floor above.

To the right were chairs and sofas with a vast circular electric blue brightening the floor that people danced on. Speakers hung on the ceiling, loudly playing Christmas songs. Not so far away from the dance floor was a small game area with little kids battering the machines, almost like an arcade.

To the left was an extra immense space with beautiful, classy sofas squaring two big pale tables. There was a waterfall of lights streaming from the ceiling.

The entire mansion was crammed with people. Lucky, the endearing Golden Retriever puppy whined at the folks, fretful, retreating between my legs.

Lucky was my Christmas present to Derek. I hope Derek will like him. No, I hope he will *love* him. When Dad heard about this, he immediately became distressed due to Derek's reputation. He insisted on having a *talk* with Derek, to "clear some things" and "get some things" into his dimwitted head.

"No worry, Lucky." Cody shielded the little dog with his body. "I protect you! Come – find Derek!" Cody encouraged the dog to leap out from the middle of my legs, but the dog merely whined once again, not in high spirits to be sociable.

I sighed, bending to lift the dog into my arms. Lucky's legs wrap around my neck, whining.

My gaze roved the throng of individuals, and I finally spotted my friends sitting on the left, far back of the grand parlour. Cody bounded after his mother to meet Luke and Neyara.

Theo noticed Lucky and grinned. "Aw, who's the little fella?"

"Guys, this is Lucky," I introduced, placing Lucky on the floor. He curled up against my ankles timidly, resting his head on his paws. "Derek's present."

"Aw!" Sophia cooed, moving from Jackson and squatting in front of the Golden Retriever. She gently tousled his fur. "That's cute. Can I hold him?"

"Sure."

She slid her hands underneath Lucky's stomach carefully, boosting him up. She sat down next to her boyfriend swiftly, and placed Lucky on her lap. Jackson caressed Lucky's fur, vulnerably grinning at how adorable the puppy was.

"Your father is back!" Jasmine cheered, standing up so Ethan can sit down and she could sit on his lap. Her dress was beyond breathtaking: halter neck and cream-gold. "You're happy, right?"

Ethan arched his eyebrows at Jas. "No, I'm horribly depressed," he responded sarcastically.

"I have to be honest." Natalia wore a grey gemmed, transparent blouse, wintry white jeans, big earrings, grey heeled boots, and a huge wrist bracelet. "Your father is hot."

Sophia gave her an exasperated look. Lucky looked peaceful on her lap.

Theo glared. "And I'm not?"

"Well, you are hot, Theo," Natalia agreed. "But…"

"But, what?" Theo fumed. "He's hero hot? Is that what you're saying? God, Natalia, you're so annoying!"

Theo stood up and walked away, provoked by Natalia's compliments.

Natalia's eyes saddened. "That's not what I meant," she whispered, jogging after Theo. "You're beautiful, Theo." The two lovers wandered off.

"Whoa, what happened to them?" Ethan asked, watching Natalia grab Theo by his hands, spinning him around and cupping his face.

"They had a small argument," said Sophia, her long grey romper dress shimmering. "Like Derek, Theo was becoming an easily jealous person whenever Natalia compliments a guy."

I understand Theo's frustration with Natalia's compliments, but either way, he should acknowledge that Natalia has eyes for him alone.

I watched Theo listen intently to Natalia's words, and the way he pulled Natalia into a passionate kiss made me beam with happiness. Theo is like another brother to me, and seeing him happy makes me happy.

"Speaking of Derek, where is he?" I asked my friends.

"He had to do something," Jackson responded.

"Something?"

Jackson shrugged smugly, smirking. "Something."

"Hi!" beamed a similar voice.

Neyara advanced to us with contentment along with Luke. Cody was in Luke's arms. Neyara is strikingly stunning in her indigo knee-length dress with white and gold fireworks.

"Hi, Neya! Hi, Luke!" Jasmine beamed back. "Hey, Cody!"

Cody grinned endearingly at us. "Hi, Jas!" He inclined towards my best friend, his fingers bending to her.

Jasmine pulled Cody into a bear hug. Jackson and Theo gave Cody a high five as I kidnapped my nephew from Jasmine's embrace.

Cody turns his eyes to Lucky. "Lucky! Come here!"

As if understanding him, Lucky leaped off Sophia's lap and bounded to Cody. Cody got off my lap and started playing with the dog, giggling.

"April, Derek's outside," Luke enlightened. "Have fun."

Baffled at Luke's words, my friends smirked, as if they knew something that I didn't.

Theo tugged Cody to his lap and began a conversation about *Star Wars*.

"You like *Star Wars*?" the three-year-old boy enquired.

"Yeah, little man! It's my jam!"

"Me too! Love Yoda! Jyn Erso mine!"

Jackson joined in. "No, pal, Jyn Erso is *mine*!"

Cody glared. "Nope! Mine. My girl."

"She's too old for you."

"Idiot, don't care…"

Walking through the mob of people, I reached the open entryway and stepped through it. I yelled when a hand pulled me backwards, and I was twirled around into a hard wall. Well, a hard *chest*.

Derek smirked, his arms around me, my palms flat on his chest. He's handsome in his jersey, jeans, and coat. His most captivating feature were his eyes. I have always had a soft spot for blue eyes—I find them so mesmerising

His warm breath fanned my face. "Merry Christmas."

"Merry Christmas."

"Do you have my present?"

"I'll give your present if you give me mine."

"Nope. Give me mine first. Then I'll give you yours. Besides, your present is longer than mine."

"Longer?" I reiterated, bewildered.

"Give my present first…" His nose and lips fondled mine. "…and I'll give you yours."

"Fine. He's in the living room. Do you want to come with me?"

"*He?*" He ~~simply~~ baffled, ambling after me to the deluxe parlour.

(handwritten: was) (handwritten: simply)

Soon enough we reached our friends at the far back. They all observed us, yet when they saw Derek, they grinned eagerly.

"What the hell?" he muttered, his eyes enlarged as he saw Lucky.

Everyone was euphoric at Derek's gobsmacked expression. Lucky's head rose up, his dark chocolate eyes drawn to Derek's charisma. His nose quivered, as if he's sniffing. Curious and fascinated by his company, the dog hopped off Neyara's lap, and cautiously padded to Derek.

Derek dropped to his knees. "You got me Lucky?"

"You did say you wanted a dog for Christmas."

Lucky halted in front of Derek, raking him with a probing glint in those brown orbs.

Derek pulled the small fluffy gold creature into his arms. Lucky barked, his tail wagging as he placed his two front ~~on~~ Derek's chest. A rumble resonated from his throat. His nose skimmed around Derek's face, absorbing his smell.

(handwritten: paw)

. Derek laughed delightfully and inadvertently ~~falls~~ backwards, permitting Lucky to explore him.

(handwritten: fell)

"Are you taking him with you?" asked Jackson.

"Why not? It'll be nice."

"But will he fit your car?"

"Yeah."

"Won't the security take him out?"

"Nah. They won't."

"What are you two talking about?" I demanded, confounded.

"Oh, nothing," said Jackson.

"But, Derek, I want play with doggie," Cody complained, advancing to my boyfriend.

Derek looked at Cody. "Will you take care of him properly?"

"Yeah!"

Derek diverted his gaze to his best friend. "Will you—"

"Sure," Theo interjected before Derek completed his question. "You and April go have fun."

I implored Derek to tell me where he's taking me as we made our way through the swarm of people. He only mumbled to me that it's a surprise.

Only a few feet away from the exits, Derek accidentally smacked into the back of a tall man. The man immediately swirled around. Seeing me, he smiled softly. "Hi, princess."

"Hi, Dad."

In his hand was a glass full of champagne, and around him were his old friends from school, Mom, Marline, and other people I am not familiar with.

"Derek!" Mom exclaimed. "Julian, remember Derek, Sam's second son?"

Dad analysed Derek. "Yes. I played basketball with him, Luke, and Mike."

"Hello, Julian," said Derek.

"Derek. How are you doing, son?"

"Fine."

"He's April's boyfriend, by the way," said Mom. Dad's friends and the other strangers amble away, leaving only him, Mom, and Marline to talk with Derek and me.

Dad's eyebrows arc upwards. "*Boyfriend?*" He crossed his arms over his chest, irately glaring at me. "He's your boyfriend, and you never told me?"

"You were busy, Julian." Mom placed her hand on Dad's muscled arm. "Besides, April told you on the phone she had a crush on Derek, didn't she?"

My cheeks burned furiously at Mom's declaration. I can't believe she said that in front of Derek.

Derek's lips twitched, self-satisfied, yet refusing to smirk in front of my father.

Dad huffed. "Fine. If Derek wants to be my daughter's boyfriend, then he must have my consent." He redirected his glare to Derek. "Tomorrow, dinner at our house, and I'll see if you're worthy of her."

Mom seemed exasperated. "Julian, you know that Derek is a sweet boy …"

"He changed," Dad said brusquely. "He became a player."

"He changed again, for the better this time."

"I don't care. Derek, if you want to be April's boyfriend, be at my house at seven tomorrow. Got it?"

"Okay." For once, I witnessed the alarm in his ocean blue eyes. His alarm of losing me all because of my father's concern and protectiveness.

Other than Mike and Ethan, Dad was the most protective one in the family. He was anxious if one of his loved ones gets hurt. He already lost Mike, and losing Mike felt as if he lost a part of his soul. He lost Mike; he doesn't want to lose anyone else.

Mom said that most fathers are like that—they're afraid to lose their girls to another man even though they know it must happen one day.

"I'm going to take April somewhere," Derek stated.

"Where?" said Dad.

"He cannot say," Mom answered before Marline or Derek could. "It's April's Christmas gift. He's very romantic, Julian."

Julian smiled. "Just like our Sammy."

Marline's eyes filled with happiness just by the mention of Derek's father's nickname. Mom was Derek's mother's best friend, and because of that Dad and Alexandra Matthew's husband, Samuel, good friends for a long time. Dad's and Samuel's friendship was another reason why the Matthews and the Levesques were so fond of each other.

Derek and I bid our farewells. Dad warned Derek not to do anything daft.

Derek's hands interlocked with mine, pulling me after him as he raced through the crowd. He hastily glanced at his watch and muttered countless blasphemies regarding the fact that we'll be late, whatever that means.

"Where are we going?" I demanded for the hundredth time. We're outside now, and the iciness seeped through my skin, numbing my bones and making my body shiver.

We got into his golden Lamborghini. To my displeasure, he did not answer or say a word. Instead, he merely smirked as he brought the engine to life and drove through the snowy roads to God knows where.

* * *

Derek parked his lush golden Lamborghini behind the fence. Alongside his superior car were other vehicles cramming the parking lot, with people hopping out and scurrying to the entryway, screaming and ecstatic.

"Adio!" A dark toffee brown skinned woman hastened after her son, who seems to be ten. "Wait up, Adio!"

The little boy called Adio whirled around. "Hurry, Mom! I can hear them speak! It's about to start!" The boy resumed his dart to the entrance.

Uncertainty marked my face. I can hear Christmas harmonies resounding from not so far away, and I distinguish the outline of what seems to be a large platform with people assembling around it. "Derek, what's—"

"Oh, shit. The kid is right. It's about to start. Come on!" He pulled me after him, pushing through the multitude of people walking to the front.

Pine trees were all over the place, budded with miniature flecks of quivering lights that suspended from one branch to another. The nippy grass was specked with ivory. As I mentioned before, people gathered in front, chanting the current song that was reverberating from the mammoth speakers on a stage, with wires, instruments, keyboards, and microphone stands. It wasn't the stage that caught peoples' attention; it was the singers, the band.

It's the Train. The band.

"Oh, my God!" I shrieked.

Jimmy Stafford, Patrick Monahan, Hector Maldonado, Jerry Becker, and Drew Shoals were here. They were all there, standing on the alluring stage with contented beams.

"Wassup, everybody!" Patrick Monahan shouted. His black hair was rumpled, wisps flying out in alternative directions as if he's been electrocuted; his eyes were similar to Derek's, except that they're much lighter. He wore a dark cardigan over a plain grey shirt and denim jeans.

A roar boomed from the crowd.

"Is everyone good? Cos if you're all feeling bored, sad, or down...we hope this song will boost up your spirits!"

Patrick bobbed his head at his bandmates. Jimmy Stafford — anchor-like beard, bald head and hooded eyes with dark shades — tugged strings of his guitar as an opening. Jerry Becker (glasses, long hair, and dark clothes) rapidly yet gracefully drummed the keyboard with his fingers. Hector Maldonado strummed his bass guitar.

"Join us!" Hector advised.

Ho, ho, ho...

Shake up the happiness

Wake up the happiness

Shake up the happiness

It's Christmas time

"Damn it!" Derek cussed when we're trapped in the middle of the cheering crowd. His hand was clutching mine securely, alarmed to let me go.

There was a story that I was told

And I want to tell the world before I get too old

And don't remember it, so let's December it

And reassemble it, oh yeah

His eyes desperately roamed above the heads. He tried to propel through to pave a small path for us to get to the front, yet in the end, we're still stuck in the centre.

Once upon a time in a town like this

He fleetingly looked at me, and then at my legs, and then back at my face. He turned his back to me, shouting, "Get on my back!"

A little girl made a great big wish

"What?"

"Get on my back and maybe try to get on my shoulders so you can see!"

To fill the world full of happiness

And be on Santa's magic list

Everyone chanted the chorus along with the band blissfully.

Shake it up, shake up the happiness
Wake it up, wake up the happiness
Come on all, it's Christmas time

"What about you? You won't see anything."

Shake it up, shake up the happiness
Wake it up, wake up the happiness
Come on all, it's Christmas time

He only smiled. "I did this for you. Not for me."

Ho, ho, ho
Ho, ho, ho
It's Christmas time

I clambered on his back and positioned my thighs on his shoulder. I yelped, edging off, but managing to stabilise my body on his shoulders.

At the same town miles away
A little boy made a wish that day
That the world would be okay
And Santa Clause would hear him say
I got dreams, and I got love
I got my feet on the ground and family above
Can you send some happiness with my best
To the rest of the people of the east and the west

His hands grasped my legs firmly. Slowly but surely, I raised my arms and screamed with enchantment. Derek and I joined the crowd and the band singers.

And maybe every once in a while
You give my grandma a reason to smile
'Tis the reason to smile

It's cold, but we'll be freezing in style
And let me meet a girl one day
That wants to spread some love this way
We can let our souls run free
And she can open some happiness with me

"Sing with me!" Patrick roared.

The throng screamed with felicity.

Shake it up, shake up the happiness
Wake it up, wake up the happiness
Come on all, it's Christmas time
Shake it up, shake up the happiness
Wake it up, wake up the happiness
Come on all, it's Christmas time

"You okay up there?" Derek asked at full volume.

"Yeah!" I smiled down at him. "Thank you so much."

"It's alright."

Suddenly, he self-consciously nibbled his lower lip, as if a thought occured to him. "I got something else for you." He sounded timid. "But I just have a feeling that you'll find it boring. Other than this concert, I tried so hard to find the perfect present for you, something that you can always keep. I asked my uncle to make something for you...something that'll always remind you of me. I just don't think you'll like it. It's lame and—"

"Show me," I interrupted. "I don't care. If it's from you, it's always perfect."

Derek didn't look at me; his eyebrows knitted in nervousness.

With his left hand on my left thigh, and since I'm tightening my legs around his neck enough not to suffocate him, he took this as a safe chance to dive his right hand into his pocket. He pulled out a superb vivid gold locket. The locket was exquisitely ~~structured~~ *made*—wings were curved over to form the shape of a heart, with lines deepening a few parts to form the feathers. I took it from his grasp, opening it to see small sentences carved inside: *DEREK'S ANGEL.*

"D-do you like it?" he stammered.

"No," I replied. His face dropped with sadness. "I love it, Derek."

He grinned. "Good. I asked my uncle to make it from pure gold—"

My jaw dropped. "Pure gold?!"

"Yeah. He crafts jewellery. He's pretty awesome at it."

"How much did it cost?"

"I didn't have to pay him. He's my uncle. He makes me whatever I want for free."

He spent his own pocket money to book tickets for a concert and a locket? Can this guy get any more perfect than he already was? What did I do to deserve such a handsome, engaging guy who helped me, put his arm around me, and allowed me to cry on his shoulders? Is this the answer from God? Is Derek the solution to my dilemmas?

I fixed the necklace around my neck, the gold chilling my skin and my collarbone. I bowed forward, my hair veiling our faces as I tenderly slam my lips on his, holding them for long enough to make our lungs burn with no air.

"Thank you," I whispered, my smile stroking his. "I love it so much."

"Any time, angel. *Any time.*"

*   *   *

The concert ended in fifteen minutes, and we spent another ten minutes talking with Jimmy Stafford, Patrick Monahan, Hector Maldonado, Jerry Becker, and Drew Shoals.

fantastic.

The band members were really fastidious. They saw Derek straight away when we entered the miniature room, and they gathered around Derek for a group hug. They asked him the basics: how is he, how is his family (yes, they know his family), and then they turned their gaze to me.

Jimmy immediately smugly smiled, as if understanding why I was here with Derek. "Who's this?"

"This is my girlfriend, April," Derek answered with self-gratification.

Patrick, Hector, Jerry, and Drew replicated Jimmy's haughty smirk.

Jerry Becker ruffled his fingers through his sleek long black hair. "That's good, I guess."

"Yeah." Patrick smiled at me warm-heartedly. "Derek is a cool man. He can be a jackass, but he has a good heart. Deciding to let go of him is like deciding to leave life."

"Aw, thanks, man." Derek cordially whacked Patrick's shoulder softly

"Are you okay now?" Drew asked, suddenly worried.

Without any reason behind his question, I directly knew what the man was enquiring about.

Derek nodded. "More than okay." He slid his arm around me. "With her, it's always more than okay."

"Make sure you're always more than okay. The last time we met, you were a little negative—"

"He wasn't 'a little' negative, Drew," Hector interposed. "You were more than negative." The lines on his forehead proved his statement. "We were concerned about you, man. You were always the happy kid, and seeing you so sad made us miserable and worried."

"Don't worry, Hector. I'll be fine. Thanks for coming to town, though. It means a lot not only to April and me, but to the people." Derek nodded at where the citizens of Peony Hallows were, tucking into their vehicles, chitchatting with their friends and families.

The Train grinned.

"It's our pleasure to make people happy. Merry Christmas."

"Merry Christmas."

*   *   *

We were famished. So, we ordered takeaway. In the car, a big bag of McDonald's chips rested on my lap.

"Give me one," implored Derek. He's driving, his eyes engrossed on the road as he ~~gyrates~~ turns the wheel.

I jostle three chips into his mouth. "So, were the Train and your family close?"

"You could say that. The Train and Dad knew each other. I don't know how, though. They didn't go to the same schools. They just…knew each other. Didn't Mike tell you about them?"

"He always blabbed about them, but not a lot."

The topic unexpectedly changed. "You know your dad?"

"No. I don't know him. Who is he?" I sarcastically muttered.

"I'm scared if he won't like me, angel."

"He will," I guaranteed. "Dad loved you. He still does. He taught you how to play basketball, remember?"

"Yeah, but that all changed. I changed."

"And you changed again. For the better. How many times does everyone have to repeat that? Derek, I know Ethan and Dad can be a pain in the ass. I understand people will get annoyed by their protectiveness, but ever since Mike died, that impacted the both of them to become more protective of us.

"Ethan hated you. Now, there's a bromance between you two." Derek chuckled at that. "And there will be another bromance between my father and you. He still loves you, Derek."

Derek sighed stressed, massaging his forehead with his fingertips. "I hope so. I'm not a good person, April."

"No matter what you did in the past, you are a good person. You're always good to me."

"What if I lose you? Because of him? Or what if I lose you...because of something else?" His voice sounded anomalous at the end.

"You won't lose me."

"I will. I'm not really good at proper relationships. The previous ones were all fake because...you know, it was all a game and all...I know I'll mess this up numerous times."

"I'll still stay with you. No matter what you do, or what you have done, I won't leave you. Ever."

He didn't believe my words.

Chapter Thirty-Nine

Promises

April Levesque

The next day, everyone woke up at past two. The party was so festive; it drained all our vigour throughout the holy celebration. I bumped into Derek's grandmother, Sandy. She saw our intertwined hands, and straight away exploded into innumerable squeals.

Last night, Sandy was dancing energetically to Nae Nae. She was pleased to see Derek and me together. She admitted that from the moment I stepped into her room in the care centre, she detected the amorous chemistry radiating from us.

Brushing my teeth with the minty toothpaste, my mind thought about the dinner tonight with Derek. I washed my face, deliberating how the dinner would turn out. What if Mom humiliates me? Oh, who am I kidding—ever since we were kids, she always embarrassed me in front of Derek! The teasing infuriated me, blinding me the candid fact that Mom shipped us from the beginning. Plus, from many novels I read, the mother always embarrasses the child.

At that moment, I contemplated ~~about~~ our relationship. From the stories I've read online, there are always those good girl/bad-boy stories, where the bad boy falls in love with the good girl. In novels, the term "opposites attract" exists. I never presumed that "opposites attract" will breathe in reality. Now, I'm proven wrong. Perhaps, if you keep on cherishing that hope, that faith…if you impatiently wait and endure life, all your dreams and your fantasies will come to you.

I guess that's what life is all about: waiting.

"We're meeting Derek tonight. Properly."

Dad, Ethan, and I were in the living room, eating our breakfast. Mom was still fast asleep. To what Dad reported us, Mom drank too much, and that's why we had to leave a bit earlier than the others.

"Ethan, what do you think of the guy?"

Ethan looked at our father. "Derek?" Dad nodded. "Well, the dude is an asshole, but then again, everyone are assholes nowadays. I'm an asshole. Derek's a good guy. Didn't trust him at first because…you know he was the player and all that shit. Now, he's fine. I don't mind him. I understand why Mike was so fond of him."

The mention of the eldest brother in the family attacked our father with contemplations. From the hazy glimmer in his dark eyes, I knew Dad was reflecting on the past, on how Dad played with Mike, Ethan, Luke, Derek, and I. "Do you think Derek is good for April?"

Ethan hastily looked at me and then at Dad. "Yeah. I mean, Mom shipped them from the minute they were born. She showed me the baby pictures of April and Derek; they're cute. Marline ships them. Mike shipped them. Theo ships them. Jackson ships them. Nat, Soph, and Jas ship them. Heck, even the people in Heaven ship them. They're destined to be together, Dad. If you won't believe that, then ask God."

Dad took in Ethan's answer, pondering. "Mia did tell me how close they were..." he whispered, his voice trailing off as Dad focuses on me. "Honey, do you know why I wanted to have a son first?"

My answer was a swift shrug.

"I wanted a son first, so he can beat up any boy who makes any of my little girls cry. Brothers are like that: they are exasperating. They make you cry, fight you, argue with you relentlessly, yet they will stand up for you, wish for you to succeed, tease you, joke around, make fun of you, laugh when you fail, help you when you're sad, make you strong, clear your mistakes. No matter how annoying they are, or how uncaring you think they are, they still love you and care about you. It's the same with sisters.

"Mike isn't here to do that, but Ethan is. And as a father, I will do those things too."

"He's right, big sis," Ethan agreed. "I know my concern for you is annoying, but I can't help it. When Mike told me about the bullying and your depression, I was so scared if you would do something that will break me. Mike is gone, and losing another one I love will be another unbearable heartbreak. I'm sorry for being annoying, sis. Sorry for being such a jackass."

I smiled. "It's alright. I can be annoying, and I can be a jackass sometimes."

"All humans are jackasses," Dad muttered. "It's how we, unfortunately, made ourselves to be. Majority of the time, we cannot control our mind. Our minds are manipulative and intolerable. It steals our power of control. It gives us incorrect theories about what is right."

"Just like how Derek's mind manipulated him," said Ethan. "Derek's parents died. He was depressed, and he blamed himself for causing their death. He called himself a murderer. A devil. The depression controlled him…it dominated him to express his hate for others, to become a bully. He admitted he regretted it, yet at the same time, he cannot control the oppression."

Ethan stirred the silver spoon around his bowl of cereal. "People will say that what Derek did was wrong. Heck, I even said it's wrong. But then I put myself in the asshole's shoes…and I understood. I empathized with him and realised his misery. Mental illness shouldn't be judged."

"Did you help him?" Dad enquired to my brother and me. "When he was depressed, did you help him?"

"After Mike's death, he pushed us away, Dad. April tried to run after him, to talk to him, but he just ignored her. I tried to do the same, but he begged me to leave him alone. So, we left him and…things changed so suddenly. He became this malicious, bleak-hearted, cold bully. He made fun of us sometimes. We hated him, well, technically *I* hated him; April disliked him. Then, all of a sudden, he returned to our lives and things seemed to go back to the good old days. We found out about Derek's depression, and we helped him. It was mostly April, though. She helped him the most."

Dad stared at me. "You're right, kid," he mused to Ethan. "Mental illness shouldn't be judged. Perhaps, I'll be okay with your relationship, April. But, just in case if something bad happens to you, tell us, and I will deal with the situation. Promise?"

"Okay. Promise."

*   *   *

The dining table was piled with plates and portions of food. Derek arrived five minutes later after seven in the evening, dressed in a dark shirt and light grey jeans. He ~~grappled~~ was holding the leash ~~that's~~ attached to the collar of his Golden Retriever puppy.

"Hi, Lucky!" I cooed, squatting to ruffle his fur. Lucky elatedly whimpered, satisfied to see me again. His snout skimmed my face, raising his two front paws to rest on my chest, his tail wiggling with exhilaration.

I stood on my tiptoes to level my lips with Derek's. "You're so tall."

"I am." Leisurely, his lips fondled mine enough to ignite heat in my blood. "I'm sorry to break this to you, baby, but you're a midget."

"I might be small, but I'm not a midget."

"You are." He cupped my face with his rough hands, pulling me closer to him. Our noses caressed, and he kissed me feverishly.

A cough sounded, and we flew apart. Dad was standing at the end of the hallway, not very pleased at the sight of us too close. He bobbed his head at the dining room door, motioning us sharply to get in.

We sat around the table. Derek to my right, Ethan to my left who offered a "Sup, asshole", and Mom greeted Derek with a motherly kiss on the cheek.

Cody grinned at Derek. "Hi!"

"Hey, buddy. You doing okay?"

"Yeah." Cody noticed Lucky. "Lucky!" He scurried around the table to incarcerate the Golden Retriever in his arms. "Lucky, I missed you!" He looked at his mother who just entered the dining room. "Mama, can I play Lucky?"

Makayla smiled. "Sure. Only if Derek allows it."

Cody stared at Derek with imploring eyes. "Can?"

"Yeah, okay."

"Yay! Come, Lucky. Up to room!"

Cody carried Lucky upstairs to his bedroom. Makayla welcomed Derek and sat down next to Dad. An unusual silent, uncomfortable atmosphere prevailed.

"Before we start this dinner," Mom spoke, her voice soft and empathetic, her eyes darting from Derek and to me, "I want to say that I'm happy about the fact that you're in a relationship. Children, please excuse Julian if he gets a little angry and will be a dick."

Ethan snorted at Mom's last words. Derek, Makayla, and I shrug our shoulders, silently sniggering at Mom's absurdity. Dad rolled his eyes whilst Mom smirked slyly at him.

"You know for a fact it's true, Julian. You are a dick, sometimes." Mom peacefully took a sip of her orange juice as she embraces Rosie on her lap.

"Enough," Dad retorted as we all suppressed shaky smiles. "Let's get to the talk. Derek, what are you interested in?"

"Meh, stuff." His hand stroked my leg under the table. I carefully dropped my hand underneath and placed it on top of Derek's hand, my fingers feeling his firm skin. "I enjoy playing sports: basketball, football...all that stuff."

"What are your plans for the future?"

Derek shrugged. "I don't really know. I think I have to take my father's business. You know, rule it and stuff."

"Ah, the Matthews Industry. Yes, Sammy did mention about wanting to start his own company to help the world."

"Yeah, Dad's company is a success in the world. We help the homeless, the unfortunate, the people in lower class cities; we campaign to stop all the immoral things: rape, murder, robbery, etc."

"The company is very popular. Everyone approves of it. There are hundreds of people from all over the world who are part of the agenda, right?"

"Yes."

"And the Falls are trying to steal the company?"

"Not only the company, but the money. We get paid more than the other companies."

"I don't like the Falls," Dad muttered. "They're very...terrible."

"Who does?" Ethan muttered next.

"Derek, is it okay if we talk about personal things?"

"Okay."

Dad warily said, "After Samuel's death — may he rest in peace; he was a good guy — things went bad, right? You were diagnosed with an illness?"

"Uhm..." Derek warily looked at me.

"You don't have to explain, son," said Dad. I sensed his body was serene and I knew he's beginning to like Derek.

"No, I want to."

"Derek, you don't have to explain," Mom said softly. "We know some of the consequences in your life. But you don't have to explain further. If it's too hard, then you can tell us another time. We'll understand."

"No, it's fine. I'll explain. Because of April, I learned that confessing to the right people is calming.

"My mother died after she gave birth to me. So, it was only Dad, Luke, Marline, and me in the house. Dad told so many things about Mom that I never knew: her charisma, her love. It's actually really sad to know that I have never been mothered before in my life. I always envied the people in my school especially when they mention their mothers. I always get angry when people don't appreciate their parents. They should be glad they have parents because a life without parents is like reading a story with plot holes.

"Luke was Mike's best friend. Because of that, I come to your house sometimes."

"You were shy when we first met," Mom reminisced, smiling at the lovely memory. "It was adorable."

"Yeah, I was shy. You were all so nice to me, I loved it.

"When I was ten, my father committed suicide. He drowned himself. I was broken. I felt so lonely without my parents. I felt hurt and miserable.

"I was diagnosed with major depression, and after a couple of months, I snapped. I snapped because I had enough of waking up, going to school and seeing the happy smiles of my classmates. It made me jealous because they had happiness and loving people when I don't. I was the one who was always breaking inside. I pushed everyone away, and they were concerned. Theo begged me to tell everything, I just cussed at him to leave me alone. I was so sad, so angry, and tired that I projected my hurt on everyone; I hurt so many people, so they would know *my pain* and *my sadness*. I wanted them to know how I've been feeling for so long.

"Mike was the first one I confessed to. He helped me, which surprised me. I thought that if I tell someone about my depression, then they'll judge me. Because that's how society is like: judgmental. Instead, Mike hugged me, telling me that so many people love me and I should appreciate it. He introduced me to Jesus, telling me that Jesus will never stop loving me no matter what I've done.

"Mike was like a true father to me. He picked me up when I fell, he wiped my tears, he gave me pep talks...He gave me everything. He's the type of guy everyone will die for to have in their lives.

couldn't

"When he died...everything fell again. I ~~can~~'t feel the happiness anymore. I got angry and sad again. I pushed everyone away—I pushed my best friends: April, Theo, Ethan...I pushed them all away. I became the bully again."

Derek had a look of sorrow on his face. I placed my head in the crook of his neck. His arm immediately went around me, as if he's frightened that I'll vanish. My fingers rubbed his sweltering eyes.

"The only thing I regretted doing in the past was not allowing April to help me. April was my best friend. I loved her. I loved teasing her, annoying her, calling her my girl, hugging her... I loved it when we read bedtime stories to each other in bed. Pushing her away was like pushing Jesus away. It's like telling Jesus to leave me alone. It broke me. It broke her. I wanted to run after her and hug her tightly, but I was scared she would judge me because I had already earned the town's title of being the heartbreaker."

"But then you two reconnected," Mom said happily.

Derek grinned, tears falling down his cheeks. "Yes. We reconnected. I thank God for that because I told her everything — my feelings, my true thoughts — and she helped me. I found out about her pain and her sadness, and I was relieved to find someone who's exactly like me – someone who has the same scars as me, who understands me and my feelings. So, in return, I helped her: I told her to stop self-harming. She did. I did all my best to make her happy: I asked my friends to become her best friends, and they did. From that day onwards, we've been there for her.

"I've always been there for her. I love her very much. She's my gift from God, my angel from Heaven. She's my miracle.

"I don't want to lose her. If you don't trust me, sir, then I respect that. But I will never stop loving her, even if we're not together. I'll keep on proving to you that I am the man for April until my last breath. I don't care if you appreciate me, I won't let go of her again. I love her. And not even God can stop me from doing so."

Derek's tears were contagious because my eyes were filling with hot tears. I slanted my head upwards to smile at him, the tears gliding down my rosy cheeks. He returned my smile, cupping my face with his hands and yanking my head closer to bring our lips together. Then, we both looked at my parents, my brother, and Makayla.

Mom was perceptibly contented. Even from the start, she approved of Derek. She knew about Derek as the callous boy, yet she also knew that there was a kind, stunning, sweet boy in him. And that kind, stunning, sweet boy was the Derek we're all seeing.

"See, I told you he's an awesome asshole," said Ethan, shattering the silence.

Derek laughed. "You're an annoying asshole."

Ethan grinned goofily. "I know. That's why we both hate and love each other. That's why there's a bromance."

Derek laughed again.

Dad leaned forward, his elbows on the table. "I believe you, Derek. I apologise if I was harsh and demanding earlier. It's just that my family means a lot to me. After all the horrible stuff I heard about April — her depression, the repeated bullying she went through, the self-harm — I don't want her to break because of a relationship. Looking at you again after a long time, I believed the rumour that you are one of those callous shitheads who love to break hearts. I thought you're a player like most guys in the world today. On the other hand, listening to the story of your life, I was proven wrong. I agree with everyone that you have changed for the better, and now you're the sweet boy I love. I approve of you. Just promise me that you won't break her. Ever."

Derek stiffened. I nudged his elbow gently. He blinked, as if he's coming out of his reverie, his world of contemplations and worries.

"Of course," he hastily replied. "I promise."

*   *   *

After we finished dinner, Mom walked into the parlour with a big cardboard box. "Derek, darling, would you like to see April's baby photos?"

I gasp. "MOM, NOOOOO!"

"Yes!" Derek said ecstatically. "I'd love to, Mia."

"Noooooooo," I whined, tugging Derek back. "Please don't. If you love me, then don't."

"They're just pictures, darling," Mom said.

"They're embarrassing!"

"Babies are cute," Derek said, "so I'm sure they're not embarrassing. I'm sure they're cute. Now, let me go."

"Noooooo, pleaaaaassseee!"

Derek shook me of effortlessly and went to sit next to Mom. Mom defiantly smiled at me. Everyone gathered around him, and I groaned. Mom drew out the beautifully decorated photo album. I sat next to Derek. Rosie snuggled into Derek's chest.

I forlornly watched Mom open the album, pointing at the first picture. It was a picture of Mom bathing me in the tub. I was looking petulant in the photo.

Cody pointed at the picture. "BAHAHAHAHAHA," he laughed, his hands clutching his stomach as he rolled off the sofa and fell to the floor with a loud thud. He didn't grimace or cry in pain, he continued laughing as Makayla hissed at him to be quiet. Mom giggled at the contagiousness of Cody's laugh.

I physically cringed. "Oh, no," I muttered, burying my face into Derek's chest.

Derek chuckled, his chest vibrating. "Aw, cute."

"She wasn't that grumpy when she was young," Dad said. "She was quieter and independent. But still grumpy."

"She's still the same, isn't she, Dad?" Ethan said in a teasing voice.

"Yup," Dad agreed, ruffling my hair.

Mom flipped the page over. The right picture was of two small babies, toothlessly grinning contentedly at the camera in their onesies.

"*Awww*," Mom cooed. "This was you two playing. Look how adorable you two were."

I was in the white onesie, leaning into Derek who's in his grey one.

Derek smiled. "We were always adorable."

The other pictures were mortifying ones of me, and then abruptly it's about Derek.

"Marline gave me some photos of you," said my mother. "When we were in high school, we promised to give each other baby photos of our children."

"Marline has my baby photos?!" Ethan and I squeaked.

"Yeah. I think it's in her attic."

One picture was of Baby Derek sleeping on an elephant teddy bear with his arm veiling a part of his face. Others were of Baby Derek and his father Samuel Matthews; he's quite tanned with sleek jet-black hair, dark ocean blue eyes with a streaked beard. Usually, Samuel was holding Derek's hand or carrying him with sunglasses concealing his mesmerising eyes, or a hat protecting his hair from the heat. A different picture was of Derek when he was seven or eight, wearing a suit with his hair combed backwards and sunglasses shrouding his captivating eyes. Standing not so far away from Derek was Samuel.

"Sam was a good guy, Derek," my father disclosed. "It's a shame he died."

"He promised me that he'd never leave us," Derek grumbled crossly. "Yet, he did. He broke his promise. I hate him for that."

"Do you know what happened to him?" Mom asked him. "In the past?"

"Yeah, he was in the foster system. A couple adopted him. Shit happened, and they abused him. Dad started taking drugs. He smoked. He drank. He became the heartbreaker."

"Do you know how your parents met?"

"Mom met Dad in a party. Mom vomited on Dad because she drank too much. Dad was so angry and cussed at her, but Mom vomited again."

"Marline and I weren't able to find her," Mom muttered.

"No, you were with me," Julian reminded. "Marline was…somewhere else."

"Dad took Mom to her house," Derek continued. "And from that day, they became friends and then a couple. Mom introduced Dad to Mia and you, Julian."

"It's like you two," said Makayla. "April is like Alexa: a nerd and a sweetheart. Derek, you're like your father: the heartbreaker who fell in love and changed."

"Like history repeating itself," I whispered.

"Yeah."

"Alexa was a beautiful woman." Mom placed her hand on Derek's shoulder. "She's proud of you. I know it. And so is your father."

"I hope so. Luke and Marline are my only family left."

Dad seemed incredulous. "What are you talking about? We're your family, too. Aren't we?"

"Yeah," Ethan agreed. "We're your family. Always was, always will be."

*   *   *

A month passed. For New Year's Eve, my friends and their families celebrated at our house, chatting, drinking (except for the underage, of course) and just having the time of our lives. It was Cody's birthday on January 21st, so we held a small party for him. Makayla started taking Cody to school. Every single day, he would come back home, blabbing to us about his friends and his school life. Dad loved Derek now. He treated him like a son.

School has been hectic. Not the bullying, I mean. No more bullying for me. Before Dad joined the army, he had qualifications for teaching. He was the head of a school somewhere in Canada for a few weeks because the normal head teacher was sick in the hospital.

Dad went to the principal of Peony Hallows High, shouted at him for not even suspecting any bullying and rudeness from the students of the school. Eventually, the principal got fired, and Dad has the title of the principal now. It's awesome. He's making the school better. Everyone loves him because of his light-heartedness. However, they're also scared of him. He's strict, especially when it comes to bullying.

The Falls will be departing from the town in two or three days. Finally. God, that boy, Owen, was bothersome.

One day, I was in my room, completing my homework. I was interrupted by a text from my friends.

Natalia: *I'm bored*

Someone talk

Now

Sophia: *Hi*

Jasmine: *Hey*

Wyd?

Sophia: *Eating*

Natalia: *I'm n de living room, trying 2 find something gd 2 watch.*

Me: *Nat, watch The Originals! It's a gre8 show.*

Natalia: *I heard that it's good*

Jasmine: *IT IS! WATCH IT!*

Sophia: *Klaus is cute af.*

Jasmine: *Ikr*

His accent *.*

Sophia: *Tbh, I suppose to ship Hayley and Klaus*

Me: *Nah, Elijah and Hayley are better.*

Jasmine: *Yup*

For an hour, the girls and I talked about TV shows, ~~competing~~ comparing which character was better, which ship was cuter. The chat was witty until the screen suddenly turned black. An anonymous number winked at me.

I declined the call. My phone rang again with the identical number as before. Baffled I answered.

"*Hello, April,*" his annoying voice greeted from the other side.

"Owen? How the hell did you get my number?"

"*I still have it.*"

"You do?" I muttered, perplexed. Why would he still have my number?

"*Yeah. Anyway, I'm just calling to ask if I can have some coffee with you?*"

I snorted. "Coffee? With a dickhead like you? Nah. I'm taken, Owen. So f—"

"*No, not as a date, I mean as friends.*"

"Friends? *Friends?*" I laughed sombrely. "Really? What makes you think that I'll have coffee with you and be friends when you bullied me? What makes you think I'll have coffee and be friends with a racist guy who has a problem with every damn thing and every damn human in the world?"

"*I know that. But I have something important to tell you, something about Derek. If you want to know, come to Starbucks, and we'll talk. I'm ordering for us.*"

"What about Derek?" I demanded, befuddled.

"*I want to tell you the main secret he kept from you for the past two or three months, about how you both are together today.*"

Chapter Forty

Dread

Derek Matthews

I quietly closed the door. "Grandma?"

As usual, my grandmother dozed in her old-fashioned rocking chair, her glasses on her pointed nose, and her grey hair in a fishtail braid. The thick odour of lavender permeated the blissful, tranquil air of her room.

I lightly lifted her into my arms with ease, carrying her to her bed and lowering her down on the mattress. I ~~wrenched~~ pulled the bulky, tepid covers over her fragile petite figure.

I kissed her forehead. "Sweet dreams, Gran." Grandma mumbled incoherent words in her siesta, inclining her head to the side.

Leaving the room and walking to the foyer, I met Kofi Okafor, the man who was Mike's best friend and companion in the war.

"Aye, Derek. You okay?"

"Yeah. You?"

"Better than ever. Your Gran?"

"She's asleep. I'll come back later."

"Kay. Have a good day, man."

"You, too, Kofi. See ya."

I advanced to the automatic doors. My phone resounded in my pocket. I took it out to see an unidentified number calling me. Accepting it, I placed the phone next to my ear.

"Hello?" I spoke first.

"Aye, Derek," his goddamned irritating accent replied.

My hand clutched my phone tighter. "How the hell did you get my number?"

"I have my ways."

"What the hell do you want, Owen?"

"Oh, I don't want anything. I'm just calling to say that I am very disappointed in you, mate."

I frowned. "What do you mean?"

"When I saw you with April, I found it hard to believe that a ruthless asshole like you could fall in love with the most predictable person: April Levesque. I know that you two were best mates, but you both stopped talking to each other, right? So how comes the two best friends reconnected and fell in love? Sure, April's mother must've encouraged your lover to spend time with you, but it seems strange. How did the opposites fall in love? And please don't say that God intertwined your souls or some other religious bullshit. God's not real."

"I never asked for your opinion about my religion, shit ass,' I snapped.

"I thought you were an atheist?"

"No. I was a Deist; I believe that God created the universe, but I also believe He left us alone. Now, what the hell are you trying to do?"

"To ruin your relationship."

"Why the hell do you want to ruin our relationship? What did we do to you? That's right. Nothing. All *you* ever did was torture April relentlessly and bully me, making me believe that I am a murderer."

"You are."

"I'm not! It was my father's decision to leave, so he did it. I hate him for doing that, but I respect his choice. My mother sacrificed herself to give me life. She loved me. My parents loved me. So many people love me. And you? Heck, no one loves you, you racist shit. Why would anyone love you when you bullied someone because of their ethnicity? Who does that? So there is nothing you can do to ruin our relationship."

Owen chuckled. "You see, that's where you're wrong. I do have a way of ruining your relationship. I did some research about how the friendship started and...I found the answer."

Countless theories made my heart race. *I hope he doesn't know. He can't. He can't know.*

"What are the answers?"

"I found out that in the beginning, April was a damn game to you. Your lad — Theo, right? — gave you a Dare to make April Levesque fall in love with you. You had five weeks to complete it, but it didn't go the way you expected it to be because instead of her falling in love with you, you fell in love with her! Again! Soon enough, she loves you, too!"

"How do you know this?" I demanded.

At this point, I visualised Owen smirking. "I have my ways, Matthews. The only way I could know the truth is if someone from the inside told me."

My heart still poignantly pulsated. I ran a panicky hand down my face in contemplation. *Someone from the inside.* Someone I know found out and has told Owen. But who?

"Jasmine?" I guessed.

"No."

"Jackson?"

"No."

"Th—" I stopped. No, Theo wouldn't do that. I know he wouldn't. He's my best friend, for God's sake. He wouldn't be disloyal. "Sophia?"

"No."

My face heated up with antagonism. I clenched my other hand compactly. I bashed my balled hand into the wall next to me in nuisance, fret, and resentment. "Natalia."

"Bingo!" Owen laughed. "I thought it would take you centuries to figure it out. By the way, she's a nice girl to be with at night."

Nice girl to be with at night...?

No. No, no, no. That little horny whore! Why would Natalia do that? Out of all the immoral things in the world, Natalia decided to cheat on my best friend — who was a very charming, understanding, and goofy guy — with Owen? Natalia knew that Theo loved her ever since third grade and always dreamed of her being his, so why the hell would she cheat? He's going to become appallingly upset once he finds out Natalia has been with another guy...Unless I don't tell him...No, I can't conceal the truth from him. It'll hurt him more. He deserves to know.

"Why the hell are you doing this? Is it because you want my money? You could've just asked! If you want a billion dollars, I'll give it to you!"

"Oh, I don't want your filthy money. I'm already rich. I just want to see you in pain."

"Why? I never did anything to you!"

"That's true. But I also want to see April in pain. The reason why is because if she never had damned feelings for me, I would still be here with Brigit today. April was crushing on me until she saw me kissing Brigit when we were young. She got hurt. She cried because she doesn't know what rejection is. I never liked her brother. Her brother, Mike, is a pure asshole, blinding his little sister with myths. I wanted to see April in pain because no one likes her. She's a bitch. Mike found out about the bullying, and he came after us. He beat the shit out of me. He told me to leave town, and I did, but not before I bullied April a little. That's when Mike saw me again, punched me again, and reported Brigit and me to the police."

"Yeah, I know. You two deserve it. You're calling me heartless when you and your bratty girlfriend are more devilish. After the meeting with the police, you both were imprisoned."

"Yeah. We were separated and then we were released. Brigit and I were in touch while I was in the UK with my foster family. We both came up with a plan to bully April so she would know the pain we felt. It's a good thing her brother died. He deserved it. She deserved it. It would also be good to see your relationship end. I mean, who wouldn't like to see the heartless player getting dumped by the girl of his dreams? Also, when April finds out, she will break. She will break so hard that she'll... Want to hear it?"

"Just say it."

"Commit suicide," Owen responded. "She'll leave this world because of one damn boy that meant so much to her. A boy who lied to her about everything."

An invisible wave of apprehension, agony, and fear roared as it battered me like a tsunami, drowning me. I paced back and forth, running my spare hand through my hair. *No. April can't do that. Oh, God, she can't!*

"Owen, please," I beseeched in a tone that's barely above a whisper. "Please don't do this."

Owen chortled. "Derek, be wise for once. It's not fair if you're going to keep this secret from April forever. She has the right to know. Besides, one way or another she's going to find out. You know that...Oh, look! She's here! Well, I have to go and destroy your girlfriend; oops, I mean your ex-girlfriend. If you think you can stop me, then try it, but I'm telling you: you'll be too late. I'm in Starbucks. Don't be late, mate. I really want to see how this will turn out."

The call ended. In the next second, I was hastening to the exit, propelling past the elderly to the doors. The automatic doors slid open, and I jogged outside, the snow falling on my clothes and chilling my already numb body.

Damn it! I didn't bring my car!

I called Theo for a drive, but the call went to voicemail. I called Jackson. "Hello?" he answered. "What's up, man?"

"Jackson, I need a favour."

"Spill."

"I need you to drive to Starbucks and quickly take April out before it's too late."

"Before what's too late?"

I was panting heavily as I ran down the white pavement, leaving footprints on the ground.

"Derek, what's going on?"

"Owen is going to tell April about the dare!"

"Oh...oh, damn, that's bad."

"Of course, it is, dumbass! Go to Starbucks and stop April!"

"It's a good thing I'm already in my car...and what about you?"

"I'll be there in a moment. Just make sure April doesn't find out."

"Derek...April is going to find out eventually. I think it's—"

"She's going to leave me, Jackson!" I shouted into the phone, my voice cracking at the statement. "She's going to leave me, and I don't want that! She's my goddamn life! So, go to Starbucks, beat the shit out of Owen if you can, and take April away! Please!"

Before Jackson could respond, I ended the call and increased my speed.

Perhaps it's the wind that's causing my eyes to get blurry.

Or perhaps it's the dreadful thought of my angel leaving me forever.

Chapter Forty-One

Trust and Love

April Levesque

"Ah, you came," Owen said with that deranged grin of his, pleased. He held out a cup of Starbucks coffee, and I took it, eyeing him cautiously. Slung over his left shoulder was a sidebag.

"What is it you want to talk about?" I asked, sitting opposite to him. "What is Derek's secret?"

Owen hesitated, his eyes wandering to my face as if he's mulling over if I'm ready to hear the truth or not. The snow outside was becoming lighter, softer. People in Starbucks were chitchatting quietly and laughing as waiters and waitresses handed out everyone's orders. Music broadcasted from the rounded speakers planted in the ceiling high above our heads.

"April, I really don't want to see you upset," he said in a sympathetic, vexed manner. "This secret will break you."

I drummed my fingers on my coffee cup nervously. *What secret has Derek been keeping from me? And for how long? Was this a trick from Owen? Or the truth?* By Owen's choice of words and the apprehension in his voice, he and I both know it will break me.

I don't want that.

"Tell me," I insisted.

Owen inhaled an unfathomable breath. "Have you ever found it strange how you and Derek are together today? Have you ever wondered how the romance between you two developed and became so strong?"

"Because of the tutoring," I countered. "The tutoring drew us together."

"Okay, but other than the tutoring, what else brought you two together?"

"Our feelings. Our once broken hearts. Our...our flaws."

"What if it was something else? Something that's very...horrible?"

I didn't answer, too confounded at where he's trying to lead me.

Owen's fingers fondled mine, and I jumped at his touch. I pulled my hand away. He held his hands up in surrender. "I won't hurt you, April. I just think you might need some comfort while I explain this to you."

"By burning me to death with your touch?" I retorted ruthlessly. "I don't think so."

He shook his head, chuckling. "Even in serious situations, that attitude of yours never dies."

"I got it from my mom. I thank her for that. Now, tell me. What is the 'secret' Derek kept from me?"

He detected the uncertainty. "You don't believe me, do you?"

"You bullied me. Bullies lie."

"Derek was a bully. He lied more than you thought he did."

"Sorry?"

"Derek lied to you for a long time, April. You meant nothing to him. You were merely a dare. A game."

I blinked. "W-what?"

"Derek was given a dare by his best friend. Derek has to make you fall in love with him so he can break you. He was given five weeks to do it. Since you're both in a relationship today, I presumed he'll crush you sooner or later in the future… in a few days, perhaps."

I stared at Owen. "No," I protested. "*No*. Derek…He…He will *never* do that!"

Owen arched an eyebrow. "Why won't he? He is a player, after all."

"He *changed*!" I shouted. "How many times do I have to repeat that? Derek freaking *changed* for the *better*!"

"Alright, alright, calm down."

"Calm *down*?" I ~~duplicated~~ *replaced*. "You're expecting me to calm down when you're trying to convince me that Derek will use me. Owen, he and I were *best* friends."

"*Were*," Owen echoed. "Past tense. He changed during those years of despair. The depression made him a cruel person."

"And you're not?" I snapped. "Are you saying that you — a racist, atrocious, malicious, sexist guy — are not cruel? Hell, Derek is better than you! I don't believe this! I don't believe this dare shit. You should never judge someone with a mental illness. It's *wrong*." I sharply stood up. "This was a waste of time. I'm going to go. I pray that you will have a shitty day."

About to swerve around and storm out, Owen grabbed my wrist, making me look at him again. "I warned you, April," he said lowly. "If Derek tells you about the dare, if you're so dim-witted to even realise and ~~realise~~ *believe* his bleak lies, then you will be trapped in a terrible position forever. I only did this to give you further notice."

"Do you have any proof?" I demanded. "I will only believe if you have proof, and from what I know, you don't."

"I do have proof. In fact, the proof is right here."

Owen unzipped his bag and drew out an iPad. "Sit." He patted the space next to him. "Sit and watch."

Desperately, I wanted to leave. On the other hand, this made me curious. I sat down not so far from him, not wanting his STDs or his caress.

Owen's fingers rapidly skimmed the monitor until he came on the messages page. "Do you know Carl Prot?"

The guy who called me ugly and who Derek hammered pitilessly? Of course. "Yes."

"Carl Prot overheard about the bet. He doesn't exactly know the specifics, but apparently, Natalia Hayes knows about the bet more than Carl and I. So, we kindly asked Natalia for further information. She idiotically ~~denied~~ said that she has no idea what we were talking about. Do you know that Natalia and Brigit were friends?"

"I won't say they were friends. More like enemies."

"Frenemies. Right, they're frenemies. Natalia hated Brigit more. Did you know they're third degree cousins?"

I blinked, astounded. "No."

"No one does. Natalia is ashamed to admit that Brigit is her third-degree cousin. Anyway, after Brigit's arrest, Natalia had Brigit's phone. In Brigit's phone, was a video that…You'll see." Owen changed the screen to the gallery and clicked on a certain thumbnail.

It's a video, ~~exposing~~ showing the two best friends, Derek and Theo. They're sitting on the bench in a park, a park that's directly next to the school building. The sunlight shone on their flawless skin. Trees danced. Derek was smoking, the cigarette dangling from the corner of his mouth.

"Theo, I have no other girl to break," Derek said.

"What about Samantha Moore?"

"Nope."

"Macy Harvor?"

"Nope."

"Daniella Willberg?"

"Nope." He tossed the cigarette into the closest bin. "Man, I think I destroyed all the girls in the school."

Theo contemplated for a moment, dramatically tapping his chin. Then, he smiled. "April Levesque!"

My heart bawled at the mention of my name. No…No, no, no…It can't be.

"What?"

"Consider it a dare, Derek. I dare you to make April Levesque — the school's nerd loner — fall in love with you. Once you did, break her or love her."

"Break her or love her?"

"You can break her, or you can love her."

"What makes you think that I'll love her?"

"You had a huge crush on her when you guys were besties."

"And that makes you think I'll love her?"

"Definitely."

He scoffed. "I won't."

"Maybe you're blind to realise this, but we can't control our hearts, too. The heart wants what it wants. So, you gonna do it or not?"

"Why, though? Why do you want me to do that?"

"Because it'll be fun."

"But..."

Theo cocked an eyebrow. "Are you refusing? Dude, it's a simple Dare. All you have to do is hang out with her for a couple of weeks, get her to fall in love with you and bam! You can break her heart and see her cry, or love her and let your heart be happy for once. And judging by the fact that *she smacked you with their bag, if she ever comes to me and asks me if I know about this Dare I'll say no so I won't get hit by her bag. I'm very valuable to mankind."*

"You're only valuable to the wall, not to mankind."

Theo rolled his eyes. "Derek, what do you have against April?"

"Nothing."

"Nothing? Is it because she's Derek-proof?"

"She's not Derek-proof."

"She is. And that's a very rare thing in this world, you know?"

He scowled. "She's just smarter than the other girls. All the girls think that they can change me because my rudeness is a way of 'hiding my true emotions'."

"They're right, though," Theo muttered. "The true Derek Matthews is just refusing to blossom. I know you had a small crush on April when Mike was still here…"

"But that all changed," I snapped. "I don't like her. She's cute. But I don't like her. Too annoying and too rude."

Tears slowly blurred my vision.

"And you're not?"

Derek ignored Theo, deliberating gradually. "Deal," he finally decided. "This is going to be easy, dude."

"Great. You have five weeks to make her fall in love with you and break her heart."

The video ended. Before I even knew it, the warm fluid desolately scurried down my rosy cheeks. I let out an unbalanced breath of wretchedness. Betrayal surged through me.

I cannot believe this…I don't want to believe this…but the proof was right there.

I've been used.

Derek never loved me.

It was all a lie.

He never loved me.

And I was so damn blind to see the truth.

I secrete my head in my hands, inhaling an unfathomable breath before I looked at Owen over my fingertips. "Why are you showing this to me?" I asked in a trembling voice.

"Because you deserve the truth," Owen replied, leaning forward and seizing my hands in his, caressing my fingers comfortingly. I instantly jerked my hands away from his grasp. I need someone to console me right now, but not him. After everything he brutally gifted me with, him trying to console me is just evil. "And you deserve to know—"

"April!"

Owen and I glimpsed where the sound of my name came from. Jackson was scurrying to me with an expression of trepidation. His eyes averted to Owen and then to me. "April, we have to go." Jackson's hand locked around my arm, tugging me up to my feet.

"What? Why?"

"It's Owen," Jackson said. "He's a bad person to be around with. He's a good liar, too. Don't believe anything he says."

Owen leaned back in his chair, smirking. "I am also honest, Jackson." He looked at me. "April, he knows about the dare, too."

Jackson went rigid beside me at Owen's declaration. He closed his eyes, murmuring a swear word under his breath. I stared at Jackson, betrayal oozing from my chest. The extra round of tears hazing my vision seeped down my chilly cheeks. My lips quivered downwards.

"You knew?" I whispered. "And you never told me?"

Jackson stared at me, wretched. I cannot believe Jackson will keep a secret from me—a very great, heartbreaking secret.

Jackson was one of my best friends, and him hiding the dare from me made me want to scream in agony.

"Why?" My voice is so shallow, so unfathomable, that the words came out quieter than a whisper. "Why didn't you tell me?"

"Because you're going to break."

"No shit, Sherlock!" I snapped. "Of course, I'm going to break. How could you, Jackson?! You...Theo...Derek." My heart snivelled at the last name. "Does Jasmine and the girls know this, too?"

Natalia knew. And she never told me. How could she?

"No," he admitted, ashamed. "Only Theo, Derek, and me."

"Who's the liar now, Gray?" Owen asked smugly, placing his chin on his propped-up hands.

I wanted to scream at him. I wanted to batter him endlessly and cuss at him, shout at him, spit atrocious, disheartening insults at him. But I couldn't. The despondent emotions clogged up my throat, restricting me to speak and restricting the air.

Suddenly, I saw the boy I always loved.

I still do.

Yet, my love for him only resulted in a heartbreaking tragedy for my mind, soul, and body.

He was standing in front of the entryway with people shuffling around behind him. His body was tense, and ten times stiffer when he saw Owen sitting down with a thrilled smirk, Jackson who was still staring at me with a sad expression, and then me.

His ocean blue eyes — alarmed and poignant — locked with mine, like a key locking the door to happiness and becoming lost in God knows where. His forehead was creased with trepidation. His dark hair was all over the place, as if he's been incessantly pulling ~~them~~ it.

My feet were paralyzed. My heart felt as if it was shattering into a thousand pieces slowly and excruciatingly. Like a heart attack. Except it's more painful and intolerable. My chest ached dreadfully, and I began to inhale shallow breaths to keep more oxygen sweltering in my lungs.

"This is going to be interesting," I heard Owen whisper.

Jackson met Derek's eyes, miserably shaking his head in defeat. "April, please listen…" he tried to rationalize, yet I turned around and fled to the other exit at the far end of Starbucks.

Stinging tears streamed down my cheeks one by one. I ignored the befuddled stares from strangers as I made my way through the labyrinth of tables, still wheezing for air. I heard footsteps pounding loudly behind me, and I ~~busted~~ burst into a sprint.

Thrusting the doors open, my feet plodded the pallid earth, my legs accelerating in a severe, exhausting speed. I rammed through the people on the road, as heart-rending sobs escaped from my already sore and cloggy throat. I attempted to swallow them back into my body, but they were feral.

I just want to get away from him. I don't want to see him.

"April!" Derek hollered after me. "April! Wait!"

Like that's going to stop me.

The recollection of the patent video shrieked in my aching mind, like a banshee forewarning a loss of life.

"Angel, please," he pleaded at full volume. I could hear him darting to catch up to me, to wrap me in his arms and talk with me.

After a few seconds, his footsteps were becoming nearer and nearer. Before I could veer into another street, his cold hand pulled my arm and swerved me around. The tears continued to gush down my nippy cheeks. My silken, searing eyes concentrated on the ground.

"April, look at me." His voice was palpably vulnerable. "Baby, please look at me," he silently beseeched. He gently cradled my chin with his index finger, slanting my head up for our eyes to meet.

I shove him away. "Don't *touch me*."

He staggered backwards, dumbfounded by my sudden unruly thrust. Even though a scarf was tied around his neck, it's slightly pulled down to expose his nude neck and the pulse clobbering violently with fear. "April...Did he—"

"Tell me about the bet?" I finished. "Yeah, he did."

"I can explain."

I laughed solemnly. "*Explain*? What is there to *explain* when I already know the truth?"

I forced myself to meet his eyes. "What is there to *explain* when I know that our relationship happened because of a damn dare? What is there to *explain* when I know that I'm nothing but a damn boring and pathetic game to you?"

"I accepted the dare," Derek admitted, exhaling precariously.

"And are you happy to know that you've accomplished it? I fell in love with you. I'm now broken. You succeeded. Happy now?"

He opened his mouth, but I continued bawling.

"I can't believe you lied to me! I can't believe that I was so blind to *believe you*, to believe that you *loved me*. I can't believe that I fell in love with you. Other than Mike, you're the only one who brought the positivity back to me. You helped me with my depression. You're the reason why I'm still living today! You're the reason why I didn't commit suicide because you told me that you needed me in your life."

I sniffed. "I just can't believe I fell for it. I don't know why I'm surprised by that. You're Derek Matthews. You're a player. You're the bad boy. You're the heartbreaker. And I was so damn blind and dumb thinking that you loved me."

"I do love you!" he shouted. His eyes were so full of melancholy; it was urging me to comfort him, to wrap my arms around him and just forgive him, but I pushed that thought out of my mind.

"Lies," I retorted. "You know how much I hate lies. Just admit the truth, Derek; you're happy that you broke me."

"No," he whimpered, shaking his head rapidly. I noticed his eyes were shimmering, vivid and burnished underneath the brightness of the dull clouds. They're diluted with tears. "No, I'm not. Baby, I *love you*." He took a step closer. "So much. You're the light in my life, April. I couldn't stop thinking about you. You're always on my mind every single second, minute, hour, day, week, and month of my life. Your smile is so heartwarming. Your laugh is so thrilling. Being with you is so calming. You finally gave me a reason to be happy after so many damn years of loneliness and despair. I love you, April Levesque."

Another hot, silent, glistening tear dribbled down my face. "If you love me then why didn't you tell me about the dare earlier?"

"Because I was *scared*!" he shouted. He looked as if he wanted to break, to curl into a ball on the floor, and just weep to himself. His body vibrated with so much regret. "I was scared to lose you!"

"I would've just let it go if you told me sooner! But you didn't.

"You lied to me, Derek. You *lied* to me. For months, you've been lying. I don't know if I can believe you anymore. I don't know if I can trust you anymore."

I can't stay here any longer. I can't be near him. He's killing me. "Just leave me alone, Derek. I need some time to...think things through."

"I can't leave you," he said, his fingers stroking mine. "Can't you see that? I can't leave you. I promised your dad that I would never leave you."

"You should never ~~keep~~ make promises that you can't keep, Derek," I whispered.

He once again tried reaching out for me, but I moved backwards, not wanting to be touched by him. He shook his head, and the tears fell from the corners of his eyes.

Bet or no bet, Derek should've mentioned to me about the dare earlier. He kept the dare from me for more than two months, and I don't know if I can believe and have faith in all his words. I recalled the Ball, to when he ~~enlightened~~ told me that he loves me.

Were those lies, too?

The snow was replaced with rain. The globules of fluid prevailed hurriedly and stridently from the lacklustre clouds, the sky clapping and snarling like a wolf. Rain beads pitter-pattered the soil, and the strong fragrance of soggy earth invaded my senses.

I walked away, lugging the hood of my bulky coat to hide my face from the rain. It's as if the weather sympathises and comprehends my sentiments, knowing how broken and shattered I was, so the weather decided to express my feeling...or, perhaps, his, too.

I just needed some time to mull over the whole puzzling situation. Theo, Derek, and Jackson lied to me. Jasmine and the girls didn't know.

Trust is very difficult to earn in a world like ours. Love too. And when trust gets slaughtered just by the truth — no matter what the circumstances of the truth are — love dies. Without trust, there is no love. Without love, there is no trust.

I peep over my shoulder to see he was still there, motionless in his spot, alone. The rain dampened him. From the maintained proximity between us, the rain made it tough for me to observe things properly. Yet, I witnessed his weeping swollen eyes that imploringly smiled at me.

"I still love you!" he shouted, his voice cracking at the end. "And I will never stop."

*   *   *

When I reached my house, my soggy hair was glued to my face, veiling my red stinging eyes.

"April?" Dad called. "Is that you, honey?"

"Yeah!" I replied, surprised that my voice wasn't hoarse.

Dad poked his head through the entryway of the kitchen. I immediately and circumspectly angled my body diagonally, not wanting my father to notice my desolate expression. "Whoa, you got soaked pretty damn hard."

"It's fine. You know how much I love the rain." I do love the rain. It's soothing. However, after what happened, I don't think I love it anymore.

"I made food. Want to eat, honey bunch?"

"I'm not hungry. Thanks, anyway."

I didn't want to tell my father about the incident. My father will become aggressive to know what Derek agreed to do. The worst-case scenario of my father having a conference with Derek will be violent and full of vulgar language. The last thing Derek and I need was another problem.

I unhurriedly ascended the stairs, hearing the music from my brother's room. Cody was in his room, watching a cartoon on my iPad. I slammed my bedroom door shut and collapsed on the floor as the endless scorching tears frustratingly continued to fall down my cheeks.

It's like there was no heart anymore in my chest. It's like a tidal wave of gloom hammering me, consuming me. Through all the negativity I felt as if I'm drowning—my lungs cold-bloodedly tearing open. The sore pulsating in my brain made me want to scream and just die.

I felt so empty. So sad.

He might've loved me. Might've not.

I gaped through the window. The glass was foggy with steam and raindrops. I reflected on my cutting days. I cannot do it. I knew I shouldn't. I promised my parents, my family, and my friends to never cut my skin again. Nonetheless, I was so tempted to do it. I just wanted these insupportable emotions to flow out of my body through my blood.

Quietly ~~Inaudibly~~, I sauntered to my closet. I grabbed a lone hanger from the wardrobe and sat on the edge of my bed. Tears on my cheeks. Heart beating roughly. I overturned my wrist and positioned the point of the hook of the hanger on a clear blue vein right underneath my palm, a vein that can kill me.

I hesitated. No, I can't do it. I can't. For my parents, I can't.

I tossed the hanger away and fell on my bed, my hair all over the place like a halo waiting to be born. My eyes concentrated on the ceiling, shimmering with the glow-in-the-dark stars that Mike gave to me as a present.

What would Mike do in a situation like this? When Mike and Makayla broke up, he cried for days...weeks...months. Losing Makayla was a tragedy to him. He admitted he felt as if he was dying.

Mike will forgive Derek. He will feel disappointed, though.

That's the thing: I forgive easily. However, in dilemmas like this, in dilemmas that involves lying...forgiving is very hard for me. Usually, I ponder about the advantages and disadvantages of forgiving first.

Forgiveness will heal the heart, the mind, and the soul, Mike said. *It will improve mental health.*

I will forgive Derek. I know I will...I just need some time alone. To think.

My eyes closed, my lips trail downwards as a wail reverberated in the dark room. I rolled to my side and curled my body, my arms firmly wrapped around my legs that were compressed to my chest.

On my nightstand, was a picture frame of Mike and me; my legs were wrapped around his torso as I sat on his back, his hands underneath my rear to be sure I won't fall as we grinned at the camera, our eyes full of dazzling joy. Underneath the picture was a small conversation written on paper. The conversation was written by two different writing styles: one was Mike's and the other was mine:

You're so annoying, Mike. I love you.

You're annoying too! I love you, Little Sis.

Don't hate me no matter what happens.

Why would I hate you? You're my gift from God.

Don't leave me xxx

I won't. I'm always there, Little Sis xxx

"Mike," I whimpered. "I need you now."

Chapter Forty-Two

Blame

Derek Matthews

"I love you!" I hollered, my voice cracking at the end. "And I will never stop."

The rain soaked me. The wind bellowed. The clouded sky clapped with thunder, as if the earth itself empathises with me.

She never looked back, never stopped, never ran up to me and embraced me. I don't blame her, though. I understood her words—I should've told her about the dare sooner before our love became zealous. If I told her later, then she'll believe that all my candid words are treacherous lies. If I told her earlier, she would hate me, yes, but I could destroy the hate and replace it with something positive.

The streets were empty. People crowded in the buildings to protect themselves from getting damp. I wordlessly and miserably strolled along the footpath, my head low, the tears mixing with the droplets of water, my hands in my pockets.

"I'm such a worthless bastard," I muttered. "I don't deserve her. I don't deserve anyone."

I can only guilt myself. A part of it was Theo's fault, yet again, he only did it to bring ecstasy into my life. I supposed he knew the consequences, yet it's mostly my fault for agreeing to the dare.

"Derek!"

Jackson was jogging to me. Surprisingly, Theo was behind him, both worried. They weren't bothered by the rain; they weren't bothered by the way the muddy water splashed their clothes and soaked their socks and shoes.

"She's gone," I whispered, feeling like a lost boy. "She left."

It was Theo who felt the most guilt out of all of us. He ran his hand through his drenched hair, his eyes reluctant to meet my face. "I'm sorry," he said quietly. "This is all my fault."

"No!" I objected. "No, don't say that! Theo, it was never your fault. In fact, I *thank you* for giving me the dare because it helped me with life, it changed me, and it made me express my feelings through words, not through heartbreaks. You were only doing a favour. You were only terrified if the sadness was too wild for me to control. You were only alarmed if I break down. Don't blame yourself. This is all on me. April was right; I should've told her earlier, because if I did, then I can fix things between us."

"Do you think she'll forgive you?" asked Jackson.

"She said she needed to think things through. She said she wanted space and some time alone. I'll give her that. I'll give her anything she wants even if we're not together. Will she forgive me? Perhaps. She can forgive people easily, but it depends on the problem. Since it's the dare...she'll forgive me later or...never."

"How does Owen know about the bet, anyway?"

"Natalia," I growled abhorrently. I looked at my best friend, aghast. "I'm sorry, Theo."

"What?" he baffled.

"Natalia cheated on you."

At first, he seemed cynical. Then, he believed me. "With Owen?" he mumbled, shocked, dismayed and horror-struck.

"She slept with him. I think more than once."

Revulsion blossomed on Jackson's face. "Ew, she's going to get STDs." I glared at Jackson, noiselessly telling him it's not the time to be light-hearted.

Theo's eyes were far away in his own world of thoughts. A tear oozed down, and his jaw all of a sudden tightened. "Is Owen still in Starbucks?" he asked Jackson.

"Probably."

Theo cursed to himself as he twirled around and thundered to the Starbucks building. Jackson and I exchanged befuddled stares and then bounded after Theo.

"Where are you going?"

"To beat the shit out of that dickhead. Why don't you come, Derek? I'm sure you would love to beat him after everything Owen has done to you—the bullying, the insults, for bullying *April.*"

It does seem pleasing.

"Whoa, whoa." Jackson grabbed Theo. "Dude, calm down. I know it hurts to get cheated on, but..."

"Jack, you just find the beanstalk while Derek and I go after Owen. That's good? Okay. Derek, let's go." Theo softly pushed Jackson away, and we both scuttled into the Starbucks building as Jackson shouted at us to *wisely stop.*

Owen was still there as I hoped him to be, sophisticatedly packing away his iPad and attempted to leave. When he saw us, he smirked.

"How did it go?" he asked me. "Did she deal with it and gave you lovey-dovey kisses, or did she mentally break down as I wished her to be?"

"Why the hell would you want a person to be mentally hurt?" Theo growled, furiously advancing to him. "And why the hell would Natalia like you? You're not even good-looking! You look like an alien." Tears flooded his eyes as he verbalized the last question.

Still complacently smirking, he shrugged. "I don't know, Theo. Why don't you ask your girlfriend that? Sorry, I mean *ex-*girlfriend."

The people in Starbucks suddenly fell silent, intently watching us.

Without warning, Theo hurled his fist into Owen's face. Owen's lips burst apart and a few cracks resounded from his skull. Gasps reverberated in the cafe.

Owen hit the wall. Blood dribbled from his nostrils and Theo grabbed his shirt, belligerently lifting him up and shoving his head into the wall as he shouted innumerable profanities to the bastard. He jammed his knee into Owen's abdomen, and Owen hollered in pain.

Theo vehemently dragged himself away from Owen, his chest irately rising up and sinking down as he puffed thin whiffs of oxygen. "Your turn," he said to me. "Beat the shit out of him."

Owen heard what Theo said because he grinned, exposing his repulsive teeth smudged with blood. "No matter what happens, Matthews, the past will always define you."

Having enough of his meaningless words, I thrashed him, mercilessly pounded him until he's grunting, hollering, groaning, and curling on the floor as blood leaked from his nostrils and hung from the corners of his mouth like ropes of drool. Theo quietly stood at the side, tears intensely dropping from his eyes. That triggered me more.

The manager of the Starbucks building thundered through the people assembling around us, shouting, "What the hell are you doing?"

The manager, a very buff man, jerked me away from Owen who's puffing out bated breaths. Owen managed to raise himself from the ground, that unhinged, rascally smirk never expiring.

Before I even realized what's happening, two cops were impeding my sight. One of them asked Owen if he's okay whilst the other glared at Theo and me. He seemed familiar; I think he's the policeman who was in the hospital to inspect April after her suicide attempt.

"You two are under arrest for assaulting the lad over there." The one staring at me — ginger hair, fair pale skin, a thick Northern Irish accent — wrenched my wrists together and handcuffed them as the other handcuffed Theo. "Let's go to the station downtown, shall we?"

*   *   *

In the reception of the police station, Theo and I quietly sat together on the bench, our hands still cuffed, our knuckles injured from the insensitive impact we gifted to Owen. The two officers spoke to their colleagues in low voices, here and then glimpsing at us.

"Who are your parents?" the Irish cop asked us after the tête-à-tête.

"Mateo and Daniella Romano," responded Theo. He gave them their mobile numbers.

"My parents are gone," I said to the cop. "It's only my aunt."

The policeman scrutinized me. "Are you that billionaire lad? The nephew of the woman who runs the Matthews Industry?"

"Yeah. Derek Matthews. Nice to meet you. Now please call my aunt so I can get the hell out of here. This place stinks. Can you control your farts or not?"

Theo sniggered next to me.

"With a tongue like that, mate, the charges will become heavier."

"I'm the nephew of a billionaire. Does it look like I give a damn?"

The cop chortled. "You're a lucky lad that I'm not strict like the other fellas. Do you know your aunt's number?"

I told him Marline's mobile number. I wondered where Marline was—perhaps she's in her office, persistently working and solving problems. She doesn't like interruptions. I winced as I recalled the time I inadvertently intruded Marline's space, and she was so mad that she thrashed her computer.

In the next twenty minutes, Marline arrived with Theo's parents: Mateo and Daniella. The two officers who arrested us explained the incident to them. This was Theo's first time getting arrested, and he sure doesn't look panicky. He seemed calm to my surprise. Me? I got arrested twice. Now, it's three times. This was just another episode of me that really infuriates my aunt.

"Really, Theo?" his mother snapped heatedly. "We raised you better than that."

"Not my fault that racist guy is a douchebag," Theo muttered. His eyes were still sore from crying. I wanted to hug him, but my hands are tied.

"Why exactly did you beat him, son?" Mateo asked.

"Because he's a dickhead who loves to see people in pain. He was the guy who bullied Derek and April."

"April?" The two adults echoed.

"Mike's little sister," Theo countered.

They negotiated with the police, and ultimately they bailed us. Marline paid the charges for Theo and me, and we all left the station after the adults signed a few papers.

Marline smacked the back of my neck. "I told you before not to get yourself in trouble! I already have so many things to deal with, the last thing I need is my little nephew to get arrested for the third time!"

I shrugged. "Like Theo said: it's not my fault the guy is an asshole."

"Is this guy Owen?"

"Yes. Now you see why I hammered the shit out of him?"

"Hmmm," she mused. "I suppose I can let you get away with this one. I don't really like the Falls."

I smirked at my aunt's gratitude. "You are such a savage sometimes."

"And so are you. You got it from your mother and me."

"Well, I thank you for that."

She placed her hand on my shoulder. "Are you okay?"

"Yeah, why?"

"You look sad."

Of course, I do. I just lost the one I love. "I'm fine," I lied.

"Don't lie to me, Derek," Marline pleaded. "You know I hate when you lie. It hurts me. Please, tell me what's wrong."

I was silent for a moment. Tears swelled in the corners of my eyes, causing Marline to become more concerned. "April and I broke up."

Chapter Forty-Three

Decision

April Levesque

It's been a day since the break-up.

One time, at lunch, I was with Jasmine and Sophia. Natalia wasn't in school because she's sick. I was still thwarted angry Natalia didn't tell me about the dare earlier. It's good she's not in school because if she was, things would be uncomfortable between us.

I told Jasmine and Sophia about the dare. They got livid and went to Theo, Jackson, and Derek, battering them with their hands and bags, grabbing drinks from random people and spilling it on them. Everyone in the cafeteria had their jaws dropped, guffawing.

"Assholes!" Jasmine scolded.

"We. Are. Done!" Sophia shouted at Jackson. "You knew about the dare, and you never told me? What the hell, Jackson!"

"I know, right!" Jasmine grabbed Jackson's plate of food and smacked it on his face. Her twin brother yelped.

Theo and Derek looked depressed. Their faces were pasty and tender. Their eyes were burgundy and bulging as if they've been crying for the entire night. I heard that the two best friends had been arrested yesterday because they were thrashing Owen and striking him until he was a gory ~~chaos~~ mess. People have been ~~rumouring~~ gossiping about the episode, some admitted they feared the two boys. They knew the boys were sometimes assholes and sweet guys, but they also knew that they could be perilous, fear-provoking, and untameable when they want to be.

Derek's clothes were withered. Our eyes united, and he gave me a distress~~ing~~ed, quaking smile. I looked away, bothered by his stare. I was still thinking about the entire dilemma, and it was tough weighing up the good and bad consequences. The ~~vista~~ sight of him smouldered my body in the most agonising way possible. His appearance just brought tears to my eyes.

It's awful enough that he's in most of my classes. For science, he wasn't present until halfway through the lesson when the door unexpectedly thumped open, everyone jumping at the clamorous noise.

"Oh, Jesus." The teacher places his hand over his heart, calming himself. "Derek, why are you late?"

"I'm just late. It's not a big deal. I'm sure you've been late to classes and school all the time, sir. So, shut up."

Ooohhhs sounded from the students, amused by Derek's savage side.

Derek hesitated, realising that he must sit next to me. He seemed tentative.

He shrugged it off, appearing emotionless as he approaches his seat. His eyes avoided me. My heart beat so ~~vociferously~~ loud that I wonder if he could hear ~~them~~ it.

Sitting down next to me, his posture relaxed to some extent. I remembered how many times he told me that my smelt

charisma calmed him. He ~~stenched~~ of something strong and pungent, filling the classroom: cigarettes. My eyes blazed at this. My lips quivered and I concealed my face with my hair, not wanting him to see me like this.

The science teacher nattered about chemical reactions in the brain, and suddenly, we're talking about love. How convenient. "What is love?"

"Love is...love," a guy responded.

"Yes, but what are the emotions?"

"Butterflies in the stomach," a girl countered. "You smile a lot."

"But sometimes, it can be a heartbreak," another girl said. "A heartbreak that feels as if your whole world is ripping apart...it's too wild to tame. The sadness, I mean."

"You're all what? Sixteen? Seventeen? You all had some crushes. So how does it feel like to be around that person?" No one answered, too mortified to speak. The teacher sighed. "Come on. It's not that embarrassing to talk about."

Silence crept into the room for a minute until that one voice said: "Being with her feels like home..."

Everyone diverted their attention to Derek. I felt self-conscious as a few of them glanced at me. Thank God they mostly concentrated on him.

"She's like a gate to heaven. I feel peaceful whenever I'm around her. She can always calm me even if I am in the deepest trouble. She inspires me to overcome my fear, my insecurities. When I look at her, all I can see is an angel. My angel. In my world, there's no one else. Just her and me.

"Being with her just brings a smile to my face. In fact, *thinking* about her always makes me happy. She can be annoying, but I love it. I love teasing her. I love being there for her. I love hugging her. All this time I was isolating myself, insulting myself, maddening my mind with misery. But just loving her...it created a new odd, different road that guided me to the light. She just makes me so happy..."

His voice drifted off. I bit my lip, the tears clogging my throat as a newly familiar weight rises up in my chest.

I can't. I can't stay here.

"But I made her sad. I ruined her world just by entering it. I ruined her."

I ruined myself, Derek.

I stood up; all eyes were on me. The bell suddenly buzzed, and everyone shot up, grabbing their stuff and walking away. My hair still veiling my face, I could detect Derek's eyes boring into me, as if he can see my soul.

"April," he whispered, his firm hands trying to caress mine and interlace them together.

I paused what I was doing, staring at our intertwined hands. The tears fell and dripped from my chin, making my black-framed glasses blurry. I pulled my hand out of his and stormed out of the room, not only irate at the world and at life, but at myself for finding it hard to forgive.

*   *   *

I closed the front door and walked into the living room. Mom and Dad were cuddled on the sofa, watching a movie.

Mom turned around to look at me and she, without delay, stood up. I could not sense a prickle of compassion on her face, empathising with the morose consuming me. "April..." She stood next to me, her hands on my arms. "Marline told me everything."

And in just that moment, I broke down crying in her arms. She cradled me, shushing soothingly as we rocked back and forth on our feet. "I-I was only a game to him. I meant n-nothing to him."

"No, baby, that's not true."

"He used me, Mom. He used me."

She patted my back. "Relationships have ups and downs, love. I'm sure everything will work out."

"Mom, I was a dare! I meant nothing to him! All I was to him was a useless game. He never loved me. He told me that he does, but I don't believe him…I just can't."

"I understand, honey. I understand how hard it is to forgive. But that's human nature—we cannot forgive straight away, we have to think about the problem first. Shhh, darling, shhh."

Dad looked tense behind Mom, taking in the sight of me weeping. I could tell Mom was mouthing words at him, trying to compose him. I didn't think he can calm down. He loathed seeing his family cry.

He tugged me out of Mom's arms and embraced me tightly, smoothing my hair. My tears soaked his shirt, and I tightened my grip around him, snivelling. It feels so good to be this close to my father.

"Do you want me to talk to him?" Dad asked. "I can talk to him. I'll be happier if I talk to him—"

"*No*," Mom and I responded in unison.

Dad heaved a sigh. "Worth a try to ask."

I wished I had never met Derek. No, I was full of gratitude about the fact that we were friends, but I wished that I wasn't a game to him. I wished I actually meant something to him. If I was, then there won't be heartbreak. No pain or tears. No broken promises. No need to cry myself to sleep. I wanted to believe what he told me on the street, that he loves me. I can't. I don't know what to believe in anymore. I don't know to whom trust other than my family.

BANG!

I turned my face in from father's arms. Ethan was in the parlour entryway, fuming. He wasn't looking at me. He was looking at Dad.

"Dad…"

"I know. I know what happened."

"Should we go after that dickhead and actually kick his dick? And maybe give something more than that?"

"I would. I would want to kick his ass and dick for hurting April but…I want to talk to him. Like, properly talk to him. Not to hurt him or punch him. Just talk to him…with a bit of anger."

"Can I come, too?" Ethan recommended. "To talk to him with a bit of anger?"

Mom raised an eyebrow. "I bet you'll beat him. I don't think it'll be best—"

"I won't hurt him. He's an asshole, but he's family. What he did – the dare and all – is immoral, I know, and I wish I could punch him for that, but maybe a guilt talk will be good. With a bit of anger. And advise him. With a bit of anger."

"I'll come," I decided.

Dad and Ethan looked at me. Mom stroked my back. "Are you sure, sweetie? You will feel bad if—"

"I'll be fine."

"April, you will break—"

"And I'll fix her if she does," Ethan interjected. "Because that's what I do: fix my big sis when she breaks. Don't worry, Mom, I'll take good care of her." Ethan looked at Dad and clapped his hands together. "Now, let's go and find that annoying asshole and talk to him with a bit of anger, shall we?"

"I want to punch him, though," said Dad. "Nobody hurts my family. April, listen: when I heard you were harming yourself, it made me mad and miserable. I couldn't handle imagining you walking with a fake smile on. However, when you started to date Derek, I was happy because you were happy. You were exactly the April I knew when Mike was still living with us. But when you told me that your relationship happened because of a stupid, ridiculous dare...damn, you have no idea how mad I am. I couldn't stand watching you cry anymore...It hurts like *hell*. I want to freaking punch that boy."

"I would love to join," said my brother.

"But you *won't* hurt Derek," Mom said. "I know Derek can be ridiculous, but give the guy a break. Now go and talk to him. *Nicely*."

"With a bit of anger," Ethan and Dad corrected.

* * *

We found Derek in a local pub. Ethan shoved the doors open, and we all entered.

We wandered around the pub, searching the place for Derek. It's not busy. Couples feverishly kissed in the corners. Some had chugging battles, others just drank by themselves. I scanned the place and finally found him. He was sitting next to the window, looking out while he sipped a bottle of beer. My heart clenched with misfortune at the scene.

Dad was the first to advance. Ethan snaked his arm around my shoulders, holding me securely as we froze in front of Derek. Derek coiled his neck sideways to look at us.

My shoulders slumped with dread. He looked awful. Like a lost, abandoned puppy whimpering to be discovered by someone loving. I wanted to sit next to him and hug him, but I restrained myself from doing it.

"Derek," Dad greeted.

"Julian," he slurred, his voice raspy. He saw me and smiled. He unsteadily stood up, circling the table and holding out his arms at my father and my brother. "I know why you're here. So just do it. Beat me. I need it."

They blinked, surprised. Then, Dad only graciously smiled. "We're not here to do that. We just want to talk regarding the situation."

Derek frowned, dropping his arms. "If we're going to sit, can April sit next to me?"

"No," Ethan responded. "Not now."

Derek heaved a sad sigh yet continued to smile at me. "At least I tried, angel."

We sat opposite to Derek. His hair was rumpled. This time, I can see tiny dots, like knots, in his hair, as if he hasn't been bothered to comb them for days. Dark bags hung underneath his droopy eyes. His clothes were ragged and worn out, and he reeked of alcohol and cigarettes.

"First, you know that drinking is bad for your liver," my father begun, "so why would you torture yourself?"

"Because I deserve it."

"You don't," Ethan protested. "Dude, you may be a dickhead, but you're a good guy."

"Exactly," said my father. "We don't like seeing you like this."

"But I broke my baby's angelic heart," Derek whispered, despaired. He met my eyes. "I deserve to torture myself."

Dad sighed. "Derek, I'll be honest with you. I am very disappointed that you broke the promise. You looked like the player as everyone thought you are, but I also saw that goofy little guy I knew when you were a kid. And today, I don't. That goofy kid is gone...died."

"Because of that shitty dare. I'm sorry, man." He looked at Ethan. "I'm sorry, idiot." He looked at me. "I'm sorry, angel."

"You shouldn't have agreed to do the dare," Ethan explained, his arm still around me. "It was wrong."

"I know...But I did it."

"Who gave you the dare?" asked Dad.

"Theo. He did it for me to find love. So love can reveal the true Derek Matthews."

"Did he run over the disadvantages of coming up with this dare?"

"I think so...I don't know, man. The dude hasn't been talking to me. He's sad."

"Why?"

"Because Natalia cheated on him." His lips curled up into a sneer. "With that asshole, Owen Fall."

My eyes ~~amplified~~ widened. "What...*Why?*"

Derek merely shrugged, enraged. "Ask the whore. Honestly, she doesn't deserve Theo. Theo deserved someone better!"

"Have you seen her lately?" asked my brother. "None of us has seen her in school."

"No. I don't care about her. She ruined her life just by hooking up with that psycho. She's probably with Owen right now."

The wind ~~weeps~~ howls outside. People put their hands in their pockets, burying their faces deeper into their coats to create warmth.

"Derek," my father spoke, "do you regret doing this dare shit?"

Sincerity filled his ocean blue eyes. They don't have that good-natured, goofy, euphoric twinkle in them anymore. In fact, his eyes weren't glimmering like before. They're drained. Drained with hope and positivity and faith. "Of course, I do. But I was happy to do it, actually."

"Happy? Why?"

"Because the dare changed me." His eyes were not on any of us. They gaped at the table, forlorn and lost in thought. "I knew the dare was cruel, but it changed me. It made me realise the mistakes I've done and fix them before they completely kill me. It made me a better person...it rebuilt my friendship with my angel...and created love. It's like a miracle. *She's* my miracle.

"But I know it's too much for her to cope with. She's right. I should've told her about the dare earlier...before the Ball...before we fell in love. Because if I did, then I could replace the hate and repair our friendship.

"I know she's having a hard time forgiving me." He chuckled soberly. "Heck, even I can't forgive. I still haven't forgiven my father for breaking his promise, and I might never will. I understand if it will take her days to forgive me, to have mercy on me, to take it easy on me...and I'll wait for her forgiveness, no matter how unbearable the distance between us can be."

He finally looked at me, his eyes pooling with tears. "Thank you for giving me a reason to live, my love." He altered his gaze to my father and brother. "Thank you for accepting me into your family."

My eyes nipped at his words; my body, mind, heart, and soul ached. The air seeped through the casements and chilled our skins and bones, convincing the revolting, vile, bitter whiff of cigarettes to molest our nostrils. This made my father more concerned as he scrutinized the alcohol bottle in Derek's hand.

flung

Suddenly, Dad wrenched the bottle out of his grasp and ~~flings~~ it across the room, the bottle shattering into a bin at the opposite end of the pub.

"The hell, man?" muttered the boy I love.

"You know that drinking and smoking are dangerous," Dad said in a low, warning manner. "It will kill you. And none of us want that. I am disappointed in you for breaking my girl's heart, but I sympathise with you. You're right. Our society finds it difficult to forgive. It will take days for Ethan, April, and me to forgive you. But if you're returning to your addiction, I will forbid a relationship between you and my daughter."

"You can't do that!"

"I can and I *will!*" Dad snapped. "If you're not going to maintain your health, then I won't allow a relationship. I'm only doing this for your sake. In fact, why are you being like this? An addict? Is it because your father was the same: drinking and drinking, smoking and smoking? Your father was a good man, yes, but his actions were wrong, and you shouldn't follow his footsteps. I know it's hard to live without parents, but you have Marline! You have Luke, Theo, my wife, my children, your friends, and other people from all over the world who love you and care about you!"

"You have a celebrity band that cares about you," Ethan added. I told him about the Christmas present Derek gave me. Just thinking about it made me sad.

"Exactly!"

"But she hasn't forgiven me," Derek said in a quiet voice, sad.

Dad heaved an annoyed, alarmed sigh, deliberately staring at Derek.

I was concerned about Derek returning to his addiction. But he's only doing this to gain my forgiveness. It's like a bait trap. In fact, it *was*. Either way, it made me silently snivel as he refused to meet my eyes, engrossed in his own contemplations.

The tears in his eyes streamed down his cheeks serenely and gracefully. He gently wiped them away, gutturally imploring, "Please leave. I want to be alone."

We were motionless in our seats, alarmingly gazing at Derek who's staring through the window next to him. He became infuriated by our company, and crossly growled, "Go away. Leave me alone. Please."

Dad and Ethan stood up and sauntered away, stashing their hands in their pockets. I noticed their shoulders sinking down, as if they're pleased with the guilt talking. Yet, I also noticed my father peeking over his shoulder at me worriedly, and then at Derek and the concern intensified.

I bit my lip in guilt, staring at Derek. He stared at me with gloom, and I frantically wanted to take his hand and squeeze it tightly with comfort and leniency, and stroke his messy jet-black hair and touch the smooth vaguely tanned skin of his. I didn't, of course.

"I forgive you," I finally whispered, taking him by surprise.

He opened his mouth to say something but closed it in the next second, flabbergasted to speak. Eventually, he stuttered, "Y-you do?"

I nodded slowly. "But…I think we should be friends."

All the hope that abruptly beamed in his eyes expired at my proposal. He considered the idea. "Will being friends make you happy?" he asked sorrowfully.

No. It won't. I want to be his girlfriend, but after everything that occurred, I don't think I can continue to trust him anymore. Without trust, there is no romance. I warned him before not to break me, to hurt my heart, yet he did. "Yes."

"April," he whispered gruffly. "If that makes you happy, then it will make me happy."

But I knew from his unspoken tears, that he was not happy with my decision. He knew that I don't trust him at the moment.

"I understand. I understand that without trust, there is no love." He opened his eyes and leaned forward, his face inches away. He unexpectedly caresses my cheek with his trembling thumb. "I'm so sorry, angel. I still love you."

He kissed my cheek. I gasped in surprise. Then, he moved away from me, leaving me all alone in the pub, pondering on his words.

Chapter Forty-Four

Endure

Derek Matthews

I wondered what was worse: having my heart ache or agreeing to be friends with the love of my life. I frankly cannot see the difference. I felt and endured both traumatizing pains. They were infinitely torturous. They're killing me slowly.

Outside was a combination of snow and rain. I paid attention to the water pitter-pattering on my windows as I stared at the passing cars, the blurry lights shining everywhere and at the sky; as if I'm trying to identify the gate to the everlasting kingdom known to be full of happiness. Walking out there in the cold only made my day ten times worse. The tears never stopped flooding my eyes just like the rain.

My room was pungent with whiffs of alcohol and cigarettes. I know, I know: smoking is vicious for my health, and I knew April would be devastated to witness me running back to my old wicked addictions, but I simply cannot help the craving. It's irresistible. Like her.

I haven't spoken to Luke and Marline since the breakup, and their concern was increasing minute by minute. Just five minutes ago, Luke was banging on the door, commanding me to open it. I cussed at him to go away. He did, and now he's out with his fiancée. Aunt Marline decided to give me some space and return to her business.

I was motionless on my bed, brutally shaking. I had no idea why. Perhaps, it was due to the cold. Or perhaps, it was due to something else.

I chucked my third cigarette into the bin and eagerly drew out another one from the packet, scorching the end of the cigarette with my lighter. I inhaled and exhaled. A puff of smoke escaped my lips, fogging in front of me like a tiny cloud. The taste was bitter, but bitter was who I am as a person.

I wanted nothing more than to forget about the world for a moment and feel like I was floating.

I wanted to forget everything.

I wanted to forget April.

I was unsuccessful. She's too alluring, overwhelming, and enticing. She's overpowering my mind. Her smile...her laugh...her breathtaking, appealing, beautiful dark eyes...her wavy, brunette hair that regularly cascades down her shoulders...her soft, smooth, warm skin... She's too beautiful. Like an angel.

She wanted to feel love. She wanted love to be the only solution to her dilemmas, and she received that love from me. Now, we both lost it because of one damn, stupid dare.

A dare that changed us both; that changed me for the better. Who knew one dare can be so magical, enchanting, and glorious yet so saddening?

Theo hasn't talked to me. He still blames himself for the dare, but most of the time, his mind was isolated from the thought of Natalia and Owen together. He called me on the phone, asking me if I'm alright. I told him no. He said he was awful too with tears quaking his throat. He cried so hard over the phone, and I desperately wished to come there and support him, but he insisted on being alone.

If a man cries over a girl, then he truly loves her, my father once told me.

Theo's crying over a girl. And so am I. This was a proof that we both truly and deeply love our girls, right?

I was tempted to find Natalia and deal with her. I don't care if I get hurt — I have always deserved it — but I do care if someone hurts my best friend. Natalia is going to pay for this.

Floating...that's how I feel like whenever I smoke...floating. Like I was in the water. That's what my father told me. Floating...Diving...Swimming...

Yet again, I felt this blazing soreness in my chest. It's as if my heart was on fire.

Sometimes, I couldn't breathe ever since April and I broke up.

The tears pooled in my eyes as the smoke spiraled up from the end of my cigarette.

This wasn't the only time I felt heartbreak. I felt heartbreak when my father shouted at me, condemning me for horrifically gifting him with depression.

You're a mistake in my life! If you were never born, Alexa would still be here, healthy and beautiful. But no, you have to come and destroy Luke, Marline, everyone in your family and me! He was drunk when he said this. Everyone knows that drunk people tell the truth. *Just die already! Go and die! Why can't you trade your body for Alexa?*

He blamed me for everything.

But he's right.

I am a mistake.

*   *   *

"You okay, brother?" Luke asked.

We're in the kitchen. The kitchen was quite big with a square-tiled pastel marble floor. There were two islands in the centre with sinks: one with a jug of orange juice, the other with a bowl of freshly baked bread Luke made a week ago. To one side was an extended counter with a sink and white cupboards above it. At the far back was an extra counter with cabinets above and large doors next to it that leads to the garden.

My silence answered my older brother.

"Still moping about April?"

"I miss her," I murmured.

Pity filled him. "You'll get her back, little bro."

"That's what Jackson and Theo said. I don't believe them. We agreed to be friends now."

"Oh. That's good, I guess."

"I don't want to be friends with her, though."

"I understand. You'll get her back."

"You think?"

"I don't think. I believe you'll get her—"

The doorbell ~~ricocheted~~ rang through the entire mansion. Luke and I exchanged confounded expressions.

"Are we expecting someone?"

"No."

We walked to the main door, and I opened it. I batted my eyelashes and repeated it twice just to check if I'm seeing things accurately. In the next second, antagonism boiled in my nerves, and my eyes roughed at the atrocious sight of her. "Why are you here?"

Her eyes were red and raw from weeping. "H-help...P-please...h-help me."

"Why should we help you? You cheated on Theo."

Her lips shuddered. She looked reluctant. Vulnerable. "W-whatever Owen told you d-don't believe it." The way she spoke in stutters felt as if she suffered so much abuse, the way she pleaded gave me second thoughts if something sadistic happened to her. "I-I t-tried calling Theo, b-but he never answered. Derek, I never cheated on him."

The wintry wind bypassed us. The sky darkened as dusk promptly takes over.

I wanted to believe Natalia, for the sake of Theo's joy, but I couldn't. Theo was hurt. No one hurts my best friend.

"There's no point trying to convince me. We don't like you. We don't want you. Leave."

"OWEN USED ME!" she screamed. "Derek, yes, I knew about the dare. But somehow, this guy called Prot knew about it. He told Owen. Owen forced me to tell him the details, but I didn't because I knew that when the truth comes out, it will break April. And after everything that happened to her, heartbreak is unfair. Owen kidnapped me, Derek. He *freaking kidnapped me* and...h-he also raped me." Her shaking hands went to the hem of her withered dirty shirt and lifted it up to expose scarlet marks and bruises. "This is what I get whenever he forces me to have sex with him."

My brother and I stared at the bruises in shock.

"Did you try to escape or call someone for help?" Luke asked.

"Owen broke my phone. I couldn't escape. He had me in a shed somewhere."

"How come your parents never suspected anything?"

"Because they don't care about me. They don't love me like how Theo does." She sobbed at his name. "Oh, Theo...I-I have to talk to him. Thank God I escaped. N-now he's running after me. He knows that I'm going to tell people about what happened. He's scared to go to jail. That guy is a mad psycho. Please help!"

We took her inside, Luke called the cops. I pulled Natalia into the kitchen and asked her ~~for~~ *if she wanted* something to eat or drink. She asked for water in a gruff manner. Her clothes were soiled with alarming blood stains. I gave her one of my shirts to wear.

I called Theo. I told him everything. He believed me. He knew that no matter how Natalia can be, she wouldn't do something wrong like that. Luke called the ambulance to medically aid and inspect Natalia just in case if something was abnormal in her body. Luke reported to me that the cops were coming.

BANG! BANG! BANG!

The garden door opened and a security guard rushed inside. "Sir, there's this young man—"

"Make sure he doesn't come inside!" Luke ordered. "Tell the others to grab him so he can't go anywhere. He's a criminal."

The guard nodded and rushed outside, hollering at the other men to ambush the boy and seize him.

Gunshots. I heard gunshots, then ragged breaths, as if people were dying. Luke and I exchanged apprehensive glances as Natalia wept quietly behind us, murmuring to herself that we're going to die.

"Do we have a gun?" I asked my brother, hoping the answer will be yes. We needed to defend ourselves from the madman. He shook his head.

We approached the main, thudding door. Natalia was shielded behind us.

"I KNOW YOU'RE IN THERE, NATALIA. COME OUT, OR I'LL DO THIS THE HARD WAY!" Owen threatened. "IF YOU WON'T COME OUT, I'M GOING AFTER THEO AND KILL HIM!"

Then I heard that joyous sound.

Sirens.

Natalia released a sob of relief as the sirens neared the mansion. Owen cursed outside. Before he could run away, I pushed the door open and tackled the criminal to the ground. We tumbled down in a roll on the hard, rough, slippery staircase, both of us grunting as each step battered our backs. When I was on top of him, I pinned his arms to the ground, preventing him from the reaching the gun that's not so far away.

The gates were, thankfully, wide open and the cars pulled to a stop in the front yard. Officers leaped out of the vehicles, grasping guns.

I jolted my hands up in surrender. "It's not me!" I informed them. "It's this guy." I nodded at Owen, who's groaning on the floor.

Paramedics scurried out of the ambulance. "Where is the girl?" one of them asked.

"She's here." Luke was carrying Natalia to the stretcher in a hastened speed.

The paramedics closed the door after Natalia was safely secured inside. The emergency vehicle rode off into the darkened streets.

Three officers pushed Owen to the floor, rolling him over to handcuff him. They jerked the psycho to his feet and shoved him in the police car, slamming the door close and driving off after the ambulance.

*　　*　　*

Theo told the girls what happened, and they scurried into the hospital. That's when I saw her. April. She's wearing a long-sleeved shirt along with dark jeans. She and her friends went inside Natalia's ward and hugged her while Natalia apologized to them for being such a horrible friend.

"It wasn't your fault," April assured. "You were kidnapped and raped. You have no fault in this. You're the victim." Natalia sniffed as a tear rushed down her cheek.

Theo stood next to me as we both looked at the girls reuniting.

"You okay?" I asked him.

He nodded. "You?"

I shook my head.

Theo sighed and placed a comforting hand on my shoulder. "You'll get her back."

"Everyone is saying that," I whispered, half-hearted. "I don't believe them. I lost her, Theo. I completely lost her. She hates me."

"She doesn't hate you."

"She does. She never looks at me. She stopped tutoring me..."

Theo laughed softly. "You're worried she stopped tutoring you?" He shook his head, smiling. "She forgave you, Derek. She wants you two to be friends. She still loves you."

"As a friend. That's not enough."

"I think she still loves you, but she's having a hard time deciding to go back to a relationship. Just give her time, man. It's hard for her to go through heartbreak."

"It's hard for me, too."

*　　*　　*

"Derek?" That velvety, modest, comforting voice that permanently makes my heart palpitate in a beautiful tempo elated everything in me.

I gradually turned around. She stood at the far end of the hallway. The propinquity was heart-rending for me. I silently implored her to come near, but she didn't seem to notice my imploring eyes. Her dark hair was made into a high ponytail.

"April," I breathed, offering her a smile.

She managed to smile, but it disappeared. Mine did, too. She inhaled an unfathomable, poignant breath, regaining her serenity to say whatever she has to say. Her fingers went to the back of her neck and unclipped the gold necklace I gave her for Christmas.

"I realised I'm still wearing this," she murmured. "I figured it's best if I return it to you since we're...not together anymore."

She gave back the necklace. I took it without hesitation, my eyes still gawking at her delicate, stunning face, captivated by her features since this was presumably the last time I'll see her.

She turned around and was about to walk away when I grabbed her wrist and tugged her to me. She gasped at the sudden action and stared at me in bewilderment. I then pressed my lips to hers and held it there for a short moment before I pulled away.

"You're always my baby," I whispered. "Always my angel. Always my miracle." I took her hand and bequeath the necklace on her palm before curling her fingers over it. "Keep it. It's yours."

"But I don't want it—"

"Just wear it as a reminder of our friendship. You do want us to be friends, right?"

She didn't reply.

"It's yours, angel. Even when we're not together, even when we won't see each other anymore like how we used to or talk anymore, you're still my angel, and I'm still your annoying asshole. I'm still your man."

Before she could speak, I left her standing there alone with a cheerless face. I glanced over my shoulder and smiled at her gloomily, but then she was gone when I turned into a further hallway, making my way to the exit.

Without her, I'm nothing.

So, what's the point of enduring?

Chapter Forty-Five

Misinterpret

April Levesque

Owen has been sentenced to lifetime imprisonment for kidnapping and raping Natalia, ~~including~~ and murdering Derek's security guards.

It's been three days since the incident. Natalia has been discharged from the hospital. Families and friends mourned the death of the men who volunteered to guard Derek's mansion.

In school, I haven't seen Derek anywhere. He wasn't in my classes. He wasn't in the school corridors or the courtyards. He was nowhere to be found. Anxiety surged through me, and thank God that Theo told me that Derek was at home.

"He's exhausted," Theo said as we walked to class together. "I came to his house yesterday, and he was asleep in the bed."

"Let him rest," I said. "He needs to sleep. Is Natalia okay?"

"Yeah. But I hate her parents. They didn't even suspect Natalia missing. What kind of parents are they?"

"All parents are different. You get the good and the bad."

"Natalia's ones are bad, that's for sure."

We entered the classroom and sat next to each other.

"I'm sorry," Theo suddenly apologised.

I was mystified. "Sorry for what?"

"The dare."

"Oh. It's fine."

"You can slap me if you want. I know how much you love to slap assholes."

I laughed. "You're not an asshole. And neither is Derek."

"Are you two getting back together?" he asked hopefully. It was more of a plea than a question.

I contemplated. "Depends. Actually, I don't know."

He nodded. "I understand. Take your time."

"But the wait is hurting him," I mumbled. "I only want us to be friends for now. Isn't that enough?"

"April you're his everything. Do you think he wants you two to be friends?" Instead of permitting me to answer, he proceeded, "Exactly, no. But take your time. We, humans, have a tough time loving again."

*   *   *

I was ambling on snowed pathways, my footsteps imprinting on the ground, while cars were driving through snow-cleared roads. People stepped into shops, restaurants, and cafes with their families, friends, or partners. On each side of the roads were undersized narrow lanes leading to a dead end. Some were filled with fretful strangers; others were vacant with nothing but hefty recycling bins. In one of the neglected roads, I became aware of a boy with a hood concealing his face, dressed in dark clothes. A cigarette was in his hands, and he raised it to inhale.

"April!"

A recognizable boy raced to me.

Carl Prot.

The guy who got on Derek's nerves.

The guy whom Derek beat up in his seventeenth birthday party.

I don't like him. Can't he just go away? "Hi…Carl."

"Hey." He stopped in front of me, grinning. Carl Prot's skin was light brown, unblemished, and tanned. He had droopy morose eyes; flabby lips; coiled, dark russet hair; and plump, sleek eyebrows with an earring attached to his right ear. His attire was an ashen grey T-shirt and cobalt lacklustre jeans. "So, you and Derek, huh?"

Word about our break-up spread through school. Some even asked me curious questions which I didn't bother to answer. "Yup. We're done."

"Owen got arrested."

"Gee, how come I didn't know that?" I muttered sarcastically.

"I'm sorry about what happened to Natalia, and with you and that asshole." He said the last word with absolute, extreme abhorrence. "Derek wasn't good for you. He never really deserved you. He's a player. A heartless, bleak, cold-blooded player."

"He's not a player anymore," I said brusquely. "He changed." I swear to God, if I repeat the "he changed" phrase one more time, I will slap that person so hard that he or she will fly to the end of the universe, and there is no end, so that's the point.

"Then why did he agree to do the dare?" Carl enquired. "Oh wait, because he's a player. I can't believe you fell for his charms. I thought you're better than that."

I can't believe it, too. I wish the dare never existed. "Well, it's in the past. The past is the past. We don't have to worry about the past anymore. Plus, we're friends now."

"*Friends?*" he repeated the word loathingly with disbelief. "You two are *friends* after what happened? What the hell, April?"

The road is now ~~uninhabited~~ empty.

"You don't know him like how I do, Carl."

"Oh, right, because you two were best friends ever since kids and are basically family." He rolled his eyes. "That bullshit."

I narrowed my eyes at him, getting a vibe off of him. "Are you...*jealous* of him?"

"No. I hate him."

"And jealous. Why? Is it because he's rich?"

His silence was the answer.

"You shouldn't be jealous because he's rich. You have no idea what his family went through to achieve that success. Don't judge him."

"It's hard not to judge him when all he's a bully. He broke girls all because of the death of his mother. That's bullshit."

I noticed something moving from the corner of my eye. I looked to see nothing, or maybe no one was there.

"The mind is deceiving."

He rolled his eyes. "Don't start a pep talk. The guy deserves to die."

The fury in me was like a lion impatiently roaring and waiting to kill its prey. "He doesn't deserve to die!"

He inclined his head to the side. "Why are you defending him? I thought you hate him."

"We're *friends*! I don't hate. I don't dislike him. I still love him, but as a *friend*!"

The last part was a lie.

I love him more than a friend.

How can I not when he was basically, and presumably still is, a significant part of my life?

"If you're going to continue insulting Derek, then I'm going to leave. You are wasting my time. Bye."

He grabbed me before I could go, and out of the blue, his flabby lips smashed onto my thin ones, catching me off guard and taking my breath away. My eyes widened and I struggled to push him off of me, but his arms trapped me, refusing to let me go. His lips forced me to kiss back, but I didn't. This was wrong. I don't even like Carl. Let alone, love him.

He pushed me into a wall, trapping me. I tried to lift my leg and strike his groin, but he pushed it down and pressed weight onto my legs to thwart them from moving. His lips left mine and travelled down my neck.

I whimpered at the way his sloppy kisses nauseated me, fiercely fighting back. "Get *off me*."

I thought he won't listen, but to my surprise, he actually stepped back, conceitedly smirking. I panted, feeling grubby at the occurred episode. My hands touched my neck where he kissed me, and I hastily wiped it, revolted. "What the *hell*, Prot?!"

Instead of saying something, his eyes shifted to his left, his superior smirk never weakening. I followed his gaze and gasped.

Dejected tears pooled in those ocean blue eyes. He was standing not so far away from us in his black clothes, his hoodie veiling his face, yet I distinguished tresses of his jet-black hair falling over his celestial orbs. His body was stiff with shock and scepticism. He saw Carl Prot, and in the next second his eyes overflowed with a huge round of distressing tears.

I immediately sprinted after him when he noiselessly turned around and walked away. "Derek!" I hollered, the propinquity expiring as I neared him. I grabbed his arm and turned him to face me.

My heart wept and died just like the last time when I discovered the dare. Although, this time, it's because of his crying face. He seemed like a abandoned, forlorn little boy—his cheeks blotched with lustrous tears, his lips quivering and thin as if he is trying to hold back the sobs.

"Derek…"

He pulled away from me, his distrusting eyes staring at me as if I'm a person he never met before. "It's fine, April." His voice was quieter than a whisper. The pongs of cigarettes harassed my nostrils. "You moved on. I understand."

"What?" I said with incredulity. Would he really presume that I will be with Carl Prot, the guy who insulted my older brother? "No! Derek, *no.*"

He only shushed me, placing his index finger against my lips. "Be quiet, baby. I understand. You moved on. I want you to be happy, and if you're happy with that guy, then I'll be happy." He stepped closer to me and kissed my forehead. "But." His breath reeked of alcohol. "If he breaks you, I'm available for you, and only you. Okay?"

"Derek—" I tried to rationalise, but he tottered away, leaving me alone in the empty street with Carl Prot.

When he was out of my line of sight, a roar of antagonism and dejection overwhelmed me. I faced Carl Prot, seeing that frustrating, self-confident smirk of his.

"You knew he was there, didn't you?" I shouted. "You knew he would see this. Why would you do that? Why would you break his heart?!"

"Because he deserved it!" Carl shouted back. "He's a bully. He deserves the heartbreak back."

"So, this is revenge? For what? What did he ever do to you? Or is this because of jealousy?"

"He's a bad person. He deserves to be in jail instead of Owen." And with that, Carl Prot left me in the around oned street.

*   *   *

I sit in the living room with my family, watching a movie, cuddling on the sofa. Ethan's arm was wrapped around me, and my head was on his left shoulder. Cody was sleeping on Dad's lap. Cody heard about what Derek did to me, and he grew furious.

"I call Star Wars help then kick Derek butt together!" Cody shouted with fury when I told him. He turned to Dad. "Grandpa, call Star Wars?" Dad only laughed and told Cody that we don't have to kick Derek's ass anymore.

In my room, I tried to call Derek, merely to make sure he's fine. The calls went into voicemail, and after ten tries, I gave up and went on my laptop to search up memes to lift my spirits.

My phone vibrated. I reached out for it to see it's Sophia calling me. I answered it and compressed the call to my ear.

"Hey, Sophia," I said with a smile on my face.

"*April.*" I heard something uncharacteristic in her voice: angst and trepidation.

My smile evaporated. "Sophia, is something wrong?"

"*Yeah,*" she whispered. I feel as if she's crying. And then I knew she's crying because I heard a sniff from the other side of the call.

"Sophia, what is it?"

"*It's Derek...*"

My heart pounded in my chest like a drum when I heard his name. "What about him?"

"*April, Derek ran away...*"

Chapter Forty-Six

Mourn

April Levesque

The rain stopped although dark clouds still covered the sky as if more rain will come thundering down. The birds took shelter in the trees. The aroma of wet soil attacked me from everywhere.

I told my parents about the news, and we ~~instantaneously~~ *immediately* drove to Derek's house altogether because Derek was basically family to them.

Up in the distance, not that far away, I saw azure and crimson blazes. The police. As the car drove nearer, there were three police vehicles parked in the front yard of the mansion. Luke sat on the front porch. Marline talked to a policeman. Jasmine, Jackson, Natalia, Theo, and Sophia gathered in a circle.

"Guys!" I called, leaping out of the car and scurrying to them with Ethan by my side.

Jasmine was the first to notice us. Her blonde hair was drenched. Her eyes sore and burgundy. Her cheeks scarlet and tender. She's shivering, rubbing her palms up and down her arms to push away the coldness. Ethan yanked off his sweater, exposing his bare chest, and offered his sweater to Jasmine which she gratefully took.

"What happened?" Ethan asked.

"Derek ran away."

"I know that. But why?"

They shrugged, confounded. However, Theo was fretful by the way he paced back and forth on the pathway. His eyebrows tucked together in disquiet and bewilderment.

I darted my gaze to Luke. "This is entirely my fault," I heard him murmur to himself. "I should've been there for him."

"No, it's not your fault." He looked at me. Remorse filled me. "It's mine. I forgave him, but we agreed to be friends which I knew will disappoint him. None of this would've happened…And then there's Carl."

"Carl?"

I explained what happened, how he kissed me to hurt Derek. I called him, but my calls went to voicemail.

"You think he ran away because of you?" Dad asked, appearing on my right side with Mom.

"It's all my fault," I said, ashamed.

"We all make mistakes." Marline looked weary, and her familiar pair of ocean blue orbs glimmered with melancholy. "Forgiving is hard, especially in a world like ours."

"You should all go inside," a policeman ordered gently as he stopped next to Marline. "We'll take care of the situation by ourselves."

"No," Marline protested. "I'm not going anywhere until I find my nephew!"

"Miss Matthews, we can handle this. We have come across dilemmas like this, and we have succeeded in finding the runaways. If we found them, we can find your nephew. I suggest you and your lovely friends go inside and enjoy something to warm yourselves. We will inform you if we find anything appealing. Meanwhile, my partner, Susan, will question you inside. Okay?"

"It's not okay!" Marline hollered at him. "He's never coming back! My little nephew isn't coming back! You must find before…" She's scared once again. "Before it's too late. Please, find him."

Luke led her away, whispering soothing things to her as Marline wailed into her nephew's shoulder.

Inside, it was warm. Cody muttered something about how he wants summer to arrive. The policewoman, Susan, was pretty with chestnut hair, rosy pink cheeks, blood red lips, dewy skin, and stunning grey eyes.

"Ma'am, I want you to fill some of the gaps for me," said the policewoman.

Marline nodded. "What would you like to know?"

"When did you find out your nephew gone missing?"

"When he came back from wherever he went. He didn't go to school today because he   didn't want to. He was sad. I don't know where he went, but throughout the day he rang me and asked if I wanted takeaway or homemade food. I told him takeaway. When I came home, the house was empty. I asked Luke if he knows where his brother is, he said no. I called Derek's cell, but it went to voicemail. Then, I immediately thought he could have run away. So, I quickly checked his room to find his clothes were still there. That's when I started to panic, and I reported the situation to the police.'

Susan scribbled down on her notepad. "Has he done this before?" she asked, glancing up at Marline. "Running away, I mean?"

Marline hesitated. Then, she nodded. "Once."

"Ma'am people have reasons to run away. Is there a reason why he ran away? Is he getting abused at home...?"

"No, he wasn't getting abused. Derek was hurting. He was feeling lonely. His depression was getting worse, so he started to have thoughts about taking his own life. When he was eleven, he tried to drown himself. When he was twelve, he did the same thing but instead he ran away. If he ran away this time, then it—"

"It's because of me," I whispered, interrupting Marline. "Derek and I broke up because I found out about this ridiculous dare. I forgave him, but I suggested we be friends, and then this asshole came along and decided to make things worse..." Tears prickled my eyes, and I furiously blinked them away. I don't want to cry anymore. I had enough of crying. "It's my fault he ran away..."

Jasmine brushed her hand up and down my back. I think this was supposed to be a comforting gesture, and I appreciate it. It didn't help me, though. Not even a little.

"Derek die?" Cody asked, his face creasing with sadness. "No. I don't want dat. Derek no die."

The policewoman thanked us for the helpful information and left the house.

A deafening silence enveloped us until a sob resounded from the businesswoman. Luke wrapped an arm around his aunt, pulling her into his embrace as her tears soaked his shirt. Next to Luke, Theo's eyes were lustrous with despondent tears as he stared at a picture frame of him and Derek, their arms around each other with their middle fingers pointed at the camera, goofy smiles beaming on their delicate faces.

"We lost Alexandra and Samuel. We lost Mike. We nearly lost April…" Marline wept. "Does this mean we're going to lose Derek?"

My heart pulsated at her words.

I stood up, not wanting to be in here anymore. I can't help it. I can't even breathe properly. I was panting. The tears I fought off succeeded to stream down my pale cheeks no matter how hard I endeavoured to blink them away.

"April," Dad called as I walked out of the parlour and ascended the stairs to Derek's room.

"Let her be," Mom told my father.

My mouth quivered. I shivered due to the frostiness curtly oozing inside. I slammed the door of Derek's room closed and collapsed on the floor, sobbing quietly to myself. I heard police sirens fading away in the distance. The rain resumed splattering on the windows unkindly as the wind howled, swaying the trees roughly.

I lost Mike. I don't want to lose Derek.

I heaved a shaky breath and banged my head into the door behind me. I leisurely lifted my eyes to the ceiling, freckled with the glow-in-the-dark stars Mike furnished. As I stared at how they flickered magically, I reflected on Derek.

I miss him.

I love him.

I wish I was there to comfort him.

I wish I never recommended us to be friends.

I wish I hugged him earlier and told him it's okay, that I will always be there for him, that I will always stay with him. Because he needs me and I need him.

Derek is unlike the other guys in the world; sure, he can be a dick majority of the time, but that's just for show. Deep

down, there is a sweet, charming, fragile boy who has been
mutely beseeching someone to help him before it's too late.

My eyes were suddenly ~~engrossed~~ *drawn* to a wall with pictures
of Jesus Christ and the Virgin Mary. I scooted to the wall,
looking at the images intently, attempting to say a prayer when I
saw something on Derek's bed.

A crinkled piece of paper. I smoothed the crinkles,
wiping my eyes to read the words properly.

Dear April,

*I really hope you will read this because I spent hours writing
this note.*

*I am so sorry for breaking your heart, angel. I am grateful that
we are friends, but friendship isn't enough for me.*

*Don't take that in the wrong way. Don't blame yourself for
causing this. It's not your fault. It's mine. It's not your choice for me to
leave my home, it's mine, and no one should shout at me for that. No
one should shout at you because you've been hurt.*

*Thank you for the memories we made together—our
childhood, our heartbreaks, our tears, our laughter, our smiles, and
our love. Thank you for allowing me to be your shoulder to cry on.
Thank you for being in my life.*

*Tell Marline, Luke, and everyone in my family I love them.
Tell my awesome dickhead, Theo, that I love him, and I am grateful
that I forced him to be my best friend. Tell your family I love them
and thank them for welcoming me with open arms. Tell Cody I love
him.*

*Don't worry about where I am. I promise I will find a safe
place to live in. I already know a safe place that is available to
everyone, and my parents and your brother are there. Don't worry;
I'm safe in Jesus' arms. He will protect me.*

*I'll give your love to Mike. I promise to tell my parents how
wonderful you are, and the joy you have gifted me with.*

I'll be fine up there. With Mike by my side, we will be your guardian angels. I promise.

This isn't the end, baby. I'm always with you, just like Mike. We'll see each other soon.

Love you so much,
Derek

Uneven breaths escape from my thin lips. I returned my attention to the holy pictures of Jesus Christ and Hail Mary.

"Please don't let him leave me, Jesus," I implored. "Please, God…Archangels…Anyone who can hear me, please give him back to us. Give him back to me."

I really do hope He heard my prayer.

*   *   *

Another three days ~~soared~~ dragged past. Still no sign of Derek. Marline arranged a search party, and literally every single person in Peony Hallows participated, which is truly and utterly heartwarming.

Marline, Luke, Theo, and I contacted the police three times a day if they discovered anything helpful or suspicious. As expected, they haven't. Yet.

Sandy, Derek's grandma, has been stressing out and going to church, praying continuously for us to find Derek soon. Students in Peony Hallows High School were starting to become more spiteful toward me, hissing at me that it was my fault Derek ran away. They're right, though. They have every right to treat me as if I'm a vermin — a vermin destined to be killed.

I've recently skipped school to search for Derek with the help of Theo, Sophia, Natalia, Jasmine, Jackson, and Ethan. We searched everywhere—the pubs, the shops, the deserted streets, the beach. We even contacted other urban areas to ask if they have noticed Derek. Their answer was no.

We even searched the meadow, every inch and area of the immense place. No sign whatsoever.

We haven't given up. We will never give up.

One night, I was sleeping with no peace. Then, I bolted upright in my bed, frightened when I heard my ringtone. I gazed sideways to see my phone vibrating. I picked it up, and on the screen flashed *Natalia*. I immediately answered the call and compressed the phone against my left ear.

"*April?*" Natalia called.

"I'm awake," I replied, my voice raspy. I subdued a yawn and wiped off the lethargy. "What's up, Nat?"

"*April, I'm on my way to Derek's house.*"

My heart thumped. "Why?"

"*April, the police finally found something that belonged to Derek.*"

*   *   *

I knocked on the door for the third time. Ethan and Dad were with me, in our pyjamas. Finally, Luke opened the door. His black hair was a rat's nest, and his eyes were somnolent. He stepped aside, so we could come in.

In the living room were Marline, Jasmine, Jackson, Theo, Natalia, and Sophia, exhausted yet anticipating to hear the news. I sat down next to Jasmine, concentrating on the policeman.

"Now, tell us," Marline demanded. "What have you found?"

"The department investigated Derek's past. We know his parents passed away. We thought that Derek could be hiding in the location where his parents were buried."

"The meadow?" I asked. "You think he's there?"

Theo frowned. "We've searched the meadow. Every part of it. The willow tree, the lake, the church...everything. No sign of him."

"Okay, but an hour ago, we received a phone call from a bartender, mentioning about a teenage boy with ragged clothes drinking and staggering out of the bar. The bartender talked to him, and he said that all the boy mumbled about was reuniting with his parents, Mike Levesque — may they rest in peace — and Jesus."

Jasmine gradually and painfully clamped a hand over her mouth.

"Then, the boy wandered away. The bartender grew worried and followed after him. To some extent, he lost the boy, but eventually found him and..." He hesitated, absorbing in our expressions, gloom filling his eyes. "He called us. We came. And right next to the lake were the boy's clothes."

Marline suddenly created a fleeting, nitpicking sound and she banged her hand on the table, her lips shaking. She dropped her head into her hands, and she frenziedly wailed. "No... No, no, no..."

"What is it?" Natalia demanded. "What's wrong?"

"Did Derek tell you guys about our father?" Luke asked. "Did he tell you what happened to him?"

My family nodded, including Theo, while my friends shook their heads, perplexed.

"Yes," I countered. "He drowned himself in a bathtub..." I paused abruptly, immediately knowing what Luke, Marline, and Theo were thinking.

I recalled three days ago when Marline mentioned Derek running away and attempting suicide.

Everybody sobbed. As much as I stopped it, the pain came out. Beads of tears fell down one after the other.

A blistering sensation ached inside me.

My heart...it's blazing. It's the same feeling I experienced when I was at Mike's funeral. My heart was burning with distress, wretchedness, and anguish.

My breathing slowed as I felt dizzy. All the voices in the room, all the sobs of melancholy and the mourning, slurred for a moment.

Derek drowned himself.

Chapter Forty-Seven

Choice

Derek Matthews

The bittersweet fragrance of smoke and alcohol emanated from me in similar waves, filling my bedroom.

Two weeks have gone away, and the memory of witnessing April kissing that familiar boy was imprinted in my brain, triggering a seething resentment that churns inside me, along with torment and misfortune.

In those two weeks, my mind has been battling the pessimistic deliberations with positive ones, yet the pessimism rose and became unfathomable.

Coughing to some extent, I reflected on my father's phrases of how he told me the truth when I was very young—I was a mistake. To him. To everyone in the family. I killed my mother merely for entering this damned world, and the death hurt him in various, indescribable ways. The death pained him and led him to take his own life. Even though it was his choice, I still blamed myself.

Dad was right. I was a mistake. I brought pain, heartache, and melancholy to others around me because I was in pain; because I envied the blissful expressions of strangers who achieved loving embraces from their precious parents. I envied them because they were happy, and I wasn't.

Then, there was the dare. I agreed to do it, and the dare's advantages were to blossom love, not in my heart, but in hers. And that love was defined as friendship at first, but then it transformed into affection, and confessions. Theo did it for me to find love and I did. Although, it hurt her.

It's killing me. Awfully slow.

I was solely too damn complicated. Maybe that's why it's challenging for me to cope with life the majority of the time. I was complicated to everyone: Theo, Mike, April... If this is how my life will be — falling in love unintentionally and annihilating that love due to my stubborn decisions; because it's my fault — then I don't want to live anymore.

What's the point? I was too complicated; too baffling. It's bizarre to even reflect on how Theo can endure my company.

I was holding a rumpled piece of paper with a pen clutched in my other hand. I thought about the ancient murky days of my depression...The depression that dominated me to take my own life. *I'm sorry for breaking your heart, angel.* The depression that oppressed me, compelled me, to run away, leave home, and discover a different place — far, far, far away from Earth — to be safe in. *It's not your choice for me to leave my home, it's mine, and no one should shout at me for that.* A place that will lift my spirits, a place that will reward me with a better life.

What would Mike do in this state? He will keep on fighting, that's for sure.

But will he understand the sentimental state I'm trapped in?

Will my parents understand?

Will He understand? *We'll see each other soon.*

Surely, it is a sin, but I had had enough of this world...enough of everything. I don't see what's special in my life other than Mike, my parents, and her. But I lost all of them, and without them, I am nothing. *Love you so much.*

I placed the crumpled paper on my bed, knowing for a fact that she will come here and read it.

Outside, a blanket of obscurity covered the radiant, fiery sinking sun, substituted with a lustrous silver crescent moon that dimly glimmered the night. Luke wasn't here. I asked my aunt if she wants something to eat: takeaway, or homemade food. She said takeaway, and she never suspected anything in that brief chitchat.

I ambled along the pathways of the roads of Peony Hallows. A cigarette drooped from in-between my lips. I blazed the end with my lighter, stashing it back into a pocket of my black hoodie.

Inhaling the smoke, I spent ten minutes mulling about going back to my house and throwing the paper away and staying there. But all I wanted to do was...just go away.

Just to forget everything.

Life.

Problems.

Wickedness.

Just *everything.*

*   *   *

Three days hastened by, and I haven't returned home, concealing myself in isolated areas from getting observed by strangers. It was night now, and the darkness of the surroundings agreed with my unenthusiastic thoughts. I walked the lanes to a local bar. Entering the bar, I sat where the bartender was working.

"One glass of vodka," I say, flopping on a seat.

He stares at me. "How old are you?"

"Eighteen," I lied. I just turned seventeen not so long ago.

He seems dubious. "Kid—"

I slammed a pile of money on the surface of the counter, jolting him at the sudden sound. "Hundred bucks. Consider this as a late Christmas present. Now, one glass of vodka."

The bartender glanced at the hundred bucks, and then at me. He immediately swirled around to prepare my glass and gave it to me before snatching the money away. I chugged the smouldering liquid down, the drink heightening my senses. The bartender stared at me with wide eyes as I hammered the glass on the counter, asking for another one.

"Isn't one glass enough?" he said, nervous. "You know it's not good for your health…"

"Coming from the guy working in a bar. Another glass, please, and I'll give you more money."

He scrutinized me fleetingly. "Blue eyes, dark hair…" He sniffed and slightly gagged. "Smells of cigarettes…bad boy look. You're Derek Matthews, aren't you?"

"The one and only." I grabbed the extra glass from the bartender and briefly sipped the vodka. I gifted him with a thick wad of money, and he took it with astonishment.

"People are looking for you," he enlightened, eyeing me warily as I slurp the drink. "Your aunt is getting worried."

Regret filled me. "Worrying about me is unnecessary. I'm a bad person."

He seemed to understand. "You're not."

"I am. There are good people and bad people in the world. I am part of the bad."

"But you changed, didn't you? That's what everyone told me about you: you were bad, but now you're good. You changed for the better."

"That's what my angel told me."

"Your angel is right."

I smiled. "She's always right." I suddenly tightened my grasp around the glass cup. "She's too good for me. I don't deserve her."

"Is that why you're here?" The bartender sat down, intrigued by this conversation. "Because of your girl? Moping about her?"

"We broke up."

"Oh. I'm sorry. When did you guys break up?"

"More than two weeks ago…No, I *think* it was two weeks ago." I swirled my finger around the rim of the glass. "I'm also considering why I'm a good person."

"You are a good man. Everyone is good and bad. It's how our nature is like, I guess. But I can say you're more on the good than the bad. Tell me, who is your girl?"

"*Was*," I corrected. "Her name is April Levesque."

"Mike Levesque's little sister?"

"Yes. I want to see him again. I want to see my parents. I want to reunite with them. With Jesus."

A stranger called the bartender, ~~enquiring~~ asking for more drinks, interfering and finishing our tête-à-tête.

As I stayed in the bar for a while longer, the bartender was unable to talk with me as he was busy with guests who were crowding the entire building. Here and then, the bartender looked at me concerned, and I could tell he was frantic to abandon his post and talk to me more.

I went out of the bar after a while and hiked the bleak, sinister, shady streets. The trees were unmoving; the branches bowing above me, cloaking the ominous air, and fabricating silhouettes to leap from the corners and devour me. The thinly covered snow-layered ground was nearly imperceptible, disguised with blotches of muck that camouflages with the colour of the earth.

My mind and body were feeling the effects of the noxious drink. Soon enough, I was lurching through a vacant road, and I knew that I was not so far from the meadow.

"Die," I slurred. "I should die. I killed Momma. I killed Dad. I am a depression to everyone. I lost Mike. I lost April. I'm useless." I reiterated those words as I tottered the stretch of road, the wintriness jabbing into my bones and triggering a mush-like feeling.

Soon enough, the memorable feeling of downy, velvety grass scratched me, and the vastness of green speckled with ivory-covered flowers, fluctuated as the unpleasantly cold breeze bristled past me, as if ghosts were pinching my skin. There were no birds, no serenading melodies.

The iciness of the immense lake was melting. The crinkled petals of the various kinds of flowers — daffodils, roses, poppies, bluebells, water lilies, peonies, primroses — perfectly arranged in the pattern of a rainbow, gradually stretched, yet cowered backwards from the nippy breeze, as if beseeching for warmth.

The ruins of the ancient church were everywhere on the right side of the Lake of Miracles. All of them smudgy silhouettes in the darkness, yet I could see a colossal cross sticking out from a curved structure of the once breathing church.

The disturbing blackness looming over the earth was now twinkling with stars, beautiful enough to ignite blissful dreams just by gaping at them. I've been wasting my time in the meadow at night before, and when I am, I feel as if I'm gazing at a kind of heaven. It makes me want to jump up and try to capture one of the stars and whisper a childlike wish.

I didn't know how long I've been walking, but I could tell it's for more than thirty minutes. An hour, maybe. Or more.

My legs were sore. My body was fatigued. I pushed the exhaustion away and concentrated on the lake. It's still icy, but there were a few cracks exposing the glossy water, reflecting the stars and the moon.

My toes stopped right at the edge, staring at my reflection mirrored on the surface.

All I can see was a seventeen-year-old boy with jet black hair over his celestial ocean blue eyes filled with nothing but hopelessness and guilt. His clothes were rumpled and worn out, as if he hasn't changed for days. There were dark circles under his eyes, as if he had no sleep whatsoever. His lips were bruised from peeling off the skin too many times.

"I killed Momma," I mumbled to myself, grabbing the hem of my shirt and tugging it off my body.

"I killed Dad."

My stomach quivered at the cold, my teeth chattered.

"I'm a mistake."

I kicked off my shoes, my bare feet stiffening at the sadistic feel of the icy ground.

"I broke people."

Discarding my clothes on the floor, I walked to the edge of the ground surrounding the lake, cautious not to angle myself accidentally into the water. Not yet.

"Why should I live?"

I was far from where I left my clothes. In fact, it's indistinguishable to observe due to the murkiness, and since my clothes were at the far opposite side to me, the only thing blocking my way to my clothes was the lake. The chilly, menacing Lake of Miracles that I once thought was stunning to look at and made wishes when a rainbow miraculously appeared.

"Jesus," I mumbled, remembering that the Saviour should be here in the meadow. Dad always told me that since there is a church in the meadow, Jesus is present. "I'm sorry, Jesus. I can't stay any longer. I don't want to live anymore. I hope you understand."

And my body collapsed into the glacial, cavernous water.

The water crashed over me like glum waves, desperate to consume me. I held my breath, stopping my lips from parting, preventing my body from swimming back up and plunging through the surface for oxygen.

I allowed myself to drift through the lake, my body motionless, my eyes slightly opened and looking at the starry sky, intently engrossed on how the stars rapidly twinkled at me, as if they're imploring me to come out and save myself before it's too late. Perhaps, the hastily winking stars were signals from the heavens, from the people of the heavens, commanding me to come up to the surface. Or perhaps, I was just hallucinating.

My tears mixed with the water of the lake, my mind replayed the memories of people insulting me.

You are a bad person.

You killed your Momma.

You with her? Please, we all know you're only using her. There is no true love for a player.

My lungs burned without air. Something jammed my throat. My heart clobbered in a sharp, relentless, warning pace, begging for sweet, heavenly oxygen. Locks of my drenched jet-black hair floated around me, like a halo, except that it's not gold or celestial, it's just black, as if I've committed an immoral sin.

Vile blemishes impeded my vision as I, at a snail's pace, turned in the water, my back now greeting the night sky rippling above the surface. The lake's graceful currents push me up…

My mouth opened, and the water overwhelmed me, stealing my last breath, surging inside me and flooding my body.

Everything around me spitefully darkened before a vivid light flared in my eyes.

Chapter Forty-Eight

Inactive

April Levesque

My fingertips dabbed my eyes. "He didn't drown." A part of my brain and my whole heart agreed with my words. "Stop thinking that he's dead. Derek wouldn't do that. He wouldn't…"

"That's what I'm trying to tell you," the policeman blurted out. "The department is on their way to the meadow right now to search the waters. There is a possibility that we can find him before it's too late."

"Maybe he's planning to," Natalia whispered. "Oh, God, we got to find him! He must be somewhere in the meadow!"

"Then let's go."

*   *   *

I came out of the police car, my feet stomping the ground. The main thing I perceived was the magnificent region of rustling dimly snow-covered grass and the leafless trees with melting snow on their branches. The sky was clear and blinking fretfully, like a warning. I presumed the serenading birds were asleep in their shelters, since no hums were reverberating in the air other than the rustling, agonising wind.

We searched the lake, and as expected, we saw the clothes lying treacherously on the ground. The first sign. Two authority figures were examining the clothes and the surface of the water, as if expecting Derek to thrust up and claw at the ground.

"He's not here," the woman informed.

Ethan frowned. "But his clothes…He must be close…He has to be."

"Did you recheck the entire meadow?" Theo asked the cops.

"Yes."

We all exchanged considering expressions.

"Then where could he be?" Jasmine whispered.

"You don't think he already…" Sophia's voice trailed off.

"No," I snapped. "No. He's not gone. He can't just go."

"He can't control his mind, April," said Dad. "We find it hard to control the pessimistic side of the mind. Like how you were unable to control your mind when you attempted suicide."

My father was right. Sometimes, it's tough to control our depressed self, our depressing thoughts. Our depression was like an evil spirit hosting our bodies, dominating us and providing us with false answers and information.

I noticed something. The snow on the floor was dissolving, but I can see outlines of footprints pressed into the soil, advancing to a particular direction. Theo noticed my gaze and followed it to see the footprints. Without uttering anything, he pursued the footprints, with me hastening after him.

"Where are you going?" Jackson asked as he, too, jogged after us with the rest behind him.

The long strands of grass irritated our skins as we shove through them. The footprints were rapidly fading, becoming imperceptible minute by minute, or, in fact, second by second.

Our jog came to a stop, and in front of us was the lake with the ruins of the church to the right. I could see a massive figure of a cross sticking out of an ashen block of the ancient church. The lake was beautifully speckled with creased flowers. The ice was melting. In fact, it's undetectable now, but underneath the torrent of the luminous light radiating from the crescent moon, I can see square-like blemishes marking the surface.

But that's not what made me apprehensive.

There, floating away from the earth was a body. A motionless body, with its back greeting the flickering stars.

"No…" I whispered.

"Derek!"

Theo dived into the water. He swiftly swam to his best friend, his forehead creased with anxiety, his eyes surging with water not from the lake, but from the fear and misery. His teeth chattered as the wintry temperature of the lake assaulted him.

Jackson and Ethan jumped into the water, giving Theo a hand when he wrapped his arm around his best friend. Jackson and Ethan bound their arms around Derek Matthews, and with the assistance of Theo, they swiftly carried the body to us.

Luke, Dad, and the two policemen grabbed onto Derek's arms, carting him out of the Lake of Miracles. The body plunged to the grotty ground, unmoving.

The world was suddenly silent. The air was still. Even the lake that was thrashing is now still. Even the stars that were twinkling seemed to stop.

I kneeled beside the others, looming over him. Beads of hot fluid raced down my cheeks. Jasmine's, Sophia's, Natalia's, and Marline's eyes were lustrous with despair. Theo mumbled incoherent words to himself. Even Ethan and Jackson were crying, and Dad was the last one to cry when he checked the pulse in Derek Matthew's pale neck.

He shook his dead, hopeless. "He's gone."

With his eyes closed, he looked like he was sleeping, but he's not.

"He's dead."

Chapter Forty-Nine

Lost

April Levesque

I struggled so strongly to stop the horrendous pain from igniting in my chest, as if needles were scratching my skin, tearing it open to dig their way to my heart. This challenge of endeavouring to extinguish the pain was difficult, so difficult that I failed and screamed in agony.

And my heart…the sentiments assaulting my heart were so familiar to the ones I've experienced at Mike's funeral: burning from the misery.

The cops were calling the ambulance. Luke tightly embraced his arm. Marline was quietly wailing, tightening her hold on Luke's shirt, as if she wants to shred it.

Jasmine and Sophia teared up together. Ethan balled his hands into fists, fighting the tears. Although, he was unsuccessful, and now small tears were leaking from his eyes. Jackson was shuddering not only from the cold, but from the muted sobs despairing him, flabbergasted as his blurry eyes absorbs the prospect of his great friend.

Derek's skin was ashen and pallid. His impregnated jet-black hair was plastered to his forehead. His eyelashes soaked. His lips, frayed and blue, parted, as if he's puffing out breaths. But he wasn't. I refused to believe that his soul left him and was now soaring up to the night time sky, passing the Milky Way and the universe all the way to what he called "his safe home".

"No." I crawled closer to him. "No, Derek!" I folded my hands together and placed them on his cold chest. "Don't you dare leave us!"

My folded hands pressed on his chest, thumping his ribcage, desiring to accelerate his heart. Theo joined, folding his hands like me and pushing on Derek's chest, shouting at him to come back as tears drip from his chin.

"Please, don't leave me, buddy," Theo begged, pressing harder on Derek's chest. "I don't want to lose my best friend."

Sirens resonated in the distance, and we knew the ambulance was getting close. The grimy ground soiled our clothed knees, shins, and ankles. The heat of his body was vanishing, interchanging with a type of chilliness.

Dad tried to pry me away from Derek. "April," he whispered sadly, "it's no use. He's dead."

"No!" I protested, thrashing out of his grasp and crawling back to Derek. I resumed battering Derek's chest, mentally screeching a prayer to the Him. *Please, please. Bring him back.*

"April," Dad tried to rationalise.

"He's *not dead!* I refuse to believe that! He's going to come back. He has to."

Dad kept his mouth shut, watching how Theo and I vigilantly pounded Derek's chest. *Please, make his heart continue to beat. Please, God. Please bring him back.*

The ambulance steered through the grass, coming to an abrupt ~~pause~~ stop. Theo and I never gave up on our desire to bring Derek back. The paramedics hastened out of the emergency van, thrusting a stretcher.

Before they reached us, I cupped Derek's face and slammed my lips to his, grasping them firmly. I puffed my breaths into his throat before I inhaled, remembering familiar scenes like this from movies where the protagonists kiss the drowned individuals, inhaling so the water can gurgle up the victims' throat. Even scientists admitted that it was possible to bring back a drowned person to life.

"We lost him," I heard Marline weep, "we lost him. We lost Alexa. Sammy. Mike. Now Derek. We lost all of them."

No.

We didn't lose him.

He's still with us.

Always was, always will.

Hands clasped on my shoulders, lightly tugging me away. I shrugged the hands off me, and the paramedic behind me heartbreakingly sighed, whispering to me that it's no use and that he's already safer up there.

I hummed unspoken illogical words to the paramedics in disagreement, my mouth never abandoning his as I continued to inhale profoundly as Theo thumped his best friend's chest. I heard him murmuring a prayer — a prayer that begged to bring Derek back.

"Derek, please come back," Theo whispered as I removed my lips from Derek's, wheezing faintly to inhale oxygen. "We love you, man. Why can't you see that? Come back. Jesus Christ, please come back. Bring him back."

No answer.

Not even a murmur.

My lips quivered after another two minutes of attempting to bring Derek back.

Ethan crouched behind me, wrenching me into a tight cuddle as I wailed into his chest, the hope dying in me.

We lost him.

We completely lost him.

Derek's gone.

He's dead.

He will never come back.

The paramedics insisted Theo to stop. Eventually, Theo did, and he bent his body forward, loudly sobbing. He shouted foul language, catching the paramedics off guard. Of course, he will be angry. When you lose someone, there is not only grief and depression, but fury as well.

Jackson embraced Theo as the paramedics lifted Derek Matthew's body. His legs that were submerged in the Lake of Miracles whilst Theo and I were attempting to bring him back were pale and blue.

The paramedics placed Derek on the stretcher. They opened their mouths to speak but were ~~interfered~~ interrupted by a phenomenal cough.

Water spluttered through his lips, his body convulsing as he coughs, his eyes lightly opening to say hello to the sparkling stars once again.

Chapter Fifty

Miracle

April Levesque

Derek's body convulsed on the stretcher, his chest thrusting up as he coughs and coughs out the water which splattered on the ground below him. His eyelids half-heartedly lifted, and those striking blue irises exhaustedly gazed at the sparkling stars that glimmered a welcome to him.

The paramedics gaped at Derek, dumbfounded, deliberating how a phenomenon like this can occur, and so did the others. Theo cried jovially, saying that his prayers auspiciously have been answered. Marline screamed elatedly, tackling Derek with a tight hug. Realising the pressure she's creating, and hearing his wheezes, Marline mumbled an apology as she moved back from his nephew, cleaning her lustrous eyes.

Derek, still lying on the stretcher, panting frayed breaths that calmed in a fleeting moment, turned his head to the side, his eyes meeting mine. He smiled. "Angel," he whispered.

I went closer, and he raised his body up, his muscular arms sheathing me as I shrouded his waist with mine; I hid my face in his neck, and he hid his in mine. My tears cloaked his soil-tarnished skin.

"I'm sorry," Derek and I both whispered in unison.

He laughed at the occurrence, and I wondered how he could giggle when there was most likely a sore pain in his lungs from drowning.

"But…" Jasmine was clearly blissful that he was back, though she was bewildered. "*How*? How are you back?"

"It is possible for a drowned person to come back," a paramedic countered. "The girl has been inhaling from his lips, which heaves the water that he inhaled from the Lake of Miracles up and out his lungs slowly. The boy has been thumping his chest, which added a better chance of him coming back."

"In all honesty, from the minutes you've been attempting to bring him back, we considered he would never breathe again," another paramedic admitted.

"But now he is breathing." A policeman was smiling at Derek, who lay back on the stretcher, his eyes quivering close, as if he was exhausted. "It's a miracle."

"Almost as if it was done by the Lake of Miracles," Dad agreed.

"It's a true miracle."

Chapter Fifty-One

Reunion

Derek Matthews

I breathed serenely, my eyelashes fluttering as I lift my eyelids. The white dawning light fleetingly blinded me before I finally got accustomed to the glare above me. I rubbed the corners of my prickly eyes, groaning.

I was in a hospital room. I can tell by the pallid walls, the cabinets at the corners, and the bitter odour of medicines filling the air of the room. My skin was scratchy, and I realised that I was wearing a medical, blue-white robe that masked my body.

The door opened, and a man sophisticatedly walked in. A dark-skinned man with curly hair and dark eyes, a beard dotting his chiselled jawline. He smiled warm-heartedly. "Hello, Mr. Little Matthews. I am Dr. Abeasi."

"Hi," I rasped.

"Do you know why you're here? Or have you forgotten everything that occurred recently?"

"I know." I remembered my suicide attempt. I drowned in the lake, and I died, but then somehow, I came back alive in the company of my beloved ones.

"It's a miracle," the doctor admitted. "We all hope you won't do it again. Will you?"

Theo, Jackson, Luke, and everyone else I know and love, including April, came into my mind. They were definitely devastated, and the thought of that made me mentally bawl at myself for being so daft to take my own life.

The doctor noticed my guilt because he hastily rationalised, "It's not your fault, Derek. You were in an emotional state, trapped in your suicidal thoughts. You cannot control them. I've checked the records of your mental health just now, and it said that you stopped going to therapy a long time ago. Do you want to continue them? It will be the best to control your depression."

"Therapy doesn't help all the time."

He heaved a sigh. "That's what you think. But I have hired a professional therapist, and he's very good. You can talk to him. He was like you—he tried to drown himself too. I considered talking to someone with the same experiences will help you."

I contemplated for a moment.

"At least give it a try," the doctor insisted. "Trying won't hurt, will it?"

Actually, trying can hurt. Trying can be painful. In the end, trying can be useless. On the other hand, it depends on what you were trying for. "Fine," I decided. "I'll give it a chance."

He beamed, approved. "Hopefully, he can help you with your depression. Now, are you sure you won't drown yourself again?"

"Yeah, I promise."

Think
I ~~pondered~~ that I can avoid the temptations; that suicidal act was egotistical, I know, and I hate being selfish. I didn't want to repeat my father's egocentric actions, but I did. And somehow, I came back. I didn't know why. I didn't know how. But I knew I came back for a reason. An important one. A reason that I am grateful for.

"You are lucky you survived," the doctor said. "It truly is a miracle you've returned. I don't really believe in God, but I like to help people who were very emotional with faithful words. And it says on your profile that you're a Christian." Just like Jasmine. "I assume He brought you back for another chance to redeem yourself. Besides, you were next to the Lake of Miracles."

"Why me, though?" I question.

The doctor shrugged. "We may not hear Him, but we simply have to trust Him and his actions. He is confusing, sometimes frustrating, but He knows what is best for us more than we do. He knows us more than we know ourselves.

"Sometimes, the Lord saves the soul and cherishes the soul in His kingdom. Other times, He gives us a second chance for redemption and to fix our mistakes. I think He wants you to rescue yourself from depression with the help of your family and friends before He welcomes you into His arms. Another chance before salvation."

*   *   *

My reunion with my friends was heartwarming. However, the reunion with her was the most euphoric.

She stood timidly in front of the door, timorous to approach me. Guilt deluged her dark irises. My heart hammered in my chest at her company, and then blubbered when I heard her soft sob.

I scrambled off the hospital bed and went~~advanced~~ to her, wrenching her into my arms and wrapping her in a tight affectionate hug.

"I'm sorry," she said with a rickety breath. "Derek, I am so sor—"

"Shh, angel." I hummed soothingly as her breath fanned my neck. "Don't apologise."

"It's my fault, though. If I just allowed another chance for a relationship, none of this will happen. I made you feel so horrible, so worthless—"

"Hey, hey, hey." I backed away for my hands to cradle her face, levelling her eyes with mine and sweeping my thumbs across the brims of her sweltering orbs. "April, it's fine. It's not your fault. It's particularly my fault for not mentioning about the dare sooner, and I am sorry for that."

"It's my fault, too!"

"Then it'll be our fault. Okay? Our fault. We'll share it. The guilt. Everything. Is that fair enough? Besides, I'm still breathing. And as I breathe, I will never decide to take my own life ever again. I promise."

"But you can't control it," she whispered. "None of us can. Our minds control us."

"I'll find help to gain self-control."

"Can I help?"

I smile. "Of course."

"Derek, I'll be honest. I don't deserve you," she disclosed.

I frown. "Why do you say that?"

"Because." She lowers her head to the ground. "I'm a bitch."

I rolled my eyes. "Men and women are bitches. Don't sound as if you're the only one, because you're not. And baby, everything is in the past now. We don't have to talk about it anymore. We've been through that road, and now we're moving into a different one. The past doesn't define us, angel."

She didn't reply, and I perceived tears forming, triggering my heart to melt. Her bottom lip trembled a little, and she inhaled a convulsing breath to tranquil her body and her mind. "But I don't deserve you."

"Neither do I."

At that, she raised her eyes to mine, and the tears leaked from the corners, saturating her eyelashes.

"I love you, April." My lips kissed her tears away. "And I think it's crazy for me, a stupid asshole, to fall in love with a beautiful, sweet girl like you. I thought I didn't deserve you. But you say that you don't deserve me. I guess we can put it this way: we don't deserve each other, but we don't care because you know why? I don't care. I want you to be mine.

"You're so beautiful, April. I never get tired of hearing your voice, looking at you or being near you. You're really my angel. You give me hope. You're a sweet miracle in my life, a rare gift to the world.

"I have and I will *always* love you. Even when we're ghosts, I will still love you."

A calm hush enveloped us. April's eyes settled on my face, absorbing my words and registering them as her eyes leisurely pool with more tears. She wanted to say something — I can tell by the way her lips twitched — but I already closed the small space between us and locked my lips with hers.

"I love you, April Levesque," I mumbled against her mouth.

"I love you too, Derek Matthews."

*   *   *

When I went to school the next morning, I was gobsmacked by the unexpected euphoric welcoming cheers from pupils in the hallways, the foyers, and the classrooms. The faces I was familiar with, yet not on first name basis with, told me that they were happy knowing that I am not gone, but alive and healthy.

Even the teachers were happy, and from what I know, the teachers hated me because of my personality. I guess they do have a soft spot for me after all.

Theo drove us to April's house, and in her house, Marline, Luke, Neyara, my friends, and April's family lounged on the sofas. Their expressions brightened at the sight of me, and they abruptly stood up to hug me once again.

"I'm glad I didn't lose my best friend," said Theo, who patted me on the back as he squeezed me tightly in his arms. He hugged me ten times today, and this was the eleventh one. I didn't mind, though. His hugs were comforting.

April's father enlightened me with: "Please don't do that again. You can tell by everyone in this room that you are loved deeply. Don't leave us. You are, after all, part of the Levesque family and like a son to me."

I blinked. "Did you just—"

"Give you my blessing?" he finished. "Yes, my blessing to allow you to be with my daughter."

"And marry her?" I asked.

He rolled his eyes. "Too young for that now, Derek. Maybe later."

Later. I smirked at the last word. The man saw my anticipation and rolled his eyes again, murmuring how lovesick I was even after a horrible event.

Cody stormed up to me, his hair a rat's nest, and he smacked the back of my head with his teddy bear.

I winced. "Cody!" I complained. "Oww, that actually hurts!"

"Idiot!" Cody scolded. "Don't like you die!"

I threw Cody up into my arms and smiled at him. "I'm sorry."

Cody's face softened, and he returned the smile. "It's okay. Don't do again, okay?"

I nodded. "I promise."

My eyes met April's. She was grinning frenziedly, and so was I. Despite all the horrendous episodes that occurred, I finally have the girl all to myself forever. No one was going to stand in our way anymore. Not anyone or anything. I will make sure of that.

I swung out my arm, and she squashed her face into the side of my chest, contented by my touch.

From now on, I vowed not to do anything inconsiderate anymore. From now on, I will only live for April because she's the one who brought happiness back to me. She's the one who's always making me smile for no reason. I love that. I shouldn't be sad — not anymore — when I know that I have April in my life forever and ever. She truly is an angel from Heaven, an angel who's destined to be mine for eternity.

At that moment, her eyes shimmered like the stars I've been gaping at in the meadow. Whatever occurred in the past was now irrelevant to deliberate about. The past doesn't define us if you let it go, and I can feel myself slowly letting the past slip away as my mind contemplates about the future with optimism and enthusiasm.

There were so many obstacles in our journey to be together: our haunting past, the bullying, our fear of love, self-harm, the dare, and suicide. But we bounced back up from everything, and still, the naked love flaring between us never weakened or died.

When she came into my life, I knew that all those puzzle pieces — full of pride, happiness, hopes, dreams and goals — were going back to finish the jigsaw.

I wanted to be with her. Even as ghosts. Imagining a life without her was challenging to visualise, and always will be.

April Levesque was the type of girl who was continuously grinning. You'll never know if her smile was fake or not. You think that she's okay, with everything that happened to her — Mike's death, her pain, *everything* — but when you properly bond with her, you will realise that she's not what people say she is. She can be an annoying brat, but then again: we are all annoying brats. Her shining eyes always cried. Her beautiful smile always tingled with the truth concealed behind them.

She was crying inside.

And I was breaking inside.

Even today, she's still crying, and I'm still breaking. But who cares? We have each other to cope with life; to endure it, and to build a sudden stamina that will take our breath away.

She came into my life for a reason, and that is to cage my heart in her chest, and for me to cage hers, because whatever happens to us, we know that we are eternal in each other's bodies, minds, and souls.

She came into my life to help me, so I can help her.

"I love you," I breathed into her ear.

"I know. I love you too."

"But I love you more. And I'll keep on saying that over and over again, even when we're dead."

Epilogue

Farewell

April Levesque

The summer ᶜᵘⁿ ardent, sizzling, magnificent orb has escalated weightlessly and fluently. And it was now situated in the light cerulean heavens, transmitting fluorescent shafts to stream into my ~~vacant~~ empty bedroom. The walls were filled with my paintings of Lucky, the Golden Retriever; and the other one of Mike and Dad, standing next to each other, saluting. My bed was basic with thick pillows and pallid sheets. My three velvety blue suitcases were cramped shut.

A knock sounded.

"April?" my father called. "Are you ready, honey?"

Ready to leave Peony Hallows? No. However, ready to leave my hometown with Derek to start a new life, to walk a new path that will include unpredictable challenges? Yes.

Without my consent, my father lightly thrust the door open. Before he can come in, a fluffy golden dog charged in between my father's legs.

I smiled. "Hey, Lucky."

"Derek's downstairs," Dad ~~enlightened,~~ said "with the others."

Regardless of the Peony Hallows' birds serenading and flapping in the morning with their pals and mates, a cosy peace enveloped us, creating a new silence that steals my father's emotions into the air of my room.

For the past year, everything went great. Derek's therapy classes were helpful to him; his therapist provided him with wise advice, to calm Derek's pessimistic mind. Here and then, his therapist assisted me with my recurring episodes, which really filled me with gratitude.

My mother was working remarkably hard in Peony Hallows High School and in the hospital. Derek's aunt's agenda became more conspicuous by the day.

Natalia was traumatised by the merciless treatment from Owen Fall. Although, she permitted Theo to relieve her. Cody was now five, and the number of friends he has pleased him. Every Friday, he brings home a girl from her school and plays with her.

My father's job as the principal of the high school was excellent. From everything that happened last year — the suicide and the bullying — was now extinct. At least, that's what he's *expecting* to do: to exterminate bullying in the town's high school for eternity.

The eyes that I've inherited from my father met with his pair, and we both knew the cheerlessness was now imperceptibly restoring the peace.

This was presumably our last encounter before I leave town. I've deliberated about the disadvantages of leaving my beloved home: the heartbreaks and the farewells. Nevertheless, I knew that leaving was only temporary.

He swung out his muscled arms. "Come here." I ambled into him, my face pushed into his chest as he embraces me tightly, as if he's implicitly and desperately requesting me not to leave. "I'll miss you." His words were slightly muffled against my dark hair.

Tears blemished my black-framed spectacles. "I'll miss you, too."

"Promise me you'll visit us," he implored.

"I promise."

Dad, Lucky, and I descended to the parlour. My treasured friends and family lounged on the sofas. We came to a decision that my cherished friends and family will assemble in my house to sombrely whisper our goodbyes. The married couple, Luke and Neyara, were pregnant with a girl, meaning that Derek was an uncle. They smiled at us before saying their goodbyes. Even Derek's grandma, Sandy, was here, dressed in vintage clothes. Theo's and Natalia's suitcases were placed in the corners of the living room, and so were Jackson's and Sophia's and Derek's.

Mom wailed as I hugged her. "Oh, God, you're already eighteen and now..." She sniffed, sweeping her glossy eyes. "Now, you're off to start your own life. Please visit us, okay?"

"Of course," I said, hugging her.

Rosie sat on Cody's lap. I kissed her forehead before I said to Cody, "Take care of your mother."

He nodded, his eyes sweltering. "I'll miss you, Aunty."

"I'll miss you too."

Cody shifted his gaze to Lucky. "I'll miss you Lucky!" he wept, offering the dog another of his endearing hugs. Lucky whimpered, as if tacitly telling him, *I'll miss you too.*

Moving to my best friend, I realised that her and my brother's suitcases weren't here. Jasmine noticed my baffled expression because she said, "We're not leaving the town yet. Ethan still needs to finish one year."

"Will you stay here?"

She shook her head. "Ethan and I decided to move to England." England. So far away from Canada, from home. "I've applied to a university there. Ethan still needs to wait for a few months before sending his application."

"Do you have any friends there? England is a very rich place—more expensive than most cities in Canada. Are you sure you can handle the new surroundings?"

"Of course. I have friends there. They can help Ethan and me. But for now, please be careful in Toronto. Okay?"

Jackson and Sophia will be moving to Salt Lake City. Theo, Natalia, Derek, and I are moving to Toronto.

"Of course. I'll see you soon."

Derek approached me with welcoming arms, pecking my lips as everyone followed us outside into the small front yard of my house. Since it was summer, the light cerulean sky was clear with only petite blotches of ashen clouds. The grass of the front yard was succulent and fresh, irritating our skins as our legs ram through them. Parked on the road was Theo's black Mercedes, Jackson's grey BMW, and Derek's golden Lamborghini.

I pulled the Lamborghini's trunk open and Derek, who carried our suitcases as his biceps attractively flexed, ~~found~~ hung them inside and slammed the trunk close. Lucky jumped into the back of the car, poking his head through the open window next to him.

"Hey, Derek," my father called. Derek looked at him. "Before you go, remember our talk, okay?"

I frowned. "What talk?"

Surprising me, an affectionate cherry glow tinted Derek's smooth cheeks. Dad, on the other hand, didn't seem bothered or discomfited. He merely smirked arrogantly at Derek's uneasiness.

"The talk about not getting you pregnant," Dad said brusquely, yet there was a hint of humour quaking his voice, knowing for a fact that he's humiliating Derek.

Theo laughed. "Julian, we all know Derek can't resist that."

Derek's blush darkened, and he glowered at his best friend. Theo laughed again, and my father rolled his eyes.

"Call us, okay?" Jackson unlocked his grey BMW and was now leaning against it. "Come visit us when you can."

"Where are you going again?" Theo enquired.

"Salt Lake City. It's nice there. What about you?"

"We're all going to Toronto," Derek responded.

Sophia winced. "Apparently, it's really cramped over there. That's why we chose to live in Salt Lake City: it's not too crowded."

Natalia shrugged. "We're only going to be there for a short while."

Derek checked his silvery watch. "We better get there soon. The roads are gonna get jammed." He hugged Jackson fondly, and I saw tears glistening in the boys' eyes. "See you later, man."

Jackson grinned. "See you later, asshole."

He hugged Theo. Theo sniffed as he patted Jackson's back.

"Be careful." Jackson looked at Lucky. "See you later, buddy."

Lucky barked, disenchanted at the farewell.

We all glanced at our cherished family standing on the porch of my house. They waved at us, shouting their farewells as their eyes were tearing up.

I slipped into Derek's car. He roared the engine into existence and drove his sumptuous Lamborghini into the road; Theo drove after us.

Derek's hand found mine and interlaced our fingers together, squeezing them. "Ready?" he asked. He's merely regarding the fact that the new path we were already driving through will be overcrowded with new dilemmas, new obstacles, new promises, and new emotions.

I smiled. "Ready."

He grinned, inclining his body sideways to bestow me a kiss. "We're going to have an awesome time. Isn't that right, Lucky?" His eyes assembled with Lucky's in the rearview mirror. The Golden Retriever barked, agreeing.

And soon enough, Jackson's car steered into a different road with only a mess of wild grass between Theo's black Mercedes and Derek's golden Lamborghini from them. They bid their goodbyes, and in less than a second, the grey BMW despairingly disappeared from our eyesight.

My eyes blurred with tears as I silently said goodbye to my hometown. I'm going to miss Peony Hallows.

*　　*　　*

We all will, unfortunately, have bad days. It's part of being human. It's normal for us to be stressed.

But committing suicide just because of one bad day? From what I've learned in the past: no matter what happens, suicide is extremely irrelevant. I understand that life can be a pain, an unbearable, treacherous pain... But feeling pain is what makes us human.

Just because we can't have everything in the world, or because our lives abruptly become so horrible, doesn't mean we won't have happiness forever.

We will. We always will have happiness. We just have to wait. No matter how impatient our desires, our hearts, bodies, minds, and souls can be.

Wickedness and sadness are only temporary.

Suicide is permanent.

And, of course, you can never undo suicide.

No matter how lonely we felt, or how depressed we are, remember that there is always someone or something out there that can turn your life upside down in a fantastic way.

It can be a lover.

A sister.

A brother.

A friend.

A parent.

A pet.

Or a deity.

Just continue enduring. Don't give up. Giving up is for losers. You don't want to be a loser, do you?

However, I cannot choose for you. If you want to commit suicide, then that's a tragedy, and you know it.

You cannot control the negativity attacking your mind. I understand that. But just stop and think for a moment — think about who you are special to and wonder how that person will feel if you kill yourself. Would they be devastated? Sad? Or worse, will they become suicidal?

We are all special to someone. We are all important for something.

Suicide only leaves the pain behind. It doesn't even fix anything. It only makes things worse.

Life is shit, yes, but learning how to overcome the obstacles, challenges, and situations in our lives makes our lives a fascinating story to tell the world. It makes us true warriors and fighters. We are all special one way or another. Most of us don't see it because we are too blind by the awful insults from the bullies.

In order to reach the rainbow and the light, we have to go through our own storms.

We are all beautiful in a way, appearance and personality wise.

That's what my older brother, Mike (who's currently in Heaven, taking care of me and my family) told me when I confessed to him that I wanted to die. He's really good at giving advice. His words are always helpful.

I followed his advice no matter how weak I can be, no matter how desperately I want to just give up.

You should too.

Important Note

Every single day, at least ten to thirteen people commit suicide due to bullying, words, pain, depression, judgment, and other atrocious things.

This book is a voice for those people. A voice that will stand up for them, to all the bullies, to all the bad people in the world:

They are human just like you. So why would you torture, abuse, insult, and bully them because of their race, beliefs, disabilities, and personal issues? Is it because you have pain and want to project that to others? If so, that's not the correct way. It'll only make you feel more guilty.

The more bad things you do, the more bad things will hit you back. And they will break every bone in your body until you think about the immoral decisions you've made.

Mental health is not a joke.

Telling someone to "kill yourself" is not a joke.

Each word has a consequence.

Bullying is a crime.

Just remember that.

Dear people, remember you will find the gorgeous light that will light up your life.

Just don't give up.

Keep on going.

Happiness is just around the corner; you just got to find a way to destroy the demons.

I know this because I was bullied in primary school and because of that, I was suicidal. I wanted to kill myself because of the people who convinced me that I'm worthless. I didn't know why they bullied me, but either way, I was still nice to them, I was still generous.

Every day, I cried in my bedroom and asked the same questions you would ask God:

"Why is this happening to me?"

"Why are people hurting me?"

"What did I do to make them hate me?"

"Why am I special to you God? Tell me why because I can't see it."

And then, I witnessed a miracle that changed my life forever, and that helped me to finally destroy my demons and reach the light and the rainbow after my unbearable storms.

The same thing happened in secondary school, except it was only a few people who brought me down and caused me to cut myself on my palms, and the scars are still there. They never fade away. Yet, I never gave up because I knew it's not worth it. I knew that if I gave up, it would only leave sadness behind to those who love me. I didn't give up because I want to help people who've been through similar situations as me.

R.I.P to all the beautiful people who unfortunately committed suicide because of bullying, depression, pain, and rape.

We love you.

We miss you.

We want you back.

Though, we're glad that you are all in the loving arms of the Lord or whatever entity you believe in.

THE END

HELPLINES

Depression, desire to do self-harm and, even the urge to commit suicide can arise at any time. It can come so suddenly that you won't even realise it. It is exceptionally important that you should seek help or information to help you during these types of episodes. It is important to take care of yourself. It is important for you to know that you can save yourself. It is important that you should never give up.

What is Depression?

Depression is a negative emotion that lasts longer than you expect it to. It can occur so suddenly and can cause wild effects such as anxiety, stress, self-harm, and suicidal ideations.

Depression is caused by bullying and judgements, or anything negative that happens in our lives, basically. But it mostly comes from assumptions and bullying from anyone.

Depression is like there's another voice in your head, shoving out the enthusiasm but permitting pessimism to overwhelm you.

It's dangerous.

It's deadly.

It's a virus.

It's a curse.

Causes:

- Bullying
- Judgement
- Family issues
- Blaming yourself
- Insecurities

Symptoms of depression:

- You feel worthless.
- You feel empty and numb inside.
- You feel confused about your emotions that you can't even describe it.
- You feel isolated.
- You feel lonely even though many people love you, yet you can't see it.
- You feel timid.
- You panic and worry a lot.
- You hate attention.
- You don't have that much of self-confidence.
- You don't believe in yourself anymore.
- You don't have any joy or interest in the activities you love to do.
- You feel as if you cannot relate to anyone.
- You felt as if there is no meaning in your life anymore.
- You get paranoid.
- You feel secluded.
- You feel tired all the time.
- You won't eat.

- You feel insecure.
- You feel ashamed even without a definite reason.
- You find sleeping difficult, or you sleep too much.
- You get unusual pains such as headaches, backaches, and stomachaches with no cause whatsoever.
- You use drugs and alcohol to comfort you.
- You hate yourself.
- People come up to you and ask if you're okay, you said yes and ask them why, they said that you look sad.
- You want to cut yourself or do things that harm yourself.
- You want to kill yourself.

How to overcome depression?

What I did to overcome with depression was that I tried to cope with it. I was bullied when I was in primary school, and because of that, I wanted to kill myself when I was 8, but then something miraculous occurred in my life and I decided to cope with the sadness. I knew that it will go away eventually; all I had to do was just continue living my life. And as promised, it did. The depression went away, and I find myself happy nearly all the time. You must think if cutting yourself or even the temptations to commit suicide is the right thing. Will this do anything beneficial to you? Because it will cause you to hate yourself even more.

The best way to overcome this curse is to talk to someone. Talking helps. All the time. Perhaps try private counselling? Because I used to do that and it helped me. Or tell the friends you trust the most.

Alternatives of self-harm:

- Get an elastic band, put it around your wrist, and whenever you feel the urge to self-harm, just yank the elastic band and let it go so it can smack onto your skin. This will cause a minor swelling, but in all honesty, I use this alternative a lot and it helped me.
- Hold an ice cube for as long as possible.
- Write.
- Draw. Draw your emotions. I know some people who draw their emotions on the area they want to cut, and they told me that it helped them.
- Cry. There is nothing wrong about crying. I cry a lot. In all honesty, crying poured out my anger, my grief, my sorrow. It helped me. It made me more human.
- Listen to music. Whenever I feel despondent, I listen to songs that I could relate to, that give me an impression of understanding. Go somewhere quiet and peaceful, somewhere where you can have some quality time with yourself, and just listen to as many songs as possible until you can feel yourself calming down. Music can be people's therapy.
- Scream and yell. Let your sorrow out. Let your anger out.
- Call or text a trusted person. Regardless of the fact that you may have trust issues, communicating with someone who is quite close to you is helpful. Or, if you want to, you can contact me for aid. I am always there to help.
- If you are religious, seek the aid of your deity. Call the person you worship and give yourself a chance to meditate and pray for peace and comfort.

Why do people self-harm?

People self-harm to express their anger and pain, to let all the negative emotions out. They harm themselves to feel something because majority of the time, they are always empty inside.

Other times, people do it to seek attention. Perhaps it is because they don't get enough attention at home or that they don't want to be the one person in their friendship group who doesn't gain enough attention or love, so they start harming themselves and tell people. Faking depression or self-harm is wrong. It is completely wrong and the only consequence you will get is more hate, therefore I advice everyone not to fake depression or self-harm because it is a very sensitive and serious subject.

Please, listen. If you are having a struggle coping with life, or if you have this need to kill yourself, stop. Talk to me if you want, and I will do my best to help you. My goal in life is to help people in many ways possible, because it hurts me a lot to see people in pain. So, let me help you □

Or, go to someone you know in real life, someone you trust.

Or, perhaps contact these helplines.

UK

https://www.nhs.uk/conditions/suicide/

https://www.nhs.uk/conditions/stress-anxiety-depression/mental-health-helplines/

https://www.rcpsych.ac.uk/mentalhealthinfoforall/problems/depression/depression.aspx

https://www.nhs.uk/conditions/stress-anxiety-depression/low-mood-and-depression/

https://www.childline.org.uk/

https://youngminds.org.uk/

https://www.itv.com/thismorning/depression-helplines

USA

https://13reasonswhy.info/
https://suicidepreventionlifeline.org/
http://suicidehotlines.com/national.html

INTERNATIONAL

http://ibpf.org/resource/list-international-suicide-hotlines
http://www.suicide.org/international-suicide-hotlines.html
https://www.nowmattersnow.org/help-line
http://www.defyingmentalillness.com/worldwide-suicide-helplines/

Can't get enough of Derek and April? Make sure you sign up for the author's blog to find out more about them!

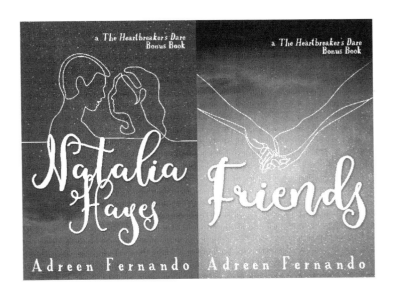

Get these two bonus chapters and more freebies when you sign up at adreen-fernando.awesomeauthors.org

Here is a sample from another story you may enjoy:

Book one
of the
*Valentine
Sisters* Series

PLAYER'S
GAME

DESIRAE CLARK

Prologue

There was nothing worse than feeling like an outcast. The loneliness and knowledge of never belonging somewhere haunted me ever since I was little.

I moved to Manhattan six years ago, afraid to be the new girl in an elite private school in this strange city. It didn't feel like home at first. There was no one I could talk to. Everyone I knew was back in Scottsdale, living their lives and moving on while I was stuck here with the brats.

Until, eventually, I became one of them.

Manhattan had been my home for six long years. But it didn't last long. The idea of living in this strange city I slowly began to love, the food I started to adore, and the friends I came to know suddenly vanished.

One sunny Friday morning, my mom excused my sisters and me from school to talk.

Instead of driving us to school, we got into her car and headed to a nice restaurant. She briefly mentioned that her boss would be joining us for breakfast.

The place was called Eleven Madison Park. It was a bit too fancy for my taste and expensive as hell. The owner was the father of one of the kids from school.

Once there, we got to our table and were soon joined by Mom's boss. She was a younger and very successful businesswoman. My mom was definitely one of her best employees and good friends.

"Samantha, you grew up quite a bit since I last saw you. And the girls!" she exclaimed as her eyes took in my younger twin sisters. Dana and Alyssa were actually my half-sisters and were nothing alike. The only thing these two had in common were their troublemaking tendencies, which seemed to run in the family.

"You grew up to be the two most charming ladies," the woman said. I never managed to remember her name.

If there ever was a case where looks were deceiving, this was it. Sure, my twin sisters looked charming, but they had my mom to thank for that. If it were up to them, Dana would come in her pink pajamas, and Alyssa would turn up in sweats.

"Thank you," Dana replied innocently.

After all the polite greetings, the conversation turned into chitchat until my mother decided to cut to the chase.

"Girls." The tone of her voice was firm, which made my sisters shut up. I was already quiet and bored beyond belief.

"Marie recently notified me that our company is expanding and offered me the opportunity to become a regional manager. In other words, it's a promotion," she informed us with a strange look on her face. "The salary is higher. We'd move into a house, and everybody would get their own bedrooms, bathrooms, and we'd have a backyard. Imagine that."

I admit, when I first heard about the offer, I was too excited to even consider where we'd be moving. *Just think about living in a house again, not having to share my room with two delinquents!*

"But there's a catch," my mom said cautiously. "We'll be moving back to Scottsdale."

"Wait. You mean you already accepted?"

My sisters remained quiet, sensing a fight was about to erupt and watching the whole ordeal without a word.

My mother, probably hoping I wouldn't embarrass our family in front of her boss, replied in a calm manner.

"We need the money."

"So, we don't get to have a say in this?" I asked, enraged, confused, and shocked at the same time. I was trying to take it all in. She was uprooting our family again so that we could live a better life—a life where my mom wouldn't have to worry how we'd pay the bills at the end of the month.

And I got that. But I had a life here! Friends, classmates, and people I loved. A boyfriend whom I wanted to spend my days with. I was finally able to fit in after her last debacle, and now she wanted me to drop everything I was doing on a whim of hers, moving our family across the country again!

"Samantha, I'm only trying to do what's right—"

I knew that, but I just couldn't listen to it anymore. Suddenly, I just felt like I was going to suffocate. That's why I excused myself and walked out of the restaurant.

"I just need to think about this," I told my mom before I left, and she nodded.

And the worst part? We had to be out in fourteen days. Which meant I had less than two weeks to explain to my friends what was going on, properly say goodbye, pack up my things, and leave.

***

Time passed in a daze as I tried to adjust to the idea of moving. At one point, my friends came over and helped.

We watched our videos together, went through photos, and cried as reality slowly sank in. I was leaving by the end of the week, and there was nothing any of us could do.

My last day in Manhattan was nostalgic and sad. I packed up the last of my things before the moving truck set off to Scottsdale where my mother already waited for the stuff to arrive.

Sighing, I grabbed my phone from the table and dialed my boyfriend Trevor's number. We made plans before I checked up on the girls.

"I'm going out. Be good, and don't make too much of a mess, okay?" I asked, and they nodded. "There's money on the table if you want to order pizza, and use my computer if you want to watch a movie. Call me if you need me."

"We're fourteen. We've got it covered, Sam," Alyssa said with a groan and practically pushed me out the door before locking it.

I felt a laugh stir up inside me as I turned away and walked down the old and creaky stairway.

My friends were already waiting for me at the edge of Central Park. I wanted to take a stroll and admire the surroundings. A part of me knew I would not be coming back here anytime soon.

The oldest among my friends was Sarah. She brought a camera with her to photograph everything. "Your last day here needs to be remembered," she insisted as I posed with my friends.

I could have sworn I saw Clara crying before she turned away. My other friend, Faith, held back some tears as well.

"C'mon, girls. We're not going to spoil this day for her." Trevor tried to keep the mood light and then proceeded to tell some jokes before we decided to catch a cab and have a last tour of New York City and all the attractions that were fairly close.

We moved on from one place to another until we couldn't anymore. Exhaustion and poor weather conditions took over, so we retired into our favorite diner in the world.

The Little Red served mean hamburgers, pies, bacon, and eggs, among other things. It was a place where we made many memories and where Trevor took me on our first date.

Who would've thought that we'd be dating for over a year? Yet that's exactly how long it was.

The thing that scared me most about moving was leaving them behind. I knew that sooner or later, they were all going to move on, and I'd have to confront my fears.

I'd have to face the people I left all those years ago. I had a secret, and it was one I had to stop ignoring.

I used to live in Scottsdale—a place where I once had a best friend, one I left without a proper goodbye. A best friend who didn't return my calls after the move and ignored me until I gave up on him.

I was moving back to my old town where I had to face my past and live in the present.

Clara went to order for us since the diner was packed.

"I can't believe the time. The day's almost over," Faith said quietly, and I knew what she meant. I wasn't sure that I was ready for this either. I felt like my heart was going to explode from sorrow and regret. I felt alone once again.

"Promise you'll call," she said, taking my hand in hers across the table. Her hand was soft and warm. We'd been through so much together. I wanted to feel some comfort in her touch, but it still didn't make the situation any easier.

"And promise to Skype," Sarah added. To which I replied with a nod. I didn't speak much, not that I didn't want to or that I was shy. It was just that I wasn't in the mood. I felt like hiding in my room and sobbing until I fell asleep.

"I love you," Trevor whispered in my ear and kissed my neck.

Clara came back with our food, and we toasted to our friendship before digging in.

As I ate, I absently looked outside the diner and just observed. I paid attention to the city life that I was going to miss—the crowded streets, the noise, the city air, and all the shops.

After we finished eating, we stayed and reminisced about our time together.

"Do you remember when you came to school in a swimsuit for Halloween," I said to Sarah who laughed at the memory. It was a dare from Clara, and Sarah did end up being dress-coded afterward. Which was not much of a surprise, as it was a stupid thing to do in the first place.

"Yeah, or when you dared Lake to walk shirtless around Manhattan," Sarah replied to me with a smile.

"I was sad he turned down the dare," Clara replied. She had a crush on Lake since seventh grade. It was so obvious to everyone but Lake himself.

"Not me, I wasn't," Faith said.

"It's time you start acknowledging the fact that your brother's hot and girls love him," Sarah said to Faith who only rolled her eyes in response.

"Guys," Clara said. "You do realize that this is our last day with Sam?"

A tear ran down my cheek because I realized that this time, I had to say goodbye to these amazing, wonderful people instead of hello.

When the time came, I hugged every single one of them and said goodbye.

Trevor escorted me back to my apartment and held my hand all the way there. At first, we walked in an eerie silence before he broke it and spoke.

"Do you think we'll be able to do the long-distance thing? I think I'm going to miss you too much," he told me before putting an arm around my shoulder.

"I don't know. I'm not really good at this whole relationship thing," I gave him an honest reply. "Probably not. A lot of relationships fall apart."

"Friendship then?" Trevor asked, and I knew it was killing him as much as it was killing me.

"I think that would be better, yes," I managed to say as the weight of my feelings crushed my insides. We stopped in front of my apartment block, and I turned to him.

"One last kiss before you go?" he asked as the idiot that he was before I pulled him toward me and gave him my most passionate kiss yet.

It was the most bittersweet goodbye we could have given one another.

Chapter 1

Our flight was in the morning. I had to make sure my sisters and I had taken everything with us before we left. We walked through the apartment one last time, deep in thought. I held my breath and grieved for the moments I spent here.

So many memories were made within these walls. Such a huge part of our lives.

The kitchen was the place where I took care of my sisters when they were hungry. Mom never made it home in time to cook, so I took over for her. I would wait for her to finally return from work and find a hot meal on the table.

The dining room was where my sisters and I did our homework. It was where I got to help them out with their problems. We never ate there.

Our bedroom was too small for the three of us to sleep in, but we didn't make a big deal out of it for Mom. She was already sleeping on the couch anyway.

Every room in this apartment was marked with at least one sign that we were here: a huge mud stain on the living room wall from Alyssa's football, the broken doorknob of our bathroom that was completely Dana's fault, the damaged door from my constant slamming. These proofs of our existence were there.

My hands shook as I lingered in my bedroom for the last time. I took in every detail of the empty bunk beds and the plain white walls. I had never seen anything so devoid of life. My hand lingered on the doorknob as I hesitated before leaving my room and closing the door behind me.

"Ready?" I asked the twins who didn't look like they were going to miss Manhattan at all. They were fourteen, four years younger than me.

"Let's go," Dana said, and I checked the rest of the apartment before walking out. I had trouble locking it because of my shaking hand, but my mind wandered off too far to notice.

Our landlord met us outside. He came to pick up the keys. "Here you go," I said and handed him every key we had. "The doors are locked and the windows closed."

"Thank you," he said and wished us a safe flight before shaking my hand.

I didn't know what was worse: the trip to the airport, getting around it to the right gate, or the wait. Not to mention the flight itself was excruciatingly long, and it consisted of me falling asleep only to be woken up again.

Once onboard, I felt relieved to have made it on time and safely at that. I hated being responsible for my sisters, but Mom always put me in charge of everything.

Alyssa and Dana didn't care that we were leaving and being uprooted again. They lived in their own worlds, daydreaming about our new life in Scottsdale and the people we were about to meet.

I thought about that too for a bit before I fell asleep. I had a dream in which I was on a roof in Manhattan with my boyfriend, Trevor. We were sitting on a bench and watching the Manhattan skyline. The city lights and the sunset illuminated the sky.

It was gone the moment Alyssa nudged me with her elbow, waking me up from this peaceful state of mind. For a moment, I thought it was real, but when I realized the plane was landing, my heart sank.

We got into a cab, and I told the driver where to go. I didn't remember that much about Scottsdale, but I knew what house we lived in, what the town looked like, and a few people here and there.

As we arrived, I started to remember things: my first birthday party in Scottsdale, the only birthday party I ever had; the cinema and the movies I saw there; the grocery store my mom always took us to.

I knew which direction we had to go and wasn't surprised when the driver took certain turns. Sooner than I expected, a yellow house came into view, and with it, a lot of other memories flooded my mind.

I remembered my best friend. Especially that one time when it was raining outside and I dared him to go out and jump into the biggest of puddles. We played until I slipped and fell into the mud. He laughed at me, so I picked up the biggest chunk of mud I could and threw it at his face. We both had the flu for the next two weeks, but it was worth it. I felt happy.

I smiled at the memory of the mud fight that happened so long ago I seemed to forget about it.

But it still wasn't okay. I didn't know anyone here anymore. People have changed and moved on, and so have I.

Our old house was three times bigger than our apartment back in Manhattan. My mom had it rented out, so a couple lived here while we were away.

When the cab driver pulled over, I gave him money, and we took out our luggage. Mom came out to greet us, but I just stood there, staring at my new home. Mom and I barely spoke a word since she sprung out the news on me. There was a tension between us that I just couldn't ignore, and I let her know very clearly I needed time to process everything.

My sisters—blind to everything around them—hurried into the house before Mom scolded them for running. I was standing in the driveway, not yet ready to take the first step.

"Come when you're ready," Mom told me and disappeared inside.

"I don't think I'll ever be," I muttered to myself and stood there like an idiot.

"Hello." A woman approached me with a polite smile on her face. "Are you okay?"

"Fine," I replied harshly before I realized it was a bit rude of me. "Thank you for asking."

"Are you with the new family that's moving into this house?" she asked, and she seemed familiar, but I couldn't put my finger on it.

"Yes, I am. Can I help you?"

"Oh, I'm just here to welcome you into the neighborhood. I'm Katherine Brady. My family and I live just a few blocks away," she explained, and I couldn't believe how stupid I was. Of course, this woman seemed familiar. She was like a second mother to me when I was younger.

"Mrs. Brady?" I asked, delighted to see her after all these years. "It's me, Samantha Valentine."

Her mouth fell before it wore the biggest grin I had ever received. "Samantha? Look at you! You're all grown up!" She immediately pulled me into an embrace, and I felt I was going to cry. I hadn't seen this woman in six years.

"How come you're back?" she asked me, and my smile fell a bit, but it didn't disappear completely.

"My mother got a promotion that demanded we move back," I explained, and she stroked my hair like I was still a little girl. Somehow, I didn't want her to stop because I felt like a child once again.

"Oh, I can't wait to tell my family. Parker will be so happy to hear that," Mrs. Brady said to me before the door to the house opened and my mom came out.

"Katherine!" she exclaimed with delight as the two women hugged and started to chat. I excused myself once I realized I still hadn't seen the house yet.

I took a deep breath and took that first step to my new home.

***

The house itself smelled like bleach and cleaning products. It wasn't like anything I'd been used to before, and it felt foreign. The floors lost its shine through the years, but the walls were definitely repainted.

I walked into the kitchen and noticed there were some kitchen appliances I didn't recognize. It was strange standing inside this house again. It felt like a weird dream.

Everything was already unpacked—no doubt my mother's work because she had been here since yesterday.

After I checked out the kitchen, I went straight to my old bedroom.

The door was open, and I saw the girls unpacking their things. I felt lost in this new yet familiar house. Alyssa came to my help as I wandered around and pointed to the stairs of the attic.

"Your room's up there," she said and disappeared into my old bedroom.

Now, Alyssa was usually a trickster, and I didn't believe anything she said, but the stairway looked new—nothing like I remembered from before. It was interesting enough for me to check the attic out.

When I opened the door, I expected it to be full of dust, junk, and my main worry, spiders plus other nasty insects. I always hated anything that crawled on six or eight legs or anything with scales (meaning snakes, not fish).

But I was met by a remodeled room. The floors were brand new, and a window was just installed. The view was absolutely amazing. If you opened the window, you could sit on the roof that was more like a balcony. It was my very own piece of Manhattan, only here in Scottsdale.

I stood there, speechless and unable to comprehend what was happening.

Then I went to work with unpacking. First were my computer and my speakers. I needed music to keep me motivated.

I had to admit that my new room was huge. Not to mention I had my own personal space.

There were still some things left to unpack when Mom stopped by to speak to me. I turned down my music so I could hear what she was saying, but I didn't stop with the unpacking.

"Sam, I know that it's hard for you to adjust to this new life. But we've only been here for a day, so please just try. For me," she said, and when I didn't reply, my mom walked over and sat on my bed.

"We have a chance to live a better life. A life where the girls will get to go to college. A life where we could afford a decent TV or a new car for you." She sighed sadly. "I hope that someday you'll understand."

"I understand, Mom. But it doesn't mean I have to like it. Just let me take in everything that's been happening. The change from Manhattan to Scottsdale was just too sudden, and the whole reality just needs to sink in first."

"I know. I'm sorry," she said and looked like she was about to cry.

"I know you are. And I know it's not your fault. I don't blame you for moving us across half the continent."

"You don't?" my mom asked.

"No. You have to think of the girls and provide for all of us. I know it's a big responsibility and not everything you do will be perfect. I know a lot of decisions you make are hard, but they're made with the right intentions. So, no, I don't blame you."

"Do you forgive me?" she asked.

"I need time," I told her.

She nodded before she stood up and walked out.

"Oh, before I forget. I invited the Bradys over for dinner tonight. Parker might be here," she said happily and left the room.

The news made my heart stop for a moment. I slid to the ground and took in what she just sprung on me.

There was a chance my former best friend would come over tonight so that we'd have a family dinner like we used to.

I felt sick to my stomach all of a sudden. Rage bubbled up to the surface, but I pushed it further down as I stood up determined to distract myself.

I cleaned the floor, arranged my desk, took a shower, got dressed, and moved on to my new bookshelf. I loved reading a book every now and then.

As a child, my mother insisted that I read as many books as I could so that I'd never stop believing in happy endings, no matter how hard life got or how much our family suffered. She wanted me to live in a world where everything was possible if I were just brave enough to reach for the stars. From my early childhood, she taught me how important reading was for the mind as well as the soul.

It took me two hours as I went through every single book I owned and found a place for it on the bookshelf. The last thing I needed to do was to take my pictures out of the boxes and hang them up or put them on my nightstand.

I completely lost track of time and was so distracted by all the work that I didn't hear the doorbell ring. I didn't hear my mother's shouts to come down or the footsteps getting closer and louder.

What I did hear a bit too late was a knock on my door that was halfway open. And when I turned around, I expected to see my annoying little sisters but was instead greeted by a familiar face. In the threshold stood Parker Brady with a devious smirk on his face and the looks of a god.

If you enjoyed this sample then look for
Player's Game
on Amazon!

Other books you might enjoy:

Outcasts
B.D. Fresquez

Available on Amazon!

Playing the Field

Kay Sh

Available on Amazon!

Introducing the Characters Magazine App

Download the app to get the free issues of interviews from famous fiction characters and find your next favorite book!

iTunes: bit.ly/CharactersApple
Google Play: bit.ly/CharactersAndroid

Acknowledgments

Thank you Mum, Dad, Rachel, and my entire family for supporting me and heartening me to pursue my dreams.

I thank my teachers for assisting me and telling me that I can do the impossible! I thank Andreja, Ayomide, Laila, Rachana, Santhiya, Sara, Bus Buddy, and all my extraordinary friends for understanding and coping with me and my personality, my dilemmas, my tears, my annoying moments, and my smiles, for being there for me and walking beside me through those atrocious, heart-breaking, and murky times we've experienced together. Without you, I don't think I will be here today. No lie.

A gratifying thank you to Shruti for merely helping me with my writing and being the greatest friend ever!

And finally, a HUGE thanks to Wattpad for the exceptional, mesmerising support and love! You all encouraged me to keep on going, helped me through the most challenging times, helped me to overcome the darkness, and always granted me with tearful advice. Without you, The Heartbreaker's Dare won't be here today!

You are all in my heart.
God bless you.

Author's Note

Hey there!

Thank you so much for reading The Heartbreaker's Dare! I can't express how grateful I am for reading something that was once just a thought inside my head.

I'd love to hear from you! Please feel free to email me at adreen_fernando@awesomeauthors.org and sign up at adreen-fernando.awesomeauthors.org for freebies!

One last thing: I'd love to hear your thoughts on the book. Please leave a review on Amazon or Goodreads because I just love reading your comments and getting to know YOU!

Whether that review is good or bad, I'd still love to hear it!

Can't wait to hear from you!

Adreen Fernando

About the Author

Hey. My name is Adreen, and I am a daydreamer, book-lover, and a Catholic. I love my friends, my family, and my supporters.

❧ Nicknames: Addie, Ren, Reen, Reenie, Renie, Adrenaline, Andy.

❧ Favourite authors: Rick Riordan, Kelly Armstrong, Josephine Angelini.

❧ Favourite books: Percy Jackson, Heroes Of Olympus, The Masked Truth, Trials of Apollo, Magnus Chase, Starcrossed Trilogy.

❧ Favourite Movies: The Hunger Games, Harry Potter, Divergent Series, Maze Runner, The Fault In Our Stars, The Space Between Us, Kingsman: The Secret Service (and the sequel), and all Marvel movies.

❧ Favourite TV Shows: Teen Wolf, Shadowhunters, The Shannara Chronicles, The Flash, Legends of Tomorrow, Arrow, Supergirl, The Originals, Vampire Diaries, Stranger Things.

❧ Favourite singers/bands: James Arthur, Sabrina Carpenter, BTS, Red Velvet, Kodaline, James Bay, Selena Gomez, One Direction, Shawn Mendes, Camila Cabello, Little Mix, Rak-Su.

Printed in Great Britain
by Amazon